Eric Van Lustbader graduated from Columbia University in 1968, majoring in Sociology. He began a stint in the entertainment industry as a journalist, then went on to work in production and marketing for Elektra Records, Dick James Music, NBC-TV and CBS Records.

He is married to freelance editor Victoria Schochet, and divides his time between New York City, Southampton, Long Island and the Orient.

Eric Van Lustbader is the author of the bestselling novels *The Ninja*, *The Miko*, *Black Heart* and *Sirens*.

By the same author

The Ninja
The Miko
Black Heart

Sirens

The Sunset Warrior
Shallows of Night
Dai-San
Beneath an Opal Moon

ERIC VAN LUSTBADER

Jian

GRAFTON BOOKS

A Division of the Collins Publishing Group

LONDON GLASGOW
TORONTO SYDNEY AUCKLAND

Grafton Books
A Division of the Collins Publishing Group
8 Grafton Street, London W1X 3LA

Published by Grafton Books 1986

First published in Great Britain by
Granada Publishing 1985

Copyright © Eric Van Lustbader 1985

ISBN 0-586-06684-5

Printed and bound in Great Britain by
Collins, Glasgow

Set in Baskerville

This is for

VICTORIA, EUGENIE AND ELI, HENRY AND CAROL,
HERB AND RONI, JUDY, SUE AND STU

Kung Hei Fat Choy!

Acknowledgments

Without my wife, Victoria's, invaluable and loving editorial contribution, *Jian* would be a far different book.

To all at the Asia Society who helped.

To all at China Books and Periodicals who helped.

Thanks to Henry Morrison for, as always, his expertise.

Editorial and psychic support: Peter Gethers.

Special thanks for their belief: Susan Petersen and Leona Nevler.

Author's Note

Except for easily recognizable characters out of history, no character in *Jian* bears any resemblance to any real person, living or dead.

Although I have been as accurate as possible, certain events have been moved up or back in the calendar year in order to conform with the internal logic of the story.

*He who is prudent
and patiently waits for an enemy who is not,
will be victorious.*

—Sun Tzu, *The Art of War*

There is no sin but ignorance.

—Christopher Marlowe

Prologue

Summer, Present

Toshima-ku, Tokyo

The old man with the bent shoulders came out of the rain, furling his *janomegasa* – his rice-paper umbrella – as if it were a ship's sail. With some deliberation he climbed the slate step, crept past the carved stone pot into which clear water flowed from a cut length of bamboo just above.

There he paused a moment, cocking his head like the most attentive of pupils, listening to the confluence of sounds: the pitter-patter of the rain at his back, the cheery gurgle of the flowing water at his side. There was within that mingling, he thought, the precise mix of the melancholy and the joyous that made life so exquisite to live. 'There is sadness in beauty,' he recalled his father telling him as a child. 'When you can understand that, you will no longer be a boy.'

The old man shook his head and, smiling thinly, pushed through the *nawanoren*'s beaded curtain-doorway.

Inside, the room was small, crowded with men drinking and eating. Smoke curled in the air like dragon's breath, dissipating slowly, leaving behind a grey haze.

The *nawanoren* was a kind of neighbourhood pub, its name derived literally from the beaded curtain that in the past served as its only entrance.

'*Irasshaimase*,' was his greeting from friends as he brushed by a tall, kimonoed figure. The old man nodded, admiring the exquisite workmanship of the black-on-black kimono. He took his seat at a table where he was expected. A waiter set an iced beer before him and he nodded his grateful thanks. He ordered what he always loved to eat here, broiled *hamachi* head. Nowhere in Tokyo, he thought, do they make this fish better.

15

The beer cooled him, the food came, and he was soon totally engrossed in heated conversation with his friends. If he noticed the movement of the tall figure as it passed through the beaded curtain covering the back doorway, he gave no sign of it.

This was no typical Japanese pub, though its front room was similar to almost every one of the thousands of such small eating and drinking establishments that dotted the islands.

Off the hallway that led from the *nawanoren* itself was a series of rooms. Since all traditional structures in Japan were built around the size of the straw mat, the *tatami* – approximately six feet by three feet – rooms were measured by that standard.

The tall figure of Nichiren paused for a moment to take in his surroundings. Here, each of the larger rooms – eighteen *tatami* or so – was filled with a single long low boxwood table. Around it were grouped men in business suits. To a man, they were leaning forward, eyes gleaming, faces sweating, white shirts open, striped ties askew. Droplets of perspiration were caught in the short bristles of their hair, sparkling like diamonds in the lamplight.

Nichiren grunted his contempt for these men. Then his eyes moved. Interspersed among the intent gamblers were men bare to the waist. Instead of shirts or jackets they wore their skin like clothing. From wrists to neck, from shoulder blades to narrow waists, *irezumi* rippled over every square inch of their flesh. The art form of Japanese tattooing was like no other in the world. The insertion of the *sumi*, the coloured ink made from pressed charcoal, was not performed with an electric needle but rather, as it always had been down through the centuries, with hand-held awls and chisels manufactured especially for the arduous task. Nichiren knew well how many years it took to complete one body. He admired the iron will of these men; he felt a certain kinship with the pain they had endured.

The inspired designs leapt out at him as he glanced from individual to individual. Here were a pair of bowing courtesans in complexly flowing robes of intricately patterned silk; there was a rampant tiger, muscles rippling sinuously, leaping through underbrush, alongside a swiftly flowing river; here a dragon's head surrounded by meticulously drawn flames; there fishermen with their skeins and boats, hauling up their catch as, behind them, Fuji-yama humbled both man and ocean with its white-capped majesty.

Nichiren was blind to the great sums of money that lay along the table. Smoke hung from the low rafters of the room. From time to time *geisha* served *sakē* and *o-nigiri*, or rice balls, from the *nawanoren*'s kitchen.

A gambler rose. Perhaps, Nichiren thought, he was tired of the table. His poor luck needed changing, so he would spend more money. Nichiren laughed silently as he watched the poor wretch stumble down the hallway. He retired to one of the small six-*tatami* rooms farther back in the complex. There a woman or, for a premium fee, two would be sent him to sate other longings.

Nichiren moved on past the two large pools and numerous baths for the clients' relaxation.

Eventually he came to a *fusuma*, a sliding door. Removing his wooden clogs, he paused before sliding back the door and, bowing formally, entering.

It was a nine-*tatami* room furnished only with a low black lacquer table. To his left sat Kisan, in the place of power. He was the owner of this establishment, and *oyabun* – chief – of Tokyo's most powerful *yakuza* clan.

Yakuza were gangsters. But, as in all things, the Japanese underworld was different from its counterparts in other countries. For instance, the *yakuza* clans were rigidly fixed,

17

bound by a moral code of *giri* – duty – as stringent as that of *bushido*, the way of the *samurai*.

If one could say that there was honour among thieves, it would be among the *yakuza*.

Inlaid into the centre of the table was Kisan's *kamon*, his family crest. It was a depiction of several interlocking *masu*, boxes of graduating sizes traditionally used to measure rice, the ancient Japanese symbol of wealth. *Masu*, therefore, also meant 'to increase' and 'to prosper.'

To Kisan's left, in the traditional place of the honoured guest, sat another man. He was whip-thin, with a sunken chest. His cheeks were emaciated, which served to accentuate his darkly burning eyes.

The three men bowed to one another and waited. Kisan had made green tea himself, serving the other men as a sign of honour and graciousness. Nothing passed between them, save polite greetings, until the tea had been made and served and the first sips savoured on tongue, palate, and throat.

'The refreshment is most delicious,' the man with the sunken chest said. He was dressed in a dark, chalk-striped suit with white shirt and striped tie. Except for the deep smallpox scars, he was indistinguishable from all the other gamblers in the eighteen-*tatami* rooms down the hall.

'*Domō arigatō,* Higira-*san.*' Kisan inclined his bald head. He was built low to the ground, like a miniature *sumō*. He was barrel-chested, with thick-thewed limbs and a bull neck. His features were powerful but coarse; some might call it a peasant's face.

In contrast, Nichiren's face was composed of delicate features. It was this curious, ethereal beauty that seemed, to the more superstitious, his almost mysterious source of power. Like Kisan, he possessed big *hara*, a centred assuredness that was as apparent when he was kneeling as it was when he was on his feet. His arching forehead and flat, planar cheeks caused him to be sought out by many

18

modern Japanese artists who wished to capture on paper or woodblock that certain magic they all found in his face.

'It is always a pleasure to welcome you to O-henro House,' Kisan said at last.

Higira smiled grimly. That was Kisan's wry sense of humour at work. Since *O-henro* meant pilgrimage, the most serious of which was *Hachiju-hakkasho*, a circuit covering eighty-eight Buddhist shrines, his use of the word in naming this establishment was ironic indeed. 'I'm quite certain that you would cherish seeing the last of me.'

'Oh, not true, Inspector,' Kisan said. 'If you were gone, there would only be another to claim the fragrant grease. We would not know him and, I can readily assure you, would not think as highly of him as we do you.'

Higira flushed at this unabashed flattery. It did not embarrass him. He never received such complimentary remarks from his superiors at the office.

'*Dōmo*,' he said, bowing deeply, deliberately wishing to conceal the extent to which he was pleased. He glanced discreetly at his wristwatch. 'Pardon me for my impoliteness, but time dictates my schedule.'

'Of course,' Nichiren said, but he made no move. A tension enveloped them, a quiet that quickly became so profound that the exhortations of the feverish gamblers came to them in waves down the long hallway, as if they were sitting near the sea.

Higira, despite the friendliness of the meeting, had begun to sweat. He felt Nichiren's glossy, depthless eyes on him with such intensity that he imagined they were causing him pain. His chest had tightened uncomfortably and it seemed to him as if he had forgotten how to get air into his lungs. Politeness prohibited him from uttering another word. But it was Nichiren's gaze that was like a talon in his throat.

Kisan watched Nichiren carefully but covertly so that his guest could not see. It was not only this extraordinary stillness that made him such a dreaded adversary, Kisan thought, but the manner in which he could, from this absolute state, explode into immediate force of such fearful intensity. Like the wind blown across the water, this power seemed elemental to Kisan and therefore that much more deadly.

In time, Higira could no longer contain himself and he began to fidget. In games of *go*, Kisan had observed that Nichiren employed just this tactic, engendering in his opponent an ill-conceived placement. Then, with an astoundingly rapid series of moves, he would cleave to the secret heart of each game, penetrating his adversary's defences, at last laying down the winning stone.

When beads of sweat could be discerned on Higira's forehead, scarring it like his concave cheeks, Nichiren's slash of a mouth curved upward at its ends.

From folds hidden inside his flowing black-on-black kimono he produced a gold key. This he applied to a lock hidden in the grain of the wood floorboards beneath the *tatami*. A section of wood came up. From within, Nichiren lifted a woven basket approximately the size of a woman's hatbox. This he placed on the lacquer table precisely over the spot where Kisan's *kamon* was embedded.

Higira was dumbfounded. 'Is this it?' he asked somewhat stupidly.

By way of answer, Nichiren lifted off the top of the basket and laid it with a certain reverence on the *tatami* beside him.

'What is in there, please?' Higira's mouth was sticky with a lack of saliva.

Nichiren pushed his kimono sleeve back with one hand while plunging the other into the basket. When he pulled it out, Higira's tongue clove to the roof of his mouth.

'Ooof!' he exclaimed, just as if he had been hit in the solar plexus. He saw, held up before him, a severed human head. Blood still oozed from the stump of the neck, and because it was being held aloft by the hair, the head twisted slightly to and fro.

'*Amida!* Shizuki-*san!*'

'Your departmental rival,' Nichiren said softly. 'You wished your own promotion assured, did you not?' His voice was high and singsong, a trait associated more with a Chinese than a Japanese.

'Yes, but . . .' The slight twisting motion made Higira queasy in the pit of his stomach. Even so, his eyes could not leave the grisly sight, like a bloody war banner before him. Thus mesmerized, his voice was as slurred as a drunkard's. 'I did not mean this. I . . . I had no idea . . . I . . .'

'Shizuki-*san* was favoured by *keibatsu*,' Nichiren said, his high, odd voice heightening the bizarreness of the scene. 'He was scheduled to marry Tanaba-*san*'s – your chief's – daughter. That would have, so I learned, sealed his fate . . . and yours. You had good cause to be concerned, Higira-*san*. The marriage would have pushed him ahead of you.'

'You came to the right people,' Kisan said, 'to solve your problem.'

'But this . . .' Higira felt as if he were in the grip of a nightmare. He wanted to feel elated, but he dared not. His terror at what his request had unleashed gripped him with iron claws.

'In another ten days,' Nichiren said, 'it would have been too late. Shizuki-*san* would have been married, part of Tanaba-*san*'s family and therefore untouchable.'

'You can see that there was no other alternative,' Kisan said. He stared at his guest. 'Higira-*san*?'

'Yes, yes.' With a supreme effort, Higira pulled himself back from the abyss toward which these revelations had been inexorably pushing him. All his training told him how evil this was. Yet he was here. He had come willingly to ask their aid in his predicament. His greed and his ambition had rendered him blind to consequences that he saw now were like ripples on a lake, moving outward from their source, affecting the whole.

Like it or not, he knew that he had stepped across an invisible but nonetheless powerful barrier and could never return to the safety and security of his previous life. Home and hearth had never seemed so far away to him. Henceforth, he would have to live according to his greed and his ambition. He closed his eyes for a moment, as if thus sealing his *karma* with a physical act would somehow reassure him.

'Now your career is free of rivals,' Kisan said, very pleased with the situation. Nichiren had researched Higira's predicament well. If Higira had not come to them seeking aid, they would have manufactured a series of events that would have manipulated him into making the request. But this way, Kisan thought, was so much less complicated. 'In several years Tanaba-*san*'s chronic illness will become insupportable even for such an iron-willed man as he. Time will force him to step down.' He smiled broadly, his small white teeth gleaming like a fox's.

'Then we shall all celebrate, eh?' He laughed. 'Chief of Police Higira. How does that sound to you, my friend?' He nodded. 'You see, we are all delighted for you. You are part of *our* family now. We will take care of you.'

The three men lifted their teacups in unison. As they drank, a discreet knock sounded. Nichiren rose and crossed the room to a *fusuma* directly behind Kisan. Sliding it open, he stood very still, as if he were contemplating a complex and slightly puzzling object of art.

He stared straight ahead at the face illuminated within the dusky semidarkness. At length he said, 'So you've come, after all. Really, I never believed that you would.'

Outside the *nawanoren*, the rain pattered dolefully, slipping off sprays of leaves bowed beneath its weight.

'*Yappari aoi kuni da!*'

From across the street, the doorway to the *nawanoren* appeared framed by a jungle of blue-green irises and hydrangeas. Hybrid gardenias of the same family of hues peeped out here and there as if shyly seeking recognition.

'It *is* a green country!'

Jake Maroc smiled to himself as he heard Mandy Choi repeat his whispered exclamation. Crouched as the two of them were in the dripping doorway directly opposite O-henro House, it was important to keep noise down to a minimum, even though the rain was a great help in that regard.

But of course it was a green country, Jake thought. It was *tsuyu*, the time of the 'plum rains.' The Japanese found pleasure in such a multiplicity of major and minor occurrences, they had created a word for that feeling. *Odayaka*. That pleasure could pertain to a person just as well as an inanimate object such as a stone, or a changeable one, such as the sea or the weather. *Aoi*, that host of varying blue-green which burgeoned beneath the early summer *tsuyu*, was the most *odayaka* of all colours in nature.

Jake glanced at his chronometer. 'Mandy, go get the others,' he whispered in Japanese. 'It's almost time.'

The small Chinese nodded and disappeared into the rain-filled night. In a moment he returned with four men. All were Chinese, trained by Jake himself at the Hong Kong Station. Though they spoke perfect idiomatic Japanese, this was their first journey here. For Jake, it was another story entirely.

He watched them as they came, as proud as a father with his sons, in their precision and expertise. They were dressed alike: V-necked white T-shirts, khaki trousers flared at the thighs like riding breeches. *Hachimaki*, wound calico headbands, encircled their gleaming foreheads. On their feet were *jikatabi*, rubber-soled boots that had a split between the big toe and the others and fitted more like

23

gloves than shoes. They were as soft and pliable as Indian moccasins, so that one could still grip with the foot.

In short, the six of them appeared to be nothing more than a group of workmen, huddled in a doorway on their way home. That was precisely the impression they wished to give.

Jake had been counting off the seconds in his mind so that he did not have to look at his chronometer again. This close to the jump, he did not want to look away from the door. His information had been exceptionally precise about the time.

'Jake,' Mandy Choi said, close by his side, 'what if he's not there?'

'He's there, all right.'

Mandy watched the manic intensity in his friend's face and felt a slight chill go through him. *I wish we had never come*, he thought. *This is the fourth day of the month.* He knew what that meant. In numerology, four was the number of death. A very bad omen.

All gods protect us, he thought now as he said, 'The danger here is acute. Did you ever think to distrust your source?'

'He's there,' Jake repeated. 'My information's accurate.'

If only it were someone other than Nichiren, Mandy thought. *Anyone. I'd sooner take on the Christian Devil himself, if he exists. But Nichiren and Jake . . .*

There was too much history between them, the river of hatred too dark and too wide. *When it comes to Nichiren*, Mandy thought, *Jake does not think clearly. Therefore I must look after him.*

Jake took three deep breaths. He could feel the tension and the accelerated pulses behind him like a tide urging him on. *Nichiren*, he thought, *at last I have you.* Black images threatened to swamp his awareness. Thoughts he had locked away securely tore from their moorings, whirling upward in anarchic disarray. And with them, emotions.

Blood rushed in his ears like a battle cry.

24

'All right,' he said thickly. 'Let's go.'

Neons turned the bed of the street to pinks and pale electric greens. Their shadows, as they passed, brought the darkness of the night back to the macadam. The few passersby were withdrawn behind the shields of their *amagasa*, backs bowed against the slanting rain. A dog barked disconsolately down an alleyway, the narrow walls lending a desperate note to the echoes.

The edge of the city, like the blaze from a hearth, seemed dulled by distance, the throbbing of its vibrant coloured lights watered down by the weather.

Jake led the way through the beaded curtains, hearing the preternaturally loud clatter they made as he parted them. He was aware of Mandy close at his side, the others behind him, and felt the brief flutters in his stomach subsiding. He was no longer an individual; he was part of *dantai*, the group. He was back in Japan.

'There's a drain break down the road,' Mandy said as patrons' heads turned and the manager came through from the tiny kitchen off to one side. He shrugged. 'All this rain. *Tsuyu*. We have to check all the buildings within these six blocks.'

Jake slid as unobtrusively as he could through the smoke. Broken conversations continued, *saké* and beer were lifted. Laughter crept again around the room. The aroma of roasting *shioyaki* mingled with those of tobacco and sweat.

They went by the manager and, abruptly accelerating, sped through the rear curtain-doorway. Two kimonoed guards drew pistols as they broke through, but Mandy and one of the others smashed the edges of their hands against collarbones, then the backs of necks. Kimonos pooled across the polished wood strips of the hallway, and the raiders stepped quickly over them.

With silent prearranged signals, Jake motioned for two of his men to take the north gambling room, two others to take the south room. He and Mandy raced down the

25

hallway toward the west room, where, his information told him, Nichiren would be.

Flinging aside the *fusuma*, Jake found himself in a kind of antechamber. It was a six-*tatami* room. Deep red and dove-grey *futon* curled on the reed mats. *Tansu* chests, their metalwork opalescent with age, crouched at the four corners of the room. On the walls were the repeated crescents of scabbarded *katana*.

At that moment he stopped dead in his tracks. Another sliding door was opening, and two men stepped into the room. For an instant the three stood at opposite ends, staring at one another.

Then the two men, bare to the waist, *irezumi* rippling with their long, sleek muscles, drew swords, advancing toward Jake. Mandy was just outside the door lintel, engaged in silent combat with another guard.

Jake darted to his right, away from the first blindingly swift strikes and toward the scabbards on the wall. He reached up, withdrew a *katana*. He knew instantly that it was old, perhaps more than three centuries. Its heft and balance were exquisite. It was a museum piece, but that did not mean it had lost its deadly edge. Over and over the pure steel had been refolded in upon itself with the master swordsmith's Zen dedication to create the finest blade the world had ever known.

Seeing him thus armed, the *irezumi*-men separated so that they could come at him from either side and so increase their chances of success.

Jake knew that time was slipping away from him. With each added beat of the clock, the likelihood of his capturing Nichiren was rapidly decreasing.

As they rushed him, he employed the techniques of *kumi-uchi*, stopping in midair the overhead blow from the thinner of the two *irezumi*-men, the one on his right, with a horizontal parry that sent a clashing ring around the room.

Within the same blinding motion, he disguised until the

26

last possible split-second the wrist-flip that now continued the horizontal slash at waist height, away from the thin man's blade and inward in a vicious arc, slicing through skin, flesh, and bone, into the second man's abdomen.

The heavier of the *irezumi*-men screamed and, clutching at the sliding mass of himself oozing through the rent, dropped to his knees. His useless *katana* clattered to the floor as Jake pushed him forward and down on his face with his left hand while his hips began the powerful right-facing swivel away from the path taken by his first opponent.

Mad-eyed leopards in reds and lurid yellows leapt at Jake, the *irezumi* bulging with the man's efforts to bring his previously deflected overhead strike down on Jake's skull.

But Jake was already in another position, swivelled enough so that he was facing the man's side, out of range of his frontal attack.

As the man's fierce momentum pushed him forward, Jake lifted his blade to shoulder height, bringing the pointed end of it outward in a shallow arc. There was a brief shout as the razor edge slashed through the meaty part of the man's arm.

Because of the fineness of the edge and because Jake was leaning his entire weight behind the strike, the steel severed the arm completely, slicing hotly into the ribcage and the vital organs it protected within.

Blood spurted and there was a fetid wind, as of a coffin briefly opened. Jake leaped over the settling corpse, turning his head briefly as he heard movement outside the door. Mandy and the rest of the raiding party were piling through the open doorway.

Using the *katana*, Jake slashed through the *shōji* into the connecting room.

He saw three men surrounding an object on a low table. Heads, shape of a hatbox – filled with what? shiny black straw? – faces turning in his direction like pale flowers to the sun. Then Jake was focused on only one person.

That man was clad in a black-on-black kimono. His obsidian eyes were quite large in a rather narrow skull. His face was triangular, almost feline. He had a long, almost feminine neck and finely sculpted features. He had small, flat ears. His thick hair was blue-black, worn long in the style of another generation.

'*Nichiren!*'

It was a sibilant whisper that Jake could not contain. His heart thudded painfully in his chest and his mouth was abruptly dry. He remembered as a youth in Hong Kong going to see a film called *The Horror of Dracula*, and being frightened out of his wits. Irrationally, he felt the same unexplainable terror welling up in him now. He was remembering what had happened at the Sumchun River and it sent a shiver through him.

Then Jake was aware of a subtle movement Nichiren made beneath the folds of his kimono. He leapt forward, the *katana* raised before him. But Kisan had stepped in front of Nichiren, his balled right fist outstretched. A honed sixth sense warned Jake and he thrust the *katana* to the vertical as Kisan's fingers unfurled like the petals of a flower.

His shouted *kiai* stunned those in the room not prepared for it. But Jake had known what lethal weapon lay within the *oyabun*'s palm, and as the metal links came hurtling at his face, he shifted the point of his blade fractionally, catching the weighted end. The *manrikigusari* whirled around the *katana* but before Jake could grab it, Kisan used the *kakoiuchi*, a circular twist, to disengage.

Immediately he was on the offensive, using a *sukuiuchi*, a vertical figure-pattern, to get inside Jake's defence. He came in hard and Jake broke away, raising the *katana*. This Kisan blocked with the *jōdan-uke*, immediately bringing his fists together for the eye strike that would end the struggle.

28

But Jake had anticipated him and he stepped through the *jōdan-uke*, freeing his upper arms. The weighted ends of the *manrikigusari* were rushing at him as he struck downward obliquely.

He grunted heavily as the blade made contact because Kisan was already twisting away. The blow cut through arm and shoulder, encountered ribs.

Kisan's eyes filled with an unnameable emotion even as he began to sink to his knees, shuddering. Jake was unsure how deep he had gone and was bringing the blade forward and down for another strike when there came a swirl of movement from just behind Kisan. A savage cry, as if reluctantly ripped from a tightened throat. Had Jake's vision not been blocked, had his mind not been fixed on the killing blow, he might have had more warning. Spherical blurred shape arcing at him.

Desperately he shouted to his men. There was a sense then of reality breaking up into tiny discrete fragments, dizzying and overlapping one upon the other until clarity was lost and only a vague impression was left, like smeared pastel hues upon a canvas.

Mandy grabbed his arm, turning him backward. He felt the other man's body close against him, felt his warmth, the protection it afforded him. But in that shifting his gaze fell upon the other people across the room, now far back against the opposite wall. Japanese faces. And the woman. Blurred sense of time shifting, of an element being acutely out of place. Then an arm was being raised and, like a brocaded curtain, a kimono sleeve rose up to shield her face from his sight.

Then the room turned yellow-white. It seemed to balloon outward at him. A ferocious howling filled his ears until it became too painful to hear. The walls split apart and shot at him; the ceiling broke apart like an ice floe and dropped inward with a sickening rush.

The monstrous percussion reached him then, hurling

29

Mandy into him, flattening them both against the floor with incredible force.

Cursing Nichiren's name, Jake went down into blackness and unending pain and it was as if the entire building followed him down, pinning him to the depths.

Book One
TZU-JAN

Summer, Present

Washington/Hong Kong/Beijing/Tokyo/
Moscow/Tsurugi

'Throw it onto the screen.'

Colour shot, eight feet by ten, made grainy by size: a human face that radiated power in precisely the way a tiger caught in mid-leap will. Curly black hair above a wide, intelligent brow. Hooded coppery eyes, extraordinary in their intelligence. An aggressive, clean-lined jaw, high cheekbones that set the eyes deeply into the skull.

'Is there an update on him?' This was another voice, somewhat warmer in tone.

'I don't think he was hit too hard,' Henry Wunderman said. 'Although we're not yet sure of the extent of the damages, it's fairly certain the worst part will be the psychological aspect of the *dantai*'s death.'

'*Dantai?*' Rodger Donovan asked.

'Yes,' Gerard Stallings said in the slightly supercilious tone he used when addressing Donovan. He was a large, rawboned man of six-four who had the chiselled countenance of an Englishman but spoke in a deceptively soft Texas drawl. Suntanned, his lined face was lean, as muscular as his body, dominated by deepset jade-green eyes below a high, freckled forehead. He had thrived in 'Nam; when Henry Wunderman had recruited him for the Quarry in 1971, he was leading the rebel forces in a small but strategic African country. Heavily supplied by the Russians and not giving a damn, Stallings had been about to mount the final assault on the capital when Wunderman had intervened. Wunderman had recognized Stallings's superb strategic mind and what had to be done to win the man over. He had selected a Soviet military cipher that had been intercepted by the Quarry. Its vowel-transposition, inconstant-double-consonant code had been broken, but despite that, no one in staff could make head or tail of it. Wunderman took it to Stallings, who had one good look at it and was hooked.

He was a student of Sun Tzu. 'To unite resolution with resilience is the business of war,' he had quoted to Wunderman that hot, sticky day in Africa, with the skulls of the government functionaries he and his raiders had killed piled all about them. He loved the business of strategy, too, moving men around the world as if it were a *wei qi* board. Like Jake.

'*Dantai* is a special kind of group,' Stallings continued, 'closer even than a family. They rely on one another completely. In situations of extreme hazard, we have found that this intimate kinship reinforces the most desirable combat attributes of courage, stamina, and clear, incisive thinking under duress.' Stallings, the only active field operative in the room, clearly disliked anyone who lacked that experience. Of the three, only Donovan had no inkling of what fieldwork was like. He often thought that if Donovan was ever called upon to do wet work, he would upchuck all over his expensive loafers.

'The *dantai*,' Wunderman went on, 'is what made Jake Maroc's unit so successful for so long.'

'Up until the time of the Sumchun River incident,' Donovan said. Occasionally he glanced down at a sheaf of computer printouts. 'It is the opinion of staff that that encounter radically changed Jake Maroc.'

Stallings shrugged. 'The Sumchun River was a bad one. Jake lost . . . what was it, Henry? Three men?'

'Four,' Wunderman said. He was a shorter man than Stallings, but a good deal chunkier. 'Henry, you look like a *sumō*,' Jake had told him laughingly more than once. He was coarse-featured, with the veined, vaguely bulbous nose of the Irish prizefighter too long at his work. His dark hair

34

was receding too fast for him, his ears were as large as a puppy's. His cheeks bore the scars of a childhood bout with smallpox, but his soft brown eyes managed to turn a decidedly heavy face into a friendly one. 'A fifth was crippled for life. That was well over three years ago, and since then Jake put together the new *dantai*. The men were supposed to be something special. I think he did not want what happened at the Sumchun River ever to happen again.'

'Yet it did. He lost them all – and almost himself – on a chaos mission.'

'He saw a chance to get Nichiren and took it,' Wunderman said. 'After what happened at the Sumchun River, can you blame him?'

'I don't, God knows,' Donovan said. 'But the Old Man does.' He was by far the youngest man in the room, of medium build, fair-skinned, thick blond hair, cool grey eyes which quietly took everything in. A graduate of Stanford and the Rand Corporation, he was the odd man out here, and knew it. He was also smart enough not to try to overcome it. 'You know better than I do, Henry, how he feels about discipline.' His voice took on the deep, almost stentorian tones of Antony Beridien. '"Discipline is the backbone of the Quarry. Without it we would have no mandate. Without our mandate, the world would have chaos."' Donovan shook his head. '*I* know what Jake was up to, but the Old Man can't or won't. I'm just trying to prepare you.'

'Shit,' Stallings said.

Tension laced the room like fog, but it was as if the three men seated across from one another at the round ash-burl table had made a silent pact never to acknowledge it overtly.

There were four seats permanently bolted to the lead-lined floor, but one was vacant at the moment.

'Where's Antony?' Wunderman asked at last.

'He's winding up the meeting at State with the President. I think they're all pretty pissed with the flap that Jake's created. Right now the Japanese government is using the *yakuza* to explain away the violence, but I can tell you they've been very cold to us today. That makes the President madder than hell, because he's spent the last nine months of his term in office creating a series of reciprocal trade agreements with Japan to help lessen our enormous trade deficit. Now only the Devil knows what will happen. And I don't have to remind you that if the President's unhappy, the Old Man will light a fire under us.'

The three men froze as the lead-lined door to their inner sanctum, far below street level, slid open with a distinctive rumble. In the doorway was revealed the small, gnarled figure of Antony Beridien, the President's advisor – and prime confidant – on all matters involving international security.

As the automatic-seal door closed behind him, the room's internal light devolved upon him, outlining his features. He had an abnormally large head with a wide, high forehead above which thick, curling hair sprouted, brushed carefully back. He had enormous eyes the colour of cobalt that could, at times, appear just as hard. His heavily bridged, hawklike nose would otherwise have dominated that face. The deeply scored lines in his cheeks and brow, like notches in a revolver's grip, were worn with pride rather than the fear of passing time.

Perhaps to compensate for his lack of height, he moved in a long, almost loping stride. Without a word he sat down, surveying them all. Then he turned his adamantine gaze on Wunderman.

'Your man Maroc took a crack Quarry unit off their preplanned assignment outside of Hong Kong and disappeared with them into the mist. He endangered a waiting

Quarry network up near the border, alerting the Communist Chinese and destroying all chance of ever running that particular mission.'

'Nichiren,' Wunderman said, his knuckled fists hard against the wood tabletop. 'He got a lead on Nichiren. The first iota of positive information we've come up with in sixteen months. He acted on that information. There was no time to notify you, to put it through proper channels.'

'For us to be implicated in the death of an inspector of police, for Chrissakes, is unthinkable!' Beridien made no effort to calm himself. 'Tell me one thing. Did he clear it with you? I mean, Wunderman, you're his goddamned superior, aren't you? You run the bastard, just like you run all our agents. That is in the job description of the head of wet section, if memory serves. Or is Jake Maroc running you, as has been my suspicion ever since the Sumchun River incident?'

Wunderman's eyes flickered involuntarily toward Donovan and Beridien, picking it up, said, 'He's not going to help you this time, Henry. Your personal loyalties have gotten in the way of the orderly running of this organization once too often for my taste. I ought to . . .'

'If we have serious business to discuss, we should get to it now,' Donovan said, with enough intensity that Beridien gave a quick, birdlike flick of his head.

'The Quarry comes first in all things,' Wunderman said. Angry at feeling so defensive, he was obliged to state the obvious. 'It always has, ever since you created us.'

Beridien took a deep breath and his voice softened. 'No one is accusing you of disloyalty, Henry. Good God, you are my mailed fist against the chaos out there in the world. But you are, like the rest of us, only human. We all have frailties, we all blunder every so often, or lose our way. In this gigantic labyrinth in which we've chosen to make our home, it's quite understandable. I was only pointing that out.'

Dismissing the subject, he turned his head in the same quick, jerky fashion that had helped earn him the long-time sobriquet 'the Owl', and said to Donovan, 'Any glimmer of what Maroc found on Nichiren, and how?'

Donovan shook his handsome head. 'Not a thing. I've been personally monitoring the Soviets' new polar cipher route over the past seven months.' He glanced at a page midway through his sheaf of printouts. 'Nothing came over our normal international routes, of that I'm certain. Whatever Maroc filched, he did it solely on his own.' He shrugged his shoulders. 'Anything we'd got would've been passed immediately on to you. Nichiren has been Code Red around here for more than three years.'

Beridien inclined his enormous head. The rose-coloured overheads threw his eyes into deep shadow, making him seem even more birdlike. 'It's clear then that Maroc received some volatile information on Nichiren. He did so outside this agency's aegis, without' – here his head swung in Wunderman's direction again – 'this agency's knowledge, support, or sanction.'

'He had a good shot, it appears,' Donovan said, 'at terminating Nichiren, which has been this department's disposition for him ever since he surfaced a little more than five years ago as the number-one independent assassin-for-hire.'

'We'll get to the consequences of Maroc's failure in a moment,' Beridien said. 'At this juncture, however, the operative's success or failure is irrelevant. I'm afraid, Henry, that Maroc's effectiveness in this agency has been permanently compromised.'

'Sir – '

Beridien raised a pale hand. 'Henry, please. We're all professionals here. This is what I was speaking of before. Maroc was under discipline. We have nothing here – nothing at all – unless we maintain discipline. The Quarry was formed fifteen years ago, with the full consent of the then President of the United States, to fight what we perceived as a growing international chaos, fomented in part by foreign governments, all of which were and still are hostile to ours. I'm not, I know, telling you anything you don't already know since you signed on with me, from the beginning. But perhaps you don't know that each President, upon his inauguration, has a period of ninety days in which to reevaluate the Quarry in order to decide on its disposition. Not one, I'm gratified to say, has ever contemplated dismantling us.

'All of that's for a very good reason. We're the best and we're rigidly controlled. So ironclad is our discipline that what happened in the CIA more than once could never occur here. We have never had to clean house and we never will.

'This crash meeting at State was difficult for the President to field. Unlike the CIA, which now belongs to the country, we are the President's stepchild. Therefore, our blunders reflect directly on him. He takes any mistakes quite personally. Let me say that right now the Quarry is not very high up on his list of favourite government organizations.' Those eyes bored into Wunderman's skull. 'As for State, they were, as usual, in a panic over a series of particularly heated exchanges with the Tokyo Chief of Police, Yasuhiro Tanaba. It seems his man, Higira, was an innocent-bystander fatality in Maroc's abortive raid, as was the businessman Kisan.

'I was not happy to be the cause of the President's difficulties today. His *cause célèbre* has been these reciprocal import-export agreements with Japan.

'In any case, Maroc broke discipline, and discipline is what makes us strong. It is also, Henry, what allows us to survive through changing administrations. The moment Jake Maroc set foot on Japanese soil, he cut himself off from us. He's totally on his own now. That's final.'

Wunderman said nothing, but his eyes dropped to his

fingers, interlaced before him on the table. Why, he asked himself, did he feel like a schoolboy called out in front of the class by the principal? He felt a momentary lick of rage at Beridien's cruel and, so it seemed to him, unfeeling summary judgment. Where was consideration for all that Jake had done for the Quarry over the years? Wunderman knew that he should speak up now, that the heroic thing to do would be to make an impassioned speech in Jake's defence on just that subject. But he remained silent. Why? Was it because he felt instinctively that Donovan was right? That somehow, in some inexplicable fashion, the Sumchun River incident had marked Jake forever? That the trauma he had suffered there had impaired his effectiveness as an agent?

The fact was that Jake *had* broken discipline. Wunderman had had no idea what Jake had planned until the aftermath of the failed raid had been relayed into Quarry HQ. Damn him! he thought now. If only he'd let me know, I could have provided some backup. I'd be in some kind of tenable position to help him now.

What really had happened at the Sumchun River? Wunderman asked himself. Was it the trauma of seeing four of his men die and a fifth become a paraplegic that had turned Jake hard and inward-directed? Wunderman recalled the debriefing. It had been an effort to get Jake to talk in full sentences, let alone to get the entire story of what had happened. And in the end, Wunderman thought now, I suspect he gave me only pieces of the story.

'Now to Nichiren,' Beridien said, and Wunderman knew that his moment to defend Jake had passed. 'Henry, do we have any leads as to what happened to him after the explosion?'

'No.' Even as he spoke, he wondered what would happen to Jake without the Quarry. Wunderman knew that he himself would be like a rudderless boat without this organization. Wouldn't it be the same for Jake? 'When the O.D.

of Ciphers relayed the signal, I ordered an emergency team in from Hong Kong, which is our nearest station. One of the *dantai* had managed to drag Maroc out of there before dying. They took Maroc back with them to Kowloon. There was nothing else to do.'

'Five men.' Beridien shook his head. 'How galling to have to add them to this long list. My God, Nichiren's a one-man abattoir!'

'I've got to hand it to him, though,' Stallings said. 'Maroc sure had the right idea about how to take out Nichiren.'

'What do you mean?' Beridien asked.

'*Huo yan.* The entire manoeuvre was like a potent *wei qi* move. Just like Jake.'

'*Wei qi?*' Beridien said. 'What's *wei qi?*'

'A Chinese game of military strategy.' Stallings was pleased to at last be in his element. 'The Japanese call it *go.*'

Beridien snorted. 'A game? Translated into real life? Oh, come on.'

Stallings ignored his tone. 'Unlike Western games, *wei qi* has a strong philosophical side. A player's *wei qi* strategy is a translation of his view of life.'

'And what is Jake Maroc's view of life, Stallings?' Beridien wanted to know. 'According to this game?'

'The raid was like *huo yan*, a move known as the "movable eye." An "eye" is created when a player's pieces surround an intersection on the board. By leaving a space in the centre, he creates a defensive formation which he then repeats across the board. No enemy piece can be placed within the "eye." Surrounded, it will die.

'But' – Stallings raised a long forefinger – 'an "eye" can also be used for offensive purposes. When it is, it is called *huo yan.* That was the essence of Jake's raid.'

'Yet it failed,' Beridien pointed out.

Stallings nodded. 'Obviously Jake was outplayed.' He shrugged again. 'Pity.'

Wunderman's coarse-featured face was set in a frown. 'We've got a somewhat more immediate problem,' he said. When he was certain he had their attention, he turned his gaze on Beridien and said, 'Jake Maroc's wife, Mariana, is missing.'

From out of the hollow silence, Beridien's baritone rose. 'What the fuck are you telling us? Missing? Goddammit, what do you mean, she's missing?'

'I think you'd better tell us all of it, Henry,' Donovan said in his calm, unhurried voice.

Wunderman squared his shoulders and did as he was bade. 'Mariana Maroc was at home in Hong Kong on the night of the chaos raid. Using Donovan's brainchild, the Random Intervention Surveillance Sweep, which we now keep on every active field operative's home base, the Janitors picked up a phone call to Maroc's apartment at 5:57, local time.'

'Local or long distance?' Beridien wanted to know.

'Long distance. As you know, the RISS is meant as a trace, not as a recording device. Therefore we can pinpoint the origin of the call, but not who made it or what was said by either party.'

'Go on,' Beridien said.

'The call emanated from Japan. Tokyo, to be more specific.'

'Maroc?' Beridien meant did Jake make the call.

'It's the most logical explanation, of course,' Wunderman said. 'But it doesn't hold. According to the ETA we've been able to piece together on the *dantai*, Jake would've been en route at 5:57. In the air, he would not have been able to reach her or anyone else by phone. All we know is that within fifteen minutes of that call, Mariana Maroc was gone.'

'Gone where?' Donovan asked.

'We've been able to trace her as far as Tokyo.'

'She or Maroc have any known friends there?' Beridien said.

'Jake did but strictly on the business side,' Wunderman answered. 'As far as we know, Mariana knew no one there.'

'How far is that?' Beridien barked.

'Far enough.'

It was very quiet in the windowless room. Beridien's dark eyes bored into Wunderman's from across the table. 'Do you have more specifics on the call's origin, Henry?'

'The Janitors are working on that now. As Rodger knows there are still a couple of bugs in the system. They tell me, however, that we have a shot at narrowing it down to at least a district and possibly even the actual number '

There was a peculiar scent in the room, as if somewhere out of their sight a fire had been lit.

'Mrs Maroc's disappearance may mean nothing,' Donovan said. 'I understand they were having some, er, difficulties lately.'

'Missing is missing,' Stallings said. 'That kind of thing's *always* serious.'

'The more so under these circumstances,' Beridien said shrewdly.

'Meaning what?' Wunderman said.

'Meaning that I don't trust coincidences. Maybe the two – Maroc's chaos raid and his wife's disappearance – are connected.'

'I don't see that,' Wunderman said, and knew it was a mistake the minute the words were out of his mouth.

Beridien's primeval head swung around. 'Oh? This – what did you call it, Gerry? – "movable eye" of Maroc's, it should have worked. It didn't. Maybe it's because Maroc isn't the operative he once was. Maybe Sumchun River has undermined his effectiveness. Or maybe, just maybe, Nichiren had some kind of inside information about the raid. If so, there could be only one source. No one within the Quarry knew about it. Only Maroc and his *dantai*. His flaming tigers.'

'Are you suggesting that Mariana Maroc could have told Nichiren?' Wunderman was incredulous.

Antony Beridien's eyes seem to pierce through him, pinning him to the wall. It was deliberate. Beridien did not like Wunderman possessing salient facts that he himself did not. 'I am suggesting nothing, Henry, merely positing a train of thought. Because of Maroc's dangerously precipitous actions, we are now under pressure. The kind of pressure that can be, if it is not eliminated immediately, the most debilitating kind for us.

'Perhaps random chance has forced us into this position. If so, we will accept it and go on from there. But the possibility exists that what we are facing here is an iceberg: an inimical design of foreign manufacture. That would put us under attack. If that is the case, I put you all on notice that I mean to get to the bottom of this iceberg in the most expeditious manner. And, gentlemen, God help the man who gets in my way.'

'All gods defecate on this weather,' David Oh said in Cantonese. Outside, rain filled the Hong Kong streets to overflowing. His mood turned blacker; he slammed the heel of his hand against the windowsill, praying to Buddha that Jake wasn't going to do something stupid, like not wake up. All the tests had been made and analysed. Physically, Jake had come away from the debacle at O-henro House with nothing more than multiple abrasions and contusions. The intervention of Mandy Choi's body between him and the blast had assured that.

Except there was the concussion to think about. EEG readings found Jake's brain patterns undisturbed. Yet he had not regained consciousness. A matter of time, the doctors had said, shaking their heads. Grey rain as dark as

David Oh's mood streaked the windowpanes, turning dust to grime.

On the fourth floor, he had stood for a time with his back against the closed door, as if wary of coming into the room itself. Shadows built a bizarre superstructure out of thin air. He heard the sound of breathing and was not certain whether it was his or Jake's.

He did not want to move, did not want to approach any closer, as if by this denial he could also deny what he knew he must eventually see.

David Oh wondered what Jake's breaking discipline would mean for Hong Kong Station. Nothing good, he was certain. He found himself afraid of that. Before Jake Maroc had joined the Quarry, Hong Kong Station had been nothing but a bunch of ill-trained errand boys scurrying about the Colony like so many ants. Without his force, it could so easily revert. Fornicate unnaturally those in Washington who control our future without taking any risks themselves, he thought. I'm sure they're bleeding inside for Jake, Mandy Choi, and the others.

At the bedside, he stared down. There was nothing much there to which he could relate. If this is what it leads to, why do any of us do this? he asked himself. But he already knew the answer. The risk was secondary to the objectives they were dedicated to accomplishing. Dedication, David Oh knew well, had many origins, but it was the one element that bound all of them in the Quarry together.

'Jake.' The whisper was out before he knew it. It hung in the air, mingling with all the other shadows spun in the room, hovering peaked and angular.

There was movement from the shadows and David started. He peered into the gloom. He heard only the steady drumming of the rain. Then he recognized the figure.

'Formidable Sung,' he said sharply. 'What are you doing here?'

'Jake Maroc is a friend,' the other man said, moving silently into the light. 'I am showing my concern as I would toward any friend.'

David Oh snorted derisively. 'Oh, I get it. Your concern about whether you will get this month's payment, more likely.'

The two men had a natural antipathy. David Oh was Shanghainese; Sung was Cantonese. The two did not mix well.

Formidable Sung's heavy moon face was as blank as a garden gate. 'The protection we provide for you and all the members of the Quarry here at your residences demands remuneration. That cannot be so difficult to understand.'

'Not at all,' David said. 'But let us not confuse business with friendship. Your money will be disbursed in the same manner as always.'

'That is not why I came. If I had required such information, I would have contacted you at your office. As I said, it was Jake Maroc's condition that brought me.'

David Oh had nothing more to say, so he turned away. Why did the Cantonese have to be here now at this moment? It had been Jake's idea to put his contacts to good use when he had been assigned here. Making his deal with Formidable Sung had been one of them, and it had proved an excellent one. David's relatives were rivals of Formidable Sung. David hated him for that. Or perhaps it was only the primitive railing of Shanghainese against Cantonese.

'Have you seen enough?'

'I have been here awhile, if that is your meaning. Good day.' Formidable Sung went out without a sound.

'*Dew neh loh moh!*' To have uttered that one word, *Jake*, with that son of a sea slime in the room. David rocked in shame. To have such a one be privy to my inner feelings!

Someday he will find a way to use that against me. Oh, gods curse my *joss*.

He made himself look down at Jake's sleeping face. In bandages. Dark bruises like thunderclouds. Say something to me, Jake. Anything.

David Oh sat down heavily in a chair by the bed. 'All gods great and small piss on all doctors.' He put down the paper cup he had been holding. The tea was cold and tasted as bitter as bile. 'What the hell do they really know, anyway? They tell us nothing, preferring to make us wait. That is what we pay them for, *heya*?'

He told himself that it was all *joss*, whether Jake woke or slept. But that wasn't good enough. David's mother was Catholic, and he had caught a whiff of the Western religion. He was like a man trapped on a spit of land between the ocean and a great lake. On the surface they appeared to be the same, but beneath they were so very different. Buddhists found contentment in living, in changing as the seasons changed, in accepting all that life had to offer . . . or take away. Catholics strove against the natural order, believing that man should be above such base instincts, that he should impose his own particular order on the anarchy that already existed.

If Jake slept on, David Oh knew that he would take it hard. How many times had they saved each other's lives in the ten years or so since Jake had been assigned to Hong Kong Station? Stupid to even try to count. They had shared death, and so they shared life with a bond closer than that of brothers. Brothers, after all, had only blood between them. Jake and David, in a way, shared minds.

Now he found himself angry at Jake for the singlemindedness of purpose that had made him risk all of it for a chance to bring in Nichiren like some great trophy from out of darkest Africa. What did a bastard like Nichiren count for, against someone like Jake?

David Oh sighed. He found hospital rooms odd, the

atmosphere so humid it seemed to dampen all coherent thought. Always, they seemed awash with violent emotion. It was as if, instead of the etching of a former Queen's clippers in Victoria Harbour and the colour portrait of the present Queen, the walls were hung with tears and wailing. Sorrow and resignation dominated here as they did in the slums nearby.

'David.'

David Oh stood jerkily. The shadows had spoken his name. He looked down at Jake Maroc's bandaged face and saw those feline eyes, a disturbing bronze-tinged topaz, staring up at him.

'*Dew neh loh moh!* Jake.' He sat down beside his friend. 'You've been out a long time. I'd better fetch the doctors. They'll want to – '

'Wait. I don't feel that bad.'

Maroc's words were crusty and brittle, as if he had lost the easy facility of speech. The tongue came out, questing along the ridge of dry lip. David Oh reached over and poured some water from a carafe. Gently he placed the cup against Maroc's mouth, allowing him to drink his fill.

'Nichiren?' The name seemed to be pulled from the very depths of him.

'Gone to ground, I'm afraid.'

Jake Maroc closed his eyes tightly. 'How long?'

'Four days now.'

'Should have had him.' There was nothing but anger in Jake's voice. 'I would've bet anything that this time he was down for the count.' Those yellow topaz eyes opened, fixing David Oh with their gaze. Not even what he had been through could dispel their fiery power. 'I want him, David.'

David Oh nodded. 'We'll get him.'

'Bullshit!' The force of emotion cost him, and he was silent for a time, regathering his strength. 'It's not wet section I'm thinking about. It's me.'

48

David Oh did not want to state the obvious. 'He's disappeared, Jake. We have no line on him at all.'

Jake's eyelids fluttered. David Oh felt as if his friend was struggling to remain conscious. 'How badly were the others hurt? How's Mandy?'

David Oh put his hands together to stop them from sweating. 'You're the only one who made it.'

'Oh, God!' Jake's eyes closed again. David Oh did not want to see the tears, but he had no choice. A searing pain tore through Jake's chest and he cried out so loudly that David Oh took hold of him, as if contact with another human being would be enough now to ease his suffering.

Oh, dear God in heaven, what have I done? Jake thought. As swiftly as the attack had come, it receded. In its wake he felt a spiritlessness, as if the very core of him, which had just moments before been filled with life, had now dissolved into bitter emptiness.

In the West, Descartes had perhaps given modern man his watchword phrase: *I think, therefore I am*. But, as with all things, in the East it was different.

We think, therefore I am. It was possible that no true Western man could fully comprehend that. Jake could. His unit, with whom he had lived and whom he had trained for more than a year, had taken on just that kind of collective presence. It was *dantai*. And it was their collective death that he had just experienced inside himself. They had been a self-sufficient entity. As was right and natural, a familial bond had sprung up between them, so that no matter what alien environment they were dropped into, they never really left the family circle. This was what gave them their almost legendary strength; it was what allowed them to do what no other unit in the Quarry was able to do: survive intact for a long time without respite from hazardous duty.

Once, when pressed to explicate further the *dantai*'s uncanny success rate, Jake had said to Rodger Donovan,

'Remember that the most famous of Japanese dramas, *Chushingura*, is not about one hero, but rather forty-seven.' But then Westerners were always asking direct questions and expecting in return direct answers. They were consequently at a loss when it came to interpreting oblique replies.

'They were all so young.'

It was like war, David Oh thought. That's what you said about the boys on the line. Time to plough on. 'Staff thinks there must have been a leak. You're too good. The *dantai* was our best unit.'

Maroc's eyes were red-rimmed, accentuating the bluish-black bruises on his cheeks. 'Betrayed? But by whom? No one in the *dantai* would have said a word.'

'There's always the possibility your intelligence was tainted.'

Jake shook his head. 'The source is unimpeachable.'

'Then I fear we must look elsewhere.' David Oh's voice had taken on a floating quality. He had no liking for what he had to do now. He saw the sweat beading on his friend's face, and suspected that his pulse rate was raised. He recognized that he did not have much time. 'At least there's no amnesia,' he said.

Jake was thinking of Nichiren's face. Had there been any surprise there? Had he been lying in wait for them? But there were others in the room with him. Two had died. One of them, Kisan, was purported to be Nichiren's only friend. None of that sounded as if he had been forewarned. 'You weren't there, David. I was. I don't believe there was a leak.' He struggled to sit up.

David Oh put a hand on his chest, pushing him back down. He wished he could say, 'Calm down,' but considering what he was about to tell him, that would be foolish. Rain drummed against the small windowpanes, gusts like angry fists.

'Was Mariana scheduled to go on any trips while you

were gone?' He forced his voice to remain even, knowing Jake would pick up any untoward nuance and pounce on it.

'None that I know of,' he said. 'If this debriefing's over, would you send her in? I'm sure she's anxious to see me up and making sense.'

'Mariana's not here, Jake.' David Oh was studying the other man. 'She was observed at Kai Tak just after your mission began. She boarded a JAL flight bound for Tokyo.'

In the flushed silence, he forced himself to continue. 'As you know, we have no one in Japan, so that's all we know. I checked your apartment for a note, an explanation, something. There was nothing. Nothing at all.'

'What?' Jake's face was white. 'What's happened to her?' He peered into David Oh's face, saw something there. 'For God's sake, tell me!'

'The consensus of opinion from staff seems to be that word of your raid was somehow transmitted to Nichiren prior to your arrival at O-henro House. Altogether we have ten people dead. That isn't easily explained.'

'David,' Jake said, shaking, 'for the love of God, what is all this?'

'Mariana got a call on the evening of your raid. We know that it came from Tokyo. Just this morning, the Janitors narrowed the origination field down to the district: Toshima-ku.'

And Jake immediately thought, O-henro House is in Toshima-ku.

David Oh went on. 'Within forty minutes of taking that call, Mariana was at Kai Tak Airport. Twenty minutes after that, she boarded a JAL flight to Tokyo.'

'Where did she go?'

David Oh shrugged. 'You know that's not our field of influence,' he said pointedly.

'It's not possible,' Jake whispered. 'Mariana knows no

one in Japan. No one at all. What would she be doing there?'

'Staff thought maybe you could tell them.'

'Well, I can't, dammit!'

David Oh leaned forward. He felt his personal anger at Jake overflowing. 'Do you have any idea what a mess your raid has made? It has jeopardized the President's entire reciprocal trade plan – '

'Fuck the President!' Jake said. 'Nichiren's more important than any – '

'It has jeopardized the entire Quarry!' David Oh let that sink in a moment before he continued. 'What are we to make of Mariana's disappearance? Is it a coincidence that of all the destinations in the world, she should choose the one to which, under a cloak of absolute secrecy, you were headed? You tell me.' He looked at Jake. 'Beridien suspects that we're looking at some kind of iceberg here.'

'Is that your opinion, too?'

'I don't know.'

'*Amida*, David, what I did, I did on my own. Like a single drop of ink on a blank page. That's all there is to it. Beridien's swiping at paper tigers.'

'Maybe so, but you know how he is. If you don't know why Mariana took off, we sure don't. He won't rest until he knows it all.'

'Neither will I.'

Rain continued to drum against the windowpanes. David walked away from the high bed, stared out and down at the rain-darkened concrete. 'Buddha, but it's foul out there.' A woman got out of a red Nissan and ran through the downpour toward the overhang of the hospital's entrance. David admired her legs, the sheen of her hair. He liked the way she ran, with strength and agility. A powerful sense of purpose.

He turned back into the room. 'Jake, how bad were things between you and Mariana?'

'I don't want to talk about it.'

'I apologize for intruding, but the answer may be vital.'

Jake closed his eyes for a moment. 'Not bad. Not good, either.'

'I'm afraid Beridien won't be satisfied with that.'

He looked hard at David Oh. 'We hadn't made love in six months. Is that intimate enough for you?'

'What happened?'

'I don't know. We drifted apart. We changed. Who knows? It's all garbage anyway.'

'It wasn't garbage when you got married.'

'We were different then.' Jake was looking at nothing.

'Well, *you're* different, anyway.'

Jake's eyes focused on David Oh. 'What does that mean?'

David Oh came away from the window. 'You're not the same person I used to know, Jake. Ever since you came back from the massacre at Sumchun River, you've been moving through life like an automaton. You only think of one thing – Nichiren.'

'I don't see anything wrong with that. The man's a machine for murder. He embraces death as if it were his lover. He must be stopped.'

'And he will be. But perhaps you cannot do it alone.'

Jake's eyes were so fierce that David Oh found himself unable to stare into them for long. 'I can and will. Don't think anyone or anything will stop me.'

'I understand. Not even Mariana.'

'What?'

'Jake, Nichiren's all you seem to care about. You have no time for her; you have no time for me or anyone else. Nichiren has crowded all of us out of your life. We used to have fun on our time off. Now all you want to talk about is your next plan to trap Nichiren. I can't remember the last time you smiled.'

'With him out there, there's nothing to smile about.'

David Oh pointed a finger at him. 'That's where you're

53

wrong, pal. You say that Nichiren embraces death as if it were his lover. I see you doing precisely the same thing. You haven't been living these past three years since Sumchun; you've been dying.'

There was a soft knock on the door. Both men turned as it opened. David was surprised to see the security guard usher in the woman he had seen running through the parking lot. Through the sliver of the opening he could see only her eyes, part of her small nose, the centre of her lips. She was quite beautiful enough to take his breath away.

'Is Jake Maroc here?'

He nodded mutely, then turned to Jake. He felt her presence acutely even through the barrier of the wooden door. 'Think about what I said, *heya*? It could be important.' He went out past the woman.

In a moment she had come fully into the room. She stood with her back against the door, stiff, almost as if she were afraid to move further.

Jake had been struggling to stay awake. He was terribly exhausted; consciousness was a gauzy layer of veils that seemed to float through his blurred mind with the inconstancy of a dream.

He sensed a presence in the room and said, 'Who's there?' A blackness full of sleep yawned like a chasm before him. His body ached all over and he wanted to escape from it. Sleep seemed like a fine idea.

The presence intruded upon him, edging back the slumber with rude hands.

'Who's there?' he said again, more softly this time.

'Don't you recognize me?'

The woman came away from the door to stand by his bed. 'Oh, Jake,' she said. She put a hand out and touched his cheek between the bandages.

His hand came up and grasped her arm, feeling along the skin. His eyes struggled to focus.

'Who?'

'It's Bliss,' she said. 'We used to – '

'Play with the snakes on Ladder Street!' His eyes opened wide in astonishment. He felt the quickening of his pulse. He tried to rise toward her, but could not. 'Bliss, how is it possible – '

'That was in the winter,' she went on. 'In the summer we'd steal dried skate from the stores in the Western District.'

'And eat pork chops and rice out of cardboard boxes along the docks at Central all year long!' A deathly slumber was fast overtaking him, but he refused to close his eyes. 'It's been so long. But I remember.' He drank her in, comparing reality with his memories. How many times had he wondered what Bliss would look like, full grown? Now he knew. He seemed to sigh then. 'You were so little – just a girl. Once upon a time.'

He held on to her arm, stroking her as if he were a blind man.

'Bliss,' he whispered. 'What are you doing here? After all this time. It seems impossible. Impossible.'

'Rest now,' she said softly. 'There will be time enough when you wake.'

Washington, like all the great capitals of the world, ran on power. The people who worked there were drawn to the city as if it were the epicentre of an incipient earthquake. The mere mortals of the world – the working stiffs who laboured from nine to five and went home to eat their meat and potatoes in front of their TVs and their squalling kids, before lumbering off to bed to lie sweatily atop their wives in comic imitation of intimacy – could discern nothing of the invisible emanations that attracted the power elite to Washington.

Power means different things in different places. In New York, America's financial capital, it means arriving at a

Broadway opening in a new Volvo stretch limo; in Hollywood, America's entertainment capital, it means playing tennis with Sylvester Stallone. In Washington – where, for those who know, the *real* power lies – it is defined in increments of perks. For the director of the Quarry, the perks were many and dazzling.

For Antony Beridien, by far the best was this sprawling 19th-century mansion in Great Falls, Virginia. Set into the lowlands of a small but spacious valley between rolling emerald hills, it was just under an hour from Quarry HQ in northwest Washington. It had once been an OSS, then a CIA safe house. It was said that Eisenhower and Dulles, as well as Wild Bill Donovan, had used its cool sanctuary during World War II, but of course that was solely rumour. That Antony Beridien chose to believe it implicitly was perhaps a measure of his love for it.

Newly repainted precisely the same shade of off-white as it had first been painted, the house was filled with arching gables, rounded turrets, and, along one side, an enormous, screened-in porch with a floor of pine planking painted battleship grey. It was filled with oversized white wicker furniture with cushions and pillows of a deep maroon background on which were printed dark green and off-white leaves in a kind of jungle pattern.

Inside, the gigantic rooms were filled with antiques that Beridien had painstakingly collected from around the world. A professional decorator might have winced at the confluence of pristine Federal-period chairs and desk with a massively ornate Louis XIV ormolu clock on the spotted marble mantel and a magnificent Chippendale breakfront beside it, but Beridien couldn't have cared less. Here within this house, he could feel time in all its grandeur.

Moving slowly from room to room, he could trace the monumental procession of the ages of Western man from Renaissance forward. Here, far from the necessarily ultra-modern blankness of the Quarry, he could stretch his mind on the wings of man's great artistic accomplishments and think through knotty problems he could never seem to unravel at the office.

Beridien unashamedly revelled in this particular perk. Though Quarry funds had bought the house, though they maintained it, though they allowed him to nurture it and its magnificent grounds filled with carefully pruned rose and tulip gardens and meticulously shorn formal topiaries, he nevertheless thought of this house as his own.

It was he who had provided it with its current name, Greystoke, since in his spare time Beridien was an avid reader of the many short novels of Edgar Rice Burroughs. It was because of Beridien that the President came here, the Secretary of Defense, a majority of the members of the Joint Chiefs. Power flowed through these old rooms like hot blood. Antony Beridien's power. He was entitled to call Greystoke his own.

This sun-drenched afternoon, he and Henry Wunderman were lunching on light fare – cold poached salmon with a lemony dill mayonnaise, a bright salad of endive and radicchio that was Beridien's favourite and, not coincidentally, a speciality of Greystoke's chef.

Because of the heat – Beridien allowed no air conditioning in the house – he had decided to dine on the spacious porch. Birds sang in the topiary and the nearby woods. Great hovering bumblebees droned somnolently in the rose garden. Beridien himself poured more Perrier for them both. There was no alcohol, not even wine, served during working hours.

'I'm glad you came, Henry,' Beridien said after a time. He had pushed his plate away from him, clearing his palate with the Perrier. Wunderman had finished before him.

A houseboy came and took the dishes away. Nothing more was said until he reappeared with small metal dishes of pear sorbet rimed with ice.

'After my outburst at the meeting last week – '

'That's all in the past, Antony,' Wunderman said, just as if he had had an actual choice in the matter. 'It's forgotten.'

'Good, good.' Beridien had lighted into his dessert, so it was unclear whether he was responding to Wunderman or commenting on the sorbet. He ate mechanically, but his face was filled with pleasure. In time he sighed, scraping the metal dish with his empty spoon. He poured himself coffee from an insulated picnic carafe. Wunderman had not touched his dessert.

'Friendship has its place in the natural order of things, of course.' Beridien was staring past Wunderman, his eyes fixed on the furry body of a bumblebee at work rubbing rose pollen all over its legs. 'However, it often slips my mind, so I know it must slip yours from time to time, that we do not live amongst the natural order of things.'

'You and I, Henry, are in the business of imposing our own brand of order on the anarchy of the world. That's a heavy responsibility. It takes all of our brainpower to keep it going, to make the shining web of our choosing work, despite' – he shrugged – 'oh, inclement weather, inhospitable terrain, the efforts of pests inimical to its creation. I think you understand my meaning, Henry.'

'Yes, sir. I do.'

'We are different from most people in the world,' Beridien went on, 'and that's by our own choosing. We're misfits, maybe. Surely we'd never be content with the humdrum. For my own self, I know that saddled with that kind of life, I'd blow my brains out.

'No, no. What we like to do – what we *crave* – is dancing in the dark. It's that edge of not knowing what's just around the bend that gets us. We're extrapolators, Henry. Seers. We look into the future and divine the strategic trends of the future.'

'By putting our hands in goat entrails,' Wunderman said, 'like the Romans.'

Beridien laughed and his eyes came back to his immediate surroundings. 'Very good indeed, Henry. Yes. I suppose there's a parallel there, somewhere.' He shifted in his chair. 'But the Quarry was created by me out of divination, pure and simple. Trends. Trends were what formed us, like a shell created out of a constant current.'

He brought out a red-bound file, opened it. His finger stabbed out. 'Do you realize what we've done with Israel? Each year we give them one-point-seven *billion* dollars in military aid, even though the country devotes fully half of its annual budget to military spending. Then we give them a further eight hundred fifty million in economic aid.'

Wunderman was perplexed. 'We both know that Israel's our only stable ally in the Middle East. If we don't prop them up, who will? I can't believe you've swung a hundred eighty degrees and are now advocating cutting aid to them.'

'No, no. Not at all.' Beridien seemed annoyed, as if he were a professor whose star pupil had turned into a moron before his eyes. 'It's not giving them the aid that disturbs me, but what that aid is doing to them.' His finger stabbed down at the file once more. 'Despite our help, there is a critical economic crisis in Israel. Inflation is running at over 200 per cent per year! Think of that, man! Besides which, the pound's value is continually deteriorating. Something drastic will have to be done there soon to stabilize the country.'

He glanced down at the sheets of paper. 'Now consider this: the industrial nation with the highest and most solid growth rate over the past two decades has been Japan. What does that tell you?'

Wunderman decided that, given Beridien's current mood, he'd be better off showing his ignorance than giving a wrong answer. 'What are you getting at, Antony?'

'Just this,' Beridien said. 'Israel, with billions in military spending each year, is on the brink of economic collapse. Japan's economy, on the other hand, is going great guns.' He hunched forward, his elbows on the parquet tabletop. 'Why? Could it be solely good management? How could it? The Israelis, as we well know, are far from stupid. In fact, we'd do well, in some areas, to learn from them. Then *what*?

'The politics of destruction,' he said, answering his own question. 'The current from which the Quarry was formed. The divination I made, way back in the dark ages, about the nature of the world in the future. And that future, Henry, is today!'

Beridien slammed shut the red folder, placed his open hand on it. 'It's all in this dossier. What it shows is that there is an inverse correlation to military spending and healthy economic growth. Japan's military spending is almost nil compared to that of Israel's.

'One of Lenin's most oft-quoted phrases is "Imperialism is the final phase of capitalism."' Beridien smiled. 'What would be a better definition of imperialism than arms sales, hmm?

'Yet the Communists engage in it, often quite heavily. There's a report here from last year's Soviet summit on economy in Novosibirsk. The consensus among those gathered was that rising military expenditures were a strong deterrent to their country's growth.

'Last year, North Korea supplied eight hundred eighty million dollars in arms to Iraq, even though it is allied with Iran, Iraq's enemy. This year the figure will increase half again. Thirty-one Third World countries increased by 100 per cent or more their military spending from 1965 to 1985. Of course, almost everyone will recognize Egypt, Iran, Syria, and Iraq among them. But perhaps you and I are the only ones not surprised by the inclusion of Honduras, Nigeria, Zambia, Zimbabwe, and Kuwait. Today, the military's the fastest-growing component of world trade.'

Wunderman cleared his throat. 'And that's mostly our doing.'

Beridien's eyes were sparkling. 'Oh, yes. You and I know that. Whether his motivations are ideological, religious, or merely political, a country's leader will surely feel safer with a bigger, better-equipped army than those of his enemies. But we know that military spending is not just destructive to economic growth but also to *political stability*.'

Wunderman listened to all this with one ear. Part of his mind was considering what Beridien had said about friendship, about how those inside the Quarry were somehow different, had chosen this life *because* of that difference. The humdrum.

But if Wunderman was honest with himself, he knew that he had not joined the Quarry to escape a nine-to-five prison. He had joined to prove to himself – and to his wife – that he could be accepted into a club filled with Ivy League MBAs with Mensa-calibre brains.

Wunderman had graduated from a state university. His marks had been middling, and when his professors were interviewed while he was being recruited by the Quarry, they had said he was an uninspired student at best. Some had needed quite a bit of prodding to remember him; several could not recall him at all.

The Quarry recruiters liked that, seeing in this vagueness the glimmering of a talent. The fact was, no one remembered Wunderman. He had that quality of being able to slip through crowds unnoticed.

His wife, Marjorie, noticed him, however. She had been Homecoming Queen at one of the Seven Sisters colleges. She was beautiful, and smart enough to finish right behind the valedictorian of her graduating class.

She and Wunderman had met at a mixer that he and several friends crashed. He had looked so out of place that she gravitated to him at once. Wunderman never had understood what she saw in him, but then he could never quite grasp the way women saw the world.

He could not possibly have understood that by her sophomore year, Marjorie had had her fill of intellectually snobbish young men, groomed in style, outfitted in Paul Stuart clothing, racing through the fallen leaves of the campus grounds in their Jaguars and Triumph Spitfires. They had spoken of clubs and polo and horseback riding as if these were the world's primary concerns.

She had seen a sweetness in Wunderman that others mistook for shyness. And, taking the time to speak with him, she found him bright, curious, and flexible, three qualities she had felt certain she would never find in a man.

By their second date, she knew that she wanted to see no one else. By their fourth, she was certain that she was in love. By then, Wunderman had needed little persuading to get married. Marjorie had stunned him from the first moment he saw her coming toward him across the gym floor. Her attraction to him seemed to him more miraculous than his winning the Irish Sweepstakes.

In this he was utterly serious. His insecurity about her love had led him into a recurring nightmare in which he woke up one morning to find out that, indeed, he was married to Marjorie but he himself was someone who wore Harris tweeds, played golf without a handicap, and spoke with a Bostonian accent.

The dream always ended with Wunderman staring at himself in the mirror and seeing a face tanned by the sun and wind, healthy and impossibly handsome. He would put his hands up to his cheeks and they would melt like putty, remoulding themselves into Wunderman's true face. Seeing this, Wunderman in his dream felt engulfed by panic that Marjorie would wake up and, seeing him, know what a terrible mistake she had made.

Their house in rural Virginia, not so very far from Greystoke, had, during their first years together, seemed lifeless. By then he had told Marjorie enough of what he had got into so that she had said more than once that the place seemed to her inhabited by shadows. For many years he had refused her the one thing that really mattered to her: having children. The uncertainty of his life made him adamant. He had lost his father – a seaman – when he was only seven. He did not want the same fate to befall his unborn children.

It had taken Marjorie's threat to leave for him to see the importance to her of having a baby. At last he had relented, terrified that his one nightmare would come true. Now, later in life than any of their friends, they had two teenaged children, a boy and a girl.

Not a day went by that Wunderman did not find himself fearful for them. But he recognized this feeling as something he felt for Marjorie as well. She had been right all along: if he wanted this life, the fear was something with which he would have to live.

'Political instability,' Beridien was saying now, 'is our bread and butter, Henry. That was how I perceived it twenty-five years ago. Kennedy agreed with me. His name is on our charter, and I'm damned proud of that. The revisionism that's gone on lately about him and his presidency is, in my opinion, disgusting. He was a President with guts, which was why he saw a need for us apart, distinct, totally separate from the CIA.

'We've used the agency as our whipping boy on more than one occasion, I can tell you. We like to let the world see what idiots they are from time to time. That kind of thing relaxes people, makes them feel superior.' Beridien chuckled. 'That's just how we like them.' He gestured. 'Then came the scandal. I imagine even you don't know that I engineered that. Some members of the press were getting too close to finding out about us. The President and I figured a smoke screen was our best defence.' He shrugged. 'Anyway, the resultant housecleaning at the CIA did them some good. Got rid of most of their most flagrant dead wood.'

He cleared his throat. 'Speaking of dead wood, Henry, I'm thinking of sending Stallings into Japan after Mariana Maroc.'

'I don't understand,' Wunderman said. 'Stallings excels at two things: planning and killing.'

'Yes, that's quite true.' Beridien tapped his steepled fingertips together as if contemplating this fact for the first time. 'This isn't a snap decision, I assure you.' He drew out a folded flimsy from his jacket pocket, handed it across.

Wunderman took it, unfolding it slowly. He felt as if a ball of ice had suddenly congealed in his stomach.

'The end phrase of the Janitors' report on the RISS phone call,' Beridien said. His voice held that peculiar note of detached calm that judges used to possess when the country as a whole condoned execution.

Wunderman looked up. 'The call she got came from O-henro House.'

'Where Nichiren was waiting for Jake Maroc, yes.' Beridien took possession of the flimsy. 'I'm sorry, Henry. But you must remember what I said before about friendship. It is a luxury for people such as ourselves. And oftentimes it is a dangerous luxury. I fear that this is just such a time.

'Mariana Maroc's connection with Nichiren must be explored. We must get to the root of it immediately. And, most importantly, we must destroy it.' He paused for a moment. 'Don't you agree, Henry?'

Wunderman felt **numb**. He remembered the times he would go to Hong Kong. Staying at Jake's. Mariana would take care of him as if he were a favourite uncle. She had taught him all about the Crown Colony, taking him out on tours of each section, explaining the history, the mixes of dialects, religions, outlooks. She had showed him the power of the Governor, the triads, the Royal Hong Kong Jockey Club. Through her, he was shown the mad whirligig world of Chinese gambling, Chinese dining, Chinese architecture. And when he had fallen ill with the flu, she had stayed up all night with him replacing compresses that his high fever quickly turned from cold to warm.

'Henry?'

Mariana Maroc and Nichiren? The concept sounded like the ravings of a madman. What sense did it make? But the RISS could not lie and the Janitors could not make a mistake of that magnitude. He had to face the truth. Nichiren had called Mariana on the night of Jake's raid. It was inconceivable that anyone else at O-henro House had placed the call. No one there was even aware she existed.

'Henry, I'm waiting.'

Betrayal was a concept that Wunderman lived with from day to day; it was part and parcel of the shadow world he had chosen to inhabit. But the sources of those betrayals never failed to confound him. He was far from the sort of cool and calculating spy portrayed in fiction who expects betrayal from his best friend, his girlfriend, even his wife. Such betrayals depressed him profoundly, the surprise sapping his energy like a bite from a vampire. He felt the shrivelling inside himself, the involuntary tightening of his scrotum, the male animal's first primitive response to unexpected danger. He felt sad and dispirited.

'I don't want to make this kind of irrevocable move without your consent,' Beridien said. 'I believe it's your right.'

'Thumbs up or down,' Wunderman said softly. 'Just like the Romans.'

Beridien recalled Wunderman's earlier reference, and nodded. 'Just like the Romans.'

Wunderman got up from the table. Outside, the day was

clouding over. All the bright colours were muted, as if the flowers were hiding their faces from him.

'So be it,' he said. The rolling hills, now a deep hunter's green, seemed far away from him. 'Thumbs down.'

Shi Zilin stepped out of the black official car the moment it ground to a halt just inside the gates of Xiangshan. These Fragrant Hills, as they were called, perhaps twelve miles northwest of Beijing, were closed to the public in 1972. Zilin loved to come here. The peace helped to drive away his increasing pain. Behind him and to the left was the main square fronting that portion of the Summer Palace known as Yuanmingyuan. The grounds there were, of course, a prime tourist attraction.

Personally, Zilin found them sad. After they had been sacked and torched by the English and French in 1860, an attempt at restoration had petered out in 1879 through a paucity of money.

After that, the few remaining pieces of marble, sculpture, sections of hand-glazed tile, and brick disappeared. All the trees, carefully cultivated over the centuries, were cut down for firewood, the larger structures dismantled to get at the iron that held the sections together.

Of the Chinese structures – made entirely of wood – not a trace was left. Some walls and remnants of a few of the European palaces remained amid the flat ricefields where once the great, intricate gardens had stretched for acres.

Zilin had deliberately turned his back on all this and was looking, rather, to the Fragrant Hills, with their purple-grey slopes running side by side with Yuquanshan, Jade Fountain Hill. Here, centuries ago, a massive geological upheaval had spewed a layer of hard sinian limestone onto the surface of the hill. In the process, the violent forces had transmogrified the limestone into marble, which had been first used by the Qin to build palaces, temples, and a park. Once there had been many Buddhist and

66

Taoist temples, along with a number of exquisite rock shrines carved into the marble hill.

Now Zilin had turned it into a military zone so that it would not be overrun by curiosity seekers as China opened its doors further to the West. Officers and infantry soldiers alike saluted him as he made his slow way up the hill. He hated the metal brace he was forced to wear on his right leg, but without it the pain would incapacitate his muscles.

He worked out every day in his villa just outside Beijing using aquatonics as well as isometrics and exercises with weights. Every other day a renowned acupressurist visited him, and once a week, like clockwork, his acupuncturist arrived to do his work.

None of this, Zilin knew, was a cure for the degenerative disease he had, but at his age, which was now nearing eighty-six, that did not matter much. Relief of pain was his short-range goal, and this his minions provided with satisfactory regularity.

Zilin turned his head to catch the summer breeze. The rice paddies were all around him, comforting him, somehow easing his pain. His eyes alighted on the edges of the buildings comprising Qinghua University, on the other side of the wide field, burnished in the sun.

That was another reason Zilin liked to come here. Along with nature, he felt closer to the young men and women who were literally China's future. It was so difficult to make his fellow ministers see that China's most precious natural resource was its young people. To a man, his colleagues mistrusted the young, fearing the treacherous influence of Western decadence, and sought in every way to inhibit the younger generation as they themselves were inhibited fifty years ago.

There was, Zilin thought sadly, more than a resistance to change within his country. There was an almost xeno- phobic fear of it. Resistance was one thing. The rushing water could eventually wear away the obdurate rock face, smoothing it to the rills and dells of its current.

But fear was another matter entirely. It was an unreasoning response and therefore immune to the effect of normal erosion. Fear insinuated itself into the very fabric of things, making them impervious, immutable.

Yet even this could not deter Zilin. If the stream, in its endless flow, could not erode an object in its path, it must then change its path, leaving that object alone to dry in the baking sun. And soon, without the stream's protection, the natural forces would crack it open, destroying it utterly.

This was the fate Zilin planned for his enemies, who were both numerous and powerful. Perhaps, together, they were more powerful than he. Like the cycles of the ages, they seemed to renew themselves, becoming ever more cunning and determined to bring him down.

Twice now within the past five years there had been a concerted effort to oust him. Once the idea had been to make of him the same kind of example that the Gang of Four had been. That failed, and just over a year later that same *qun*, a group of ministers, had sought to retire him quietly on the grounds of his advancing age and illness.

Just after that second failure, two of the more virulent members of the *qun* had met with unfortunate and fatal accidents just a month apart. At least the official investigation findings had labelled them accidents. Perhaps the remaining members of the *qun* felt otherwise, for since that time, Zilin had encountered no interference from any of them and the opening of China to at least some capitalist profit methods had begun.

That is, until six weeks ago. From one of his many sources, it had been made clear to him that a rising young – in Chinese terminology, that meant fifty-two-year-old – bureaucrat by the name of Wu Aiping, who had within the past year been appointed as the head of the Scientific and Technological Institute for National Defence, had contacted one of the members of the *qun*. Wu Aiping, as Zilin knew well, had the ear of the Communist Party Chief and the Defence Minister. Tremendous amounts of money were being siphoned into the Institute because, they were all agreed, a modern defence was of paramount importance for the new China. That made him powerful indeed, much more so than any single member of the *qun*, who were, nevertheless, all high-ranking ministers. It was Wu Aiping who was spearheading the fight against China's turning away from strict Marxist-Leninist ideology.

Zilin was passing graveyards on either side. It was as if the entire history of China were buried along this road, endless families who had endured it all: weather, changing dynasties, invasions by the Manchus, the Japanese, and the *gwai loh* of so many nations. And still China endured. It had been battered and beaten, decimated by the stupidity of the Manchu government and, much later, the warlords like Chiang and the demigods like Mao.

It occurred to Zilin now that, despite his best efforts to the contrary, his beloved country had been regressing in almost every area since the end of World War II. And still regression threatened.

Was there to be no end to it? he asked himself.

The silent spirits of those buried all around him seemed to fill the air with a concerted murmuring. *No more*, they seemed to whisper in his ear. *There must be an end for China to survive into the 21st century.*

There were tears in Zilin's eyes as he came to the crossroads and took the right fork. Around the turning stood Wofosi, the Temple of the Sleeping Buddha.

The place, once renowned through all China for its rare trees, was among the oldest in the Beijing environs. The temple itself was built by the Tang, and although it was said that a sandalwood statue of the Buddha already rested in the spot, in 1321 the Yuan used 500,000 pounds of copper to cast a new and more splendid one. Seven

69

thousand workmen were involved in the task. It took them two attempts and a total of ten years to accomplish what would be impossible to do today due to the prohibitive costs.

True to the heritage of the spot, Zilin had brought a very up-to-date School of Forestry to the long deserted annex building. But as for the temple itself, that was left intact for him.

Inside, he became utterly lost within the tranquillity of the place. There was no door, thus birds and small forest animals made use of the interior. Birdcalls echoed from the rafters, seeming to hover in melody on the bars of thick sunlight.

There might have been a great many places that Zilin could have used for such moments of quiet contemplation. But in none of the others did he feel the manifestation of the Buddha with such strength of purpose.

What validity had communism, he thought now, in the presence and power of such universal law?

He sat with some difficulty on one of the two camp chairs on either side of a stone table in which a *wei qi* board was set. A game was already in progress. Zilin turned his eyes to its familiar configuration but his mind was still elsewhere.

Wu Aiping's solicitation of the *qun* coincided to the week with Zilin's initiation of the final phase of his Hong Kong schemata. That did not bode well. Zilin was too old to believe in coincidence, at least anything on this scale. Though his security had been excellent, the schemata had been running for many years. It would, therefore, be foolish to assume that some hint of them, no matter how small, would not have leaked out.

Zilin addressed himself once more to the *wei qi* board. It was composed of nineteen vertical and nineteen horizontal lines. The game was played with small oval stones of cool shell with a curiously silken texture that never failed to

70

delight him as he scooped them up from within their side bowls, fingering them between the pads of thumb and forefinger as he thought. Black and white, they were arrayed much like armies in ancient times. Here, on the board, they were placed on any one of the 361 *lu* or intersections of lines.

In this complexity of territories, routes, liaisons, strong and weak lines, in which the two contending forces must strike, unite within themselves, extend, and recover if each was to seal off sections of territory and thus gain the winning advantage over the other, Zilin saw a microcosm of the real world.

There was a stirring from the mouth of the temple, and Zilin looked up to see a figure in silhouette against the sunlight streaming in obliquely behind him. Even without any visual details, Zilin could imagine the slightly dumpy body, almost comically wreathed in its ill-fitting, rumpled suit.

'Come on, come on, Zhang Hua,' he said. 'You're so late, I almost started without you.'

The other man hurried to the chair opposite the one on which Zilin sat. He wiped his wide Mongolian face with a linen handkerchief, then blew his nose into it. He pushed his wire-rimmed spectacles back up the almost nonexistent, flattened bridge of his nose. 'I must make a note to myself not to be late,' he said apologetically.

'One of these days.' Zilin laughed good-naturedly. Then, seeing the look on the other man's face, he said, 'Look here, Zhang Hua, we are friends as well as senior minister and junior minister. We have worked together on official as well as clandestine affairs for – how long – twelve years now? It seems to me that lateness is your only vice. So be it, then! All men should have one vice – so long as it's a minor one. Don't you think so?'

'I wish I had none, Shi Zilin.'

'But, my dear Zhang Hua, that is pure foolishness. I do

not trust the man who professes to have no weaknesses. I think, What does that protestation hide? No, no, you must understand that minor vices protect us from the major ones.'

He reached out to place a black stone on the *tian yuan*, the single most important of the nine *xing* or stars, intersections that divide the battleground into territorial zones. *Tian yuan* was in the belly, the middle of the road. In its new position, a series of consequences rippled forth from the piece: heretofore hidden strategies were revealed, new possibilities opened up, others closed off.

Each piece could have up to four *qi*, or breaths. To surround an enemy stone on all sides was to deprive it of all its *qi*. This was the move Zilin had just made. The dead white stone stared up at the combatants.

'You'll have to take care of your casualty, Zhang Hua.'

'A message was delivered to your office this morning,' the aide said as he removed his stone and scanned the board for his next move. He recognized the upper right and left quadrants as veritable minefields of *huo yan*. At first glance, they appeared inviting, seeming only to be innocent *yan*, 'eyes.' But Zhang Hua recognized them as lethal traps. The difficult *huo yan* were a trademark of Shi Zilin.

'This Friday at nine you are summoned to appear before the Premier.'

Zilin grunted. 'Bad news. Did the summons give a reason, or name anyone who might be present?'

'No.'

'Even worse.' Zilin looked up from the board. His eyes locked with Zhang Hua's. 'My friend, we must assume this summons is at the instigation of Wu Aiping.'

'I am afraid so.'

Zilin glanced down. 'You haven't moved.'

Zhang Hua had not taken his eyes off the senior minister's face. 'Shi Zilin, I am frightened. That man terrifies me.'

'I understand,' Zilin said. 'And it is good that Wu Aiping frightens you. It means that you understand the full depth of his threat to us, and all we have worked so long to create.' He smiled his confidence. 'Terror is a human emotion, my friend. You must learn to respect it rather than be afraid of it. When you come to understand even such a primitive emotion as terror, you can then use it.' He nodded. 'Yes, Zhang Hua, use even that.'

'Fear paralyses me.'

'Yet,' Zilin confided, 'we both know the meaning of real fear. It was bad enough when we had only to deal with the Russian navy and air force in Vladivostok and several other lesser Far Eastern ports. These threats, along with Soviet forces in Siberia, have been a hammer over our heads since the end of World War II.'

Zilin's ebon eyes were deep and lustrous, reeling Zhang Hua into the whirlpool of power that emanated from the old man like a furnace at peak power. 'But now comes a series of more frightening developments. Over the last three years the Russians have begun upgrading their fifty-odd divisions, seven of them armoured, along our northern frontier. In Eastern Siberia, where we are particularly vulnerable, they have deployed just under one hundred TU-22 bombers and one hundred fifty SS-20 mobile missiles with nuclear warheads. The bombers, by the way, known as Backfire by the Americans, have a range of five thousand miles carrying nuclear weaponry, either bombs or air-to-surface missiles.

'And that is not the worst of it. The United States, in its infinite wisdom, built the largest airfields and naval installations in the entire Southeast Asian region in Cam Ranh Bay and Da Nang. Now that they have fled Vietnam, the Russians have taken over those bases. From them, Soviet personnel now administer manpower and material, overseeing the entire region.

'For a time, only reconnaissance aircraft were launched

from there. But recently you know we have photographed TU-16 medium-range bombers at the airfields. Naval patrols from Cam Ranh Bay have increased from eleven thousand five hundred ship hours at sea in 1981 to twenty-seven thousand just last year.

'Now the Soviets can strike at us from the north *and* the south. They have a virtual ring of military strength surrounding China. We are in a noose, my friend.

'And in a worldwide view, the Russians also have striking power into the Straits of Malacca, should there be more of an escalation in the Mideast war. It is through that strait that all the oil tankers bound for the South China Sea sail. Under air cover from six expanded and modernized airfields in Afghanistan, the Russians can send battleships and destroyers into the northern Indian Ocean. They also have a potentially huge auxiliary ground force in the Vietnamese army, which numbers roughly one million soldiers.'

Zilin spread his hands over the battle arrayed upon the *wei qi* board. 'This China noose must be our first concern, Zhang Hua. How unimportant a presence is Wu Aiping, compared with that mailed fist so brilliantly designed and executed by General Anatoly Karpov.'

'I wish I had your confidence, minister.'

No, Zilin thought, I do not believe that you would want this crushing pressure, my friend. But then, he knew that everyone wanted to sit wherever he was not. That, too, was human nature.

In truth, Zilin wondered whether he had as much confidence as the younger man was giving him credit for. Certainly he had fended off attacks against himself before. He was the last scarred warrior from the old days. True, he had had some close scrapes, had run up against any number of cunning opponents. But Wu Aiping was some-how different from the rest. Perhaps it was because he was from another generation. The thought that men such as

74

Wu Aiping might form the generation of China's future caused Zilin to shudder inwardly. How different this man was from the legions of the country's youth, at Zilin's own School of Forestry or even at the nearby University, preparing themselves for China's new tomorrow.

Indeed, there was good reason to fear Wu Aiping. Perhaps in all of Beijing he was the only man who could undo the years of work on the Hong Kong schemata.

And, given the ghost of a chance, Zilin knew he would do just that.

Zhang Hua had taken a white stone from the shallow dish on the side of the board. On the lower quadrant he found what he was looking for and placed his stone on an intersection. He had completed *zhang*, an extension, giving back two sources of breath to a stone of his that had been under attack on the adjacent intersection.

'Why should Wu Aiping bother you, my friend,' Zilin said, 'when you move with such precision and daring?'

'Because this is *wei qi*. When my stone is deprived of its four breaths, I only take it off the board. I am still alive.'

You are wrong, my friend, Zilin said silently. And that is the difference between you and me. You cannot see beyond the board; you do not understand the life-applications of this strategy. That is why you are a fine player, but not Jian.

He selected a black stone and in the lower left corner of the board was about to place his piece on the 5–19 intersection. He did not look up, and his keen ears heard no sound, but his sixth sense picked up Zhang Hua's increased tension.

By playing this stone here, Zilin would have 'struck lightly.' This *pu* would prevent six white stones from uniting. But after due consideration, he decided to play his stone elsewhere on the board.

Zhang Hua took no time for his next move, playing his white stone on the 5–19 intersection to prevent his opponent from returning there. He breathed an inaudible sigh of relief.

'But General Karpov is not all we have to worry about, Zhang Hua,' he said now. 'Behind and above Karpov is another man. In his way he is far more dangerous to us. Yuri Lantin. It is he who sees China's destruction as a necessary first step in Russia's goal of world domination. If we cannot neutralize Yuri Lantin, then we are doomed. But our assault on him must be delicate, consumed by stealth, from a quarter impossible to defend.

'We must discover his killing ground and get him there while his mind is focused elsewhere.'

Zilin took up his black stone and struck it at the open 7–19 intersection, thus creating *huo yan*, a 'movable eye'. He had taken all six of Zhang Hua's stones. He could not have accomplished that, had not Zhang Hua played at 5–19.

I see the parallels, Zilin thought. Each moment of each hour of each day brings change. Change frightens most people, but in change I see the essence of strategy. Like an artist putting colour to canvas, I observe that often movement in and of itself is enough of an attack. I have learned to use everything. Not moving can sometimes be an attack. I have just proved that.

Yes, *wei qi* and life are inseparable. For those who can see it. For those who can use it. For those bold enough to Steal the Light. As Laotse wrote, the Jian excels at saving: there is no useless person; nothing is rejected.

Jake chased shadows down a narrow, twining street. He heard exotic birds calling from feathered fans of darkness. This became the sound of his mother beckoning him; he leaned close to hear the thick phlegm blocking the back of her throat, the peculiarly chilling aqueous rattle as she died.

Around her dirt-streaked neck the talisman, enclosed

within its soft chamois pouch. Its power could not save her. Shadows and light played over it. Holding it up to the light, he could almost see through it. Almost. The sky was lavender. He saw clouds in its carved face, an animal's cloven hoof on the obverse. Cool to his touch.

A long time ago, chasing shadows. Down a narrow, twining street. Littered with rubble and paper snakes. Watch them move! Turn and twist. Gyre upward as the wind took them. Chattering of treed monkeys, hanging and swinging. Baring their yellow teeth. Mandarin's ivory.

The chattering became laughter, light and liquid. He saw the girl outlined in a patch of pearl grey. Followed her down. Chasing her shadow to land's end. The sea beckoned. Wavelets crashing against rotting pilings. The scent of salt and phosphorus. Fish scales. Innards drying in the sun. Gulls wheeling. Calling.

Aboard the ferry, he lost her in the crowd. Shadows milling. Black sunlight falling. A sense of motion, of shoving, pushing. Heard her laughter and followed it down the length of the boat. Another shadow.

Resistance was thinning, the undertow of the crowd slackening enough so that he found he had gained some semblance of forward momentum.

Saw her near the bow, long hair flying in the wind, soft lips half parted, a glow in her eyes. The gentle rise of her breasts, the outflung length of one leg. Her slender ankle and the pointed toe of her shoe. The innocence of her pose created the eroticism of the moment. Intensifying so that he felt the stirring inside himself. Not merely in his groin. All over. He was suffused with longing. His penis was stiff and quivering. As if it were his whole body.

Her browned arms were bare. She stood naturally, but the rail pressed against the small of her back, arching her ribcage. Her breasts.

Her eyes were so full of promise.

His mind was full of Mariana, and as he approached, he opened his mouth, her name on the edge of his lips.

The pulse in the vulnerable hollow of her throat revealed her longing. He pulled her to him, his longing overwhelming. It was as if he had stared at her from afar for all his life but had never possessed her. Her heat set him on fire. Her mouth opened under his, lips so soft, tongue hot and questing, curling around his, stroking. He was so hard it hurt.

Groaned into the abyss of her, calling out her name at last.

Bliss.

Sat up in bed, gasping like a fish out of water.

She was the first thing he saw.

'Bliss!'

'It's all right, Jake. I'm here.'

He blinked as she came over to him and used a towel to wipe the dripping sweat from him. She did this as though she had done it often.

'It's easier now,' she said, as if divining his thoughts. 'There are fewer bandages.'

He watched her with his hooded copper eyes. She was Eurasian. She could easily pass for pureblood Chinese among the *gwai loh*, but subtle fillips here and there about her face betrayed her ancestry to the discerning eye. Was it her grandfather or her grandmother who had been Austrian? He could not recall. But seeing the hint of the steel-grey motes in her ebon eyes, the strong sweep of her jawline, the shape of her ears, he could discern the Caucasian artist's brushstrokes.

Her long, thick hair was drawn back from her sleek head in a wide, gleaming plait. Her large eyes were turned up sharply at their outer corners. Her cheekbones were high, her lips thick and sensual. He started as he felt their kinship to the lips in the dream. A quick pang of guilt struck him like a sharp slap to the face.

'Could I have some water, do you think?'

She turned away to pour from the carafe, and he put his palm up to feel the burning of his cheek. She revealed her bare neck to him, and he felt the flush increase.

She wore a simple sleeveless silk blouse in teal green, collarless, with a scooped neck. The flesh between her collarbones was creamy. Below, her waist was cinched in a blue leather belt. Her green linen skirt looked fresh and neat.

Drinking the water she handed him, he tried to find in this stunning woman the little girl he had played with so many years ago. Felt the guilt again like a sharp adder's bite. His stomach roiled.

Why have you come back? he asked her silently. Why now? Why at all?

'What day is this?'

'Thursday,' she told him. She cocked her head to one side, giving him a judicious look. 'You look infinitely better.'

'Better than what?'

She laughed and he saw her small white teeth. Everything about her made him long to draw them both back into his dream. 'Than yesterday's *dim sum*.'

'I've got to get out of here.'

'Are you hungry?'

'I'd eat you if you were a step closer,' he said; then, realizing the second, sexual meaning, he became embarrassed. The dream. 'That is, I'm starving.'

'Then the prognosis is excellent for your getting out of here.' If she had picked up on the unintentional *double entendre*, she gave no sign of it.

Or *was* it unintentional? Jake asked himself. Freudian slip seemed a better definition. 'I mean right away.'

Bliss leaned over, rang for the nurse. 'I think you'd better get some solid food in you first.'

Jake sighed. He was already restless. The four white

walls seemed to crowd in on him. He thought of the *dantai*, the black, empty space inside him. Was that the loss of the *dantai* he felt, or his estrangement from Mariana? Was it that he no longer loved her, or was David Oh right? Was it that he was no longer capable of loving anyone?

What had happened to him along the blackened banks of the Sumchun River? It was possible that he no longer knew. Probable that he did not want to know. It was as if he had taken a surgeon's burning scalpel and cauterized his own terrible wound, sealing all the emotions attendant to it away in some dark, cobwebby corner of his mind.

Mariana. From the day he had returned from the Sumchun River, they had not touched each other emotionally. They had kissed, made love, even on occasion exchanged kind words. None of it meant a thing. Ashes in his mouth, a taste he was never rid of. *Well*, you're *different, anyway.* Wasn't that what David had said? Wasn't that what Mariana had implied when, night after night, she had whispered to him from the dark, *Jake, what is it? What happened to you in the north? Whatever happened, don't you think I can help you with it?*

He had made no reply. Again and again. How could she know that he had already taken care of it? Put the surgeon's implement to the wound. Seared it down and away. Away.

Jake, away from Mariana.

Was that what had happened to them? Sumchun River? Or was it Nichiren?

Now she was gone, and he searched inside himself for an answer. Found none. Only felt the added coiling in his guts, nipping at him. Where was Mariana? Only knew he wanted to find out. What had happened to her? He wanted to know that as well. What was waiting for her in Tokyo, in Toshima-ku? O-henro House?

Who was waiting for her there? Nichiren?

His worst nightmare come true.

* * *

Darkness revolved around her like a top. Set in a window-less space, she felt as if she were blind. The darkness was absolute. Until it became a pressure against her forehead and her eyes. For a time she had had trouble breathing. That was when her panic was at its height, when she was convinced that she had somehow been traduced. She had gasped into the darkness.

Later, when she had settled down, talking to herself in calm, rational sentences, she had begun to hear the soft hum of the air conditioner, and it was a little less like being buried alive.

Senses returning, she decided to work on the Zen exercises Jake had taught her when they were first married. She got off the wooden chair, and sinking into the lotus position on the bare floor, she began by ridding herself of as much carbon dioxide as she was able. Increased her breathing in increments.

Try to emulate a baby. She could hear Jake's voice, strong and firm. *A baby breathes deeply, fully. It is only when we become adults that we forget how to breathe We breathe shallowly, at the tops of our lungs only. Relearn the way of breath. Inhale as deeply as possible, then exhale with your mouth open. Hear yourself sigh. Continue even after you feel you have expelled all breath. Go further. You will not die.*

It wasn't funny. That was precisely how Mariana had felt the first few times she had tried it, breaking off, gasping. Now she breathed fully and felt herself calming even further.

In the absence of the babble of her terror, she began to think more clearly. She remembered the tremendous noise. The percussion against the walls of her dark world. Sounded like an explosion. The floor had moved slightly, she had been certain of that. What had happened?

She had expected him to return to her, to explain it all. But there had been nothing. Silence. Darkness. And finally the pressure provided by her rising terror. Like being buried alive.

He is my husband's enemy, she thought. Why did I believe him? But she knew the answer to that one. It was obvious. He had proved the truth of his words to her with a startling and terrifying example.

And in that electric moment he had turned her world upside down. She no longer knew who her enemies were. Where was Jake? What were they doing to him?

A month ago she would have wondered if she really cared. They had drifted so far apart. He had built a shell around himself, a love-proof box impervious to anything she had used to get through. Until she had come to hate it, resent it. She had thought she hated Jake.

But the danger to which she had been witness showed her how much she still loved him. Whatever had happened to him in the north, she knew that he had not changed underneath. She was committed to him forever. She had taken her marriage vows with full recognition of what they meant, the depths of responsibilities they entailed. In her youth she had imagined that she would be daunted by those responsibilities. But when the day of her own marriage dawned, she was certain in her heart that she welcomed them.

And she still did. What she had been shown that dreadful night had proved to her that it was the shell he had erected that she had resented, not the man behind it.

'Jake, where are you?' she whispered into the darkness. Abruptly, she felt a million miles away from him. She reached down, underneath the hem of her dress. Extracted the chamois pouch from inside the waistband of her panties. Opened the drawstring with fumbling fingers. Poured out the contents into her cupped palm.

The jade was slightly warm from her own body heat.

'Jake,' she said, closing her hand around the object, feeling closer to him now, knowing how important this artifact was to him. Why was I told to bring it? she asked herself. What is its importance? Why do his enemies covet it so?

There were no answers to her questions. Only more questions unscrolling along the horizon of her mind.

When will he come for me? Mariana wondered. When will he answer all my questions as he promised he would?

Where is Nichiren?

General Daniella Alexandrova Vorkuta was putting the last of her papers into her slim briefcase when there was a polite knock on her office door. The general's office was on the fifth floor of the enormous, dirty, ochre-façaded building at 2 Dzerzhinsky Square, built, ironically, in neo-Renaissance style, home of the *Komitet Gosudarstvennoi Bezopasnosti*.

The room was less of an office than she felt she deserved. It was nothing more than a ten-by-twelve-foot rectangle with two windows of four panes each, which overlooked the square dominated by the bronze image of Felix Dzerzhinsky. This Soviet hero, a Pole of aristocratic upbringing who had turned revolutionary, became the first head of the Soviet Secret Police, founded in 1917, just after the Bolsheviks toppled the Tsar of Russia. Today his statue served as a reminder to the masses of the true state of man; the notion of the revolutionary ethos still served the KGB well, though its practical applications at home had long since been interred deep in the frozen earth, with not even the salute of one soldier to mark its passing.

General Vorkuta's office was much the same as those of the other high-ranking functionaries of this most powerful bureaucracy in the Soviet Union. It was small, dark, drab, furnished with several depressingly heavy wood items poorly made in Rumania or Czechoslovakia. The ceiling was low and in need of repainting. Dark whorls and spots marked its surface, the accumulated result of cigar and cigarette smoke emitted through endless hours of meetings, interrogations, and solitary strategy sessions. For the past nine months she had sent a series of requisitions through channels, requesting new furniture. It had been promised. It had never arrived. Still, like clockwork at the beginning of each month, she sent in her requisition forms.

Daniella Vorkuta ground out the last of her black-tobacco cigarette in the unlovely gunmetal ashtray that lay like a wart on the mahogany surface of her scarred desk. The day was heavily overcast, with low, racing clouds, dark with the precipitation that the morning broadcaster had predicted. As if to underscore this gloominess, she had left only one lamp burning, a black metal floor model with double shades. Pale light spread across her desk, but no farther. The general herself was in shadow.

'*Vchodite*,' Daniella said, and the door opened inward.

A uniformed courier stepped smartly across the room to her desk. He was carrying a small leather briefcase. 'This just arrived for you, Comrade General,' he said in clipped tones. He was looking at a spot just above her head.

General Vorkuta signed for the case. She waited until the courier had departed before using a small brass key she carried on a long chain attached to her belt. Inside she found four stiff sheets of paper covered with what looked like an archaic hieroglyphic scrawl. In fact it was a cipher that she had devised herself some years ago, when she was with *Sluzhba Aktivnykh Meropriyatiyi*, the Active Measures Service, involved in disinformation and ciphers. It had been just an exercise then; now it had become much more.

Daniella's heart beat fast. It was the latest report from 'Medea'. Her attention narrowed. She had been waiting for this. Her excitement level doubled. Now to settle down and mull over the new intelligence.

Dark shadows poured through the opening, filling up the small office. 'Good morning, Comrade General.' The words were spoken in a deep bass. Taking the cue, Daniella smiled and returned the friendly, informal greeting, ignoring the ice particles flurrying in her lower belly.

Anatoly Decidovitch Karpov came through the door. For a moment his bearlike bulk hid the figure just behind him. But then the second man's superior height came into play.

Daniella carefully put her hand over the four sheets of precious paper. General Karpov, head of the First Chief Directorate, walked silently across the bare, worn floorboards, sinking down into the hard seat of the single chair that crouched like a gargoyle directly in front of Daniella's desk. He was not a tall man, but he was an impressive one nonetheless. He had broad shoulders and a barrel chest. His muscles bulged impressively, even though he had just celebrated his sixty-second birthday.

Karpov's thick, straight hair was pitch black, though Daniella knew it remained so, because of his twice-weekly diligence with the dye bottle. His powerful face was lined and pitted with age, his high, prominent forehead feathered by his thick eyebrows. His clear brown eyes peered out from behind wire-rimmed glasses, penetrating and intimidating. But when he smiled there was an ingenuousness about him to which Daniella responded.

He wore a dapper, dark blue suit. Pinned to the left lapel were the army medals he had earned on the line, of which he was so proud. She was pleased to note that his tie was tethered by the black onyx tack she had given him for his birthday last week.

Her eyes shifted to the other man as Karpov said, 'You know Comrade Yuri Vasilevitch Lantin.'

'I have heard of him, of course,' Daniella said carefully. Lantin was a member of the Politburo and the Central Committee, one of a handful of Muscovites who held positions of stratospheric power within the highly structured Soviet hierarchy.

Daniella knew her boss well. Knew that he had not idly

made the trip in from the First Chief Directorate's modern headquarters of glass and steel, along the Moscow Ring Road. His own office, on the top floor of the half-moon-shaped structure, with its views of the surrounding forest, was far more impressive, Daniella knew, than her own cramped and musty office. That Karpov had chosen to bring Lantin to Dzerzhinsky Square was important. Power was on parade here. Power with incalculable dimensions. And it was very clear on which side of the room Comrade Yuri Vasilevitch Lantin was standing. She steeled herself for what was to come.

Patiently, Karpov lit a cigar with a solid gold lighter. This was not an imperialist luxury. Daniella had been acquainted with Karpov long enough to know its significance.

Karpov and Yuri Andropov had been in command of the Red Army forces in Hungary in 1956. Ruthlessly, fearlessly, so Daniella had been told, the two of them had dealt with the complex and highly volatile situation.

To commemorate that bravery, the two friends had exchanged gifts. Now, whenever Karpov flicked up the flame, he kept Andropov's memory alive inside himself.

Karpov blew out a cloud of aromatic Cuban tobacco smoke and peered at the end of the cigar, pursing his thin lips after a moment to see it briefly glow cherry red.

'I have brought Comrade Lantin here today because he has a special interest in certain matters that fall within Department S's sphere of concern.' By that Daniella knew he meant KVR interests of which she was in charge. But even the initials KVR were never spoken aloud, whether within these thick walls or without, so Karpov's rather heavyhanded circumlocution was perhaps understandable.

'Specifically Nichiren.' Lantin spoke for the first time, and Daniella spent some time analysing the tones. One could, she had learned, tell much from voice tones.

Lantin was standing against the wall, his head obscuring

the centre of a standard-issue portrait of Lenin hung there either by one of the previous tenants or, more likely, Daniella thought, by some cretin in the Supply Bureau. His long legs were crossed at the ankles, his hands clasped loosely behind his back. He wore a charcoal-grey suit that made Karpov's appear old and out of style by comparison. He might, for all the world, be watching a sculling contest on the banks of the Thames.

Daniella watched his face. It was long, slightly saturnine. He might be in his middle fifties, quite young for such an exalted post, but it was impossible to be certain. His long, thick hair shone in the feeble lamplight. He had a mole on one cheek that made him seem even more attractive than did his deepset eyes, the cut of his jaw, the almost rakish line of a superbly manicured pencil moustache. Only his lips, thin and somehow cruel even in repose, conflicted with this magnetism.

'Nichiren is run by General Vorkuta,' Karpov said, careful to keep the upper hand in this three-way conversation. 'I devised the idea of employing a known lone-wolf terrorist to further our own ends. In this way, I felt sure, we could get, er, extractions accomplished that otherwise might have the potential to cause us a certain degree of international embarrassment.' Daniella shot him a sharp look as he went on. 'Nichiren's a damn sight more efficient than the Bulgarians, and more reliable than any of our Arab contacts.'

Daniella pushed the blob of an ashtray across the wooden expanse towards him. 'We have had an astounding rate of success with him over the short term,' she said in her best businesslike tone. 'In Ghana, Chad, Angola; in Lebanon, Syria, Egypt; in Nicaragua, Guatemala. In all these places and more we have run him in and have used him to extract certain revolutionary leaders, exacerbating hatreds, ensuring polarities, fomenting further stages to the incidental revolutions that will one day combine – '

'"Ideological combustibility,"' Lantin broke in. 'I believe that is the term General Karpov uses in his monthly reports to the Central Committee. It has a certain ring to it. My colleagues are pleased with it.' He inclined his long, sleek head slightly. 'As they are with the work your singular agent has accomplished.'

Now was the time to concentrate hardest, Daniella knew. Compliments were rare within the *sluzhba*, or 'the service', as it was colloquially known among its constituents. She also knew that if the Politburo had wanted to congratulate her on her direction of Nichiren, Karpov would somehow have managed to interpose himself between her and those above, preferring to seem the angel. That he had allowed Lantin to come to her office was a bad sign.

'Thank you, Comrade,' she said, putting on a smile. 'I work hard for the *sluzhba*. It is good to hear that one's accomplishments are appreciated in other, more rarefied circles.'

Karpov studied the dark end of his cigar, its frozen ash. 'You know, Comrade General, we often have a tendency to believe that there is no power outside of this building. "We are Russia." I myself have heard this phrase used often along these corridors.' He nodded his head. 'And perhaps there is some truth in that.' He looked into her face, his dark eyes locked on hers. 'Up to a point, Comrade.' He rolled the ash off his cigar. He did not have to elaborate that Yuri Lantin represented the larger power outside the walls of the *sluzhba*. The real might of Mother Russia. Daniella understood his implicit warning.

'Your agent,' Lantin said, 'was almost extracted himself in a raid last week. On his own home ground. This is most disturbing.' His forefinger probed at the lower edge of his thin moustache. 'Especially since it was via a Quarry team led by Jake Maroc.'

'Maroc, Maroc.' Karpov almost sang it, as if he were learning a new language. His eyes studied the ceiling. He pulled deeply on his cigar, blew smoke upward in a lazy spiral.

'Nichiren destroyed five members of the team,' Daniella said.

'But not Maroc.' Lantin's tone had turned hard, and Daniella opened her ears. She wanted to know what that meant.

'Damaged but not down,' Karpov said in a tone that managed to be an indictment.

'Considering the past track record of this man Nichiren, I find it unsettling that he allowed this team, inimical as it was to him, to get so close. And on home ground.'

Daniella felt Lantin's eyes like a flashburn on her skin and shifted her gaze from Karpov. She saw something there, something odd, something that did not belong in this room, which she filed away for study at a future date. She did not want to muddy increasingly difficult waters at the moment.

'One would have thought his sources better than that,' Lantin went on. He seemed never to blink. Daniella found herself wondering whether he wore contact lenses. That would at least partially explain the extraordinary presence of his eyes. 'Accomplishments are one thing. But most of his have been in the past. I believe, Comrade Vorkuta, that it is time to subject your Nichiren to a test of sorts.'

Daniella was about to protest, but, remembering Karpov's warning, she bit back her harsh words. 'What sort of test would you suggest?' she said instead.

'Something definitive.' Lantin possessed a languorousness she found impossible not to admire. 'A possibility presents itself that is as time-saving as it is elegant.'

'And what might that be?' Daniella said, matching his tone.

Lantin came away from the wall. He seemed to fill up the room with the aura of his persona. No one could fail to listen to his words. 'This is what you will do, Comrade,' he said softly. 'Send agents into his vicinity. Have them stay close to him, observe him. On audio and videotape if you deem it necessary. I want to know conclusively that he still has the killing instinct. Then you will give your order: Have Nichiren extract Jake Maroc.'

General Karpov's cigar had gone out. He placed it in the ashtray on Daniella's desk.

Three Oaths Tsun stared out across the harbour at Aberdeen. Leaning against the railing of his great high junk, he watched the swells of brackish water, the low black sky hanging like a shroud over the South China Sea, the aftermath of the all-day squall. He was undisturbed by the weather.

In his left hand he gripped a slip of fine rice paper that had been carefully folded four times. Despite that obvious care, its outside was stained here and there a terracotta brown, bespeaking its long journey from creator to recipient.

On the paper were five vertical lines of calligraphy that might have been Hakka but were not. Just like me, Three Oaths Tsun thought. Unconsciously his huge fist contracted, crushing the thin paper with its grip. His heart beat faster in his chest and his blood sang in his veins.

Dragon's Heart. That was what they had called it then. It held a special meaning for them, a meaning no one outside their circle could possibly fathom.

So it has begun, he thought. But perhaps it is already too late.

Dragon's Heart. That was how the coded calligraphy was headed. It was what had galvanized Three Oaths Tsun. It was what had caused him to send Number One Son to fetch Formidable Sung with all due haste. Protocol demanded such an honour for one such as Formidable Sung.

All the bobbing lights strewn throughout the harbour

had no effect on Three Oaths Tsun. Rather, his thoughts returned to the urgency of the oath he had sworn long ago.

Dragon's Heart. His summons to the final act had commenced the moment Number Two Son had come aboard, the stained rice-paper message curled like an adder in a metal tube sealed with a gob of red wax. Or perhaps, he reflected, it had actually begun the moment the tube had first been sealed so far away.

He shrugged. No matter. What must be, would be done. Well, he could tell himself that from now until the sky dragons ceased to wake and in their battling give forth thunder and rain. The truth was, it would be a hollow victory.

Family, Three Oaths Tsun thought. Life is nothing without family.

At that moment he heard the slight sounds behind him, felt the infinitesimal swaying of the junk as they came on board. Silence and the lapping of the tide, which was, he knew, no sound at all. He looked down at what he clutched so tightly in his fist. The fingers on his left hand seemed suffused with an abnormal strength. Fire from the words inscribed on the paper.

'By the spirit of the White Tiger I will do what is required. I honour my obligations.' He convulsively ripped apart the thin paper, so delicate a medium for words that could, perhaps, change the world. Into the bay with them, floating like motes of moonlight out into the trough of the South China Sea, lost for all time. Yet indelibly etched in his mind. He took three deep breaths and turned slowly from his water view. Soon, he knew, he must be off, if he was to make his rendezvous. No one, not even his Number One Son, knew whom it was he met within the maze of jungled waterways upriver.

Po-han Sung, known for some time only by his triad name, Formidable Sung, stood silhouetted in the moonlight. He was a pear of a man, with wide hips, almost no neck, and legs so bowed they might have been comical on another man. Not on Formidable Sung. He was 489, the head, of the 14K triad.

He came now over the creaking deck, turned, and spat heavily over the side of the junk. 'The Dragon Boat race on Sunday,' he said. 'My brother says bet, bet, bet on T. Y. Chung's boat. I say no, we will make money with Three Oaths Tsun's.' He stood in front of the other, watching carefully, all true emotion hidden away far behind his mask of a face. 'I think I had better come to the source and find out where to play my hard-earned taels. After all, Chung's boat won last year.'

Three Oaths Tsun held his face expressionless. 'By the Celestial Blue Dragon, T. Y. Chung's captain cheated to gain that win. This year my men have orders to keep their lane clear under all circumstances.'

'This is beginning to sound very fornicating serious.' Formidable Sung sat on top of a large coil of rope. 'The way you two are going at it, there may be nothing left of either of you for any of the *tai pan* houses to pick over.'

'I think you exaggerate.' Three Oaths Tsun struck a match to an ivory pipe he had been tamping down. He took several quick puffs. Then, satisfied, he said, 'Feuds are a way of life here. They're often a good way to stimulate competition.' He said this carefully, because there was so much hidden emotion behind it. Business feuds were one thing, and he was correct, they were a way of life in Hong Kong. But this matter with T. Y. Chung was something different. It was quite personal. Quite terrible to contemplate.

Formidable Sung grunted. 'You acquire Donnelly and Tung's tanker fleet, T. Y. Chung acquires Southchina Electronics. How much money, I wonder, did he spend in trying to block your acquisitions? How much money did you spend in trying to block his acquisitions?

'There must be a limit to what even *tai pan* such as you

and T. Y. Chung can expect. At some point your cash reserves will become dangerously low. Stretched as thin as that in waters made so perilous by the dung-eating Communists' dire warnings of the future is courting disaster. And the sharks circling all around make it a lethal proposition.'

'Sharks such as Sawyer and Sons, Five Star Pacific, and Mattias, King, you mean.' Three Oaths Tsun took his pipe out of his mouth. He was most pleased to lead the conversation away from the difficult subject of T. Y. Chung.

'Fornicate unnaturally all *gwai loh tai pan*,' Formidable Sung said. 'As sure as a dog will defecate in the middle of the road, you will have to contend with the first two. But as to Mattias, King and Company, that is another story entirely.'

Three Oaths Tsun said nothing.

'I have heard a rumour.'

He wondered what price the Cantonese would exact for his information. He leaned down. 'Would you care for a drink?' He produced a bottle of Johnny Walker from out of the shadows.

'This fornicating weather makes a desert of one's mouth,' Formidable Sung said, taking the bottle by its neck and drinking from it as a sailor would do. He passed the Scotch back to his host, watching him as he tilted the bottle up.

The formalities over with, Formidable Sung said, 'I have a third cousin who is not a part of the triad. He is, in fact, a captain of a trading ship. Recently he came to me with a problem. It is this: his voyages are being plagued by a series of cargo thefts. Nothing too serious, he made it clear to me, but enough so that his masters have said they will take the future losses out of his pay. Now my third cousin assures me that he has done everything in his power to track down this thief or thieves. To no avail.

'Accordingly, he came to me. I told him that I would

93

help him, even though this was far from my own business.'
Formidable Sung gave a bray of a laugh.

'Rumours,' Three Oaths Tsun said, knocking out the
dottle of his pipe on the outside of the rail. 'One often pays
a high price for something that, in the pure light of day,
turns out to be worth nothing at all.' He blew into the
stem to clear it of tobacco residue. 'One must be most
circumspect, I have found, when it comes to rumours.'

Formidable Sung nodded in commiseration. 'Without a
solid source, a rumour is as useful as fornicating rats
aboard ship. I myself would not consider paying a copper
for a rumour such as that. That is why I consider sources
before I consider rumours. I would not allow my friends to
do otherwise, either. That is a strict rule.'

'I think another drink is in order,' Three Oaths Tsun
said.

When they had finished the round, Formidable Sung
said, 'I have heard that Mattias, King and Company will
be leaving Hong Kong, perhaps as soon as this autumn.'

'Leave Hong Kong?' This interested Three Oaths Tsun
so completely that he feigned indifference. 'That is
ludicrous.'

'Perhaps so. To you and me. But we are not *gwai loh*. If
the *tai pan* of Mattias, King feels sufficiently threatened by
the Communists in our future, despite their assurances of
this fifty-year reprieve, he might deem it the prudent move
to make.'

'It would cause too much instability here; their holdings
would be at risk. By the spirit of the White Tiger, think of
what it will do to the Hang Seng! The market will plummet
like a stone. It will be the autumn of 1983 all over again.'

Formidable Sung nodded. 'The Hang Seng dropped
almost two hundred points in ten days when the Communists began their scare campaign regarding our future. It's
recovered quite a bit since then, of course, but what if that
gwai loh tai pan knows something we don't? It's possible,

heya? If I've learned one lesson in my sixty-seven years, it is that anything is possible. What if the fornicating Communists don't honour their word? What if they march in here before 2047? Then where will we be?'

Three Oaths Tsun considered this for a time. His eldest son would soon be on his way to America to be educated properly. And to get his Green Card. This was one of Three Oaths Tsun's hedges against the forces of Communism. He asked the Cantonese for the name of his third cousin's ship and counted himself the winner in that exchange. Behind him, noisy *walla-walla*s made their way between the junks of the Hakka floating city. 'If what you have heard is the truth, then we should prepare by decreasing our stock holdings.'

'But slowly,' Formidable Sung said. 'Too swift a move will set off panic selling.' He lit a cigarette, threw the match overboard. 'We'll also see a scramble between Sawyer and Sons and Five Star Pacific.' He was speaking of the two most powerful Western-run *tai pan* houses behind Mattias, King and Company. 'You know as well as I do that under those conditions, Five Star Pacific will make a run at Sawyer. Five years ago they attacked Sawyer through proxy acquisitions via dummy corporations. The old man just about fended them off then.' Don't I know it, Three Oaths Tsun thought. 'Who knows whether he's still got it now. Personally, I think he's vulnerable.'

Three Oaths Tsun almost yawned. But inside, his heart was beating fast. 'Yes? How so?'

'Utilities,' Formidable Sung said in a knowledgeable tone. 'Five Star's got the New Territories all sewn up, now that they're about to sign the Pu Lo agreement. That area's been hotly contested for almost seven months now. Barring a lightning bolt from Buddha, I think Sawyer's utilities can get eaten up, using the right moves.'

Three Oaths Tsun crossed his arms over his chest, put his head back against the cabin bulkhead. He might have been falling asleep. There's much to pass along this night, he thought.

'But all this is beside the point, it seems to me,' Formidable Sung said. 'All very interesting, *a mi tuo fo*. But not what I was sent for, I have no doubt.'

'No.' Three Oaths Tsun was staring out to sea. A tanker, black as pitch, broke the silver line of the South China Sea as it lumbered on its way, perhaps to Japan. Moonlight spangled its path fore and aft like a deserted highway. 'I have at last heard from our Source.'

'But we are not yet ready,' Formidable Sung said.

'I have also had word that the next summit has been postponed a week,' Three Oaths Tsun said, seemingly changing the subject.

'That is bad.' The 489 rose, stretched his arms over his head. 'Plans have to be set, commitments made.'

'I agree, it is unfortunate. But I am afraid that it is unavoidable.'

'Not for the 14K, it's not. It's fornicating bad enough to deal with Shanghainese, Chiu-chow, and the rest of that pack of diseased hyenas. *Dew neh loh moh*, do you expect me to jump through hoops as well? This idea has been madness from the first.'

'Is it madness to want a future for ourselves?' Three Oaths Tsun's eyes blazed. 'Do you think I would commit myself to something I thought the ravings of a madman?'

'Of course not, but – '

'Trust, Sung Po-han,' he said, using the 489's childhood name. 'If we are to have any future at all, we must all trust the Source. That is the only thing that can bind us together, that has a prayer of making us whole again. You have been witness to the power. Would you willingly turn your back on such a chance?'

Formidable Sung turned his head and spat heavily over the side. 'On whom should I place my taels, come Sunday?' he said by way of an answer.

'My boat will carry the day.'

Formidable Sung grunted and turned away, thinking, Perhaps I should be on T. Y. Chung's craft as well. Just to be on the safe side.

When Three Oaths Tsun heard the car door slam as Number One Son drove the Cantonese home, he lumbered to the rail of his junk. He rubbed his leg. The weather was changing, his wound told him that.

He thought of Formidable Sung. Holding all of them together is like trying to take hold of the four winds, he thought. Especially now. It is all as fragile as a house of straw. Dragon's Heart. It could blow away in any sudden gust, and it will be over. Just like that.

By the Eight Drunken Immortals, that must not happen.

Climbing down the rope ladder with some difficulty, he settled into the small *walla-walla* that Number Six Son was holding at anchor by the side of the junk. In the shadows, out of sight of everyone. Especially Formidable Sung.

Time, Three Oaths Tsun thought. There is just enough to make the rendezvous.

'Where is he?'

'Where is who?'

David Oh watched the volunteer make the bed. Someone had taught her how to make hospital corners. 'He has not been moved; he has not checked out.' He turned to face Bliss. 'You know fornicating well who I'm talking about. Jake Maroc.'

'He's not here.' Bliss smiled sweetly.

'I know that. I can see his clothes are not in the closet. Where did he go?'

The fu *is missing.* That was what she had come to tell him.

Missing? Jake had said. *I don't understand.*

It's gone from your flat, she said. *Mariana has taken it.*

But why?

Bliss did not know; that was why she was here. The *fu* was more important than any single life, save Jake's.

The *fu* was no secret from her. Jake had let her play with it when they were children. It had been precious to him then, too, but for different reasons.

You must retrieve it, she had said.

He had stared at her. *That is why you've come back.*

It is in Japan now. Toshima-ku.

Yakuza *territory.*

Nichiren's, as well.

Won't you tell me who you are? he had asked.

You know who I am.

I want to know who you have become.

She had laughed at that, perhaps out of self-defence. *I am Bliss. Here I am.*

But he had only shaken his head. *I know only a little girl.*

If your memories are strong, Jake, then you know me.

Bliss –

For now, you must trust that I am a friend. I do not think I would know about the fu *otherwise.*

If Nichiren knows of it, if he has it now . . .

That is why you must go to Japan. Now.

What about David Oh?

I'll take care of things here.

He stared hard into her eyes and Bliss knew he was deciding whether to trust her. *What do you have to lose?* she had said.

'Whatever I know, I've told you,' Bliss said to David Oh.

'You've told me nothing.'

'Then you already know the extent to which I am involved. Jake and I grew up together. We were childhood friends.'

'And you came back now. Just like that.'

'I'll tell you something sad, Mr Oh,' she said sincerely. 'Death and injury have a way of breaking down the barriers of time. They also reveal to us our own mortality. Life is infinite. So are the fruits of friendship. It is a pity that tragedy causes us to see that.'

'You'll pardon my suspicious nature,' he said, lighting a cigarette. 'I was born with it.'

Bliss smiled. 'I am not offended.'

'You don't know where Jake went?' It was as if he had switched gears, another preset tape loop running.

'I came in just before you did.' She spread her hands. 'This is what I found.'

David quizzed the volunteer, but she knew nothing at all. Excusing himself, he went back out into the corridor. At the nurses' station, he put them all through their paces. None of them was even aware that Jake had left the room, let alone the hospital. One phoned the doctor in charge of the case to inform him.

Nothing. It was as if Jake had vanished off the face of the earth. David Oh turned back, saw Bliss emerging from the now empty room. She smiled at him, shrugging.

He flipped the powerful transceiver on, a bright light on the ether, zooming across the curve of the globe. Crackle and hiss in his ears and he adjusted the earphones.

When the settings were fully adjusted, he began the complicated phases of the recognition code for this hour, day, week, month, year. He waited with patience until he heard the string of numbers spewed out in return.

Contact!

'Nichiren,' Source said, 'have you secured Mariana Maroc?'

'Yes.'

'Where is she?'

'Still in Tokyo.'

'I want her out of there. Too many potential leaks in a city that size. Moving her around from place to place, someone's bound to see her.'

'I know where to take her, then.'

'Good. See to it.' Crackle of interference. ' – right?'

'Say again. I missed the first part.'

'Is she all right?'

'I assume so. Yes.'

'Haven't you spoken with her?'

'I haven't been with her much.'

'Is there a reason for that?'

Nichiren hesitated, and the voice picked it up immediately. 'You should have no personal feelings about this.'

'That's not possible. She's his wife.'

'What of it? One cannot bend discipline to one's whims. Discipline either is or is not.' There was a pause, during which Nichiren felt sweat spring out along the back of his neck. 'Tell me how you feel about her. If you lie, I will know it.'

'Keii Kisan is dead. Her husband is the reason for that. I cannot stand to be in the same room with her.'

'All the more reason for you to do just that.' There was no admonishment in the voice; that was one of the reasons Nichiren never lied to his Source. 'Stay with her until the resentment leaves you. You have been taught to feel nothing but the game when you play *wei qi*. It is just the same with this. Think of the game.'

The *usagigoya* was two blocks off Yasukuni-dori. It was tiny, as befitted its name, rabbit hutch, but it overlooked the Sumida River where it was crossed by Ryogoku-bashi.

This was Kamisaka's place of sanctuary, and in all the world the only other person who knew of its existence was Nichiren.

Kamisaka, who was, in Nichiren's opinion at least, a glorious mixture of shy and aggressive, had debated for months before finally capitulating. Still, she was hesitant as she took his hand and led him up the stairs to the apartment door. She would not let the key out of her hand;

she was the first over the threshold. Then she had turned around and, bowing as a true host should, formally invited him inside.

Of course, she could not have afforded the rent on even this small *usagigoya* on her own. And there was no question of going to her father for the money; it was to flee his autocratic rule that she had need of such a sanctuary in the first place. Besides, he would have interrogated her for hours about her reasons for needing such a large monthly sum of money.

Kamisaka was a clever woman, though she was only nineteen. She had gone to her older brother, a very successful lawyer. In exchange for his patronage with no questions asked, she had agreed to apprentice gratis in his understaffed office three days a week while she finished school. She had only one year to go. Whatever burden it placed on her, she remained uncomplaining.

Her greatest joy – once she had got used to the spirit of another human being sharing her sanctuary – was to make Nichiren bitter green tea. She had learned the art of *chano-yu*, the tea ceremony, early – her mother had seen to that. Kamisaka had taken to it like a carp to a sparkling pond.

In it, she said, she experienced an utter peacefulness. And with Nichiren she found it particularly comforting. He was a mysterious figure in her life, more than twenty years her senior, obviously well-to-do – she had a superb eye for tailoring and the manner in which people spent money – and perhaps most important of all, he had the bearing of the ancient upper-class traditionalist. Sometimes she felt positively bourgeois in his presence, as if she were back in the 18th century and she, a merchant's daughter, had, through some cultural aberration, come in contact with a *samurai*.

But when she made the tea ceremony, matters of money

and class distinction faded. Only the appreciation of an exquisitely detailed courtesy held sway.

On the other hand, Kamisaka was crazy about his body. The muscled presence of him against her silken smoothness was like a balm to her frazzled nerves. The pain in her lower stomach, which glowed like a fierce and unrelenting sun all the while she was forced to kowtow to her father's dictatorial whims, was totally obscured by the cloud that was her lover.

Though she was but recently engaged to be married, she had been to bed with no one other than Nichiren. Her husband-to-be was not of her own choosing, but rather had been another of her father's iron-willed dicta. It was to be a marriage of families. '*Keibatsu*,' her father had said in response to her reasoned protests, 'will make both our families stronger. Your marriage to Shizuki-*san* will be good for everyone involved.' As a last resort, Kamisaka had tried hysterics, but her mother had soon put a stop to that, pulling her aside to admonish her that 'no civilized lady of culture and breeding would think of acting that way toward her father and her husband-to-be.'

Now Kamisaka did not have to be concerned with marriage. Shizuki-*san*'s horrible death on the subway tracks a week ago had put her entire family in mourning. Inwardly, Kamisaka had blessed her *karma* while she said her silent thanks to the *kami* of her ancestors, to whom she had prayed for deliverance.

Dusk in Tokyo. The neons threw back the encroaching darkness, turning their corner of the sky the pale, streaked hues of the inside of a calm shell.

When Nichiren was with her, she lighted only the bedside lamp. Its low-wattage bulb through the rice-paper shade produced a glow that warmed them both. But now, when she was here alone, she was obliged to keep all the lights on even in the middle of the day. And no matter what she did, it seemed cold.

102

In fact, within the past week, Kamisaka had become frightened of her own feelings. At class, whether it was during lectures or exams, she found herself thinking of Nichiren. Like woodbine, he seemed to have entwined himself about her spirit. She did not feel lifeless without him, merely dull and purposeless.

But these were concerns for her own soul; she knew that she must never articulate them to him – or anyone, for that matter. So it was with a terrible shiver of fright that she received his news.

'Kamisaka-*san*,' he said softly, 'I must go away. It is likely to be for a long while.'

Kamisaka's heart froze and her tongue clove to the roof of her mouth. He had told her this before – he was always going away on one of his mysterious journeys. Somehow this had added to his appeal, for she would create her own romantic fantasies of what he was doing, heroically righting some wrong, or some such that she knew in her heart to be absurd. Yet these simple daydreams of him had made her love him all the more on each return.

As she stared into his extraordinary eyes, Kamisaka saw that this trip was different. Somehow she was able to penetrate all his careful layers of metallic deceit. She knew that 'a long while' might very well mean 'forever'.

She felt her pulse in her throat and she fought the urge to open her eyes wide, like a panicked animal. Emotions gyred so intensely inside her that she felt abruptly nauseated.

She longed to close her eyes; she felt the desire to weep at his feet and, at the same time, rail at him like a harridan. She did none of these things, however, recalling her mother's words that such behaviour was not within the province of a civilized lady of culture and breeding, which Kamisaka certainly was.

Instead she bowed her head and murmured, 'I wish you good fortune.'

103

Nichiren watched her. 'Kamisaka-*san* . . .' He paused for a moment, and in the silence he could hear the mournful hooting of a barge on the Sumida over the muted clatter of rush-hour traffic. The sound made Nichiren melancholy, longing for the countryside where he had been brought up. 'Will you speak to me? Kamisaka-*san* – '

She shook her head, the cascade of her long, thick hair coming down across her shoulder, obscuring part of the front of her kimono.

'But I must – '

Her long, slender forefinger against her pursed lips stopped him. She came against him on the bed. Her flesh was hot beneath the thin skin that slithered sinuously between them, a barrier to their awakening desire.

Nichiren's calloused hands came up, resting lightly on her shoulders. With great care he moved them down, taking the kimono with them.

His lips left hers still wanting, his tongue licking out into the hollow of her neck, then down to her bare breasts. They were small and high, with exceptionally responsive nipples. Under his tender ministrations they seemed to grow to the length of a finger joint.

Kamisaka moaned with her open mouth. Her eyelids fluttered closed. She had the neck of a swan. The lamplight burnished her taut flesh. As Nichiren's mouth moved downward, her eyes opened. She loved to watch him while they made love. Her own pleasure seemed to soar while she watched his muscles ripple. The sight of his naked body was such an erotic stimulus to her that she often found herself flushed and wet with excitement while he was dressing, shaving, or climbing into the shower.

His body was the stuff of which Kamisaka had dreamed. While at school she had watched the male athletes working out in their uniforms of shorts and sleeveless mesh shirts: long, flat muscles much like those of a *kenjutsu sensei* or

104

a distance runner, rather than those of a wrestler or bodybuilder. Kamisaka had often seen the mountainous musculature created by pumping iron – it seemed that many of her female classmates carried with them magazines filled with colour photographs of such oiled figures, posing like self-absorbed peacocks – and she could not see the attraction.

She loved to dig her fingers into Nichiren's muscles, feeling with detailed precision, almost as a doctor would, just how far they would give and at what point they resisted her absolutely.

When they were joined, she liked nothing better than to bite him. The twin satisfactions of being hotly penetrated while at the same time feeling his firmness between her bared teeth never failed to open up her orgasm like a giant flower within her, turning her limbs and her pounding heart to liquid.

She would not allow him to make love to her with his mouth unless she could slide his thick length between her parted lips. She adored the sounds he made when she withdrew him, slick and quivering, from her prolonged kiss, and blew her hot breath upon his engorged crown. Too, she loved to feel his scrotum tighten at the onset of his storm. She would then clamp her fingers around the base of him, using her searing tongue to lick all around the purple head until he thrashed upon the bed, entangling them both in the flowered sheets. He would spray her with the beads of warm sweat that flew from his hair as his head whipped back and forth on the pillows before returning to its place high up between her shadowed thighs.

She would feel his own tongue flicking out, tracing her feverish inner flesh, opened to him like the petals of an *asagao*. The heat would infuse her just as if she had stepped into a *furo*, a hot bath, and she would relinquish her hold on him, plunging her mouth down to the root of him, feeling the shock waves rippling through him, multiplying until they became a part of her own tidal wave of lust.

Kamisaka was not a passive lover, and she detested women who were; she was certain that she could tell this fact about them just by engaging them in a conversation of her choosing. She did not believe in lying back in wait for anything in life – especially pleasure. Though she had been trained well, and therefore, to a *gaijin*, might appear meek and acquiescent on the surface, nothing could be further from the truth.

It was just this surety that had drawn Nichiren to her. Before Kamisaka, he could not have imagined spending the night with a girl of her tender years, let alone seeing one regularly.

But Kamisaka had reminded him of a basic tenet in life, and that was that everything was mutable, just as anything was possible.

This night, her ministrations were more tender than usual, her murmured words to him sweeter even than he could remember their being before. In the midst of his driving passion, gripped as he was by her fingers and her working lips, tongue, and palate, Nichiren felt an entirely different emotion ascend within him. Instead of distancing him from his ecstasy, it rather plunged him deeper into it. He felt more passion, more pleasure than he had ever before experienced – more, in fact, than he had ever thought possible.

Kamisaka's serpent tongue flicked out, curling around the huge crown of his member. He felt ineffable softness gliding all around him, bringing his passion to a peak without allowing it to overflow.

His mouth was filled with her most delicate flesh. He was suffused by her scent, which was musky and fresh at the same time. With every breath, he inhaled her in with him so that he was reluctant to let go and exhale.

Her velvety thighs rose up like the columns of Buddha

on either side of his head, the fluting of the muscles along their inner faces transmitting her excitement to him in palpable waves. He moved in even deeper, so that he engulfed her as she did him.

With this new emotion's ascendancy, Nichiren entered Kamisaka in a wholly different fashion from what he was used to. Now he was inside her without having penetrated her. How was this possible? It was not often that Nichiren asked himself a question, relying on his fully developed instincts to provide him with answers as he moved through life.

And in this totally open state, Nichiren felt her fear as tangibly as if he had come upon a bird with a broken wing in the midst of a dark forest. He held it up to the light, peering at it as the curiosity it was.

He hit upon its nature at the precise moment that understanding of his own emotion flooded through him. Then the building storm of sexual release of his and Kamisaka's manufacture overcame them both and, for a time, drove all thought from his mind.

In the aftermath, Kamisaka, exhausted emotionally, slept. She did so on her right side, lying slightly curled up, facing Nichiren.

For a long time he lay awake beside her. He did nothing but watch her, tracing with his eyes the lines of her body, providing from memory the completion of some where the inadequate light could not. He felt her breathing as if he were on a shoreline, stretched in the surf, at the mercy of the suck and pull of the tide. The gleam of her long hair held the same mysterious glisten of sunlight spread upon the ocean at the horizon.

He wanted very much to touch her, but he did not. He feared that he would wake her, and he could not bear to bring this moment to an end. He contented himself with feeling the warmth of her breath upon his wrist.

But he knew that feeling could not last long. Time was

racing past too fast. Slowly, carefully, so that he would not wake her, he rose. In absolute silence he dressed. Outside, on the Sumida, the barge, or another one like it, hooted, sounding like the cry of a child.

In a moment he was gone.

Embracing anonymity, Jake took the bus in from Narita Airport. He had had no problem clearing Immigration under his passport name, Paul Richardson, a salesman for a New York insurance firm in Japan on holiday.

Rain pearled off the windows as the crowded bus rocketed in almost absolute silence on its way into Tokyo.

It felt odd, coming back here so soon after the explosion. Memories of the *dantai*'s high spirits were strong inside him. At times over the past several days he had felt their absence so acutely that he had become momentarily disoriented.

In Tokyo, Jake took the subway into Toshima-ku and checked into a small, inexpensive hotel he knew that was quite out of the normal traffic flow. Though this was a Western-style place, it had only one john on each floor and no shower at all. That was all right with Jake; he had decided the best place for him was in a *sento*.

As was the case with most cheap *hoteru*, this one was located just around the corner from a public bath. He passed through the sliding glass door marked MALE, bought a ticket and a small, thin towel that would double as washcloth. He went into the first of the tiled communal rooms, where a female attendant handed him a wicker basket in which to place his clothes. This was then put on an open shelf. No one here thought about theft.

In the next room were the open showers and, lower down on the white-tiled wall, two sets of faucets for washing. It was important to do all one's cleaning up here, before stepping into the pool room.

Naked, he padded over to the line of faucets, scrubbed

108

himself carefully. He felt the places where his body was still sore and swollen. Though all the bandages were gone, along with the worst of the discoloration, he made a complete inventory of his aches.

His mind felt dislocated, almost as if he were in another man's body. Surely, since the raid at O-henro House, he felt as if he were living someone else's life. What had happened to his own? His wife was gone – perhaps, inexplicably, to his archenemy; his *fu* was missing; a girl – no, scratch that, a woman! – he had not seen for years had come back into his life, also inexplicably.

And the *dantai* – gone, gone, gone. His fault, alone. Blindly they had followed him and he had shown them death. The shock and fear were like the taste of raw gunpowder in his mouth. Mandy Choi had saved him from death. Who had pulled him from the rubble? Which one of the *dantai* had died to free him? He would never know now, and somehow that one slim fact seemed more horrible to him than any other.

He winced as he soaped across his temple. The worst place. He touched it again, gingerly, to get a sense of its depth. He closed his eyes. He had to remind himself where he was, what he was doing here.

Mariana.

Find Mariana. Find the *fu*.

He went through into the next room. It was quite a bit larger. Here, excruciatingly hot water was fed into the bottom of a pool by an open pipe. At the far end, a faucet dripped cold water. Only the faint of heart congregated there. Of course, all *gaijin* were expected to sit near the cold water.

Naked, Jake chose a spot midway down the pool and eased himself into the steaming bath. He groaned softly to himself as his tense muscles reacted to the heat.

On his right was a high wall above which sat an attendant in a high chair who, like a magistrate, oversaw both the men's bath in which Jake was soaking and, on the other side of the wall, the women's pool.

Sweat drifted through his thick hair, sliding down his damp cheeks and chin. He was aware of the other bathers around him only dimly, through the haze of steam rising from the almost still surface of the pool. When he shifted position, the temperature of the water dictated that he do so with the exaggerated slowness of a drunk. And, indeed, he felt lightheaded from the intense infusion of heat.

Disconnected, except from the heat. Followed that down, through the tunnels of his memory . . .

In his seventh year, in a spring unseasonably hot, he and several friends had used the opportunity a holiday had afforded them to flee the Island. It was Ta Chiu, the time of the Spirit-Placating Festival, and they had taken the ferry out to the tiny fishing island of Cheung Chau.

Jake and his friends had plunged off the old, rickety wharves the first chance they had. While barebacked men erected the sixty-foot bamboo shelters for the festival, the children had engaged themselves in a cannonballing contest, seeing how far each could leap out into the water.

After lunch, they had walked up the dusty paths toward the line of bamboo shelters. Inside, they could see men constructing nine-foot-high papier-mâché images of the festival's triumvirate of reigning gods. In the centre was the white-bearded sage. He was flanked on the left by the fierce-looking demon-god, and on the right by the glowering warrior-god in full battle dress. So cleverly worked were the papier-mâché pieces that the children were held spell-bound as the figures came to life before their eyes.

In the hazy twilight, lights came on and torches were lit. A procession of women brought the long poles on which were placed the freshly baked buns. With a great deal of cheering and commotion, the poles were lifted on high so that the buns rose into the darkened heavens, there to be consumed by the hungry souls of the island victims of 19th-century pirates.

Children gathered around the bases of the poles in increasing profusion. The climax of Ta Chiu was almost at hand. The souls had been given their time to feed, now it was the living's turn.

At a signal from one of the old men designated as judges, the children were loosed to scramble up the poles and, if they could get that far, take what was left of the buns and eat them as their prizes, thus gaining good luck in the year ahead.

Jake and Bliss leapt up adjacent poles. The firelight sparked and crackled all around them as if they were in the midst of a fireworks display. Far off, the glinting of the ocean brought them a sense of the world outside their *juk saan*, bamboo mountains.

Bliss was agile but Jake had strength and, more important, stamina. At the top of the *juk saan*, he grabbed at the bun, tore it from its stake. Then, putting it between his teeth, he shinnied back down. On the ground, he was surrounded, congratulated. But Bliss had no such welcome. She had managed to climb three-quarters of the way up when her strength had given out.

Jake broke away from the crowd and tore his bun in half. Reluctantly, Bliss took the piece he gave her.

'This means you will have only half the good luck you have earned for the year.'

Jake shrugged. 'Maybe good luck should be shared,' he said, pressing the baked dough on her. 'Maybe that way it multiplies itself.'

Happy with that thought, Bliss bit into her piece. They munched together. Later, when they had missed the last ferry back to the Island, Jake called home and gave his mother a list of all the children who were with him, so she could pass the word to their families. She had been calm-voiced, but even through the phone line, Jake had recognized her concern. He told her not to worry.

Because of the unseasonable weather, there seemed no need to seek shelter. The festival had broken up. Inside the bamboo shelters only the tall gods stared out, unseeing and immobile. The children found places to lie down and make themselves comfortable.

Jake and Bliss fell asleep together, but something awakened him several hours later. It was deep in the night. The lights had been extinguished and only the remnants of the torches remained, guttering and briefly flaring.

Jake looked around as if expecting to hear a repetition of the sound that had brought him out of slumber. Or had he dreamed it? It was not certain. No one was about. He stared upward. The stars, hard as diamonds, glittered down on him with the ethereality of dragon's eyes.

Heard a sound.

He turned his head. It seemed to have come from within the shadows of the bamboo shelter. Moving Bliss's arm, which had been draped around his waist, Jake got up. Cautiously he went toward the shelter.

Inside, he walked around the bases of the statues, peering in every corner. Perhaps a dog, he thought. But there was nothing. It was as if he alone was awake on all of Cheung Chau.

Then he caught a slight movement and looked up. Had one of the statues moved? But that was impossible. They were made out of papier-mâché. Jake had seen them being constructed himself. And yet . . . had not the warrior-god been looking straight ahead all through the Ta Chiu? Now his gaze was lowered, almost as if he were looking straight at Jake!

'You look at me as if you knew me.'

Jake jumped. The warrior-god had spoken!

'Have you no tongue, young tadpole?'

'I – ' Jake peered upward. 'You cannot be alive. I saw you being built.'

'You saw my image. Now I inhabit that image.'

'You are made out of paper and glue,' Jake insisted.

'Oh, pragmatic child. Is there no more room in this world for miracles?' With that, the warrior-god's right arm moved. 'There, you see?'

Jake reached up and, pulling on the fingers of the warrior-god's right hand, tugged until the arm broke free, bouncing down beside him. 'God, god,' Jake said. 'What god! There is only one God.'

Shadows moved as the armour plating of the statue swung open. A man stepped out from the hollow innards of the image. 'One God?' His expression was perplexed. 'And who taught you that, young tadpole? It is certainly not a Chinese idea.'

'My parents.'

The man clambered down until he sat upon the papier-mâché foot of the god. He had a narrow face and a high forehead. What was left of his hair was very long and wispy. Jake had seen the style before in a picture book, and knew it was from another age.

'I am Jake,' he said. 'Jake Maroc.'

'Jews,' the Chinese said softly. 'Your family is Jewish.'

Jake nodded. 'Do you have a name?'

'Fo Saan.'

Jake peered hard at the man. '*Fo saan* means "volcano". '

'Is that so?' Fo Saan said. 'What does *your* name mean?'

'I don't know.'

'Well, perhaps it is time you found out.'

Now his head hung with the burden of the bath's heat and his thoughts. He felt entangled in a vast web of a design beyond his knowledge. He was moving with painful progress from one delicate, shining strand to another without a glimpse of the overall pattern. He knew he was doomed unless he could discern that pattern and make it work for him instead of, as now, against him.

Jake closed his eyes, sinking down into the past again. Fo Saan was an artist, but one unlike any he had met since. Fo Saan knew about the ocean, for instance. He had shown Jake what lay beneath to create the changing colours; he had described the merging of sea and shore, the gradual rise of stone caused by the grinding upheavals of the earth.

They were, Jake had soon discovered, the sources of Fo Saan's power. He knew how to harness the forces of nature, to draw upon them when he needed them.

'Do such things have interest for you?' Fo Saan had asked him that first hot night.

Jake had thought of how difficult it sometimes was, being raised a *gwai loh* in Hong Kong. Of course Bliss was his friend. She was Eurasian. Who else would play with her?

How many alleys had Jake walked out of his way to avoid after the first beating he had received in one at the hands of the Chinese?

What was it, really, that Fo Saan was offering him?

'If you pick up a weapon,' Fo Saan had said some time later, 'you must first know what it is you wield.' He had drawn a long sword, its edge so sharp that Jake could not see it. That was the first thing Fo Saan had taught him about it. There were many others to come before he would allow Jake even to wrap his hands around the hilt.

Jake was to learn breathing, balance, form, grounding, before he ever took hold of any weapon. He had to learn to think of his body as if it were an army. To understand its weaknesses as well as its strengths, its limitations as well as its frontiers.

As he worked daily with Fo Saan after school, his body filled out, stretching and hardening, the muscles building themselves around flexible bone and tough sinew. It was not that his parents did not notice the changes in him. Just the opposite, in fact. But his mother, fearful from the first street fights he had inevitably got into, saw another person emerging, and, wisely, she was loath to interfere with its progress. That this was perhaps an atypical response from a parent is not surprising, since she was far from being a typical mother and had, from the first, seen in Jake the kernel of uniqueness she now saw budding daily in front of her.

'If you possess allies,' Fo Saan said, 'unite with them. If you find yourself in enemy territory, do not linger. If you find yourself imprisoned, you must hold your body still and concentrate with your mind until a way out presents itself to you. If you find yourself in death ground, you must fight to the end. But in all of this you must remember that there are some roads not to follow, some enemies not to strike, some cities not to assault, and some ground that should not be contested.'

Years later, Jake had come to realize that Fo Saan had been paraphrasing Sun Tzu's *The Art of War*. Jake wondered now whether he was striking out on one of those roads not to follow. If so, he knew where it would inevitably lead: to death ground, where, ultimately, the only possibility was to fight to the end.

Jake felt a stirring of the scalding water, looked to his left. He saw a young Japanese with a weasel's face. Tattoos covered his chest, shoulders, upper arms, and back like a fantastic shirt.

'I shouldn't be here,' Weasel Face said. 'Not after the mess at O-henro House. That information was costly.' He glanced around, even though there was no one in their immediate vicinity. 'You should have told me why you wanted to locate Nichiren. I didn't know it was to blow him halfway to Hiroshima.'

'He was the one using explosives.'

Weasel Face guffawed. 'Buddha, I would, too, if you were coming after me.'

'I need your help again,' Jake said.

Weasel Face looked away. '*Neh*. No way.'

'It's important, otherwise I wouldn't be after you so soon after the last bit I bought from you. I know what you've got to contend with.'

'See, I don't think you do. You haven't a clue. What makes you so smart, anyway?'

Jake recognized the Japanese's nervousness and decided to back off a bit. 'The thing is,' he said carefully, 'it's become personal.'

'I'm not surprised,' Weasel Face said. 'What do you expect after you killed Nichiren's best friend? He's not going to do any bowing in your direction for a while.'

Jake had no response to that. 'Ten thousand US.'

'No soap.'

'If it's a matter of money – '

'It's not,' Weasel Face broke in. 'It's a matter of my own neck, see?' He sniffed. 'There's nothing more I can do. You're lucky I met you. I figure I owe you that much.'

'I can't do it myself.'

'That's tough. You should have thought of that before you let him slip through your fingers.'

Jake thought a moment. If the Japanese's source could locate Nichiren once, it could do it again. 'How about I guarantee not to involve you? You get ten thousand US in your locker today. You walk out and that's it.'

Weasel Face turned his head.

'You're already here,' Jake said, sensing that he was close. 'You've made this commitment. I'm asking for nothing more.'

'Yeah? So what *are* you asking for?'

'The name of your source for the information you sold me last time.'

'About Nichiren?'

'About Nichiren.'

'You must think I'm dim.'

'No. But you'll be a helluva lot richer in ten minutes.' Jake shrugged. 'What do you have to lose? I can't go to your source. I can't involve you in any way.'

'Fifteen thousand.'

Have him! 'Ten. That's my limit.'

'Okay.' Weasel Face knew that he would never make so much money so easily again in his life. 'My source for that info was inside the Komoto clan.'

'Who inside the clan?'

'Now you're getting to the nub of my livelihood. That name hasn't got a price.'

Jake nodded. He knew the boundaries as well as the next man.

Nearly two hours after entering the *sentō*, he emerged, feeling at least more resolved. This was ground that he knew in his heart must be contested. If it meant that for the first time in his life he would forsake Fo Saan's teachings, then so be it. Whatever the price, he must accept it now, while there was still the option to turn back. His *joss* was his, just as his resolve was his. He was its creator.

It was still pouring, the murky afternoon having given way to a dull, featureless twilight. Neons streaked the pavement and streets, but the insistent rain washed all colour from the reflections. With a pang, Jake was reminded of the moment when the *dantai* had crossed the road to enter O henro House.

He passed up the Biggu Makku at the local McDonald's, but he did look with some nostalgia at the teenage Americans who, despite the inclement weather, were grouped around its familiar bright yellow and red façade. They seemed so carefree as they laughed raucously, the boys clumsily flirting with the girls.

He dined on *sushi* washed down with Kirin beer and,

later, the steaming hot, slightly fishy tea typically served at *sushi* bars.

It was dark when he finished, late enough for him to begin. It did not take him long to find it. Such gambling establishments abounded, but were accessible only to those who knew about them. Because he was unknown to the place, and perhaps also because he was a *gaijin*, he was required to pay a heavy entrance fee.

Inside, Jake fought his way through the billowing pall of cigarette smoke mingled with the sour stench of sweat and, in the losers' case, fear.

Around a low cypress table that gleamed from hours of hand-polishing, the gamblers knelt like penitents before the altar. These were mostly middle-aged businessmen, still in their dark suits, crisply starched white shirts, and dark ties. It was hot and close in the room, but none of them appeared to notice.

Those who ran the game were bare-chested, their spectacular *irezumi* rippling as their muscles flexed with the rapid motions as they raked in money or paid it out.

Jake, fighting *déjà vu*, found a place at the table and began to play. He started out cautiously and within an hour's time was slightly ahead.

Then, in the opinion of those Japanese around him, he got bitten by the gambling bug and, seeking to increase his winnings, commenced to bet heavily and imprudently. Within three hours he was wiped out but not yet ready to quit.

He rose rather shakily from the table and spoke softly into a waitress's ear. She shifted her tray of hot *sakē* and pointed the way through a curtained doorway in the rear of the room.

The *sarakin* was just three blocks away, his late-night office lights washing out into the rain-slicked street.

He was an enormous man. Fat hung from beneath his jowls and his eyes seemed lost within the heavy folds of his

118

wide, round face. He had small, pudgy fingers that he kept laced across the globular expanse of his great belly.

'How can I help you?' he inquired in English.

'I need a loan,' Jake said in Japanese.

The *sarakin*, whose name was Fujikima, grunted heavily. His small brown eyes squinted as he scowled. 'What have you for collateral?'

'I've got plenty of cash in the bank,' Jake lied. He put an apologetic smile on his face. 'But considering the hour, it is not available to me. Tonight, my luck is about to change. I know it.'

'Ah,' Fujikima said, 'a gambler.' He smiled. 'I have a special fondness for gamblers.' The smile abruptly dropped away. 'Have you your bankbook with you?'

'I'm afraid not.'

'Uhm. You are living here? You have a permanent address? A job?'

'I come through four or five times a year,' Jake said. 'That's why I need the account here.'

'What bank?'

Jake told him.

The *sarakin* shook his head. 'Poor risk. You have nothing at all to give me. I don't think it would be wise for me to
'

'My passport,' Jake said, digging into his jacket pocket. He placed the document on Fujikima's scarred desk. He grabbed up a paper and pencil. 'This is where I'm staying. I guarantee I'll be here at ten tomorrow morning with the cash.'

The huge Japanese stared down at the passport and the printed address.

'Look.' Jake put a note of pleading into his voice. 'I can't go anywhere without that passport. And you yourself said you had a soft spot for gamblers.'

'The price will be high.'

'I understand.'

119

Fujikima's hand covered the passport, sweeping it off the table. 'Ten A.M. sharp, tomorrow.' He looked into Jake's face. 'Now, how much do you need?'

Ten minutes later, Jake was back at the table. For a time, his fellow gamblers saw, he was able to hold himself in check and he made a number of sensible moves. Then he became overeager and, following on the tail of a winner, lost everything he had borrowed from the *sarakin*. The veterans all about him observed that he left white-faced and shaken, and they gossiped among themselves, speculating about him for some time, until those running the table reminded them of why they were there.

The gambling resumed, at an even more frenzied pace, and Jake was forgotten by all but a few.

He was not, however, forgotten by Fujikima, and when, at eleven-fifteen, he had still failed to show, the *sarakin* picked up the phone. He dialled a familiar number and when he heard the '*Moshi-moshi*' on the other end, asked for Mikio Komoto. Komoto was the man for whom Fujikima worked. He was also the man who ran the gambling establishment in which Jake had lost so much money the night before.

Mikio Komoto was a *yakuza oyabun*. He had a reputation to protect, as did the *sarakin*. Using information provided by Fujikima, he immediately dispatched two of his men to Jake's hotel.

Thus Jake awoke from a deep and dreamless sleep to find a silenced .38-calibre automatic pressed muzzle-first against his temple.

'Get up,' one of the men said in harsh, guttural Japanese. 'Get up now.'

The road not to follow. He was on it now, and there was no turning back.

The Quarry maintained a number of extensive rural properties in Virginia. They existed for a variety of purposes, ranging from combat-simulation training to what the agency liked to call 'recuperative reorientation,' where agents were treated for everything from shock to sprained backs.

The Movie House, where unfriendlies were shipped if they proved recalcitrant, looked more like a dude ranch than anything else. A wooden fence in the Western style surrounded the sixty-acre property. There were stables, two riding circles with jump bars for English-style horsemanship, and a plethora of winding, shady trails through the surrounding hills for Western riding.

With all this equestrian paraphernalia, it was quite possible to miss the low, windowless concrete structure, built as solidly as a bunker into a hillside, that gave the place its name.

Gerard Stallings, however, made it a point to watch the concrete monstrosity as he urged his chestnut stallion out of its stall. The Movie House served as a constant reminder to him of the darker side of his profession. It both frightened and reassured him. It was a symbol of the Quarry's ultimate might, and the proof that good triumphed over evil. That made Stallings feel very good indeed.

Until several months ago, his only recreation had been riding. It was a passion he had grown up with as a kid in Texas. He rode a horse better than he drove a car, and he was tops at handling any auto made by machine or hand, not only in his own view but in the opinion of Quarry staff as well.

Lately, Wunderman had begun teaching Stallings how to work a computer. At first Stallings had balked. He disliked on principle any activity that did not take place outside, in fresh air. But Wunderman had persevered, pointing out that Stallings could quadruple his problem-solving capacity by delegating some of the complexities to the computer. He had given Stallings a hands-on demonstration, and Stallings was hooked. Now he used it as

121

an intellectual toy, devising new ways around seemingly unsolvable problems.

However, Stallings had vowed not to take time away from his horses, so when Rodger Donovan wanted to get hold of him, he was obliged to drive out to the Movie House, sign out a horse, and ride out after the agent.

Donovan was uncomfortable on horseback. He had never had anything to do with horses as a child. Consequently, he had an adult's innate fear of something so large, which could, at the drop of a hat, throw him into the tall grass.

Nevertheless, he was determined to get it done this way rather than use his beeper to call Stallings in. Donovan knew full well that was the coward's way out and would decrease his already low standing in Stallings's eyes. In Stallings's view, you weren't a real man unless you rode, and rode well.

Eventually he found Stallings sprawled beneath the shade of a mature oak, cowboy hat pulled low on his face. He appeared to be asleep, unmindful of his untethered horse, which was cropping contentedly at the savoury grass.

Donovan decided to take the unobserved moment to dismount, which for him was rather more of an ungainly slither. He took the reins of his horse and walked her to Stallings's stallion, where he bent and took those reins as well. He began to walk the horses over to the tree.

'Don't do that.' Donovan stood stock-still. 'He doesn't like to be tethered.' Stallings lifted his hat, stared straight at Donovan. 'Why don't you leave well enough alone?'

Donovan dropped the reins of Stallings's horse. Because he did not know what else to do, he patted his own mount on the side of the neck. Startled, the animal snorted, swinging her head so hard against Donovan that he staggered back a pace.

'Always let your horse know where you are,' Stallings said, getting slowly to his feet. 'They don't see the way humans do. You've got to remember that, or one fine day you'll get kicked right in the butt. That's something you're not likely to forget, not with six weeks in the hospital with a broken thighbone.'

Donovan stood a bit apart from his horse now. The thought of getting back on it filled him with dread. 'You're moving out,' he said, glad to change the subject.

'Where to?'

'Tokyo.'

'Japan, huh?' Stallings spat. 'Well, I haven't been there in six years. Time I stretched the muscles of my Japanese, anyway.' He came into the sunlight, reaching out to give his stallion a sugar lump. The horse lifted its head and whinnied. It nuzzled Stallings's palm long after the treat was gone. 'What's up?'

'Jake Maroc's wife, Mariana.'

Stallings stood as still as a statue. The stallion nosed him several times, perhaps wanting more sugar, but Stallings ignored him. 'You'd better explain yourself. We're talking about a Quarry dependent.'

'It's unfortunate, I know,' Donovan said, trying to make this as easy as possible. 'The Old Man made the determination. The call she got that night was from O-henro House.'

'Nichiren?'

Donovan shrugged. 'Maroc himself told David Oh that his wife had no friends in Tokyo. Form your own conclusion about the call.'

'It's still all circumstantial.'

But Donovan could see that Stallings was not at all sure. 'It's too dangerous a situation for us to take a chance. Remember the Old Man's iceberg. He's made the determination that it's real. The computers helped us on that one. Mariana Maroc must be terminated.'

'If we're under attack, I'm off.' With a leap, Stallings mounted his stallion. Jerking the reins, he brought its head up. Its nostrils flared. Even Donovan, unschooled in horses, could see that it was a magnificent specimen.

'The Travel Agents have your instructions, along with all the other normal stuff: passport, visa, currency, backup documents.'

'Who am I this time?'

'Get rid of that cowboy hat,' Donovan said. 'It won't fit.'

What General Vorkuta liked least about Moscow was its landlocked status. She had been born in the thrumming port of Odessa, on the extreme northwest edge of the Black Sea. Her father had been captain of a fishing fleet that consisted of sixteen vessels used for fishing and four used strictly by the KGB for what they liked to call 'external security,' but which was nothing more than spying. Rumania, Bulgaria, and Turkey constituted their sphere of influence.

The Committee for State Security had contacted Nikita Makarovich Vorkut soon after his acute business acumen increased his fleet from eight to sixteen. In the beginning it was he who had trained the KGB *apparatchik*s to sail and fish as professionals would. Afterwards, they had merely asked for his advice from time to time. He was not, strictly speaking, KGB but he was vetted just as if he were. They trusted him, they said. But all along they had his daughter.

So it was not surprising that she enjoyed coming to this *dacha*. It was on the water, though not in Odessa itself. The *dacha* with the sea-blue tile roof was just outside Yalta, on the Crimean peninsula that jutted, squarish, tailed, south into the Black Sea. It was just about equidistant from Bucharest, Istanbul, and Rostov, which gave General Vorkuta the sensation of being at some kind of nexus point. But perhaps that was only a consequence of her childhood. In comparison to Moscow, this place seemed small and isolated. Every time she came, it seemed, she enjoyed the quiet and salt air more.

But this morning, as the general alighted from the black Zil limousine that had picked her up at the military airport at Odessa, she cursed the changeable Crimean weather.

It was raining, a steady downpour as thick as wheat. The sky was close and as grey as slate, houses and trees indistinct through humid mist. Everything inside the *dacha* was clammy; the atmosphere had about it an unpleasant, unused quality.

The general called for the windows to be thrown wide open despite the downpour. She ordered the heat put on to dispel some of the pervasive dampness. Then she stepped outside, onto the wide, screened-in porch that overlooked the sea.

Wind and rain had whipped the water into a white-capped froth. It too was grey, totally indistinguishable from the sky. As she stared out, south to where the beginnings of Turkey lay nearly three hundred miles away, she saw a gull wheel high above, slanting down through the rain. It cried out, diving close to the skin of the unquiet sea. A windblown wave rose up and flicked at it. Immediately the bird rose and vanished into the grey film that passed for sky. General Vorkuta stared after it, certain she had seen it shudder at the moment the chill water spattered it.

'Comrade General.'

'Yes.' Daniella Vorkuta turned around.

General Karpov stood in the centre of the dark living room. He wore the brown and red army uniform that was his dress outside 2 Dzerzhinsky Square. In this space he seemed powerful, magnetic. He filled up the room the way Yuri Lantin had filled up her office.

'So pleasant to see you here.' He cracked a smile. '*Danushka.*'

He held out his arms to her and she came into them. His lips settled over hers. Her body melted into his.

In 1971, Daniella had been working in Department S, an enormous unit within the First Chief Directorate in charge of the recruitment, training and direction of KGB illegals sent to be set in place in foreign countries. She had been in charge of the Werewolves, the legend-weaving division responsible for creating credible cover fictions for the agents.

In that year Oleg Lyalin, a high functionary of Department V, in charge of assassination and sabotage, which had recently been absorbed by Department S, defected and went to ground in London with some of the KGB's darkest secrets. On the Square, that was a hard enough blow, but when, some two months later, Daniella spotted a brace of facts, minor but curious, in Lyalin's dossier, she began to dig deeper.

Perhaps only she, a Werewolf trained to spin lies of a certain kind and therefore able to spot them, could have noticed the discrepancies. Three weeks of increasingly furious work led her back to an inescapable conclusion. Amassing her damning evidence, she took her bulky dossier to General Karpov, then head of Department S.

Within twelve hours he acted decisively and ruthlessly. What Daniella had discovered was that Lyalin had been a British mole for more than two years before he defected.

Soviet xenophobic paranoia swept Department S, concentrating itself on the high-ranking officers of Department V, who were either summarily executed after intensive 'debriefing' beneath the same high-intensity lamps under which they had formerly interrogated exposed aliens, or were reduced to training raw recruits from the Foreign Intelligence School.

Comrade Karpov made certain that Department V was no more, and for his heroic services to the State, the

General was given an added star for his shoulder boards and the chair of the First Chief Directorate.

It was Karpov, of course, who took all the glory and honours for the discovery of Lyalin's treachery. But he did not forget from whence his information stemmed. And, as soon as was practicable, he moved Colonel Vorkuta into the newly formed Department 8, which was taking over the functions of the now disbanded Department V.

But it was not merely gratitude that had motivated Karpov. Nor was it solely the recognition of her talents. He had lusted after her from the moment she was first brought to his attention by a member of his staff. She had been nineteen then, a clerk in the Active Measures Service. But already she had devised several brilliant ciphers for agents to use.

She had dazzled him with her thick blonde hair, cool grey eyes, and soft, inviting lips. At the time, Karpov had never been unfaithful to his wife. He had been married for thirty-odd years, and in all that time had never contemplated having an affair. The sight of Daniella Vorkuta had changed all that. However, the general was too canny a career man to be swayed merely by lust. His ambition was his all-consuming master. Only within its service would he take Daniella Vorkuta for his own.

From time to time he called upon one of his aides to check up on her progress. He was informed when she was sent into Europe to recruit for the First Chief Directorate. She had the talent and the spirit to rise on her own, but occasionally the general deemed it prudent to put in a quiet word here and there, moving her from service to service as it suited him. Within six months he had her sent back. He did not like it when she was so far from him. Also, he enjoyed the way she ferreted out the bad seeds and deadheads from her working environment. She was a pistol, and he admired that. In a sense, he was moulding

127

her in his own image, though neither she nor, oddly, he himself, realized it.

Daniella's coup allowed him to rush her upward openly. He placed her in a subordinate but – and this, to his way of thinking, was the crucial element – adversary position to the man he had chosen to be the new head of Department 8, a man who Karpov was not at all certain could do the job.

Within eighteen months, Colonel Vorkuta was in a position to become the new head of Department 8, just as Karpov wished. She had already proved her ultimate worth to him and, even better, she was in the precise place to do him the most good. The Politburo took a dim view of a great deal of lateral movement within an *apparatchik*'s career, and Karpov had no desire to attract their attention at this stage.

Accordingly, Karpov had called her into his office one morning and outlined his plan for her. Head of Department 8. And that, of course, was to be only the beginning.

If . . .

The general had waited his good time to have her. Now, totally in the service of his own career, he had his opportunity. He was determined to make the most of it.

Daniella declined.

The more she demurred, the more the general became inflamed. His gaze went back and forth between those pouty lips and those cool grey eyes. She seemed to him a wild mare of dazzling strength and agility. He needed to tame her. He found, much to his surprise, that he had never wanted anything so badly in his life. He found, in fact, that when she left his office he could do nothing but think about her. For a man in his position, that could be disastrous.

I must have her, he thought. *I must.*

He could, of course, have ordered her into the affair. But he had to admit to himself that he would soon have loathed

128

and discarded any female so totally acquiescent. He knew that Daniella was far too important to him to risk that kind of situation.

In his heart, he wanted her to say yes of her own volition.

That day he cancelled all his appointments and, extracting her dossier from the Library, took it home to his flat. His wife was off for two weeks, visiting her sister in Riga. Karpov had the place to himself.

He fixed a drink and, carrying it into his small, homely study, sat in the leather wingback chair and cracked the file. Three hours and two drinks later, he thought he had found the answer.

Daniella had been born and raised in Odessa. As it happened, her *dacha* was nearby, on the Black Sea. A return home. That's just what she needs, he thought.

For Daniella's part, she had every intention of sleeping with General Karpov at the very first opportunity. She found his power, his size, and his manner very attractive. But, as her father had taught her, one should never give away what one can sell. She had marked Karpov as a high bidder. She would have to be deaf, dumb, and blind not to have recognized the passion of his gaze.

She liked that, more than she cared to admit. For Daniella was also driven by ambition, and she knew full well that personal passion could easily deflect discipline. Karpov's inky eyes sliding over her made her shiver inwardly. The idea that this man, who embodied so much absolute power within Russia and without, melted inside when he saw her was a heady aphrodisiac indeed.

'Odessa,' he had said expansively, late one Friday afternoon. 'I have not been near the water for a very long time.'

Daniella, amused at the tack of the conversation, said, 'My *dacha* overlooks the Black Sea.' She shrugged. 'But I rarely get time enough to make use of it.'

'What about this weekend?' Karpov said, as if it were a spur-of-the-moment thought.

Daniella sighed. 'Unfortunately, I have far too much work.'

'Work,' he said. 'Take it with you, if you must.'

Daniella laughed. 'Do you mean you are inviting me to spend the weekend with you at *my dacha*?'

Karpov, unsure as yet of her personal preferences, was careful, therefore serious, in his reply. 'Is that too revisionistic for you?'

She had another good laugh at that.

On Sunday morning, Karpov had offered her Department 8. Daniella wanted the KVR *and* a promotion to general. She told him that she would not settle for less.

As it turned out, she did not have to. In his youth, on his way up, Karpov had had many women spread their legs for him. None, however, had the effect on him that Daniella did. He had never thought of himself as a crude man in bed. Certainly his wife had never complained; neither had any of the girls of his youth.

Daniella showed him that he had a lot to learn about the art of making love. She did not shame him; rather, he was awed. It was as if she had taken him by the hand up to a familiar door and, going through it with him, had showed him a whole new universe. The depth of pleasure he experienced with her seemed boundless. Then she showed him how to do the same thing to her.

After that, he gave her everything she wanted, and counted himself blessed at that. She was brilliant at her new work, brilliant in the bedroom as well. Karpov was on a roll.

Then Moonstone, the general's plan for the encirclement of China, was approved, and he was given limited jurisdiction over certain select elements of the GRU in order to carry out the directive. Yuri Lantin's oratory within the Politburo had helped carry the day for Karpov. Now the two worked closely together, since Lantin was heavily connected with the GRU and had personally cleared the way for the general's crossover responsibilities within Moonstone. It had been Karpov's lucky day when Moonstone had crossed Lantin's desk.

'Comrade General,' Karpov said again. He whispered it into Daniella's mouth, laughing. It amused him to hold secrets from Lantin. That was one of the main reasons he wanted to take him into Daniella's office. He wanted that undercurrent flowing all about the other man. He wanted to call Daniella '*Comrade General*' while thinking *Danushka*. *He* knew; Daniella knew. Yuri Lantin, for all his prodigious power, did not know. That gave Karpov a degree of control in the face of a power that he, quite frankly, might otherwise find overpowering.

He swung Daniella around, watching her face as her cool grey eyes caught the slate-grey light. Her cornflower hair was pulled tightly back from her pale face, accentuating the flat planes of her cheeks, the narrowness of her strong chin. Her ears were bare of ornament, though at one time they had been pierced.

'Now you have met the other end of Moonstone,' he told her. 'Oh, but I almost split a gut when you first saw him, Comrade General.'

Daniella seemed less amused than he. 'Moonstone is one thing,' she said. 'Nichiren's quite another. What does Yuri Lantin have to do with the KVR?'

Karpov chuckled, swinging her back and forth from the fulcrum his laced fingers made at the small of her back. 'Yuri Lantin has to do with *everything* inside the *sluzhba*.'

'You are head of the First Chief Directorate,' she said, eyeing him.

'My dear *Danushka*, surely you understand that there is an authority above the First Chief Directorate. Remember what I said. The *sluzhba* is a world unto itself, but only up to a point. It is important for you to know our limits.'

She turned away and, pulling apart his fingers, contemplated the sea. She felt lightheaded at the thought of someone alien peering over her shoulder. She shivered slightly.

Karpov came up behind her, pressing his warmth into her back. 'What is it? Why such black thoughts out here, so far from Moscow?'

'Not so far from Central,' she said.

'Is that it?' He spun her around so that she faced him. She saw the concern on his face. 'Is it Lantin? *Danushka*, he was always there. Isn't it better that you're aware of him now?'

'I don't want him screwing with my operatives.'

'But Nichiren belongs to all of Russia, my dear. His prowess and fame have spread too far for you to hold on to him for yourself. Don't you see that he has become a kind of celebrity outside the *sluzhba* as well as inside it? Do you think Lantin picked up Moonstone and read it with the care it deserved, rather than throwing it into his "out" tray by accident? He recognized my name from the monthly reports. He remembered me because of Nichiren.'

'Operatives should not become celebrities,' Daniella maintained. 'Certainly not *my* operatives.'

'You'll have to learn to live with it,' Karpov said. 'Just as you'll learn to live with your new knowledge of Yuri Lantin.' His hands came up, cupped her breasts lightly. In a moment he began to squeeze until he felt her nipples come erect. She loved having her breasts caressed.

Daniella's head came back until the thick sheaf of her hair was draped across her shoulder. Karpov's tongue licked out at the side of her neck, following down the soft line to the point of her shoulder.

'I don't want to talk about him any more,' Karpov said thickly.

'About whom?' Daniella whispered.

He pulled apart the front of her blouse, reached in, and

scooped her breasts out. He rolled her nipples between his fingers until he heard her breath panting through her open lips.

He dropped to his knees, and Daniella hiked up her skirt. He smoothed his palms over her stockinged thighs. He licked the tops of them, sucking at the bare flesh. His broad thumb stroked back and forth across her mouth, making her moan. When her pelvis began to roll toward him, he grasped the waistband of her panties and pulled them down to the middle of her thighs.

His head lifted and his mouth settled over the core of her. Daniella held her breath. At first she felt only his hot breath tickling her hair. Then, little by little, she became aware of his active tongue as it opened her up, petal by petal. When he reached her innermost layer, she was already lubricating furiously.

Her fingers pushed through his wiry hair as she brought his head harder against her. She rocked against the stimulation, feeling the buildup of pleasure through her veins and muscles, the ecstatic engorging of her tissues. Her thighs began to tremble and the hard muscles of her lower belly to ripple with the onset of her orgasm. She was breathing hard, her nostrils flared. She rolled her hips.

At the last instant, as she hovered on the brink, with her contractions already beginning to build up, he took his tongue and lips away. Daniella gasped in frustration. He moved lower, his tongue flicking out at her other orifice. Daniella groaned deeply and pulled apart her buttocks with her own fingers. She felt her pleasure double, quadruple.

'Oh, yes,' she chanted. 'Oh, yes.'

She felt as if a fire were consuming her loins, an erotic tickling racing all through her insides. She could no longer keep from touching herself, used her fingertips high up in her folds, finding just the right spot . . .

She screamed, a short, high cry as Karpov's maddening tongue replaced her fingertips. Then his whole mouth was

133

encompassing her and she felt herself being sucked up into him. The wet friction was too much.

She cried out to the rhythm of her body's contractions as wave after wave of ecstasy engulfed her, her hips lurching heavily against him in searing contact.

She sank down, half conscious, sliding her hand inside his trousers. She found him as hard as iron. He trembled as her hand closed around him. She felt for his scrotum, then drifted her fingers over the entire length of him. As she reached the head, she heard his thick groan, felt his penis give a warning lurch.

Quickly she drew just the head out of his trousers, slid her lips over its silky girth. Just in time. At the contact, he reared up and she felt him wildly inundating her mouth and throat as her tongue continued its soft whipping.

Afterwards, unthinking, she encircled him within her arms.

'Don't!' he said, his eyes flying open. 'You know I cannot stand restraint!'

Daniella wondered how he could think her holding him lovingly in her arms was a form of restraint. She watched him while he fell into a thick slumber. She thought of love, sad that she had not felt that pure emotion since the last time her mother had kissed her cheek.

Karpov began to snore and she sat up, staring past his furry shoulder to the Black Sea. But the beautiful view seemed full of ashes.

Perhaps I'm tiring of him, she thought. Or was it the weight of Medea, the razor edge of the terrible, deadly game she had constructed for herself?

She spun and went inside, to her study. She sat beside an inlaid stone table she had had clandestinely imported from Beijing some years before, when Medea had begun. Its face was an inlaid *wei qi* board. She took up a black stone and played it judiciously. Now she switched sides, searching for a counter for white. But the war game was complicated enough when one was concentrating only on one's own strategy. Taking both sides, she had never completed a game; what was displayed before her now was the same one she had begun over three years ago.

Daniella felt a shiver roll down her spine. Lantin. She saw him in her mind's eye, standing in her office in that offhand, almost negligent manner of his. She wondered what was locked away behind those charcoal eyes. If he was insinuated this deep inside the *sluzhba*, would it be long before he sniffed out Medea? Daniella knew that she could not afford that.

Idly she took a handful of stones, shook their coolness back and forth in her hand. She put her head back and closed her eyes. Sex often had an interesting effect on her: it allowed her to concentrate deeply. What to do about Lantin? There had to be a way to neutralize him. His absolute power made that a problem. But Daniella knew that all problems had an answer. One only needed to discover it.

The thing to do with Lantin, she knew, was what her father had taught her. *An enemy's strength is more quickly defined than his weakness,* he had once told her. *If time is of the essence, you will not be able to afford to search out his weakness. Instead, determine his strength and then devise a way of using it against him.* The grey pall was lifting. Through the windows, patches of cerulean sky could be seen high up as the clouds began to tear themselves into tatters.

In a moment, Daniella's eyes opened. She stared down at the board, wondering if she had found the answer. Reaching out, she made white's last move. In the next round, the one-hundred-and-sixty-second move, black would win by five points. The game was, at last, over.

And a new one had begun.

The minutes ticked slowly by. Jake used the time to deepen his breathing, slowing it as he did so. He centred his being, sinking down into a lower layer of consciousness where, Fo Saan had taught him, all six senses were heightened. When one used one's eyes in this state, for instance, one could take in the whole room. One could react and move faster as well. It was a state he strove to maintain throughout all potentially dangerous situations.

He knew this was one of those. The two *yakuza* had had a car waiting. They took him further northwest, deeper into Toshima-ku. Through the clutter of Ikebukuro, skirting the sprawl of Rikkyo University on the left. Right on to the Yamate-dori for just about a mile. A left into Kaname-cho.

Immediately the blocks were bigger, the houses more expansive. Lawns appeared, stone gates, high bamboo fences. Within sight of the university's baseball grounds, they had turned through an iron gate in a three-metre bamboo fence. Boxwood trees and cryptomeria rose above the martial-seeming fencetop. They were old and well cared for.

Jake had had the barest glimpse of a house before thick foliage screened him out. They got out and he walked on round stones of varying diameters, through an expanse of carefully raked ochre pebbles. He passed one cluster of three rocks, all of varying but complementary sizes.

He had been hustled into the house as if he were late for an appointment. Down a narrow corridor papered in grey and white. He passed several *fusuma* on either side, but all the doors were closed. Outside the lintel of a room, he was made to take off his shoes. He went through an open *shōji* into a six-*tatami* room. The walls were painted a traditional natural clay colour. The ceiling was of cedar planking. Along the right wall was a *tokonoma*, an alcove. On its slightly raised platform stood a slender vase of clay with a mauve glaze containing a single white and crimson day lily. Behind it, hanging on the wall, was a scroll. Its calligraphy read: *Where flies the general's banners, there is his army*; *where points the general, there advances his army*; *when the*

*general punishes a criminal, the heart of the army is sternly
controlled. In this way are battles won.*

Jake wondered if he was about to meet the general.

A *shōji* along the left wall opened, and one of the *yakuza*
who had come to the hotel appeared. He held it open as
another figure emerged into the room. This man took
short, exceedingly athletic steps as he crossed the lintel
track of the sliding screen. He stood in front of Jake with
his legs slightly spread, and, in so doing, managed to turn
a simple room into a court of law. He possessed an
undeniable presence.

Jake studied him. He was thick-shouldered and narrow-
waisted. His barrel chest gave grudging way to a thick
bull's neck and a scowling moon face with just a hint of
stubble from shorn hair. He had small ears that lay close
to his head, dark triangular eyes below startlingly thick
eyebrows. His mouth was wide and almost lipless.

He was nattily dressed in a dark sharkskin suit of sleek
European cut, striped rep tie, and pale pink shirt. A small
gold lapel pin was the only ornamentation Jake could see
until the man lifted a hand. A gold band in the shape of a
dragon encircled the marriage finger of his left hand.

'My name is Mikio Komoto,' the man said without
preamble. 'The *sarakin* from whom you borrowed the
money works for me. You have caught me at a most
disadvantageous time. I have very little time for the likes of
you, Mr Richardson.' He lifted Jake's passport, flapped it
back and forth as if he were fanning himself. 'What am I
to do with you? You ask for a favour and then have the
bad manners to refuse to pay that favour back. You
gamblers are all alike. Like gluttons, your eyes are always
bigger than your stomachs.' Here he had used the word
hara, which meant both stomach and a kind of overall
attitude that the Japanese respected most fully.

Jake's heart beat fast. He had been right. This was the
man he had come to see. '*Oyabun*,' he said, bowing in the

traditional *yakuza* manner. 'Will you allow me to apologize to you and to your *sarakin* in the proper fashion?'

Mikio Komoto said nothing, so Jake began to move toward the other man. The *yakuza* at the *shōji* reacted. Komoto made a cutting gesture with the edge of his hand. His black eyes looked at Jake as if he were a lizard on a rock.

Jake dug into his breast pocket and produced his wallet. Carefully he counted out enough yen to repay what he had borrowed from the *sarakin* the night before including the usurious interest. He added another one hundred thousand yen. This pile of bills he set before Komoto.

'I apologize for the inconvenience I have caused you, *oyabun*,' he said, bowing again in the ritualized *yakuza* manner. 'But between the money I lost last night at your gambling den and the repayment of the loan, I believe that I have paid well for a moment of your time.'

Komoto signed for his man to take the bills, and when the man had done so, the *oyabun* said, 'Toshi-*san*, show this *iteki* out.' He dropped Jake's passport on the *tatami* where Jake had left the money. He turned to go.

'I know who you are, *oyabun*,' Jake said. 'It is important that I speak with you.'

Komoto turned partially back. 'You think I am impressed with your grasp of my language? You think I am impressed that you know some of the rituals? You are *iteki*. A barbarian. I do not have conversations with barbarians. I take their money, if they are weak as you are weak.'

'It is about Nichiren that I am here, *oyabun*.'

'I know nothing of Nichiren.'

'Keii Kisan was *yakuza oyabun*. You are *yakuza oyabun*. Your clan and Kisan's are bitter rivals for Toshima-ku. Hadn't you better listen to me?'

Mikio Komoto's eyes sparked, and Jake could feel his intrinsic energy building dangerously. When the *oyabun* spoke again, his voice was cold enough to freeze the room. '*Yakuza* business is *yakuza* business. Perhaps you think that you are clever in having been brought here. Let me disabuse you of that thought. You have been quite stupid. In certain extreme cases, I have been known to do more than merely take a stupid barbarian's money. If an *iteki* crosses me, I kill him.' He almost spat out the last sentence.

The sneer was clearly etched across his face. '*Iteki*,' he repeated. 'Toshi-*san*, take this barbarian and his passport and get them both out of here. There's a smell in this room I don't like.'

His disconcertingly high voice seemed to travel only the distance it needed to reach her. It was perfectly modulated. She had been moved several times, always blindfolded. Consequently her sense of disorientation ran deeper than the darkness.

'Where am I?' Mariana said. Unlike Jake, she spoke no Japanese and only a smattering of Cantonese.

'Have you eaten today? Have you been fed well?'

'Yes to both questions,' she said. 'But I haven't much appetite.'

There was silence for a time.

'I feel like a rat in a cellar,' she said.

'I don't understand.'

'I have seen no light in some time.'

'I'm sorry.'

A flare like a sun, and Mariana threw her arm across her eyes. She heard him moving away from the door. Through her slitted eyes, she saw nothing but the crook of her arm. So many questions chased themselves through her mind. She did not want to ask any of them until she could see properly. It disturbed her how vulnerable she felt without her sight.

'It is important to maintain the utmost secrecy,' Nichiren

said. 'That is the reason for all the movement, the window-less rooms. The danger was very great.'

'And now?'

'Nothing has changed.'

What was he doing? All sound had ceased. 'Where am I?' she asked again.

'The answer is irrelevant to you.' His voice was matter-of-fact. 'Somewhere in Tokyo.'

She heard him closer to her. 'I am beginning to regret doing what you told me.'

'I don't understand,' he said in his heavily accented English. 'You are alive. The *fu* is safe.'

'I have been incarcerated in pitch blackness for days, without companionship or explanation,' she said with some vehemence. 'How else do you expect me to feel?'

'Frankly, I never gave it any thought,' he said in an almost puzzled tone. 'I have done what I had to in order to protect you from your enemies.'

'And what if you're lying to me?'

'I did not lie to you that night. You saw what you saw. That is the truth.'

'I don't know what is the truth any more,' she said raggedly.

'Will you cry now?'

Her head lifted. The glare was almost totally gone now. 'Do you think I'd give you that satisfaction?'

'It seems to me that is what women do when they are under stress.' He was dressed in a soot-grey lightweight linen suit of superlative lines. The conservative collar of his snow-white shirt seemed to dig into the muscles of his neck. His black hair was thick, brushed straight back from his wide forehead. He had a feline, almost triangular face. Besides Jake's, he had the most extraordinary eyes Mariana had seen in a man. What she saw swimming lazily in their depths frightened her, though she would admit such a

140

thing to no one. He looked neat and trim. She could see that he was very fit.

Despite her fear of him, or perhaps because of it, she felt anger rising in her. 'You're an idiot,' she snapped.

Then she noticed his hands. The edges were so over-grown with callouses they were positively yellow, patinaed like ancient ivory. This was in sharp contrast to his fingers, which were so long and delicate that she found herself filled with envy to look at them.

Nichiren regarded her with a disconcerting calmness of spirit. 'We must go now,' he said after a time.

'Go?' she said. 'Go where?'

'Away from Tokyo,' he said, as if this in itself were a sufficient explanation.

There was nothing for Jake to do now but wait. He had walked several blocks until he came to a stationery store. There he had purchased a small notepad and a ballpoint pen. Nearby he found a *nawanoren*. Pushing aside the beaded curtain, he went in and sat at a table in the corner. Near him a couple of old men were drinking beer and playing a spirited game of *go*. It was the time after lunch and before dinner; there was no one else about.

Jake ordered a Kirin and *shioyaki*. Midway through eating the salt-crusted roasted fish, he called for another beer. The old men were far along in their game and play was slowing.

Jake took out the notepad and pen and set about drawing an outline of Mikio Komoto's house from memory. Before seeking out the stationery store, he had taken a complete tour around the environs of the estate, so he knew roughly its size and, more specifically, its shape. Inside, he placed the halls and rooms he had passed going in and going out. Toshi had escorted him out through the front door. Next he assigned each room a function. Then he began to take educated guesses about the rest of the house.

141

This was not as impossible a task as it seemed on the surface. Traditional Japanese homes were built within a rigid structural system. Space was at a premium; even the richest businessman was limited by the land available to him. Too, each room was some multiple of the size of a *tatami*, so it was easy enough to break down an interior; there could be no odd-shaped rooms or surprises. The Japanese sensibility, moreover, was centred on confluence: clean lines moving, one to the other, in uncluttered fashion. Given these absolutes, the possibilities were reduced to a strict set of definites.

One other fact in Jake's favour was that Komoto's rooms would be in a separate wing of the house. No woman, save perhaps the cleaning lady, would be allowed in there. This was the area that interested Jake the most.

When he had finished his diagram, he studied it for some time. He wondered now whether this was all worth it. What if Komoto did not know where to find Nichiren? But obviously he had done so before; why not again?

There was no use worrying about it, Jake decided. He'd find out soon enough. He got up, paid the bill. On his way out, he took a look at the setup of the game the two men were playing. He saw the road to victory that they did not. He wished real life were so easy to define.

Outside, it was still light. He walked until he found the several shops he was looking for. In each, he made purchases. When he emerged from the last, he found that he was near a movie theatre. He went in and watched a revival of a film about the last great Japanese tattoo *sensei*, who apparently found his female client's skin more receptive to his needle if she was engaged in sexual intercourse while he was working his magic on her.

It reminded Jake of the difference between fiction and reality. 'Fine-sounding words,' Fo Saan had once told him, 'are not true. Beware the man who has honed his ability to talk; he is a liar.

142

'On the other hand, art is truth. Art takes nothing – a blank page, a white canvas – and makes of it something affecting. Art can only be defined by the emotion it engenders in the viewer. It does not presuppose; it does not contend. Like the great seas and rivers of the world, art is one of the Lords of the Ravines. Its power stems from keeping low.'

Jake had expected Fo Saan to whip out brush and ink at some time, but such had not been the case. Instead, when Jake asked if art was so powerful, wasn't it to be a part of his training, Fo Saan said, 'It *is* your training.'

It had taken Jake some time to understand that. That was all right. One learned in increments, anyway. That was the meaning of *chahm hai,* to sink in. Absorbing lessons, Fo Saan contended, was the only way to learn. 'One thinks,' he had said one morning, ' "I learn with my eyes; I learn with my ears; I learn with my nose; I learn with touch." One even thinks smugly, "I learn with my mind." ' He pointed. 'Go down the incline. Keep going.'

Jake did as he was bade. The fog was so thick that Jake soon lost touch with all landmarks. He felt the earth beneath his bare feet turn to dry, loose shale, then to thin, strawlike grass, and finally, as the incline increased, to sand. The sand, too, changed in texture as he descended, from coarse to fine.

With a start, he found himself in the water. He sniffed heavily, wondering how it was that he had not scented the sea before entering it. Then he looked up and saw that he was surrounded by an opalescent swirl. He saw no sky, no cloud, no sun. He turned fully around and found that he was out of sight of land. The fog.

He called out to Fo Saan, tentatively at first, then, cupping his hands beside his mouth, more loudly. His voice sounded strange and muffled, an odd tone he recalled from nightmares when he was trying to shout and only a raspy whisper emerged.

With his feet and the bottoms of his legs submerged, he could feel nothing. With sight, smell, hearing unreliable, he concentrated on touch. But he soon found that he could not even tell at what level the water had risen about him until, with a gasp, it seeped over the waistband of his shorts. How had he managed to go out so far? He had no idea. Until that moment he had been certain that he had moved only a step or two. He decided that the tide must have taken him. But why, then, hadn't he felt its insistent tug?

Panic welled up in him. Deprived of the use of his senses, he felt lost and isolated in the most absolute sense. He tried to calm himself by the use of reason, but with its reliance on the usual flow of sensory data, his mind seemed to have shut down. He could not think. He did not know what to do.

He shouted for Fo Saan.

The odd sound of his voice frightened him. The resulting silence frightened him further. He began to thrash around, trying to make for shore. But the tide had him too deeply and now would not so easily let him go. He felt trapped in quicksand.

The ocean lapped around his chest, then at his neck. When he felt it rising above the level of his chin, he shouted at the top of his lungs.

'You cannot learn with your eyes,' a voice said in his ear, 'because you cannot trust what you see.'

'Fo Saan!' he screamed. 'Where are you?'

'You cannot learn with your ears,' the voice went on, 'because you cannot trust what you hear.'

'Fo Saan, I'm drowning!'

'You cannot learn with your nose or from touch, because you cannot trust what you smell or touch. Therefore, do not think.'

'*A mi tuo fo*, Fo Saan!'

'*Ba-mahk!*' Feel the pulse!

What pulse? Jake thought as he snorted salt water out of his nose. His eyes stung and he felt heavy beneath the water, in the grasp of the tide. I will die, he thought.

'*Ba-mahk!*'

He went under then, just as if the tentacle of some monstrous sea creature had clamped him about the legs. Desperately he kicked out, holding his breath. The tide spun him. It was dark. An inchoate roaring in his ears sounded like absolute silence. He wanted to take a breath and could not. He was in an alien world, inimical to life. His life.

In that moment he felt the balance of life and death. It was as if he hung suspended between two massive entities. They had no physical form, merely a psychic presence. The darkness and the light. He knew from which side emanated that anarchic roaring. He wanted no part of the darkness and thus he turned away from it.

Ba-mahk. Felt the pulse.

Not from any of his senses, not from his mind. From his heart. Suspended in the heaving, primeval darkness, he had let go all his senses. He had ceased to think, and had begun only to feel. And had found the pulse.

It was like a river of silver in the darkness. It was like a monkey bridge across a violent chasm. Unthinking, he followed it and it brought him home.

Gasping, on the shore, he had felt Fo Saan's presence close beside him. He had felt the blanket settling over his shoulders and, gratefully, had wrapped it around his shivering self.

'You found the pulse.'

Jake wanted to respond, but his teeth were chattering too much.

'Now you know where you must look to find the truth,' Fo Saan said.

Now, surrounded by the night, Jake moved silently around the perimeter of Mikio Komoto's compound. 'If you invade another man's house,' Fo Saan had said, 'you must not rely on any one sense, or on senses at all. *Bamahk.*'

The pulse that Fo Saan had caused him to find was, of course, *qi*. If one could describe it, one might say that it was the ineffable combination of *i*, the will, and *qi*, intrinsic energy.

What Fo Saan had been intent on teaching Jake to achieve was *hao ran zhi qi*, the immensely great, immensely strong power.

Jake sought the pulse now and, finding it, entered Mikio Komoto's domain.

The elements were with him. The moon was a pale, inconstant shadow, alternately blurred and snuffed out by low-riding clouds that hinted of more rain. The old trees seemed to spread their branches, welcoming him into pitch blackness.

Crouched in the deepest shadows, Jake wound a piece of gauzy black cotton around his nose and mouth to muffle any breathing sound. He rubbed lampblack beneath his eyes, across his forehead, down the exposed upper part of the bridge of his nose. He took off his shoes and socks.

He listened to the wind in the willows and cryptomeria. He emerged from his impromptu hiding place, using *seuhn-fung*, or 'steps with the wind,' which Fo Saan had taught him. Rather than trying to make no sound and failing, he sounded like the soughing of the wind through the trees.

In this manner he came to the west side of the house. This was where he had been brought earlier in the day. Mikio Komoto's wing. He passed up the side entrance after several moments of contemplating it. It was bathed in a powerful overhead mini-spotlight. That way was certain suicide.

He moved farther along, past the manicured hedges. Beyond, he saw what he had not this afternoon: an exquisite private garden. It was narrow but far longer than the length of the wing. A tall, closely linked copse of mature cryptomeria rustled at the far end.

Jake crossed the garden, using the steppingstones to negotiate the pebbles. This path ended at a flat, rising stone. This was the last step up onto the *engawa*, a porch of cedar planking. Jake crept up onto it. The wall directly in front of him was a *fusuma*. Beside it was a window. The lights were out in this room, though they blazed in other areas of the house.

Jake took out a small jar of liquid silicone and applied it with a *mimikaki*, a Japanese earpick, something like an outsized Q-Tip, to the upper and lower tracks of the sliding door. Using a knifeblade inserted between the door and the wall, Jake quickly found the hook catch and flipped it up.

Cautiously he slid back the *fusuma* an inch or two. The moon emerged from a cloudbank and he ceased all motion until its wan, watery light faded before another onrush of clouds.

When he had opened the door just enough, he went in, sliding it shut behind him. He sat with his feet in the air, wiped the dew off their soles with a cotton rag. Then he donned a new pair of *tabi*, Japanese socks worn indoors. Wearing them, he would leave no footprints.

He flipped on a penlight. In the electronics shop where he had purchased it, the salesman had cautioned him against its flagrant use. This culture, the creators of the miniaturized, the portable, the tiny electronic marvel, was becoming increasingly alarmed at its accumulated fallout: discarded-battery pollution.

Jake played the narrow-beam light around the room. Nothing here for him. It was a long shot that there would be. He would now have to go out into the hall.

He went silently across the *tatami*. With his hand on the *shōji*, he took a deep breath. Centred himself. Sought again the pulse. Finding it, he drew the screen toward him.

And came face to face with a diminutive, wrinkle-faced Japanese. His eyes opened wide. Then, in perfect parody, his lips mirrored his eyes. He was just about to speak when Jake grabbed him by his shirtfront, pulled him over the threshold and into the room. Slid the *shōji* shut at his back.

He used his thumb, which was far more effective than the multipurpose knife he carried, sliding it under the small man's chin. Found the arterial nexus and put pressure on it. The man's eyes bulged.

'Name?' Jake said in Japanese. Eased off with his thumb.

'Ka – Kachikachi.'

'Files.'

'I don't – ackk!'

The ball of the thumb had disappeared in his flesh. Jake kept up the pressure for a sufficient amount of time.

'Files,' he repeated.

Kachikachi's oversized head bounced up and down. He winced with the pain.

'Take me to where they are.'

Together they went out into the hallway. It was dark and deserted. It was long past the time when business would be conducted in this house, save for an emergency. It was doubtful whether Komoto himself was even here, at this hour.

Jake had been two rooms away, as it turned out. He drew out a length of nylon cord and, placing Kachikachi on the *tatami,* bound him hand and foot. He used the cotton rag to gag the Japanese. Then he set about finding out all he could about Nichiren.

There wasn't much. That was always the risk. He had known that the information concerning Nichiren was volatile. There was always the chance that it was communicated through the clan strictly verbally.

He read with mounting disappointment through the sparse notations: Nichiren's womanizing, his frequent, erratically timed trips out of Japan, his comings and goings

148

within Kisan territory and, more specifically, within Keii Kisan's compound. It was clear from the last, at least, that Nichiren did not live there or even stay overnight. Scratch that as a potential hiding place.

Then he came upon a handwritten notation. The others, above, were typewritten. It took him some time to decipher the cramped *kanji*. Nichiren had been observed twice coming down from the Japan Alps, north of Tokyo. The first time, it seemed, he had been seen totally by accident. One of Komoto's *yakuza* on vacation had spotted him from a roadside restaurant as Nichiren stopped across the highway for gas.

Canny Komoto had then kept a watch, and sure enough, eleven days later, Nichiren had been spotted along the same road. This time it had been determined that he was descending the road out of Tateyama. But apparently further than that Komoto had not come. Nichiren had disappeared for three weeks, and when he returned to Japan, he stayed more or less within the Tokyo environs. At length, Komoto had given up the stakeout, deeming it too costly in time and manpower for a more than dubious end.

Yet this was just the chink in Nichiren's armour that Jake had been seeking. He returned the file and, leaving Kachikachi bound on the *tatami*, went back down the hall, exiting the house as he had come in.

He retrieved his shoes and socks just in time. It had begun to rain.

Uniformed soldiers were everywhere. The Premier had a thing about them. Zilin considered it a fixation. The Premier had been the one who gave the orders to bring down the Gang of Four. Zilin remembered it well.

The Premier had watched while the dispatched soldiers did their work. Ever since he had ascended in rank, he had made certain that everyone knew he had not forgotten the incident.

Power is fleeting. Like a Roman emperor, the Premier had his Praetorian guard. No doubt, Zilin thought, the Premier was safeguarding himself from what had happened to his predecessors. What had occurred once in China could occur again.

Well, that wasn't so far off the mark. If Wu Aiping had his way, there would be more ideological blood spilled across Tian An Men Square. Mine, Zilin thought.

Tai He Dian, the Hall of Supreme Harmony, the hall of the Premier, was so vast that it was chilly even now, in the middle of summer, when all other places in China were hot and sticky. The ceiling was so high it was lost to view. The mist of the centuries seemed to hang in the air, to film the hard wooden furniture as if with a new coat of lemon oil. It had an odd, distinctive smell that rippled at Zilin's memory, brushing against the past – *his* past. But at the moment he could not bring it to mind.

As he approached the far end of the room, he could see that Wu Aiping was already present. The minister sat folded up on a carved ebony chair, like a praying mantis, all angles and sharply delineated lines.

The Premier, on the other hand, round and squat, sat behind the high wooden desk that had the appearance of a Western judge's banc. This physical elevation he affected as a personal manifestation of his power. It was in the purest sense, Zilin mused, an anticommunistic gesture. We will mouth the word 'Comrade' to each other when we are obviously nothing of the sort. The hierarchies of power are ubiquitous; they defeat us all, in the end, if we are not cautious, most cautious.

Poor Karl Marx. What an unquiet time his spirit must endure, considering the liberties his followers have taken with his precepts.

As Zilin settled himself upon the mean seat of an ebony

chair, he reflected that never had the Communists and the Roman Catholic Church been so close, not in spirit but in the interpretations of their precepts. Historically, both of their ideologies had been corrupted in the name of purity by those who craved power. Death and destruction were wreaked under their aegis. They were both bastions of sanctimonious power.

And I, Zilin thought, am hardly blameless. A sudden wave of despair overcame him with the intensity of pain. Though I did not lift a hand, my guilt is the same. I looked on mutely as blood was brutally spilled across these streets I now walk. I remained silent when voices of righteousness were raised, explaining the bloodshed as right and necessary to expunge ideological disease from the corpus of modern-day China. Death in the name of holy purity! That has been our crusade for so many years. We are a poor, self-deluded people.

In that moment he thought of abandoning the *ren*, the plan he thought of as his harvest. Despair was a powerful emotion; it could undo the work of decades. And it would, here and now, Zilin knew, unless he could find his way through it. Certainly, he had known despair before. Zhang Hua knew that he was subject to bouts of profound melancholy and, knowing Zilin as he did, would put it down to a lack of family. For he knew that Zilin had no one.

Then, once again, as he always did, Zilin remembered that it had been his silence that had brought him this far. Only he, of all the old leaders, still lived; only he, of all the old men of his youth, still retained a grasp on the slippery reins of power.

Nonaction is action. He had been taught that long ago when he had learned how to play *wei qi*. Silence is a voice heard somewhere, interpreted by someone. Without it, he knew that his *ren* would never be on the verge of fruition. He knew the personal rewards it would bring him as well as the lasting benefits for his country. He could not allow anyone to stop him. Not even Wu Aiping.

'Ministers,' the Premier intoned, 'I greet you in the name of China and the Revolution. We are here today to discuss business that is both vital and difficult.' He cleared his throat, shuffling papers in the interim.

'Shi *tong zhi*,' he continued, 'Wu *tong zhi* has asked for a formal hearing regarding your external policies in Hong Kong. Rather than reiterate what he has submitted to me, I will ask him to address the issue himself.'

Slowly, Wu Aiping unfolded himself from the chair. He was tall for a Chinese, just under six feet. He had the kind of odd extension of his ribcage that, in this part of the world at least, might be construed as a deformity. His large eyes were like beacons flashing in the night. He was the junior of the other two in the room by at least three decades, but that did not decrease the forcefulness of his personality. Quite the contrary, in fact, since few in China would expect such intelligence from one of his age.

'The public announcement of our compromise policy – so called by Shi Zilin – with the *faan gwai loh* British regarding the future disposition of Hong Kong has been a source of great concern to me and the leading members of my academy.

'As you are aware, we were against capitulation to the foreign devil in any manner at all. This so-called compromise smacks of the myopia of the Manchu dynasties, which allowed the invasion of the Middle Kingdom's sovereign territory in the first place.

'It seems to me and to my colleagues as well that the longer we delay in taking over Hong Kong, the more face we will lose, and the more unlikely it is that we will succeed in our takeover. Bad enough to lose face to a civilized man, but to do so to *faan gwai loh* is intolerable.

'Comrade Premier, since you have allowed the formulation of Hong Kong policy to be dictated by Shi Zilin, we have been giving nothing but mixed signals to the West. The impending defection of Mattias, King and Company is just the latest example. I don't believe we can afford that kind of vacillation. If we are to make Hong Kong our own again, we must be allowed in there as quickly as possible, to ensure that businesses will run smoothly as we move our troops in and make of it a special administrative control district.

'In this, the Party Chief and the Minister of Defence concur.' He produced sealed packets. 'Here are their signed statements.'

The Premier took time to read both documents. At length his head lifted. 'Shi *tong zhi*?'

With an effort, Zilin rose. He had not wanted to bring his walking stick in here, so he was obliged to grip the arms of the ebony chair with both hands.

'Comrade Premier, with all due respect to the minister, Wu *tong zhi* knows nothing of policy inside Hong Kong. He knows nothing of the millions of Chinese there born and raised under the capitalist system. He has no conception of the difficulties that await us in inculcating those millions, should we decide to impose an entirely different social and economic structure on them. We would be – '

'Does that mean we may not turn Hong Kong into a part of China?' Wu Aiping had spun on Zilin. 'We are all dedicated to a certain way of life, Shi *tong zhi. All* of us. There is no room for a compromise when it comes to Hong Kong. That part of China was stolen from us by the barbarians. They have it still, to this day.'

'With all due respect,' Zilin said, 'Hong Kong is already ours.'

'Nonsense!' Wu Aiping exploded. 'It is a den of capitalist vice and corruption!'

'Which provides us with millions each year. Funds we desperately need for heavy industry. Funds, I might add, that go in no small part to Kam Sang.'

'Ideology, Shi *tong zhi*,' Wu Aiping hissed. 'Purity of purpose. All this talk of money smacks of heresy and ideological backsliding. You have opposed me in this just as you have obstinately refused to back the Kam Sang project. I – and many like me – find your views objectionable in the extreme.' His eyes blazed. 'That is why I have petitioned the Premier to have you dismissed from your post as the head of the Hong Kong policy unit. Huang Xiao is more than qualified to replace you.'

Huang Xiao, Zilin thought to himself, is one of the *qun*.

'Comrade Ministers,' the Premier said, 'there has been much turmoil of late within the government regarding these issues. So much so that we have reached a dangerously divisive state.

'Wu *tong zhi* is correct. I see a return to the days of 1900 when the Manchu were in power, feudal lords bickered among themselves, the militant Boxer *tong* rose on mighty wings to power previously unimaginable.

'In the meantime, the *faan gwai loh* stole our land from us.

'This cannot be allowed to happen again. It has been decided. Although the work of Shi *tong zhi* for the State over a span of many decades is admirable, there are particulars in Wu *tong zhi*'s petition worthy of merit. Therefore, it has been decided that Shi *tong zhi* will have a period of thirty days to resolve the problems inherent in the present Hong Kong policy. At that time a second hearing will be convened on these premises. If the present work of Shi *tong zhi* is not deemed satisfactory or is proved in some manner deficient, then Huang Xiao will be appointed in Shi *tong zhi*'s place. It is so ordered.'

On his way out of the Tai He Dian, Zilin saw the smile of satisfaction on Wu Aiping's face. Zilin could feel the noose tightening around his throat. He knew he was under attack as surely as if Wu Aiping had lobbed a grenade under his desk.

At that moment, Zilin felt his age. He wondered if his twin enemies, time and the proximity of power, had conspired at last to bring him down. He had been so long with both. Wu Aiping could be their agent.

Perhaps my time has come, he thought. If so, my *ren*, my harvest, was only the dream of a dying man.

The Japan Alps run almost directly through the middle of Honshu Island. Unlike the European Alps, whose current foliage was in large part dictated by glaciation during the Ice Age, their Asian counterparts were only slightly affected. Indeed, their narrow V-shaped gorges were sculpted by heavy rains and melting snow. Thus their exquisite heavy foliation, rich in broad-leafed deciduous trees such as oak and beech. Too, the Japan Alps are a haven for a wide variety of species of flora, as opposed to Europe's Ice Age-ravaged alpine region.

The northernmost of the Japan Alps is the Hida Range. To the south, where its mountains abut the Sea of Japan, is some of the most treacherous terrain in all of Asia. The range consists of twenty peaks, six of them major, averaging over ten thousand feet.

Sacred Tateyama is one of these. It is bounded in the north by Shiroumayama and by the immense five-peaked massif of Hotaka, or Highcrest, a Matterhorn-like monster to the south.

Tateyama, too, has many peaks. One of them, Oyama, is the home of an 8th-century Buddhist shrine. Another is known as Tsurugi. Its eight sharply jutting peaks gave rise to its name, the Sword. Among Japanese mountain climbers, it is the origin of the phrase 'to climb the Sword,' which is akin to crossing the Rubicon. On Tsurugi, it is said, there is no turning back once you have begun.

Today, parts of the Sword are accessible by car, bus, and even cable car. It is still, however, a remote and, many say, an unfriendly place. Certainly none of the tourists who daily are driven up the single narrow, tortuous road to the series of overlooks would contemplate staying overnight, let alone building a residence there.

For this reason, among others, Nichiren had decided to make Tsurugi his retreat from the world. Which meant that it was his only true home.

It was to his stone cabin on the north face of the Sword that he took Mariana now. He had chosen the site because it was away from the tourist routes. It was also the most forbidding. What glacial remnants were still to be found in the upper reaches of the Hida Range were here. Winters brought swirling winds, heavy snow and shrieking ice storms. Drifts could easily reach six or seven feet in January and February. But the clear days were a pearlescent blue that could be matched nowhere in the world. And when the sun struck the rugged, pitched slopes of the Sword, the resulting rainbows off ice and snow made his heart soar.

Wounded by the world, Nichiren periodically had to return here to heal, to be made whole again.

In the summer, it was a dream. The oppressive weather that blanketed Japan was left far below in valleys indistinct with heat and humidity. The direct sun was extremely hot at this elevation, but it was a clear, piercing heat, like the first step into a *furo*; one felt cleansed by it.

And within the dappled shade of the stands of oak and beech, the crisp coolness never left the slopes even in the middle of August.

Nichiren had brewed tea. He sat drinking it out of a rough clay mug as he sat on the edge of his house's *engawa*. This traditional part of any Japanese house was a loggia-like porch. It was just such a spot on which he used to play as a child. Only one stone step up from the outer garden, the *engawa* served many purposes. It was left open in summer to catch the warm breezes that, at lower elevations at least, cooled the interior of the house. In winter it was closed off from the elements, thus increasing the house's floor space. But it had a further, more social function. It was bad manners ever to let someone pass by – the mailman, for instance – without offering a cup of tea or a bit of sweet cake to lift the spirits. To ask a casual acquaintance inside the house was to begin a long train of formalities that would both violate the privacy of the house and be wildly inappropriate. The *engawa*, then, served as a middle ground or neutral territory where casual courtesies could be observed.

All these multiple layers of meaning passed through Nichiren's mind as he sat gazing out at the majestic mountains to the north. Occasionally he dipped a pair of chopsticks into a jar of homemade *umeboshi*, soft pickled plums, red from fermentation with the mintlike *shisho* leaves. These he put on a bed of white rice to make *hinomaru bento*, the 'rising-sun lunch,' eating with quick, sharp flicks of his chopsticks.

Presently a second shadow crossed the polished wooden floor of the *engawa*, mingling with his own. He did not turn but said, 'Are you hungry? I have lunch for you here.'

'I'm tired,' Mariana Maroc said. She wore a kimono that Nichiren had found for her inside the house. Because of her small size, it fitted her well. It was in earth tones: umber, sienna, rust. The autumn equinox displayed through the superb weaver's art. On her feet were snow-white *tabi* and dark wooden *geta*.

She moved and Nichiren turned. He watched her.

'You are not clumsy,' he said. 'You do not walk like a Caucasian.'

'Is that a compliment?'

'An observation only.'

She came and sat down next to him, carefully folding her kimono beneath her knees. The bowls of rice and *umeboshi*, the tea mugs were between them.

'Drink,' Nichiren said softly. 'You must be thirsty.'

'I want Jake.'

157

Mariana's pellucid beauty was marred now by the dark circles beneath her eyes, as livid as bruises. Worry and lack of sleep had combined to defeat her natural loveliness.

Nichiren pointed. 'Do you see that great peak to the north? It is called Shiroumayama. White Horse Peak. In winter it takes on an equine shape, but that is not how it got its name. Early in May, the snows along its slope retreat, leaving what the farmers below see as a horse-shaped patch of rock. Each year, when they see this natural seasonal clock, they know it is time to plant their rice.

'Long ago, they gave it the name Mountain of the Paddy Horse. You may not know that *shiro* has associated with it two *kanji* characters. One means "paddy field", the other "white".

'Some clerk somewhere long ago made a mistake, and so we call it by a name it was never meant to have.'

Mariana shrugged as she took up her tea and sipped at it. 'It seems easy enough to have it changed back.'

'Nothing in life is easy.' Nichiren put aside his bowl. 'Least of all attempting to correct one's mistakes.'

Mariana looked at him. She had the sense that he was speaking about something else entirely. She felt in him an odd kind of melancholy that sent a tiny shiver, an undefined ache through her, the kind one gets by hearing an owl hoot on a silver autumn night.

'When will I be able to see Jake?' she asked, holding herself with her elbows.

'There is danger all around,' Nichiren said obliquely.

In the time she had been with him, Mariana had got used to this odd manner of his speech. She had learned quite quickly that one could not cut through his tangents; rather, one had to learn to interpret them.

'That was what you told me when you first contacted me in Hong Kong.'

'I told you the truth,' he said, pouring more tea. 'Enemies are generated from the unlikeliest positions. In *wei qi*, as in life, that is a difficult lesson to learn. You showed good judgment in following my directions.'

'I simply had nothing to lose.' Mariana held herself more tightly. 'But Jake must be out of his mind with worry.'

'Perhaps that is not such a bad thing.'

Mariana's head whipped around. She glared at him, putting into her eyes all the anger, bewilderment, and fear she had been feeling ever since his call had pinned her into this nightmare.

Nichiren must have felt something, because he stirred as if abruptly uncomfortable. 'If you would use your mind instead of your emotions, you would see the wisdom of my words.' He paused deliberately, as if to allow her to come to her own conclusions. 'If your husband does not know where you are, then his enemies cannot, either.'

Mariana was silent for a time. It was impossible to refute his logic. Nichiren put his head back against the square wooden post, one of six that ran the length of the *engawa*. Filtered light played upon the smooth planes of his face. He was quite handsome, Mariana thought. His was a proud face, with lines somehow purer than any human face had a right to have.

'I want to know something,' she said. 'Were you at the Sumchun River when Jake was there?'

He sipped at his tea. 'Is that important?'

'It might be,' she said. 'It might explain a lot of things.'

'I see.' He placed the cup between them. 'If I said yes, it would wrap it all up in a neat package. You would have the easy answer to your problem.'

'Nothing in life is easy,' she said, meaning to mock him but somehow failing. She was angry at his intransigence, but he restrained her harsh tongue in some manner unfathomable to her. She found herself wanting to understand him, as if, by this, she would be better able to understand Jake.

'You have a good memory,' he said, 'to go along with your good judgment.'

'Why won't you tell me anything?' she said, abruptly exasperated.

'For the same reason adults don't tell their children everything they want to know.'

'I'm a child,' she flared. 'That's how you see me?'

'If you continue to jump to conclusions,' he said reasonably, 'I will not be able to speak with you at all.' In the silence, the *fūrin* at the end of the *engawa* turned as the breeze took it. Its light tinkling showered them with sound.

'Words are only words,' he said, after a time. 'They can be believed or not.'

'What are you saying?'

'That you would not believe my answers to your questions.'

'Why don't you try me?'

'I have no desire,' he said, 'to be called a liar.'

Jake, she thought, what are you in the midst of?

To their right, the *fūrin* moved again in the sudden wind, its three slim metal bars coming together below the ellipse of the bell in a tinkling cascade that echoed softly all along the *engawa* and out into the garden. In the stifling heat, this ethereal chiming was a sound on which to concentrate. Its otherworldly presence was like a repeating *mantra*, an escape from the debilitating lethargy.

All around them, the *fūrin* sang its song of summer.

The air conditioner in the Nissan was inadequate. Jake's suit jacket had long ago been laid out like an exhausted warrior along the back seat. His shirt, with open collar, was dark with sweat stains under the arms, down the front and back.

About midday, already far north of Tokyo's urban sprawl, he stopped at a roadside stand to eat a lunch of eel *teriyaki*, the traditional summertime fare because it was

160

'stamina' food. He stretched his legs while he ate. He was on a small thoroughfare lined with wood-frame houses. Many of the doors were thrown open in an attempt to lessen the heat. Old men sat in their underwear along the *engawa*, fanning themselves with slow, automatic motions while their minds were engaged with games of *go*. Beneath a large boxwood, where he stopped to be out of the intense sun, the stirrings of the *fūrin* could be heard, lacing the air with melody, lightening the oppressive humidity.

As was the common custom, he urinated into the bushes at the side of the road before climbing into the Nissan. The stop had done nothing for the temperature of the interior. Though he had been careful to park it in the shade, it was stifling as he started up. Still heading north.

The Japan Alps dominated the horizon ahead of him. Jake watched the countryside flash by in varying shades of green. He felt a sudden lessening of the heat at the same moment the hues outside cooled down to a more subdued level. Clouds had come in behind him, darkening the sky.

Jake knew he was taking an awful chance. If Komoto's information was false or odd, he would not find Mariana. If Nichiren was in hiding somewhere else, he would not find her here. Yet the more he thought about it, the more logical this mountain retreat seemed for the situation. It was isolated and therefore more easily defensible than any quarters in Tokyo. Also, after the raid on O-henro House, it would be logical for Nichiren to be wary of another such penetration.

He hoped he was right. But he was aware, too, that his desperation was forcing him to take immediate choices that, in more normal situations, would have required some deliberation. He was, he knew all too well, in the wrong terrain for this kind of spontaneous action. Thus, the danger was acute.

The mountains rose up all around him now. Several times he was obliged to pull onto the verge, horn sounding, to race around the slower tour buses that were becoming more frequent as he headed into the Hida Range.

Rain's coming, he thought, turning down the howling air conditioner. He was already several thousand feet up, and there had been a palpable change in the humidity as well as the heat. He opened the window gratefully, despite the threat of a downpour. Cool air fanned his face, and he felt immediately refreshed.

The first drops began. *Potsu-potsu*, Jake thought. It was said that the Japanese were a tactile race, their language more concerned with describing how things feel rather than how they smell or taste. *Potsu-potsu* was one of those words, meaning 'a few drops here and there.' Jake knew that if it got bad he would have to stop. This road was not made for travel in slick weather. Too many of the verges were far too near the cliff face.

He grunted, squinting upward at the roiling cloudbank. The sky had darkened considerably, low and fulminating. In a moment, deep rumblings began.

'Shit,' he said.

With a crash, he seemed to hit a wall of water. The world turned grey-green and indistinct all around him. He switched on the wipers at high speed.

Zaa-zaa, he said to himself. It's raining cats and dogs. Time to seek shelter.

Several miles up, he pulled into a small village. Apparently, others on their way up had the same idea, for the street was jammed with silver tour buses and cars parked or idling in the midst of the downpour.

Jake pulled into a space between a Toyota and a sleek Mercedes. He cut the engine and rolled up his window enough so that he would not get drenched.

Summertime, he thought, glancing skyward. How I used to love it as a kid. Now it's different. He shrugged resignedly. Well, it's not a season for adults.

He watched disinterestedly as the door to the Mercedes

162

swung open and, beneath an elegant blue-and-green striped umbrella, a young blonde woman in a white sleeveless blouse and navy linen skirt herded a six-year-old girl made in her image across the pelted street and into a tea shop, its windows steamy with humidity.

Thunder rolled again, crossing from left to right like writing across a page. Two cars down from the parked Mercedes, four men got out of their rented Subaru. They were large, and it appeared that they needed to stretch their legs. They passed a cheap black nylon umbrella from one to another as they did leg stretches, knee bends, twists, and the like. They could have been mountain climbers or . . .

Jake felt the tension come into his frame. He wiped away the mist that clung to the interior surface of the windshield like fog.

He started the engine. The wipers came on at once, clearing the windshield further. Now he was certain, and his heart beat fast.

He had recognized one of the men getting back into the blue Subaru. They were all back in the car now. The rain was lessening and it began to back out of its space.

KGB. First Chief Directorate. KVR.

For hours now they had heard the deep basso rumblings of the thunder emanating from the deep blue swirling clouds below their eyrie. The storm filled up the crevasses and valleys like a surging tide, obscuring all but the Alps' upper peaks.

Nichiren had gone inside to work on the three games of *wei qi* he had set up. They were all in complex middle stages, and after a few moments of superficial study, Mariana had abandoned any idea she might have had of working out the vectors of attack and defence. Besides, the boards and pieces reminded her of Jake.

She returned to the *engawa*, though the air was cooler now and, in the long oblique bars of shade, even chilly.

The crimson sun seemed impaled on one of Tsurugi's bloodstained spires. She stood leaning against one of the wooden pillars, staring down into the murk of the storm. At length, she realized it was rising up from the valley floor, along the ridged sides of the peak. Soon they would be engulfed in rain.

The Nissan slewed around a corkscrew and began its slide outward toward the void beyond the rock face that shot down to the floor of the valley, six thousand feet below.

Steering into the slide, Jake began to finesse the car back onto the pavement. He kept very still, not wanting to add his shifting weight to the forces already in play.

Back on the road, he floored the accelerator, muscling the Nissan upward. In heavy weather like this, he knew, there were likely to be mudslides, falling rock. At the very least, the shoulders would begin to crumble away.

He had lost some time and now could not see the Subaru hastening up the mountain. The storm seemed to be following him, reintensifying as it rose up Tsurugi's face. Premature night had settled in, its embrace heavy and cloying. Hissing rain beat down, defeating even the wildly arcing wipers.

At least he knew they could not pull over. There was only one road to the series of lookouts. He could not lose them. The car screeched around another hairpin turn, his stomach wrenching with the centrifugal force. In this weather, he knew, they would not see him even if they suspected they were being followed. He cursed as he nearly spun out again. Weather's getting worse. He was almost talking to himself.

He leaned over, turning on the heater and the defroster to help clear the windshield.

* * *

164

'Rain's on its way up.'

Mariana stood in the open doorway, looking in at Nichiren, who was bent over the middle board. He took a black stone, settled on the move. He placed it down, removed a white piece from the board. Then he looked at her.

'Storms have a way of gaining in intensity this far up,' he said. 'But don't worry. We'll be safe enough here.'

Mariana laughed softly. She was not immune to the irony of his reassuring her about a storm, after what she had been through. A storm could not kill her.

'Even as a child I loved lightning,' she said. 'My father would often have to come and get me out of the fields in the middle of a storm. If I had not yet seen the flash for which I had been waiting, I would cry. My brother always said I was a brave child.'

'You were attuned to nature more than he,' Nichiren said in such a neutral tone that Mariana did not know whether she had been complimented or rebuked.

'Nichiren,' she said. He watched her as carefully as if she were a doe in a forest glade. The silence stretched itself, and still she said nothing. He did not prompt her. She changed her mind several times before she said, 'Perhaps it's time to leave.'

He shook his head and her heart sank.

'I cannot bear this enforced isolation any more. I cannot bear to think of what Jake is going through.' Her eyes beseeched him. 'I want to be with him. Don't you understand?'

His head swung away into the shadows of the room, but not before she caught a glimpse of his eyes. A curtain had fallen, as heavy and secure as lead. What is he thinking? she asked herself.

'If you leave here now, you will surely perish.' She could not see his mouth moving, there was so much darkness within the house.

Her agitated mind was snagged on the spike of one phrase. 'I don't understand. Why is my life important to you? I am the wife of your enemy.'

'I have my instructions.' He knelt on the *tatami*. Shadows poured across him. He looked towards the doorway, saw her small figure outlined in kimono and *geta*. With some astonishment he realized that his resentment had faded. Outside, she might be Jake Maroc's wife. But this was Tsurugi, and here she was something else. He did not know what.

'Instructions?' she echoed. 'Perhaps you are not a man, after all. Perhaps you are only a marionette. When someone pulls your strings, you jump.' She regarded him levelly. 'In school, in biology class, I was once given a frog. It was dead, but I was taught that when I poked it with a sharp instrument, I could make its muscles work. That's you. A dead frog.'

'Words,' he said, returning his gaze to the game board. 'Words mean nothing. Actions are everything.' He played a move.

'You play this game. Jake plays it as well. I cannot understand why. Life is to be lived, not to play games with. You cannot move people around in the same way you place these black and white stones on the board. Life just doesn't work that way.'

Nichiren looked up. 'But that is precisely what someone is doing. Your death, the capture of the *fu*. That was how they were planned.'

'And didn't work.'

'Because of a judicious countermove.'

Mariana was becoming claustrophobic. 'Just what is Jake's *fu*?'

'In ancient China,' Nichiren said, 'the emperor created a *fu* to his specifications. It was carved out of jade or ivory in the design of his choosing. Often, more than one would be made. The *fu* was a royal seal imparting, to a great

166

extent, all of the emperor's power. He gave them to his most trusted ministers so that they became his arms. Thus his power was extended ten-thousandfold.'

'And Jake's *fu*?'

'All *fu* are created in power. Those who wield them are given the power. I assume it is the same with this *fu*.'

'Assume? Then you don't actually know.'

'How could I?' he said, turning away. 'I am a dead frog.'

Stallings had picked Jake up in Tokyo. Toshima-ku. It was the logical place to start. It was where O-henro House was, where the confluence of the Kisan and the Komoto *yakuza* clans' territories created violent eddies, where Nichiren was most protected and most powerful while in Japan.

Jake's presence had startled Stallings somewhat. As far as he had known, Jake was still in a Kowloon hospital. Yet it had made sense to him to find him here.

Though it was the biggest break Stallings could have hoped for, it had also presented a problem. Stallings did not make the mistake of underestimating Jake's abilities, and he had wondered how long it would take Jake to tumble to him.

It had been a source of worry that Jake had not become aware of him until he thought about the crushing pressure the other man must be working under. To have his wife disappear, perhaps with his enemy, was a burden Stallings was grateful to observe from afar.

It was a curious feeling for him to be on the other side of the field from Jake Maroc. It disturbed him. More, it frightened him. But he felt the fear was a healthy emotion. His fear would protect him from making a mistake when it came to Jake, and he was grateful for it.

He had had a bad moment when Jake stopped in town. It was so crowded that he had had to park in a spot that

167

gave him only a partial view of the Nissan's rear. But it had been enough for him to see Jake pull out.

Now, as he followed Jake's Nissan into the Alps, he grinned with the sheer exhilaration of the moment. He manhandled the car, slewing it around a sharp turn. He was driving without headlights. It would have been safer to use them, but he could not afford that luxury. Jake's Nissan was being driven at erratic speeds. For long stretches of time, it was out of his sight because of the road's many switchbacks. He knew that if Jake slowed through one of the blind spots, his own headlights would glare in Jake's rearview mirror. He might as well send him a warning signal.

The narrow road, the slick tarmac, the soft shoulders, the increasing possibility of a mudslide, the poor visibility all combined to bring out his skills. His grin widened. It was all he thought about. That and the kill.

Outside, it had gone quite silent in the interstices between thunder rolls. The wind had died in deference to the swiftly oncoming low-pressure system.

'I asked – '

'Shh!' The harsh, sibilant sound checked her. She saw him silently uncoil, like some lethal animal. In an instant he was standing by her side. She watched his eyes, which seemed focused on the middle distance. After a time she realized that he was listening intently.

'Sometimes,' he whispered, 'the rocks carry the oddest soft sounds upward. I can hear animals foraging as much as a thousand feet below, or birds crying.'

She was certain these were not what he was listening for now. 'What is it?'

'A car,' he said, moving out into the deepening twilight. 'I hear a car where there should be no car.'

* * *

As soon as he had pulled in, Jake jumped out of the Nissan. The downpour drenched him immediately. He scrambled up the rocky scree to where the Subaru sat at the very lip of the last and highest outlook. It was deserted.

They've gone up, Jake thought. It's the only direction possible.

This far up, there were still patches of icy snow, now beginning to break up with the soaking rain. Gusting wind howled all around him. It flung sleet into his face. The temperature had plummeted, and his soaked shirt clung to his goosefleshed skin in icy sheets.

Often he was obliged to grasp the bases of tree trunks as the wet weather undermined the icy crust of the mountainside. He was not dressed for this kind of work, and this made the going even slower.

Jake was now desperate. If Mariana was with Nichiren, then the KGB team would find her. He could not be concerned as yet with the question of why the KGB would want Nichiren dead. Mariana was all he thought about.

He scrambled upward, his clothes shredding along the way as he stumbled and fell. Layered shale crumbled beneath his scrabbling soles, tumbling down the mountainside with a clatter silenced by the ferocity of the storm.

Eventually he reached a kind of plateau, and stopped so abruptly that he was almost pitched headlong into the void.

This strenuous exercise combined with his anxiety over Mariana's safety to weaken him. He was not yet over his bout in the hospital. He took several deep breaths as he began to climb again, skirting a shallow glen to the left. Here the mountain wall was not so steep and seemed to be composed of firmer rock, so that he had little trouble negotiating the humped incline.

It was quite a bit darker now, but lightning had begun to flicker, illuminating the landscape for seconds at a time with the incendiary light of a dragon's fiery exhalation.

Jake's head was pounding, and his shoulder had begun to pain him with short, sharp jolts like surges from an open electric line. He kept his breathing deep, even though he felt a disconcerting tendency to pant in rapid, shallow spurts. This frightened him more than anything else in this rapidly deteriorating situation, because it meant that he could not fully depend on his body. He knew that if he did not have control of that, he was surely lost. And so was Mariana.

Don't think about such things! he berated himself. But as he felt the fire in his chest, as he continued to fight the urge to bark out his breaths in order to suck in more oxygen, he began to lose faith in himself. I'm too old, he thought. Ten years ago, or even five, that stint in the hospital would have meant very little. But now . . .

Don't think, he told himself fiercely. Just get yourself up there where the long gun rests. Go on! Don't look up! Just concentrate on the next step! And the next! That's right! Keep going, old man! Old man! Old man! Old man!

And with this goad like a litany in his head, releasing all the anger and pride in himself, he gathered his reserves of energy and struggled up the remaining feet of the rocky cliff.

Jake threw himself over the last outcropping, rolling in the sleet and freezing rain along what seemed to be an endless meadow. He kept himself low and squinted into the gloom, searching for shadows, and found the Russians, sooty wraiths crouching within a clump of foliage just a foot back from the lip of the meadow, which, at that point, fell away into the canyon far below at an almost vertical drop.

Already chilled to the bone, he snaked his way towards them on his belly and knees. He used his elbows to drag himself forward without raising his body up at all. The grass here was thick, but certainly not tall enough to hide him completely.

He was within a hundred feet of them when he heard a series of shots. He jerked his head to the right, and dimly saw, across the chasm to the other escarpment, the outlines of a house. A figure running through the grass beyond the chasm. Who was it? The sleet made identification impossible. He rose up.

Then a gun spoke with a report like the rolling thunder hanging suspended far above.

Nichiren had pushed her back inside the house with a calculated admonition to stay there under all circumstances. Mariana had watched him steal through the garden and into the meadow that led to the edge of the deeply veed chasm three hundred yards away.

She strained to follow his route as he began to fade into the sleeting evening, moving cautiously out to the edge of the *engawa* to keep track of him until the very last instant.

When she was totally alone, she turned and, following his direction, went back inside, bolting the front door. She stood in the centre of the room, shivering, alone with the three unfinished *wei qi* games.

For some reason, now, she wanted desperately to understand the game. Jake had told her that a player's strategy in the game was the same as his strategy in life. She circled the boards slowly, narrowing her concentration.

Thus the fusillade of shots that slammed through the wood of the back door caused her to jump violently and cry out. Her mind, numbed with terror, blanked out entirely, allowing the animal organism to take over. To protect itself, it ran.

With a harsh shout of anxiety, Mariana ripped off the bolt on the front door, threw it back so violently that it rattled on its track. She stumbled in her *geta* and, moaning in frustration, kicked them off. In *tabi-claó* feet, she ran out into the storm, her blind instincts taking her on the same course she had seen Nichiren use minutes before.

The KGB stalkers, catching sight of her, followed along behind with cool, unhurried steps, guns in their right hands, hanging loosely down at their sides.

Across the chasm, the storm was still making a great deal of noise, but even had it been a silent evening, they would not have heard Jake's approach.

Fear and the adrenaline running through him caused him to grin, his lips pulled back as if in a terrible rictus. He reached them where they knelt at the crest of the ridge.

The heavyset man nearest him turned just as Jake went into *irimi nage*, the entering throw. They crashed together. The Russian towered over him, gaining false confidence in his illusory position of strength.

Jake moved into the other's rush instead of resisting it. This motion of evasion metamorphosed smoothly into one of centralization in which *irimi nage* began to control the adversary's energy, transferring its force to Jake.

The full weight of the Russian's two-hundred-plus pounds was against Jake, who, following the dictates of the manoeuvre, used the energy thus transferred to him like a wave, dipping his upper body down and then rising with the increased energy flow, locking his right arm beneath the left of the Russian. This rising up put the Russian off balance, and his upper torso began to bend backward against the inviolable force of Jake's strength combined with his own energy turned upon him. Now, at the apex of his upward thrust, Jake kept his torso erect but swiftly bent his knees, lifting and uncoiling in a blur like an arrow shot from the bow.

The Russian had no balance left. His legs still drove forward in a momentum that was now false as Jake bent his upper body painfully backward. As he collapsed horizontal to the ground, Jake delivered a vicious liver kite to the unprotected area, and the Russian did not rise when he struck the ground with a heavy thump.

172

Jake whirled, groaning with pain, his left hand arcing upward and across in a bowstring strike that swept the second Russian's aimed weapon from him. He grabbed the other's still extended right hand with both of his. At the same time he stepped backward with his left leg, leading the Russian towards him in a circular motion. The Russian, recovering his wits, drew back his left fist to deliver a blow to Jake's head as he passed close to him. But Jake's left hand had dropped away from his hold and now he lifted it at the last instant, blocking the heavy strike.

While the Russian was thus occupied, Jake jerked smartly down on the other's right arm and, using his right leg as a fulcrum, stepped forward with his left leg, beginning a reverse spin that pitched the Russian forward.

Swinging quickly around, Jake chopped heavily at the exposed neck, and the Russian stumbled as if over a stone. He slammed face-first into the rock-strewn grass. Jake was already up and running toward the smeary grey outline of another figure crouched at the edge of the ridge.

Nichiren felt a presence behind him. He was concentrating so heavily on the figures several hundred yards away across the expanse of the hazy canyon that it took him some extra time to believe what his senses were telling him.

He was very close to the verge of the cliff face, having spent some considerable time working his way through the underbrush that curled like hair along the edge. He had not found the Russians, and he had just made the decision to back away towards the cover of a long stand of cedar, when he heard the shots. He wanted desperately to return to the house, but he was caught in this trap. Any overt movement on his part would put him squarely in their sights. He was in the process of moving slowly back from the edge.

Mariana changed all that. Her terrified charge out toward him caused him to rise up involuntarily. Because of his intense concentration, he had not sensed her until she was quite near him. Now he feared that she had lost all sense of where she was on the escarpment and, in her frenzy, would hurl herself into the abyss before she could stop herself.

He saw them then, two bears coming after her in the standard semi-crouch. They were armed. One carried what appeared to be a long-bore assassin's rifle. There was very little time. Nichiren threw two *shuriken*, small steel blades, and the Russians went down, one, two, like cardboard soldiers in a shooting gallery.

He turned and ran after Mariana. She was far ahead, twisting through the underbrush. Now and again, lurid lightning illuminated her headlong flight. Nichiren was faster than she, and he knew the terrain. He made up the distance between them with astonishing rapidity. He was very near now, and he knew he would be able to get to her.

In that instant he heard the charged explosion of the rifle and – it seemed to him later – in the exact same instant saw Mariana hurled sideways, crashing into the heavy thicket of beech trees and underbrush at her side. Buddha, he thought, the shot came from across the chasm!

Sleet had turned pink. The frozen rain on the breast of Mariana's kimono was running in red rivulets. Nichiren saw where she had been hit, and his eyes closed briefly. There was a flutter at the side of her neck. Her eyes opened, fixing him with their intensity.

'Mariana-*san*.' It was the first time he had spoken her name.

She opened her lips to say something, but at that moment earth turned to mud by the storm gave way beneath their weight.

Instinctively, Nichiren lifted an arm, curling fingers around the bole of a pale beech. Mariana had fallen to a stone outcropping no more than two metres below him. With his free hand he strained forward for her. She thrust

174

something into his fingers. He stared at her. Those eyes. Their depths revealed to him her spirit, a colour dancing in the gloom. The ferociousness of her emotion fluttered his core like a leaf.

He reached for her, knowing that he did not want her to die.

'No!' Jake cried.

In a frenzy he leapt upon Stallings, wrenching the weapon from his slickened hands. He tried to drive the open steel stock into the arched throat in order to crush the larynx and the cricoid cartilage at once. But he felt as if he had been beaten for a week with a billy club. His mind was fuzzy, his reflexes nonexistent.

Stallings butted him, then followed it up with a vicious rabbit punch that sent Jake to his knees. Mud filled his eyes. He made a blind grab for his adversary.

Stallings, who had no time for this, swept up his rifle and loped down along the mouldering scree. Christ, he thought, what a mess. What the fuck are the Russians doing here, anyway?

But there was no one to answer his question, and anyway he had completed his mission. This was no time for problem-solving. He knew Jake would be up in a moment, and he had no desire to tangle with the man again.

With a sharp intake of breath, he started down the slope into the glen. In a moment he had disappeared into the sleety rain.

Jake coughed and spat flecks of blood. He was panting and dizzy. There was a ringing in his ears. A wounded animal, he fell back against the bole of a tree. When he had recovered sufficiently, he rose up, scrambling forward towards the edge of the escarpment. He heard a roar, saw part of the far mountain wall give way.

The storm was lessening now, and visibility was grudgingly returning. He saw the woman in the stained kimono tumbling in a tangle of arms and legs. Six feet down, she hit an outcropping and lay faceup in the freezing rain, arms outflung as if embracing the storm.

Jake's heart lurched painfully in his chest, and his bowels turned to water.

Mariana!

How he wished now that Komoto's information had been wrong. He saw her, bloody, slowly losing consciousness, pinned to the rock face, dying for his sins, his omissions, his selfishness. All the days since he had returned from the Sumchun River pressed back down on him. All the time they could have spent together and had not, all the love they could have shared and had not, all the life she had offered him that he had not taken.

He had ceased to love her at the moment he had ceased to like himself. It had begun at the Sumchun River, and it was ending here. Mariana was dying and he was impotent to help her, separated from her by an abyss, as he had been for the last three years. He was not close to her, but someone else was. Who?

He saw a hand reach out toward her. To push her over the last brink? He saw her slip a little bit further toward the void. If only she would look up and see him. Then he heard a sound as of a great wind rushing.

'Mariana!'

His scream echoed into the diminishing storm, falling away into the abyss. Mariana's body followed it into the deepening gloom, no more than a mote in the air, suspended on the rushing winds.

Jake lifted his tear-streaked face from the awful empty space yawning below him. His clawed fingers dug into earth turned to mud. He slipped a bit as he focused on the second figure climbing like an ape from an outthrust beech.

The figure stopped in its journey to safety, and their eyes locked across the eternity of the chasm between them.

Jake and Nichiren.

Suzhou/Shanghai

In 1895, precisely five years before Shi Zilin was born, the Chinese sued for peace with the fanatic, superbly disciplined Japanese forces. As set forth in the Treaty of Shimonoseki, Japan gained possession of the island of Formosa and freedom for Korea. In breaking up the solidity of the Chinese Empire, Japan had emerged from war as a powerful nation, one with which the whole world was now forced to contend.

If, through the intervention of Russia, Germany, and France, Japan did not retain her hard-fought foothold on the Liaodong Peninsula, not so very distant from Beijing itself, still they perhaps gained something more important. A key clause of the treaty allowed the Japanese to establish industries along the China coast at the designated treaty port cities.

Even the usually astute English *tai pan* who had set up immensely profitable companies in Shanghai had not thought of such a thing. The *tai pan* were in the business of trading, buying goods from the vast interior of the Asian continent, passing them on to the rest of the waiting world while taking their chunk of the profits.

Factories in Shanghai! It was a fantastic concept, for at that time, save for a few foreign-owned silk shops, industry was totally unknown in the International Settlement. Sanctioned by the 'most-favoured nation' clause of Britain's own treaty with China, signed in 1842, the *tai pan* of Shanghai rode on the coattails of the canny Japanese, turning to industrialization with enormous zeal.

Thus the Japanese were highly significant in China's

history, just as they were to be in Zilin's life. Though he and his two brothers had been born in Suzhou (or Soochow, as Westerners called it then), he had migrated to Shanghai by the time he was in his teens.

Always Suzhou was in his memory, however. It was a city of the most spectacular gardens. He had been born near one of the most famous of these, and had been named after it: the Forest of Lions.

Nowadays, of course, these gardens all belonged to the public. But in Shi Zilin's younger years they had all been privately built, maintained, and enjoyed. They were owned then by mandarins who had retired from the stressful conflicts surrounding court life to the north, or were simply rich local officials.

In either case, they had bought plots of land in Suzhou and had proceeded to build their gardens. These *yuan lin* were, naturally, much more than gardens. They were villas. But there were villas of this sort scattered throughout the country. What distinguished the villas of Suzhou were the *yuan*, the gardens.

The gardens were made for contemplation rather than for show. The same Buddhist tenets that found their way across the South China Sea to Japan in the formulation of the Zen gardens there were already at work here.

The garden that Shi Zilin remembered best was at the end of a shaded narrow lane barely wide enough for two people to pass one another. One entered through a wooden door set into a stone wall that ran entirely around the *yuan lin*.

Truly great *yuan* were rare. The Jian of such a one was required to be architect, poet, painter, sculptor, all in one. Such men, even in China, were scarce indeed. Throughout the ages, the term *Jian* had had many meanings. In other times it could have meant 'general of the army', 'grand champion of *wei qi*', 'celestial guardian'. In this period of China's history, it meant 'creator'.

178

The object of the *yuan* was to establish as many varying perspectives as one could within the boundaries of a severely confined space.

This particular *yuan* seemed at first dominated by a *ting*, a summer pavilion of exquisitely delicate beauty near its westernmost edge. It was, Zilin had once thought, like a tender young girl caught in contemplation. And like a natural and therefore imperfect reflecting surface, such as a lake, it revealed more of the underlying spirit of the subject than ever a manmade mirror could.

But as one spent more time in this *yuan*, one began to see the *ting* not as an isolated element, but as one of many ways of experiencing the profound peace of this place.

Zilin had often heard the refrain, *Shang you tian tang, xia you Su Hang*. 'In heaven there is paradise; on earth, Suzhou and Hangzhou.'

Not far from the summer pavilion was a gently sloping hillock from which one gained another – and entirely different – perspective of the *yuan*. Originally, Zilin had thought the Jian incredibly fortunate to have found a piece of property with such a feature, since Suzhou was set in the middle of a plain and was otherwise entirely flat. Only later did he come to understand that the hillock was artificial. Stones had been dragged here, then covered with soil and vegetation to give a perfectly natural appearance.

These surprises were part of the *yuan*'s charm as well as part of his growing-up process. *Hu shi* were another such. These 'stones from the lake,' so pleasing because of the natural erosion that had pocked and scarred their surfaces, softening them, were also not what they seemed. They had been placed at the bottom of Lake Tai Hu by the Jian's own hand when he was a young man.

For many hours, Zilin would sit by the small pool surrounded by stands of dwarf bamboo and miniature lemon trees. In the tranquillity of the spotted carp that swam lazily therein, he began to see through the artifices of the world to its sacred inner heart.

Here, though he was not to know it for many years to come, his philosophy of life as well as his future business acumen was formed. Had the Jian of the *yuan* known that such a process had sprung from his own creation, his joy would have known no bounds.

As it was, it would be altogether fair to say that he had at least an inkling of the changes beginning in the young Zilin. Certainly he knew of the boy's specialness.

One hot afternoon in the torpor of summer, he stepped from the shade of his *ting* and walked in dappled sunlight to where Zilin sat by the side of the carp pool. The cicadas were singing their shrill song in hard, sharp bursts. Stunned by the stifling heat, birds clung to branches. Even the high, fleecy clouds were unmoving in the white sky.

The Jian crossed over the crimson-lacquered bridge he had painstakingly constructed by hand, went across the islet on which he had set the pool.

In the distance, now slightly hazy in the heat, he could make out the line of *hua chuang*. These polygonal lattice windows were his pride. Made of earthenware, dried, fired, then carefully whitewashed, each had taken him nine months to produce. Each was as dear to him as a child. Perhaps this was because he had no progeny of his own, his wife having died in unsuccessful childbirth many years ago. He had never remarried.

'Everyone who comes here now,' he said, 'believes the *yuan* is entirely natural. In years gone by, when I would attempt to explain my art, I found the reactions not to my liking.' He smiled at the openness of the boy's upraised face. 'All preferred to believe in the perfection of nature.' He took Zilin's small hand in his. 'Except you, of course.' His face screwed up. 'Why do you suppose that is, hm?'

Zilin thought for a time. He watched the carps' sinuous movement through the murky waters and wished that he

180

had their facility in moving through life. 'Perhaps, Elder Uncle,' he said, using the honorific, 'it is because I prefer to believe in the perfection of the human mind.'

For a long time, then, the Jian continued to stare at him. The boy spoke more like an elder scholar than did many of the elder scholars of the Jian's acquaintance.

'I think,' he said finally, 'that you will find perfection an entirely elusive commodity in this world, Younger Brother.'

Zilin lifted a hand. 'But is this *yuan* not perfect, Elder Uncle?'

The Jian smiled. 'To you, perhaps, Younger Brother.' He squeezed the boy's hand. 'And that pleases me greatly.' He shook his head. 'But as for me, I have been around far longer than your ten years. It is possible, therefore, that we have differing ideas of what perfection may be.'

'Then you are not happy here?'

The Jian smiled again. 'Happy, yes, Younger Brother. But not content. There is a vast difference between the two.' He let go Zilin's hand and, picking up a smooth pebble, dropped it into the pool. The carp moved as they did at feeding time, then, finding no food, returned to their laze. 'You may find, after some time, that life is a continual seeking.'

'A seeking after perfection?' Zilin wanted to know.

'Well, perhaps for some, yes. Others understand that perfection is not of this world and is therefore impossible to attain.'

'Should that stop you from trying, Elder Uncle?'

'I don't believe so, no.' He lifted a finger. 'But there are some – much like myself, I imagine – who do not wish to find perfection.'

'Why not?'

'Because only in a state of contention can life exist. I sometimes think that death is the only state of perfection of which we are all capable.'

'What of the Buddha, then?'

'I am not the Buddha,' the Jian said thoughtfully. 'And neither, Younger Brother, are you.' He seemed sad now, as if darkness were falling over him like the mantle of night. 'You will make mistakes as you grow up. Everyone does. But always you must remember to go on, and to learn from your mistakes. You are a fool only if you repeat them, not if you make them.'

The sun baked them for the rest of the afternoon. Neither spoke again for those long hours, each preferring the silent contemplation for which this special *yuan* was built.

Summer edged into autumn, and soon school studies occupied all of Zilin's waking moments. Too, there were rumours within the family that they were moving south in the winter, perhaps all the way to Shanghai.

When he next had a chance to come down the narrow shaded lane, Zilin found the wooden door to the *yuan* locked. This was most unusual, and with a beating heart, he ran all the way around the walled villa to its front entrance.

A strange man opened the door in response to Zilin's knock. He was dressed in the robes of a priest of the local monastery.

'Yes?'

'Pardon me, Elder Uncle,' Zilin said, trying to peer around his bulk, 'but I am looking for the Jian of this villa.'

The priest smiled. 'But you are looking at him.'

Zilin was stunned. 'I don't understand. I used to come here all the time. I – '

'Oh, you must mean the previous owner.'

'Previous?'

The priest nodded. 'He was a rather ferocious gambler, I understand. He lost this *yuan lin* in a game of *fan tan*. Subsequently it was purchased by the monastery.' He stepped back into the doorway. 'But you will still be

182

welcome here, Younger Brother.' He smiled shyly. 'Perhaps there is more learning for you here than there is in school.'

Zilin was appalled. 'But the Jian,' he said plaintively. 'Where is he?'

The priest shrugged. 'I have no idea.' His round face broke into a smile again. 'Now shall we come inside? There are always lessons to be learned . . .'

But Zilin was already running down the dusty road, a dog barking at his heels.

Though he had made every effort, he had never been able to find the Jian. Perhaps it was just as well. The Jian belonged within his *yuan*, and Zilin preferred to envision him there, amid his bamboo and lemon trees, his irises and oleander. He had the long, lean face of a sage, but always there was brown earth beneath his nails, embedded through his constant pruning. The knees of his trousers were always wet with soil.

As a child, Zilin had despaired that he had not taken something tangible – even something as small as the smooth stone the Jian had dropped in the pool that steaming August afternoon – away with him as a remembrance. Now he was glad that he had not. What the Jian had planted within the *yuan* was meant to stay there. Besides, he had brought away with him something far more valuable than a child's trinket of the past: he had his ideas.

Spawned by the *yuan*'s very concept, these ideas had made Shi Zilin into a very rich man. In his *yuan*, the Jian had skilfully used artifice to create something more powerful and more lasting than illusion. That was what most people had failed to see; that was why they had been so disappointed when he had revealed his secrets: now they saw only illusion.

But Zilin had seen the truth. The Jian's artifice had

created moods and feelings. Those who entered the *yuan* ignorant of its secrets were moved and, thus, changed.

The young Zilin grew to understand that he could apply the same skilful methodology to his entire life. If one gave people what they wanted, he had decided, it did not matter one whit if it was all artifice. Left to their own devices, people believed what would benefit them the most. All this thought stood him in good stead when it came time for him to leave Suzhou.

Shanghai was perhaps the most fortuitously situated city in all of China. It was the only major port in central China that was not cut off from the interior by mountains. Further, it was the natural seaward outlet, and thus the gateway to the lush Yangzi basin, one of the richest regions on the entire continent.

It was fortuitous, too, that Zilin's father, a brilliant industrial engineer, had been promoted out of Suzhou and transferred to the one place where his skills would be most efficaciously utilized: Shanghai.

Until the Treaty of Shimonoseki, the demand for industrial engineers was necessarily limited, and perhaps one could say that Zilin's facility for being ahead of his time was something of a hereditary trait.

In any case, the economic revolution the Japanese had begun in the city in 1895 enabled the Shis to journey from the tranquillity of Suzhou's relative backwater to the bustling, modernized eastern metropolis, already China's most populous city.

Besides more money and prestige for his father, Shanghai provided excellent schooling for Zilin and his brothers. He and his youngest brother attended Futan University, while the middle brother preferred the Shanghai University of Science and Technology.

Zilin's horizons were greatly expanded, he learned English, his friends became many, he was exposed to foreign devils and to the opinions not only of his elders but, importantly, of his peers. None of this information, however, superseded that which he had garnered in the Jian's *yuan*. Rather, it reinforced it.

The Chinese did not rule all of China, and had not done so for some time. To Zilin, the opinions of his peers regarding the intrusion of the foreign devils were as useless as those of his elders. The older men believed in a kind of Confucian patience. The Middle Kingdom belonged to the Chinese, they believed, and eventually Chinese would again hold sway throughout the country. In the meantime they counselled tolerance when it came to dealing with foreigners.

On the other hand, Zilin's contemporaries were almost universally militant, preferring to strike back at the foreign devil in revenge for humiliations both real and imagined.

Privately, Zilin saw them all as myopic fools. He had another idea entirely. The Jian had taught him to contemplate mistakes rather than to dwell on them – to use them, in effect, as history lessons. And as he grew and gained in knowledge, that was precisely what Zilin did with the recent history of his people.

What struck him immediately was that the Chinese had, through their own weaknesses, lost control of their country to the foreign devil. The Westerners had been clever enough to take advantage of every internal rift within the factionalized Chinese political system and thus bend the Chinese like a willow to suit their own needs.

In the middle of the 18th century the Empire was experiencing almost unprecedented prosperity. The population had ballooned by approximately 130 million within the space of forty-odd years. Agricultural reforms were instituted, and new crops, such as maize and tobacco, were introduced. Both state and individual business began to employ enormous numbers of salaried workers in silk, metalwork, pottery, and the like.

But along with prosperity came the desire to expand,

and this the Empire did, waging war in the southwest against the Burmese and in Central Asia against the Eleuths.

Wars, for underindustrialized nations like China – even successful ones, as these were – can often produce more negative results than positive ones. In this case, the power of the ruling Manchus was severely weakened. And, in response, opponents to their regime grew in strength, feeding off the Manchus' weakness. The secret societies were rising.

Now China had more than internal strife with which to contend. The Tsars of Russia had but recently invaded Siberia. To the south, England had founded the Empire of India, and the Dutch had formed the Netherlands East Indies. Both areas, long-time havens for emigrants fleeing the poverty of the Chinese provinces of Fujian and Guangdong, were now, due to the recent population explosion, inundated with Chinese.

Through these emigrants and via other sources, China's new neighbours were well aware of its plight, and they sat poised to take advantage of the cracks beginning to break apart the Manchu dominance.

The English, who by 1839 had been in Canton for quite some time, were busy illegally exporting opium, the profits from which helped to balance their heavy trade deficit.

That year, a mandarin by the name of Lin Zexu decided to make an example of the foreign devil. By so doing, he hoped to shore up the Manchus' swiftly eroding hold on the country. The English, who were well acquainted with war, wasted no time in retaliating. Western gunboats sailed up the Xijiang, levelling Chinese forts at its mouth. By June of 1842, the English had taken Shanghai and Nanking. The ensuing treaty opened five strategic ports to English trade and, perhaps more importantly, ceded them Hong Kong.

It was at this point in their history that, in Zilin's

opinion, the government should have asked the foreign devils to keep their forces in China proper to help return political stability to the country. The Manchus could have used the British then, just as the British had used them, but the court had never paid much attention to foreigners and there seemed no good reason to do so now.

It was far too busy handling the Moslem uprisings that broke out in Yunnan and Turkestan near the end of the decade. Soon it had an even more serious threat to its existence with which to deal.

A Chinese faction known as the Tai Ping was rapidly gaining power. So well led were they that soon they had taken over Guangxi province and by 1852 the violence had spread into Hankou. Just a year later, the Tai Ping leader, Hong Xiuquan, declared Nanking the capital of the Tai Ping Tian Guo, the Heavenly Kingdom of Great Peace. He began to issue edicts and soon was leading his army north to take Peking.

While the Manchus were thus occupied, the British and the French, having already decided to expand their lines of trade in China, used the country's inner turmoil to mount another military campaign.

The court in Beijing had just time enough to repel the Tai Ping when they found themselves face to face with the loaded guns of the foreign devil. In the south, the Tai Ping were massing once again. In October of 1860, the British and French troops marched on Beijing. Still the Chinese did not fully comprehend the European threat.

Thus, the foreign devil's forces were ordered to sack the summer palaces. A friend of Zilin's was there and related to him later what occurred moment by moment. The most valuable art objects and pieces of highly wrought furniture were methodically set aside, to be shipped at some later date, it was subsequently learned, to Queen Victoria and Napoleon III. That done, the soldiers were let loose to plunder the rest at will. But the looting got somewhat out of control, and in order to stem the madness, the English officers ordered the buildings torched.

After that, the court had no choice but to accede to the foreign devil's demands. It had been brought home to them, at last, that their sacred capital, so far to the north, away from whatever was occurring in Hong Kong, Shanghai, and Canton was just as vulnerable to attack as its southern cities.

The Treaty of Peking called for eleven new ports to be opened for foreign trade. In addition, foreign residents were granted certain privileges, such as the right to organize concessions, freedom for missionaries, and extraterritorial rights.

In return, the Europeans used their own military might to join with the government's in defeating the Tai Ping revolt. By July 1864, Nanking was once again back in Manchu hands. But the government's hold on its country was severely weakened.

Again, Zilin was convinced, the Manchus were guilty of not understanding their foe. Had they planted a sufficient number of spies within the Tai Ping, they would have found the faction riddled with internecine rivalries after its defeat at the gates of Beijing. They would have seen that they had no need of the foreign soldiers now.

Sun Tzu has written that one who confronts his enemy, yet who, because of the arrogance of exalted rank and honours, or for a few hundred pieces of gold, fails to employ secret agents, is no general, and no master of victory.

The Manchus were obviously no students of Sun Tzu.

Meanwhile, the court became concerned with the progress the French were making into another neighbouring country, Annam. War erupted in China's southwest provinces in 1883. Two years later the French were granted trade rights in two towns on that frontier.

Now the dissection of a once-great country was all but

complete. Increasingly, the Europeans were controlling the country's customs. They now had land on lease, and their concessions won at Peking included the building of railway lines throughout China. The last step was for the country to be carved into 'spheres of influence'. This was done just before the turn of the century. The Russians got the north, the Germans Shandong, the British the Yangzi valley, the French the southwest.

But the Yi he tuan, the most powerful and xenophobic of the Chinese secret societies, was on the rise. The Westerners called them 'Boxers.' Their revolt in Peking on the eve of the turn of the century led to foreign powers, for the first time, occupying the Imperial Palace. That, in turn, led to the Revolution eleven years later, and the founding of the Republic of China.

Zilin's views differed markedly from those of his peers. He was neither xenophobic nor complaisant when it came to the foreign devil. For he saw their presence in his homeland as perhaps no other Chinese did. There were ways in which the Europeans could be used just as they had used the Chinese. Zilin had learned that in the Jian's *yuan*, where the ultimate power of artifice was brought home to him.

Why, he thought, should I wish to be rid of them, when they can be so useful to me and to my country?

After the Boxer Rebellion had been put down, Europeans in China experienced a period of unprecedented prosperity. But in 1906, everything changed irrevocably.

The Japanese victory over the Russian Empire was like the tolling of a great temple bell. Its reverberations were heard in China, giving new spirit and determination to the revolutionaries there. The chief of these was Sun Zhongshan, whom Westerners came to know as Dr Sun Yat-sen. He was born in Canton and had the support of the southern Chinese bourgeoisie. But, far more importantly, he had the backing of Chinese students who had been educated in the West, and of the expatriate Chinese who were rich enough to fund him and the association he founded, the Tong Meng Hui, and then his party, the Guomindang.

Sun Zhongshan was clever, and he utilized every blunder of the government, every discontent of the common man to his and his party's advantage. Thus the Guomindang's power waxed as the Manchus' in Peking waned.

When the Qing Empress, Cixi, died in 1908, the government could not have been in poorer shape. No adult Qing existed to whom she could pass the reins of power. Instead, she designated the two-year-old Puyi as her successor.

It was inevitable that such an ill-conceived notion should throw the court into the most intensive bout of infighting it had seen in more than a century. Supporters of the Regent, the tiny Puyi's father, contested bitterly with those of the court's most powerful general, Yuan Shikai.

In August 1911, the government, such as it was, decided to nationalize the railways. It was a direct blow aimed at the hierarchy of Chinese capitalists. Like a shot from a pistol, the move was a signal for revolt. So widespread and virulent were their uprisings that the court was forced to appeal to General Yuan Shikai for support. But the general, scenting the changing winds of fortune, preferred to side with the revolutionaries.

He knew whereof he spoke, for in December of that year, a delegation of officials from all the far-flung provinces met to elect Sun Zhongshan President. But just over thirty days later, he willingly gave way to the general. He was seemingly proved correct, for Yuan Shikai was able to effect the abdication of the last of the Qing emperors just one month later. For this deed, he was appointed temporary president of the new Republic.

But then the good general betrayed the Revolution. The fantastic lure of ascending the Emperor's throne himself and founding a new dynastic line proved too much for him to resist. He dissolved the Guomindang and the parliament that had been formed in early 1913. Yet renewed internal strife ultimately denied his ascendancy, and in 1916 he died, still nothing more than a coarse military man.

A paper government was formed in Beijing. Again, warring factions kept it from being of much use or strength. Several times, Sun Zhongshan tried to form what he called a 'national government' in Canton. Finally he was able to stabilize Guangdong Province, winning it over to his cause.

All this served as a backdrop to Zilin's love affair with the wild Mai. That night, July 1, 1921, as the Westerners reckoned it, he met her in Shanghai amidst the heat and high emotion of the first rumblings of the Revolution that was not to be realized until eighteen years later.

At that meeting, the Chinese Communist Party was founded. But even the fact that history was being made all around him did not dim Zilin's burning image of her so near yet so far away from him in the audience. He fell madly in love with this uncharacteristically wild-spirited revolutionary woman.

She was very young, not yet twenty, and an orphan – which, Zilin always felt, had accounted for her decidedly unfeminine attitudes. But instead of shunning her, as most other males within the Party did, Zilin – at the meeting more out of curiosity than any real revolutionary spirit – found himself drawn to her.

He was twenty-one, and in almost all ways more worldly than she, but he had lived a highly cultured, rather upper-class life. She had not, and perhaps her ability to live by her own wits formed much of the bond between them. She knew of artifice herself.

That night, even Zilin did not suspect the true role the Communists were to play in the future of his country. But his uncanny nose for history had led him here, and although at the time he was more smitten by Mai than he was by the spirit of communism, still he was here all the same.

Afterwards, as he plucked up his courage to approach her, he got his first good look at her. She was small, with a tawny litheness that reminded him more of a young boy than it did of a woman. Not that she was unfeminine; it was just that there was so much power within her. And power was the sole province of men. At least Zilin had thought so until that night.

'Are you a member?' he said, shouldering his way up to her. It was the only thing that came to mind; he had had very little experience with women.

'I am Sun Zhongshan's assistant.' Her eyes were shining with the absorbed heat of the meeting, but she lacked the fanatic's glossy fervour that had previously caused Zilin to shy away from those possessing the revolutionary spirit.

'I didn't see him here,' Zilin said. 'But I observed many Russians.'

She cocked her head. 'Do you find that odd?'

'I find it interesting. I would like to know more.' He flashed her a quick, nervous smile. The hall was rapidly emptying out, leaving behind only the sour smells of sweat and overexcitement.

'Why don't we go somewhere and talk?' Mai said.

'Soon,' she said, her hands around a large porcelain teacup, 'the Guomindang will merge with the Chinese Communist Party. It will make us strong. It will make us unstoppable.'

The table was littered with the remnants of rice and sautéed *garoupa*, flash-fried shrimp, chicken with straw mushrooms.

Mai laughed abruptly, looking at the debris between them. 'This is the best I've eaten in years.' She patted her narrow waist. 'I am stuffed.'

'It's a good feeling, isn't it?' Zilin said. 'There's a certain contentment after a fine meal.'

She eyed him, her face lost its smile. 'I'm not so sure that *is* good. Contentment breeds complacency. There are

192

far too many wrongs being perpetrated in China for that ever to occur.'

'Would you lose your dinner, then, and insult the chef? It is his handiwork you pass judgment on now.'

For a moment Mai thought he was serious, and a severe rebuke was on her lips. But as she let her eyes roam his face, she saw the merriment slyly surfacing and she was obliged to laugh. 'Perhaps you are right, Zilin,' she said. 'There is a time for everything. But when you have been forced to flee your homeland, as I have done with Zhongshan, humour becomes brittle and an almost forgotten commodity.'

'I would think that a time of adversity was the ripest time for humour.'

She nodded, silently acknowledging his thoughts. 'In Japan, where we were forced to flee when Zhongshan's bitter battle with the traitor, General Yuan, went against us, there was little in the way of humour. We found the Japanese to be a strange and terribly cold people.'

'Yet they gave you asylum when even your own people feared to do so. They must, at least, be courageous.'

'How is it,' Mai said, 'that you have an answer for everything?'

Zilin laughed. 'Not everything. Else I would already be a *tai pan* of enormous wealth and power, instead of what I am.'

'And what is that?'

He looked from her beautiful face to the bobbing lights along the crowded quay. 'Just a man filled with all manner of strange ideas.'

They both experienced the clouds and the rain with exquisite intimacy. Though Zilin had never before made love, he found that he was not frightened. With Mai there was a certain comfort, as if her fierce power, which spilled over into this quarter as well, held enough courage for them both.

If she was fiery in her approach, he was tender, and this mixture, this true *yin-yang*, thrilled her utterly. Previously, her demeanour in bed had caused her male partners – who, to a man, were unused to such aggressiveness in a female – to either lose their rigidity or attempt to match her spirit with a transparency she found totally repugnant.

Thus, though Mai had previously experienced sex, she had never before that night been lifted up to the ecstasy of the clouds and the rain. Her cries at being so transported caused Zilin to lose all control himself, filling him with the most divine pleasure.

Afterwards, lost within each other's limbs, they spoke in the most honest manner, free of all traces of artifice, of which they had never before been free, even with people they had thought close to them.

It would not, therefore, be incorrect to say that each found the meaning of true love at the same moment: Mai, who had, for as long as she had known Sun Zhongshan, been in love only with the concept of the Revolution of the Three People's Principles – nationalism, democracy, and livelihood – and Zilin, who had known as his only love the concept of artifice.

Each now saw, deep within that hot summer night, that their concepts of the world and of life had been somewhat parochial, that instead of only one burning, overriding love in one's life, rather a hierarchy of loves could exist, each in harmony with the other. To two so highly self-motivated people, it was a revelation of the highest order.

Within three months, Zilin had been introduced into the world of Sun Zhongshan; within six months, he and Mai were married.

For Zilin, Zhongshan was another revelation. The doctor of medicine had been educated in such diverse institutions as an Anglican boys' school in Honolulu and a medical college in Hong Kong. It was apparently at the former academy that he had come under the influence of both Western thought and Christianity.

Zilin did not know the man well enough at that stage to talk to him openly of his own private plans for the foreign devil. But in heated discussions among the three of them – though sometimes other party leaders, such as Hu Hanmin and Wang Chingwei, sat in – Zhongshan often took the Western point of view. It was especially during these times that Zilin absorbed his words like a sponge. It was particularly fascinating to him to hear Western philosophy and economic and political theory filtered through an Eastern mind, especially one as brilliant as the Doctor's. Thus it was not surprising that Zilin soon fell under his spell.

These discussions, however, were not without their abrasive side. When it came to the subject of the Russian Communists, Zhongshan and Mai disagreed violently. Perhaps it was the Anglican teaching that had – as Mai said – 'corrupted' this side of him.

The fact was that the two of them approached this admittedly emotional issue from different levels. Zhongshan saw the Communists almost from a religious point of view. Mai, on the other hand, saw them merely from a historical perspective. The Russian Communists, she argued over and over, held the true revolutionary spirit of the times. They were superbly organized, they wielded incalculable power, and they were willing to aid the Guomindang through the newly formed Chinese Communist Party.

There was never bitterness between the two; they had far too much respect for one another. But the Doctor was often exasperatingly resolute in his position, often citing the opinion of his military assistant, Chiang Kai-shek, who was virulently opposed to what he saw as Communist intervention in the internal affairs of China.

One evening, late in autumn, with rain pounding against

the windowpanes and the sky devoid of stars or moon, Mai finally threw up her hands in disgust. 'You're impossible!' she cried angrily. 'Why, even Zilin has come to see the light about the Communists.'

The Doctor had turned his head, his clear eyes regarding Zilin. 'Oh? So you tell me, young man, just what it is you see in this godless group.'

Zilin was thinking of artifice again. 'Well, sir, it seems to me that the Russian Communists possess two valuable commodities that, in my opinion, the Guomindang cannot obtain anywhere else.'

'And these are?' Zhongshan said coldly.

'First, they can organize the Guomindang as no Chinese is now able to do. Your organization will thus be more efficient and at the same time more streamlined. Money continues to pour in from overseas, I know, sir, but any measures of economy that we can adopt can only be for the better.'

He paused to clear his throat. 'Second, and I think even more importantly, communism can become a powerful rallying cry for the poor. You were born in Canton, sir, so I don't have to reiterate how terrible the economic conditions are in the southern provinces. Hong Kong, Annam, Burma, India are all being flooded with emigrants from China, seeking a proper means of livelihood. This has been so for decades.

'Perhaps if the Guomindang merged with the *Chinese* Communist Party, that would give you the added centrism to rally the majority of the country to your cause.

'Frankly, I don't believe you can wrest control of China any other way.'

'I was proud of you tonight.'

'Proud?' Zilin did not understand what Mai meant. They had returned home from their meeting with Zhongshan, and Mai had immediately wanted to make love.

196

The clouds and the rain was particularly piercing, Mai particularly frenzied.

'Yes, dear.' She stroked his cheek. 'I was watching him while you made your speech, even though I was almost as surprised at it as he was. I think you broke through his armour.'

'Good,' Zilin said. 'I like him; I believe that what he wants for China is right. I'd like to see him succeed.'

Mai laughed, squeezing him. 'I knew I'd win you over. You are a true Communist behind your façade.'

Zilin had sobered. 'Don't misunderstand me, Mai. I have no allegiance to communism. I'm purely neutral about it as a concept. But as a means to Zhongshan's ends, I think the Russians can be tremendously useful.'

'Then it's all a fake. Your zeal is just part of your theory of artifice.' There were tears in her eyes.

Zilin sat up, pulled her to him. 'Listen, Mai. What does it matter how I feel? The important thing is that Zhongshan be made to see that right now the Communists can be his saviours in China. *That* is the only thing that is real.'

After a time of silence, Mai half-laughed, half-cried into his chest. 'And I thought,' she whispered, 'that I was getting to know you.'

Later, when she had had time to think about what he had said, she turned to him in the darkness. 'The real obstacle to the Guomindang and the Chinese Communist Party merging is not Zhongshan himself but Chiang Kai-shek.'

Zilin thought about that for a time. He had met Chiang several times, had spoken with him at length twice, and had come away from both meetings with a bad feeling in his stomach. 'Tell me what you know of him,' he said softly.

'He's thirty-four,' she began. 'He was educated at a Japanese military academy, and got his field experience in a Japanese regiment of the line. He returned here in time to take part in the revolution against the Manchus. He fought with Zhongshan against General Yuan. They are very close. Too close, in my opinion.'

'Why do you say that?'

'Because,' Mai said thoughtfully, 'I sense another loyalty in him beyond the one he evinces for Zhongshan.'

'Do you think he is in the employ of an enemy of the Guomindang's?'

'No, I am certain he's not.'

'Would he betray Zhongshan?'

'Not while Zhongshan was still alive,' Mai said. 'I think what Chiang learned in Japan, besides the art of warfare, was a loyalty to Chiang Kai-shek. I think his ambition ranges far beyond this revolution. Privately, he does not hold with Zhongshan's ideals for the people, though he says he does. He is a strong man, with a strong man's visions.'

'Zhongshan needs a strong man now. He will need one once he gains power. He will always need protection, Mai.'

'Yes.' Mai nodded, and her dark hair flowed down across her face, obscuring one cheek. 'But protection from whom? That is what I continually ask myself.'

They tried to sleep after that, but it was impossible. The clock on the mantel across the room kept them awake as if it were the tolling of a bell. Outside, on the street, the cries of the fishermen along the quay floated in the rain-heavy air like passing clouds.

After a long time, Zilin rolled over. 'Mai?'

'Yes, darling.'

'If, as you have said, my words have opened the door, then you must make certain it stays open.'

'You know that I will try.'

'Good,' he said. 'Because I have an idea that will take Chiang out of Zhongshan's hair and perhaps make him change his ways all at the same time.'

'*Dew neh loh moh!* By all the gods, how?'

198

Zilin laughed. 'Once Zhongshan is made to see the wisdom of using the Russians, you must suggest to him that he send his most trusted military aide, Chiang Kai-shek, to the USSR to learn proper military organization. Borodin will be only too happy to comply. If Chiang balks, as he most assuredly will, suggest to the Doctor that he tell Chiang that it would be far better for Chiang himself to learn the new organization, and return here to implement it, than to allow the Russians to come here and do it for him.'

Mai was already laughing. It continued unabated until the tears were rolling down her cheeks. She threw her naked body onto her husband's, hugging him.

Laughing again, like thunder rolling off the walls of their small room.

In 1923, Zhongshan, using the argument Zilin had proposed to Mai that night, indeed sent Chiang Kai-shek to Russia to gain knowledge of their manner of organization. And a year later he merged the Guomindang with the Chinese Communist Party.

With the aid of Soviet advisors and material, a new, better-equipped revolutionary army was created, its constituents also members of the Party. The revolutionary spirit was in the air, and renewed optimism buoyed them all.

Because Mai was increasingly tied up in working on doctrine with Zhongshan, Zilin set about getting to know other key members of the Guomindang. His own work as a clerk in the harbourmaster's office was sufficiently nontaxing for him to spend his off hours any way he pleased.

It did not take him long to attach himself to Hu Hanmin. Hu was already forty-two, much closer to Zhongshan's age than most of his other followers. He was a tall, slender man with a gentle face and a normally soft voice that he could transform into the orator's fierce shout when the need arose.

He was a lawyer who had met Zhongshan and Mai while he was at school in Japan. His keen, analytical mind had been caught immediately by Zhongshan's revolutionary spirit, and they had become fast friends. Because of this, and because he was so good with people, Hu had risen quickly within the Guomindang.

Of all of Zhongshan's major supporters, it could be said of Hu that he was most like the Doctor. He was, like Zhongshan, essentially a humanist. He felt for the people of China even as he believed in them. His failing, if it could be said to be one, was that he failed to perceive the campaign for victory in military terms. He was often derided for this by Chiang Kai-shek, who, perhaps quite accurately, perceived in him his most serious rival in the natural succession of the Nationalist government.

What Zilin liked best about Hu was his quick mind. He was most often the one at the protracted political meetings who was able to wade through all the tangled webs of various arguments to get right to the heart of the matter. But in fact what he responded to most in Hu, on the subliminal emotional level, was the man's openness of spirit.

Zilin's father had had little time for his family as the rapidly Westernizing city of Shanghai put more and more pressure on his time. For many years he was the only Chinese with enough training or the expertise to get many major projects done. In fact, for the first three years after he and his family had moved to Shanghai, he was in constant demand by the Japanese and the Europeans as well.

Consequently he left the house early and returned late, almost always when the rest of the family had long since finished dinner. It was quite an untraditional family in that regard, and he had had to prevail upon his wife to obey his wishes in this and not wait for his return to get the children fed. Still, she herself would not eat until he had come home. She felt scandalized enough that the children did not wait. The elder Shi did not see it as a sign of disrespect, but merely as a signature of the changing times.

In any case, Hu had time for the young Zilin, seeing in him, no doubt, the spark of genius that was already beginning to surface. Thus it was that many evenings the two would stroll the twisting back streets and long, curving dockside known as the Bund, discussing every subject under the sun.

Late one afternoon near the end of 1924, Hu broke off their conversation. He had turned uncharacteristically melancholy, staring out at the harbour forested with black masts, spars, and rigging. It was cool and relatively dry, though far warmer than the 23-degree weather under which Beijing was suffering. To the north there was snow, coming out of the Siberian steppes, but here the swollen red sun, sinking like a thrown stone, turned the ships to spiky silhouettes. Zilin could see the mighty dredgers still at work at the mouth of the harbour, where they had been all day long. Out of necessity, trade had been halted for them. But none of the *tai pan* raised a word of protest. Vast sums of money were spent each year to keep the constantly building silt from making the harbour floor impassable for the oceangoing steamers so vital to the China trade.

Zilin returned his attention to the older man. His affection for Hu had grown steadily since they had first met, and he did not like to see him so low.

'Elder Uncle,' he said after a time, 'Zhongshan tells me that it is a Western custom to share a burden among friends.'

Hu turned, refocusing his eyes on Zilin. He smiled, but there was a grimness to his gesture that chilled the younger man. 'It may be the custom, Younger Brother, in other, more barbarous cultures to be so disrespectful of a friend's feelings as to share pain.' He shrugged. 'The ways of the world are odd indeed.'

'Yet there is, perhaps, some good I may perform,' Zilin said gently. 'In matters of internal Guomindang policy, it might prove useful to turn to someone on the outside, someone who is able to render a fair and impartial opinion.'

Now Hu was forced to laugh. 'By all the gods, Zilin, you are quite a remarkable young man. Are you certain you never studied before the bar? You would make a superb lawyer, with your powers of persuasion.'

'I would like to help, Elder Uncle,' he said seriously.

The dredgers were packing up now. Dusk had fallen across the city. Within its murky mauve light, the muddy water seemed pristine and full of promise. An opalescent glow had risen along the sweep of the Bund as the night lamps were lit and the cooking fires from the houseboats flared up. It was overhung by a smudge of smoke that painted a newly risen crescent moon bluish-purple.

They began again to walk. 'There is truth to your words,' Hu said at last. 'Yet I do not wish to involve you – '

'Have no fear on that score,' Zilin prompted. 'Mai has already seen to that.'

'All right,' Hu relented. 'How well do you know Ling Xichu?'

Zilin shrugged. 'Enough to talk to him now and then. In my opinion, he's something of a bully boy. He employs force without being fair. But he has taken to the Bolshevik methodology quite well, it seems. He's a quick study, at least.'

'He also perceives himself as my chief rival. You and I, I think, understand that to be Chiang, but Ling does not believe Chiang can muster the support to become head of the Guomindang.'

'And you do.'

'Well,' Hu said, 'what is your opinion?'

'I think Chiang's dangerous. But I must admit that my opinion may be a bit weighted on this matter. Mai hates and distrusts Chiang. She fears that he is capable of betraying the Revolution.'

'Chiang,' Hu said, echoing Mai, 'thinks only of Chiang.' He shrugged. 'But I think that is a function of a military officer. A commander in warfare cannot think too much about his men, or else he would never send them out into battle to die.

'On the other hand, Ling has no cause to feel that way. Yet he does, all the same. He opposes me now in the Guomindang's central committee. He has sided with Chiang in pushing for an all-out military campaign northward through the provinces to take Beijing.

'Though the army has made great strides since Chiang returned from Russia, I feel we are still unprepared to take on the government. And if we fail now, after so many past defeats, I fear it will be the end for us. Zhongshan has just so much stamina left in him. He puts in twenty-hour days; he pushes himself beyond the tolerance limits for even a much younger man than he. Leading a major military campaign now must surely kill him.'

Young boys passed them, running, calling to one another. Great sacks of rice were being laded, to be ferried off to one of the *tai pan*'s great, swift steamships. Tea, as well, was piled high upon the docks, awaiting its turn to leave Shanghai. And somewhere inside those cases was, no doubt, a fortune in opium.

Zilin watched this activity while his mind whirred through all that his friend had told him. 'You must continue to oppose them in the committee,' he said. 'Do not use rhetoric that might inflame them to retaliate in kind, but rather use cool words that prove your levelheaded response.' He looked at Hu. 'Then, privately, you must meet with Zhongshan. Tell him just what you have told me. If he takes on this campaign before the army is ready, before all the support is coalesced, and if he perishes on the long northward march, his dream of revolution will die with him. For if he begins the march at the head of the army and cannot finish, all the spirit will fall from his soldiers and the power of the Guomindang will ebb away. Zhongshan knows well the wisdom of patience.'

Hu stared at the crates of tea as if he had never seen such cargo before. 'You know,' he said with great deliberation, 'I was supposed to chair a committee meeting tonight. But at the last moment it was cancelled. All gods bear witness, it was a good omen. Otherwise I would not have been able to meet you.'

There was no need to say more. Zilin smiled and they strolled on around a turning, out of sight of the myriad ships that lay at anchor, resting for the night.

A week before the Chinese new year – in the beginning of 1925 – Mai woke him out of sleep. It was deep within the night. A full moon bathed the street outside in blue light. A drunkard was singing a garbled shanty, and farther away, voices were raised in argument.

'Zilin!'

'Yes? What is it?' He fought to clear his mind of sleep.

'I am worried about Zhongshan.'

'Hu's cleverness has saved him from attempting the long march. What has happened now?'

'He's ill.' There were tears in her eyes. 'Seriously ill.'

Now Zilin was concerned. 'But I've heard nothing of this. Even from Hu.'

She shook her head. 'You wouldn't. He's kept it from everyone except me. Now I've told you. I don't know what to do.'

'Mai,' he said, holding her, 'you're not a doctor. There's nothing you can do except bring him to one.'

'It's all been done.' She turned to him, and in the cool

half-light he saw how pale she was. 'There's nothing any of them can do.'

'He's dying?'

She nodded. 'Zilin, I am so afraid. If Hu Han Min does not take over, I fear for the Revolution. Chiang is an animal who will do everything in his power to destroy the Communist Party as soon as Zhongshan can no longer hold him in check. I don't even want to say it.' She broke down then, sobbing against him, her body shaking like a leaf in a storm. 'He'll be gone soon,' she whispered. 'I cannot believe it. It's too soon. Too soon.'

For the moment there was nothing Zilin could do but hold her and give her what comfort he could.

In a while she had calmed enough for him to say, 'Then you must use all your expertise to ensure that Hu gets the support he needs to take power. There's not only Chiang to be wary of, but Ling Xichu as well.'

Mai was weeping again, shaking her head back and forth. 'I don't know, Zilin. I don't think I have the strength left. Without Zhongshan . . .'

'Now think, Mai,' he whispered harshly. 'What would he say if he heard such antirevolutionary words? He'd most surely reprimand you. His strength flows through you. I know. I feel it. So do the others. That is why they are jealous of you. Well, the time has come for you to wield that power to its fullest.' He stared into her pale, tear-streaked face, thinking that he loved her more now than he ever had, and finding that a most wondrous feeling 'Your enemies are just waiting for you to falter. They will say of you that you are of no use, after all. Like all women, you fall apart at the first crisis. You break into tears as no man would, and kneel, sobbing, broken, before Zhongshan's memory.

'This is not the course he planned for you, Mai. It is not why he has brought you close to him, why he has shared all his innermost thoughts with you, why he has trusted

205

you above all others, even his beloved Chiang. Do you not see that Zhongshan leans on you fully as much as you depend on him? And perhaps now it is *your* strength that helps sustain him. Perhaps without that his disease would already have finished him.'

'Yes.' Mai's voice was but a sigh. Her head bent until her damp forehead pressed against his collarbone. She was like a long-distance runner who, at the edge of exhaustion, was beginning to find inside herself the courage to go on, to draw on her conviction so that she could finish what she had had the audacity to begin.

'Thank you, my husband,' she whispered. 'Yes.'

In April of that year, Zilin received a promotion to chief clerk at the harbourmaster's office. At the end of the workday he hastened home to share his good fortune with Mai. He had been diligently setting aside a portion of his pay, and instead of donating it to the Party as Mai had often suggested, he had begun to invest it. He and his two brothers had pooled their money, purchasing land in areas of the city not yet fully developed, but that they felt would soon become valuable. In this manner they had already sold off two lots within six months, tripling their seed money. With the profits of a third chunk of real estate, combined with Zilin's increased salary, he had an idea to buy a quarter-share in a clipper ship. His brothers did not think that such a thing was feasible, but Zilin was already formulating a plan.

Mai was not yet home when he arrived at dusk. He went immediately to his desk and, taking up pen and ink, began again his calculations, estimating the potential profits from part ownership in one of the great oceangoing ships.

Thus absorbed, he did not immediately hear Mai when she came in. But the absolute silence at length caused him to raise his head from the orderly rows of figures he had written in his neat hand across the page.

'Mai?'

Her face was white, her body rigid. Zilin came around from behind the desk and gripped her hands in his. They were as cold as ice. 'By all the gods, what has happened?'

Mutely her eyes sought his, and there was within them such a depth of sadness and despair that he knew without her telling him that Zhongshan was dead.

'He went to Beijing alone,' she said tightly, after a long time. 'I wanted to go with him. I pleaded with him, but he was unshakable in his conviction.' Zilin saw then the immense courage inside her, the determination not to weep. 'It was as if he went there to die, as if he felt death coming and did not wish to die here among his family.'

Zilin felt a loss in the centre of his being. It was as if some comforting hand to which he had grown accustomed over the years had abruptly disappeared. 'Perhaps, as always, he was thinking of the Revolution,' he said thoughtfully. Mai looked at him. 'Our memories of him are all the more powerful, I think, since we were not exposed to his last frailties, his inevitable last weakness. Rather, we remember him strong and whole and eager to continue the battle.'

'Still,' Mai whispered, 'I fear for us all.'

With Sun Zhongshan's death came the inevitable quest to succeed him from within the ranks of the Guomindang. As was expected, Hu Hanmin emerged as the strongest candidate. His voice, raised in the forum of the central committee, was one of reason and patient common sense. Of course, Ling Xichu opposed him at every turn, speaking out for immediate military mobilization. But, curiously, Chiang Kai-shek, a most vocal proponent of such a move, was silent. He sat stolid and unmoving in his seat, surrounded by his retinue, in an almost judgmental attitude as he observed the two rivals in constant debate.

Zhongshan's widow, of course, had no say in anything,

but Zilin felt disturbed by this most uncharacteristic stance of Chiang's. He was, after all, a man of action, and he, Mai, and Hu had all expected the general to make his move immediately.

But other events conspired to take time away from Zilin's contemplation of the internal struggle within the Guomindang. Negotiations had begun with the American *tai pan*, Barton Sawyer, with regard to buying into his fleet of steamships.

Thoughts among the Shi brothers had settled around one of the British *tai pan*, who were generally more powerful by dint of having been in China the longest. But in the course of his work, Zilin had observed that one *tai pan* had been, over the past six months, consistently late in his harbour duties: Barton Sawyer of Sawyer and Sons. This, he argued with his brothers, was the soft spot they had been seeking. At length, the three of them agreed, delegating Zilin to make the approachment.

Thus, while the debates raged within the Guomindang, Zilin, dressed in his finest clothes, sat in the vestibule of Sawyer & Sons' offices in the American Concession.

An officious young Westerner sat at a desk, making portentous motions to convey the importance of his position to the barbarian Chinese seated in the waiting area. After a suitable amount of time, the young man, who was unsuitably dressed for the climate, told Zilin that he could go inside.

Barton Sawyer was a large-shouldered, beefy-faced man. His colouring was so red that it momentarily disconcerted Zilin. Zilin bowed, then quickly took the American's proffered hand as he had seen Westerners do many times, and squeezed it – which, he had found in his careful observance, was the proper response to the pressure he felt. Most of his brethren would merely have winced at having their hand squeezed and pulled it away.

Sawyer smiled. 'Well, you sure know how to shake

hands.' He had a loud, bellowing voice that privately disturbed Zilin's sensibilities. But outwardly he showed nothing. 'Where I come from, in Virginia, a man's known by his handshake. My daddy was known not to do business with anyone 'less he had a good solid handshake.'

It was the Americans' conceit to believe that everyone they came in contact with knew the location of their birthplace. As if a continent on the other side of the world would be an open book.

'Come on,' Sawyer said jovially, raising a hand, 'let's sit and be comfortable.' He directed Zilin to an overstuffed sofa that had obviously been imported from the West. Zilin found it exceedingly uncomfortable, but he was determined to make the best of it here inside the foreign devil's world. He must learn to acclimate himself, he told himself.

'Now,' Sawyer said, his voice still booming though the two were close together, 'how can I help you?'

No tea, no civilized conversation to stabilize relations, to get a feel of the spirit of the other man. Zilin was momentarily astounded. But then, as he recovered, he vowed that it would be the last time the coarseness of a foreign devil would so nonplus him.

'It has come to my attention that certain, er, monthly tithes required by the city of Shanghai have not yet been paid by your firm. I – '

'Now I recognize you!' Sawyer snapped his fingers. 'You work in the harbourmaster's office.' His face darkened. 'Since when are the mandarins sending clerks to make their collections?'

'I am not,' Zilin said softly, 'here in any official capacity.'

'You're not?' The American began to eye him more carefully. 'You mean you're not here to demand payment?'

'No, sir.'

Sawyer leaned forward, withdrew a cigar from a perfumed humidor. He bit off the end, spat it sideways onto the carpet, and lit a wooden match. He puffed heartily for a time, savouring the tobacco. 'Well, hell, son, it seems to me, then, you've got a nerve wanting to see me.' He began to rise. 'I haven't got the time – '

'You'll have no time at all,' Zilin said, 'if you can't make next month's harbour tithe.'

'That's none of your business,' Sawyer said coldly. 'I don't discuss the affairs of Sawyer and Sons with a Chinee.'

'Westerners call this pride,' Zilin said calmly. He had not moved. 'Or perhaps it is prejudice. I had heard that the Americans were somewhat less provincial in their thinking than their British brethren.'

'The British are no brethren of mine,' the American said quickly.

'No,' Zilin went on, 'I imagine not. The English *tai pan*, with their new, faster steamships are beating you at every turn. Consequently, your profits over the past years have dwindled so drastically that for the last six months you have been paying overhead with bank securities. Now you are having difficulties making your loan payments.'

Sawyer squinted down at him. 'You sure know a lot for a little Chinee.'

'I may be small in stature,' Zilin said, 'but my mind's another matter altogether.'

Sawyer stared openmouthed at him for a moment before he burst into a fit of laughter which turned his face so red that Zilin feared blood vessels had burst.

'Ah, oo.' Sawyer wiped at the corners of his eyes and sat back down beside Zilin. 'Well, well, well,' he said, 'I do believe we have a rare find here. A Chinee with a real sense of humour.'

Zilin nodded. 'Thank you,' he said. 'But really, I would prefer it if you called me by my name.' This thinking and speaking like a foreign devil was taxing indeed, he thought.

'All right.' The American tapped his cigar ash. 'What's your business, Mr Shi? That is, besides clerking.'

'My brothers and I have a certain amount of seed

money,' Zilin began, pausing almost immediately to take a breath. *Dew neh loh moh*, he thought, my heart is beating so fast it is sure to burst. 'We would like to use it to buy into your shipping line.'

For a moment Zilin was certain that Sawyer was going to hit him. All colour drained from his face, and Zilin was appalled at how ghastly he looked.

'Now look here, Mr Shi – '

'Naturally,' Zilin hurried on, 'there are certain guarantees my brothers and I are prepared to make as our first contribution to the firm ... and as a gesture of our goodwill.'

'This is all out of the question,' Sawyer said. 'Sawyer and Sons is an American firm, pure and simple. If I sell out, there'll be nothing for my son, Andrew, and his son after him.'

'If you *don't* relinquish part of the firm now, Mr Sawyer, I fear that your debts will eat it all up long before control passes to young Master Andrew. What kind of a legacy is a bankrupt firm?'

'It's out of the question.'

'As compensation for the share in Sawyer and Sons,' Zilin went on, 'my brothers and I are willing to infuse the company with more than much-needed capital. First, we can guarantee that the firm's property will not be touched by the Communists or the revolutionaries. There is going to be some kind of explosion throughout the country in the next several years. Quite naturally, foreign concerns will be a primary target of such unrest.

'Second, because I have access to all the harbourmaster's records, Sawyer and Sons will be privy to every shipment offloaded and laded in the port of Shanghai. You will, in effect, know who is shipping what – and how much of it, and to where – before any of your competition.

'Third, we will guarantee the safest and fastest method

of bringing opium from the interior of China through Shanghai and into Hong Kong, where you ship it overseas.'

Sawyer spent some time grinding out his cigar. When he next spoke, both his bantering tone and his anger had fled him. 'Taking the last first, Mr Shi. How in the name of hell can you guarantee such a thing?'

Zilin smiled. 'My youngest brother makes his living now captaining a lorcha along the rivers. He knows them all, knows the growers, the best fields and how to get the best prices out of them. Currently he is a free-lance, but that will change, of course, when we sign the deal.'

'How much money are you prepared to kick in?'

Zilin told him. Sawyer did some rapid calculations, his pulse racing. Zilin knew the sum to be inadequate. It would just about cover the next two months' overhead, including loan surcharges and harbour taxes.

Sawyer's answer was predictable enough. 'Sorry, Mr Shi. Some of the deal sounds fair enough. But the capital falls far short of what I'll need. In thirty days' time, I'll be back in the same position, only the poorer for it, for having signed over to you a percentage of the firm.'

'Not,' Zilin said, 'if you get the harbour-dredging concession within the next ten days.'

'Now you're talking nonsense,' Sawyer said. 'Mattias, King, the oldest and largest of the British *tai pan* houses, has that locked up. They've done so for as long as I can remember. You can just forget about that one.'

'I'd prefer not to. You see, I am privy to information that even *tai pan* do not possess.'

Sawyer noted Zilin's tone and nodded. 'We *are* in your country, Mr Shi. I take your point. Please continue.'

'The dredging is not yet complete. Tomorrow morning, when the English captains wake, they will find their dredgers deserted. Not a crewman will be found aboard.'

'That won't stop 'em for long. Mattias, King know your

people. Money buys an awful lot from the coolie, Mr Shi. He'll die for an English shilling.'

'Yes, of course he will,' Zilin agreed. 'So the captains will find makeshift crews, and taking them on board, they will also take a number of young revolutionaries whose zeal for destruction is frightening in its singlemindedness. In short, there will be fires on board. The dredgers will be lost or surely have to shut down.'

'Pardon me for saying so, Mr Shi, but the scheme's not worth its weight in nuisance value. Sure, the *tai pan*'ll lose money and time.' He shrugged his beefy shoulders. 'But so what? They'll get the ships back in working order sooner or later.'

'Unless it's sooner — so soon that they will have no chance to do it — the dredging concession rights will revert to the harbourmaster. You see, there is a time limit in the contract. It was put there by mutual agreement between Mattias, King and the city when the contract was originally awarded. The job must be done within six days' time or too much business is lost.

'Once the rights return to my office, the harbourmaster will call for sealed bids among the *tai pan* who are interested. With my assistance, Sawyer and Sons cannot fail to receive the concession. Since the job must be finished immediately, money will be forthcoming within a fortnight of completion.'

The *tai pan* stared at Zilin as if he had suddenly grown wings. 'Well, I'll be goddamned if you haven't thought of everything!' He sat down slowly, lost in thought.

When he judged that the American had had sufficient time, he said, 'There is one additional provision.'

'I knew it,' the American said. 'Now comes the kicker.'

'Nothing of the sort,' Zilin said. 'I wish only that you take my middle brother into the firm. You may interview him and so determine which position and at which level you wish to start him. Thereafter, he may move up in the firm solely on his own merit. Within two years, however, if he should prove satisfactory to you, I wish him to be transferred to your offices in Hong Kong.'

'I can live with that,' Sawyer said. 'But look, if he slacks off or can't learn the trade or is caught with his hand in the till or passing company information to a competitor, he's out on his ear. That's my decision, as *tai pan* of Sawyer and Sons.'

Zilin smiled. 'I leave his fate in your capable hands, Mr Sawyer.' He stood up. 'A last stipulation of our deal is that the firm's name shall not be altered in any way. We shall be silent partners at Sawyer and Sons.'

Now the American could not keep the smile off his face. 'Hell, let's go out and get the best meal money can buy, eh, Mr Shi?' He knew Shi would like that, since that was how the Chinese sealed a successful business deal between themselves. He laughed, and this time it did not seem nearly so loud and coarse to Zilin. 'You just may turn out to be the best business partner a man could have.'

Zilin looked up from his work at the harbourmaster's office as he heard a clatter at the front door. Voices were raised. Seeing Mai, he put down his quill. Over the shouts of others, she ran to him. She was out of breath, as if she had been running a long distance.

'Husband,' she gasped, 'it is disaster! A total disaster. We are all undone!'

He held her trembling body. 'Mai, what has happened?' Everyone in the office was gaping at them.

'Ling Xichu was found murdered late last night. This morning, the authorities arrested Hu Hanmin's first cousin. He is being accused of political murder.'

'What of Hanmin?'

'You know him as well as I. He just spoke before the central committee. I felt certain that this week they were going to elect him president. Now he has withdrawn his name from nomination.'

There was a breathless silence. 'And?'

Mai was weeping. 'The worst has happened. Chiang at last spoke up. He denounced all political murders. He spoke out for a strong, united leadership. No one, not even Hu, raised his voice against him. The committee is voting this evening. They want a president and, oh, husband, I am sure it will be Chiang!'

Of course, Mai was quite correct. The central committee of the Guomindang elevated the general, and thereafter, the Canton National Government came under his control.

As had been his intention all along, he consolidated power around himself, and when he judged it sufficient, he announced in June of 1926 the Northern Expedition. Both Mai and Hu tried to oppose him, rationally preaching caution, but the forward momentum that Chiang's militarism had injected into the movement was too infectious. Thus the Long March toward what many hoped was freedom for the Chinese people was begun.

During that year and the beginning of the next, Chiang's Nationalist army rolled through the central provinces, picking up support as it went. By the beginning of 1927 it had taken an additional three provinces to the east.

All the while, Mai worked with Hu and the Communist Party in trying to ensure that Zhongshan's ideals would not be lost in the growing imperialism of the general's victorious army.

Zilin, on the other hand, had steeped himself in his growing assets. In view of the increasing unrest of the country, he prevailed upon his brothers to sell all their land holdings, and though their profits were perhaps not as large as if they had waited longer to divest themselves of these assets, still he felt more secure with their money elsewhere.

215

That 'elsewhere' was an increasingly larger share of Sawyer and Sons. With the Shi brothers' help, the Sino-American company had prospered to the point where it now outshone all but two of the firms held by the British *tai pan*.

Zilin's brother inside the company rose even more quickly than Zilin had anticipated. Sawyer, who Zilin had learned was an excellent judge of character, soon insisted that the young man work directly with him. And when Zilin reminded him of his promise to send the man to Hong Kong, the American was reluctant to do so.

'He's invaluable to me here, Mr Shi,' he said.

'Think, then,' Zilin said, 'how much more valuable he will be, heading up the Hong Kong offices.'

In the spring of 1927, Chiang returned to Shanghai in triumph. Yet he came back to find that the Guomindang had a new president, elected in his absence. Still, Chiang's power had increased to such an extent that his return sundered the Guomindang into two separate factions.

Mai was distraught to see the flower of Zhongshan's dream thus rent, and she did all in her power to bring the two warring sides together. To no avail. Bad blood had been spilled, and there was no way to reverse the tide that was pulling the Revolution in two.

Just after the Chinese New Year, Zilin awoke in the middle of the night. He had been dreaming, but, as was sometimes the case, he did not remember of what. He was in a sweat. He turned to Mai for comfort, but she was not there.

He got out of bed and, pulling on a robe, went through the rooms. He found her at the front door. Two soldiers and an officer in the Nationalist army were with her.

'What is this?'

'This is nothing to concern you,' the officer said imperiously. 'General Chiang wishes to speak with Mrs Shi.'

'She is my wife,' Zilin said, responding to the look in Mai's eyes. 'Everything that concerns her concerns me.'

'This is the business of the central committee of the Guomindang.' The officer spoke as if by rote. 'In the name of the general I enjoin you from interfering.' He turned on his heel. 'Now, Mrs Shi, you will come with me.'

'I wish to speak with my wife before she – '

But the soldiers already had hold of her, and she was out of the apartment.

'Zilin!' He heard Mai's voice. 'My husband!'

'Wait!' he cried. But the officer levelled a pistol at his chest.

'Be good enough to return to sleep, Mr Shi,' he commanded. 'Your wife will be returned home when the general is quite done with her. She is safe in our hands.' He closed the door behind him.

In a moment the paralysis wore off and Zilin rushed to the window. Out in the street he could see the soldiers hustling Mai into the darkness. Just before he, too, slipped from sight, the officer glanced upward. His white teeth gleamed in the streetlight. He lofted the barrel of his pistol as if in salute or warning. Then he was gone.

Zilin was in a fever. His heart was constricted as he rushed into the other room to dress hurriedly. His mind was in such a whirl that it was not until he returned to the front room that he heard the pounding on the door. Thinking that it had all been a mistake, after all, and the officer was returning Mai, he leapt at the door and threw it open.

Hu Hanmin stood there. His face was as white as rice paper. 'I have just come from the Party headquarters. We have Chiang's army at our front door. They are making arrests and gunning people down as they flee. Executions, they are calling them. Chiang's broken with the Party. He's taken the Guomindang on its own. Mai's worst fears have come to pass.' He glanced at Zilin. 'Where is she? I fear she's in danger.'

'Buddha!' Zilin cried. 'The army's taken her!' He grabbed his friend. 'Come on, Hanmin, we must stop them before she gets to Chiang!'

They clattered down the steps and ran out into the street. A voice from the shadows halted them in mid-stride.

'Going somewhere, gentlemen?'

Zilin recognized that voice even before he saw the figure of the officer emerge from the shadows of the street. His pistol was pointed at a spot just between the two men.

'In this as well, General Chiang was correct. He felt certain that, given time, Hu Hanmin would show his face here.' He smiled. 'And now he has.' He gave a barking command, and his men appeared. They held Mai between them.

'Let her go,' Zilin said. He took a step toward them, but the officer pointed his gun and he stopped.

'Let her go,' Hu echoed. 'Let her go, and I will go with you willingly.'

'Those are not my orders,' the officer said, obviously enjoying his position of strength. He smiled. 'Besides, I don't care if you come willingly or otherwise.' He redirected his voice. 'Hold her up!'

His men obeyed, tightening their grip on Mai's wrists. They stood apart from her, and abruptly, Zilin knew that the officer had never had any intention of bringing her to Chiang.

'No!' he cried, springing forward even as the officer discharged his weapon.

Mai's eyes were upon him, and there was no fear in them as the bullet pierced her heart. Zilin thought she sighed.

'No!' he cried again, breaking into a stumbling run. The officer made no attempt to stop him; he was enjoying Zilin's grief too much.

Thus he did not see Zilin change direction at the last instant and veer toward him. In his rage, Zilin grabbed the pistol out of the officer's hand and pulled the trigger point-blank.

The explosion echoed in his ears and he felt the heavy recoil. Then he was staring at what was left of the officer's face, a raw red pulp. Muscles jumped in useless reflex as the corpse tumbled to the ground.

With the unconscious precision of the cornered animal, Zilin turned and squeezed the trigger twice more as the soldiers let slip their dead charge to come to the aid of their commander. After they fell too, Zilin emptied the weapon into them.

Then he went to where Mai lay in the dust and knelt beside her. Her eyes were closed and there was very little blood.

If he closed his mind, he could pretend that she was merely asleep.

Book Two
WU-WEI*

* To refrain from contention

Summer, Present

Hong Kong/Crimea/Beijing/Tsurugi/ Tokyo/Washington

Andrew Sawyer awoke with the dream still fresh in his mind. He sat up in bed, stared at himself blankly in the large, marbled mirror on the opposite wall. He saw a long face, his father's cornflower-blue eyes. The meticulously clipped moustache was as snow white as was the thinning crop of hair on his head.

Vaguely, he ran a liver-spotted hand over his face. When, he wondered, had his hair receded so much? Had it been at the same time his moustache had turned from the dirty blond it had been all his adult life? Where had the years gone?

He rolled over the satin sheets, fumbling for the china carafe of water on the night table. He poured himself a glass and drank thirstily. I must call Peter Ng right away, he thought, as he gulped down the liquid. Peter surely must know a good *sam ku*.

Sawyer put the glass aside. As he did so, his gaze fell upon the back of his hand. How fragile the skin appeared, how marked by time. How deeply the visible veins pulsed, how close to the surface.

He was not a man normally given to thoughts of mortality. As *tai pan* of Sawyer and Sons for more than forty years, he had always been concerned with the running of the family business. Not even the death of his first wife, Mary, in the '48 typhoon had stopped him for long.

Today, at seventy, he would have had no thoughts about the passage of time, had it not been for the dream. And the death of Miki.

He had been twenty-eight when Mary was taken from

him. *Joss*. One could call it that, but Miki had been only eighteen months old when she died. For many years the thought of remarrying had not entered his mind. He surmised that but for the urging of Peter Ng, his *comprador*, his chief and most trusted advisor, he might never have thought of it again. But Ng had argued for the family. A *tai pan* needed an heir to whom he could pass on the reins of power.

But it was not until ten years ago that he had met someone for whom he felt anything. Susan Welles had been thirty years his junior, and their marriage had caused something of a scandal in the Crown Colony. It made Sawyer remember the potential scandal from which Zilin Shi had saved him, many years before in Shanghai.

Of all his extended family inside the company, only loyal Peter Ng had been genuinely happy for him. But the marriage had little happiness to it. A year later, Susan died in a difficult childbirth. The baby girl, whom Sawyer had called Miki, lived for eighteen months before succumbing to the plethora of infant diseases with which she had been born.

It was about Miki that he had dreamed.

Sawyer reached for the phone and dialled a familiar number.

'I'm sorry to disturb you so early, Peter,' he said into the mouthpiece, 'but I must see you immediately.' He listened for a moment. 'No, the office will be fine.' Then, angry at himself that his distress had made him forget his manners, he added. 'How is Jocelyn? And the children? Good. Forty-five minutes, then?'

Showered, shaved, and powdered, dressed impeccably in a lightweight linen-and-silk suit the colour of *café au lait*, Sawyer waited for his chauffeur to open the Rolls's back door. He stepped out onto Sawyer Place, the only street in Hong Kong named after an American. Around the corner was the wide thoroughfare of Connaught Road Central, already busy even at this early hour of the morning.

Sawyer looked up at the Sawyer and Sons building. Across the street, to his right, was Connaught Tower. To his left was the building that housed the firm of Mattias, King and Company, rivals from the founding of Hong Kong by the West.

As he went up the pink marble steps to the brass-fitted, solid mahogany double doors, Sawyer was never more aware of the mutability of life. When he was young, he had seemed immortal. Lately it had seemed as if only the company would be immortal. For the most part he had ignored all the hysterical talk of the Chinese takeover in 1997.

He had taken his lumps with all the rest when, in 1980, the Hang Seng dropped a hundred points virtually overnight. But unlike many of the other *tai pan* who continued to sell in the days that followed, Sawyer had instructed his firm to buy. His wisdom had been apparent a year later when the Hang Seng surged upward, following the real-estate scare, and Sawyer and Sons found themselves major shareholders in a dozen new ventures, all beginning to prosper again after the year-long economic tailspin caused by the Communist announcement.

Privately, Sawyer thought the Chinese were mouthing a lot of hot air. They had face to recover, and they were going about it with a vengeance, making the Queen grovel before them. Well, that was all well and good – as far as it went. But the truth of the matter was that the Communists could no more run a complex business community like Hong Kong than they could walk on the moon. If the Colony should close down, the amount of revenue that China would lose yearly was enough to stagger the mind. The Communists were not fools, whatever else they might be.

Sawyer had been proven right. The announcement this

year that an interim period of fifty years had been granted to the Colony, during which nothing would change, had come as no surprise to him. Yet the jitters within the Colony had increased since the second announcement, not decreased as Sawyer had felt certain they would.

Privately, many businessmen did not believe the Communists, did not trust them at their word. Even the new signed agreement meant nothing. After all, they argued, practically speaking, what was to stop the Chinese army from ignoring the fifty-year interim period and moving in on the stroke of midnight, January 1, 1997?

Others were calmed by the fifty-year reprieve. They felt that whatever would ultimately befall the Colony after that time could not possibly hurt them. Sawyer knew that was a false hope. Hong Kong had always prospered on the backs of family-run trading houses. That meant the continuity of succeeding generations building on what had been accomplished before.

In his heart of hearts, this fifty-year hiatus did nothing to assuage his fears for Hong Kong's future.

If the rumour that Mattias, King are moving their operations out of Hong Kong is true, then God help all of us, he thought – including the Communists. To see the oldest and most prestigious of the *tai pan* houses abandoning the Colony could not help but sound a death blow for investor confidence.

In his office, which took up nearly half of the top floor of the building, Sawyer let himself through the outer doors into his inner sanctum. Through the plate-glass windows that stood ten feet high across the northern end of the room, all of Kowloon crouched at his feet, hazy through humid grey mist. Across Victoria Harbour, a Star Ferry pulled away from the pier beneath the old clock tower where, years ago, the trains had come and gone.

Sawyer turned, hearing soft footfalls in the anteroom. In a moment, Peter Ng entered the room. He was a small, dapper Chinese with a wide Cantonese face and clever eyes that saw everything. As usual, he wore a charcoal-grey raw-silk suit and black patent-leather loafers.

'Good morning, *tai pan*,' he said in his high, singsong voice. 'I brought us breakfast.'

'Good morning, Peter. Thank you.'

Ng placed a pair of styrofoam boxes down on Sawyer's rosewood desk. He dug out plastic chopsticks and they sat across from each other, rapidly eating rice, gravy, and bits of tender pork. They drank tea out of plastic cups. This was ritual with them. Being at the office so early often meant a crisis was at hand, and Sawyer had found that calm and orderly thinking were the best ways to combat a crisis.

'Bad news, *tai pan*,' Ng said, setting aside his empty box. Chinese never talked business while eating. 'I have just heard that Mattias, King will announce their relocation to Bermuda this afternoon.'

Sawyer closed his eyes. He sat very still, but his mind was whirling with the possibilities now laid open to him.

'The Hang Seng will take a nosedive on Monday, that's for certain,' Ng said. 'The only question is how far it will plummet and whether we should be ready to sell Monday morning.'

Sawyer's eyes flew open. 'Never sell, Peter. Never. This Colony is our lifeblood. Mattias, King is running scared. I can't believe that they've so overreacted, but there it is. They can get an enormous tax break in Bermuda, being servants of Her Majesty's Government, so from that point of view they'll lose nothing. But otherwise, my God! Think of the opportunity it affords us. With Mattias, King gone, Sawyer and Sons will be the largest and most prestigious of the Western *tai pan* trading houses.'

'They are going to say that the move will in no way affect the amount of trading they will be doing here in the future.'

'Face,' said Sawyer coldly. 'You and I and every trader in the Crown Colony know that they'll no longer have the clout they once had. Once they pull up stakes, they'll be outsiders. The best deals will be closed to them.'

'There are still the Chinese houses to worry about,' Ng pointed out. 'Between them, T. Y. Chung and Three Oaths Tsun have the shipping and warehousing industries just about sewn up here. And Five Star Pacific's heavily committed to utilities both here and in the New Territories.'

'At a guess, the fluctuating market will be harder on Tsun. He's got some tricky financial problems. He's gone into this Kam Sang nuclear power plant with Mattias, King in China. Their pullout might put him in a precarious position.'

'The Communists as well,' Ng said, 'if the Hang Seng nosedives on Monday.'

'Oh, it will. Of that you can be certain. And we must be prepared to take advantage of it. The war between T. Y. Chung and Three Oaths Tsun may be to our benefit. Wars – of any kind – drain their participants' resources.'

'Pak Hanmin?'

'Tsun's utilities arm, yes. Through Pak Hanmin and the Kam Sang deal, Tsun seeks a foothold in that area. Only a project having the size, scope, and longevity of Kam Sang could hope to do it for him.' Sawyer's eyes were alight. 'Perhaps we have found an Achilles' heel in our powerful enemy.'

'Don't you think Chung and Bluestone will have the same idea?'

Sawyer finished up his breakfast. 'Why don't we wait and see, hm?'

Peter Ng began to clear the remnants of the meal off the *tai pan*'s desk. 'How stupid the Communists are, to vacillate this way. A fifty-year grace period is no decision at all. It certainly will not help property values.'

'I think,' Sawyer said, 'that they have no clear idea how

228

to handle this situation. It is new to them, and the Communist Chinese historically cannot deal with new situations. Will they send troops in or won't they, will they become involved in the running of the Colony after 1997 or won't they, will they eventually nationalize all industry or won't they? Personally, I don't think they have a clue.

'But they'll come around eventually. They're great pragmatists, after all. They need us as much as we need Hong Kong. They have no need for the land; they have no expertise in business administration, nor, even worse for them, in dealing with the rest of the world. No, for the time being, at least, they require middlemen to do their business for them. That way, face is saved all around.

'They need the device of this new administrative district that Hong Kong will come under when the lease expires. The British will have to bring the Governor home. No matter. Governors here have no power whatsoever. The Chinese have it all, anyway. But Hong Kong is China's only real channel to the wealth and the industry of the West.'

'Mattias, King's decision must be an unmitigated disaster for them.'

'The important thing is that we make it a triumph for us.'

Both men were silent for a time. Around them now they could hear the office awakening. Phones burred softly, lights blinked on banked PBX consoles, hushed voices could be heard, doors closing softly, heels click-clacking down corridors.

'Tai pan?'

Sawyer's eyes were closed again. 'Yes, Peter?'

'What was it you wished to talk with me about?'

Sawyer sighed. 'Miki.'

'Miki?'

'Last night she came to me in a dream. Her spirit has met another spirit whom she wishes to wed.' Though Miki

229

had been a baby when she died, spirits were, of course, ageless. To the Chinese way of thinking, even spirits became lonely, craved happiness, desired completeness. This was what Sawyer meant.

'But that is wonderful, *tai pan*,' Ng said, leaning forward. Dreams such as the one Sawyer had were fairly common in China among parents who had lost children. Ng thought it interesting, though hardly surprising, that his *tai pan* had had such a dream. *Gwai loh* were not supposed to be in touch with such ephemeral emotions, but Sawyer, Ng knew, was very attuned to Chinese culture. 'Her spirit will be happy now. Did she tell you whom she wishes to marry?'

'Here is the man's name,' Sawyer said, pushing a slip of paper across the desk. 'We shall need a *sam ku* to tell us the address of the family as well as to make the arrangements for the ghost wedding.'

'This is a fortuitous sign,' Ng said, taking the slip. 'A most favourable omen, *tai pan*. I know just the *sam ku*. With luck, this dead man's family may have already come to her about Miki. It happens that way sometimes. The dreams occur to members of both families simultaneously.' He got up. 'I'll phone her right away.'

When he was alone, Sawyer put his hands flat on the polished rosewood. When, in a moment, he lifted them up, he could see their imprints, a part of him slowly fading into the air. Just like Miki.

Sei An, his secretary, stood in the doorway. Obviously she had just come in.

'*Tai pan*, is there anything I can get you?'

Andrew Sawyer shook his head slowly. 'Nothing.'

The *dacha* was so still that she could hear the water and the wind. It was late but still light, something for which she had always treasured the summertime. A bird cried, its sound seeming to echo like thunder across the vast bowl of the sky.

Down in the cellar, she recovered her notebook from its hiding place behind a pair of bricks in the west wall. It occurred to her that the dark niche beyond was just such a spot as those in which Russians often hid their religious ikons. Daniella's mother had been a practising Russian Orthodox, a fact she had never dared reveal to her husband. It was not lost on Daniella that what she was doing now was precisely what she had seen her mother do many years ago; it was no accident that she had chosen this type of hiding place for her most precious possession.

The danger, also, was akin to that which her mother had endured in her long years with Daniella's father. Never to tell him of her innermost beliefs. Her bastion from him. Now, in a way, it was the same with Daniella and Karpov.

She sat at the wooden refectory table and, placing the sourcebook and the cipher side by side, began her translation. An overhead lamp with a green steel shade cast her in a cone of concentrated light.

She worked swiftly and efficiently. Because it was a code of her own design, she required a minimal amount of time. Again she was reminded of her mother who, so clandestinely that she even managed to fool her husband, toiled for the church. Inside the religious underground, she joined others who were determined to reestablish the power of the Russian Orthodox Church by installing a Patriarch who would be independent of the will of the Communist Party.

On occasion, Daniella's mother had taken her to her meetings. This religious inculcation, a secret shared by mother and child, drew them together. It was as if Daniella's mother had taken her to the opera or the Ballet Russe. Slowly, Daniella had developed an appreciation for religion. Perhaps, even at that age, she had been fascinated by the enormous power an idea could wield. Capitalism, and perhaps communism too, were passing things; God was not.

That was not something her mother had had to tell her. She had discovered it all by herself. And had never forgotten it. Because history confirmed it. All political systems were temporary because they were creations of man. She did not think God was.

When she was finished transcribing, she closed the notebook and returned it to its sanctuary, careful to make certain that she put back both bricks precisely as they had been. Then she returned to the table and began to pore over this latest of her Medea intelligence reports.

Medea was a project that had been running for just over three years. Its chief operative was a man whom Daniella had herself recruited. She had made contact with him in the course of another, much more routine project. It had concluded satisfactorily. At that time she had researched all members of the opposition. One, Zhang Hua, a ranking Chinese Communist official, had, as it turned out, a younger brother in Hong Kong. Daniella immediately put him under surveillance. Within a span of ten days, she had a complete, detailed picture of the family's movements.

With that in mind, she contacted Zhang and made her pitch. He refused. That was no surprise. Daniella then ordered the brother's wife picked up and held. Zhang held out for forty-eight hours before, terrified, he capitulated.

Daniella had not released the brother's wife until she had received and evaluated the first piece of intelligence. Still, she had been sceptical. That was only natural. So Zhang had fed her three further bits of intelligence at roughly month-long intervals. All had proven to be of a very high grade indeed.

In the beginning, Daniella was tempted to take her triumph to Karpov and thus earn herself a medal. But almost immediately she had second thoughts. And the more she thought about it, the more she was certain that she could have her kudos and her own private pipeline into Beijing as well. As the Medea intelligence was transmitted, she first very carefully screened it, passing on one tiny chunk at a time, testing the waters.

The day she ran the raid on the heavy-water installation in Sinkiang was her most serious test. Her people arrested three engineers who had somehow been turned by the Chinese. That put her under Karpov's scrutiny. Of course, he wanted to know her source. It was easy to lie, and the fabrication she gave him – that suspicions had filtered up the line and had eventually been reported to her office – was perfectly plausible.

She did, indeed, get her medal. And kept Medea to herself. Now, as she read this latest report, she was very glad that she had. It told her that there was a bitter internal struggle being waged within the Chinese government over the eventual disposition of Hong Kong. Basically, there were two camps. The traditional hard-liners wished to assume complete control of the Crown Colony in 1997. They still smarted under the way in which sovereign Chinese soil had been 'extorted under the most heinous duress' from the Empress in 1842. They felt shamed that others ran a corner of their country so successfully, and that it was assumed worldwide that the Chinese Communists could not. It was imperative, if China was ever going to stand shoulder-to-shoulder with the other major powers, they felt, to prove that it had the modern business wherewithal to do it.

On the obverse of this coin stood the so-called modernists. These, the Medea intelligence reported, were more basically Chinese in nature – that is, truer to the spirit of the nation than to the Communist ethos. They believed that because the trappings of communism afforded them power in the most populous country on earth, they were reconciled to using it. But only superficially. The modernists were convinced that if China was ever to rise into the

20th century as a viable power, it had to adopt the ways of the West – at least for some time to come.

It also needed vast infusions of capital. To disrupt the freewheeling, day-to-day dealing of the Chinese in Hong Kong was to risk cutting off this supply of money into China, or, at the very least, to severely hamstring it to the point where it would be all but useless. Over the past six years or so, Daniella knew from her own research, the Communist Chinese had become much more active in business within the Crown Colony. Their profits were burgeoning.

As were hers, since she had instituted her pilot programme there. But that, she had known from the beginning, was merely a start. Which was precisely the reason for her institution of Medea.

Now she came to the kernel of the report. One of the modernists, an official of the 'highest rank,' was mounting a Hong Kong operation. Its objectives appeared to be twofold, according to Medea. One was to ensure that the modernists would eventually have their way in the Crown Colony. The other was 'purportedly to gain control clandestinely of all monetary and bullion transactions passing through Hong Kong and Macao.'

To control Hong Kong! It was Daniella's fondest dream. But until this point it had, in all reality, been an untouchable one. Karpov's almost obsessive drive to get Moonstone on line disturbed her, even more so when Lantin's intervention had begun to make it a reality. The Soviet Union's wanton display of military force throughout Asia was, in her opinion at least, a dangerous course to take. Karpov and Lantin seemed like a pair of teenage hoodlums playing 'chicken' in an old jalopy. Only the car they were up against was the property of China, and the vehicles were loaded with nuclear warheads.

Daniella knew there must be another way to gain control of China besides threatening her borders. Hong Kong was that way. As soon as she had made sure of Medea, she was certain of it.

If Medea could get her inside the Communist Chinese operation, she knew she could gain control of it. Once she was overseeing the bullion traffic in and out of the Colony, she could have it all. All that wealth flowing into and out of Macao! It went unreported; it was untraceable. Trading-house profits – at least partially – were 'washed' that way. Vast amounts that bypassed even stockholder dividends, and which found their devious way into numbered Swiss bank accounts that could be opened only by the *tai pan* themselves – this was how trading had been done in Hong Kong for more than a century.

To have at one's fingertips the ebb and flow of such wealth was a dream come true. With such knowledge, Daniella could tap into the resources of any trading house in Hong Kong. Their secrets would be open to her; the *tai pan* would do her bidding rather than be caught out.

Daniella reread the passage. Her pulse rate began to climb. Oh, she thought. Oh, oh, oh. Dare I believe this at all? The thought of gaining control of such an operation and turning it to her own ends – to realize her dream – dizzied her. She fought to catch her breath. This is pure gold, she thought. If it is correct. *If*. What proof was Medea offering?

She took several deep breaths so that she could finish the report without the Cyrillic letters swimming before her eyes.

Information sketchy as yet, she read, *but I caution you not to confuse lack of detail with lack of veracity. Intelligence gleaned from highest possible source. Operation somehow revolves around non-national: Westerner named John Bluestone. He is one of the five* tai pan *heading Five Star Pacific, one of the top trading houses in Colony.*

Bluestone! Daniella thought. Good God, how is that

235

possible? She read on. *This fact photographed directly from official's file. Print enclosed.*

Daniella turned to the last sheet, a high-resolution black-and-white photograph, enlarged to eight-by-eleven-inch size. From a drawer she extracted an oblong magnifying glass. Carefully she ran it over the blowup. She stopped when she came to the chop, the signature seal of the 'official of the highest rank' whose brainchild the Hong Kong operation was.

Carefully she copied out the ideograms, reading the result over to herself.

'Shi Zilin,' she said out loud. Now she had her proof.

Three Oaths Tsun was seated at the best table at the Chiu-chow restaurant in Causeway Bay. At his right hand sat a stunning Chinese woman with a flat, high-cheekboned face that successfully rose to dramatic heights, employing only a minimum of makeup. It was a face that looked equally as wonderful in bed in the early morning as it did beneath glittering lights at night.

To Three Oaths Tsun's left was the seven-metre-long case filled with row upon row of swallows' nests, whose prices ranged anywhere from four to one hundred Hong Kong dollars. As he had done, many patrons picked out their choices, which were then made into the most indescribably delicious soup. Picking the right nest was, of course, an art, as was every culinary element in China, and Three Oaths Tsun prided himself on being a master.

He had just presented his mistress, Neon Chow, with an emerald necklace. Neon Chow worked for the Governor, and during the day she was as demure as her job demanded. One of the things she adored about Three Oaths Tsun was that he seemed to enjoy her in her natural state.

She had squealed uninhibitedly when she opened the box, and had not waited to put her present on before launching herself across the littered table, throwing her arms around Three Oaths Tsun.

'*Eeeeya*, but it's beautiful!' she cried. A lock of thick black hair had come undone and now swept dramatically across the side of her wide brow. Three Oaths Tsun looked at her and felt a stirring not only in his sacred member but further northward, in the area of his heart. He was constantly amazed at how this young girl – she was just 23 – affected him. Just by a movement of her exquisitely graceful arm, just by touching his shoulder in private, or by laughing and thus filling a room when they were out, she could elate him past his wildest imaginings. And when, he thought, we experience the clouds and the rain, *oh ko*!

Three Oaths Tsun summoned the waiter and barked an order for *tie guan yin*, a fine oolong tea known as Iron Goddess of Mercy. It was so strong and expensive that it was served in cups the size of a thimble.

'I'm glad we have this time together,' she said. 'I was beginning to think that you were tired of me.'

'What does that necklace tell you?'

'Presents are all well and good,' she said, drawing her lips into the pouty shape that drove him wild, 'but you have been spending so much time with Bliss, I was becoming concerned.'

'Business matters need not concern you, *heya*?'

'What business could you have with your own daughter?'

'What are you, deaf?'

The pout intensified, but now he was inured to it. His mind had switched gears, which was bad for Neon Chow, and she knew it. 'You treat me like a child sometimes. I am not a teenager. I have a very responsible job.' She tossed her head. 'I do not think the Governor would speak to me in this way.'

'Then open your jade gate for the Governor,' Three Oaths Tsun said shortly. 'Governor or no governor, he is still *gwai loh*. I had no idea you were so enamoured of their fornicating barbarian ways.'

Neon Chow knew that she had pushed him over the edge. 'I am sorry that I am jealous.' Her voice dropped to a husky whisper. 'When I am not near you, I think about you constantly. If I wish to be near you more, do I deserve to be treated like a sack of garbage?'

Three Oaths Tsun grunted. That meant he'd think about it. If she was good.

Neon Chow drank in the look on his face and put one perfectly sculptured hand over his. Her eyes were as dark as the night, as lustrous as the gemstones in her new necklace. The nails scratched his skin with great delicacy, even a certain amount of modesty.

'I love my present,' Neon Chow said, fingering the emeralds where they lay, glowing and mysterious, in the hollow of her throat. 'I love you.'

Beneath the table, Three Oaths Tsun's sacred member began again to unfurl.

Rage. The red heart of darkness consumed him. In the aftermath of the storm, he gathered his strength about him. Rage was like a cloak, warming him, healing his wounds, or at least soothing their pain.

He saw the outlines of the stone lodge on the far side of the chasm and knew he wanted to be there. He followed the ragged lip of the scree to his left for several hundred yards. When he was certain there was no way around there, he retraced his steps and eventually found the rubble and mud-strewn slope down into the shallow glen.

Grey mist clung like coils of gauze, and he went down into it, skinning the heels of his hands as the loose earth gave way beneath him. He fell back, continuing his slide downward.

Reaching the floor, he went quickly through the mist.

His breath was hot and his heart hammered mercilessly. Rage.

There was no sky, no horizon. The world had turned nacreous, giving him the sensation of being inside a shell. Echoes, piling one atop the other, of his progress, a falcon's cry, the *dree dree dree* of insects, the swift rustling of a stoat or badger through the underbrush. A mosaic of elementalism.

Jake was oblivious to the beauty all around him. Climbing out on the far side of the glen, he went across to the spot where he had first seen Mariana. On the way, the blood on the high grass stained his trouser legs. He saw the flat rock where she had fallen. The rain had washed it clean.

He lifted his head. 'Nichiren!' He howled like an animal. 'I'm going to kill you!'

He stopped before the house. The front door was open, the *engawa* was deserted. A soft tinkling, and Jake turned his head. *Fūrin*. The bells of summer, children playing on the shoreline, laughing, carefree. Alive.

Hot tears slid down his face. *Mariana*, he thought. *Mariana, I've killed you.*

Inside, he looked around. He saw two *wei qi* boards set up in mid-match, saw a third on the floor, the black and white stones scattered to the four corners of the room. He went to one, lifted off a white piece. It was so easy to kill a stone. Just take it off the board. But a human being was another matter. The thought that Mariana was gone confused him. What would life be like without her? For three years he had all but ignored her. They had made love infrequently. Never once in all that time had he felt anything save a certain localized relief when he came.

The stone man. Isn't that what she had called him once? Finally she had turned her confusion and frustration into rage to try to get through to him. *Why am I here if you've got nothing to give me, Jake?* she had screamed. *When we got*

*married, we were in love. I with you, you with me. Or at least I
thought so. My God in heaven, don't you see what's happened to
you? The Sumchun River has destroyed all the love, all the humanity
you had inside you. Whatever it was that made me fall in love with
you is gone. Jake, do you understand? Jake, the stone man. The
Quarry's the place for you, all right.*

Better by far than the filthy streets of Hong Kong.
Would the Marocs have felt the same way? He did not
know. They had spent so much time talking to him about
his dead mother and father. He had had a sense of them,
though he could not even bring the image of his father to
mind.

They had given him the piece of the *fu*. It was his legacy,
they told him. His link with his past, proof of his parents'
love for him. Whether the Marocs had made up much of
what they told him, he never knew. He suspected that it
made no difference. His sense of what his parents had been
like was all that mattered. How he wished that they were
here now! His sense of their loss flooded through him
again, mingling with the pain he felt for Mariana.

Oh, Buddha! he thought. I have nothing. Again, I have
nothing!

Darkness all around him. This place was filled with
shadows. What it needs is a little light, he thought. Just a
spark. In a corner he found a stack of kerosene cans. All
but one was full.

Rage. It made coherent thought an impossibility. He
ripped open the cans, hurling the liquid all over the place.
Again and again, until there was no more left. Then he
backed to the front door. Out onto the *engawa*. Only the
slight tinkling of the *fūrin* to keep him company. Memories
clawing at him.

Lit a match and threw it.

Boom like thunder. Echoing down the mountainside.
Greasy ball of black and crimson rising upward, dissipating
the clinging mist, turning it lurid colours.

Jake sat on the shaking ground, hands clasped around his drawn-up knees. Watching the flames lick up, engulfing the stone as they ate away at the ancient wooden beams. The house groaned in giving up its long life.

Jake was crying again. He was sorry for what his rage had made him do, just as he was sorry for what his spite had made him do. He felt ashamed. Once, as a very small boy, long before he met Fo Saan, he had stoned a frog to death. He had come across it on the bank of a river. It was huge, ugly, squatting like an idol, unmoving. At first, Jake threw a stone at it simply to see it move. But when the creature did not oblige, Jake grew inexplicably angry. He threw another stone, and another. His anger turned to rage at the stupid frog. Now he threw the stones to hit it. And still the animal refused to move.

Then, quite suddenly, it couldn't move. It was dead. That same feeling of shame and remorse now engulfed Jake, and he put his head down, resting it on his forearms.

How much time passed, he could not say. Perhaps he slept. In any case, nightmare images rode his mind: Mariana wreathed in flames, calling to him; Mariana on the rock, bleeding, he reaching out to her, straining, shoving her off into the abyss; Mariana watching him as he made love to Bliss, squeezing her breasts, opening her thighs, nuzzling her mount with his lips; Mariana at a river ford, twisting thigh-deep in eddying water, her blood flung into his face, blinding him, his hand around a smooth stone, his arm arcing, his fingers letting go, the stone striking her, splitting her face open.

No!

His head started up. Had he screamed out loud? Had he been dreaming? His face was covered in sweat and he had begun to shiver. Night surrounded him. Starlight covered him in luminescent blue.

He sat still. He listened to the crickets' hum, the foraging of nocturnal predators. He heard the wind through the grasses, rustling the treetops. He began to gather his thoughts.

He saw that it had been foolish to come here on his own. It was obvious that he needed help. But this wasn't Hong Kong. He had no real friends here. No one he could turn to. Certainly he could not allow anyone in his network of informants to see him in this state. They needed to respect him if they were to continue working for him.

He breathed deeply and thought of Fo Saan. What was it that he had once said? *There will come a time, my son, when you will find yourself in enemy territory, pitted against overwhelming odds; when even your friends have become your adversaries.*

Enemy territory was surely where he found himself now. Hadn't Stallings killed Mariana? Stallings and the Quarry? *Why?* Why was Mariana with Nichiren? The two impossibilities seemed linked. Stallings was not the villain; he was a company man. Who had given the orders? Beridien? Donovan? Wunderman?

The last thought was chilling, but Jake could not discount the possibility. How much was he ignorant of? With so many unanswered questions, he could make no hasty assumptions, take no rash actions. He had a score to settle with the Quarry, but there was a tangled web to be unravelled first. Patience.

And Nichiren. His first target.

Only one thing was certain: he was effectively cut off from Quarry headquarters. If you don't know who to trust, trust no one. The filthy, dangerous backstreets of Hong Kong had taught him that important lesson early on.

When you find yourself in enemy territory, pitted against overwhelming odds, Fo Saan had counselled, *seek aid. If you believe there is no one to help you, that is the time to change your patterns of thought. Know that aid may be found in the most unlikely places.*

Jake pondered this. He sought every avenue, old and new. Each time, he arrived back at the same conclusion. There was only one person in Japan to whom he could go for help. On the face of it, it seemed an absurd notion. But he thought again of Fo Saan's words and they buoyed him. Well, what do I have to lose? he asked himself.

At first light, he was already making his way back down the mountainside known as the Sword.

Zhang Hua pushed his thick-lensed spectacles up against the bridge of his nose as he came into the drab office. The gesture did no good; the glasses slipped down his wide nose a moment later.

Outside, through the poorly made panes of glass, the steamy expanse of Tian An Men Square wavered as if seen through the haze of a mighty truck's exhaust.

'Are you feeling better today, Comrade Minister?' he asked as he dropped a sheaf of dossiers into the wire basket on the desk.

Shi Zilin grunted, all but ignoring him. He was engrossed in a raft of communications flimsies that Zhang Hua had observed had been hand-delivered to him a moment ago by a uniformed courier.

'You look well,' Zhang Hua said, watching Zilin carefully sorting the flimsies into two stacks. In truth, he thought, the minister looked decidedly unwell. His colour was pale, and Zhang Hua was certain he detected an increase in the tremor in the old man's hands. Perhaps the acupuncture treatments were no longer working.

Zilin's eyes darted upward, clashing with Zhang Hua's intense gaze, and like a child caught out, the assistant averted his gaze slightly.

'You are sweating, my friend,' he said, focusing his attention. 'Are you unwell?'

'I'm quite all right, Comrade Minister.'

'Come, come,' Zilin said, reaching out a hand. 'We needn't be so formal among ourselves, eh, Zhang Hua?' He saw the direction of his assistant's gaze. 'Close the door and sit here near me, my friend.'

243

When Zhang Hua had complied, Zilin closed the dossier cover on the flimsies he had been reading. His old black eyes studied the younger man's face. The passing years had dimmed none of their intelligent lustre.

He lifted up a cloisonné pot and a matching cup from a low wooden table at his side. 'Have some tea, that will serve to restore you.' He poured, handed over the cup. The tremor in his hand was particularly noticeable. 'It is tepid, I'm afraid. I no longer tolerate the heat as well as I did in my youth. The tea cools me now as it used to warm me years ago.'

The two men drank together.

He looked into Zhang Hua's eyes. 'I made a decision early in life to become a Celestial Guardian of China. Those who follow me must accept that burden.'

'I know, *lao* Shi, but this situation with Wu Aiping cannot fail to generate dire consequences for us. I fear that he is too powerful for us. He is so young for one with such enormous power. He is the head of the most powerful academy in China. Their sole purpose is to find the military deterrents to the danger from the Soviets all along our border. The *qun* aligned against you could not have found a better leader. His militancy has an appalling following in Beijing. It appears to be growing each day. If Wu Aiping should prevail . . .' He shuddered openly as his words drifted off.

Zilin sighed, putting aside his teacup. 'I saw this future, my friend. Oh, I don't mean Wu Aiping specifically. But certainly someone like him. Yes, he is strong. He may even defeat us. But we must not stop trying. Without us, China is doomed. We are its future. I knew that a long time ago, just as I knew that I was needed to help share it. But I also understood that to do so required enormous concentration. And sacrifice. I could not have it all, as those others who rose and fell on the hubris of their self-aggrandizement did. Chiang, Mao, all the others felt that their selves could encompass the world. They were wrong.

'Only I have survived from that time, Zhang Hua. Because of my dedication. Not to myself. Like a Buddhist monk, I had my God to which I dedicated my entire life. To serve China as I did, I was required to divest myself of, as it were, all earthly possessions. All.'

For a time the only sound the two men heard was the whirring of the metal fan standing atop the filing cabinet across the room. As it swivelled, they, in their turn, could feel the clammy air brush across their faces.

'Sometimes,' Zhang Hua said with a slight tremor in his voice, 'it is important to know when one is outmatched.'

'My friend, is that what you believe of us now? After all our time together, have you so easily lost your faith?'

'Faith is something one must never give up,' Zhang Hua said. Out of the corner of his eye he watched the tremor in the senior minister's hands. 'I did not mean to give you that impression.'

'Good. Now finish your tea, Zhang Hua. I promised your father I would take care of you, and I am a man of my word.'

He closed his eyes again and thought about sacrifices. All the manipulation he had done, and still continued to do. All the human lives he had set dancing to a rhythm only he controlled. Was this the future he had truly envisioned for China? He knew that it was. Talking of sacrifice was all well and good. But one only understood its true nature after one acted.

How long has it been, he wondered, since I have experienced true happiness? He considered this for some time, but still the answer eluded him.

Stallings had wanted to go riding. He had even gone so far as to call the stablemaster at the Movie House to prepare his stallion.

Then he changed his mind. Right in the middle of a spoonful of Wheaties and strawberries, he got up and

245

cancelled his appointment. Left his half-eaten breakfast on the table and drove to the office on H Street.

He had slept on the flight back from Japan, but not soundly. He had dreamt of being pursued. He was in a dark forest. On horseback he was making his way from the scene of a termination. Somehow he had been found out. Branches whipped at his face and shoulders. Though he tried to duck, the trees continued to scourge him until he was raw and bleeding on every exposed area. Then his shirt began to be flailed away.

He became convinced that he was being punished. But for what? He had carried out his assignment without a slipup. He had killed again.

Then it occurred to him that he had killed the wrong person. The thought terrified him. And that was the moment when he became aware that he was being pursued. How was that possible? He had been so careful. As always.

Still, he could hear the clatter of horses' hooves behind him. He urged his own mount on. This served only to intensify the scourging. He made no swifter progress.

With the pounding of the pursuit loud in his ears, he dug his heels into his horse's flanks. Bending lower over the creature's whipping mane, he shouted to it, striking it on the side of its neck to increase its gait.

Shadows climbed his back, pressing in on him from all sides. He could not see the sky. Blood was flowing freely from his lacerated skin in hot streams. The faster he went, the more severely he was punished. Why?

The sounds of pursuit grew louder, and Stallings turned his head to look back. Saw the riderless horse, nostrils flared, eyes glowing demonically.

He had screamed so loudly that two flight attendants came running. One of them, the young woman with the auburn hair and the beauty mark at the corner of her mouth, stayed and eventually gave him her phone number, so it hadn't been a total loss.

The dream haunted Stallings: at home, taking a hot shower to wash the grime of travel off him; eating indifferent Chinese food out of cartons sticky with soy sauce and monosodium glutamate; making love with Donna, the auburn-haired flight attendant; at the health club, as he worked out with free weights and Nautilus.

Unlike other dreams of his, it had not faded away into the night or even into the clear light of day. That was why he had cancelled his ride, had leapt into the car before finishing his breakfast.

The dream would not let him be. It had somehow struck a familiar tone even as it had engendered a deep-seated fright in him. Why?

He was about to find out.

Seated in his windowless office, Stallings activated his terminal. The Quarry had had built for it a Xicor computer several generations beyond what was normally in business use. The GPR-3700 mainframe was housed in a temperature- and humidity-controlled, dust-free environment deep within the bowels of the Quarry building.

Stallings closed his eyes for a moment, recalling the long line of access codes that would pass him into the deeper and more secretive layers of the computer's memory.

He thought of the riderless horse. He thought of catching Mariana Maroc in his sights, of pulling the trigger, one, two, three, the bullets popping in the sonic static of the storm, squeezed out into the night. He saw her flung across the heath, surprise in her wide-open eyes.

Lost her in the storm for moments, then found her stretched against the rock, Jake on him now. Saw her take the long plunge into darkness.

He thought of the riderless horse. And the Russians up on the Sword. It was ironic, Stallings thought. If Jake hadn't taken care of them so efficiently, Mariana Maroc might still be alive. Maybe.

The riderless horse. The Russians. What the hell were

they doing there? If they had penetrated the operation . . . but Wunderman had made no comment at the airport when he picked Stallings up, debriefing him in the car on the way to Stallings's Federal-period clapboard house on S Street in Georgetown. It was just a block away from Dumbarton Oaks, and Stallings had very much resented the senior officer's intrusion on his **own** peaceful turf. His home was his home, period. He never took his work there. Besides, the auburn-haired flight attendant was on her way. Although, as it turned out, the spectre of the riderless horse had made that encounter something less than sublime.

Stallings opened his eyes, saw the **MONDAY ACCESS OPEN** graphic glowing on the screen. The GPR-3700 had seven access levels, graded by the day of the week. 'Monday' was the least sensitive, 'Sunday' the most sensitive. Agents and officers obtained access codes to more sensitive levels as they rose within the Quarry heirarchy. Stallings, as one of the inner council of five, which included the President, had access up to and including the seventh level, though he had never bothered to delve that deep.

'Thursday' was his most familiar ground, the area he used most often when deliberating one of his thorny field problems. Now, after three hours at that level, he found it inadequate. He could find no answer for the presence of the Russians.

He sat back and pressed his thumbs into his eye sockets, massaging gently. Looking into those phosphor lights still bothered him.

It was that they were not just Russians, he thought now. Or even KGB operatives. There were always a contingent of those, wherever he was. He had learned to live with them, as a poor man learns to live with cockroaches in his tenement apartment. No, these men had been something special. Department S. KVR. That was General Vorkuta's area, and Stallings, macho man though he was, had learned to respect that particular woman's intelligence and field acumen.

Units under her command had ruined two of his prior operations – and tried for a third – over the last two years. In Angola, Lebanon, and – which was it? – Guatemala, yes; he had difficulty with those Central American countries, they all looked alike to him.

The first time had been the most hair-raising – that race down the Guatemalan mountainside in a car ten years past the time it should have been condemned. But the third time, in Angola, had been the worst. Two .38 slugs in him, shoulder and upper arm – a third missing his head by a fraction.

All KVR. All designed by General Vorkuta.

Stallings had quickly learned respect for her. He swivelled his chair around, punched out another access code: **FRIDAY ACCESS OPEN**. His fingers flew over the keys. Like stroking the flank of a horse. He went through the procedure of accessing KVR operations. 'Backtracking,' Wunderman had said to him, 'is often the best way to work the memory bank. If you've got a problem in the present, it's often got a tail in the past.'

Thirty-six in this list, and he began the tedious task of going through each file in detail. Found the Guatemalan operation, rechecked the date to make certain it coincided with his operation. Routine information until he came to the end and discovered an electronic footnote. Did a search but could find no trace of it on this level. Fingers dancing. **SATURDAY ACCESS OPEN**.

Found it down here. **MATAS SANDINAR DIES** – here the readout gave a date of some three days after Stallings's operation had gone awry – **OF ACICOTE POISONING**. Stallings stopped there, disconcerted. He had read the news reports of the death of Sandinar, who was then the republic's President. It had been of a massive myocardial infarction. Heart attack. What was this about a poisoning?

249

Stallings thought this over. Sandinar had been a strong and bitter antagonist of Carlo Guerrerra, Stallings's target. After Sandinar's death, Guerrerra had gained in power, fully doubling his ragtag insurgent army – until, six months later, Stallings had reentered Guatemala and terminated the rebel leader.

He went on accessing the KVR operations on this level. Found Angola. And, again, a footnote not on this level. He quickly checked for Lebanon, could not find it, and went deeper.

SUNDAY ACCESS OPEN.

The electronic asterisk surfaced like a cork: CHOJO MTUBA DIES OF ASPHYXIATION DUE TO CRUSHING OF CRICOID CARTILAGE. Date given was one week after Stallings's operation. Published reports had Mtuba's death due to a fatal fall from a horse that had reared unexpectedly, shying from a snake.

Again, as in the Guatemalan operation, Mtuba had been the general of the faction opposing insurgents led by Stallings's intended target. These were but two of Stallings's many operations, but what stuck out for him were the notations of assassination. They were so written and so placed as to seem to be at the instigation of the Quarry. But that was patently impossible. To order the termination of Sandinar and Mtuba was unthinkable. Totally against Quarry policy.

Stallings remembered the Russians on the Sword. The riderless horse. He went on.

And found Lebanon. It was buried in a series of noncompatible files, like a gemstone in rubble. If he hadn't been still learning to use the computer, he doubted whether he would have found it at all.

He wondered why it should be here. As far as he was concerned, it had been little more than routine. Yes, he had discovered the KVR team on his tail. But after

Guatemala, he had been on his guard and he had picked them up shortly after he arrived.

He had planned a feint and had employed it to perfection, using the Russians' own favourite weapon: disinformation. Thus, while the KVR team was waiting for him to show at what they believed was the rdv point, he was across the city, putting a bullet through Mahmed Al-Qassar's head from three hundred yards. Termination complete. The end of one of the most powerful and feared pro-Soviet faction leaders in the Middle East. In and out in thirty-six hours, and how do you like that one, General Vorkuta?

Why was it here on the seventh and most sensitive level?

Eventually, through more donkey work, he found out. He wished he hadn't. The answer was buried in an adjacent file. Another electronic asterisk. Since this was the deepest level, there was obviously nowhere else to put it.

MAHMED AL-QASSAR, he read, TERMINATED – here it gave the correct date – AS DIRECTED. DOUBLE AGENT FOR TIMOTHY LAINE.

Stallings's eyes bugged. No! he thought. It can't be! Timothy Laine was Director of the Central Intelligence Agency.

In a kind of cold frenzy, Stallings returned to the Lebanon file, thinking, Could I have killed one of our own agents? How could it have happened? Went to the end of the file. It stopped in mid-sentence. He tapped the access file key over and over but got nothing. He scrolled the screen. It went blank.

Then, remembering his lessons, he tapped the CONTROL bar and was confronted with this:

CONTINUATION OF FILE STRICTLY CLASSIFIED *EYES ONLY, QUARRY DIRECTOR.* USE ACCESS CODE FOR *YAHU.*

What, Stallings asked himself, in the name of Christ is *Yahu?*

It took him three calls, the last to a linguist, and a trip to the Library of Congress to find out.

Yahu, it seemed, was a Burmese word. In their culture it was the term for the eighth day of the week.

What came into Jake's mind now was a fragment of the calligraphy on the scroll hanging in Mikio Komoto's house. *When the general punishes a criminal, the heart of the army is sternly controlled.*

He suspected now that it was the general's mentality, so expressly spelled out on that banner, which controlled Komoto. He knew he desperately needed to understand the man before he was to confront him. Otherwise, he knew, after what he had done inside the *yakuza oyabun*'s house, he would have no chance in the encounter. Komoto would punish him as an example to his troops.

It was to Komoto's house that Jake had come as he drove out of the Alps. This was because the *oyabun* was the only one of Jake's enemies who had the potential of being turned into an ally.

Much of this depended on what kind of man Komoto was, beneath his outer mask. And this was what would make the next several hours so tricky and so hazardous. Jake would have to play much of this by ear, changing his tactics as Komoto revealed more and more of himself. If he was a greedy man, Jake could use that. If he was a moral one, that too could be an advantage.

Michi. The path. Jake would have to find the right one if he was to have any chance of finding Nichiren and the *fu* shard that Mariana had taken from him.

It was somewhat earlier in the evening than when Jake had last been here. He approached the house the same way. This time, however, he saw two cars at the side of the house. One he recognized as Komoto's. This one was nearest the light-bathed side entrance.

Now he came again to the manicured hedges. Beyond,

he found the private garden. Curious about its unnatural elongated shape, he detoured down its long length. At its far end he found the answer; it was not a total surprise. Beneath the boughs of a slender cryptomeria, Jake discovered a *marumono*. It was strung up by a length of cord. He raised a hand, set it in motion, swinging back and forth like a pendulum. It set off memories in him, like the ripples made by a stone thrown into a still lake.

The *marumono* was one of three traditional targets for *kyūjutsu*: a dowel stuffed with straw or cotton batting, then covered with tanned hide.

For centuries, the bow and arrow had been the chief weapon of the Japanese soldier. The *samurai* alone were allowed to use sword and bow and arrow; the common man used pike and staff as his weaponry.

Kyūjutsu was the martial art of archery. The reason the *marumono* was hung stemmed from archery's origins which, according to Fo Saan, at least, emerged with the warrior on horseback. Thus, in training, one learned to hit a variety of targets, including moving ones. This was *marumono*, the most difficult of all of them.

In feudal times, every *samurai* household had a variety of *yaba*, or archery ranges, for target practice. Jake saw that times had not changed all that much.

Making a sudden decision, he returned to the front of the house and, after walking steadily up the stone pathway, knocked on the door.

In a moment it opened. Toshi stood framed in the doorway. He blinked when he saw Jake. He looked as if he had seen one of the guardians of hell.

His hand went to his waistband. He pointed a snub-nosed .38 at the centre of Jake's stomach.

Jake stood very still. He thought about raising his hands over his head, but, keeping careful watch on Toshi's face, he decided to make no move at all. Instead, he worked on his breathing. He did not like guns. He had never trained with one, but this was not why he had a healthy fear of them. It had been his experience that men did not use guns; rather, boys played with them.

In the hands of an accomplished assassin, the long gun was an effective tool of the trade. Otherwise, Jake had found firearms useless. Handguns were bulky, difficult to smuggle through airport security, erratic, and, worst of all, addictive. They were the lazy person's solution to managing perilous situations. With a gun, one didn't have to think. One pointed and shot. The same solution for all problems. Lazy thinking.

Besides, it was dangerous to rely so heavily on any mechanical system. The boy's attitude again. It was reflected most heavily in the mystique of the gunfighter.

Regarding Toshi, Jake saw that he was no different from all the rest. He was in love with his gun – in love with the power it gave him over others.

Always seek out the weakness of spirit in your opponent, Fo Saan had said. Jake knew he had found it in Toshi. That did not make him any less dangerous, only somewhat more manageable.

'I want to see Komoto-*san*,' Jake said.

'You'll see what I tell you to see,' Toshi said. '*Iteki*.' He waved his .38 in Jake's direction. 'Maybe I should shoot your kneecaps, one by one.' His smile was like the rictus of a corpse. 'That way you'll understand how you must look up to us.'

'Tell Komoto-*san* that I have an urgent message for him.'

Toshi laughed. 'Tell him yourself.' The muzzle of the gun described a circle, up to Jake's heart, down to his groin. 'You apparently consider this house open to you, so go on past me. See how far you get.' His face was getting darker as blood began to suffuse it. Jake thought that soon he would have to intervene or risk getting shot.

'Tell Komoto-*san* – '

'Tell Komoto-*san* what?'

Jake saw a figure in the darkness of the hallway just behind Toshi. He saw the *yakuza* stiffen, but he had already recognized the voice.

'I do not seek to cross you, *oyabun*,' Jake said, remembering Komoto's threat.

'Now you whine at me, Mr Richardson. What next? Will you grovel at my feet and ask forgiveness?' The distaste in his voice was obvious.

'I thought that you did not have conversations with barbarians.' There was silence. Jake knew he was playing an exceedingly dangerous game. Komoto could have him killed here on his doorstep, and no one in Japan would ask a question. But Jake knew he had no choice. Time was precious to him, and he needed to prick beneath the traditional armour of the man.

'This is hardly a conversation,' Komoto said. 'I hear only the sounds of the crickets and of my own voice.'

'This is what I came to tell you,' Jake said, knowing he was playing his last card. 'My name is Jake Maroc. I killed Keii Kisan.'

With a jerk of his shadowed head, the *oyabun* said, 'Bring him inside. Take him to the six-*tatami* room and hold him there until I'm ready.'

Toshi did as he was told, his cold eyes staring hard at Jake, daring him to make a move against him. When Jake did nothing, he reached out with his free hand and violently dragged Jake over the threshold.

He kicked the door shut and said, 'Shoes.'

Jake took them off and, stooping at Toshi's silent direction, stowed them in the wooden closet beside the door. When he looked up, Komoto was gone.

Toshi took him down the dimly lit hallway, through an open *fusuma*, into the same room to which he had first been taken. Toshi stood him opposite the *tokonoma*, no doubt on purpose.

There was an extraordinary stillness throughout the house. It was as if the night had closed in all around them. He became aware of a small purling and, looking across the room, saw the bottom of the scroll fluttering. He shifted his gaze, saw that the *shōji* screens out to the garden were open.

The darkness had a physical presence. There seemed to be no stars, no moon. Rather, a velvet blanket flowed into the room from outside. The heat of the day had not yet dissipated, and that too seemed an element of the blackness.

Jake closed his eyes. He could hear his own breath and, in a moment, Toshi's. He tried to judge the other's emotional state by the depth and rhythm of his breathing. He could feel the tenseness coming from the *yakuza* in waves. He would have to remember that.

When Komoto entered the room, he was dressed as a *samurai* from the 18th century would have been. He wore a loose-fitting, dark-coloured silk blouse and the traditional black *hakama*, the divided skirt of the archer.

He did not even look at Jake, merely jerked his head at Toshi and said, 'Outside.'

The *yakuza* reached out with his free hand and pushed at Jake's shoulder. Jake went across the room, the other two men following. Outside, he found himself in the *kyūjutsu* garden. He was at the near end. He saw several bows lined up on a rack. They were all between two and three metres tall, the traditional longbow made out of sections of bamboo. Beside them was a *yadate*, a cylindrical stand bristling with arrows.

He felt Toshi coming up behind him and, feeling the other man's hand on his shoulder, wondered whether he should take him now. But he saw no point in that.

It was to be *kyūjutsu*. He had already learned several important things about Komoto. Jake knew him better now than he had before. If he took Toshi down now, he

256

knew that source of information would come to an end, and he could not afford that.

They took him down to the far end of the garden. The *marumono* swung slightly from the cryptomeria.

'You know what to do,' he heard Komoto say. The voice seemed odd and floaty in the darkness, as if it emanated from a wraith.

Jake felt a cord being wrapped around his wrists. He grimaced as Toshi jerked it tight, knotting it. Then Toshi turned him around so that he was facing the other end of the garden, so far away. The end where the bows and arrows stood at attention, waiting patiently.

Toshi no longer held his gun. Instead he had a length of rope in his hands. He backed Jake just behind the *marumono*, so that his back was against the bole of the cryptomeria. Then he bound him to the tree so tightly that there was no possibility of movement.

The *marumono* hung just in front of Jake's face, obscuring his vision.

'Lying is a punishable offence.' He heard Komoto's voice drifting towards him. 'As is breaking and entering, assaulting a clan member. *Yakuza* business is *yakuza* business.'

'*Oyabun* – '

'Do not grovel, *iteki*.' Komoto's voice had turned disdainful. 'You were warned and you ignored that warning. I cannot say that I am surprised. You are a barbarian. Now you must take your punishment.'

Jake felt Komoto's presence moving away from him. But not Toshi's. In a moment the *yakuza* reached out, set the *marumono* to swinging in its arc. Across the plane of Jake's face. Back and forth, ticking off the seconds.

The night was still. Hot. *Tick-tock*, the *marumono*'s arc. An endless time when there was nothing to see, nothing to hear. Jake felt himself back on Cheung Chau, thigh-deep

J.–I

in the South China Sea. Surrounded by mist. Calling for Fo Saan.

Then he heard the sharp buzzing, the sound quickening with terrifying rapidity, until it cut through the heaviness of the night.

The first arrow struck home.

David Oh put the key into the lock of Jake and Mariana's apartment in Hong Kong Island's Mid Levels. The door swung inward and he stepped over the threshold.

He smelled a commingling of scents: hints of past cooking, of Mariana's perfume. A light film of dust lay here and there. Out the windows, dusk was almost done. Streetlights shone, and far below in the harbour, slow junks were moving back to port, their sails black wings against the last amethyst light. It was dinnertime.

He went slowly through the rooms. David Oh was at a loss to say what he was looking for. Something out of place, perhaps, a clue to Mariana's motivations, a hint of where Jake had disappeared to. Surely Jake had maintained security with Mariana. Therefore, what could she know? What secrets could she tell Nichiren about their inner workings? Still, David Oh's stomach would not stop its uncomfortable fluttering; the coppery taste of fear would not leave his mouth. He felt as if he had been swallowing blood all morning. He was praying to all the gods that Jake had not gone off to Japan on his own.

He came out of the bathroom. Nothing. He wandered into the kitchen. Through the panes of glass he looked down on a small driveway below which the garage entrance lay. The expanse of oil-stained concrete was unutterably ugly compared with the mist-shrouded view of the Island and, beyond the harbour, Kowloon, a great dusky jewel glowing in its setting of the South China Sea.

He turned back into the room. Glassware and china sat in the sink, unwashed. There was one plate with bits of

258

food still stuck to it at the round wood table. Beside it was a wineglass still partially full. Taking hold of the thin stem, he lifted it up to his nose and sniffed. A full-bodied red. Mariana. Jake would have preferred *sakē*.

She left in a hell of a hurry, he thought. That wasn't like Mariana. She was neat and very disciplined. No dirty dishes in her sink. Yet here they were. He peered again into the sink. The food scraps in these plates seemed less dried out. He poked a finger and broke the scummy skin. Definitely less dry. Someone had eaten here after Mariana left. But who? Not Jake. He would already have been in Tokyo.

David Oh leant over, peering more closely at the jumble of dishes. Greasy and oily spots were always the best places to start. Around food, that made it easier. He took a roll of professional-width Magic tape out of his jacket pocket, ripped off the five-centimetre strips. These he placed judiciously over the raised rim of two of the plates.

He counted off thirty seconds, then peeled each off with a slow, steady tear. It was important not to jerk, since this could distort the tape. Quickly now, he reapplied the tape strips to a clean plain white index card. He returned to the window and stared at his handiwork. What he saw beneath the protective covering of the tape were two perfect finger-print impressions.

He pocketed the card and went out of the kitchen, thinking, Maybe this is nothing at all. Something in his gut told him otherwise.

'Fornicate unnaturally all our enemies,' he said into the empty rooms.

Grinning, Toshi came to pull the *marumono* away from the left side of Jake's face. The arrow that Komoto had loosed at him in the darkness had punctured the target with such force that it had pushed it back. Because it had struck the *marumono* at the point in its swing where it had just cleared

Jake's face, the target had thunked heavily against his ear and cheek.

Toshi's hand reached out, feeling at the back of Jake's trousers. 'How are you doing, brave *iteki*?' he said. 'Have you soiled yourself yet?' He grunted. 'No? Well, we have time to prove you the barbarian you are.' He withdrew from Jake's sight, set the *marumono* to swinging again. This time, because of the added weight of the arrow, its arc was through a narrower range. It barely cleared Jake's head on either side.

Darkness. The oppressive night closing down. The heat seeping up off the ground. Jake could feel the beginnings of dew wetting his toes. *Tick-tock*, a leaden pendulum before his eyes.

Silence. Jake thought of the South China Sea lapping at his legs. He thought of Fo Saan. And wondered if what he was building for himself was a house of illusions. Terror lurked just around the next dark corner of his consciousness. But if it was an illusion, it was all that stood between calmness and fear. He drew it to him like a steel curtain, cloaking himself.

Angry whirring, splitting apart the night. Scarcely time to breathe. He could feel his body closing down at its extremities, and it worried him. That was the result of the tendrils of fear creeping through the interstices of his illusion. Perhaps he was not safe at all. Don't think! Breathe, he told himself. Breathe.

But it was difficult, knowing what was buzzing its way towards him through the blackness.

THUNK!

Like a pistol's report. And an instant before, he had felt the stirring of the tiny breeze presaging its arrival. Death.

The *marumono* slapped him sharply on his right ear. Two arrows were now in its centre. He was certain the point had missed his cheekbone by only a millimetre or two. He felt the sweat trickling down beneath his arms, across the small of his back.

Someone was laughing. Toshi stepped into his field of view, drew the heavy target away from him. 'Hot night,' he said, and laughed again.

Jake felt a stinging and blinked his eyes rapidly to rid himself of the sensation. Sweat rolling into them.

Toshi felt at Jake's crotch. This time he could not keep his disappointment from showing. 'Sweat, *iteki*,' he said.

Jake could feel another presence. Komoto came slowly down the long lane of the garden. He held a longbow in his left hand. He said nothing, merely watched Jake with hooded eyes as Toshi checked to make sure the bonds were still secure.

'This time,' he said at last, 'I will use this.' He held up a length of cotton. It was a blindfold. Then he turned and went back down to the far end of the garden.

'This will be good,' Toshi said, setting the *marumono* swinging, and stepping away. The target was now so heavy that its arc did not clear Jake's head, but merely swung from one side of it to another.

Jake tried not to focus on them, but he kept seeing the serrated blades of the two arrows sticking through the centre of the target. If he extended his head forward, his nose would brush against them.

He felt the tunnel that both separated him from and linked him with Komoto. He was totally at the *oyabun*'s mercy. Perhaps that had been the point of this from the beginning. A lesson in humility. An example of power. Jake knew that Mikio Komoto held his life in the palm of his hand. But he had known that from the moment he presented himself at the *oyabun*'s door this evening. Now the moment of truth was at hand.

Beneath it all, what kind of man was Mikio Komoto?

Jake could guess at it, but in a moment he knew he would come face to face with the answer.

Calmness, Fo Saan had said, *will eventually teach you all you need know about victory*. He thought of that now, repeating it as if it were a *mantra* that would keep him from harm.

Heard the far-off rustling. Rushing up on him with appalling speed. Heard the sound equally with both his ears, and knew that it was headed at the centre of his face.

Tick-tock, the *marumono* swung. He marked its movements in increments of darkness: lighter, darker, lighter; side, centre, side. If the arrow struck during one of the lighter moments, he was dead.

Tick-tock ...

Lighter, darker, lighter –

Thock!

Utter darkness, and Jake felt the target swinging in towards the bridge of his nose with less of a motion than before. He focused, saw the point of the third arrow aligned with the two others. Dead centre.

It was some time before the *marumono* was taken away from in front of his face. And when it was done, it was not Toshi standing there.

'Perhaps we have allowed the punishment to fit the crimes,' Mikio Komoto said.

'If I committed any crimes at all,' Jake said in a reedy whisper, 'it was desperation that drove me to them. Nichiren had my wife. I needed to know where they were. That is why I went to the *sarakin*, to get to you. I hoped that you would help me.'

'More lies,' Komoto said coldly. 'What could an *iteki* like you have to do with Nichiren?'

'I want him. Now my wife is dead. It happened last night, up on the Sword.'

'Tsurugi?' Komoto seemed surprised. 'You were up on Tsurugi during the storm?'

Jake nodded. 'I found Nichiren's hideaway.'

'Stealing into my house,' Komoto said. 'Attacking one of

262

my men. That is what you did. I do not want to hear any more of your *iteki* lies!' He began to turn away.

'It is the poor general who refuses to listen to information that could be vital to him.'

The *oyabun* spat. 'Who are you to talk of what generals do and do not do?'

'I know that a good general must use all the resources available to him if he is to taste victory.'

Komoto's black eyes narrowed. 'What talk!'

'I killed Keii Kisan in front of Nichiren's eyes.'

'Words,' Komoto said shortly. 'All I hear from you are words.'

'Then let me prove my words by deed.'

Komoto stood stock-still. He did not want to show his consternation. He was canny enough to know that he had been outmanoeuvred. He had no choice but to honour Jake's request now; otherwise he would lose enormous face.

He called to Toshi. 'Unbind the *iteki*.'

'Yes, *oyabun*.'

'His wrists as well.'

When Toshi had complied, Komoto grunted and said, 'Bring him along.'

At the other end of the garden, Komoto stopped and faced Jake. 'You will show me in deed now. Only a *samurai* could have felled Keii Kisan. Only a *samurai* could have penetrated O-henro House under the nose of Nichiren.'

Jake chose a longbow. Toshi made a move to stop him, but Komoto waved him off.

'A *samurai* should be adept in many disciplines,' Jake said. '*Kyūjutsu* is one of the most important. But I am not telling you anything you don't already know, *neh*?'

He selected an arrow with a serrated tip, went to stand in a line with the hanging target. 'Will Toshi-*san* set it to swinging?'

Thinking this a bluff, Komoto signed for the other man to do as Jake wished.

263

'But *oyabun* – '

'Do you think me incapable of defending myself?' he snapped. 'Do as you are told, then come back here.' Komoto turned back to Jake. 'At this distance, with no light and using the *marumono*, I think this is a feat that the student of a fine *sensei* could perform. Even that man would be eaten alive by Keii Kisan.' He held out his hand. 'You must use this.' In it was the blindfold.

Jake took it just as Toshi returned. He considered the challenge for a moment before replying. 'It is obvious that you are *kyūjutsu sensei*, *oyabun*. Tell me, could you have taken on Keii Kisan one-on-one?'

'Without doubt,' Komoto said. 'Your ignorance is showing again, *iteki*. Don't you feel embarrassed?'

'It seems obvious to me,' Jake said, ignoring the other's remark, 'that you will not be convinced by a feat any less awesome than the one you have just now demonstrated.'

Jake stared hard at him. 'Will you then, *oyabun*, stand against the tree in the spot where I am standing?'

Komoto felt himself suffused with rage. The bastard *iteki* has done it to me twice, he thought. Very neat. I cannot possibly refuse him.

The *oyabun* willed himself to relax. 'Such a deed,' he said, 'would surely convince me of the truth of your words. However, I must insist on one stipulation. Toshi-*san* will stand by your side. His pistol will be against your left ear. If you cannot duplicate my feat, he will blow your brains out instantaneously.'

Jake watched the small smile spread across the *oyabun*'s face. Their eyes locked. He felt the power struggle within which they were waging a psychological war. But also, for the first time, he felt another emotion emanating from the *yakuza* chief: respect. Grudging, yes, and tentative, but genuine nonetheless. It was a foothold.

Jake gave a slight bow. 'I accept your stipulation.'

'Of course you do, *iteki*!' Komoto said. 'Of course you do.' He gave a sign. 'Toshi-*san*, affix the blindfold.'

As the *yakuza* moved to obey, Jake said, 'Tell me your exact height, *oyabun*.'

'Five feet six inches. Tall for a Japanese, *neh*?' He seemed suddenly in good humour. Jake wondered whether it was the *oyabun*'s own form of illusion. He had no way of knowing whether Jake knew the first thing about *kyūjutsu*, let alone whether he was of *sensei* calibre. Jake stared at him, fixing his form in his mind.

'All right,' he said to Toshi. The blindfold settled across his eyes.

'Make certain it is not too tight,' he heard Komoto's voice say. 'We do not want anything to discomfort the *iteki*' – he laughed again – 'in his last moments of life.'

Jake held his breath. 'What do you mean?' He could feel Toshi close behind him.

'Whatever you do, I think I shall have Toshi-*san* blow your brains out.'

'That was not our agreement.'

'Agreements are for civilized folk,' Komoto said, his voice diminishing as he went down the garden lane. 'Not for *iteki*.'

'Even an animal possesses honour,' Jake said, but he could not be certain that the *oyabun* had heard him.

He felt Toshi moving around to his left side. In a moment he felt the cold steel of the gun muzzle nestling in his ear.

'*Iteki*,' Toshi said softly, 'you are doomed, no matter what you do. My orders are to shoot before you even release the arrow.'

Jake made no response. He fought to ignore the other's words. He suspected that they were putting all the screws to him now, working on his fear. Komoto would dearly like to see him break, to prove the inferiority of the barbarian. Jake vowed not to give him that satisfaction. Even so,

265

there was a nibbling at the back of his mind. They might not be lying. These might be his last moments.

He closed his mind to all outside influences. He concentrated on feeling the longbow in his hands from its centre all the way up to the *kata*, the shoulder at the end, against which the *tsuru*, the bowstring, was wound for some distance. The string was of hemp, and very hard. This was a war bow rather than a ceremonial one. So much the better.

Jake stood very still. He began his breathing, centring himself. His mind expanded as he sank into his surroundings. With his mind he felt the surrounding trees, the tunnel down which he would in a moment loose the arrow. He felt the stirring of the night, a shallow, inconstant wind that he need factor in only at the last possible instant.

He heard the chirruping of the insects, the buzzing of the white moths around the house lights. He became one with the garden. And in so doing, found *ba-mahk*, the pulse. It pulled him forward in a line straight and true to the spot where Mikio Komoto was standing. Jake felt the short-arced swing of the *marumono* from its piece of hemp.

He took up *ashibumi*, the archer's stance. He breathed deeply and rhythmically from deep down in his lower belly where the Japanese believed all power dwelled: *hara*.

He raised his left hand, fitted the fletched end of the arrow to the bowstring: *yugame*. He brought the bow up into the firing position, then allowed it to float down, following the dictates of *ba-mahk*. He could feel Komoto's presence as clearly as if he were only a step away instead of a hundred metres.

Jake began to draw the string back so that the arrow was parallel with the line of his mouth. This was *kai*, the last of the three most crucial steps in *kyūjutsu*. Concentration was at its most intense now while the muscles strained to keep the bow drawn to its maximum, the mind centred on the target swinging back and forth, back and forth, *tick-tock* . . .

Steel moving in his ear, Toshi's sibilant whisper, 'So long, *iteki*.'

Ignore everything but the arrow, the bowstring quivering with tension, the power building in the bamboo. *Ba-mahk*. Feel the pulse.

Tick-tock, the *marumono* swung with its bristling cluster of arrows across Komoto's face.

Henare! The release!

Zanshin was now operative. That quality which allowed the *kyūjutsu sensei* to guide the flight of the arrow all the way to its target. It was akin to follow-through in the other martial arts, in sports. The release meant little if there was no follow-through after it.

Zanshin.

Heard the *ziikk!* of the arrow hitting home, then the satisfying *thunk!* Jake had been waiting for. He released the bow and took the blindfold off. The tickling in his left ear was gone. He looked first at Toshi, who stood with his gun pointed at the ground. His eyes were wide and staring.

Jake turned his gaze to the far end of the garden. The *oyabun* stood in front of the slender cryptomeria. At his feet lay the *marumono*, on its side, like a discarded ragdoll.

Its cord had been neatly severed by Jake's arrow, which was embedded in the tree a millimetre above Mikio Komoto's head.

The gleaming black Zil limousine hurtled down the Chaika lane left open along major Moscow thoroughfares for such official government traffic.

In its back seat, General Karpov and Yuri Lantin sat side by side. It was dusk. The streets through which they passed seemed dusty with a surfeit of sunlight, as if this city were uncomfortable with such largesse. Could it be that, instead, it longed for the heavy blue snow of the long wintertime, the rimed beards of those on line to visit Lenin's Tomb, the crystal exhalations of breath in the chill black mornings?

It was the end of the working day, even among the elite of the KGB. One night a week, instead of returning home to his bachelor apartment on Kutuzovsky Prospekt, Lantin would invite General Karpov to dine with him.

Lantin had the reputation within the *sluzhba* of being something of a gourmet. Though he was a Muscovite, his taste in food was eclectic. His current favourite restaurant was Aragvi, named after the coursing river that was well known and loved by all Georgians.

But Lantin, it seemed, was not the only one enamoured of the place. Each night, regardless of the weather, long lines would form just after work and on into the deepening night as Muscovites waited for a chance to eat at this excellent restaurant. Of course, Lantin and Karpov were weekly led directly into the place. Always they found their table waiting, gleaming with spotless cutlery.

Lantin ordered *lobio tkemali* as soon as they sat down, and the two of them munched on the tender kidney beans in a sour plum sauce redolent of fresh coriander while they perused the menu.

Thick, ice-cold vodka was poured, the bottle placed in an ice bucket at Karpov's left elbow.

'Well, Yuri,' Karpov said, taking off his glasses as he set aside the menu, 'what will you have tonight?'

'The *satsivi*,' Lantin said, selecting the most famous of Georgian walnut dishes, made with room-temperature poached chicken smothered in a rich sauce combining ground nuts, coriander, cinnamon, vinegar, and egg yolks. For his part, Karpov chose a lamb dish made with the fiery *adzhika*, a combination of hot and sweet red peppers, blended with coriander and garlic, and the inevitable *khmeli suneli*. The recipe for this last marinade varied from family to family, its secrets guarded as closely as any KGB dossier.

Basically it consisted, so Lantin informed his guest, of varying amounts of black and cayenne pepper, mint, basil, dill, parsley, savory, dried coriander, and dried ground marigolds to impart to it its characteristic golden hue.

Karpov downed vodka, reached for the bottle to refill his glass. Lantin gave their order and the waiter left. He drank only mineral water. He sipped at his glass with a kind of affectation that, in Karpov's mind, at least, was a wholly feminine trait. Secretly he wondered how he could rid himself of Lantin. Despite the other's help, he did not think of him as an ally. Personally, he despised the man. He was using Lantin to ensure that Moonstone would be put into action.

Karpov knew that it was one thing to install all that firepower around the circumference of China, quite another to implement it. Karpov was no fool. He knew that what he was proposing as Moonstone's ultimate aim was fraught with danger. But the risk was a calculated one. As a military man, he had to deal with calculated risks every day. He had been trained to make such decisions and, further, to trust implicitly in his own judgment. He knew that even with Lantin's support there was still opposition in the Politburo to Moonstone's ultimate use.

Old men and frightened wives. That was how he thought of them. The power inside Russia had too long been in the hands of elderly men who had the timidity of women. *They should leave the running of this country to us.* How many times had he said that to his wife?

Karpov abhorred having to align himself with someone like Lantin. He had no respect for the man. Look at his hands, Karpov thought now, pouring himself another vodka. They are soft. A woman's hands. All he knows is a desk and the old halls. What does he know of command? Of fighting? Has he ever killed a man? No, never. He would shit his pants at the stench, at the sight of blood leaking, the filmy, sightless eyes. Yet he has the power I need to take Moonstone to its end phase.

To just that end, he said now, 'I trust you are pleased with Moonstone's penultimate phase.'

Lantin continued to contemplate his mineral water, as if it were the elixir of life. 'I did not mention that? Forgive me. My colleagues and I were quite impressed with the latest havoc wreaked in Malipo County in Yunnan by the Vietnamese army. How many Chinese casualties were inflicted?'

'It's difficult to say with any degree of certainty,' Karpov said. 'While the Vietnamese are excellent at carrying out the orders we give them, they nevertheless have a perhaps forgivable propensity for exaggeration in the area of their prowess on the line.'

'Nothing should be forgivable when it comes to soldiers and war,' Lantin said crisply. He put down his glass and looked at Karpov. 'I agreed to this phase of Moonstone because I could see the vision behind it. Using the Vietnamese to invade certain designated border districts of China – areas chosen by us for their strategic purpose – has a certain elegance about it. It's easy enough to send out propaganda via Thach' – he was speaking of Vietnam's foreign minister, Nguyen Co Thach – 'regarding Chinese aggression in Malipo and Ha Tuyen province. Since all foreigners are unilaterally barred from these areas, independent verification is impossible. Using our word against theirs is a time-honoured tactic we can easily exploit to its fullest potential.

'However, any degree of unreliability from the Vietnamese could be detrimental to the entire Moonstone timetable. We cannot afford any defections or dissatisfactions. Before that occurs, I would expect you to send your executioners in there and weed out the troublesome elements.'

Karpov winced inwardly at the word 'executioners.'

That was but one example of what he detested about the man. He bandied about terms without a full understanding of them. He was preparing his answer when the food came, and he waited until they were alone again.

'You need have no worry concerning the Vietnamese. I – '

Lantin lifted his head. 'Let me correct a notion of yours. *I* have no worries about the Vietnamese or even about Moonstone. Those worries are yours and yours alone.'

'As I was saying,' Karpov ploughed on, 'I have placed my own people as observers within every Vietnamese unit ordered into action. Each agent has explicit instructions on how to deal with dissidents. The terminations' – he put some emphasis on the word in order to gently correct Lantin's erroneous terminology – 'are to be public and instantaneous.'

'I imagine with the native population, that kind of vulgar display is needed to get the message across.'

Karpov stared at Lantin for a time. He was thinking of the mortar blasts, the cannon and small-arms fire that had, just hours before, levelled two towns, killed hundreds of men, women and children. He thought of the crippled soldiers drowning in their own blood, the maimed children, the pregnant women – the loss of two lives at once. Then he contemplated this smug creature savouring his dinner just across the table. Hatred clawed at him like the talons of an animal trapped inside his belly.

'So far,' he said with all the calmness he could muster, 'there have been no incidents. Not one.'

'Good,' Lantin said, clearing his plate. 'I want it kept just that way.' He looked up from his food. His face was flushed, as if he had recently had sex. 'Can I interest you in dessert? There are some most enticing selections here.'

Karpov, who had been mostly pushing his food from one side of his plate to the other, declined with extreme politeness. He wondered whether he should send a team

271

into Lantin's apartment tonight and do away with him forever. But for the fate of Moonstone, which would thereby hang in the balance, he found himself sorely tempted.

Over thick, chocolate-brown coffee, Lantin said, 'I want to talk about General Vorkuta.'

Karpov sat very still. A tiny ball of ice began to form inside him. A voice whispered that they had come to the crux of tonight's dinner meeting. Karpov, like a child with his hand in the cookie jar, wondered if he had been caught. Did Lantin know of his affair with Daniella? If so, how would he use it against him? But it seemed he was wrong.

'I have yet to make up my mind about her.' Lantin sipped at his coffee, allowing his pause to become a silence. It was as if he were assuming that Karpov knew what was in his mind from the outset.

'How so?' This was at last squeezed out of Karpov, and he hated himself for it – hated Rantin even more.

'Hmm.' It was not clear whether this was a sound of contemplation or a simple clearing of his throat. 'I remain unconvinced regarding her attitude.'

Again, Lantin was saying too little. Now Karpov was truly on his guard, knowing that by supplying an answer to these minuscule interrogatives, he would be unearthing a wealth of information for Lantin to pore over. Alternatively, saying nothing would be even worse.

Karpov finally settled on as noncommittal an answer as possible. 'I have always found her to be a loyal and intelligent agent.'

'Perhaps,' Lantin said. 'But that is no answer. She guards her department with a zeal I find disturbing. To me, it borders on xenophobia. Either that or she has something to hide.'

'Nonsense,' Karpov said immediately. Watch it, he told himself. No telling what he's searching for. 'Yuri, the department I have put General Vorkuta in charge of is among the most secretive in all the *sluzhba*. I need not remind you of that. I have given her a difficult row to hoe, as it were, and she has performed admirably. I really think you have overreacted.'

Lantin shrugged as if it were of no real import to him. 'Perhaps. But I have had no small experience with the manifestations of the guilty consciences of my fellow man. Just to make certain, I am sure you won't object if I have my office keep an eye on her for a month or two.'

'Of course not. If that is your wish.' Speaking of guilty consciences, Karpov wondered whether Lantin was indeed unsure of Daniella's loyalty or whether this was his way of flexing the parameters of his power in Karpov's direction. Certainly he would be foolish to suspect Daniella, and if the latter were the case, Karpov could see no better method than Lantin had selected. Damn to hell his meddling, Karpov thought. I cannot possibly go that long without touching her.

On his way home, in Lantin's Zil, he considered telephoning Daniella to at least warn her. Immediately he thought better of it. That was just the kind of activity he could not afford at this stage of the game. He had Moonstone to consider. Lantin was the key to Moonstone. Until that unfortunate circumstance changed, he would have to stay in line every step of the way.

But, Karpov vowed, when the final phase of Moonstone is under way and I no longer need Lantin's backing, I will have my revenge. I will not only have it, but I will savour it as I saw him savour this rich meal tonight. I will feed him poisoned meat – a fitting way for Comrade Yuri Lantin to die – and then I will take Daniella and together we will dance on his grave.

'Hello, Rodger,' Antony Beridien said. The shades were down in his office, and through the regular interstices between, the White House, lit up like a fountain, could be seen glowing in the Washington dusk.

Beridien's huge head turned like a hawk at his assistant's approach. The lack of light in the office threw his heavily browed eyes into deep shadow.

'I've been wanting to talk with you about our iceberg,' he said. 'I've been at the computer since five this morning.'

Donovan sat down in a leather chair that looked like a sling and was about as comfortable. 'What have you come up with?'

Beridien grunted. 'Quite a bit. Here, take a look at these.' He slid an accordion sheaf of computer printouts across his desk. His eyes watched his assistant's expression as he flipped through the maze of lists, tables and charts. 'It appears to me as if our iceberg might be Nichiren himself.'

'How could that be? He's a known free-lance.'

'That's just what we've been supposed to believe!'

Donovan's head came up. 'Disinformation? That means that the Russians – '

'Precisely!' Beridien's fist hit the desktop with a resounding thump. 'This iceberg's beginning to have shape as well as size, Rodger, and the more it becomes visible, the more recognizable its source becomes.'

'Karpov?'

'A good guess, but a wrong one.' Beridien was obviously enjoying his position of power. This was, Donovan had discovered, what to a great extent motivated the man. He did not like it, but in time he had learned to live with it. 'You're still just learning the intricacies of the KGB bureaucracy. Those two and a half years when State had you stationed in Paris may have been fine for other international matters, but not for this one.'

This oration, spewed out in Beridien's familiar dark basso tones, was a familiar trademark, one of his most successful attributes, according to the President. Beridien, he had often said behind closed doors, could sell anyone anything, at any time. Even normally hostile Senate subcommittees.

But living with it every day, Donovan knew that it helped mask a mind capable of taking every opportunity, no matter how minute, and turning it to his advantage without letting you know he had done so.

'No,' Beridien continued, 'Nichiren is far too elegant a dupe to have been manufactured by Karpov.' He picked up a crystal owl and held it in his palm until the glass warmed to his touch, then he put it aside. 'It appears that, far from being the free-lance assassin he has appeared to be, Nichiren is being run by a specific source. And I believe that source to be General Daniella Vorkuta. The KVR was nothing before she took it over. Now we must fight it tooth and nail for every minor mission.' He shook his head as if he had just made up his mind. 'I think General Vorkuta has submerged an iceberg under us, and day by day is allowing it to surface.'

Donovan glanced down at his watch. 'It's time for your weekly physical. If we could continue this on the way, we'd save time.'

They went out into a corridor with bare walls painted the colour of clay. There were no doors off it. At its far end, a brushed-bronze elevator door opened at the touch of Beridien's palm print. Inside, there were only two buttons. Beridien pressed the lower one and they dropped down the shaft.

Six floors below, the door opened onto a sterile white suite of rooms, one of which was a fully outfitted operating theatre with all the latest equipment, including laser scalpels, cryonics, and pathology facilities.

The agent on duty took their plastic ID cards and fed them into the slot of a terminal, then watched impassively as the two men went into a cold white room containing an examining table, a crash cart filled with innumerable vials, bottles, and tubes, all mysteriously labelled in the language

275

of the physician, a small semicircular sink in one corner, and a foot-pedal garbage can. Beside a Breuer bentwood chair on which to hang clothes were a doctor's scale and an optometrist's eye chart.

A young nurse in a crisply starched uniform greeted the two men. 'Right on time, Mr Beridien,' she said, as if he were a child. 'Doctor is ready for you.'

'She's always ready for me,' Beridien growled. 'Vulture.'

'Did you say something, Mr Beridien?' the nurse said, just as if she hadn't heard him.

Beridien waited coldly until she went out. 'Now that we know Nichiren's source, it's more imperative than ever to terminate him with all due speed,' he told Donovan.

'How do we accomplish that? Maroc was supposed to be our great white hope when it came to Nichiren.'

'He was,' Beridien said. 'Until the Sumchun River. I'm beginning to suspect he came back from that mission only half an operative.'

'His men were massacred – by Nichiren, I suppose, although his debriefing was difficult and ultimately – for us, anyway – inadequate. Perhaps we should have suspected sooner and had him replaced.'

'All that speculation is useless now,' Beridien said coldly. 'You cannot bleed for your soldiers and expect to lead them into battle at the same time. I want you to remember that, Rodger, the next time you feel the twinge of empathy.' Donovan thought he made that phrase sound like the plague. 'What is really important is what happened up there. I mean apart from the massacre.'

Donovan was curious. 'How do you know anything did?'

'Because of Maroc's attitude,' Beridien said simply. 'I know my operatives. Maroc was always a well-adjusted misfit.' He laughed shortly. 'I know. That sounds like a contradiction in terms. The President certainly thinks so. But then he hasn't had the experience I've had in this shadow world.

'Anyway, Maroc was, with Stallings, our best agent. In fact, in many ways, he was better. He had a curious flair for administration as well. We never got such a wealth of first-class intelligence from our Hong Kong Station as when he ran it. He was a born leader. Operatives flocked to him, just to have a chance to be in his units.' Donovan noted how Beridien constantly spoke of Jake Maroc as if he were dead.

'All that changed, however, the moment he returned from the Sumchun River mission. He lost personal contact with David Oh and apparently with his wife. It was as if he had cut himself off from those he loved most in life. If I didn't know better, I'd say that he had been preparing to die.'

'Maroc's psychological profile makes no mention of a death wish,' Donovan said. 'In fact, if memory serves, the conclusion our doctors came to was just the opposite. His will to live was exceptional.'

Beridien nodded, beginning absently to undress. 'All the more reason to wonder what really went on up there.' He turned, hung up his shirt. 'That brings us back to square one: our iceberg. Nichiren. We go after him, then we get to General Vorkuta. Rodger, I want her out of that position. She's turned the KVR into a lethal weapon. I think we'd better try a little disinformation of our own to see if we can rattle Karpov's cage enough so that the discomfort compels him to do something he'd rather not.'

'Such as get rid of General Vorkuta.'

'That would be good,' Beridien acknowledged. 'But it's going to take some research and quite a bit of time. Meanwhile, we've got to terminate Nichiren with all possible haste. Send Stallings back out again. He likes to be in the middle of all those midgets.' Beridien lifted himself up on the examining table. 'This is a pain in the ass, you know that?'

'I would think,' Donovan said as the doctor appeared

through the door, 'that you'd be used to it by now. You were the one who made it mandatory that the head of the Quarry have a physical exam every week and that he be accompanied during the examination by a ranking officer.'

The doctor, a woman of forty whom Donovan secretly desired, drew the hospital gown through Beridien's white arms. She had a fine, strong Slavic face, heavy breasts, and good long legs. Donovan wanted to climb those legs one day. She presented them both with a professional smile, but otherwise gave no indication that she thought of them as anything but objects. She poked and prodded at Donovan once a month, a day he kept circled on his calendar.

'I think I'll make a note to myself,' Beridien said. 'Next week I'll send Wunderman down to be examined in my place.'

The doctor gave him the same stern look she would give to an overly rambunctious teenager. Beridien laughed, finally feeling as if he had put something over on her.

There was one light left burning. In its amber glow, the planes of Mikio Komoto's face appeared as hard as rock.

'Maroc-*san*.'

The words were the extent of the change in his attitude, but for a Japanese that was significant. He had come back down from the utter darkness at the far end of the garden like a stone emerging from the depths of a well.

Jake was aware of his coming presence, then the outline of his bearlike body. The light illumined the loose shirt and *hakama*. Finally, as he stopped a pace in front of Jake, the features of his face resolved themselves out of the night.

His face was closed. There was an idiomatic Japanese phrase for it, but Jake could not bring it to mind. He carried his *hara* – his intrinsic power – in tangible form. Nothing else was required.

278

He showed his hands. Crossing them was the arrow that Jake had fired. 'I believe this is yours.'

As if in a dream, Jake reached out, took the missile from the *oyabun*. He had not fully thought out his actions. It began to dawn on him fully what he had set out to do and, more importantly, that he had succeeded.

This arrow was part of a *samurai*'s specialized weaponry – *this* particular *samurai*. In quite a real sense, it was part of his heritage. Certainly it was never given away except in acknowledgment of a deed of extraordinary merit. Jake recalled that in feudal times it was said that *sensei* – that is to say masters – of particular martial arts who met for the first time exchanged bits of their personal arsenal to seal treaties for the *daimyo*, their overlords.

Jake bowed. '*Dōmo arigatō*, Komoto-san.'

He noticed that Toshi was no longer around. He and Mikio Komoto were alone in the night. The high black trees overarched the pair. Filled with nesting birds and chirruping insects, they swayed in the night wind, giving motion to the garden as if it were a trough in some vast, moonlit sea.

'Time,' the *oyabun* said, 'to drink.'

They got drunk on Suntory whisky. Inside, seated on the *tatami* with a small, well-oiled boxwood table in front of them, they talked of matters great and small, just as if they had been friends all their lives and not, as they had been an hour before, adversaries.

'Keii Kisan,' Komoto said, 'is well gone to his ancestors. He was aggressive, tough, and by far the smartest member of his clan.'

'He was giving you trouble.'

'I think,' Komoto said in a judicious tone, 'it is safer to say that Nichiren was giving us trouble. Toshima-ku had become a source of friction between my clan and Kisan's. It is my belief that this was Nichiren's doing.'

'Why?' Jake poured them both more whisky. 'What does Toshima-ku possess that is worth this bloodshed?'

'Other than traditionally being an extension of Komoto territory, nothing.'

'Then I seriously doubt that Nichiren would have been involved. He'd have no reason to counsel an aggressive policy and every reason to keep the situation calm on his home ground.'

'I doubt it,' Komoto said. 'Our information is that Nichiren is a deep-cover agent of the KGB.'

Jake stared at him. He tried to control the fluttering of his heart. 'My intelligence is that he's a solitaire terrorist.'

'Then you're a little behind the times.'

Jake thought about this for a time. At length he said, 'How long have the Soviets been running him?'

Komoto shrugged. 'I'll show you the entire file. Three, four years. We're not absolutely certain. But we know his control. General Daniella Vorkuta.'

KVR, Jake thought. Buddha! No wonder they were up on the Sword. Fleetingly he wondered why the Quarry had failed to pick up this intelligence.

The *oyabun* stared into Jake's face. 'I would say that either you're very drunk or very surprised.'

'If I was any drunker,' Jake said, 'I wouldn't even understand what you were saying.'

Mikio Komoto laughed. 'This is barbarian whisky!' he cried. 'We're just beginning to get to the real stuff! Toshi-san, bring on the *sakē*!'

For Nichiren, it was *meinichi*, the death day.

Dressed in a sea-green kimono with a snow-white double-wheel pattern, he trudged with deliberate slowness up the steep, winding dirt path. Through the pines and cedars – their summits, like Fuji-yama, lost in grey mist – he ascended from the tiled roof of the railway station to the northwest of Tokyo. At his back the great metropolis spilled across the island in shades of hard, insensate grey, compared with the mist swirling through the branches above his head.

Here and there, boys in Shinto robes swept away the dust of the centuries with bamboo whisks, their first duties at the temple. One first had to learn humility, the first step on the path to oneness with all things.

Near the summit of the hill, he turned to the left, away from the crimson-and-black temple buildings. Here the path ended at a stone gate. Beyond was the graveyard.

Though it was yet early morning, he could discern through the mist the kneeling figures at prayer before the stone markers of their ancestors. The chanted prayer lifted up, penetrating the mist in a way the sunlight could not.

He let the holy words inundate him as he trod the narrow paths until he came to the familiar stone marker. There he knelt and placed just in front of the stone the sticks of incense he had carried with him from the city. Carefully, with a prayer on his lips, he lit them one by one until their burning essence melted into the mist.

His head was bowed. His thoughts were only with his mother. On the stone before him were two lines of ideograms, but he had no need to look at them; their message was engraved upon his heart forever.

Meinichi, though its meaning was 'death day,' was composed of two ideograms that, separately, meant 'life' and 'day.' This seeming contradiction was easily explained in that in choosing to remember the anniversary of an ancestor's death, in making the physical pilgrimage to the burial site, by thought and deed, one had in effect returned the dead to the world of the living, at least for this short period of time each year.

It was also a time for the family to gather, to renew ties perhaps stretched by the far-flung migrations of various members. Nichiren felt a great sadness that there was no one else here. Family, which, as with all Japanese, meant so much to him, was reduced to one.

Bitter tears squeezed out from beneath his lowered lids, lay trembling for an unspeakable moment on his cheeks before sliding down, staining his kimono.

Yumiko had been dead for many years, but through the miracle of *meinichi* she was alive again within Nichiren. He remembered her face, which, over the years, had lost none of its porcelain beauty. Rather, the youthful, exquisite features had softened, the skin gradually becoming patinaed just like a treasured *ningyo*.

As a child, he had seen many of these dolls within their glass cases in shop windows against which he had pressed his nose, staring until his eyes crossed. He could remember inexpensive dolls of rice paper hanging in his room during the years that he was sick. Much later he had learned that these were Yumiko's guardians against the evil that she was certain had befallen him. During those long days when he lay besieged by high fever, her hands would be busy constructing new paper dolls to help ward off further illness.

Then, when he had recovered sufficiently from his bouts of illness, she had set about to make him so strong in body and in spirit that sickness would be unknown to him in the years afterward.

For Nichiren, Yumiko had been both mother and father. She had never remarried. In fact, he could not remember her having a lover in the house. Rather, she had buried herself in the arcane texts she often spent weeks tracking down in the far corners of Japan.

Often he would lie in bed at night with her hypnotic chanting in his ears, an odd kind of susurrus that mingled with the insects' percussion and the nightbirds' alto trilling to bring him sleep.

Small and beautiful, she had nevertheless possessed a fierce, indomitable will. *Tetsu no kokoro*, her iron spirit.

282

There was, even in the golden glow of remembrance, only the barest vestige of gentleness about her. Though she was loving with him, she never coddled him nor fondled him overmuch. In fact, she barely touched him.

Nichiren could recall only one time with any clarity. He had come home carrying a dog he had kicked either in anger or in frustration over his ostracism at school. He was already under Mitsunobu's tutelage, and had lashed out with the toe of his shoe only once and broken the poor creature's neck.

Yumiko had taken one look at the animal and had ordered him to drop it outside their property. Then she had taken him into the house and beaten him. She had no physical strength to hurt him, but something, perhaps a fingernail or a ring, had caught in his skin and he had begun to bleed.

When she saw this, a look of the most profound horror had transfigured his mother's face. She had cried out from the depths of her spirit and, pulling him close to her, rocked him with her arms close about him.

In time, he had felt the hotness of her tears crossing his lips. He heard her unearthly shout ringing in his ears and he shuddered. Never had he heard such an exclamation from a human throat. It had contained such a degree of despair and self-loathing as he had thought it impossible for one person to contain.

That moment was, perhaps, more significant for both of them than either knew. It bonded their spirits in some unfathomable way. What Yumiko required of him, he did. But he had always done that. Now he did more. What she believed, he believed. He did so with at least some knowledge of what he was doing. He loved her. To him, she was life. He would do anything to ensure that she never cried out like that again.

His mother remained in his memory the most beautiful female he had ever seen. Time had not diffused his memory.

Rather, he recalled Yumiko with a clarity that one usually reserves for picking through old photographs.

It was not until she died, when he took her to be prepared for burial, that he saw her naked. The one memory of her he wished he could expunge was when he drew back the shroud and saw, below a face that even death could not ravage, the hideous disfigurement of her small body.

Meinichi. On this day, for as long as he knelt here beside her grave, Yumiko lived again. He felt close to her, felt her spirit settle about him like a mantle across his shoulders.

Awakening to the pale sunlight of the early morning, he had been uneasy. As he dressed in his ceremonial outfit for this occasion, his unease had remained unabated. He had dreamt of Mariana Maroc. In his dream she had kissed him. She had held his head tenderly. She had spoken into the shell of his ear with such tenderness that in his dream he had wept.

And had awoken with a start, ears straining mightily to hear her words. What had she whispered to him that moved him so? He found that he very much wanted to know. The syllables floated tantalizingly just beyond his recall. He could actually feel them; but he could not hear them.

Now that he felt Yumiko's spirit girdling him, he was no longer aware of the unease and he sighed a little as he used to do as a little boy. He recalled again the day she had cradled him, crying. After a time, she had asked for an explanation.

Why did you kick the dog to death? she had asked him.

He had taken some time with it, not really knowing on the surface of it, but understanding that his answer might be important. *I got angry,* he said at last.

Angry at what, at whom? Yumiko's liquid eyes had searched his depths.

The kids at school. They tease me because I am an outsider. They

284

say that I am not Japanese at all. Always, it is them on one side and me on the other.

Yumiko had looked at him steadily. *Did you make your feelings known to them?*

Over and over. They laugh at me, call me names, throw stones at me, sometimes.

Then why did you not take your anger out on them? Why take the life of an animal that has never harmed you?

He had hung his head in shame. *I am afraid of them.*

Fear, Yumiko said sternly, *has nothing to do with it. It is solely a matter of honour. Sensei would tell you the same thing. You know it in your heart.* There were no more tears now, no touching. Yumiko's *tetsu no kokoro* had returned with such force that each word she uttered seemed to him like a burning bullet implanted in the centre of his brain. *You will have no honour until you have faced them, until you have made them see the error of their ways.*

Meinichi. Nichiren breathed in the death day, breathed in the memory of Yumiko, breathed in *tetsu no kokoro*, the living legacy with which she had provided him.

He had not needed his Source to remind him of this day. It had surprised him that the subject came up at all when he accessed the overseas line late last night.

'At the grave of your mother, you will kneel to light the incense sticks and say the prayers for the dead,' Source said, just as if this was to be a business rendezvous.

Nichiren had bridled. '*Meinichi* is a private ritual, an affair for family only. You have no right to intrude.'

'On the contrary,' Source had said, 'I have every right. There is another ritual that you must perform, and only I can guide you.'

Nichiren listened very carefully to what Source said next. After it was done, he said, 'How do you know this? It is incredible.'

'I know everything there is to know about you,' Source said in the electronic tones that made it impossible to determine even the gender of the voice. 'That was, after all, how you were recruited in the first place. I control you. Being under discipline has given you purpose other than the dubious function of an assassin. Life cannot be measured in the number of people one has terminated. That is purposelessness: pure chaos, the end of all things.'

Nichiren had said nothing. He was, oddly, thinking of Mariana, of how close he had come to saving her life. Of how he had failed by the merest hair's breadth, betrayed by the wind and the rain and the crumbling earth: nature. It was obvious that he was far better at taking lives than he was at saving them. He heard echoes of his mother's words in that thought.

Sunlight stroked his back like Yumiko's strong hands bathing him when he was too ill to do it himself. He looked up, past the small stone monument. He saw the rows of others. Here and there, like dots of colour placed by a careful painter, people moved along the narrow aisles. Otherwise the cemetery was all greys and greens.

Nichiren glanced to his immediate right. As Source had said, there was an open plot. Reserved for him, someday. How did Source know? *I know everything there is to know about you.* Nichiren moved closer to the empty plot, digging out a small gardening trowel from beneath his kimono. He measured precisely six centimetres from the left corner of the plot along the bottom edge, another six into the plot.

Dug his trowel into the grassy loam.

No one was watching. Everyone possessed inward eyes at a cemetery: lost in memories. He dug down to the depth of the tool's blade, then he used his fingers, not wanting to damage that which Source told him lay beneath the earth. Waiting for this day. Waiting for him.

He came to the top of the package, dug carefully around its edges like an archaeologist nearing his find. At last he unearthed it: an oblong perhaps eighteen centimetres by twelve, wrapped in rice paper. The outer layers, he saw, as

286

he dusted the package off, had been painted with some preserving substance, because they were decomposed only here and there. It occurred to him that this artifact must be quite old, dating perhaps to just after World War II, because there was no plastic sealer, which surely would have been used had the package been from a later time.

He opened it. And found inside a *ningyo*. It was a paper doll such as Yumiko used to make. In fact, it was undoubtedly one of hers. Though it was yellowed with age, he recognized her style of handiwork.

Break the doll.

That was what Source had told him to do last night. But how could he? The *ningyo* had been made by his mother. Could he destroy that?

He was under discipline. *You are a killer,* Source had told him years ago, when he was recruited. *You destroy life with a heartlessness that is awesome. It is also quite terrifying. That is not, I can tell you, why you were brought into this world. You are not the avenging angel your mother thought you were and taught you to be. You are not a beast in the night.*

I am Nichiren, he had said.

She gave you that name as well.

She believed in me. She was the only one.

She believed in death. In death alone. I believe in you.

Nichiren broke open the doll.

And inside, found the haunch of a tiger. It was a piece of lavender jade, the carving deft and flowing. With his breath hot in his mouth, he took the chamois pouch that Mariana Maroc had pushed into his hand and opened it. Dropped what was inside into his palm, beside the haunch of the tiger.

Shoulders, neck, fiercely grinning head. The two pieces of lavender jade fitted together, forming a whole animal, one half of the *fu*.

Power, growing.

* * *

'I must humbly apologize on behalf of the *tai pan*,' Peter Ng said. 'But it was impossible for him to accept your invitation himself tonight.'

Three Oaths Tsun smiled. 'It is of no matter,' he said in his most civilized tone. 'I have known you almost as long as I have known Andrew Sawyer, Mr Ng. I know that you speak for him.' He flipped his hand, palm to back. 'In any case, it was imperative that this meeting take place before Monday.'

Peter Ng nodded. 'The *tai pan* caught the sense of urgency in your invitation and acted accordingly. I trust these arrangements will be satisfactory.'

'Oh, most satisfactory, Mr Ng. Most satisfactory indeed.'

It was just past nine. The two Chinese were sitting in Three Oaths Tsun's office-stateroom aboard his junk, moored in Aberdeen harbour. Above their heads, the summer night was vying for dominance with the confluence of neon and incandescent light with which the Colony glowed.

Three Oaths Tsun closed his eyes, felt the gentle rocking of the junk beneath him. All will be well, he told himself through the triphammer beat of his heart. Have faith.

In a moment one of his daughters appeared, carrying a tray filled with teapot and cups, small plates, chopsticks, and platters of steaming seafood.

'It is said, Mr Ng, that Hakka food fortifies the spirit as no other in the world.' Three Oaths Tsun opened his eyes, watching his Number Two Daughter set out the meal with perfect precision. I have trained them all well, my children, he thought.

'I hope that you are hungry, Mr Ng.'

Peter Ng, dapper as always in a charcoal-grey linen suit with white shirt, white-polka-dotted dove-grey tie and black tasselled loafers, inclined his head. 'I am always hungry this time of night, Honourable Tsun,' he said, despite the slight queasy feeling in his stomach. It happened every time he stepped onto a boat. No matter that the junk was at anchor, no matter that there was only the most infinitesimal rocking motion. Just the thought was enough to give Ng the jitters.

As a small child he had been thrown into the water by his older brother. It had been a harmless prank, but Peter could still recall with supraclarity the sensation of swallowing water, of sinking down into the trough of a wave, of drowning in airless darkness.

The *tai pan*, who had become aware of Ng's affliction – an odd one for an island-bound Chinese – on a business trip during which the two of them were obliged to take the ferry to Macao, had once suggested he see a psychiatrist. Ng could never bring himself to do so. He could not see how a *gwai loh* invention could be of use to him.

Now, as he set himself to eat his host's food, he steeled himself – or, more accurately, his stomach – against the inconstant fluttering.

As was the custom, they spoke only of trivial matters while they dined: the weather, Tsun's children, Ng's family, and so on. Both carefully ignored any business matters, even ones that might not directly involve either of them.

At length, Number Two Daughter returned to clear the dishes and replace the empty teapot with a full one. She also brought a full bottle of Johnnie Walker Black and a pair of old-fashioned glasses.

Now, Peter Ng thought, it is just a matter of time. The *tai pan* had called him into his office just after he had received the call from Three Oaths Tsun.

'Things are beginning to heat up,' he said to Ng. There was a soft smile on his face, an indication that he was in the midst of serious thinking. 'It seems the Honourable Tsun wants to meet me tonight.' He looked hard at Peter. 'I want you to go in my stead. This will serve two purposes. It will indicate to Tsun that I am willing to listen but am not necessarily eager. It will also put him off guard. He may reveal something to you – either deliberately or inadvertently – that he would not to me.'

'And if he has a proposal for us?'

'Oh, he has a proposal,' Sawyer said, sitting back in his chair. 'I have no doubts about that. Remain noncommittal, Peter. This is, I think, essential. Tsun will want to make a deal as quickly as possible. I believe Monday, when all the commodity markets open, is his deadline. Even if his offer seems good, make no positive response. If we decide that what Tsun has is of interest, we will wait until the last possible moment – late Sunday night – to indicate our interest. By then we will no doubt be able to negotiate better terms than the ones we might get right away.'

Now, as his host poured chrysanthemum tea sweetened with rock sugar into their cups, and three fingers of whisky into the glasses, Peter Ng fought for control. The food he had ingested, though light, weighed on his uneasy stomach like a lead weight. He took three deep breaths and downed the sweet tea, feeling better at once.

'Mr Ng,' Three Oaths Tsun said, 'your company and mine have never had much in common. That is public knowledge. In the areas where our trade has overlapped, we have been vigorous competitors. There has never been a hint of animosity, however. Correct me if I am wrong.' His pause went unanswered.

Three Oaths Tsun gave a little nod of satisfaction. 'I believe that both our houses have remained strong competitors for many reasons, not the least of which is our resiliency.

'Times dictate a constantly changing business environment the world over. This is especially true here. I think you will agree with me. Over the past ten years we have seen a succession of business and political upheavals that have literally changed the face of Hong Kong.

'They have also obliged us to alter our perception of our future. The defection of Mattias, King and Company will force other, even less palatable changes on all of us, I am afraid.'

'It is a certainty,' Ng said, 'that at least the short-term effects will be disastrous for the entire business community.'

Oddly, Ng thought, Tsun smiled at that. 'Well, perhaps not *everyone* need suffer, Mr Ng.'

'I beg your pardon?' Peter strained to gather in every nuance hidden within his host's words.

'I am prepared to let you in on a secret,' Three Oaths Tsun said. 'But first I would appreciate a, er, token of your *tai pan*'s sincerity.'

'I think my presence here at such short notice would indicate that.'

'Perhaps.' Tsun's tone, however, indicated that he was acceding nothing. 'However, I would also wish to know whether or not Andrew Sawyer is willing to risk . . . a great deal in order to make a fortune – a literal fortune – in the coming months.'

Ng considered a moment, thinking of his instructions. 'Money,' he said at length, 'is the source. A businessman who does not want to make money is dead and buried in the ground. Yet one learns over the years, by painful process, to temper one's – shall we say – quest for capital with the wisdom of caution.'

So, Three Oaths Tsun thought, you have said nothing. But that in itself tells me a great deal. We shall have to go on from here. When a river finds a rock in its way too large to move, it alters its course. 'Of course,' he said now, 'temperance, forbearance, patience: the rich man's credo. I understand completely.' He turned to look at the clock on his desk. 'Well, I see that I have kept you late into the night. That was not my intention. Please accept my apologies.'

Ng panicked. He knew a dismissal when he heard it. He knew, too, that if he returned to Sawyer empty-handed – knowing that there was a deal in the offing – he would be handed a red envelope containing his severance. Trusted member of the house or no, the *tai pan* would find no forgiveness in his heart for such a foulup.

'Honourable Tsun,' he said a bit too hastily, 'it occurs to me that perhaps I have not made myself sufficiently clear. You must forgive me. I am not as quick on my feet as is my *tai pan*. My ancestors were slow and patient men, and they taught me to behave as they did.'

By the Eight Drunken Immortals, Three Oaths Tsun thought, this one has a golden tongue. His humility would send any *gwai loh* digging into his pockets for money to offer him.

'Patience is all well and good,' he said easily, to show there was no offence taken, 'but every so often we see *kai ho*, and recognizing this Gap, we must enter swiftly or forever be left behind.'

'It is my opinion that the *tai pan* thinks along similar lines,' Ng said, holding the relief he felt close inside him.

'Good.' Three Oaths Tsun nodded. 'Then let me tell you in all confidence that Mattias, King's decision to leave the Colony has augured a change in certain business plans of theirs. Particularly long-range plans.'

Ng's pulse rate picked up considerably. He thought he knew what was coming, and he sought to rein in his excitement at the prospect.

'As you may know,' Three Oaths Tsun continued, 'Mattias, King and I are each one-third partners with the Communists in the Kam Sang nuclear project in Guanong Province. Mattias, King have informed me that they are pulling out. Of course, they offered me a buy-out price first through my Pak Hanmin arm. But, quite frankly, the expense over the long haul is just too great a risk to my other business.

'Therefore I am offering their one-third interest to your trading house.'

Ng's mind whirled with ten thousand questions. Why

Sawyer and Sons, out of all the houses? Why not, for instance, Five Star Pacific, the major utility in the New Territories? Weren't they the first logical choice? Had Mattias, King really offered their share to Tsun? Was he lying about why he hadn't taken it himself? On and on. But Peter knew that he could ask none of these questions – could, in fact, evince no interest whatsoever.

'Kam Sang,' he said carefully, 'has quite a large price tag, if I understand correctly.'

Three Oaths Tsun nodded. 'Six billion dollars, US.'

Ng nearly choked on the whisky he was drinking. *Dew neh loh moh!* he thought. That is an unbelievable price tag to put on an energy source.

'But,' Three Oaths Tsun went on, 'the potential for profit is literally unlimited. *If* we can get Kam Sang built and on line.'

Ng's eyes narrowed. 'Is there a problem?'

'The future of Hong Kong and of much of southern China depends directly on the Kam Sang project,' Three Oaths Tsun said. 'Our energy sources are limited at best. You know as well as I do the disaster that can befall us without the water piped in to us. Kam Sang is designed not only to provide us with electricity, but also with water. Unlimited water.'

Ng sat up straight. 'I have heard nothing of this.'

'You would not have. It is a closely guarded secret. Kam Sang is designed to provide us with inexpensive desalinization.'

'Sea water into drinking water!'

Three Oaths Tsun nodded. 'No more rationing for Hong Kong. No more shortages. Water all the time.'

'And the problem?'

'The Soviets,' Three Oaths Tsun said. 'They have already tried twice to sabotage the project. There is no reason to think that they will not try again. There is your major risk. But it would increase a hundredfold if the

293

Soviets should discover Kam Sang's secret.' He looked at Ng. 'You can see why I must have an answer from your house immediately.'

Ng's mind was reeling. 'I must, of course, discuss this with the *tai pan*.'

'Mr Ng,' Three Oaths Tsun said, rising, 'I am speaking of hours, not days.'

Peter nodded, rising too. 'I understand completely.'

'Good.' Three Oaths Tsun gestured. 'My Number Three Son will see you off the vessel.'

Ng bowed. 'Thank you for your hospitality, *tai pan*.'

'I am always grateful for interesting companionship at dinner, Mr Ng.'

Three Oaths Tsun watched Peter Ng as he was led up the companionway to the deck. In a moment he called softly. A figure came down the narrow passageway, wreathed in shadows.

'I am sorry you were obliged to wait, *bou-sehk*.' *Bou-sehk* meant 'precious stone.'

'No matter,' Bliss said, coming into his stateroom. 'I had a delicious meal with *a-ma*.' Bliss had fallen into the habit of referring to his Number One Daughter, and therefore the oldest, as 'mother.'

'You have information for me.' It was not a question. He poured them both whisky into fresh glasses he pulled from a drawer in his desk.

'Jake Maroc is in Japan.'

'Ahhh!' He turned. 'We have set him on his way.' He handed her a glass. 'To Jake Maroc's *joss*.' They drank together.

'I feel odd about it,' she said. 'As if we have manufactured Jake's *joss*.'

'What an extraordinary thought. *Bou-sehk*, you know as well as I that *joss* is not manmade. It is, rather, part of the intrinsic nature of all things.'

There was some fear in her eyes. 'Perhaps . . .' She

hesitated a moment. 'Perhaps you would tell me now why you instructed me to send him to Japan.'

His face darkened. 'You are an instrument of the *yuhn-hyun*.' Used thus, the word could mean either a ring or a circle. 'I could not love you more if you were my own flesh. I consider you my daughter, *bou-sehk*, but at the same time you are special, unlike my other children. You were brought to me to raise and to train. You are on the inside as my other children are not. To them, I am only what I seem to be. Only you, of all of them, know the truth.'

He stared hard at her. 'Nothing must alter the *yuhn-hyun*.' He held her eyes for an interminable time. Then he glanced down at the calendar on his desktop. 'By now,' he said, changing the subject, and so sparing her a vocal rebuke, 'Nichiren has no doubt found his piece of the *fu*.' He seemed to make up his mind about something. 'I did not lie to you. He was sent to regain his piece of the *fu*.'

'But why? What significance could it have in today's world?'

'It is power. Power that was set in place long ago.'

'Power for what?'

'That I truly cannot say. Perhaps it will create its own answer to that question.'

There was some silence for a time. Bliss put her head down as if in this posture she could think more deeply. When her gaze came up, she said, 'Father, who else is included in the *yuhn-hyun*?'

For a moment she thought that he would explode with anger, then something seemed to strike him as if with a mighty blow, and he collapsed into a camp chair.

'I wonder,' he said softly, 'what is happening to this world. No one, of all my family, would ever dare ask me such a question. And now you do. A woman.'

He shook his head.

'Father,' she said, going to him, 'I did not mean to anger you.' She knelt before him, her head bowed.

'No need,' he said. 'No need, my dutiful daughter.' But just the same he felt a glow inside him at her filial piety. It was a two-edged blade, the warmth of her devotion blended with the independence that was part and parcel of her training.

'Even though,' he said now, 'you are a vessel of the *yuhn-hyun*, there are matters that cannot be revealed to you.'

'Why? It is inevitable that Jake will begin to ask questions. The longer we are together, the more questions he will ask. Is it not important to feed him the answers?'

For a long time she believed that he had not heard or that he did not choose to answer. 'For now, at least, it is important for Jake to know as little as possible. That is part of your job and it won't be easy. But those are your orders and they must be carried out without question.

'You know me well, *bou-sehk*. Better than any of my other children. Better than my wife ever did, I daresay. I am a man of tradition. If one abandons one's heritage, one holds nothing but ashes. Keeping alive the traditions that have made us what we are today is all that stands between us and the end of our culture. Already, over time, the *gwai loh* have taken so much from us. And still they want more. They are insatiable. Like omnivores, they are not satisfied until they have it all.'

Three Oaths Tsun looked down at her with old eyes. He wished to touch her, even though that was not the Chinese way. She was so precious to him, he held so much affection in his heart for her that, like his sorrow for China, it sometimes threatened to overflow the boundaries he had built around it. His hand twitched but otherwise did not move from its position on the chair's armrest.

'You must never abandon tradition,' he said at last. 'There will be temptation to embrace the business practices of the Golden Mountain' – he was speaking of America – 'the affectations of proper English "society." You may wake up one day to find that you covet Western men,

296

their hard-edged Occidental looks, their fast cars, their philosophy. You may yet find that you yearn to be accepted by them and, in so doing, forget the land that spawned you.'

Bliss felt Three Oaths Tsun close beside her. That should have comforted her, but tonight she trembled in response to the fear and worry she felt emanating from him. 'I will do what the *yuhn-hyun* asks of me.'

Three Oaths Tsun looked at her. He tilted his glass, finished his whisky. 'That, *bou-sehk*, I know.'

When Stallings awoke, it was already after eleven. He blinked, staring at his watch face for a moment. Then he realized that he had not got back to the hotel until after three. A very late night of frustrations among the haunts of the *yakuza*.

He swung his legs out of bed and sat up, running his fingers through his rumpled hair. He could not recall just how many people he had spoken to, how many differing lines he had dropped. It did not matter, really. He had got nowhere. Well, he should not be surprised. Even though he spoke fluent Japanese, he was a *gaijin*. As a foreigner he was entitled to nothing that concerned the inner workings of Japanese society. Oh, hell, he thought. Another day in Tokyo, banging my head against a stone wall.

As he rose, he noticed that his message light was blinking. He picked up the phone and asked for the front desk. He was told that a written note had been left for him.

'When did you receive this?'

'I'm sorry, sir. I came on at nine. It was already here then.'

Stallings hung up, making a mental note to query the night concierge this evening. He padded into the bathroom and stood under a cold shower for ten minutes, until he began to feel vaguely human again.

He dressed in khaki linen trousers and a blue and

brown striped Izod shirt. His feet were clad in lightweight moccasins. He drew on a lightweight nylon shell jacket. Downstairs, he picked up the note on his way into breakfast.

He ordered orange juice, toast, three eggs over easy, and a half-gallon of black coffee. He was never more grateful that his tour had checked into the Hilton.

After his first cup of coffee, he opened the note. It was in a plain white sealed envelope. 'It has come to my attention,' he read, 'that you are seeking information of an extremely specific and sensitive nature. Undoubtedly you are aware that this is difficult to come by and that certain precautions must be taken to ensure that repercussions will not arise should answers be provided to your questions. Also, because the answers are as dangerous as the questions, they will be expensive. Please, therefore, be good enough to be standing on the platform of the Ginza station of the Toyoko Line subway at 12:30 P.M. today.'

There was no signature, no other information on either the sheet of unlined paper or the envelope as to whom it had come from. There was no stamp and, of course, no postmark, as it had been hand-delivered. He had not been stopped on his way into the hotel late last night, though he had walked right by the concierge, who had given him his key out of his box. No note then, so it had to have been delivered some time between three and nine this morning.

There was one other thing. The writing was definitely in a masculine hand.

Stallings glanced at his watch. It was already after twelve. He'd have to hurry if he was to make the deadline. He thought about that for a moment. Was there a reason not to go? He couldn't think of one. If he ignored this summons and went on with his nighttime questioning, he knew he'd be in Tokyo until doomsday.

Still, it paid to be cautious. He quickly signed the bill, leaving his food uneaten. He had more important things to do, up in his room, and very little time in which to do them.

Wu Aiping was feeling a bit peaked after his long, exhausting week marshalling the resources of the *qun* in a furious attempt to penetrate Shi Zilin's Hong Kong operation. So at dinner, in addition to ordering *ban hai zhe*, dried jellyfish; *chao ou*, lotus root; and, to end it, *zhu dun tang*, bamboo-marrow soup, he requested *hai shen*, the strongest tonic known in China. These sea slugs, caught off the south coast and flown daily north to Beijing, were sun-dried and soaked in spring water for a week. On the second day they were cleaned in order to make them dilate and thus tenderize their otherwise rubbery flesh. At the very last moment they would be combined with *yu du*, carp stomach, and the whole flash-seared in a soy-based sauce seasoned to bring out the delicate taste of the treat.

As Wu Aiping lowered his oversized body into the chair at his reserved table, his enormous eyes locked on those of the cowering waiter. He called for *tie guan yin*, Iron Goddess of Mercy tea, the rarest and most expensive black tea in the whole country. He invariably drank it, ignoring the common custom of switching from Dragon Well tea in the summer to jasmine tea in the winter.

Wu Aiping, over six feet tall, with the kind of odd extension of his ribcage that in a Chinese could be called a deformity, sat with his back ramrod-straight. The peculiarities of his body combined with his huge eyes to give him the appearance of a giant insect. This mien in turn combined with the razorlike brilliance of his mind to make him one of the most intimidating people in his government.

The ministry restaurant was located in the basement of the bleak concrete building just off Tian An Men Square. It was often pointed out to visitors as the National People's Congress Building, which was only half a lie. Wu Aiping's office looked south; Mao's mausoleum was always in his direct sight.

Though his guest had not yet arrived, Wu Aiping went ahead and ordered. It was not, strictly speaking, the polite thing to do, but tardiness annoyed him. The white-faced waiter bowed deeply and swept away, no doubt grateful to be away from the high-ranking minister's baleful presence.

The ministry restaurant was, as was the case with all government-run businesses, drably decorated with furniture and accessories that were purely functional. But its chefs were among the finest to be found anywhere. Though images of sight and sound meant little to Wu Aiping, his appreciation of the principles of gastronomy were legendary.

Now he turned his head as a tendril of smell invaded his space. At the next table, a minister whom he knew only slightly had lit up a *Tai Shan*, a miniature cigar whose smoke Wu Aiping found particularly disgusting. He glared unblinkingly at the man until he became aware of the scrutiny and turned. He blanched, quickly stubbed out the *Tai Shan*, and, calling for the bill, made a hasty retreat.

At that moment, Wu Aiping's guest entered the restaurant and was shown across the colourless room.

'*Nin-hao-a*,' Wu Aiping said, nodding slightly. Good afternoon.

Zhang Hua, slightly dumpy looking in his ill-fitting, rumpled suit, pushed his thick-lensed glasses back onto the flat bridge of his nose. He was sweating profusely and he extracted a white linen handkerchief as he sat, wiping his wide, flat Mongol face with quick, practised swipes, neatly avoiding disturbing his glasses.

Wu Aiping lifted a hand. 'Please,' he said. 'Sit down.' Then, when the other made no move, he looked up. 'I won't bite, you know.'

The tea came, and Wu Aiping went at his as soon as it had been poured. In time, he poured for Zhang Hua.

Though inwardly terrified at having complied with Wu Aiping's telephoned summons, Zhang Hua would not give the other the satisfaction of seeing his shock. He therefore made a great show of finishing mopping his face, folding away his handkerchief, and pulling out a pack of *tian shan* – black-tobacco cigarettes – so that he would not have to touch his tea yet. He shook out a cigarette.

Wu Aiping stared at it as if Zhang Hua himself were of no import. 'If you insist on smoking,' he said, 'perhaps you would be good enough to do so at that table on the other side of the room.'

Zhang Hua flushed, and spun the cigarette in his fingers before breaking it nervously in two. 'It's just as well,' he recovered. 'I'm trying to quit.' He swept the broken thing into his pocket.

'Admirable,' Wu Aiping said in a tone of voice that implied he did not for a moment believe the other's lie. In the space of thirty seconds, Zhang Hua had lost an incalculable amount of face. He found that intolerable and began to struggle to reverse the process.

'I haven't much time,' he said. 'If you would be so good as to come to the point as soon as possible.'

Wu Aiping nodded. 'As you wish.' He folded his long fingers in front of him. 'I'll be frank. So long as Shi Zilin controls his army generals, it doesn't seem to matter a whit what I or the other members of the so-called *qun* do to reverse his dangerous policies. Therefore I have struck upon an entirely different tactic.' He smiled slightly. 'You, Comrade Minister, will provide me with – how shall we refer to it? – an inside view of Shi Zilin's Hong Kong operation. I want to know everything, and as soon as possible.' His hands opened like the petals of a malignant flower. 'Now would be as good a time as any to start.'

Zhang Hua felt as if all the breath had gone out of him. Never in his life had he encountered a Chinese such as this man. In reflex, he jammed his cup of tea against his trembling lips. He was far too agitated to taste anything. He swallowed convulsively, abruptly aware that his mouth had filled up with liquid.

'You must face facts, my friend,' Wu Aiping went on. 'Shi Zilin is an old man. Worse still for you, he's sick, his condition deteriorating every day. This is our time. The *qun* will win out. You can go down with Shi Zilin or . . .' He shrugged.

'What – ' Zhang Hua was obliged to moisten his mouth with more tea before he could go on. He was so filled with righteous indignation that he could barely see straight. 'What you propose is a monstrous distortion of honour and trust! You ask me to throw over everything I have ever believed in and worked for all my adult life. Shi Zilin has been more to me even than a mentor. He is as my father.'

He began to get up. 'Your proposal fills me with such disgust that I can no longer bring myself to sit in the same room with you, let alone share tea.'

Wu Aiping almost stifled a yawn. 'It is your choice, Comrade Minister,' he said, his tone casual. Then he threw a brown paper packet on the table. It was sealed and stamped. 'By the way, would you be kind enough to drop this in the mailbox on your way across the Square? I'd like it sent right away.'

Despite his rage, Zhang Hua could not help but look down at the package. His heart seemed to stop beating. He could hear the rushing of the blood in his ears. Echoes magnified, climbing the walls of his mind.

'Here,' Wu Aiping said, extending a hand to the other as he slid raggedly down into his chair. 'You look decidedly unwell. Some tea, perhaps?' He pushed a cup into the other's trembling hand.

Zhang Hua got the liquid all over himself. He did not feel it. His eyes were stuck on the name and address printed carefully on the outside of the packet.

'This – ' The breath was sawing in his throat. 'This is addressed to my wife.'

Wu Aiping stretched his long neck. 'Have I got the street number wrong?'

Zhang Hua looked up. He ran his fingers through his hair. 'What are you sending to my wife?'

The younger minister shrugged. 'If you are that interested, I suppose you can look for yourself.'

Zhang Hua hesitated a moment, then quickly ripped the seal. Inside he found a simple typewritten note addressed to his wife. 'I believe these may hold some interest for you,' Zhang Hua read. It was clipped to a dozen eight-by-ten photographs.

He emitted an oath. All showed him in bed with a woman in her twenties – young, nubile, and quite acrobatic.

'Your secret life. Your mistress.' Wu Aiping sighed. 'The intense indignation you so profoundly expressed some time ago interests me. It means I have been correct in my interpretation of your personality.

'You are a righteous man, Comrade Minister. You live your life guided by certain distinct tenets. You are rigidly controlled. As you say, honour and trust are paramount in your life. Your kind ultimately make the best spies, and I will tell you why. No one would think of suspecting your integrity. Further, once caught out by your *hubris*, you are bound to me. Self-loathing and guilt ensures my hold over you. Absolute in your righteousness, absolute in this as well.'

Wu Aiping smiled a little. 'But you can prove me wrong, Comrade Minister. All you have to do is put the photos back in the envelope and reseal it. I made a joke before; I can mail it myself.'

Instead, Zhang Hua ripped the eight-by-tens in two. Then he tore the pieces again.

'That's right,' Wu Aiping said softly. 'Now to business.'

'The negatives.' Zhang Hua could barely get the words out. 'When do I get the negatives?'

'Why, I thought the answer to that was self-evident,' Wu Aiping said. 'When Shi Zilin is either defeated or dead.'

The food was coming, and Zhang Hua grabbed the opportunity to recover some of his lost equilibrium. He felt so numbed that he found it hard to think clearly. He ate with apparent gusto, but really, he might as well have been chewing straw. His heart was hammering so hard in his chest that he thought he might have a coronary right here at the table. His imagination swept him away: Wu Aiping calling for medical assistance, the ambulance arriving, the attendants giving him oxygen, heart massage.

He knew why he was fantasizing this way. In hospital, he would not have to go through with this. As an invalid near death, he could relinquish all responsibilities. He would be free.

'Why are you doing this to me?' he said. 'The Premier has Shi Zilin under the gun. What more do you need?'

Wu Aiping's smile chilled the junior minister. 'Your master has been under the gun before. He has not only survived, but has managed to put his enemies six feet under the ground. This time I mean to give him no such leeway. As I told you, I have studied his methodology. I *will* crush him, Zhang Hua, be assured of that.'

Immediately the dishes had been cleared and they had finished their final course of fresh *pi pa*, a variety of yellow loquat imported from the south, Wu Aiping continued.

'Shi Zilin's ideas are leading China down a disastrous path that will eventually cause the total Westernization of our country. He would crumble our ideology, the very core of what makes us strong. He would undercut that which allows us to stay in power, to control the destiny of six hundred million souls. Without us, there would be utter anarchy in China. Death and destruction, looting and rioting. The Boxer Rebellion all over again!

'Now, in order to put a stop to him, what I need to know first is the basis of his Hong Kong operation.' He poured himself tea, waiting. When Zhang Hua refused to respond, he said, 'Come, come, Comrade Minister. The hardest part is already behind you. You have already taken the first step in compromising your integrity. The second step cannot be nearly as difficult.'

Zhang Hua seemed to give a little shake. Then he said, 'Shi Zilin has set me up as the conduit for disinformation to the Soviet KGB. Together we decided to make me vulnerable to blackmail through my brother's family in Hong Kong. Now I report directly to General Daniella Vorkuta, chief director of the KVR within Department S.'

'I will need to see all communications between you and this KGB functionary,' Wu Aiping said, immediately. 'It will be necessary for me to study this dialogue in detail. You will provide me with the documents.'

'That will not be easy. There are no photocopies – only the originals.'

'Your guilt will provide you with the spur you need to find the answer,' Wu Aiping said. 'We might as well get something straight at the outset. You will do as I say and tell no one about it. As far as problems that arise and your attempts to shovel excuses at me, forget it. Keep them to yourself. Now get on with it.'

Zhang Hua trembled in rage at how this creature was treating him. He opened his mouth to say something, then changed his mind. He knew that he had absolutely no choice but to go on with it. 'Because the Soviets seem to be in such a sweat over Hong Kong,' he said, 'Shi Zilin has determined to allow them to do much of our work for us. The core of the operation revolves around the disinformation we are providing the KGB to act on, and instructions to our own highly placed agent there.'

'Who is he?'

'Code name "Mitre". His real name is Sir John Blue-stone, one of the five *tai pan* who control the trading company of Five Star Pacific.'

'I will need the communications pertinent to "Mitre" as well. The sooner the better. Now, what about these disconcerting fluctuations in official policy that Shi Zilin has been authorizing?'

'That I do not know. He does not tell me everything. I am not privy to the workings of the overall operation, merely a number of the pieces. But perhaps the documents I shall procure for you will provide at least part of the answer.'

'They had better,' Wu Aiping said sharply. 'You will meet me tonight at eight o'clock. Take the Line Nine bus all the way to the end. Hong Miao. I will be waiting for you at the tea shop three blocks west of the depot. Bring everything I have asked for with you. Otherwise a duplicate set of prints will be sent to your wife by special courier.' His bright eyes caught Zhang Hua's. 'I trust I make myself clear.'

Zhang Hua nodded mutely.

Wu Aiping laughed as he paid the bill. 'Cheer up, Comrade Minister. Becoming a patriot is always hard work.'

Stallings had spent considerable time in New York, so he thought he was used to crowds and subways. New York had nothing on Tokyo. He had not been underground in this city for years. While there was no dirt and almost no noise, the sheer number of people jamming the platforms was staggering. He was soon lost within the madly jostling throng.

He looked at his watch: 12:28. A train was approaching on his side. He watched its gleaming metallic face rushing at him with awesome speed. It pulled to a halt and its door sighed open. He jumped back as people hurled themselves forward before those passengers inside seeking egress could make a move. Chaos ensued as the doorways were turned into brief battlegrounds.

Stallings stared as uniformed platform attendants began to jam their white-gloved hands against passengers' backs to fit them all into the cars. A warning buzzer sounded and the train doors began to close. The attendants continued their hard shoving until everyone was in. With a hiss of well-oiled hydraulics, the subway began to move out of the station, picking up speed.

When it was gone, Stallings was for that instant almost alone on his side of the platform. His gaze drifted across the tracks and he saw a young woman in a pink and orange kimono, with a pattern of gold chrysanthemums embroidered across it, standing directly opposite him.

She was in wooden *geta* and carried a *janomegasa*, an oiled rice-paper umbrella. Even from this distance it was clear that she was wearing the heavy makeup of the *geisha*. The skin of her face was dead white, her lipstick a brilliant crimson.

She beckoned to him.

Stallings was momentarily taken aback. It was most unusual for a woman to gesture in public that way. Then he glanced down at his watch and saw that it was precisely 12:30. He took the note from his trousers pocket and displayed it. The *geisha* beckoned again.

It took him just ninety seconds to find his way to the other side of the tracks. By that time a train was on its way into the station. The *geisha* led him into it without a word. Inside the car, he created a path for them. There was one empty seat and she demurely took it. He stood over her. He tried not to stare. She was very beautiful.

They were headed north, in the direction of Kita-Senju. Stallings had taken the schemata for the Tokyo subways that had been waiting for him in his room, courtesy of his tour company, and had done his best to study it on the short walk to the Ginza station.

Just after the Naka-Okachimachi station, the *geisha* rose and went to stand near the door. Stallings followed her. Ueno was the next stop. They had been travelling for just under eighteen minutes.

They went up out of the artificial light of the station into the sunlight of Ueno Park.

'*Yappari aoi kuni da!*'

They were the first words she had spoken since he first caught sight of her. Stallings nodded, more on the lookout for any person who might be following them either on his own or by electronic means than he was for the lush foliage of early summer.

Children filled the park. Babies sitting up in carriages, being fed sweet *tofu* by their mothers, toddlers taking their first tentative steps outside between mother and grandmother, three- and four-year-olds racing each other down park paths, their shoes banging like bell clappers against the stone paving.

They walked on, leaving the children behind. The high, piping voices, however, continued to float through the afternoon, tingeing the atmosphere. Cherry and plum trees rose up on either side of them, their wide, sweeping branches now bereft of blossoms.

Along a steep turning the *geisha* paused in front of bushes whose flowers were past their prime or perhaps merely still dormant.

'These are *tairin*,' she said in her pleasing husky voice. 'They are a large-wheeled variety of *asagao*, the face of morning. I think you Americans call them morning glories, *neh*?'

'Yes.'

'This particular one is known as Crimson Dragon. A Chinese name, because they were imported from China during the Nara period, approximately the middle of the

308

'8th century A.D. by the Western count.' Her delicate hand extended, the crimson nails gleaming in the sunlight. 'These, unlike your own varieties, which bloom until noon, are in fullest blossom at four in the morning. By nine they have faded.'

'That's too bad,' Stallings said, somewhat distractedly. He was still on the lookout for ticks who might have picked them up coming out of the underground.

'On the contrary,' the *geisha* said. 'We treasure the extreme ephemerality of the Crimson Dragon above all others, for it mirrors life's fleeting moments, imprinted so strongly on our consciousness but so soon gone.'

'Can we get on with our business, miss?' Stallings had had enough of this botany lesson; he had far more important matters to discuss.

The *geisha* bowed her head. Her blue-black hair shone, the intricate coif perfectly held together by mother-of-pearl *kanzashi*, sticks stuck through her hair. 'We have already begun,' she said.

Stallings looked around him, startled. 'I see no one else here,' he said.

The *geisha* laughed softly. 'Should there be?' Her tone was mocking.

'*Yakuza* never use women to do their work. I assumed you were working for someone who did not wish to contact me himself. The note said . . .'

The *geisha* had moved to a stone bench, half hidden by the furious growth of the *asagao*. She sat down. 'Why do you wish this information?'

Stallings crossed to where she sat, two fingers on the shaft of her *janomegasa*. He felt uncomfortable and edgy, as if he had already lost control of the situation. 'I'm not here to answer questions, but to ask them.'

The *geisha* said nothing for a time. Her eyes held his enigmatically.

'I don't even know your name,' he said at last.

309

'Eiko.'

'Eiko what?'

'What do you wish from this man Nichiren?'

He stared at her wide-eyed. 'You don't really expect me to answer that. I'm paying *you* for providing all the answers.' But now he was beginning to suspect that she did not have any. Instinctively his hand went inside his jacket, his fingers wrapping around the grips of a pistol.

'I think it would be prudent to return to a more populated section of the park,' he said as he drew the gun.

But the *geisha*'s hands were already moving in a blur. The haft of the *janomegasa* had been laid bare. Instead of the bamboo, a thin steel blade now slashed towards him, its pointed end piercing the fleshy part of his gun hand just below the thumb.

Stallings's hand went numb and the pistol clattered over the stone path to land at the *geisha*'s feet.

'I think we should stay where we are,' she said, keeping him skewered as she rose. She kicked the gun under the bench and into the foliage. 'Come with me.' She leaned on the sword and Stallings felt searing pain race up his arm into his shoulder socket. She must be right next to a nerve, he thought, furious with himself.

He walked where she led, behind the bench. In the midst of the *asagao* they were in dense foliage, totally screened from the turning path.

Already the sounds of the park and of the city had faded away as if beneath a heavy snowfall. Stallings, still connected to the *geisha* by her slender blade, was getting ready to make his move. No woman is going to get the better of me, he thought.

Mentally gritting his teeth, he bore down on his skewered hand, feeling hot flame exploding up his arm as he forced the steel to slice further through his flesh and free him. He came at the *geisha* then, crouched low, the fingers of his

310

good hand searching for purchase along the *janomegasa*'s haft.

Instead of opposing him, the *geisha* allowed his attack, ceded control of the blade to him, and, in his moment of surprise, delivered a vicious liver kite that left Stallings dazed and without strength.

He found himself on his knees, his head bent so far forward that he could feel the folds of her kimono brushing back his hair. He tried to rise but felt her hand on his shoulder, the fingertips digging in to find the neural plexus. His entire left side went numb. He held his bleeding right hand on his thighs. It lay there like a broken bird, incapable of movement.

Stallings was breathing heavily. It seemed as if he could not get enough oxygen into his lungs. There was a blackness around the edges of his vision, and as he recognized it he became afraid.

Many times during combat he had come to comfort fallen comrades as the battle raged on around them. They had spoken in whispers over the screams of the falling shells, but he had heard them well enough. They had told him what it felt like to fight for life, what it felt like as that life was ebbing from them. How they had struggled to reach out and regain it. How they had striven to hold on to life even as death overcame them.

There was death in the air now. With a feverish shiver, Stallings recognized its dank presence, knew that it was close. Death had come in the form of a *geisha*, an unlikely enough figure. The *geisha* stood above him, her right hand cutting off the life from his body.

Stallings wanted with all his might to rise up and slash her down. He wished to see her sprawled in front of him. He felt humiliated that such a frail creature had brought him down. He was a warrior, after all, and if he was to die, he wished a warrior's death. Not this.

Then Stallings felt a hand in his hair, and his head was

jerked upward so that he was staring into the *geisha*'s painted face. My God, he thought, she's beautiful. Beautiful and deadly.

Her eyes were darker than the night, her lips a perfect bow. Behind her he was aware of the clouds racing by, the sky changing from a deep cerulean to a grey as heavy as lead, losing all depth. It was as flat as painted scenery.

'Whatever you know,' the *geisha* said, 'you won't tell me. You're a professional.'

'There is nothing to tell you.' Even to speak this much caused him excruciating pain.

'Nothing?' Thus twisted, the *geisha*'s features turned hard and ugly. 'There is everything.'

Stallings coughed. Breath like flames rising up into his throat. The woman's grip felt like the jaws of a steel trap. Then the *geisha* reached down between his legs. Her long, delicate fingers unzipped him. Uncomprehending, he watched as her hand disappeared from view. Then unimaginable agony enveloped him for a time that seemed to him an eternity, until he began to wish for death.

And in the cessation of that exquisite pain, head bent, sweat rolling from him like water, he confessed his sins just as if he were in the sanctuary of a church. 'They wanted Mariana Maroc dead.' His voice was as cracked and dry as a winter reed. 'They sent me after her.'

'You are her murderer,' the *geisha* acknowledged. 'Did you not ask the reason for your proposed act?'

Appalled at what he had done, Stallings murmured his expiation: 'I didn't ask; but I suspect that it was because she was with Nichiren. They suspected her of tipping him off to her husband's raid on O-henro House.'

'She was murdered because it was suspected she was with Nichiren?'

Again that pain, so acute that it electrified every nerve ending, so intense that it seemed to come from the very core of him. His chest was heaving in great, erratic bursts when it was over. The sound of his heartbeat was like painful thunder in his inner ears. All he could do was shake his head.

'Though you were the agent, Nichiren was the cause of her death.' The *geisha*'s voice was as ethereal and tender as a night wind.

Through sweat-streaked, bleary eyes, Stallings watched with horror the change coming over his adversary. Her free hand went to her perfectly coiffed hair and tugged on it. The wig fell, smothering the sleeping *asagao* blossoms beneath it.

'Ahh!' The hoarse cry was tugged from Stallings's throat. He could see through the heavy makeup now as if a window had abruptly opened into the other's soul.

This was no *geisha*. This was no female at all.

'Who . . . ?' His words stumbled over his whirling thoughts. 'Who are you?'

The black eyes shifted back into focus. 'Your discreet queries were heard last night, Mr Stallings. I have many friends in this city. They brought your interest back to me.'

There was an electric fierceness in those eyes that held a certainty of purpose. 'I am Nichiren. And I am your death.'

Stallings watched with stupefaction as those long crimson nails clove the intervening space. When they touched his flesh, he closed his eyes for as long as it took all feeling to flee him.

Shanghai

What Zilin remembered most from that frightening time were the rats. And the stench. In the deep shadows at the back of the *godown*, the wharf rats were everywhere. Their constant squealing was a miniature cacophony, reiterating the tiny boundaries of his world.

In the bleak aftermath of Mai's death, Zilin had taken his only true friend, Hu Hanmin, with him to Barton Sawyer's back door for refuge. He would not endanger his family by going near them now, and no one knew of his business affiliation with the *tai pan*.

The American had been loyal to his beleaguered silent partner, and had conducted the two fugitives through the maze of alleyways surrounding the Bund. Into one of Sawyer and Sons' myriad *godown*s they had gone, threading their way carefully through the rows of crates and fifty-pound bags of opium.

During the days, the intense, humid heat liquified the poppy resin, causing it to ooze here and there through the burlap casings, filling Zilin's small world with the sickly sweet stench.

Twice a day, one of Sawyer's coolies – always the same one – would bring a bag on his shoulder that looked just like the ones stored in the *godown*. He was always careful to coincide his visits with the periods of maximum activity within the warehouse.

There was no opium or tea inside his bag, but rather food and drink for Zilin and Hu, which the two consumed with almost greedy intensity. This sustenance constituted their only physical contact with the outside world, and they were determined to absorb it wholly.

Barton Sawyer never came to see them, but every so often the coolie would deliver to them a note in his handwriting. In this way he kept them abreast of outside events. He informed them when the hunt for them was at its height, and as it slowly diminished.

Within six weeks General Chiang had more to worry about than two hunted men, missing for so long. According to Sawyer's reports, the Guomindang's leftist leaders under Wang Jingwei broke away from the mainstream as Chiang's faction had done some months before. Chiang was far too busy rallying support for his cause within the splintered group to care about them.

Thus there came a time when the coolie appeared without his customary burlap burden. From the dense shadows he called to them, beckoning them outward.

Slowly they emerged into the dense, stifling night. The coolie led them, blinking heavily in the flaring streetlights, to the office of the *tai pan*, where Sawyer was waiting with a ten-course feast in celebration of their release from sanctuary. It was almost six weeks to the day since they had been incarcerated.

After the joy of reunion and freedom, harsh reality set in. The time was long past when Zilin's absence from his job at the harbourmaster's could be explained away. Three weeks ago, another man had been hired to take his place.

Sawyer offered Zilin a job in the firm, but under the circumstances and after careful consideration, he declined. His middle brother was already securely ensconced in the company's Hong Kong office. Zilin had no wish to put all his eggs in one basket. The essence of good business practice was to diversify.

But, he had no desire to take a job without prestige and, even more importantly, connections within the city. Thus he bided his time, carefully scouring the list of opportunities as they presented themselves. Money was no problem.

Since he and his brothers had invested in Sawyer and Sons, the company had returned to profitability.

Having been handed the dredging concession by Zilin, the *tai pan* had taken the opportunity to heart. His system was more efficient and more economical than the one employed by Mattias, King and Company for years. Thus the harbourmaster's office was delighted with the firm and, as a result, bestowed upon them three new shipping routes.

Too, Sawyer had used to maximum effect all the inside information Zilin had brought him while he was still within the harbourmaster's office.

All of this combined with the uninterrupted runs of opium traffic Zilin's younger brother was providing the firm and the constant innovations Zilin's middle brother was creating in the south to take Sawyer and Sons from a middling sixth among the *tai pan* companies, to second only to Mattias, King and Company within the space of three years.

Per the contract Zilin had worked out with Barton Sawyer, the Shi brothers owned twenty per cent of the firm with an option to buy ten more within five years from the date of the contract's signing.

In August, the Chinese Communist Party began an organized and quite militant plan to drum up support within the army. There was an uprising in Nan Chang in which many Chinese were killed and wounded but almost nothing accomplished.

Near that time, Zilin found a job. It was in the Customs office, a spot on which he had set his eye for some time. Customs, he had known from his days within the harbourmaster's, could be an almost explosively profitable department to be in. He had tried several times to gain a transfer in the old days but there was never any room.

Now the unrest and the killings had made room and Zilin was swift to answer the call. His credentials and experience made him an ideal candidate, and he was chosen from among more than fifty applicants.

Long ago, Zilin had fashioned for himself a business personality as meticulously constructed as an exoskeleton. It was all tied into his theory of illusion that the master had taught him in a faraway Su-zhou garden.

He exuded the essence of the earnest and hardworking young man, quick to learn and to adapt new principles to old. None of this was, in reality, false. It was simply not all of him. Of his burning ambition, which drove him constantly, he showed just a trickle. And it was always for the firm for whom he worked at the time – never for himself as an individual.

In truth, Zilin's new job was neither difficult nor particularly demanding for him. And yet, as in all things, he was able to make the most of it. Because he was so swift to learn, his superiors acquired the habit of giving him more and more of the work they themselves should have been doing. In this manner, Zilin became privy to all the most closely guarded secrets of Shanghai trade.

And as had been spelled out verbally in their agreement, he regularly passed on many of these tidbits to Barton Sawyer, thus increasing both their profits.

Certain choice snippets, however, he kept for himself and his brothers in order to build their own company. Diversification, Zilin thought. It is the only road to success.

By 1935 he was a wealthy man. By that time, a central Nationalist government had been declared at Nanking, following the Communist Party's abortive attempt to take Canton.

General Chiang was coming under increased attack as he tried to solidify his support among the fractured remnants of the Guomindang, dissidents, provincial political leaders, and the Communists. As may be supposed, the latter opposed him the most virulently. They had gained new-found vitality from two new leaders who had recently

317

surfaced with the power in their fists: Mao Zedong and Zhou Enlai. In the middle of 1935 they had set out on the Long March that covered more than 20,000 miles from the south to Yenan in the north.

Perhaps it was fitting that Zilin should have met his future wife on a bright, sunshiny Sunday, the very day Mao and Zhou led their victorious army into Yenan. The air seemed scrubbed, as fresh as spring. One of those quite rare days in China when the oppressive summer heat is temporarily banished.

It was an odd day, perhaps, to be at a cemetery, but since Mai's death, Zilin made this pilgrimage fortnightly without fail. After conducting Zilin and Hu Hanmin to the sanctuary of the *godown*, Barton Sawyer had made certain inquiries and at length had gained custody of Mai's remains. According to Zilin's wish, she had been buried here.

It was a picturesque spot, south of the central district, quite near the ramparts of the labyrinthine Old Town. Across the river, the Long Hua temple rose, its central pagoda the only one within the precincts of Shanghai. In the other direction, beyond the Ziccawei or southwestern district, the Quixiapu, the Garden of the Purple Clouds of Autumn, stood solemn and somehow gaunt.

The Long Hua temple had drawn Zilin from the moment he had discovered it as a teenager. It consisted of four buildings. His favourite was the Hall of the Celestial Guardians. Perhaps later it occurred to him that that was how he saw himself.

In any event, he came here now to be closer to Mai. Since her death he had not looked twice at any other woman; he had not felt the rain and the clouds. Often his body ached in the secret places where Mai used to caress him, as if with a singleminded will of their own; did they not know that she was gone?

This particular Sunday, with a brisk, cool wind blowing

in from the Huang Pu River, Zilin, dressed in a dark pinstriped business suit, entered the precincts of the cemetery clutching in his white fists the *joss* sticks that he ritually lit in front of the grave while he knelt, reciting the Buddhist *sutras* that should have been said at the funeral Mai had never had. She had been interred without ceremony of any kind during the black days of Zilin's incarceration with the rats and the opium. Now he felt that he must make up for that indignity.

The cemetery was rarely crowded. This was not the favoured place for the dead, being so far from the bustling central district. Also, many *gwai loh* had been buried here, missionaries and the like.

As he walked to the site of Mai's grave, Zilin became aware of another presence. He turned his head, saw a slim woman standing with her head bowed before a stone marker with a Christian cross surmounting its crest. In her hands, held before her at her waist, she grasped a small but exquisite bouquet of pink and purple flowers. She was dressed in black. She was a Western woman with dark eyes and hair.

Ordinarily, Zilin was singleminded in his duties here. He rarely saw or thought about anything else but Mai during these painful journeys.

Nevertheless, he paused there on the stone path, staring openly at the woman, just as if he were a mannerless *gwai loh*. What was it about her that caught him? Was it the gentle arch of her spine that threw her shoulders back as if in defiance of her sorrow? Was it the way several strands of her pulled-back hair fluted against her cheek in the summer breeze? Or was it perhaps the way the soft sunlight struck her at precisely the right angle, throwing into relief her high cheekbones, her sensually curving lips? All or, again, none of these things.

Zilin had never before found beauty in a Western woman. It had simply not occurred to him that he could be attracted to a *gwai loh*. In truth, the thought frightened him. He had long ago put away any qualms he might have had about moving among Caucasians, doing business with them, or even, in one or two cases, becoming friends with them. But this was another matter entirely.

With a concerted effort, he tore his eyes from her slim form and moved in almost somnolent fashion to the end of the curving pathway, where he knelt and lost himself in the ritual.

With a start, he realized that someone was standing just behind him. The shadow rippled across his shoulders, eclipsing the slowly smoking *joss* sticks. How much time had passed? he asked himself stupidly. All the *sutras* were done.

He lifted his head and stared directly into the smokily burning eyes of the slim woman. He was immediately lost.

'Pardon me,' she said in passable Cantonese, 'I hope I have not disturbed you. I wanted to wait until you were finished. Are you?' Her eyes searched his face, and when there was no reply forthcoming she plunged bravely on. 'I seem to be lost. A taxi brought me here, but I have lost my bearings. Are you going back to the Central district?'

She smiled slowly. She pointed back to where he had first seen her. 'My brother is buried here. He was a missionary . . .' Her voice trailed off. She was terrified that she had somehow intruded on a private moment and had offended him unalterably.

Zilin came out of his daze slowly. He cleared a throat abruptly clotted with emotion. 'Don't worry. I am quite finished.' He got to his feet. 'My wife.'

'I'm so sorry.'

He saw that she was, and this threw him even more. He swallowed heavily. 'And I, about your brother.'

She smiled again. It was the shy smile of a little girl. 'He was very happy here. His work fulfilled him.'

They were through speaking for the moment. The silence

that engulfed them was thick and uncomfortable. The hooting of a boat came to them over the water.

Zilin took it as an omen. 'Certainly, I will take you back to Central with me. But if you have some free time, there's a temple near here. Long Hua. A beautiful place from my youth. Perhaps a brief tour through it will relieve us both of mourning's heaviness.'

The slim woman looked at him. 'Do you really think that wise? What would people say?'

Zilin was a rarity in that he was almost unconscious when it came to the subject of gossip, which was such a passion of the inhabitants of Shanghai – in fact, all of China – that it had developed into something akin to high art. For instance, it never occurred to him that because of his stature within the city, as well as his considerable wealth, there were constant rumours circulating about him, speculation on his private life and the like.

'What *could* they say?' he said, a little bewildered. He was coming to realize that she had this kind of effect on him.

She laughed outright, and the sound pierced to the very core of him. 'Oh, any manner of thing, knowing the Chinese passion for gossip-mongering.' She smiled easily. 'A clandestine lovers' tryst, perhaps.'

Zilin reddened. 'But that is preposterous!'

'Yes,' she agreed, still smiling, 'isn't it?' She shrugged. 'But one cannot control the minds of others – or their tongues.'

Of course, Zilin knew better. His whole life was dedicated to the science of doing just that. It occurred to him that their roles had somehow become reversed during the course of this conversation. She was speaking to him as if he were the *gwai loh* and she were a Chinese. How odd, he thought. And unsettling.

'Are you afraid of what others say about you?' he asked.

She laughed again. 'If I were, I would never be here

now. China, it is said, is no place for a proper lady, which, my family and my friends suppose, I am.'

'Are they wrong?'

'In my country, no gentleman would dare ask that question.'

'Perhaps that is why you are here,' he said, half joking.

'No.' She was abruptly quite sober. 'I came to bury my brother, who died of malaria.' But is that the truth? she wondered. I buried him more than a month ago. My mourning period is over. Besides, Michael was happy; his life fulfilled. That's more than I can say for my own. She thought of what Zilin had said.

Abruptly she made up her mind. 'How can I go anywhere with you, sir? We have not been introduced.'

'A thousand pardons,' he said, reddening again. 'My name is Zilin Shi.' He deliberately Westernized his name, putting his surname last, so as not to confuse her.

'Well, Shi Zilin,' she said, using the proper Eastern form, 'I am pleased to meet you. My name is Athena Nolan.'

She had dark skin for a *gwai loh*, deeply tanned and free of wrinkles. Her eyes were almond-shaped and the deepest pure brown he had ever seen. She said they were hereditary, her mother's eyes. Her mother was Hawaiian, descended from the family of the Islands' first sovereign, Kamehameha I. Her father was an expatriate Englishman, a strong-willed man who, like his father before him, had travelled extensively throughout the world. But it was his political bent that had led him to the Sandwich Islands, as Captain Cook had named his discovery in 1778 some thousand years after Polynesian explorers had settled them, with Sanford B. Dole, the current territorial Governor.

All of this Zilin learned some eight days after their initial meeting, which ended in the trip back to town. After all their bold talk, neither of them had wished to compromise the other, even if only in appearance. For his part, Zilin was disappointed with himself. From the time of his youth, he had known that he was a maverick. His ideas always ran ahead of his contemporaries. Now he was ashamed that he seemed trapped within the web of his society's mores.

This feeling was short-lived, however, for just over a week later he met Athena again at a Sawyer and Sons gala. In fact, it was Barton Sawyer's eldest son, Andrew – now eighteen and a working member of the firm – who introduced them.

It gave them both pleasure to take this formal introduction completely straight-faced, as if they had been total strangers.

Zilin bowed formally to Athena. Then, taking her hand in his, he kissed its back in true Western fashion. Athena appeared delighted.

'It is a pleasure, Mr Shi.'

Their eyes laughed at one another, but not their mouths. And forever after, their first meeting at the cemetery was to be their secret. Somehow, in Zilin's mind, at least, it made up for their timidity that clear sunny day.

Athena saw in Zilin everything for which she had escaped her stultifying life in Hawaii. Lately, the rolling turquoise surf, the lemon sunshine, the whispering of the palms, the lime-green sunsets of the Islands had begun to cloy, sticking in her throat like syrup. She could not sleep. She was restless and irritable all the time. She was interested in no one. The new of Michael's death had been her reprieve. She had used it as an excuse to get out and, over the protestations of her family, sail to China. Had her father been at home, she knew she would never have had the nerve to go. But he had been on the mainland on a political mission.

Zilin represented the embodiment of the exoticism she had avidly read about since she had first entered school.

323

He was supremely intelligent and not a little bit unknowable. She felt his inner strength as if it were a palpable caress on her arm and, always having wanted such a core of power within herself, prized her proximity to it now. Too – and perhaps most important of all – she was bathed in the glow of his own captivation with her. She saw her effect on him reflected in his ebon eyes, and inwardly she trembled at its depth. She was in love with him and with the fact that she could so immediately tame such an arcane and potent personality.

Now she could admit to herself just how frightened she had been to take this journey. Because she had seen it as her only salvation, she had closed her mind to the fear. Her many years of study had made her feel as if she could embrace any nation on the globe. She had read in fascination about many, delving into the myriad manners and mores of the cultures of the world.

Actually being in China had been another matter entirely. But now, basking in the heat of the emotions in Zilin's eyes, she realized how silly she had been to worry at all. China wasn't really so strange, after all. Basic emotions were the same in people, no matter where they lived. Love could bloom in the most exotic of climes.

He said something and she laughed. As she did so, her arm brushed against his. The contact was like electricity racing through her. She laughed again, drunk on this marvellous feeling.

Of course, he wanted to know about her name.

She smiled at that, and he marvelled at how such a small movement could transform a face. 'I am often asked that question, Mr Shi. It was my paternal grandmother's name. She was Greek. She met my grandfather in Asia Minor. They were archaeologists following after Schliemann at Hissarlik. Troy.'

Zilin looked blankly at her. 'I am afraid that I have not heard of Troy.'

'Or Homer, either?'

'Homer?' He turned the odd word around on his palate as if it were an unfamiliar wine. 'No.'

She brightened. 'Good. Now, while you teach me about China, I can read to you from Homer and teach you about ancient times in the West.'

He did not so much care for the *Iliad*, not because of the poetry, which he could certainly admire, but for the story line, which reminded him too much of the warlike past of China.

On the other hand, he loved the *Odyssey*, revelling in the long, convoluted quest. He delighted in Odysseus's cleverness at outwitting his plethora of foes, insisting that Athena stop before reading him the solution to each puzzle, so that he could match wits with the ancient hero. And he sighed with knowing contentment when Odysseus' revenge was consummated.

'Altogether a fantastic tale,' he said when, on a cool night some months later, Athena at last set aside the book. It was an old and frayed copy in the original Greek, from which she had been translating as she read aloud to him.

But he was not so much thinking about Homer's poetry as he was about Athena. She absorbed information like a sponge and, what's more, retained it all. There was nothing she had learned from him concerning Chinese history that she could not repeat to him at a moment's notice. He had encountered no Chinese woman – or man, for that matter – with her thirst for knowledge in all areas of human endeavour. He was used to specialists who stuck to their particular fields. And now it began to dawn on him that his list of true friends – not acquaintances or business associates – was so short because none of them were like him. But Athena was. Her knowledge was of the *world* – her concept of life truly global in nature. In an odd way, Zilin found himself contemplating her as the practical embodiment of his Buddhism. Buddha taught that the individual was one with all things. The reason, he saw, that Athena was so at home in China – he knew then that she would be so, no matter where she lived or travelled – was that she felt as one with the world.

Zilin was convinced that China's eternal weakness was her insularity. That stemmed from the traditional Chinese horror of the *gwai loh*. Rather than seeing that there were important things to be learned from the foreign devil, the Chinese had closed their eyes to anything and everything not indigenous to the Middle Kingdom.

Thus had they failed to understand. Thus had they been defeated. Thus had the feared *gwai loh* come to China and taken all that they wished.

Zilin knew he was in love with Athena. He knew that he had lost his soul to her. This frightened him more than when he had stared death in the face that night when Mai was murdered. For all his ecumenical thinking, he was, after all, a Chinese at heart. He had never been with a Western woman before, had never felt the clouds and the rain with one. It was no wonder, then, that he trembled constantly when he was in her presence. He drank little, yet felt as if he had consumed a vat of rice wine.

It was the physical contact that terrified him the most. He felt, quite irrationally he was sure, that when he touched her, his love would shoot right through his fingertips and his very essence – the history, the uniqueness that made him Chinese – would be lost forever. In short, he was convinced that in loving her he was sacrificing something else dear to him.

Yet he could not break away from her. By day he was able to maintain his concentration at his job; his obsession with his life's work ensured that. He regularly met with Barton Sawyer and, increasingly, Andrew as well, delivering to their safekeeping the valuable secrets he had gleaned from Customs. Too, he regularly met with his younger brother – the middle brother was too far away in Hong

Kong to attend – to make business decisions that would swell the coffers of the Shi business.

His father died and, some weeks afterward, his mother. Now the family consisted of the three brothers and . . .

By night, this was what Zilin dreamed of. Already, in his subconscious mind, Athena had been made family. This was the source of his disturbance. Not an evening went by when he did not see her that she was not on his mind. One could only think about business so long.

He saw Hu Hanmin rarely now. The scholar was back with the Communists, and though he had made several attempts to bring his friend with him, Zilin had no taste for it.

Again Zilin's unusual mind allowed him to see what others could not: that communism was no better or worse than any other form of government. Its theories, thought so innovative by Hu and his lot, were in reality meaningless. Communism was devised by men and had to be implemented by men. Long ago Zilin had come to the conclusion that pure theory and the human being were two mutually exclusive elements.

This had been proven to him again and again during his tenure as a Communist when Mai was alive. The Party was not ruled by adamantine theory, but by men who had about them all the vices other men had. They were avaricious, self-aggrandizing, venal, callous, and, worst of all, monomaniacally power-hungry. Perhaps Sun Zhongshan had been different. But he had been plotted against, opposed, and, in the end, defeated by those inside his own ranks.

Man was not content to read theory and act on it. He felt obliged to *interpret*. And Zilin had learned that interpretation meant corruption. Communism was an ideal that could never be achieved. At best, he thought, it was an imperfect tool through which a small band of powerful people could control a vast number of less powerful people.

Its tenets could defeat the masses far more easily than it could exalt them.

He told this all to Athena one night over dinner. He had never done anything like this with anyone. Certainly he would never have exposed Mai to these thoughts; they would have hurt her too much. For much the same reason, he had not done so with Hu, either.

At the time he had no idea why he did so, but later he knew that he had been testing her. He had wanted to see if she would react at all negatively. He had wanted to see if she would fail to understand. Had either thing occurred, he could have broken off their relationship in good conscience.

'You are not an idealist, then,' she said, after he had spoken his piece. Her eyes had about them the peculiar soft focus that he had noticed in them now and then when she was deeply involved in a puzzle or in communicating to him a particularly thorny Western concept.

'Michael, my brother, was an idealist. As I told you once, he was a missionary. He loved what he did.' She looked away, out the window at the boats bobbing at Pudong. 'On the other hand, I could not accept what he did. I don't believe in proselytizing. The Catholic proselytizers accompanied Pizarro to Peru; they came with Cortez to Mexico. In both cases, entire civilizations were destroyed wholesale. Don't forget, I come from a family of archaeologists.

'The problem with proselytizers is that they leave no room for those who disagree with them.' She turned her head back from the watery, wavering lights of Pudong. 'I suppose the same could be said for your small band of powerful people.'

At that moment, Zilin knew that he would marry Athena.

When, in 1931, Manchuria became a Japanese protectorate by dint of military perseverance, Zilin again had occasion to take note of the Japanese. In some ways, they had never been far from his thoughts. In studying them, he had seen how clever they were at picking over Chinese culture and mores, lifting what they felt was the best from this area and from that, incorporating these elements into their own society.

Zilin felt certain that a culture this intelligent bore watching. Also, he was vitally interested in them from a historical perspective, since they, like his own country, had shut themselves off from the Western world for centuries.

However, unlike in China, the Meiji Restoration had changed all that. Zilin had seen how this 'cultural revolution' had at once freed the country to embrace the attitudes and thus the business opportunities of the new century, and had doomed the traditional *samurai*-dominated culture.

For these formerly elite members of Japanese society, it was adapt or die. Those who did adapt were properly emasculated within the new bureaucracy. Compounding their problems was the swift rise of an altogether new stratum of Japanese society, the merchant class. The Restoration was making of them the new heroes of Japan as trade increased and they became the *nouveaux riches*.

There were lessons to be learned there, Zilin was certain, both positive and negative. But increasingly he was disturbed by a concomitant development within Japan's expanding infrastructure. That was the new militarism.

Japan's relations with China had never been anything less than hostile. But now Zilin perceived that the greed of the mercantile class, so vital to the new Japan's continued economic growth, was causing a rise in militarism that used as its fuel an insular – almost fanatic – patriotism.

Zilin saw this as particularly pernicious, since the true genesis of Japan's aggressive expansionism lay within the business sector, adherents of which were already well established in both the powerful bureaucracy and the weak government.

He was certain that blood would be spilled in China when, early in 1936, Hu told him stories of a series of secret meetings between Mao and General Chiang. The fact that the two most bitter enemies within the internally riven country should feel the need for a rapprochement chilled his blood. Only an outside threat of the magnitude of imperialist Japan could cause them to share a concern.

But, as Zilin had expected, the talks broke off abruptly and with a good deal of rancour. The Guomindang and the Communists were still at war.

It occurred to him that since the turn of the century his country had known nothing but internal strife, that even if his countrymen had possessed his foresight, they would be too busy battling each other to pay any attention to the long-range future of China.

It was a sobering thought but, he had to admit, one that mitigated his antipathy to communism. A united China was the first step towards the future, *any* future. He was as certain that Chiang's despotic road was wrong as he was about his lack of faith in the implementation of the principles of Communism. Already he suspected the Russian leadership of betraying the Revolution; and, further, he was beginning to see them not as the Communist ally Mao claimed them to be, but as a future antagonist poised at China's vulnerable northern frontiers. Still, in many ways, communism seemed to him to be the only viable road toward the consolidation of power and, thus, internal order and stability.

At about the same time Mao and Chiang broke off talks, Zilin and Athena were married. He wanted a Buddhist ceremony. Athena said that she had no religion, and so the nature of the ceremony did not matter to her. Zilin was vaguely disturbed by this, but he was otherwise in such a state of euphoria that he did not give it much thought.

The ceremony took place in the Long Hua Temple, at Zilin's request. In the Hall of the Celestial Guardians, they took their vows. At the celebration afterwards there was much talk among the assembled guests about Mao's increasing power, Chiang's new defensive posture, the Japanese in Manchuria. Zilin was appalled at how little real concern was voiced. These events, so vital to him, seemed part of another world to these people. He turned away, glumly staring out the window, seeing nothing. He thought of Japan and Russia, and it frightened him just how vulnerable a disunited China really was.

Later, when he told Athena of his concerns, she said, in her entirely rational manner, 'You are a businessman, Zilin. What you speak of now are political problems. They require political solutions.'

'Does that mean that I cannot become involved, then?' He was thinking of the Celestial Guardians of his youth. 'Perhaps it is up to me to help.'

'Frankly,' she said, 'I think events have gotten too far out of hand for any one person to change their course now. It seems to me that China is in the grip of a massive current of water. Where that river rushes, so will China be taken.'

'But we are not helpless!' he protested.

'True enough,' she said softly. 'It is you and I who are helpless.' She watched him at the window. He had bought her a new house for a wedding present. For three weeks a *feng shui* man had padded up and down each hallway, making certain the house was situated correctly upon its plot of land (one did not want to live inside a house placed upon the back of the great Earth Dragon); making certain that each room was situated correctly; making certain that each hallway had a turn to the right (since it was well known that demons could not turn to the right); making certain, after their bed was installed, that it faced correctly, to the east and south, not the north or west.

'Zilin,' she said now, 'come to bed.' And when there was no response, 'I need you.' She trembled as she said it. The words had almost stuck in her throat. What an effort of will that had taken! Now, once launched on her chosen course, she was unable to stop. She threw off the bedcovers. 'Do you not find me desirable?' She watched his back carefully. There was no movement from him, no indication that she even existed. He was locked within his fear of her. Now that the moment was at hand, he felt her physical presence like a bar of iron across his chest. His insides turned to water and he felt the beating of his heart as a painful reminder of the seconds passing. He wondered at his core whether he could survive this, whether his ancestors would ever forgive him his weakness for losing his heart to a *gwai loh*. Was that what he was terrified he would lose to her: his family, the tradition that bound him to China? What of the family he would start with her? Would they be separate from the Shis who had come before? That was a notion he could not tolerate. The family – the dynasty – was paramount and absolutely sacred.

'Zilin, look at me.'

He turned at last to her call, and knew that he was undone. Whatever would befall him in the next moments, he could not resist her. She lay upon the pale peach sheets, her thick black hair unbound, curled like the inky sea at night against the pale pillows. She had fooled him. She wore no nightdress or covering of any kind.

In the warm lamplight of the room, her dusky skin glowed with topaz fire. It was the first time he had seen her naked, and he was stunned into immobility. She was like a pool into which he longed to plunge headlong. He was amazed and terrified at how deeply he wanted to lose himself in her essence.

She was petite, but formed as no Oriental woman ever could be. Her breasts were larger, her waist smaller, her hips wider. In China, there was the peasant woman who, with her calloused hands and feet, her stocky frame, was built for the fields, and at the other end of the spectrum,

332

there was the fine lady whose skin never felt the sun, whose hands were softer than silk, whose feet were bound painfully in childhood so that they would be tiny and thus beautiful.

Athena fell into neither of these categories. She was fine-boned, her flesh glowing with health. Her hands were strong and capable, and her feet were not golden lilies. She was an alien.

She was smiling beguilingly at him, and seeing the direction of her gaze, he looked downward. He was horrified by the distinct bulge in his trousers.

'Your body has answered me,' she said huskily, 'even if your mouth will not.' She raised her naked arms to him, and Zilin thought he had never seen such an erotic gesture. 'Come here to me.'

He felt as if his mind had been numbed. He felt himself moving toward her across the rug, but he had no sensation of conscious volition. He was walking in a dream, like the men old before their time lying insensate on filthy pallets, pipes gripped laxly in wooden hands, eyes glazed, in the grip of opium.

He stood next to the bed, staring down as Athena unbuckled his belt. As she, piece by piece, divested him of his Western garb, he felt more and more a stranger to himself. Until he was as alien as she.

Naked, he stood before her, barely breathing, his sacred member as hard as a pillar of teak. His shame was not carried over into her eyes. Curiously, this increased his feeling of dislocation. He could not have exposed his maleness so brazenly to Mai, or any Chinese woman, for that matter.

Then Athena reached out, enwrapping him with her fingers. She moved them lightly up and down the shaft. It felt as if he were being caressed with a satin glove. His chest shuddered, filling with oxygen, and it seemed his body was working normally again.

While her left hand stroked him, her right spread across

333

his abdomen, rising upward, travelling with light curiosity over his ribcage, the fingertips making circular patterns across his chest. She connected with his nipple and he felt an abrupt lurch between his thighs. Heaviness began to suffuse him.

There was a sensation growing within him, riding his emotional currents. It was unexplainable to him. It was like a patch of darkness at noon; it should not be there, but its presence was irrefutable nonetheless.

She drew him gently onto the bed, into her perfumed precincts. With a deeply felt groan, he bent over her, his lips opening to kiss the inside of her thigh.

Athena would not let go of him. He crouched over her in a position that was almost worshipful. His hands encompassed her waist and, moving lower, felt the hip-bones, the cage of her pelvis. She had fuller buttocks than most Chinese women, and somehow this inflamed him. He kneaded them with passion as his tongue caressed her.

Abruptly, he was mad to enter her. He moved around, kneeling between her legs. Her curled fingers drew him forward.

'Come into me,' she whispered in precisely the same way she had said, 'Come here to me,' moments before.

Her fingers slid up his quivering shaft as he moved the last several inches. His flaring crown touched her moist lips and she groaned. She was breathing hard, her lower belly rippling with her efforts.

He entered slowly, gently until she had encompassed his crown with her wetness as before she had done with her fingertips. He slid in and out with just the very tip, teasing her with the promise of what was to come. He rose above her, his eyes drinking her in, watching the effect of the eddies his hips made on her flesh, as if he were the moon and she the sea.

He found that he was skilled at control. Mai had tutored him as best she could in the pillow arts. She would have remembered him as a gentle and understanding lover, but hardly a passionate one.

Would she have recognized this Zilin, who felt as if he had plunged into the heart of a great tangled jungle, enmeshed within wildly sprouting emotions that, before now, he had been unaware of in himself?

Though his pillow skills were highly honed, he felt their almost mathematical precision deserting him. The deeper he penetrated Athena, the less sure was his grasp upon the positions, pauses, deliberate caresses with which he brought himself and his partner to culmination.

Rather, he felt an acute sensation of racing headlong, recklessly, heedlessly, wantonly. He felt his own hot breath inside her as he moved up her, felt the perfume of hers entering him as he withdrew. He was intoxicated with her, out of his mind. He had ceded control to an abruptly wilful shadow inside himself that enmeshed him in pleasure beyond his imagining.

Thus it was that when Athena, her smoky eyes lidded, raised her arms to him, her fingers gripping his shoulders as she moaned, 'Come down on me. I want to feel your weight on me when I come,' he mindlessly crushed himself down onto the hot pillow of her breasts.

'Oh, now, yes, now!'

Merged with her, he came upon the clouds and the rain, shooting in ecstatic bursts, endlessly into the furnace at the core of her being.

War with Japan was in the air. It was the beginning of 1937. In Shanghai, business went on as usual. The city's inhabitants were used to living with tension.

Zilin had been doing his best to keep as much of the news as possible of the worsening situation from Athena. Hers was a soul unused to the strife of war. Besides, she was a woman, and there were matters one just did not

335

discuss with the female of the species. But Athena confounded him at every turn. She was intelligent and inquisitive and, in her way, far bolder than any Chinese woman could ever be. She learned most of the news – mixed, of course, with far too many rumours – despite his attempts at shielding her. She asked questions endlessly, and in the end, Zilin went against his better judgment and told her most of what he knew, if only to dispel from her mind some of the more outlandish gossip.

He and his youngest brother had had a meeting in which they had decided to begin selling all their nonliquid assets – *godowns*, manufacturing plants, and the like. If war did break out, Zilin did not have a great deal of faith in the Chinese army. Not against the Japanese.

One cold, blustery February day, Andrew Sawyer came to see him at the Customs office. This was a somewhat rare occurrence, since Zilin and Barton Sawyer sought to keep their business association as secret as possible.

Andrew had grown into a strong, long-limbed young man. He had his father's ice-blue eyes and his mother's straw-coloured hair. He had towered over Zilin for some years now. He seemed acutely aware of this height difference, for he was always careful to sit in Zilin's presence. He did this now, pulling a slat-backed wooden chair up to Zilin's desk. He had not bothered to remove his heavy overcoat. His cheeks were flushed from, Zilin supposed, the winter wind sweeping in off the Bund.

'Excuse me, Elder Uncle, I would not have come to your place of business unless I had no other recourse.'

Andrew Sawyer spoke a better idiomatic Cantonese than even his father did. It was the language in which he invariably chose to engage Zilin.

'Please think nothing of it,' Zilin said, immediately centring his concentration on the young man. 'My work is such that interruptions are often welcome. Especially from you, Andrew.' Zilin genuinely liked the fellow. Though he

336

was young and thus prone to making mistakes, he learned from every one and never once repeated them. Too, he did not have the *gwai loh*'s usually inherent superior attitude towards the Chinese. He never had to be reminded to whom this country belonged. All the Chinese with whom he came in contact liked him because they were comfortable in his presence.

Andrew nodded his handsome head. 'That is most kind of you, Elder Uncle. I know how busy you are during the day.' Here he hesitated like an engine abruptly bereft of steam, though Zilin knew that he had meant to continue the thought.

Zilin thought it was time to help him. 'You seem troubled, Andrew. Is there something I can do?'

The young Sawyer sighed in obvious relief, and his wide shoulders sagged a bit. 'I was wondering . . .' Again his voice trailed off. He clasped his hands together, rubbed his palms as if they itched him. 'That is, Elder Uncle . . . I was wondering . . . I know this is a terrible imposition, but I . . .' His head came up, and Zilin was startled to see the amount of pain in the young man's eyes. Carefully he buried his astonishment. 'Would it be convenient if I came by to see you tonight . . . at home . . . privately?'

'Is it all right with your father?'

'My father knows nothing about this, Elder Uncle,' Andrew said quickly. In his tone there was pleading. 'It must be kept that way.'

For a moment Zilin did nothing but watch the young man. But this attitude so upset Andrew that he began to tremble in anticipation.

'Of course, of course,' Zilin said, smiling. 'You are always welcome in my house, Andrew.' Again, relief was apparent on the other's face. 'Would nine o'clock suit you?'

'Oh yes. Yes indeed, Elder Uncle.' Andrew jumped up. 'Thank you.' He forgot himself for a moment and grasped

Zilin's hand. 'My apologies for intruding on your busy day.'

Zilin watched him hurrying down the wharf, towards the Western structures ranged along the Bund.

Sleety rain the colour of lead rattled against the shutters of Zilin's study as Athena led Andrew in. Zilin was hunched over his private papers, busily totting up the Shi brothers' assets in an attempt to make some sense of what to do with them during the impending military storm.

He turned around in his chair when he heard Athena's cadence in the room. He stood and bowed, smiling. He had changed out of his Western work clothes. He wore a night-blue quilted silk coat over traditional Chinese blouse and trousers. 'So good of you to come, Andrew,' he said, just as if it was he who had issued the invitation. He spread an arm outward in an arc. 'Come, let us be comfortable over here. Athena already has tea brewing.'

They sat on Zilin's hand-carved dragon chairs. The bamboo shutters were drawn against the inclement weather. At their side was a lacquer screen on which a pair of tigers, lords of the earth, leapt over lush foliage. Above their heads, unconcerned by their power, a brace of herons spread their wings, moving through white, curling clouds.

Athena returned in a moment, carrying their tea on a small, exquisitely wrought red lacquer tray. She did not stay and they did not ask her to.

In honour of the occasion, Zilin had called for Black Dragon tea instead of the usual winter jasmine. This did not go unnoticed by Andrew; nor did the fact that because this was *she*, the Hour of the Snake, they sat facing southeast. He was now more grateful than ever that his Elder Uncle had agreed to receive him.

The hard rain rattled the bamboo shutters, moving them minutely as if wishing entry into this sanctuary. Zilin had had his study built in the rear of the house. During the day, it had the best view of the water; at night, it was the quietest, insulated as it was from the other rooms by a long hall with two right-hand turnings.

Zilin held his porcelain cup in both hands, feeling the heat penetrating his flesh. He sipped, savouring the tea's special flavour, before allowing its warmth to steal through his insides.

Covertly he watched Andrew. The handsome Western face, so much an amalgam of his father and his mother, was slightly drawn. The flickering lamplight picked out growing circles beneath the young man's eyes.

'I saw Wiqin last week,' Zilin said. 'I was up north for a few days and ran into him. He sends his best regards and hopes he will be able to travel south in the spring to see you.'

Andrew nodded. The mention of his old school friend had failed to rouse him out of his morose mood.

'Your mother is well?'

'Yes,' Andrew said. And a moment later, 'Thank you for asking, Elder Uncle.'

'One needs always a strong and united family.' He sipped at the Black Dragon tea. 'Such a network is what makes an individual strong, Andrew. Without family, a man sinks to a level below that of the animals. A man can survive without a family, but he can do nothing more. He cannot live according to the tenets of Buddha.'

Zilin put his hands in his lap. 'This storm. It is already *li chun*, the Beginning of Spring. In just over a month, *jing zhe*, the Waking of Insects.' He shook his head. 'This violent weather does not seem right.'

'Elder Uncle . . .' Andrew lifted his head. He put his teacup aside, having sipped but a little. 'I am in a terrible dilemma.' It came out all at once, like the first burst from a cannon.

And he has come to me, Zilin thought. Why did he not go to his father? He recalled Andrew's words of this

339

afternoon: *My father knows nothing about this, Elder Uncle. It must be kept that way.*

Zilin also now put his teacup aside. The time for serious talk was at hand. But he said nothing, knowing that prompting would only increase the young man's embarrassment.

'For some time, Elder Uncle,' Andrew began, 'I have been seeing a girl.' He wrung his hands as he spoke; his eyes were lowered. 'I am not . . . I am not a promiscuous person. I saw this girl in good faith. I had feelings for her. Genuine feelings. But all the time I . . . well, I suppose I was unsure. No one knew I was seeing her. That is to say, no one within the family. Some of the servants – no doubt Ah Xip was one – may have known or suspected.' Here Andrew paused to take a gulp of tepid tea.

All this was fairly standard, Zilin thought, assuming he had divined the ending to Andrew's sad little adolescent adventure.

With a trembling hand, the young man set down the cup. It clattered noisily in the still room. 'Now the girl has told me that she is pregnant.' He looked up. 'Elder Uncle, I have searched inside myself for the aspects of love. They are not there. I do not love her. I do not want to get married.'

Zilin tapped his arched fingertips together in an internal rhythm. 'Pardon me for voicing the obvious, Andrew. But it seems to me that this is a problem that is easily solved. Go to your father and – '

'No!' Andrew fairly shouted it out. 'My father – no one in my family, for that matter – must ever know any of this happened. Elder Uncle, my ascension to *tai pan* is at stake.'

'You must tell me why, Andrew.'

'Because,' the young man said, averting his head, 'the girl is Chinese.'

Buddha! Zilin thought. 'I take it, then, there is a family involved.'

'Very much so. Yes.'

Zilin took several deep breaths to calm himself. It was one thing for a *gwai loh* to visit a brothel, he knew, and feel the clouds and the rain with a Chinese courtesan. It was quite another to have a clandestine affair with a Chinese girl of the mandarin class. Especially for the scion of one of the leading *tai pan* houses in Shanghai. The family had stature, money, influence. Perhaps Barton Sawyer dealt with the father in business. Perhaps he was a distributor. Whatever the case, he would demand retribution. Andrew would have to marry the girl. And Andrew was quite correct. If Barton Sawyer then handed over the title of *tai pan* to Andrew, the house would be put into the bride's family's debt. That the elder Sawyer would never allow. Reluctantly he would come to the conclusion that Andrew had already reached and that Zilin was reaching now: the new *tai pan* of Sawyer and Sons would have to be one of the younger brothers. Zilin knew them both well; neither was Andrew's equal in courage or business acumen. Neither, in short, were *tai pan*.

'What is the family name?'

'Chiu.'

'Jiu Ximin?'

Andrew was grasping his ears with his fists. His voice was but a whisper. 'Yes, Elder Uncle.'

Oh, oh, oh, Zilin thought. Jiu Ximin was a worker organizer. Fully seventy per cent of the Chinese labour force employed by Sawyer and Sons came under his influence. He could, if provoked, cripple the company.

'It's a mess, Elder Uncle. I admit it.' Andrew was rubbing at eyes squeezed shut. 'An irretrievable mess.'

Zilin watched the minute tremors of the bamboo shutters, pelted by the howling winter storm. This seemed to him to be the last straw, the embodiment of the creeping dread he had been feeling during the buildup of what he knew to be the coming war. He had sensed all along that this holocaust would in some way irrevocably change his country. Andrew's crisis had brought his fears for his country to the forefront. He recalled Athena saying, *It is you and I who are helpless*. At that moment he knew that she was wrong.

He returned his gaze to the young man weeping before him. His mind was running at full speed. 'Come, come, Andrew,' he snapped in the harshest tone he could muster, 'that is no way for a future *tai pan* to act! One must be strong always, even in the face of blackest adversity. One must never show one's fear. A *tai pan* cannot be thought to be weak; he has too many enemies who would seek to take advantage of that weakness. After all, a *tai pan* has an entire house to think of, a history of growth and expansion that is sacred.'

'Yes, Elder Uncle.' Andrew took one last swipe at his teary eyes.

'Lift your head up.'

'Yes, Elder Uncle.'

'The master of a noble house must never be seen to lower his head. It is a sign of defeat. There will be no defeats for you, Andrew. Not if you hope to take your father's place one day.'

'I understand, Elder Uncle.'

'Good,' Zilin said. 'Now to Jiu Ximin's daughter. You do not love her?'

'No, Elder Uncle.'

'Then a marriage is out of the question. And rest assured, Andrew, marriage is what Jiu will demand of you.' He gave the young man a penetrating stare. 'Rightfully so.'

Andrew swallowed hard, but he did not take his eyes off Zilin.

Zilin thought, What an opportunity this young man has presented me with! He has put in my path a chink in the *gwai loh* armour. I must be careful as I insert my blade to open it further. Such a gap may only come to a man once in a lifetime. Be careful, he cautioned himself, not to squander such a treasure

Holding his mounting exhilaration in check, he began to think of Jiu Ximin, a black-eyed dragon of a man, inflexible and greedy to a fault. Greed, Zilin, thought. Perhaps, yes, perhaps we can trap him there. He has coveted my Huangcheng *godown*s for years. Why, every time he passes them, he almost drools. A prudent, forward-looking businessman such as myself would want no part of Shanghai real estate these days. But there are few who understand this as yet. Yes, the Huangcheng *godown*s might be the answer. But I must be careful. Jiu Ximin is a difficult and clever man. He will surely make us pay dearly for what Andrew has done to his daughter.

Giving no hint of these thoughts, he said, 'There are always ways around such difficult situations, however. It is a matter of careful negotiation. And money, of course.'

'I haven't enough money, Elder Uncle.'

'Nor do you yet have the ability for such subtle negotiation. But you shall accompany me on all meetings. Your posture will be one of abject humility. Jiu Ximin will like that. It will give him a sense of power over your father.'

'That must not happen, Elder Uncle!'

'Of course not, Andrew. Set your mind at ease on that score. I will deal with Jiu Ximin, and while I do so, you will be gaining invaluable insight into conducting negotiations. But' – Zilin held up a finger – 'such extraordinary lessons as these do not come without a price.'

'I will pay you whatever you – '

Zilin's upheld hand gave him pause. 'Never transact business in such a crude fashion, Andrew. Besides, I do not want money. I rather desire a pledge from you.'

'I will give you anything, Elder Uncle.'

'Anything,' Zilin smiled, 'but not everything. Remember, you must think of Sawyer and Sons first now.'

Andrew nodded.

'Your pledge is for future services. There may come a time in the future when I will come to you – or contact you by messenger. You will know him because he will carry the rest of a token, a piece of which I will give you. At that time you will remember this moment and will do whatever is asked of you.'

'Anything, Elder Uncle?'

'That was your word to me, Andrew. Anything.'

Andrew Sawyer bowed deeply from the waist. 'It is as you wish, Elder Uncle. I so swear to you on my honour as future *tai pan* and on the honour of my ancestors in Sawyer and Sons.'

All gods bear witness, Zilin said to himself, I will make this boy into one of China's great *tai pan*. I am bound to him as closely as he is now bound to me. Because of his blunder I have been liberated from the inaction that was threatening to destroy me. By all the gods great and small, he has given me my bridge to the West.

Great Buddha, I may yet ascend to the role of Celestial Guardian of China. Today I have begun a lifelong struggle to lift China up from the mud into which the foreign devil and her own insular stupidity have dragged her.

Jiu Ximin was an immense mountain of a man, dour in countenance, with smouldering button eyes. By turns taciturn and fiery in his responses, he sought continually to catch Zilin off guard by these apparently contradictory moods.

However, his intense traditionalism soon made itself manifest to Zilin's searching mind. Lian Hua, the girl who Andrew had made pregnant, was his child and he was properly angry about her situation. But, after all, she was a daughter and therefore not particularly important to him. His sons were his life; their future would continue the Jiu line.

Cleverly, Zilin had selected a suitable Chinese whose

family were clearly delighted to have their son enter into marriage with the illustrious Jiu. Their own wealth was sufficient for Jiu Ximin to feel immediate relief at the mention of their name. He would not show it, of course – and Zilin had seen no reason to inform Andrew of this, feeling that the scare would serve him better in the long run – but despite all his bluster about Andrew having to marry his daughter, he would never have allowed such a thing. A *gwai loh*, even one on the exalted level of a future *tai pan*, was anathema to Jiu Ximin. It was enough that he had to deal with them on a day-to-day basis. Taking their money assuaged much of his anger. But allow one to enter the family? Never.

Jiu Ximin saw *gwai loh* not only as barbarians but as cultural children. The Chinese had been cultured for more than four thousand years. In the face of that, what were two or three hundred? He wanted no part of them.

He wanted the Huangcheng *godown*s.

On the fourth day of their meetings, when he at last allowed a thawing note to enter the negotiating session, they were served jasmine tea by a young woman. She could not have been more than nineteen or twenty, a year or two older than Lian Hua.

Zilin watched her carefully because she was the only other person of the household whom Jiu Ximin had allowed them to meet in all their time at his house. By definition, that made her important. Zilin felt certain that she was not here by accident.

His suspicions were confirmed when the girl did not leave after she had served them, but rather knelt by the side of the low table with her hands in her lap and her head bowed.

'This is Sheng Li,' Jiu Ximin said casually. 'She is a friend of Lian Hua's. A childhood friend.' Deliberately he took a sip of his tea. His eyes never touched her. 'Now that my daughter is a grown woman' – his gaze bored into

Andrew with an almost palpable venom – 'she must put aside childish needs.' It occurred to Zilin that Jiu Ximin had ordered Sheng Li to remain simply in order to shame her. He spoke of her as if she were no more than his daughter's dog-eared stuffed animal, which now must be consigned to the pyre.

'Lian Hua will have far too much to do and to learn in her new life, her new family, for her to carry any excess baggage. Therefore, as part of our arrangement, Shi Zilin, I suggest that you take her. Do with her what you will, it does not matter to me. I will tell my daughter that you have offered Sheng Li employment at a rate of salary above what I am willing to pay her. That will be the end of it.'

Zilin, feeling that the girl would be better off as far away from this man as possible, agreed.

It was not until sometime later, after he had installed Sheng Li in the home of a Chinese friend of his, that he came to understand Jiu Ximin's true motives in wanting to be rid of the girl.

'I came to the Jiu household with my mother,' Sheng Li told him one afternoon when he came to see her. 'In those days I was too young to do much of anything in the way of real work, so I became Lian Hua's companion.' She wore a brocaded silk robe that flattered her slim-hipped figure. Her thick, night-black hair was pulled back in a ponytail that cascaded down her back. When Zilin had come to the door, she had met him there and kowtowed. When she spoke his name, she always used 'Shi *zhu ren*,' which meant Shi, the man in charge, and used the *nin* form of 'you' that one used in addressing a person of clearly superior rank.

'We became friends,' she continued, 'much to Jiu Ximin's chagrin. You see, he eventually found out that my father was Japanese. My mother was dying, and he went through her papers to see if there was family to whom he could ship her back, so that he could avoid the expense of a doctor and later a funeral.'

To all this, Zilin said nothing. He walked beside her, his hands clasped behind the small of his back. The cool spring wind caused him to bend lightly into it so that he gave the appearance of being lost in thought.

'We had no such family, and Jiu Ximin was forced to pay for her care. This sum he took out of my pay, so that for the last six months I received no payment from him. I did not mind. It was my duty to care for my mother as she once so lovingly cared for me. I would have felt somehow soiled, had I been obliged to take his money for my mother without being able to replace it.'

Boats bobbed along the Pudong, and everywhere the industry of the city was in evidence.

'You have been exceptionally kind to me already, Shi *zhu ren*. I felt obliged to tell you of my stigma. I do not expect you to keep me or to pay my way. Now that I am on my own, I am prepared to go my own way. You will never see me again.'

Zilin watched her face. It was a perfect Oriental sculpture. Large almond eyes that seemed somehow always heavy-lidded, a wide, intelligent brow, flat Mongol cheekbones, and a bow of a mouth. She did not have the typical Chinese moon face, which he attributed rightly to her half-Japanese ancestry. He saw a fierceness of spirit – a brightly glowing spark that somehow reminded him with painful acuity of Mai – commingled with her feminine pliancy.

At that moment the sun slipped out from behind a bank of blue-grey clouds and bathed them both with a golden light. Zilin felt a plangent chord struck inside him, and all his longing for a return to his Chinese nature, which had been complete with Mai, struck him full force. For this time, as he strolled with Sheng Li, as they spoke in low tones, he felt totally divorced in spirit from all *gwai loh*.

And abruptly he knew why he had instinctively not brought Sheng Li home to live in his own house. There was a point at which, despite all efforts, East and West

347

could not meet. There was a particular nexus – perhaps it was the simple concept of *yin* and *yang* that an Oriental couple implicitly understood – around which Chinese and *gwai loh* could only circle like moths about a flame, never merge.

Sheng Li, he thought, stealing another long look at her. The name meant Victory.

At the end of the long Saturday, when at last he returned her to the family residence and, in the gathering twilight, himself returned home, Athena met him at the front door to tell him that she was carrying his child.

For a long time Athena suspected nothing. She knew, of course, that her husband had interceded in some important way for Andrew Sawyer, and that it must be kept a secret. But nothing more.

During her pregnancy, she kept up her studies in Chinese history, politics, and culture. Several times Zilin attempted to teach her about Buddhism, but perhaps because of her background, she could grasp nothing of the innate concepts. She was far more interested in pursuing her ongoing study of archaeology, the field of endeavour that had fired her paternal grandparents' lives.

She got a small crew together and began a dig to the southwest of the city, near the Old Town. By the sixth month she had cut down her hours at the site from six to three, mostly because of Zilin's concern. By the seventh, he insisted that she suspend work altogether. By then she had enough of a supply of shards and bones to keep her occupied at home.

Athena was not aware of any lessening of Zilin's passion towards her, even as her belly expanded to its fullest. She did not feel the lack of an inner connection between them, because she had no idea that such a thing might exist. This was not so much a failing within herself as it was a lack of understanding within a broader cultural spectrum.

To his credit, Zilin tried. His attempts at explaining the unexplainable concerning Buddhism were therefore bound to fail. Though Athena could embrace the world – a remarkable enough achievement for a *gwai loh* – she could not perceive the underlying oneness with the universe that was the essential skein of life.

He did not love her any the less for it. He just could not love her as completely as he wished. Or as he needed to.

Athena felt a shift in the forces surrounding her. She did not know what was the matter, just that the atmosphere around her did not feel the same. At first she put it down to her pregnant state. The baby was fully formed inside her, she knew that, and was very active. So near the birthing process, her body was changing itself for what was to come. Nothing seemed the same to her.

Why or when she began to suspect it had something to do with Zilin, she could not say. With the new life so complete inside her, the enormity of the change in her own life was finally sweeping through her. Long days at home with her shards and bones no longer held her interest, and she brooded about her new life. She was angry with everyone and everything. She suspected the world of clasping her in its heartless fist.

She suspected Zilin.

Of what, she did not immediately know. She thought she felt a lessening of the force by which she had known him ever since they had first met. She found herself thinking often about that sunny Sunday at the cemetery. She recalled how the sun had felt on her cheek, how sweetly the birds had sung, how openly Zilin had looked at her. And with the recalled rush of that wild stirring would inevitably follow the horde of her present suspicions.

She wanted him around her more, and when he was not there, she grew wild with longing for him. Her hands would cup her swollen belly as if she felt the need to protect her unborn child from her husband's desertion.

The thought that he would somehow leave them filled her with unreasoning terror. The black spectre of being alone with her baby in the vast tumult of China – a China stirring towards war – was more than she could bear.

But then she would close her eyes, breathing deeply and evenly until she forced herself to sigh. What is wrong with me, anyway? she asked herself. Zilin loves me; he will love the baby. Where could he possibly be going? Sleep would come to her on that note.

For his part, Zilin felt no guilt in being with Sheng Li. For one thing, mistresses abounded in the China of that time. But for another – and far more significantly for him – he felt no estrangement from Athena or their newborn baby, whom she had named Jake, for her father's father. In fact, because a side of him that Athena could not understand was now being nourished, he was a happier, more alive person.

Since Sheng Li had come into his life – since they had felt the clouds and the rain together – his inner fear of Athena had faded away. He no longer felt as if he were losing something precious each time he pierced her jade gate. For whatever his love for a *gwai loh* took away from him was returned by Sheng Ri's deepening devotion to him.

Less than two years after he had taken her from Jiu Ximin, she delivered to him a boy. He was a premature child by more than almost six weeks, and he came into the world dangerously underweight and yellow with jaundice.

Sheng Li cared for the infant night and day, dozing fitfully perhaps an hour or two a night when the child did, but no more. Zilin tried to be with her as much as he dared, but he knew it was not enough. More than a year ago he had taken her out of his friend's residence and placed her in a small house of her own, which he paid for.

But there were other problems to surmount, and the

child's birth only compounded them. The war with Japan had finally come like a stormcloud at last breaking over China. The battlefield encompassed Shanghai and much of northern China. For the time being, at least, the army was bravely holding its own against the massed Japanese military machine, but Zilin knew what the inevitable end must be.

The outbreak of hostilities quite naturally made Sheng Li's parental secret all the more volatile. So much so that Zilin had refused to hire an *amah* for the infant and to help Sheng Li, for fear that word of her half-Japanese heritage would somehow come out. In the city's current paranoid climate, nothing could be more lethal to Sheng Li.

Also, now that Zilin had two sons to think about, the enormously important decisions facing him were being made even more painful. It was now October 1936. The Japanese army had taken a majority of the larger towns in the north. More ominously, they controlled the lines of communication. In the south, they were holding the Yangzi valley as far as Canton and the Yichang gorges. What stability was left in Shanghai was slipping fast.

The nexus point for his country that Zilin had foreseen was at hand. It was time to make his move. He knew that he would have to do it now, or it would be gone from him forever. He thought he understood the enormity of the sacrifices he would be asking of himself. But of course he knew that their effect could not be calculated ahead of time, and that he would not truly know their toll on him until afterwards. He also knew that, as in *wei qi*, once having been made, his move was irrevocable.

When he was with Athena and Sheng Li and held the babies against his chest, his resolve would waver. His thoughts would selfishly centre on the pain he would be inflicting on those he loved most in the world. But weighed against that human suffering was the agony of China. He

351

knew that if he could help to relieve his country of its self-destructive, divisive bent, then any sacrifice was worthwhile.

Yet, whether he was with Athena or Sheng Li, he would often rise in the depths of the night, moving silently away from their warmth and the comfort of their bodies. Alone and apart from the world, in the soughing silence of the great darkness, he would weep tears of self-pity.

He was a man with two families, but all too soon now he would have none. There would be no time for self-pity then. China was calling out to him.

As they had done almost all his life, it was the Japanese who finally undid him. Because of them, because of Sheng Li's secret, he would have no one in the house with her.

Li Qiu – Sheng Li had insisted on calling the child Beginning of Autumn because he had been born on Wednesday, the day of the August demarkation – had, with difficulty, recovered from his infant's jaundice and gained in weight. But he remained a sickly child, and Sheng Li or Zilin was always feeding him some medicine or other.

On a night when Zilin was with neither woman, Li Qiu became ill. His temperature rose alarmingly until at the Hour of the Dog, near eleven o'clock at night, he seemed to Sheng Li to be burning up from inside. His skin was hot to the touch and dry, pulled so tightly across his flesh that she could see the veins pulsing and distended just beneath the surface.

She used cold water, then alcohol to rub him down, but nothing seemed to help. She began to panic. She had no friends to whom she could turn, and with her mind clouded with fear and a mounting dread for her son's safety, she wrapped him in blankets and fled with him into the night. Now all the shapes and configurations of streetcorners, shop façades that had once been so comforting to her, seemed menacing.

From open doorways and windows through which pale, flickering light splashed, she heard the hard, brittle click-click-click of abaci totalling the week's take, or mah-jongg tiles boldly slapped down on baize tabletops. Tonight these sounds, so integral to this city's rhythm, took on a sinister quality, like the snapping of giant insects' mandibles.

The sounds made her bolt all the faster down the twisting streets, past dark, dank alleyways thick with the breath of the poppy, past the locked and bolted faces of Shanghai's greatest businesses: Mattias, King and Company, the Asiatic Petroleum Company, the Hong Kong Bank, Sawyer and Sons, Ewo Brewery, the British-American Tobacco Company, Gibb, Rivingston and Company, and Standard Oil's Mei Foohong subsidiary, which nightly lit most of the lamps of China.

Sheng Li's mind was filled with terror for the safety of her Li Qiu. She did not think of herself or of the consequences of her headlong flight. She thought only of getting her child to safety.

Only dimly did Athena hear the pounding. She did not stir out of bed until the *amah* came in to wake her. Scrubbing the sleep from her eyes, she drew on a silk gown and dutifully padded behind the old woman through the darkened house.

Sheng Li stood shivering with cold and fear just inside the front door. The *amah* wrung her hands and chattered like a monkey in a dialect that Athena had never been able to penetrate.

Sheng Li, even more terrified now at having to confront this *gwai loh* who, she knew, was mistress of the house, tried to kowtow. But the baby bawling in her arms would not permit her to.

'My lady,' she whispered. 'Oh . . .'

'What is it you want here?' Athena asked.

'My baby . . .'

'Ah Han,' Athena commanded, pointing. The *amah* took

the child from Sheng Li, began to examine it with great care and tenderness. Sheng Li stared at her with wide, unblinking eyes. She sucked in deep breaths and tried to still her panting.

At last she turned to Athena and said, 'I wish to see Shi *zhu ren.*'

But Zilin was at that moment far from Shanghai. He sat in a darkened lorcha, anchored along the east bank of one of the myriad northern tributaries of the Huang Pu. There, amid the cacophonous calls of the night birds, the engine-like whirring of the insects, he sat with his youngest brother.

With great ceremony, Zilin handed over the thick packet covered in red cloth.

Zilin's brother's calloused hand closed over the packet, automatically weighing it. 'By the Eight Drunken Immortals,' he said, 'this is a great deal of money.'

'All I possess,' Zilin said in a shivery voice, 'save for the two houses and the money I've set aside for the women and my sons.'

Zilin's brother looked carefully at him. 'Nothing left for you, then.'

'Where I'm going, it will be far better. Money could only be suspect.'

The younger man slipped the packet beneath his shirt, inside his belt. 'It is very dangerous, what you contemplate.'

'All life is dangerous,' Zilin said. 'I do this for all of us.'

'You and I,' the other said carefully, 'may never see each other again. We are family. Is that right?' Zilin said nothing, staring out along the skin of the faintly phosphorescent river. Somewhere a fish splashed.

'You'd better take care in your dealings with Mao. He might eat you alive, Elder Brother. I've heard many stories. Usually I discount these rumours, but the ones concerning

Mao are too numerous to ignore. He will never allow you to lead.'

'I do not want to lead,' Zilin said. He leaned forward, elbows on knees. 'If we are victorious against the Japanese, if we can unite China under communism, we will have gained a measure of success. Naturally, Mao will reap the immediate benefits. His self-aggrandizing and his ego will cause him to become a hero to the country, a living legend. But as you know, Younger Brother, legends have a way of falling to dust here. Everything is mutable; China thrives on change.

'I think the qualities within Mao that make him a born leader will also eventually destroy him. His ideas are far too radical. After the Revolution will come a time of reappraisal, perhaps even of reactionary retrenchment.' He shrugged. 'Who can truly say? But I will not die with him when his time comes.'

'By the Spirit of the White Tiger, what of me?'

'You are to sail to Hong Kong,' Zilin said. 'But do not join your brother. He will know you are coming. He has his instructions from me. Use the money I have given you wisely. Invest and prosper. But give yourself another name.'

'Another name? But why? By the Celestial Blue Dragon, not even my ancestors will recognize me then!'

Zilin laughed. 'They'll know.'

'By the Eight Drunken Immortals, I hope so!'

'All right,' Zilin said. 'I'll name you myself. That way they will hear and know.' He looked at his brother and laughed again. 'A nickname is what you need, Younger Brother. Nicknames are common in Hong Kong, and I've just the one for you: Three Oaths. Three Oaths Tsun.'

Of course, Athena did not understand. Until that moment she had been certain that Zilin loved her completely. Now she knew that was not true.

355

Somewhere inside her, perhaps, she was appalled that she could not understand what Zilin had done, nor find it in her heart to forgive him. She was well acquainted with the custom of men keeping mistresses; she just was not able to accept it in her husband.

She simply could not comprehend his need for another woman. She felt utterly humiliated, as if he had pushed her face in the mud. She wondered if that was truly what Zilin craved – to be kowtowed to. Then why had he married her? Surely he understood that kowtowing was for Chinese.

Again, part of her was appalled by what she was thinking. How could she possibly consider herself a citizen of the world if she could not accept another culture's customs as her own? And at last she knew that she could absorb all the data, could understand from a distance exotic customs and mores, but when it came to living according to those different tenets, she was as much a prisoner of her own background as were her parents or her grandparents. Her father, for all his love of Hawaii, had never integrated himself into his wife's culture. None of the children had been given Hawaiian names; they were not versed in Hawaiian culture. Athena felt ashamed.

She fought against it, just as she fought against the feeling of humiliation. But it was a losing battle. She could not stand the sound of the alien infant's screaming; she could not bear the sight of Sheng Li, slim and spare and delicate, standing with her head bowed, as docile as a lamb.

Athena felt red rage suffusing her. This woman was everything that she was not. And she had stolen Zilin away from her. Athena's worst fears had come true.

With a cry, she sent all the servants out of the house. The bawling baby was left on a chair, settled in a silk pillow. Then she turned back toward Sheng Li.

Fury was in her heart. She was like an animal mother

who finds her family injured or missing. Zilin, had he been there, would certainly not have recognized her.

For the first time in her life, Athena felt all rationality desert her. The Chinese woman's docility only enraged her all the more.

She struck out with her fist, and Sheng Li's head whipped on its slender neck. Athena hit her again. Her chest was heaving like a bellows.

She glared down at Sheng Li, stretched out, insensate beneath her wide-apart legs. Sheng Li's coat was thrown back, and Athena saw the long, perfect legs, the delicate curve of her rump, the sweet swell of her hip bared and glossed in the lamplight.

With an animal cry, she whirled, running into the kitchen. When she returned, she held an iron bar in her white fist. It glowed red hot at its end.

Grey smoke curled lazily off its tip, the ghost of a dragon in the charged air. With a great rush of wind like the breath loosed from its gaping jaws, it uncoiled itself, rushing downward just behind as the iron made searing contact with smooth flesh.

Book Three
HSING-I

Summer, Present

Hong Kong/Tokyo/Moscow/Beijing/ Washington

'Five hundred on Fa Shan!'

'Eight hundred to cover that! Clubfoot Su will carry the day!'

'You're both wrong, by all the gods! Their oarsmen are as weak as infant's piddle! Three Oaths Tsun's craft will win, and here's one thousand that says so!'

'How inconsiderate you are of our host,' a fourth voice cried. 'A fornicating week's profits say the Dragon Boat of T. Y. Chung will emerge the winner!'

This set off another round of betting, more furious than the first.

Slit-eyed, T. Y. Chung watched them from the cockpit of his sloop, *Loong wang*, the Dragon King. He was a moon-faced man who looked to be anywhere from his mid-sixties to his early eighties. He was slim, though not tall. His raw-silk Savile Row suit, the colour of mint tea, was impeccably tailored to gain him a semblance of height he otherwise would not possess. His feet were clad in comfortable moccasins hand-stitched for him in London to his own last.

It was Sunday, the Double Fifth, the fifth day of the fifth month according to the Chinese calendar, and T. Y. Chung had organized this outing of friends, business associates, and enemies aboard his yacht, picking them up at Central and sailing south around the Island for the traditional Dragon Boat races. Though they were also taking place at Stanley, Tai Po, and Yaumatai, the most important of the races was being held here in Aberdeen.

'Two thousand on Fa Shan! His boat won the first and

361

third heats! Just now a great gull dipped down over his boat! I have a feeling in my sacred member!'

'That's how you make all your decisions!' There came a chorus of raucous laughter. 'Twenty-five hundred says the gods of rain are with Clubfoot Su this day!'

'Another three thousand on T. Y. Chung! He won last year, didn't he? All gods bear witness, he'll do the same again today!'

No one spoke of the whispers that had raced like sheet lightning last year. Though no official protest was raised, it was claimed by some that T. Y. Chung's craft had illegally veered, causing a neighbouring boat to run into Three Oaths Tsun's, one hundred yards from the finish line. That delay had ensured Chung's victory. To a man, all the guests wondered whether this would be the moment of Honourable Tsun's revenge.

It was said that the Dragon Boat races dated back 2,300 years. Legend had it that a poet-statesman named Chu Yuan had turned himself into an instant folk hero by throwing himself into Lake Dongting in a province now known as Hunan to protest the inhumane policies of the ruling prince.

Fleets of local fishermen took to the waters in a vain attempt to find and save Chu Yuan. At last, giving up their search, they contented his spirit by throwing packets of cooked rice into the lake to turn away any evil spirits who might seek to harm him.

There were, of course, other stories of the origins of the Dragon Boat races, but this was the one that T. Y. Chung liked the best.

Now, as the long, slender boats with their brightly painted dragon-head prows lined up at the starting position, he began to focus his attention on the building excitement of the race itself. The craft had fifty oarsmen. At the centre of each was a drummer who would set the pace for the others. The owners of the boats were either shipping magnates like T. Y. Chung or Three Oaths Tsun, fishing families, cargo-vessel associations, or sports clubs. There was even a police boat, but each year one of the other entries was designated by all the others to see that it did not win.

During the last several years the rivalry between T. Y. Chung and Three Oaths Tsun had spilled over into this annual sporting and betting event, adding, for those who watched, a certain delicious piquancy. The vying of these two mighty *tai pan* in the arena of high finance was the stuff of vicarious gossip; their rarefied world could never actually be experienced by the crowds in the street. But the Dragon Boat regatta was an event for everyone, and because, as in almost all things Chinese, there was an enormous amount of betting – because of the *tai pans'* participation more here, in fact, than in the other three races combined – they could feel a part of the intense and bitter rivalry and thus elevate themselves for the time of the festival.

It had also become a tradition that the principals not wager on this race, and this heroic feat of abstention seemed to heighten the frenzy of betting from all other parties.

All, that is, save Sir John Bluestone. His tall, angular presence was like a shadow standing beside T. Y. Chung. From time to time they spoke, as if unconcerned with the confluence of gaudy tension and gaiety rising all around them. With almost clockwork regularity they broke open bottles of ice-cold San Miguel beer, drinking from them in long, hard swallows.

The line of Dragon Boats was bobbing in Aberdeen harbour. At the other end of the eight-hundred-metre course opened up between the masses of high-sterned junks at permanent anchor here, red and gold pennants were fluttering.

'The wind is rising,' one of T. Y. Chung's invitees said

judiciously. He squinted into the face of the high, rising clouds. 'Northwest and building.' He spat heavily. 'It must affect the race. But, by all the gods, how? Which craft will benefit and which founder?'

'We'll see now how the captains fare,' another said. 'Fornicating rain! How can any real determination be made now?'

'A captain's skill will be in evidence, no matter the weather,' the fourth man said. 'Will he not have the gods with him? The fornicating weather means nothing to gods. It will mean nothing to the winning captain, either.' He laughed. 'Perhaps your guts have turned to water. Perhaps your sacred member is as limp as a worm. You can still change your bets.'

'A blind pox on your words,' the other responded. 'I've made my choice, and by all the gods I'll not be swayed now, fornicating bad weather or no fornicating bad weather!'

'*Oh ko*, that's the spirit, Honourable Wo! Shall we double our wager in accordance with the onset of the rain? I say it will hold off until the leaders have rounded the last turn. What do you say?'

The Honourable Wo cast his thick forefinger aloft. His tongue came out, getting a taste of the wind. '*Eeee*, in this you are wrong as well, Honourable Soong! All gods bear witness, I'll take your side wager.'

T. Y. Chung laughed silently to hear these men so frantically involved. They are like children, he thought mockingly, playing at *fan tan* or dice. I have more important places to put my money. Only the prospect of a good wager and the exhilaration of a fine race, he knew, could bring so many rivals together. The harbour waters took the bad blood and washed it away for as long as they all stood upon these decks. That, and the fact that these men all fear me. All save Bluestone, I think. The *gwai loh* is powerful, though not, perhaps, quite as powerful as he believes.

'*Ayaa!* They're off!'

'And the wind is coming on! Now it is in the leaders' faces!'

'The boats in the second tier are gaining! Fornicate all *gwai loh*! Look!'

T. Y. Chung's Dragon Boat had got off to a poor start. But the driving wind was slowing the craft ahead of it. Now T. Y. Chung's craft was passing that of Clubfoot Su. It was just behind and alee of Three Oaths Tsun's. The race was already half over; it should be making its move.

'Look how it lies there! It cannot make any headway on Honourable Tsun's boat!'

'Defecation and piddle!' Soong exclaimed. 'He is not full out! He hides from the wind! As the Honourable Tsun's shadow, he is protected!'

'Yes! Yes!' cried the others excitedly. 'By all the gods, he's right!' They were clustered at the rail, gesticulating and sweating profusely.

The sky had turned a dense slate grey and they could all feel the warm wind on their faces. The pressure was dropping fast, and a dankness had come into the air.

Three Oaths Tsun's and T. Y. Chung's boats were sweeping around the last turn, the other Dragon craft not far behind. At that moment they all felt the first spatters of fat drops of rain.

'*Ayeeya!*' Soong called. 'The gods have favoured me!'

Now the Dragon Boats were nearing the finish line. The men aboard the *Loong wang* could see the straining backs of the oarsmen, wet with sweat and rain. Fireworks were crackling, building as the race shot to its close.

T. Y. Chung remained beside Sir John Bluestone, content to drink his beer and speak in low tones as if he had not a care in the world or, as Wo said quietly to Soong, 'As if he already knows the outcome of the race.'

'If Honourable Chung's boat does not make its move –'

'But it is! Now!'

365

They could all see it clearly, though just beyond the skyline was a purple-black bruise as the heavy rains swept down across Victoria Peak.

'*Dew neh loh moh!* The fornicating storm will destroy the very end of the race!'

'One thousand says it doesn't!'

Now it could be seen that the beater in Three Oaths Tsun's Dragon Boat had picked up the pace considerably. It was impossible to hear anything but the barking fireworks and the increasingly frenzied shouts of the betters.

T. Y. Chung's craft began its final spurt. With powerful unison work, the fifty closed the distance until they were nose to nose, the two flamboyantly painted dragons' heads duelling into the voracious forefront of the whirling storm.

The rain hit them all like a green-grey wall. The Island slipped away from them, and for a time they were isolated from the rest of the world. Even the black junks in the harbour had become merely a dark grey mass, their bulk turned into the horizon.

Still the men did not seek shelter but rather bent over the railing, their hands above their eyes as they strained to be the first to announce the winning vessel.

'Who?'

'Which has won? The Honourable Tsun or the Honourable Chung?'

'Fornicate all bad weather and all those who forecast all weather! I cannot tell!'

'It is T. Y. Chung!' came a shout from out of the steady drumming of the downpour. 'T. Y. Chung by a fornicating whisker! An oar on Honourable Tsun's boat broke at the last minute!'

'Praise all gods forever!' Soong shouted. 'Today I am doubly blessed!'

Not as blessed as I am, T. Y. Chung thought triumphantly. *Hsun-feng Teh-li*, 'temper the winds and gain profits.' Mentally he rubbed his hands together.

The downpour had lessened and their world was again reappearing. The Dragon Boats in the water rode the choppy waves listlessly, the oarsmen slumped over their seats while the rain pummelled their bare heads.

Firecrackers were exploding with renewed intensity, forming a flickering, smoky glow through the steaming rain. Champagne was being served all around, and the banker, Soong, flushed with his good fortune, lifted his glass. 'To T. Y. Chung, master of the Dragon Boat races for the second straight year!'

There were cheers all around while the day grew fuzzy with rain and drifting smoke from the fireworks.

In a moment Sir John Bluestone found a lull and eased T. Y. Chung out of the knot of businessmen.

'Was it merely your good *joss* that won your boat race today?'

T. Y. Chung shrugged, squinting up at the tall *tai pan*. 'What else but *joss*?'

'Last year a boat swerved into the leader's lane; this year an oar on the leader's boat cracked. Both incidents occurred near the finish line. In both instances your boat benefited.'

'In many cases, *joss* is seizing opportunity by the throat,' T. Y. Chung said calmly.

'And when there is no vulnerable area available?'

T. Y. Chung brushed lint from his superb suit. 'One must, Mr Bluestone – how shall I say it? – create that which a throat would otherwise provide.'

They were both being careful – testing the waters, as it were. That was only right and proper when one began a new business alliance.

He's brought all these *tai pan* here to lord it over them, Bluestone thought, looking into T. Y. Chung's eyes. He's gained great face by doing so, especially with me here. Serving me notice. His power is on display for me to review as if I were in an art gallery. But is it all of his power? That is what I must find out.

'Did you make money this afternoon?' Bluestone asked in his most careful tone of voice.

'How so?' T. Y. Chung had a quizzical look on his face that could be hiding anything. 'You know that principals in the race cannot bet.'

Bluestone smiled. 'Just conjecture on my part. I thought you might have been "creating" again.'

'Do you think I would concern myself with such a paltry sum?' His face had darkened appreciably, and Bluestone noted this.

'Why, then?' Feeling for the nerve he saw coming into the light.

'To win, Mr Bluestone.' There was anger written across T. Y. Chung's face. 'To ensure that Three Oaths Tsun gains no face on such an important occasion. This face I can take into business. It is worth bullion. It – ' He was about to go on, enraptured by his rage, when he caught himself. He shrugged. 'Face is face.'

But Bluestone knew that was not what he had meant to say at all. The light in T. Y. Chung's eyes had meant, 'It is worth everything.' Now Bluestone had to ask himself why.

The answer, he thought, is Tsun. It must be. But what happened between the two to feed the hatred so? And how can I use that enmity in the weeks to come?

When Kamisaka opened the door to his knock, she gasped to see him. 'Buddha!' she cried, clutching him to her. 'You look like you've just returned from the land of the *kami*!'

Nichiren knew that it had been a mistake to come here. Yet he had come anyway. He would have been much better off travelling across town to the Kisan family villa. His mind knew that, but his heart felt something different.

He had shied away from the Kisan compound because

368

he did not feel safe there. Here in the tiny *usagigoya*, amid the eternal bustle of Tokyo, he felt a semblance of peace returning to him.

Ever since the attack at his lodge atop the Sword, he had felt periods of despair engulfing him. During the execution of Gerard Stallings it had come to a climax. He should have felt some satisfaction in destroying the man who had murdered Mariana Maroc, but he had not. Instead, within the depths of his mind, he was preoccupied with Mariana herself, spinning like a top, set in hideous motion by the high-powered bullets. He could feel the spatter of her blood like hot brands across his face. He felt himself scrambling over the muddy earth in desperate search of her, his determination to reach her.

At the very edge of the world, he reached out, certain that he could pull her back to safety. But she had instead pushed the *fu* shard into his hand. Why? And why did he now possess a second piece of the same *fu*, linking him to Jake Maroc?

But he knew that the two of them had been linked long before this. From the moment he had found his mother's diaries among her personal effects and read them, incomplete though they were, he had known that he and Jake Maroc must be mortal enemies as their mothers had been before them.

It was Jake's mother who, in trying to take Nichiren's father away, had beaten Yumiko senseless and then used a white-hot poker to brand into her flesh for all time a reminder of barbarian cruelty.

Had not that moment blossomed into fruition at the Sumchun River?

But now the *fu*: source of immeasurable power. Jake had a piece, now he had one. From the same source. Who? Yumiko? Had Jake's mother stolen a piece of Yumiko's *fu* during the attack? But how would Yumiko, a Japanese, come to have a *fu*?

Just as importantly, whose power did it represent? Jake Maroc's Source? Then why did he, Nichiren, also have a piece? Their Sources were poles apart.

These were questions he had put to his Source after relating the incident atop Tsurugi.

'You are the future,' Source said. 'Can you accept that?'

'I can accept anything but what the two pieces of jade seem to indicate.'

'Which is?'

'I want no part of Jake Maroc. I suspect that the *fu* shard I unearthed did not come from my mother at all. I suspect that you somehow planted it. This has been your idea all along, to somehow link me with Jake Maroc.'

'If that is to be – '

'No!' He had fairly yelled it through the overseas line. 'I will not have it!'

'You have no choice in the matter.' Source's voice was calm, almost emotionless. 'First, the *fu* shard was your mother's. Second, you are under discipline. Did you think I began to lead you away from the future your mother planned for you in an aimless manner? That is not my way. There is a reason for all action, a role for each individual to play.'

'But this is too much,' Nichiren had said, Mariana falling through the spaces of his mind, tumbling, bloodied, her blood still on his face and shoulder. The look in her eyes. 'You cannot play the god with people in this way. This manipulation – whatever it is – is far too vast in scope. It cannot hope to succeed.'

'For all our sakes,' Source had said, 'you had better pray to whatever form of the Buddha touches you that it *does* work. Otherwise, destruction will engulf us all.'

'From what quarter?'

'From what quarter will it not? America, Russia, China, they will all be caught up in it. The entire world.'

'What has all this to do with me, and with Jake Maroc?'

370

'When you meet, all will be made known to you.'

'We've already met,' Nichiren had said, 'a number of times. Only death has been the result.'

'The *fu* will change all that. It will bind you together. It will provide you with life. Have faith.'

He wanted to say: But I do not believe in Buddha. I have no faith, therefore I cannot believe you. Instead, he had been silent.

Thoughts chased themselves like golden fish amid bewildering coral shoals. Exhausted, he accepted Kamisaka's gift and fell into her open arms, staggering them both. She kicked the door closed and on *tabi*-clad feet led him into the minuscule living room.

With some difficulty she leaned down and threw her text books off the *futon* that had been folded into the shape of a sofa. Together they collapsed upon it.

She made a move to leave, but he clung to her.

'Tea.'

'No,' he mumbled, his face buried in her shoulder. 'Not now. Don't leave.'

Kamisaka felt worried and elated at the same time. She lifted her hand to stroke the back of his head as she had seen her mother do with her younger brothers. Her heart constricted to see his obvious pain, but her emotions soared to know that he had come back to her. That he needed her. She knew there were other sanctuaries to which he could run. He had come here. To her. 'Nichiren-*chan*,' she whispered. She kissed the side of his head. She held him close. What had happened to him? His world was a mystery to her. She read the papers; she had heard of the assassin named Nichiren. But she could not relate that creature of the outside world and the media to this man whom she loved with all her heart and soul.

But now, for the first time, seeing him in this state, she found herself wanting to know – to know everything. She wanted to understand what could cause such anguish in a human being. Now she wanted to know what he did. She wanted to know why.

And at last she knew that only by understanding the core of him could she stop him from leaving her again. Would he kill someone when he left? She did not know or care. His leaving was what mattered most to her.

She understood that her ignorance of this part of him had been deliberate. With a child's stubbornness, she had not wanted to face the darker parts of him. Once she could have accepted their relationship – this partial happiness.

Now she could not. She realized that she had grown up in the last six months. Sometime when she had not been looking, she had become a woman. Nichiren was her responsibility. If she wanted his love, if she wanted a completeness to their relationship, she had to deal with it all. And she sensed that it would somehow also be better for him.

But how to go about it?

She knelt on the wooden floor beside his body. She wore only a light cotton day kimono, beneath which was a thin silk under-kimono. Though she most often wore Western clothes in the street, she much preferred the comfort and freedom that traditional Japanese garb afforded her at home.

She knew there was nothing she could tell him that would ease the pain or make him speak. Therefore, there was nothing to say.

Now into her mind came a *haiku* her mother had turned into a kind of lullaby when she was a child: *Yari tatete/toru hito nashi/hana-susuki*. Of those who pass/with spears erect, there are none./Plumes of pampas grass.

All through childhood, that peculiar litany of words had followed her down into sleep. She had never truly understood the meaning of the lullaby, she had merely been cradled by the confluence of Shiki's poetry and her mother's homespun melody.

Years later, however, at a small Tokyo museum, she had come upon a woodblock print of Ando Hiroshige's depicting a procession of a *daimyo*'s retainers toward one of the Fifty-three Stations of the Tokaido, one of the two main thoroughfares that had linked Edo to the provinces of Japan in the days of the Tokugawa Shogunate.

In this scene she saw reborn Shiki's poem and immediately understood its meaning. Instead of the *daimyo*'s *samurai* passing in regal array, today only the pampas grass grew, its stately plumes taking the place of the soldiers' spears.

Now that same poem made her think of Nichiren, and she suspected that Shiki had been wrong, despite the sad beauty of his thought. For here before her was a *samurai* from the days of the Tokugawa Shogunate. Perhaps he was the last one; perhaps he did not even understand what an anachronism he was. Perhaps he needed to know.

Still, there was nothing to say.

Through the open window she could hear the sounds of modern-day Tokyo: the susurrus of rushing traffic, the waxing and waning of the klaxons of emergency vehicles. The neon glow of the Tokyo night infused the *usagigoya* with an opalescent mixture of pink and blue, tinting the walls and ceiling, her cheek, his hair. An electric fan whirred like a nocturnal insect. Outside, in the hall, the click of shoes, a brief splash of conversation, then a door slamming shut.

Silence.

Though Tokyo was all around her, Kamisaka made herself shed her modern day self and enter into the world of the past. In Edo there was only flowing, patterned silk, meticulously coiffed hair, and the precise manners of a *samurai* lady with the pliancy of a courtesan on the outside, the fearful shades of steel on the inside.

A stillness had crept into the room, dispelling the cacophony from outside in the stone-and-glass night. There was a sense of *ma*, of space, a pause.

And because there was nothing to say, Kamisaka injected into this interval the only thing she could.

She reached out across the space between them, lit by the ghostly reflections from the neons, and touched him. It was a gesture of such infinite tenderness and caring that Nichiren, even though his eyes were closed and his face turned away from her, could not fail to understand its nature.

Slowly he turned over on the *futon* until his eyes found hers. She had not taken her hand from his hip. This connection spoke like the greatest shout in the silent room. It possessed a depth unknowable in voice communication.

Kamisaka was stunned to see that he had been crying and that, furthermore, her touch had caused him to reveal this to her. That acceptance of her melted her heart. Tears welled up in her eyes, but with an act of will she forced them back. It would not do at all to show him his naked emotion reflected back at him. He would construe that as a sign of weakness in her and a mark of shame within himself.

She wished to speak now, but seemed incapable of breaking this fragile *ma* that enveloped them both in its shell. She felt that just by her touch she had drawn much of his agony out.

'If I came back here,' he whispered, 'it was for a purpose.' He closed his eyes to better feel the strength of her flowing into his hip from her palm, fingers, nails. 'Someone died in the mountains. High up. The weather was bad. There was rain. There was blood.' His voice was breathy and thin, as if he were talking in his sleep. 'She spun away from me. Her blood flew at me like rage. For just a moment we were connected by that essence of her. Then she was gone into the storm.

'The ground had been weakened by the rain. A mudslide began, taking us both down. I grabbed at the bole of a

374

tree. I wanted to save her, too.' His eyes were squeezed shut. 'I wanted to save her, too.'

Now all Kamisaka could do was rock him as her mother had done to her when she was a child.

'*Yari tatete*,' she sang to him. '*Toru hito nashi*.' Her voice almost broke before the end. '*Hana-susuki*.'

Jake awoke with his head full of glass shards. He had been dreaming of Mariana. He had been in a room filled with a sourceless light. He was naked. It was cold in the room, obliging him to keep moving even when he became exhausted. Ceiling, floor, and three walls of the room were a featureless slate grey.

One wall was a thick slab of glass. On the other side of it was Mariana. He saw her moving around their apartment quite naturally. She arose from bed, relieved herself, washed, brushed her hair, dressed. She sat at the wood refectory table in their living room and wrote letters. She fixed herself breakfast, read *Through the Looking Glass* in her favourite easy chair, stared out of the window. She appeared to be waiting for something.

After a time Jake became aware that she was waiting for him.

He moved until his nose was flattened by the glass barrier. He spoke to her. His own voice echoed back at him as if he were in a tunnel. The reverberations picked up speed, clashing noisily against one another.

Mariana ignored him.

'I'm right here!' He shouted until he was hoarse. And woke up with a head full of glass shards. His throat felt sore.

He groaned, remembering his drink with Mikio Komoto. There was a discreet knock on the *fusuma*. He rolled off the *futon* and said, 'Come in, I'm up.'

The sliding door opened and the *oyabun* came across the threshold. He was shaved, dressed in lightweight slacks and short-sleeved cotton shirt. His *tabi*-clad feet made no sound on the reed mats.

He grinned. 'You call this "up"?'

'Ugh!' Jake said.

Komoto held out a glass full of a liquid the colour of ox-blood.

'What is that?' Jake took it, sniffing.

'If you have any respect for your body, you'll drink it down.' He nodded. 'That's it. All in one swallow. It's the only way.' He laughed as Jake almost gagged on the thick, fiery stuff. Jake's nose began to run. 'Clears the sinuses, too,' Komoto said, taking the glass back. 'I'll meet you in twenty minutes. Toshi-*san* will show you to the bath.'

In the space of that time Jake felt, if not perfect, then at least halfway human. The short-sleeved shirt that had been left for him fitted fairly well, but he was a bit too tall for the Japanese-made trousers.

It made him sad, this defect, a reopening of the wound his dream had made in him. Mariana dying on the Sword. Japan. He thought that he hated this country now, and that, too, saddened him.

They ate an abstemious breakfast of rice cakes and tea. Neither felt inclined to put more in his stomach at this hour.

'Where are we going?' he asked Komoto as they went across the garden.

'It is important, I have found, to leaven one's life.' Komoto opened a car door and they got in. He started the engine. 'Knotty problems are often solved in the most creative atmospheres. I am tired of the gloom of my house and our weighty talk. So' – he pulled out into the street – 'we will have some fun.'

Mikio Komoto's idea of fun, Jake soon discovered, was to play *pachinko*. They went down to the Ginza, losing themselves in the crowds and the enormous neon signs.

376

Colour ran rampant, flowing across the street, sidewalks, building façades, climbing even into the sky.

Together they stood before the chrome-and-glass doors of a *pachinko* parlour. As a teenager, in Tokyo for his secondary schooling, Jake had been taken with them, playing the steel-bearing balls that click-clack-clicked down the vertical glass-encased field of play as they bounced off strategically placed metal nails.

One bought a handful of balls and, using a lever, snapped – this was the derivation of the word *pachinko* – them one by one up into the playing field. The object was to win balls, which one would then trade in for various prizes.

Jake had never won anything, but that had not stopped him from playing for hours on end, fascinated by the garish colours, the blinking lights and whizzing buzzers, the strident bells and electronic tickering that were part and parcel of the game.

For Jake, it had a particularly poignant quality. He had been playing *pachinko* all one bleak winter afternoon. He had cut classes, as he seemed to do more and more as the term wore on. Restless and lonely, he gave himself up to the game, seeing in this mindless symphony a form of release different from the one he found at the martial arts *dōjō*.

That afternoon was filled with light as heavy and metallic as zinc. He trudged home through a layer of frosty snow. On campus, he found the telegram waiting for him like an adder on his bed. He ripped it open to find that the Marocs had been in an automobile accident. A head-on collision with a drunk driver had killed them instantly.

Now I have nothing, Jake thought. Reflexively, his hand gripped the chamois pouch. Only his piece of the *fu* remained: the last link to his personal history. Though the Marocs had instilled in him a sense of his past, of his mother and what little they knew of his father, it was not enough to sustain him now.

The school term was only half over, but Jake packed up what few belongings he had and flew back to Hong Kong the next day. He had no more interest in classes of any kind.

But it had been three long years since he had been back in the Colony for any length of time. He had lost touch with what few friends he had. He was utterly alone. The stateless Marocs, having moved through Shanghai, had moved through Hong Kong in the same manner: unobtrusively and alone.

In desperation, Jake, now stateless himself, took to the dangerous Hong Kong streets. There he made new acquaintances, and as he practised the expertise that Fo Saan had so painstakingly taught him, he made more. In time, he even gained something of a reputation.

Which was, of course, how Wunderman had found him.

'*Pachinko* took off the moment it was introduced,' Komoto was explaining now, as they walked through the aisles lined on either side by eager men, women, and youths snapping balls with glassy-eyed concentration. Music as garish as the colours on display blared from loudspeakers.

'Some say that it was created by an industrialist gone bust in the aftermath of the war. There was, of course, no more use for the munitions his factories had produced, so the story goes, and he was left with a stockpile of thousands of cases of steel ball bearings.'

Komoto laughed. 'In truth, I cannot say if this was so. In any event, *pachinko* was just what we needed after the war. The colours and the sounds lifted us away from the years of drabness and sorrow. The entertainment was cheap and addicting. It absorbed the excess time on our hands.'

They paused to watch an old lady feverishly snapping her lever. The lower half of her face was covered with a

378

breathing mask, indicating that she had the good manners not to want to spread her cold.

'In the old days,' Komoto said, 'the *yakuza* clans, mine included, fought bitterly over *pachinko* territories.'

He took up station beside the old woman, drew out a ball. He began to play, but not in any manner Jake had ever seen before. First he grasped the machine and shook it, as if getting the feel of its weight. Next he took a long, hard look at the set of the nails on the playing field. He adjusted the lever. Then, placing the ball against it, he snapped it. The ball flashed upward, then, encountering the first nail, bounced from one to another. Lights flashed, bells rang. Komoto won an entire slide of balls.

He produced another ball, played it with the same result. Jake watched in fascination. Finally he had to ask, 'How do you do it?'

Komoto was pleased that he had entertained his guest. 'When I was a boy, I went to all the parlours with my father. He was *oyabun* then. Some of the technicians began to teach me the tricks of the trade. They were known as *kugishi*, nail men. Every night after the parlour closed, they'd go into each machine, set the number of balls inside, realign the nails.' He shrugged. 'In *pachinko*, balance is everything, because offsetting the weight of the machine will affect how the ball in play performs, bouncing from territory to territory.'

Jake thought of Toshima-ku, the territory of contention between the Komoto and Kisan clans. What made it special? Blinking lights, whirring sounds. A bell was ringing somewhere close at hand as someone won a slide of balls.

'Is there anything you can think of,' Jake asked, 'that occurred around the time of my raid on O-henro House? Anything out of the ordinary that might have affected the balance of power within Toshima-ku?'

Komoto thought a moment. 'Only Shizuki's death.'

'Who was he?'

'A high-ranking police inspector. Departmental head of a newly formed anti-organized-crime unit. Very smart cookie. Had good taste, too, from what I'm told. He was all set to marry Police Chief Tanaba's daughter.'

'How did he die?'

'Nothing very interesting, though it was bloody enough. He was pushed by the crowd in the subway at rush hour. A train decapitated him.'

Jake could not see any connection. 'What happened to the unit?'

'Well, now I don't know,' Komoto said. 'Held in abeyance, I suppose. Higira-*san* would have been the next in line for the job. But he died at O-henro House in your raid.'

Jake flushed on scarred, sunken cheeks, black eyes burning as with fever. 'That was a cop?' he said, somewhat incredulously. 'He acted as if he were a friend of Nichiren's.'

'Impossible,' Komoto said.

'But if it's true, then it follows that perhaps Shizuki's death was not accidental.' Jake was staring at the *pachinko* the old lady was playing. The ball bounced and bounced from nail to nail, territory to territory. Something there for him.

'It's a moot point,' Komoto was saying. 'There is no way to know whether it was murder. Not after all this time.'

'Did you see the pictures of the incident in the papers or on TV?' He had found the edge of *ba-mahk*, the pulse. In this state Fo Saan had taught him to concentrate on nothing. He did the opposite of focusing his attention: he allowed it to diffuse to the point where he took in sensory data as impressions, patterns of dark and light, colours and sounds commingled.

The old lady's ball bounced from nail to nail. It reminded him of something. An impression. What?

380

'Sure. I took a great delight in Shizuki's death. That had been a personal score I would have settled myself in time.'

Enlarge the field. Follow *ba-mahk*. Darkness and light, a pattern forming another image in his mind. An image of . . .

'Funny thing, though,' Komoto said, 'that decapitation. They never did find his head.'

. . . the top of a head, thick stiff hair like a brush, the edge of a forehead, the tip of an ear. Stuck in a box on a table. In Kisan's office in O-henro House!

'Buddha!' Jake whispered. His eyes were glazed with the aftermath of *ba-mahk*.

'Jake-*san*, what is it?'

'Shizuki was murdered. I know it. I saw his head inside a hatbox. Kisan, Higira, and Nichiren were grouped around it when I burst in. I got only a flash of it, then all hell broke loose and there was no time to think.'

'What brought it to mind now?'

'*Ba-mahk*,' Jake said. And the pattern of nails in the *pachinko* playing field, the black stippling the same as that of the hair on poor dead Shizuki's head.

'I have had a chance to go over in detail the papers you gave me,' Wu Aiping said.

Zhang Hua nodded. 'And what have you concluded?'

'Actually, I'm elated. For the first time, the *qun* has a real chance of destroying Shi Zilin.'

Above them loomed the two-storey watchtower with its thickly enclosed guardroom below and its lofty observation eyrie above. It was, Wu Aiping thought, a most excellent example of Ming Dynasty military architecture.

He rustled the flimsies, copies of the documents Zhang Hua had delivered to him in the Hong Miao tea shop at their previous rendezvous. On top of the Great Wall, he had no qualms about security.

'I have given up my mistress,' Zhang Hua said, and winced at the senior minister's sardonic laugh.

'And now you are saved, eh, Comrade Minister, is that it?' Wu Aiping shook his head. 'Comrade *lou sin* – the mouse – that is what I shall call you from now on. Oh, you are really quite entertaining. Come, come, you have already made your transgression. The eyes of Buddha, or whoever it is you pray to, have recorded your sin. Recanting now will not save you. Not from me.' He bared his teeth in a kind of horrific grin that made Zhang Hua recoil slightly. '*Lou sin, lou sin,*' Wu Aiping chanted like a bully in a schoolyard.

Humidity gave the atmosphere a cloying heaviness, so that there was a tendency to want to move as little as possible. The sky was vast but without any discernible colour. Heat haze had blanched all blue away, leaving cloud and heavens nearly the same shade of oyster white.

Wu Aiping, who towered over the heavyset junior minister, strolled on. It was Zhang Hua who was sweating, not he. He was rapidly coming to detest this man. Which made his control of him all the more satisfying. Mouse, he thought. I have trapped you. Now I shall slowly crush the life out of you.

It amused him to have arranged this rendezvous here; the irony of this spot appealed to him. It was commonly assumed by uniformed foreign devils that the Great Wall had been built for defensive purposes only. That was not the case. An important function was to provide communication and, since the broad avenue along its top could easily accommodate horse-drawn wagons, the transshipment of food and essential materials to and from outlying regions where the otherwise mountainous terrain would prove inimical to such rapid transit.

'The answer to Shi Zilin's defeat,' Wu Aiping said, 'lies within these documents. You see' – his laugh now was all heartiness and good cheer – 'I was correct in recruiting

you. The patriot's role suits you, though you fight against
it.

'Much of Shi Zilin's plan, his *ren*, has been revealed to
me. This "Mitre", Sir John Bluestone, is his primary funnel
into Hong Kong. The problem seems to trace itself back to
Kam Sang. This concerns me, but I'll come back to that in
a moment.

'It seems clear from the intelligence traffic that the
pullout of Mattias, King and Company has caused a
change in the *ren*. Now fifty per cent of the Western share
of the Kam Sang project is up for grabs. The Pak Hanmin
Company has half. Mattias, King have divested themselves
of the other half – reneged on their commitment at the
worst possible moment, just when we've come to the final
phase.

'It is clear that Shi Zilin has decided to push Five Star
Pacific, his agent's trading firm, into the breach, a double-
edged move. It provides the additional capital needed to
begin the project while keeping more control of it than
would otherwise be possible.'

They continued along their route. They had come as far
as Badaling. They passed beneath an arched gateway
that had obviously been restored but was nonetheless
magnificent. They were heading towards Zhangjiakou,
more commonly known as Kalgan. The name was taken
from the Mongolian *kalgha*, which meant 'pass'.

Wu Aiping went to their left and they ascended a steep
flight of stone steps. Now they were on the very ramparts
of the wall, at a level with the guard tower's eyrie. To the
north they could just make out parts of the newly built
Guan Ting reservoir.

'Of course, that would be how Shi Zilin would see it. It
is essential,' Wu Aiping said, 'that one learns to think like
one's enemy. Crawl inside his head, study his tendencies,
find the pattern. The pattern, *lou-syu*. Everyone has a
pattern, and I'm beginning to discern Shi Zilin's.'

He grunted, leaned against the dusty battlements out of the enervating sunlight. His eyes roamed the horizon, tracking the lines of umber and cerulean that were the demarkation between land and sky. In between was the uniform drab grey of the modern Chinese institutional structures.

'I see the danger here that he does not. This Bluestone may be Shi Zilin's agent, but he is *faan gwai loh*, a foreign devil. He is therefore beyond being unreliable; he is suspect. It occurs to me that he has played along with Shi Zilin just on the chance that has now come his way: to get in on Kam Sang.'

'But he cannot know Kam Sang's secret,' Zhang Hua said.

'I see that you *are* a patriot, after all,' Wu Aiping said judiciously. 'Well, in any case, I share your concern. The Kam Sang project is vital to our future survival. It's been extremely difficult to keep its secret from the *faan gwai loh* investors. We require their money, not their inquisitiveness. Of course, Kam Sang will give them what they want, what Hong Kong needs. But it will also provide us with our mighty sword to cut down the Soviet menace that surrounds us like a malignant growth.'

Wu Aiping waited until a straggle of three or four foreign tourists passed them by, their cameras clicking away like a field of crickets. In the hazy distance he could just make out the rising topography that led to the twin mountains of the Tiger and the Dragon, between which was the great red archway leading to Shi San Ling, wherein the remains of the ranking members of the Ming Dynasty were entombed for all eternity.

'Bluestone's and, I suspect, Shi Zilin's immediate problem is debt. According to the intelligence documents, it seems that Five Star Pacific was caught out hard by the Colony's financial nosedive in 1982. Mitre reminds Shi Zilin in three separate communications of his company's short-term debt load. Now this opportunity comes and Bluestone is concerned with divesting Five Star Pacific of almost all its liquid capital to buy up shares of Pak Hanmin and thus wrest control of that company while buying cheaply into Kam Sang. It could, he pointed out, make Five Star Pacific itself vulnerable. Shi Zilin, ignoring his warnings, has ordered him to go ahead.'

'All well and good,' Zhang Hua said. 'Do nothing and you will be assured that Bluestone cannot stick his nose into Kam Sang. That part, at least, I agree with.'

Wu Aiping shot the other minister the kind of withering look he would give to an underbright bureaucrat. 'Now I know why you never rose above your current level. I don't want to destroy Five Star Pacific; I want to destroy Shi Zilin. Five Star Pacific is obviously the key to his *ren*. It is his way into the Kam Sang project. *My* project. I know he opposes our clandestine use of Kam Sang. Through this trading company he expects to get close enough to Kam Sang to sabotage my part of it. So I want Five Star Pacific left alone. I want him tied into the *faan gwai loh* trading company so deeply that it will be impossible for him to extricate himself.'

In a moment, he laughed. 'Oh, yes. I do believe I have found our solution. We will trap Shi Zilin inside his own company!'

'I don't understand.'

'Of course you don't,' Wu Aiping said, so bitingly that Zhang Hua winced again. 'But if you think that I am stupid enough to explain it to you, think again. I want to make absolutely certain Shi Zilin is caught unprepared. I will take no chances now.'

He was figuring furiously. What he had not told Zhang Hua was that he had already called upon the other members of the *qun* to research the names of the banks and lending companies that were holding Five Star Pacific's short-term notes. There were an astounding number of them. Though, on the surface of it, the trading company appeared to be in good shape, it was overloaded with five- and ten-year notes.

Now the *qun* would, in secret, through a dummy company they had dubbed Yau Sin-Kyuhn Services, H. K., buy up those notes one by one. It would take millions, he knew. None of the members individually could come up with the money. They all needed to borrow from their ministry funds and, in Wu Aiping's own case, the Science Institute's government research allocation. The risks were great, but the reward would undoubtedly be greater. Then, Wu Aiping thought, when he makes his move against Kam Sang, I will expose Shi Zilin as the traitor he is *and* control Five Star Pacific all in one breath.

Coming down off the Great Wall with Zhang Hua, the *lou sin*, by his side, he laughed. 'Enjoy these days, Shi Zilin,' he said to the heavens. 'They will surely be your last.'

Mikio Komoto caught up with Jake at the *yatai*, the nighttime food vendor near the Kannon Temple in Asakusa, Tokyo's old quarter. Kannon, the Goddess of Mercy, attracted tourists as well as adherents day and night. The park out front was always filled with young and old.

It was just dusk. Shoppers were hurrying home to their dinners, children were being swept up by their parents after having played in the open air all afternoon, the old folk were still engrossed in the idle gossip that fuelled their days while they observed the several *go* games which had slowly developed through the afternoon.

The haze, an incongruous confluence of water particles and exhaust fumes, had turned sapphire with the lowering of the light. The dark, sweeping lines of the temple itself lent the scene a heavy, brooding quality.

At the *yatai*'s mobile cart, travellers, weary from the day, sat at the small wooden pull-out table. Into its copper recesses were doled Chinese or Japanese noodles, pungent barbecued chicken, or – what Jake was eating – *oden*. This last was a savoury stew consisting of a delicious broth filled with an assortment of vegetables, boiled eggs, seaweed, fried bean-curd cakes, a variety of thick fish pastes, and a dab of fresh, bitingly hot mustard.

Mikio pulled up a stool and ordered the *oden*. There was a great deal of talk all around them. As was often the case in Japan, the normally reticent citizen was eagerly rabbiting on to the stranger sitting next to him, revealing secrets about himself that he dared not even tell his wife.

'What have you found?'

'Nothing,' Jake said morosely. He added a bit more mustard, took a pair of cheap plastic chopsticks from the vendor, and began to dig in hungrily. He had left Komoto outside the *pachinko* parlour, heading into the Roppongi district after making a call to the weasel-faced Japanese he had met in the public baths. But three hours spent in grilling him had turned up nothing. He stirred the remains of his *oden*. 'That leaves us back at square one.'

'Not quite, Jake-*san*.' Komoto was eating like lightning, his bowl tipped just beneath his lips. 'I have been as busy as you. Like a firefly, I have been darting from flower to flower, picking up tidbits. Just before I arrived here, I gathered in a most interesting one. It's possible that Shizuki-*san* had a rival for the affections of Chief Tanaba's daughter.'

Several stools down, a patron who had been drinking *sakē* with his bowlful of noodles since before Jake had arrived began to sing a melancholy melody. He had a pleasing tenor voice, and he obviously knew how to sing. Perhaps once he had been a professional. His drunkenness did not stop him from staying on key.

As the song unwound sinuously, it reminded Jake of the night of the raid on O-henro House. The green world, the heavily dripping foliage, the smears of neon caught in the wet pavement of the street. He felt an enormous wave of sorrow welling up in him at all he had lost since that terrible night.

He looked away from the singer, as if that would also put his song aside. 'How did you come by that?'

Komoto shrugged. 'I have some small real-estate interests about town. A landlord who works for me remembers the girl because she's got a *usagigoya* in one of his newest buildings. One I put up, by the way. He's sure she doesn't spend all her time alone in the apartment. But the interesting thing is he's never seen Shizuki-*san*. I showed him a snapshot. He was certain. The man he described was of another physical type entirely.'

Jake thought about Shizuki-*san* being pushed off the crowded platform, the terror as the onrushing train lit up the tunnel with blinding light. He thought of that bristly hair, the gentle curve of the ear lying in the hatbox on the lacquer table. The three of them around it as he burst in, the *irezumi* men on his tail: Kisan, Higira, and . . .

'Did you show that landlord another snapshot?' Jake asked.

Komoto grinned, holding up the black-and-white photo. Head and shoulders, in Jake's memory for all time, smouldering there.

Nichiren.

Daniella discovered she was being followed the moment she went out of the office into the street. Across from her was the Square, mothers taking their children by the hand or allowing them to run after the pigeons beneath the low, watery sun. An almost pastoral scene in the heart of Moscow.

As Daniella moved, a car moved. It was almost dinnertime and the streets were clogged with traffic, much of it official in this area. Everything was regulated by the lights,

so it was easy for her to spot the anomaly. She w
at that. Someone wanting her to know she wa
watched?

Instead of walking away, she approached the car,
model Volga sedan. She got a good look at the dr
sandy-haired thug. She'd seen the type before, living a
them now and almost all her life.

She stopped before his rolled-down window and pu
hard face on. That was not difficult; she did not like b
followed. She was obliged to lean down slightly, movin
avoid the sun-glare spinning off the hood.

'Who are you?'

The sandy-haired man glanced her way as if only no
focusing on her. 'Get in.'

Daniella bridled at the tone. 'Which department do you
work for?'

'None,' he said.

He reached behind him, opened the rear door on her
side. 'Please get in, Comrade General. I have been sent to
fetch you.'

'By whom?' But she got in anyway, intrigued.

'It is not such a long drive,' he said in an odd, friendly
voice. He spoke to her familiarly, as if passing the time of
day in the same manner as they had done for months or
end.

He switched into the Chaika lane and they picked
speed. Daniella was careful to watch where they w
going. They went through the heart of the city, the sa
haired man driving well. They hit the highway, the M
River glittering in the twilight and the reflected lig
the new residential towers along its far bank.

The sandy-haired man turned the Volga off the F
skaya Embankment, crossing the river over one of
stained bridges. Behind them was Gorky Park.

They hit the highway doing better than on
k.p.h., outrunning the lightening traffic by a go

t seemed they were heading into the countryside as they progressed this way for more than fifteen minutes.

From time to time, Daniella caught the driver glancing into the rearview mirror. Still, she was unprepared for his sudden turnoff. He slid them over three lanes within the space of sixty metres, cutting off a blue Zaz in the process, hearing the squeal of brakes and, almost simultaneously, the blaring of a horn, dopplering quickly away as they took the S-curve of the off-ramp at almost the same speed.

Dark trees rushing by, then abruptly braking, a sharp turn to the left, and they were back on the highway, heading into the city.

Lights of Moscow creating the horizon, bright and lemon-rich, the deep dusky sky behind them, reaching down to purple as the haze tinged it.

The sandy-haired driver turned them away from the Moskva soon after they recrossed the river, this time using another bridge. Heading north through the city, staying away from the larger arteries; no Chaika lanes here, few official eyes.

'Who was on our tail?' Daniella asked.

The sandy-haired man glanced at her in the rearview mirror, shrugged. 'Perhaps no one,' he said in his laconic manner. 'Precautions are mandatory.'

She recognized these streets. They led to Red Square. Soon he turned off, paralleling them until they were just north of the Square. At Kutuzov Prospekt he turned east, slowing now, cruising down a street lined on either side by orange brick and grey stone private houses, well maintained, though they all dated back to the middle of the 19th century or earlier.

Stopped in front of one and got out. He opened the door or her, bowing just as if he were a uniformed chauffeur.

'Up the steps, Comrade General,' he said in his friendly ice. 'If you would be so kind.'

Daniella looked at him a moment, then turned and went

390

up the stone steps. Warm light, muted behind translucent curtains, bathed the stoop. She felt very naked on the landing. The door opened before she could ring the bell, and she saw his tall, lean frame, his long, handsome face. She watched his light eyes, so curious in his otherwise dark, saturnine countenance. She wondered what was beneath his surface coolness.

'Comrade Lantin,' she said. 'You have an odd way of issuing invitations.'

'Come in,' he said, stepping back a pace and closing the door behind her. He turned down the hallway, forcing her to follow after him in order to hear. 'Are you hungry? I hope so. I've been preparing *blini*.'

He took her into a surprisingly large, bright, spotless kitchen, obviously custom-built with its imported Vulcan stove, marble-topped workspace, stainless steel commercial refrigerator-freezer. Copper pots hung from wire racks chained to the ceiling. He resumed his work, turning his back on her again. He wore lightweight wool slacks that had been tailored in Europe, a newly pressed cotton shirt, and black polished loafers without socks.

'You look quite decadent, Comrade,' Daniella said somewhat archly. She was annoyed at having been pulled so mysteriously from pillar to post.

Lantin was laughing, and she was surprised at how open his face looked at that moment. Almost like a little boy's, save for the pencil moustache.

'Yuri,' he said. 'Yuri and Daniella. There are no "Comrades" here inside these walls.'

When she made no reply, he decreased the heat on the stove burner and turned around. 'What is the matter?'

Daniella looked around the room. She peered into corners, behind cabinet doors.

'Are you looking for this?' Lantin took a portable tape recorder from a hidden drawer in the centre island. He handed it to her. 'As you can see, it's not on.'

Daniella examined it carefully. She took out the cassette and placed it on the countertop, handing him back the instrument. 'Where is the camera?' she asked

Blank-faced, Lantin pointed. Daniella followed his direction, discovered the video lens behind a mirror that had been altered to allow the picture-taking. She followed the cord down, underneath the sink to the videotape recorder.

She bent down, removed the cassette from that as well. She placed it beside the audio cassette.

'That wasn't necessary,' Lantin said. 'The thing's not working.'

'I'm not surprised,' Daniella said. 'All that moisture's very bad for the works. You'd best move it.'

They stared at one another for a time. When Lantin smelled the butter beginning to brown, he turned back to the stove. 'I have no intention of recording this conversation,' he said. 'You are too suspicious.'

'There's no such thing,' she said, peering over his shoulder. His hands moved deftly, kneading the *blini* dough. 'Where did you learn to do that?'

'My mother,' he said, adding a few drops of cold water. 'I have a Cuisinart somewhere, but for *blini* there's really no comparison. One must use one's hands.'

They ate at the small wrought-iron table in the kitchen, as informally as husband and wife. The meal, however, was anything but ordinary: buckwheat *blini* filled with Beluga caviar, drizzled with clarified butter; iced vodka, spiked with buffalo grass. To Daniella, it had the aspect of a celebratory feast. On the other hand, it brought to mind an article she had read about American women, who, it was purported, began their seduction of a man by serving him his favourite food.

Her own body, and the effect it had on most men, was never far from her mind. How could it be otherwise? She was a supreme pragmatist. Early in life she had recognized her assets and had determined to use everything in her arsenal to climb the difficult Soviet bureaucratic ladder.

Daniella was no whore. Rather, she had determined to use sex as the bright men around her used power. They, she found, connived with their wits. Since they were unwilling to believe she could compete with them in that manner, she used what she had to get to a point where she could whisper in their ears.

It had worked with Karpov; it had worked with Colonel Valentinin and Lieutenant Tolkchin before him. It might work with Yuri Lantin as well, but she was acutely aware of the different arena in which she now found herself. This was, after all, what she had been striving towards. But the danger – that, too, confronted her.

'You must congratulate me,' Lantin said when they were through. He had brewed them thick, black Turkish coffee, the kind Daniella loved best. Coincidence, or had he ferreted that out? 'Our robot war against China is going splendidly.'

'You mean the Vietnamese clash along the Yunnan Province frontier?'

Lantin nodded. 'Just this morning the New China News Agency issued a further warning against what it terms "these armed provocations", and indicated that the army command was deploying thirty more divisions along the border.'

'This is your doing, I take it?'

'Karpov will say it is his, but yes, it is my idea. Just as it was my idea to send a Department S team into Japan to terminate Nichiren.'

Daniella felt as if she were about to gag. The rich food threatened to rise back up into her throat. Through the heavy beating of her heart, she said, 'You ordered me to send in a KVR team to observe and record Nichiren's movements.' She was desperately trying to regain her equilibrium. 'Does Karpov know what you've done?'

'Karpov is – how do they say it in the West? – part of my hip pocket. He's in there with the lining, the lint, and a couple of kopeks.' He smiled at her. 'Drink your coffee, Daniella, it really is quite good.' He poured himself another cup. The clock on the mantel in the living room ticked stertorously, like an old man ill with asthma.

'So you walked in and took over one of my teams,' she said after a time.

He shook his head. 'I merely had them reprogrammed.'

'Usurped my authority, diddled with the chain of command.'

'Rearranged their objective.'

She saw that he enjoyed this kind of dialogue. 'They're all dead,' she said in a tone that assured him where she was placing the guilt.

'Yes, well.' He thought a moment. 'I hadn't counted on the intervention of the American agent.'

'Jake Maroc.'

'That's the one.' He looked out of the window, into the night. 'I wonder what he was doing there.'

Daniella did not rise to that one. Instead she said, 'The affairs of my department are my own.'

He might have been waiting for her to say that – even, perhaps, baiting her. He took an object from beneath the table and placed it squarely between them. 'This, too, is the affair of your department, I take it.'

Daniella willed herself not to stare. Holy Mother of God, she thought. He's found the Medea book.

Peter Ng waited in the vast, almost baronial foyer of Andrew Sawyer's house in the mountains above Shek-O Beach. The place was done up in flamboyant American style: furniture in old oak, great knotty-pine sideboards, paintings on two of the walls. One depicted Andrew Sawyer's grandfather, Daniel Martin Sawyer, in hunting gear. Behind him were the verdant, rolling hills of his beloved Virginia. Across the two-storey foyer hung a painting of Andrew Sawyer's father, Barton. He was also in hunting gear. Behind him were Victoria Harbour and the Kowloon settlement of seventy years before.

Ng knew well that hanging in the inner study was a painting of Andrew. Though he was not in hunting gear, he had chosen to have Victoria Peak in the background, keeping at least one-half of the tradition alive.

Though Ng had much to discuss with Sawyer, he was stuck here in the cool dimness of the anteroom, waiting. In time he heard the sound of a car pulling up the gravel drive. He left his chair.

When he opened the door inward, he was prepared, already bowing.

'Excellent evening,' he said in his best obsequious tone.

'An excellent evening to you, Younger Nephew.'

A tiny Chinese in baggy pants and a suit jacket seemingly three sizes too big for him walked with him over the Oriental runner. With bright, inquisitive eyes, he squinted up at the stuffed bison's head on the wall above the doorway to Andrew Sawyer's study.

'Is this another unfathomable *gwai loh* tradition?'

'You mean the bison, Elder Uncle?' This was a term used outside the family as well as inside when an older and a younger man who knew each other well spoke. Here, however, it was literal as well as figurative. The two were nephew and uncle. 'It is an animal native to the Golden Mountain. The Honourable Sawyer's father shot it when he was but a boy. He brought this trophy here with him when he sailed here nearly one hundred years ago.'

'A trophy.' On Venerable Chen's lips, the word had an obscene tinge.

'A rite of manhood, it is said,' Ng went on. 'Such rites are common to all peoples of the world, *heya*?'

Venerable Chen lowered his button eyes to Peter Ng. 'Foreign devils are foreign devils, *heya*, Younger Nephew?

They still hoard their money in a bank; they have minds like animals. But we need them, we need them.' Again his gaze rose to the shaggy head on the wall. 'But never forget that that is how they view us. Just like trophies to hang in their boardrooms.

'Tell me, Younger Nephew, if they exploit us, should we merely bow our heads and murmur *joss*? Should we give up life with a callow sigh?' His eyes burned. 'You are Chinese, never forget that.'

'I am Shanghainese,' Ng said, 'just as you are. But what about the Cantonese? The Chiu-chow? The – '

But there was no point in going on. Venerable Chen had already delivered his answer by spitting into the corner.

'That is why we have been exploited, Elder Uncle. Because we are not united. If Chinese stood with Chinese – '

'Never!' And Venerable Chen thought, This summit is a proposal that is doomed. Shanghainese, Chiu-chow, Cantonese can never work together. There is not a shred of trust between us. Now, more quietly but no less forcefully, he repeated, 'Never.'

Peter Ng bowed his head. 'Honourable Sawyer is waiting for you.'

'I will tell you this, Younger Nephew. If the *gwai loh* Sawyer had not come to Macao for our last meeting, I would not be here now.'

'We work together, the Green Pang and Sawyer and Sons, to our mutual benefit. It is important to show that mutuality in tangible fashion.'

For a moment Venerable Chen stiffened. He wondered whether Peter Ng was giving him a lecture in manners. Then he dismissed the thought. The young man was simply devoted to Andrew Sawyer. Personally, Venerable Chen did not understand it, but he had been able to accept it. Besides, Ng was correct, this alliance was benefiting both parties. It might not pay to be so antagonistic. Long ago he had learned to smile with his mouth, leaving his heart untouched by such false emotion.

'That is why I have done as you suggested. Do not expect me, however, to relax my standards. All dealings between my triad and Sawyer and Sons must continue to be effected through you.'

Andrew Sawyer was waiting for them in his spacious study. As the two Chinese came in, he bowed deeply and ushered Venerable Chen to the best seat in the room, Sawyer's own spacious leather chair. It was part of a grouping on the other side of the room from the office accoutrements, and included a comfortable settee and a low cocktail table of green jade squares inlaid in a brass frame.

'I'm so happy you could come, Honourable Chen,' Sawyer said, deliberately using the Shanghainese dialect. He carefully watched Venerable Chen's brittle smile and knew he was on thin ice with this man. He poured them all Johnnie Walker Scotch. None of them used ice.

Pleased with the choice of drinks, Venerable Chen refused to be impressed by the other's good manners. It was a well-documented fact that foreign devils possessed nothing but bad manners. Though it was certainly true that he had had little personal contact with Andrew Sawyer, Venerable Chen could not think of any reason why this man, *tai pan* though he might be, should be any different.

He drank and tried to relax. It wasn't easy. Foreign devils still made him nervous. He had never met one he could trust. Not like Younger Nephew over there, he thought. He is Shanghainese; he is family. There, trust is implicit and absolute.

'I have taken the liberty of having prepared a bite to eat,' Sawyer said. 'I dislike discussing business on an empty stomach. I find that hunger impairs the reasoning process.'

'Just so,' Venerable Chen said grudgingly. How many times had he said the same thing to his sons? Educating the impatient young in the traditional ways of business, he thought, was an arduous and largely unrewarding task.

As he spoke, Sawyer was busy at the gleaming stainless-steel-and-teak sideboard and service area that took up half of one of the room's walls. In a moment he returned to where the two Chinese sat, holding a tray filled with small bamboo steamers.

'*Dim sum*,' Venerable Chen said, with no apparent emotion. 'Most unusual at this late hour.'

'Just so,' Sawyer said. 'At restaurants I frequent, which serve *dim sum* at this time, it is invariably soggy. However, my chef is always on hand.' He was well tuned to the Chinese way of acting. He knew the other's response was as positive as he could expect.

When he had proposed this meal to his *comprador*, Ng had indicated that he would be happy to heat and serve the plethora of small dumplings. Sawyer would not hear of it. 'It's important that I serve Chen myself,' he had said. 'Face, Peter. After all, we have asked him to come here, on our territory. That could not have been easy for him.'

Now, as the three of them ate, Sawyer knew that he had been right. Watching the tiny man in his oversized clothes, he had had to suppress a smile of delight. Sitting in the huge chair gave him an even more diminutive quality. It struck Sawyer that Venerable Chen appeared to be a doll that, by some alchemical process, had been brought to life for a time.

Sawyer was reminded of a story his father used to tell him at Christmastime. All year, Sawyer recalled, he would wait to hear this story retold until it became more important even than the presents laid out for him beneath the brightly decorated tree.

Venerable Chen was a character out of that tale, 'The Nutcracker.' It was all too long since Sawyer had last heard the story; he could not remember any names beyond the Sugar Plum Fairy. The thought saddened him. If his daughter had lived, he would have had some reason to read the tale again so that each Christmas he could relive the magic all over again through her.

When they had finished the *dim sum* with sticky rice wrapped in fragrant lotus leaves, Sawyer poured chrysanthemum tea.

Venerable Chen licked his lips and belched, thereby showing his pleasure. He looked at Andrew Sawyer and thought, Perhaps I have misjudged this one. His manners are very good indeed.

He smiled, and this time it was from the heart.

'I don't like it,' Sawyer said after Venerable Chen had left.

'Which part, *tai pan*?'

'Any of it.' Ng had related the details of his meeting with Three Oaths Tsun.

Sawyer moved slowly around his library, touching things: the corner of a filigreed silver frame, the gilt edge of a leatherbound volume of Bruce Catton's Civil War history, an agate paperweight, and so on. He was a tactile man, as many Americans and few Britons are; he thought better when he could run his fingertips over a succession of surface textures.

Peter Ng stirred. 'I thought you wanted into Pak Hanmin and Kam Sang.'

'Perhaps,' Sawyer said in an almost dreamy voice. 'Perhaps.'

'Well, here it is. I gave you all the details that Three Oaths Tsun outlined to me. It seems a fair deal.'

'Yes, it does.' Sawyer's eyes caught a hint of the soft lamplight as he passed briefly through its pool of warm illumination. Beneath his feet, the umbers and pale gold of an antique Tabriz. 'Assuming one wishes to invest almost two billion dollars in the future of Hong Kong.'

'If that is not what we wish to do,' Peter Ng said matter-of-factly, 'we should join Mattias, King and Company in moving out of here.'

Sawyer ceased his circling of the room long enough to say, 'I take it, then, that you are for the deal.'

He could almost feel the other's shrug, though he could not see it in the darkness of the room. 'It's what we've wanted. "Seize opportunity by the throat", that's a well-known Chinese saying.'

'I am familiar with it,' Sawyer said, commencing to circle again. 'I'm also familiar with an old American saying: "Give a man enough rope and he'll hang himself".'

'What does that mean?'

'It means,' Sawyer said seriously, 'there's a fool born every minute.'

'You think Tsun's hiding something about Pak Hanmin?'

'Or Kam Sang. Either one, it doesn't matter much.'

'What makes you say that?'

'If I could answer that one succinctly, Peter, I could tell you how to go out and make your own fortune.' Sawyer grunted. 'Maybe it's only that Tsun's so anxious to unload it.'

'His reasons make sound business sense.'

'Absolutely. Otherwise, the whole thing would blow up. You've got to make it look legitimate as well as enticing. But it's all happening too fast. There's no time to think rationally. He wants us to jump, to make an emotional decision based on I don't know what – greed, envy, pick one. Something smells.'

'Too bad we can't get a closer look at the both of them, then,' Ng said. 'It would make life a lot simpler.'

'Frankly,' Sawyer said, 'I'm not concerned with what's going on with Pak Hanmin and Kam Sang. It's after midnight. Call Tsun. Tell him we're passing. If he starts in on you, fend him off politely and hang up.'

'Then what? Just forget about it?'

400

'Not so fast.' Sawyer sank down in his favourite wingback leather chair, soft with age and ground-in oils. 'Let's see if he calls us back. By my reckoning, he's only got until the Hang Seng opens in the morning. If no one's picked up Mattias, King's share of Kam Sang by then, he's going to be twisting in the wind. Pak Hanmin stock will be out on the line. That being the case, we might be able to pick it up for a song, and get in for far less money than this deal he's proposing would cost us.'

'Would we want that if, as you said, something smells?'

'I meant the deal, not the assets themselves. After all, we're fairly familiar with Pak Hanmin's dealings and administration ourselves, and when it comes to Kam Sang, we have the assurances of Beijing; the government of China's not likely to screw up a project they need so desperately.'

'He's not going to give it away. He can't afford that.'

'He can't afford what will happen to him on the Stock Exchange floor tomorrow morning, either.'

'That's conjecture,' Peter Ng said.

'Better the devil you're not sure of, eh?'

'I don't understand.'

Andrew Sawyer laughed. 'Don't worry. I doubt that Three Oaths Tsun would, either.'

'The sphere of influence of the KVR does not extend that far. I want to know,' Lantin said, 'what you are doing with the Chinese.'

Out of the corner of her eye Daniella saw the code book swimming up through her vision. What would have happened, she asked herself, if my father had ever found out about my mother's secret life? How severe would have been her punishment?

Lantin gathered up the book and rose. He walked to the window, leaned against the mullioned sash. 'When my men discovered this, the first thing I did was to take it to a

psychiatrist of my acquaintance at the Serbsky Institute.'
Lantin was speaking of the psychological corrective arm of
the *sluzhba*.

'I told him of the circumstances under which this was
discovered, where it was discovered. I filled him in on the
overall picture. Then I asked him why.'

Lantin's thumb was stroking the cover of the book. He
held it very close to him. 'Do you know what he replied?
He told me it seemed clear to him that in some unconscious
fashion you wanted to be found out.'

He turned from the blackness beyond the pane, his light
eyes catching her unawares. 'I can take that further. You
knew that the only way you would be found out was if
someone smarter than you entered the picture.

'Well, you obviously had no fear of Karpov. Which, I
suppose, shows good judgment on your part. He never
would have found it. Why would he even look?'

'Why did you?'

'Because I thought I had caught a glimpse of you that
day in your office. Some sliver that had evaded Karpov all
these months since the two of you have been bedding
down.'

'No,' Daniella said. 'That's a strictly male fantasy. You
saw nothing at all except a new place to thrust yourself.'
Lantin grinned. 'I learned a lot at your *dacha*. That you
and Karpov were intimate, for one.' He held up the code
book. 'This, for another.'

'How did you find it?' She did not want to ask, but
could not help herself.

His smile broadened. 'Your mother.'

Daniella steeled herself. 'What about my mother?'

'It would be where she would hide such an object, don't
you agree, Daniella? An important secret. An ikon.'

'You know about her?'

'Oh, yes. It's all in her dossier.'

'But she was left alone. Why?'

'Because of you, Daniella. You were always the one who was important to us. Actually, we have Karpov to thank for that. He wanted you to remain happy. He did not wish to disturb the relationship you had with her. It was obvious that you would turn against us if we took her in as a subversive.'

'She was no subversive!' Daniella said compulsively. 'She loved Russia.'

'She loved *a* Russia,' Lantin corrected her, the smile now off his face. 'Not *this* Russia.'

'Why are you telling me this now?'

'You asked how I found the book.'

But she suspected that was a lie. Rather, he wanted her to know the extent of his power over her.

'When one harbours secrets,' he was saying now, 'one flirts with a kind of irrevocable danger. Secrets give their owner power only so long as they remain solely in his or her domain. Discovered, their power often boomerangs.'

She had been preparing herself to bring at least part of Medea to Lantin. She wanted to be rid of Karpov. He had become a millstone around her neck. She knew that he was impeding her career. He wanted her just where she was, where she could benefit him the most. But she had outgrown her position. She wanted more than Karpov could provide now.

It saddened her to know that Lantin had coerced her into giving him what she had been willing to offer up to him. He had spoiled everything. She tasted ashes in her mouth, saw in a flash how she had been used by everyone around her. Even while she had gulled herself into believing she held the upper hand, it was always the men who won out. She was fighting a losing battle. But even so, she thought, it was still important to end up on the winning side.

With nothing further to lose, she set out to beat him at his own game. She told him only as much as she felt she needed to regarding Medea's information. She spoke at length about the internecine warfare among the ministers in Beijing because she intuited that this aspect of the intelligence would appeal most to his sensibilities.

She was rewarded with a positive response. He wanted her to pursue that part, and though they skirted the Hong Kong issue, he did not ask her to amplify. He was too busy figuring the angles in Beijing.

'Does Medea know which faction will win out?' he said after she was through.

'He cannot say for certain yet.'

'This is important,' Lantin said. 'I would say crucial. If we can get advance intelligence as to which faction will grasp controlling interest in Beijing, we could step up our robot war with China without fear. If we know who they are, we can control them by giving them just what they want. They'll be like donkeys to whom we feed carrots.'

Daniella was watching the light coming on behind his eyes as much as she was listening to his words. She needed to understand what made him tick, or she would stand no chance against him. He was more powerful than she; and he was a man.

She needed to know what he wanted most, and she knew words would not get the job done. What she had to do was somehow alter the balance of their relationship. She was aware that Lantin thought of her now much as he did of Karpov: as part of his hip pocket. That would have to change if she was to have any chance at all.

She got up and went into the living room. It was done in dark, masculine colours, heavy leather furniture. There was no relief, no airiness at all. When she had completed the inspection of the entire apartment, Daniella was certain that no feminine mind had been at work here. That in itself was intriguing. She wondered how Lantin felt about sex. She knew, from her dealings with him, just how he liked to manipulate people, finding their weak spots and then treading on their faces while they were paralysed.

He reminded her of a dentist her mother had taken her to see when she was a teenager. He had pretended there was no Novocaine left in his office, and had then proceeded to drink in her cries of pain as he drilled out the cavity he had found in her lower molar. She saw him get hard, but it was not until years later that the haunting memory had made any sense to her.

Now Daniella had an intuition that Yuri Lantin was the same way as that dentist. To prove it, she decided to use the code book. She told him she wanted it back. When he refused, as she knew he must, she insisted. Again he refused. It was not in her nature to beg, and she did not want to arouse his suspicions. So she slapped him.

Lantin hit her with the book. Then, as she reeled back against the bookcase, he reached out with his free hand and gripped the bodice of her blouse. He jerked her hard towards him, and the cloth ripped in his fingers. He twisted, shredding it, denuding her.

She wore no bra; she never had. Now she watched through half-closed eyes as Lantin stared at her nakedness. She had beautiful breasts, and she knew it. She was bent backwards by his strength; she whimpered softly.

He struck her across her breasts and she cried out. He dropped the book and dug both his hands into her flesh, kneading her. He pulled heavily on her nipples, so that she gasped and tried to twist away from him. He liked that even more.

He insinuated one hand inside the waistband of her skirt, felt the top of her panties. He brought her to him and lowered his mouth to her breasts. He was rough with that as well, but Daniella could not say she did not enjoy it. She would not let him know that, however, since that would spoil his illusion.

He wanted to take her. It was not rape, precisely, that

405

was on his mind, but close enough. Daniella allowed it. It was easy to do, and, she thought, somewhat enjoyable to play-act the helpless female. She could fit herself into the role without much trouble. She was hot, as well.

She wanted to be taken, charged by the onset of emotions, the excitement of deceit and the danger. And when she saw his long, lean body come undone from his tailored clothes, when his rampant animal body was revealed to her, she felt the wetness between her thighs. So close to his power, she wanted to become one with it.

Each groan pulled from his throat, each twitch and tremble of his body, each inarticulate cry was a victory for her on this odd battlefield. And when she felt his spasms begin, the hot pumping of his seed deep inside her, her inner muscles rippled of their own accord, milking him and herself at once.

And, half insensate, she knew she had found what she had been searching for all her life: power and the key with which to unlock it.

Jake wanted to go alone to the *usagigoya*. Mikio found this a particularly foolhardy notion, and made no bones about voicing his opinion.

'At least wait for her on the street,' the *oyabun* said. 'I will have one of my cars parked. When she emerges, we will pick her up cleanly, without any fuss. You can talk to her in complete privacy and safety.'

Jake shook his head. 'That's not the way. I'll never get anything out of her if we kidnap her off the streets like a common criminal.'

'He could be waiting there for you,' Mikio said. 'I know I would, if I were in his place.'

'There's risk in everything that pertains to Nichiren,' Jake said. 'In this case, I don't think I have a choice.'

Mikio was annoyed; his anxiety for Jake's safety made him so. 'For a *gaijin*, you certainly have an anachronistic sense of honour. You should have been a *samurai* in the service of the Tokugawa.'

Silently he held out a hand. Lying in his palm like a gleaming black blotch was a snub-nosed automatic.

Jake smiled and shook his head. '*Dōmo*, Mikio-*san*,' he said. 'It is not necessary.'

Dusk. Getting on towards dinnertime. The streets of Tokyo were choked with clouds of people rushing homeward.

Jake stopped in a store and bought a fresh fish, which he had the clerk wrap with a sheet of special rice paper he had bought moments before. He handed the clerk seven paper cords in white and crimson, with which the man tied the package. He was an old man and understood the nature of what he had been asked to do. A younger man might have had to be told.

In the upper right, just above the cords, Jake affixed the *noshi*. As in olden times, he used a piece of *awabi* – ear-shell – stretching it tightly. It was a symbol of long life – which was why it was stretched – and protection from harm: *awabi* does not decompose. Nowadays, one most often found the *noshi* printed on the wrapping paper as a design. Jake was taking great pains to wrap the traditional visitor's gift in the traditional manner.

With the package under his arm, he walked the rest of the way to the *usagigoya*. There was no point in looking for a taxi at this time of the evening; even if he found one, he'd be mired in the traffic for his efforts. On the other hand, he had no desire to be forcibly squeezed into a sardine box below Tokyo's streets in the subway. Rush hour was no time to ride the trains.

At the front steps, he looked up. He knew what apartment she was in. He walked around to the side of the building. Mikio had shown him a layout of the complex before he had set off on this journey. Lights were burning inside. Perhaps he was expected. *Joss*.

407

Shrugging, Jake went back to the front and entered. The tiny elevator took him up. He could hear his shoe soles echoing hollowly along the narrow hallway. He stopped at her door.

From beyond the walls he could hear the rush of the traffic. A barge hooted. Nearer at hand he heard the muffled chatter of familial conversation. The last of the daylight was coming down. Soon the coloured neon would take hold, spangling the night, banishing the darkness to the somnolent countryside.

He found that he was unaccountably hot. Above the muted sounds of the city he could hear the hard beating of his heart. Or was it just that he felt its throbbing in the centre of his chest? He took several deep breaths, centring himself as he had been taught over and over.

He felt a peculiar itching just below his hairline, and when he lifted a fingertip to investigate, it came away with a warm bead of sweat. He put it on the end of his tongue, as if tasting its biting saltiness would prove to him its true nature.

He stared straight ahead at the blank door. It was painted a shiny black, and in its uneven surface he could just discern a ghost of a reflection.

With a start that sent a tiny shiver through him, he realized that he was frightened.

He watched, fascinated and detached, as his right arm came up and, seemingly of its own volition, rang the bell.

For a moment he could hear nothing but the thunder of his heart. Gone was the soughing traffic, the melancholy calling of the boats along the river, the tiny, homely sounds that wafted through the hall from behind closed apartment doors.

Nothing existed now but himself and his coal-black reflection. When that disappeared he would, perhaps, stand face to face with Nichiren. Everything would change in the blink of an eye. He would have his answer.

With a jerk, the door opened inward.

'Yes?'

His reflection was no more.

'Kamisaka Tanaba?'

'*Hai.*'

He bowed, showing her the top of his head. 'I am Jake Maroc. Nichiren and I are acquainted with one another.'

He could see the fear like a dark flame flickering in her eyes. Did that mean he was here with her? 'Who are you?'

She wore a celadon-green silk kimono with a wave pattern woven through it. At collar and sleeve cuffs he could see peeking through a tomato-coloured under-kimono. On her feet she wore snow-white *tabi* of lightweight organdy. Would she be so dressed, he wondered, if she was alone?

'I have brought you a present,' he said, extending the package towards her. His awareness extended behind her into the *usagigoya*. Questing for any sign of Nichiren's presence. 'Only friends bring presents.'

She watched his face as if she believed that at any moment it would explode. 'He has no friends, this man you speak of. Not now. I have heard that.'

'I did not say I was *his* friend,' Jake said, smiling. And then, when she made no sound or move, 'Please, it is vital that we talk.'

She hesitated a moment more, then bowed formally, taking the present from him. Jake bent, slipping off his shoes.

His muscles tense, his mind alert, he took the fighting position, his knees slightly bent, moving swiftly on the outsides of his feet, body weight centred in his *hara* – his lower belly, where the wellspring of all physical strength dwelt – leading with the right side of his body. The miniature kitchen, the sleeping alcove with its cloudlike *futon*. All taken in in a flash. Then into the bathroom. Nothing there, either.

He returned to where she stood watching him. He bowed again. 'I had to be certain. *Sumimasen*, Tanaba-*san*.'

Kamisaka stared at him a moment as if dumbfounded. In Japan, *gaijin*, that is, foreigners, said 'Thank you' in only one way: '*Dōmo arigatō*.' On the other hand, natives often used '*Sumimasen*,' a word almost impossible to translate accurately. While it also meant 'Thank you', it held within it overtones of other feelings, such as an apology for prevailing upon a stranger to do one a favour; a sense of honouring one's obligations, knowing that one could not as yet reciprocate the kindness extended.

'You might have asked,' she said.

Jake was intrigued. Kamisaka might be dressed as if she were a *geisha* from the celebrated days before the war, but she spoke like any modern-day Japanese girl. But for her words, he would have believed her to be a *samurai*'s concubine from Edo-period Japan. She did not, for instance, open her gift in his presence. That was the traditional way to forestall jealousy and to keep hidden the emotions that went into the choosing of the gift.

'Would you like tea?' she asked. Her eyes told him that she was still wary. Perfectly understandable.

'Thank you. Tea would be wonderful.'

They sat on opposite sides of a low ebony table. It was hand-carved, its elegance odd and overpowering in the tiny apartment. Kamisaka knew how to serve. She set out rice cakes and sweet *tofu* confections with the tea.

'You will forgive me if my questions are blunt?'

'Whether or not you are forgiven, Maroc-*san*, will be totally up to you.'

That gave him pause. *Always*, Fo Saan had told him, *gauge your opponent well before you engage him. Remember that if you underestimate him once, you will never be allowed the opportunity to do so again.*

Jake had no inclination to underestimate Kamisaka. A girl she might be, but she had already demonstrated to

410

him her keen mind. He had a healthy respect for her — and, most reluctantly, for Nichiren. This was, after all, his lady.

'When was the last time you saw Nichiren?' he asked her.

She smiled. 'I think you must give me a reason for answering such a blunt question.'

'Nichiren has something that belongs to me. A piece of lavender jade carved in the shape of the hindquarters of a tiger. He acquired it from my wife, who is now dead.'

'Oh! I'm so sorry. Was it recent?'

'Last week,' Jake said, thinking, How many days ago? How could I have lost track so quickly? What is happening to me? 'She was with Nichiren.' He saw in her eyes that he had hurt her, and realized that that had been his intent. He was immediately ashamed. Why should this bright girl take the brunt of his rage and frustration? He turned the anger in on himself.

'I understand now why you look so exhausted,' she said, surprising him. 'Your cheeks are so gaunt, your eyes so darkly hooded. When you first came to the door, I mistook you for a marathon runner.'

If it was not the truth, then it was an artful lie, made for his benefit. He felt his cheeks burning with his shame.

'I *am* tired,' he heard himself saying, as if from the far side of a tunnel. 'I happen to be in a business where that is an occupational hazard.'

'Bad business,' she said, refilling their tiny cups. 'I had an uncle like that once. I loved him so. He used to buy me presents; he could get me out of the bluest moods. He died suddenly. Overwork, my father said, when I asked him why Uncle Teiso no longer visited us.' Her eyes filled his vision. 'I wouldn't want the same thing to happen to you.'

'Why would you care?' He was inexplicably filled with self-pity.

Kamisaka sat very still. In that stillness Jake observed

the exactitude of her manners. 'I think,' she said, 'that your life has inured you to emotion. It seems sad to me that this is so.' She looked at him. 'Do you have so little faith in humankind that you assume you are being lied to constantly?'

She said this with no rancour or harshness. Rather, her voice was soft and melodious, gently questioning. It caused Jake to reflect on her words. It was true, he saw. He lived his life within a web of lies. And that life had hardened his heart. He saw with a momentary shiver of terror that he could no longer differentiate truth from fiction. Saw, too, that his rage stemmed from the beauty and warmth of this woman. Nichiren's woman.

Mariana, his woman, was as cold as a winter frost – lost to him forever.

'I don't – ' He paused, not quite knowing how to put it. 'You're not at all what I had expected.'

'Did you expect me to come at you with a hidden knife?'

He said nothing, admitting to her the truth of what she said.

'There is violence in your heart.'

'And in Nichiren's.' The bargaining had begun.

'I do not pretend to understand him completely. Or to be perfectly content with our relationship. But he is *samurai*, an anachronism who would be more at home in another, more ancient age. I forgive him much because of that.'

'Can you forgive his killing?'

'I am a Buddhist. I can tolerate no killing,' Kamisaka said. 'Yet I am flexible enough to seek an answer to it.'

'But you live with him!' Now her calm, rational, almost meek manner disturbed him profoundly. He found himself reacting to it with an irrational, blind anger. 'You sleep in the same bed, you feed him! For God's sake, you have surrendered your heart to him! How can you, knowing what he does when he is not with you!'

412

'How can I continue to live in this imperfect world?' Kamisaka said.

'That's no answer!'

'Like the man who demands perfection in his garden, you ask the impossible from yourself. Therefore it is natural that you expect it in others. And also natural that you find yourself disappointed when they fail to live up to your expectations. You find yourself betrayed. But not by those around you, Maroc-*san*. You have been betrayed by your own values.

'You must learn to accept the world as it is, not as you wish it could be. There is so much anger in you, as there is in him. The same kind of deep-seated anger. From whence does it come that it is so difficult to exorcize? How different the two of you would be without its terrible burden.' She smiled. 'You see, whether you choose to believe it or not, I wish the same for both of you.'

'We're cut from completely different cloth,' Jake said hotly.

'He is a killer,' she said, 'and you are . . . what?'

'I am not here to talk about myself.'

'Of course. How foolish of me.' Was there something about her expression that was slightly mocking?

'Will you answer my question?'

'But I have already done so. It is you who have not listened.'

'I've heard every word you said.'

'I am speaking now about your heart, Maroc-*san*.'

He snorted. 'Now you're giving me homilies as old as time.'

Awareness dawned across her face. 'Ah, I understand!' she cried. 'It is worthless without the struggle. If Nichiren were here and you fought a pitched battle with him, killing him in the process, then you would feel that the knowledge you gained in the process was worthwhile.

'If I turned out to be a rough-and-tumble *samurai* lady

413

with *wakizashi* in my hand beneath the table, ready to puncture your heart, you would know for certain the worth of what you had wrested from me.'

Jake saw the pity in her eyes, and it rocked him to his very core. She was right in everything she had said about him. Secretly he had yearned for a struggle. In his world, anything easily given up was next to worthless.

His world. There it was again. He saw now that he and Kamisaka came from different worlds – just as he and Mariana had been separated by the gulf of emotionlessness with which he had deliberately surrounded himself. It was a condition brought about by the Sumchun River. It had destroyed much of his effectiveness as an operative. It had made him into a nonentity as a human being.

He thought of that floating ghost, the reflection of himself in the lacquer of Kamisaka's door. That was all he was, his sum and substance. Abruptly he was overwhelmed by sorrow. His heart felt hollow and wooden, as if, though it would continue to beat, it would never again even feel pain. What good was this revelation, now that Mariana was dead?

With blurred vision, he saw Kamisaka reach into the wide sleeve of her kimono. She put a tiny package on the table between the uneaten rice cakes and *tofu*.

'I believe this is yours,' she said simply. She had the priceless gift of never judging. She always spoke her mind, but that was all. Someone else might have added caustically, 'You may not wish to open it, even though I guarantee it will not explode in your face,' but she said nothing else. Instead she remained motionless, her hands on the table. Jake saw the folds of her kimono sleeve, its pattern green on green like a painting of the sea, drawn from life, taking that essence, then, like all true art, adding another quality, creating something new where before only the old and ordinary had existed. He was acutely aware of her long fingers, of the gentleness inherent in them. They were like the kimono she wore, possessing an inner structure at once surprising and moving.

For a long time Jake sat as still as a statue. He smelled her scent, pine and musk commingled, as fresh as a summer's evening. He stared at the tiny package, at the cheery gift wrap. He saw the glint of silver and gold in the rice paper. It reminded him of the strings with which he had wrapped Mariana's wedding gift. She had wanted them to exchange gifts then, as if their giving of themselves was not enough. Jake thought he knew now why she had needed that tangible assurance from him.

He at last reached out and unwrapped the package. At first he thought that Nichiren had unaccountably given him back his piece of the *fu*. It was a shard of lavender jade, all right. He recognized the style of carving by the same skilled hand. Then he turned it over and his hands began to tremble.

What he saw were the powerful head and shoulders of the beast. It was unarguably part of the same tiger. Holding it up to the light, Jake could further discern from the depth of colour and the degree of translucency that this piece was part of the same whole. *Another* part.

My God! he thought. What is happening?

Jake suppressed a desire to scream at her. But he could not keep the slight tremor out of his voice when he said, 'Kamisaka-*san*, have you seen this before?' He held the piece of the *fu* at the ends of his fingers.

She turned her head just enough. She nodded.

She could be quite maddening. 'Whose is it?'

Her dark, gleaming hair, thick and blue-black in the lamplight, framed her open, intelligent face. Jake watched her eyes for any hint of guile. But there was none. 'Nichiren's,' she said. 'He told me that it had been his mother's.'

But Jake had ceased to hear a word she said.

* * *

Monday brought typhoon warnings to Hong Kong. The shelters in Causeway Bay and Aberdeen were teeming with preparations, as were all the settlements on the periphery of the Island. But inland, the Hong Kong businessmen were preparing themselves for a different kind of disaster, as the bell for the opening of the Hang Seng sounded.

Immediately there was a panic rush on the floor. The official announcement of Mattias, King and Company's impending move out of the Colony had been broadcast. The ragged edge of terror was in the air, and as the bidding reached a crescendo an hour after opening, it was clear that everyone's fears were being realized. Unless a reverse of the trends could be found, more than a score of prominent businesses within the Crown Colony would be bankrupt or near bankruptcy by day's end.

Feverish eyes watched as stock prices of key issues began to drop and then to plummet. One pair of eyes belonged to Three Oaths Tsun. Because of the vulnerability of his position with the Kam Sang project now that Sawyer had declined his offer, his Pak Hanmin stock was declining at an appalling rate.

Dizzy with anxiety, Three Oaths Tsun clung to the back of his chair overlooking the Exchange and closed his eyes. He swallowed hard, cursing his *joss*. He was under discipline; his hands were tied. He had been ordered not to call Andrew Sawyer back, even though his instinct told him that if he did not, Sawyer would pass on the Kam Sang deal.

Dawn had come, and he had been proven correct. Now he knew that his meeting with Peter Ng had been business suicide. Deals such as the one he had offered Andrew Sawyer were almost impossible to keep secret for very long in a climate such as Hong Kong's. The Chinese loved only one thing more than gossiping, and that was betting.

It was clear from how violently the Pak Hanmin stock was reacting that someone at Sawyer and Sons had passed

416

on the Kam Sang information to the other *tai pan*. News other than Mattias, King's announcement was driving the stock down.

Pak Hanmin was falling down around his ears and he was certain it was because he had proposed that deal to Sawyer. He would never have done so on his own. Far better to keep a closed mouth, the secret of his vulnerability deeply buried for those final hours before the Hang Seng opened. Those had not been his orders. He insisted that the others inside the *yuhn-hyun* have faith. He could do no less, especially considering the source. Yet he was here and the source was not. He was privy to customs, information the source was not. Oh, *a mi tuo fo*!

He sought to calm himself, but when he glanced back at the board, he blanched to see that his stock had fallen another two points! It was impossible! Two points in ten minutes! By the Celestial Blue Dragon, he thought, if this keeps up, Pak Hanmin will be finished!

Faith or no faith, his hands turned into fists. He bent, gave the order to buy up his own stock. If he did not do that, the decline would feed upon itself. But he had only a finite amount of resources, and as he glanced down at his notebook, he saw with a fluttering in the pit of his stomach that he had just bought the last bloc of stock he could.

His eyes were drawn again to the Hang Seng board. His stock was where it had been five minutes before. It had lost seven and a half points since the opening, since the news of Mattias, King's pullout had become official. But it was holding now.

He was sweating. Certainly a bad sign. But even so, he refused to use the linen handkerchief clutched in his white fist. By the Eight Drunken Immortals, Three Oaths Tsun mouthed silently, I will not show my enemies my fear.

Pak Hanmin was holding tight. If this is all I lose today, he thought, I will be happy. I will light *joss* sticks and pray to the memory of my ancestors.

Still there was pandemonium on the floor of the Exchange. Three Oaths Tsun stared down, wide-eyed, as if he were witness to the caves of hell. He remembered well the same kind of activity in '71 and '72, but then the Hang Seng was in the process of doubling each year. Now the reverse seemed to be happening. There had been a mini-run three years ago when Britain had announced that there was no way they could retain control of the Crown Colony after 1997. But it was nothing compared to this.

Three Oaths Tsun's uncomfortable *gwai loh* suit was sopping under the arms. He detested being so enshrouded. Hated, too, that a rolling deck was not beneath his feet. He looked at the board again, had to squint. Pak Hanmin was still steady. Well, not so bad as it could have been. He let out a long breath. Perhaps the worst was over.

Now the time of waiting had begun. Because of its depressed price, his stock was vulnerable to a takeover. It was in just this fashion that he had acquired a controlling interest in the Xiu HK Ltd Companies. He had bought hugely while the stock was depressed, becoming the majority stockholder because the Xiu family lacked the ready capital to buy back the required shares at the inflated price that Three Oaths Tsun's bloc purchases had raised the stock to.

Now he was fully aware that the same thing could happen to him. Three years ago the Xiu line of *godown*s seemed a good buy, and indeed they had proved a money-maker as part of Pak Hanmin. Then he had been ordered to turn them over in order to get Pak Hanmin into the utilities market in the New Territories. Bad business decision, he had thought at the time. Illogical, because the *godown*s were extremely profitable, and entering the already tightly contested utilities market with the threat of 1997 looming was risky by anyone's standards.

Faith.

And belief in the *yuhn-hyun*.

One and the same, really, when you thought about it.

Though he owned the largest individually owned commercial tanker fleet in the world, T. Y. Chung was heavily into banking, refinancing real estate, and gold; Sawyer and Sons were, now that Mattias, King was leaving, the largest manufacturers in the Colony; Five Star Pacific was the leader in utilities.

Any one of these three would have reason to buy into Pak Hanmin. It would be like them to run in on him, scoop up the remaining shares at bargain-basement rates, then turn around after they had driven the price sky-high and offer to sell them back for three or four times their cost. Or stay in and force Pak Hanmin to pay its share of the Kam Sang project out of cash flow.

Three Oaths Tsun gritted his teeth. His eyes were blurry from staring down onto that pandemonium. He blinked rapidly to clear his vision. He did not know what he wished to see least now, the price of the stock dropping or rising. Either way, it would be bad news. Only a modest fluctuation would be good for him.

By noon the stock had made no serious move one way or another. It had hit a support level and, like a patient whose fever had run its course, seemed to be recovering.

Three Oaths Tsun took some time out to have tea and cold sesame noodles brought up to his seat. He had been on the phone all morning with his office, conducting business he would normally have directed from his shipboard stateroom.

At one-fifteen, the stock was up a half-point. Three Oaths Tsun mentally blessed his good *joss*. His orders had been right, after all. His early heavy buying had scared everyone else off. They were staying away now because they feared that if they started buying, he would match them share for share. If he possessed enough shares, he would not need to buy theirs back and, further, they could not wind up with a majority position in the company.

They would be committing economic suicide. That is, if they believed his bluff. He felt himself relaxing. The worst was over, he was convinced.

Just past one-thirty, the phone connected to the floor of the Exchange rang shrilly. Three Oaths Tsun snatched it up. 'Someone's just bought fifty thousand shares of Pak Hanmin,' his broker said.

'Who?' Three Oaths Tsun said. He felt a warning quiver deep inside him.

'I don't know. I'm making inquiries now.'

'Call me back when you have a name,' Three Oaths Tsun said brusquely. He slammed down the phone. By the Spirit of the White Tiger, he breathed silently, let it be a one-time thing.

He watched the board like a hawk, unable to sit any more. The quote had not changed. He felt time break up into discrete fragments with each heavy pump of his heart.

The ring of the floor phone was like a noise in his brain. He started, lunged for the receiver. The plastic slipped. He was astounded to find his palm slippery with sweat.

'Yes?'

'Another fifty thousand have been bought just this moment.'

Buddha! 'Same source?'

'Yes.'

Oh, gods, we were wrong. They're coming after me. The sharks smell blood. I haven't bought in hours. Now they've made two smallish forays to see if they can bring me out. Do I have the capital to cover, they wonder? 'Who?' His voice was a dry croak.

'We're still checking, sir,' the broker said in his ear. 'They've been blind buys.'

'Get me the name!' Three Oaths Tsun said down the line.

On the Hang Seng board, the quote was changing. Three Oaths Tsun felt his heart skip a beat, and he put a clawed hand up to his chest. To anyone watching, it would seem as if he were smoothing his vest. Pak Hanmin was up two full points!

It's begun, he thought dully. Someone wants in, and I have not the power to stop them.

The telephone began to jangle.

David Oh had secured himself in front of the glowing emerald computer terminal that linked him to the GPR-3700 mainframe monster deep within the bowels of the Quarry's Washington base. This network included a secure-line telephone modem that could handle all printed and graphic material. With this setup he could tap into every nook and cranny of the Quarry's vast files, using his series of access codes, which, like a castle's iron gates leading to the keep, would pass him through to deeper and deeper levels of classified information.

No one was in the small, stifling room with him. The door was closed and locked and had been so since he had sat down at the terminal forty minutes ago to feed the two fingerprints he had lifted off the plates in Jake's apartment into the graphic modem.

Since then he had been passing through classified sections of the Quarry files to get a fix on them. Almost immediately he had received a 'Go Forth' response from the system, which was an indication that somewhere within the mainframe, half a world away, the identities of the men infiltrating Jake's apartment were known and had been stored away.

A half-hour of reaching for files of known unfriendlies had, however, proved fruitless. As David Oh eliminated possibilities, the 'Go Forth' response stayed maddeningly lit at the top of the screen. He had gone through the most obvious KGB operatives, all the 'organized' terrorists, that is, members of the Red Brigades, Black September, Baader-Meinhof, the Red Star, Japanese extremists. Now he set to work on bringing the 'singletons', the unaffiliated terrorists-for-hire, to the fore. File after file was reviewed and rejected. Nothing.

'Damn it!' he said aloud.

The terminal's silent response was GO FORTH.

What was left?

Tried KGB operatives from left field. Nothing.

GO FORTH.

Tried retirees, figuring an old grudge. Nothing.

GO FORTH.

Punched up the menu to review again his dwindling list of options. There was only one he had not yet plumbed. Using yet another access code, he extracted the dictionary of names, certain that this could only be another dead end. His mind was already devising computer-language methods of getting beyond the pre-set menu when the name list disappeared, leaving two names pulsing on the screen.

FOUND AND MATCHED, read the terminal's top line.

'*Dew neh loh moh,*' David Oh said, his hands automatically working the keyboard to double-check the findings. Within thirty seconds he knew there was no mistake. He ran a hand through his hair. He was dripping wet.

What the terminal showed was that the two men who had been in Jake's apartment just after Mariana left were a Quarry extraction team. These men were not sent to question or as messengers. Their particular skills made them far too valuable for that.

They were assassins.

That meant only one thing: that the order to terminate Mariana Maroc had been given *before* the suspicion of her betrayal of Jake and the Quarry had arisen. How could that be so?

David Oh's head came up, and even though he knew that he was alone in a locked room, he could not help but look over his shoulder. For the first time in his long career, security had fled him within his own organization. He felt totally naked, a child again.

The typhoon warnings came down as the violent storm veered to the southeast, whipping water into eighteen-foot waves, grey and trembling beneath its fury. To the northwest, the outer wing of turbulence sent a summer squall racing through Hong Kong. The light changed to sapphire, then a kind of grey-green peculiar to the Colony at this time of year. The atmosphere, already thick with humidity, turned aqueous, so that it seemed one moved underwater.

Activity across the sluicing decks of Three Oaths Tsun's high junk continued unabated, despite the downpour that rattled windows and shuddered ratlines.

Belowdecks, in Three Oaths Tsun's master stateroom, there was activity as well. But it was of a very different nature. When Neon Chow was on board, all movement was dictated by her.

She crouched now over her master's thighs. Her bare back glistened in the strange reflected light. Her black hair cascaded down her buttocks. Stray strands caressed Three Oaths Tsun's knees as she worked over him.

Sweat lay on him like sea water. He seemed oiled with it. It was always thus when Neon Chow gave her tender ministrations to his sacred member.

He groaned out loud, feeling it swell beyond its natural girth. How it loved her. How it quivered for the release she would bring it.

Slowly, delicately, even magically, Neon Chow used nails, fingertips, lips, tongue, hot breath, stiffened nipples, the wet cleavage between her breasts to take him upward into the realm near the clouds and the rain.

He savoured each moment, feeling his heart pounding against his ribs, his breath short and hot at the back of his

423

throat, barked out intermittently when Neon Chow added a delectable fillip here or there.

His eyes were closed. He felt immersed in the heat of his own desire. He sank in with a groan. He felt the weight, like gravity, pooling in his thighs and lower belly. He felt too heavy to move, to think, even to breathe.

He felt the clouds and the rain coming for him, and he reached down and gently drew Neon Chow away from his engorged sacred member. Now he opened his eyes and drank her slick nakedness in as if he were seeing her thus for the first time. Her long legs, her marvellously carved thighs, so strong and soft at the same time. Her narrow waist, the flare of her ribcage and those quivering, upthrust breasts riding atop. Her long neck and well-defined jawline.

Her eyes smouldered, heavy-lidded with lust. Her eyes inflamed him, and he brought her like a doll upwards towards him, until he could bury his mouth against her core.

She cried out at the contact, her long fingers frantically entwining in his hair as she pressed her hips forwards and back, establishing a rhythm.

It was slow at first as she savoured the hot lick of his tongue, the nibbling of his lips. She was dripping with need, her upper body shaking in anticipation as he invaded her all the deeper. He pulled the groans of ecstasy from her as he extracted her nectar.

Now she held her pelvis immobile, feeling the pleasure dancing through her, rippling her musculature in uncontrollable waves. She felt the tide pulling her onwards, and at last she gave herself over to it completely, bucking her hips against him with frenzied need, her hair flying out behind her as if she were in the midst of the storm raging above their heads.

The clouds and the rain touched her and she gasped heavily. It was the signal for which Three Oaths Tsun was waiting. He pushed her away from his mouth, down his torso, and onto his sacred member.

Neon Chow gave a wail of delight as, with one long, ecstatic stroke, he plumbed her to the depths. The heated contact was all he needed in his aroused state to push him up the last several notches.

Engulfed fully by her intimate flesh, he felt the onset of the clouds and the rain. Convulsing inside her, he drew her to him, feeling the scrape of her nipples against his, feeling it all the way down into the sac of his celestial jewels.

They never kissed before making love, only after. To Three Oaths Tsun, kissing was among the most intimate of gestures for lovers. It heightened and prolonged his pleasure in the aftermath of the frenzy of the clouds and the rain.

Neon Chow sighed contentedly. Her fingers stroked his cheek while their tongues duelled wetly.

'Come here,' he said thickly. He turned them on the bed. 'We mustn't face west, or else we will wake the Earth Dragon by lying on his head. His anger will bring bad *joss* down on both of us.'

At length they did nothing but listen to the rain drumming against the hull and cabin bulkheads. It diminished with the same slowness their pulses took to return to normal.

She sat up before he did. She plumped pillows, set them at her back. She lit a cigarette, got it going, and transferred it to his lips. Then she lit one for herself.

'Will you keep control of Pak Hanmin?'

Such directness would once have angered him. No longer. Perhaps this was Bliss's doing. Like Bliss, Neon Chow was different. She was part of the new breed of changing Chinese. On the one hand, Three Oaths Tsun did not know what to make of such boldness. On the other, it excited him.

He sighed inwardly. One had to face facts. It was a foolish man indeed who sought to stem the ocean's tides. Perhaps his acceptance of the way women could relate to men stemmed from the fact that he himself had trained Bliss to function as competently as any man in the modern world. He had carried out his orders concerning her future in unthinking fashion. But in doing so, he had been exposed to the soul of a woman's mind. It had amazed him how much knowledge she could absorb, how well she reasoned, how, in certain instances, she out-thought him.

He thought about the last phone call he had received before leaving the Hang Seng. He had heard the voice in his ear identifying the dummy corporations that had scooped up the vulnerable Pak Hanmin stock.

'Powerful as I am,' he said to Neon Chow, 'I do not have unlimited capital.' But then, neither did Five Star Pacific. That had been the real surprise. He had been certain that Five Star Pacific's short-term loan situation would preclude them from expending so much cash in buying the blocs of Pak Hanmin. But there it was. Five Star Pacific owned all the dummy companies engaged in buying his stock today. Where had all the money come from? What could the source have had in mind when he proposed this madness?

Neon Chow looked down at him, her gaze traversing his body like a caress. 'You must have some plan in mind,' she said. 'You always do.'

'I want to keep Pak Hanmin very fornicating badly.' Three Oaths Tsun did not bother to keep the concern out of his voice. 'Sun the Monkey knows I could do wonders with that company. But the *gwai loh* who run Five Star Pacific have bought too much already. *Dew neh loh moh* on all *gwai loh*!'

Neon Chow crushed out her cigarette. She bent her head before his words and placed her palm against his heart. 'Then it is as you say.'

* * *

Rodger Donovan called for a change in venue for the afternoon meeting. It was just as well. Because a heat wave was blanketing the entire Eastern Seaboard of the United States, Washington was a steambath. The streets, choked with tourists, were weeping moisture. Industrial fumes settled into the heat inversion, sending ripples of sooty, metallic particles through the atmosphere. The entire city took on the appearance of a pointillist painting.

Which was partially why Donovan reconvened the meeting at Greystoke. The clean grounds, the large, cool house had never seemed so inviting. It was also true that Donovan loved the old house. Save for the time he was stationed in Paris, where he lived in the Sixteenth Arrondissement in an apartment in a turn-of-the-century building, he had been used to the space of Los Angeles living. It was natural for him to prefer life at Greystoke.

Too, there was a spot on the third floor where a Seurat hung. It was not *the* Seurat, the one in Paris with which Donovan had fallen in love. But it was a Seurat nonetheless, and like all his paintings, it fascinated Donovan, evoking in him a great longing along with the envy. He loved the way the artist fooled you. He placed two dots of different colours side by side and your eye saw a third. It was there and not there at the same time. To Donovan's way of thinking, Seurat was a prestidigitator of the highest order.

Henry Wunderman's surprise when he drove up the crushed blue gravel drive was that he saw only one other car in evidence: Donovan's pride and joy, his 1963 Corvette, with the original design body, which he had had shipped east from California when the Quarry took him on. He was constantly working on it, either cleaning its outside or tuning its inside.

As Wunderman parked his battered Cougar, Donovan came down the wide wooden steps of the old house. The younger man had an attitude that Wunderman secretly envied. Wherever he was, he appeared as if he belonged.

He was like a chameleon in that respect. Well, what do you expect? Wunderman thought as he climbed out. Wealthy family, good breeding, the finest schools. Christ, you should at least come out with *something* from that background.

Wunderman had never fitted in anywhere but the Quarry. He had been a fat kid, always teased at home and at school. Now he was an overweight adult. He owned one good suit, which he used for all formal occasions with crass indiscrimination. But then Wunderman's idea of formal was going to any governmental function that began after the hour of five in the afternoon.

He wore a pair of mud-brown polyester trousers picked up at Sears and, despite the heat, a long-sleeved dress shirt. He detested short sleeves, a prejudice he had picked up in his unhappy teenage years, when his heavy, unmuscular upper arms were a source of unbearable embarrassment to him.

Donovan, dressed in greyed-out white ducks, a forest-green Ralph Lauren polo shirt, and scuffed Top-Siders, appeared slim, tanned and fit. All that good life in LA, Wunderman thought. Well, he couldn't very well blame Donovan for that. The man had tried his best to get him interested in tennis, offering to teach him from the fundamentals on up. That was another thing Wunderman detested: tennis.

'Where's the rest of the crew?' Wunderman asked.

Donovan indicated the rose garden. 'Let's take a walk.'

They strolled in silence down the narrow aisles of beaten earth, between flowering bushes and fat, furry bumblebees. The scent was so strong it tickled the back of Wunderman's nose. The colours were exquisite.

On the far side of the regimented garden was the topiary. Donovan took them into the deep green hedgerows that climbed to a height of three metres and, in some places, quite a bit more.

'Antony's over at State. Lunch with the secretary at Lion d'Or.'

Wunderman made a sound. 'In this weather?'

Donovan smiled, nodding. 'Yes. It's a bit heavy for my taste as well. The French food's not great for Antony's cholesterol level, either, but I'm afraid he had no choice. It's the secretary's favourite restaurant. He likes to be seen, I imagine. Since State is still touchy over Jake Maroc's unsanctioned raid, Antony wisely opted to concede the point.'

They came upon a hedge carved in the shape of an animal. Wunderman had been through here before. He could never tell which animal was which. There was a stone bench between two hedges. He sat, wiping his face with a handkerchief. 'Whew, I'm glad we're out of the city.'

'It was my idea, this meeting.'

Wunderman picked up on the other's tone. 'You mean just the two of us?'

Donovan sat, nodded. 'I spoke to Antony about it just before he went off to his luncheon meeting. He approved of the idea.'

'The iceberg?'

'The iceberg.' Donovan ran his fingers through his thick blond hair, making Wunderman think of the models on old cigarette ads on television. Donovan could be making a mint inveigling the American public into buying diet soda through his wide smile and wider shoulders. Advertising executives could always use the All-American boy on TV.

We all have our separate reasons for joining the service, Wunderman thought. He wondered what Donovan's was.

'With Stallings's death, the iceberg's breached to the Quarry's core. I am concerned. Properly so. So is Antony, but you know how he is. His regard for his personal safety is overshadowed by his concern for the Quarry itself.'

429

'What are you saying? That the object of this iceberg is to terminate Antony Beridien?'

Donovan's eyes were ice-blue. 'Can you think of a more effective way to cripple the service?'

Wunderman was already shaking his head. 'No. It's impossible. The risk's just too high for an objective that would have, at best, short-range effect.'

Donovan rose. 'Can we continue our stroll, Henry? Lately, staying in one place too long makes me nervous.'

Wunderman watched him carefully as they went on through the odd sculptures. 'The heat's got nothing to do with why you moved this meeting's venue, has it?'

'Not enough, I'm afraid.'

They made a turn to the left, came out on the rolling Virginia hills. Horse country. The thought made Wunderman sad. Stallings had finally got him to agree to his reciprocation of Wunderman's teaching him how to use the Quarry's computer. Next week, Stallings was to have given him his first lesson: how to mount without terror filling his heart. Now Stallings's stallion would never again be ridden in that hard, aggressive manner he had become used to.

'The computer has provided some suspicion that security has been breached.'

'By whom?'

'We don't know as yet. But it's certain that several programmes have been activated and infiltrated.'

'How deeply has it gone?'

'That's another thing we're working on.'

Wunderman took a long look at the grassy knolls that used to fill Stallings with such a sense of joy and freedom. He wondered what it would be like to feel that kind of ecstasy. He resolved to visit the Movie House this week and have one of the grooms teach him how to mount a horse.

'What you said before about security,' he said now.

'We'd better get on it right away. Get the Engineers in the first thing in the morning.'

'Good.' Donovan nodded. 'I've made certain that Antony won't return to the office again today.'

'I think we'd better have him stay here until the changes are complete.'

'All right. I was nervous about him being in Washington, anyway.'

'What about out of the office?'

'Oh, that's covered all right.' He glanced around. 'I think another dozen men here will do the trick.'

Wunderman began to turn back towards the topiary. Donovan's voice halted him.

'There's one other thing that Antony asked me to take care of with you.'

'What's that?' The westering sun was in Wunderman's eyes, obliging him to shield his face with his hand.

'Jake Maroc.' Donovan, seeing the other's discomfort, moved to block the sunlight. Wunderman dropped his hand. The sound of the cicadas was very strong. 'He slips off to Japan. An entire KVR extermination team winds up dead. Antony has no idea what he's up to. Neither does David Oh. What about you?'

'I haven't heard from him either.'

'Antony thinks we'd better reclassify him.'

Wunderman's stomach turned over. 'To what?'

'Henry, Antony and I spoke of this at length. I wasn't sure, but the Old Man was adamant. It's possible that Maroc has invaded the computer's memory. Frankly, Antony believes that to be the case. He thinks Maroc has been on the edge since the Sumchun River incident. His wife's death, he reasons, has pushed him over the edge. To tell you the truth, I'm in no position to argue otherwise. You know Jake Maroc better than either of us. What do you think?'

Wunderman wished that he could refute everything

431

Donovan and Beridien had come up with. The fact was he could not. It was useless to deny to himself, or to anyone else for that matter, that Jake had changed after he had returned from the Sumchun River.

Wunderman could recall reading the intelligence flimsy recording Mariana Maroc's death. He should have felt something, but the sad fact was that his first thought had been, Jake will go nuts now.

'The memory bank invasion,' he said softly. 'What programs were touched?'

'KVR priority, Nichiren, restricted lists of Quarry's former agents.'

'KVR priority.' Wunderman said it with a sinking feeling. Jake had taken over that KVR team, all right. With help from the computer.

'Jake terminated the entire KVR team himself. That's the kind of reckless abandon that's dangerous. Furthermore, it's obvious to all of us that he must've seen Stallings kill his wife. Stallings is dead, but we at the Quarry's inner core, we who made the decision, we who sent Stallings into Japan, are not. We're still alive.

'The Old Man thinks that Maroc's intention is to terminate us. First him, then us.'

Wunderman was rolling something over in his mind. 'If it *was* Jake,' he said at last, 'how did he access the information?'

'Isn't *that* a good question?' Donovan said. 'You and I know the closest terminal access that's open to him.'

'Hong Kong Station.'

Donovan nodded.

'That means David Oh.'

'The Old Man brought his name up. Maroc and Oh are very close, isn't that right?'

'David Oh would put his arm in the fire for Jake Maroc.' Oh, Christ, Wunderman thought. It's all falling apart.

432

First Jake and now his whole network is following him down. 'How could this happen?' he wondered out loud.

'Our architect is General Daniella Vorkuta, as Antony suspected. She's been using Nichiren, it seems, to get at Maroc. Now we know she's succeeded.'

'Nichiren, working for the KGB?'

'The confirmation came in today,' Donovan said.

The sun was orange. Its thick rays seemed to drip onto the surrounding countryside, destroying the purity of the afternoon's colours. Wunderman let out a long breath. 'Jake's new status?'

'The Old Man won't do it without your approval. I must say, I feel the same way.'

'How will you classify him now?' Wunderman demanded, knowing what the answer must be.

'Rogue.'

Still he was obliged to close his eyes. 'Rogue' meant Jake was now an outcast from the Quarry. Further, he was judged dangerous to security. The orders to Quarry personnel would be to bring him in for interrogation at the Movie House. If he resisted or there was any indication that he might lose them, they were to shoot to kill.

Wunderman turned his head away from Donovan. That was all the indication he would make.

Donovan nodded. 'Henry, for what it's worth, I'm sorry.'

Daniella at work. The model Soviet bureaucrat, in and out of meetings concerning budgets, departmental responsibilities, appropriations; finishing her weekly paperwork on manpower reassignments, debriefing updates, mission progress, expense reports, assets, human and otherwise, lost in the field; pulling computer hard copies of field data, success rate probabilities, status evaluations, three-, six-, and twelve-month projections based on specific departmental goals, making five copies now instead of four: two for her files, two delivered to Karpov, as usual. One smuggled to Lantin.

Daniella, her cornflower hair shining with extra strokes from the British brush that Lantin had bought her, wearing satin tap pants, lacy garter belt, stockings of real sheer silk beneath her stern *sluzhba* 'uniform' of stiff skirt and high-necked cotton blouse.

Daniella feeling wicked, almost wanton in those dreary, smoke-filled meetings, bending over the printer terminal to pull her hard copies. Imagining Yuri's palms on her buttocks, fingers spreading slowly into the crack between. He had promised her a pair of French-made, midnight-blue pumps with four-inch heels, and during the appropriations debate, she found herself wondering what those extra four inches would do for her figure – the arch of her ribcage and abdomen, the thrust of her breasts. Startled, she felt a warmth between her thighs and shifted in her uncomfortable chair, recrossing her legs while the interminable meeting wore on.

At lunch with three other female *sluzhba* officers, she found herself wondering what Yuri was doing with the reports besides reading them. Was he passing them on to someone else in the Politburo? Had he been doing someone else's bidding, or had he asked for them on his own? Why? Was it to keep an eye on her or on Karpov?

The success of the intermediary phase of Moonstone had set Karpov off. In the office today it was all he spoke of, the girls said. He never mentioned Lantin or the support he got from above. It was only Karpov this and Karpov that. 'I was right and now they know it' was becoming a familiar refrain. Lantin had said the idea of the puppet war with China, using Vietnam, had been his contribution to Moonstone. He told Daniella that he had seen just this potential in Karpov's plan, and had decided to seize the initiative. Karpov, on the other hand, claimed the glory was all his. He was becoming something of a bore.

What did Lantin have in mind? If she had heard of Karpov's boasting, it was logical to think that Yuri knew, too. He had not brought it up with her, but she would have been surprised if he had. Yuri, she had discovered, was composed of a series of façades. *When one harbours secrets*, he had said, *one flirts with a kind of irrevocable danger*.

That had been meant to tell her two things: first, that ferreting out other people's secrets was his stock in trade; second, that he had none himself. Daniella, however, knew that to be a lie. Yuri Lantin's secret lay in his façades. She was beginning to suspect that there were many Lantins. She was certain, for instance, that the one she knew was definitely not the one Karpov was familiar with. Also, the Yuri she knew now was far different from the Yuri she had been introduced to in her office.

Because she was unnaturally quiet at lunch, the officers began to tease her about her rather startling new habits: she had begun to smoke Egyptian cigarettes and wear her long hair down, rather than tied tight at the back of her head. Both were done at Yuri's suggestion.

Somewhere along the line, Daniella caught on and, listening to their gibes, smiled good-naturedly. Secretly she felt only disdain for these creatures. That also was new for her. Formerly these women – had she once really considered them comrades-in-arms? – had been her friends. As much as anyone could be a friend inside the *sluzhba*.

Daniella took a hard look at them. They might as well have been three jabbering monkeys, for all the sense they made. Their minds were filled with useless effluvia. They seemed as contented as cows grazing along a hillside. Happy and satisfied with their own productivity.

They made her want to be sick.

This, too, seemed a product of Lantin, but she could not quite grasp how it had come about. It was as if her affair with him had elevated her to a point where she felt

435

estranged from the people, habits, haunts she had known and felt comfortable with for the past three or four years.

She excused herself and went to the ladies' room. At the cold porcelain sink, chipped and smelling strongly of disinfectant, she bent, throwing cold water on her face. She heard the door opening, closing again, went on with her washing. She stood up, taking paper off a shallow shelf, wiping her dripping face and the back of her neck.

'The others couldn't understand why you weren't yourself out there,' Tanya Nazimova said. She was a squat, plain-looking colonel whom Daniella had pegged as a lesbian. She had her head cocked at an angle. 'It's because of the vigil, isn't it?'

Daniella, her pulse rate up, had the presence of mind not to stare or blurt out, What vigil? As calmly as she was able, she threw the matted paper away. She turned to the mirror and, under the guise of fixing her hair, watched Tanya Nazimova. She had green eyes, as bright as a bird's, and a mole at the corner of her mouth. Like Zsa Zsa Gabor, they used to tease her.

'Why should the vigil worry me?' Vigils were conducted by select surveillance teams to build up a record of habits of a suspected person. Daniella had no idea why a vigil should be ordered on her, but she was going to let Tanya Nazimova tell her.

The other woman shrugged. 'Well, no. I just thought that since this one originated outside the *sluzhba*, you might be nervous.' She smiled. A colonel in Department P, handling liaison between the KGB and the rest of the Kremlin bureaucracies, Tanya Nazimova was always on the alert for situations that could curry favour with her superiors and thus get her promoted out of what she termed 'the armpit of the *sluzhba*.'

'But considering its source, I don't think there's anything to be concerned over. Yuri Lantin and General Karpov are as tight as this.' She held up two crossed fingers. 'Since it's

Lantin's vigil, you can assume Karpov knows all about it. It's just routine, Daniella, that's all.'

No, you idiot! Daniella wanted to scream at her. It's not routine at all. Why has Lantin ordered a vigil on me? And, more important, why hasn't Karpov warned me?

She was still wondering the same thing late in the day, in between calls to two of her field directors who were experiencing problems. It took her mind off concern over the arrival of the next bit of intelligence from Medea, which she was expecting at any moment.

Near quitting time, Karpov appeared in her office, and before he left she had her answer. It was not the one she had been expecting.

He slid into her office as silently as he often did. He did not startle her, though she was on the ciphered, eavesdrop-proof overseas line she often used. She continued to speak in a normal tone of voice while her eyes tracked his progress. He sat out of the light, but still his dyed hair gleamed with pomade, one that contained a thickener he preferred. His cheeks were red and shiny, his skin glowing, indicating that he had just come from his daily facial. Daniella could not see how it was possible, but until this moment she had not realized what a vain man he was. She continued to watch him as she would any outsider in her office while she finished her conversation.

'Well, Comrade General,' he said in his rumbling basso, 'you've had a busy day, I imagine. This is my third trip down to your floor.'

She smiled, indicated the phone. 'You could have tried a call, Comrade.'

He hiccupped or laughed, she could not tell which. He took out a cigar. 'Visits, I think, have a certain piquancy that is lacking in phone conversations.' He spent some time examining his gold lighter. He turned it around and around in his palm, an archaeologist with his find.

She thought then that he would tell her about Lantin's

vigil. He had not come here to smoke a cigar. He could do that anywhere.

'Comrade General,' he said in the tone of voice he used in situations where there were observers from outside the *sluzhba* present, 'your name came up today during a Department S executive meeting.' He continued to stare at the lighter, and now Daniella knew that he had come to deliver bad news. 'There had been some thought of elevating you into Department 12.' Department 12 was directly responsible for infiltration of Britain and associated territories. Quite a large step up from her current position. 'I'm afraid that was vetoed today.'

'And you were delegated to tell me.'

He looked up. 'Better from me than to hear it thirdhand, Comrade General.'

Which was bullshit, Daniella knew. He had been ordered to do it.

'May I ask the general why?' She was peculiarly calm.

Karpov rose. He did not want to get too deeply into this. He shrugged. He had not bothered to light his cigar. He had pocketed the lighter. 'That Japanese disaster might have played a role in the matter. Five men murdered in the field.'

'Four.'

'A simple operation botched.' Karpov's eyes glittered. Daniella was familiar with that look. He was enjoying this. 'Was it lack of preparation or a failure to command?'

She opened her mouth to say that it was Yuri Lantin who had superseded her orders, turning what was basically a surveillance team into a termination squad, but closed it immediately. She saw that even if Karpov believed her – which was doubtful, because he had already cut his deal with Lantin – he would inevitably ask her for the source of her information. What was she to say to that? Oh, it came up while Yuri Lantin and I were fucking?

In any case, she had missed her opportunity to defend herself. Karpov was already out of the door.

This is the last straw, Daniella thought. I've had my fill of him. Her contempt for him exceeded her anger, which was fortunate. Anger never did anyone any good, but contempt, she had found, was, at least in her case, an excellent spur to serious thinking.

What an idiot Karpov was, she saw. He was head of the First Chief Directorate, the largest and most powerful single entity within the *sluzhba*. If she had been in his shoes, she would already be making a run on the Politburo. But Karpov was either too thick to see his job as a springboard or he was clumsy enough to have run into a roadblock like Yuri Lantin. Either way, Daniella decided, she had no more use for him.

For a time she sat quite still, contemplating the darkening streets of the city through the tiny panes of her window. She hated these old-fashioned panes. They were like prison bars. She decided that she hated this entire office. It was altogether too small. She would have to get out.

Perhaps, she thought now, it was time to use Chimera to activate Valhalla. Chimera was a secret she had recruited overseas strictly on her own. *Sluzhba* policy had dictated that she report this asset to her superior within twenty-four hours either in person or via an eyes-only broadcast cipher. This, Daniella had not done. From her mother she had learned that one must have an escape valve, one last card to play. Chimera was hers, the Valhalla plan her ultimate weapon in the game she had been trained for by the State. Once activated, she knew, there was no turning back. She would have made her choice. But what glory its success would provide her!

She felt her heart fluttering. She wiped a thin line of sweat off her upper lip. She was suddenly so hot that she was obliged to get out of there. In Dzerzhinsky Square, she walked on stiff legs between the children running after pigeons. Their faces were so innocent, filled still with the afternoon's light, their cheeks as round as apples, their lips red and sticky with sweets.

Unconsciously, Daniella touched her fingertips to her belly. She wondered whether she would ever know what it felt like to have a child growing inside her. Somehow the thought of carrying a tiny life, of feeling its every move from the inside out, frightened her. It meant thinking more about someone else than she did about herself. She did not think she was capable of that. She knew she was a selfish person; she just did not understand the depths of that selfishness.

The children decided her. She saw in their faces the passing of time. Saw, too, the crack in a door she had believed would always be closed to her. The Politburo.

Yuri Lantin had inadvertently provided that crack.

Now she would use Chimera to force it all the way open.

With a small nod, she strode across the Square. A rubber ball painted red and white bounced her way. She caught it while it was in the air, threw it back to the waiting child who had missed the catch. She caught the toss and laughed in delight. It was infectious, and Daniella laughed with her.

Four blocks distant, she found a shop that would give her sufficient change. Then she found a public phone. She would not dare make this call anywhere else, even over the cipher line in her office. Too many eyes, too many ears.

Though the Soviet telephone service was abominable, she did not want to entrust this to any other means of communication.

In a kind of euphoric daze, she made the call, plugging into the *sluzhba* circuits that would automatically reroute her overseas. It took fourteen minutes to make the connection. In the meantime she calculated the time in Washington, DC.

The ring of the telephone at the other end of the line

startled her. America. The ringing stopped and a voice answered, 'Hello?'

'Chimera,' she said, speaking up as if talking to someone hard of hearing, 'this is your great-aunt Martha.' She often wished that her conversations with Chimera could last more than ninety seconds at a time; she enjoyed speaking English with an American. But the ninety-second deadline was absolute in order to maintain one-hundred-per-cent security. Beyond that, any electronic scanner buzzing along the lines, as they often did throughout Moscow, could record and store the call. 'Martha Washington.'

'I remember.'

'This is the wake-up call for Valhalla.'

'Would you repeat that, please, Auntie?'

'Valhalla.'

'I see.'

'Yes,' she said into the receiver. 'I know you do.'

Shi Zilin was tired. When he was young, he could have fought the Celestial Dragon across the clouds of heaven. Now he felt the weight of the world on him with each breath he took.

He lay naked and sweating in Beijing's summer heat in the centre of a small room in his villa, waiting for the acupuncturist. Not so long ago, he remembered, this had been a weekly occurrence. Now it was daily.

The pain. The pain.

Lying on his stomach, his loins draped modestly with a square of white cotton, his head cradled in his bent arms, Zilin thought of the long war he had waged on China's behalf. A Celestial Guardian should not feel this age. Or this pain. A real Celestial Guardian was immortal; he would still be able to chase the great, gold-scaled dragon across the skies.

This he did not quite grasp. Age was never a concern to him. His *ren*; only his harvest. The *ren* crowded his mind

441

like a flock of plovers wheeling in flight. So many personalities with which to contend, so many changing situations to which he must adapt, so many destinies in the palm of his hand.

Late yesterday he had heard of the appointment of Deng Zhaoguo, one of his enemies from the *qun* being led by Wu Aiping. Deng would be the new head of the Communist Party's propaganda wing. Immediately he had announced a far-reaching campaign against 'spiritual pollution' among China's youth, as Zilin had known he would.

Zilin had petitioned the Premier. To him, this potentially dangerous course harked back to the dark days of the Cultural Revolution that had crippled China from 1966 to 1976. He had argued that Deng's reactionary policies would be derided abroad by the very nations whom China sought as modern-day allies.

To no avail.

'No matter what I might feel personally,' the Premier had said, 'there is far too much power behind Deng Zhaoguo for me to consider blocking the appointment.'

Zilin wondered anew at China. Was this the country he had spent fifty years trying to direct? For what purpose? So that dangerous fools like Deng Zhaoguo could gain power? Perhaps, he thought now, it is I who am the fool.

Zilin stirred as he heard a soft rustling in the room. In his position, with his head away from the door, he could not see who it was.

'Doctor?' he said. He was abruptly afraid.

'It is I, Comrade Minister.'

Zilin relaxed, recognizing Zhang Hua's voice. 'What news, my friend?'

'Five Star Pacific is making its run at Pak Hanmin. It has already bought up close to one hundred thousand shares.'

'Ah,' Zilin said. 'And this is only day one. It seems our

ploy worked. Someone leaked the news of Three Oaths
Tsun's meeting with Peter Ng.'

'Undoubtedly.'

'Is Five Star Pacific the only one?'

'It appears not. Sawyer and Sons is in for thirty thousand; T. Y. Chung for fifty.'

'Lots of pressure.'

Zhang·Hua nodded. 'It will get worse.'

'So it must.' Zilin stirred on the table as a jolt of pain
went through him. 'The pressure must get to strangulation
level, otherwise there will be more than one route to
pursue. That we cannot allow.'

'I understand, Comrade Minister.'

'Perhaps, then, you should begin now.'

'Yes, Comrade Minister.' He turned to go.

'Zhang Hua . . .'

'Yes, Comrade Minister.'

'Any news of Jake Maroc?'

'He is at this moment en route to Hong Kong.'

'Bliss will meet him at Kai Tak?'

'She has been alerted, Comrade Minister.'

'Good.' He allowed himself a long sigh.

'Sir?' Zhang Hua took a step towards him. 'Are you all
right?'

'Mariana,' Zilin said. 'That was tragic.'

'*Joss*, Comrade Minister.'

'*Joss*, yes.' Zilin turned his head with some difficulty.
'Her death serves to remind us, Zhang Hua, that nothing
ever goes precisely as planned. The discovery of the *fu* by
the mysterious Chimera was the start of it. Then came
Jake Maroc's raid on O-henro House, Mariana's death,
and Wu Aiping's elevation to the leader of the *qun*.' He
sighed again. 'I am afraid, my friend, that I am beginning
to lose touch with the mutability of the world. When I was
younger, I could juggle all these permutations and still
have room in my mind for more, should they arise.

'Lately I find myself preoccupied with matters of the family.'

'Under the circumstances, Comrade Minister, that is perfectly understandable.'

'But not excusable, I'm afraid. If I make one slip now, so close to the edge, we will all go down: you, me, China, the USSR, America. It will be a chain reaction that is quite unstoppable. The Soviets have pushed us too far; we have allowed them to reach a level of readiness that is frightfully dangerous.'

'There is always Kam Sang.'

'Yes. There will always be a Kam Sang, Zhang Hua. It seems that the human race needs such terrible spectres glaring over its shoulder in order to keep its finger off the trigger to annihilation.'

'The Soviets will not see it that way.'

'The Soviets will have no choice in the matter, Zhang Hua, that I can guarantee you.'

'Wu Aiping.' It was a whisper.

'Yes. First we must defeat our enemies at home.' Zilin closed his eyes. 'Take care of that matter for me, Zhang Hua.'

'Yes, Comrade Minister.'

'Zhang Hua . . .'

At the doorway he paused, his hand on the knob. 'Sir?'

'You understand the critical importance of every message at this stage.'

'Yes, sir. I do.'

'There can be no mistakes.'

Zhang Hua went out of the room.

When he was alone, Zilin said, 'I feel Wu Aiping's evil presence everywhere. He is close. Very close.'

He was filled with anxiety. Not for himself. He had no fear of death. But he knew that his work had not yet been completed. Fifty years was a long time to toil tirelessly in the service of one's country. A long time in the context of a

444

mortal's life. A blink of an eye in terms of the history of China.

He stirred on the table, impatient for his treatment to start. Pain laced him. He was used to that by now. But still one could yearn for surcease.

At length Zilin heard the soft padding of the acupuncturist's bare soles on the carpet. He felt the strong, capable hands on his back, searching for the meridians.

'Where does it pain you most today, Minister? Here?' The hands moved in concert. 'Here?' And again. 'Here?'

Zilin gave a little cry.

'Ah,' the voice said. 'Ah, yes.'

In a moment Zilin felt the cold brush of the alcohol across three separate spots on his body: the small of his back, over his left hipbone, behind his left knee.

'Now.'

Expertly the long, gleaming needles pierced his flesh. In a moment the pain subsided to a throbbing ache. Then it was gone altogether.

Zilin slept.

Jake flew into Hong Kong's Kai Tak Airport just after 7:00 P.M. He would have been in hours sooner but for the squall. To his surprise, Bliss was waiting for him at the airport.

He saw her standing there, slim and beautiful, just after he and his bags cleared Customs. She came across the crowded floor towards him and he found himself watching the liquid sway of her hips. In the movement he saw a motion that was both innocent and sensual. She might have been a college student welcoming her older brother home.

They stopped a foot from one another. She was silent. He saw the look on her face and recalled Kamisaka's words to him: *I mistook you for a marathon runner*. Do I really look that bad? he wondered.

He had slept fitfully on the plane – a shallow, unrestful slumber in which the image of Nichiren dressed and made up like Kamisaka beckoned him onwards to Hong Kong. For what reason?

'He is in Hong Kong,' Kamisaka had said to him. 'That is all I can tell you.'

'Why?' he had persisted. 'Why has he gone there?'

'He goes often. Three or four times already this year. I don't know why.'

Despite everything she had said, everything he felt from her, he was still suspicious of her answers. He told her so.

Her eyes seemed to drink in his soul. They were standing very close, at the door, his shoes just across the lintel in the hall. The last moment before he would depart. There was nothing sexual between them, yet he felt a connection. It disturbed him as much as it confounded him.

'You have a piece of the *fu*,' she said simply. 'Nichiren also has one. I've seen them both. They comprise one-half of the whole. So the two of you are linked. You cannot be enemies.'

Which just went to show how wrong a person could be.

'A name,' Jake said. 'You may not know why he travels to Hong Kong, but you may have heard a name.'

'He never speaks to me of his business.'

'An inadvertent reference.'

'Pillow talk? There is none of that. Not, at least, of the sort you mean.'

'Actually, I was thinking of something you might have overheard. A telephone conversation, for instance. Has he ever called Hong Kong from here?'

Kamisaka's brow wrinkled in thought. Then she nodded. 'Yes, I think so.'

'Remember anything? A name? A place? Anything at all?'

'Well, it wasn't too long ago. Let me see.' Her eyes, lost in thought, were luminescent in the dim light of the *usagigoya*. When she refocused, Jake felt that odd connection like a heat in his chest.

'Does the name Formidable Sung mean anything to you?' Kamisaka said.

'Was your trip profitable?' Bliss asked him now. The babble of Kai Tak was all around them.

A very Chinese question, Jake thought. He replied in kind. 'Yes and no. I made a friend who is powerful. That is always profitable. On the other hand, I watched my wife die.'

'Oh, how terrible!' She came a step closer. 'I am so sorry.' She kissed him on the cheek, pressed him to her as if he were in need of solace. Now it was his turn to be silent.

'Let me take your bag.'

'It's all right,' he said quickly. Defensive. 'I'm not a cripple.'

'I didn't – ' She tossed her head, angry with herself. Her night-black hair swung in a heavy arc away from her cheek. 'I'm sorry. We seem to have gotten off to a bad start.' She smiled as if nothing had happened. 'My car's outside.'

She took him to her apartment. Jake was too tired to utter a word of protest. It was near the top of Victoria Peak on the Island. Below, one could see the Mid-Level towers, the mostly dark skyscrapers of Central. The harbour was beyond, always filled with ships of every description. Both the living room and the bedroom overlooked this spectacular view. From the bedroom one could see a bit of Wanchai, lit up like the inside of a circus tent.

She fixed him dinner – flash-fried salt-and-pepper prawns; chicken and mango; *chao fan*; fried rice – and he ate silently, with short, rapid movements of his chopsticks.

'You eat like a Chinese,' she said, watching him gorge himself.

Afterwards they went into the living room. Jake collapsed

onto the sofa. It was a soft jungle print, peaceful, calming. He put his head back and Bliss brought them brandy.

Jake did not drink. He stared out of the window at the glitter of nighttime Hong Kong. The squall had washed the air clean, so that all the lights sparkled like gemstones: rubies, emeralds, sapphires. Diamonds.

Back in Hong Kong. Yet Japan clung to him like a foul mist. Memories would not let him go. He was engulfed by greyness.

He felt something, saw Bliss's palm over his heart.

'*Hai-ma-hai nisiu dong a?*' she said. Is this where it hurts?

He could do nothing but look at her.

'Excuse me,' she said. In a moment she had returned. She knelt down beside him and he heard the striking of a match. A moment later the plangent spice of a *joss* stick wafted his way.

'Please forgive my forwardness,' Bliss said, 'but I thought out of respect I would say a prayer for the spirit of your wife.'

'She was *gwai loh*,' he said, defensive again.

'I cannot see how that would matter.' She set the glowing *joss* sticks between them. 'A spirit is a spirit, is that not so?'

With that, she began to pray, using a Buddhist *sutra* of ancient heritage. Jake put his head back against the sofa, listening to the words. Slowly they penetrated, until he began to feel caught up in them.

At length he opened his mouth, found himself speaking the prayers with her. Eventually he felt the wetness on his cheeks.

He thought they were silent tears until he heard himself sob. Then he felt soft arms enfolding him, a gentle perfume surrounding him. He felt her warmth pressing against him, and the comfort it transmitted was at that instant ineffable.

Still sobbing, he put his arms around her, pressed close to her golden skin.

* * *

The Exxon terminal screen of the GPR-3700 mainframe was gravid with information. None of it was good.

COMMAND ACCESS CODE: GARGANTUA
UNIT ACCESS CODE: BLIND BOY
RESPONSE: GO FORTH

'Goddammit!' Chimera said as his fingers paused over the keypad. 'Gargantua' was the current Quarry access code for all known KGB operatives in the massive Mother File. 'Blind Boy' was this fortnight's code for the operative requesting access to the files. There were nine letters and spaces in the code name, indicating that the Quarry operative was part of the Hong Kong Station personnel.

But it was worse still, Chimera thought, as he hit the RETURN key.

COMMAND ACCESS CODE: WATERSNAKE
UNIT ACCESS CODE: BLIND BOY
RESPONSE: GO FORTH

Tuesday Level, he thought. Organized terrorists known to the Quarry. The second letter of the Hong Kong alphabet belonged to David Oh.

Hit the RETURN key.

COMMAND ACCESS CODE: HERMES
UNIT ACCESS CODE: BLIND BOY
RESPONSE: GO FORTH

Wednesday Level: unaffiliated terrorists for hire.

'Shit!' Chimera said to himself. 'What the hell is that bastard up to?' What worried him most were the last three letters of the nine. There were innumerable suffix ciphers within the Quarry computer language. The confluence of B-O-Y was the ultimate access code into the bowels of the data banks, places where there was more shadow than light.

In fact, it was the generation of the B-O-Y suffix code that had brought Chimera's terminal to life. He had spent many hours outside the office perfecting this relatively simple override to the ironclad directive for total autonomous secrecy within the organization.

Stabbed at the RETURN key.

COMMAND ACCESS CODE: FURIES

UNIT ACCESS CODE: BLIND BOY

RESPONSE: GO FORTH

Next, he saw, David Oh had begun viewing the list of lone-wolf KGB operatives. Where was this all leading? he wondered. There had been no terrorist activity in the immediate vicinity of Hong Kong. And no KGB activity that Daniella had not already apprised him of. Then what? He began to sweat. Had she become impatient? Had she put some of her Chimera network people into the field? Had David Oh picked up their scent?

Punched the button, saw the access code for Quarry retirees emblazoned across the screen. 'Now what?' he wondered. What could David Oh possibly want with a list of the Quarry's recently retired operatives?

Hit RETURN and his mouth dropped open.

COMMAND ACCESS CODE: SPHERE

UNIT ACCESS CODE: BLIND BOY

RESPONSE: FOUND AND MATCHED

'Jesus Christ.' He was staring at the names of the two operatives he had assigned to Mariana Maroc in the first place. The ones who had somehow botched the job.

Found and matched? His fingers flew over the keyboard until the computer provided him with what David Oh had been searching for all along.

'Fingerprints,' he murmured. 'They left their fingerprints all over Maroc's apartment! Damn David Oh!'

He swivelled in his chair, snatching up the phone. He dialled the regular Quarry-installed scrambled outside line, then jabbed at the phone again, switching to one of his own lines, which were fully secured against any kind of infiltration. Once assured of that, he dialled the overseas number.

'Yes?' the Taiwanese said. He had snatched up the phone after the first ring.

'Your services are required for a specific purpose,' Chimera said.

'I know the purpose,' the Taiwanese said. 'To whom shall I bring the deliveries?'

'David Oh.'

Half a world away, the phone was set quietly down. That was all the answer Chimera required.

Bliss was breathless with longing for him.

She heard the sound of the shower. In her mind, the image of the needle spray cascading over his naked body. She desperately wanted to be that needle spray.

Watching with twinkling lights climbing up to the Peak, she played a game with herself. Trying to imagine his body, the contours of his flesh. Ridged muscle and the shadowed places between. She had seen dozens of photographs of him after they had lost touch. She still remembered his child's body, close to hers. His warmth that night on Cheung Chau. How she had missed it when he was gone!

But even then, so young, she had had a job to do. The *yuhn-hyun* had dictated that she ensure that Jake got to the fishing island for the Ta Chiu festival. She'd had no idea why at the time, but as she grew up, Three Oaths Tsun had explained it in two words.

Fo Saan.

He had been another part of the seemingly endless *yuhn-hyun*. Perhaps, she had thought, that was how it had derived its name: the ring.

Fo Saan had trained her as well. Out of sight of Jake, not in the same ways. She had her own skills to perfect.

Bliss had been in love with Jake from that night they had spent together on Cheung Chau. As she grew older, she put it down to a childhood infatuation. Perhaps that

451

was because it was not part of the *yuhn-hyun*. Contact with Jake at that point was forbidden.

He had never been out of her mind or her heart, and later, when Three Oaths Tsun had shown her the first photo of him, she melted inside. She was lost to him, utterly and irrevocably. But by then Jake was already married.

Now, as she sat on the edge of the jungle-print couch, she shook with longing for him. Stuck in the corner of her vision: the guttering *joss* sticks. Even in death, Mariana stood between them.

She wanted him so badly, desire was a taste in her mouth. Life was but a dream without him. But there was Mariana to think of. At least his memories of her. Bliss's prayers to the dead had not been a mere gesture. Mariana was a part of Jake; that meant she was important to Bliss. Her body might be buried somewhere in Japan, but her spirit lived forever. That was something Bliss would not forget.

Water like rain in her apartment. Jake in the shower, his long muscles flexing, his coppery skin gleaming, half-hidden in the steam.

The lights of the harbour were smeary in front of her eyes. Bliss wept openly, wept as she had not in years. She experienced her desire now as a tightness in her chest. She fought to breathe, but her weeping made that difficult. She fought for control and could not find it. Her conscious mind closed down. Frightened, she sought out Jake. Ran to the rushing water, just the beat of a heart away.

Through the translucence of the pebbled glass door, Jake saw the shadow of rapid movement. His first thought was for the *fu* shard. Still soapy, he pushed open the door, stood on the slick tiles. Dripping steaming water.

He had had the hot water on as high as he could stand it, and the small bathroom was alive with tendrils of mist.

The doorway was filled. Backlight turned the figure to

452

silhouette, made the outline as fuzzy and glamorous as a photograph in a slick fashion magazine. By the shoulders and hips he knew that it was Bliss.

Jake was conscious of his nakedness, but to make a move to cover himself would have made him feel even more foolish. He was aware of blood suffusing his face. He was certain it wasn't from the hot water.

'Do you have a reason for skulking around like a spook?'

'But I *am* a spook,' she said. 'Skulking is one of the things I do best.' Her first sight of him coming out of the shower had taken her breath away. Smoke curled from him as if he were some mythical creature, rare as a dragon. He seemed full of power.

She moved into the bathroom light and he saw that her lips, partly open, were trembling slightly. He came all the way out of the shower. She wore what she had had on when she picked him up at Kai Tak, a black and white silk dress with a crisscross bodice and no back to speak of. She was barefoot.

'You didn't answer my question.'

'I thought I had.' It was so hard for her to speak. Raw emotion was a fist in her throat.

'What are you doing here?'

'I wanted to see what you looked like.'

'And you came in. Just like that.' His voice was getting tighter and tighter.

'Yes.'

'Goddammit, I am naked!' he exploded. 'It's not . . . it just isn't . . .'

'Don't,' she said. Her eyes were full and glittery. 'Please don't yell at me.' Her voice was thick.

'Bliss, really.' He was at a total loss for words. 'This isn't fair!'

She took a halting step towards him. She was so close now he could see the faint tracks her tears had made down her cheeks.

'Bliss . . .'

'Jake.' Her voice was a reedy whisper. 'Don't take my heart away, Jake.'

No one had ever spoken to him in this way. No one had ever spoken his name the way she did. A caress.

'Forgive me, Mariana.' He heard her faint words and the rustle of fine silk against flesh in the same suspended moment. One sound blended with the other so that later he was unsure if he had actually heard either. In an instant, Bliss's dress was a soft halo around her ankles.

Jake had the good sense to stare. He could hardly have done otherwise. The sight of her robbed him of all volition. She was as tawny as a great cat, her skin lustrous and firm, gently muscled, so well formed that it was as if the years had barely touched her. She was lush and small at the same time. Her waist and ankles were slender. She had the shoulders of an athlete but the hips of a woman, flaring and sensual. He saw a muscle rippling along her thigh; he could see its power.

She put her extended arms over her head, drawing up her breasts even higher. They were full and firm. Her large nipples were already hard. She put her hands underneath them.

'Do you like me?' That reedy whisper again.

This time he shivered in anxious response. 'Bliss,' he breathed.

'Even if it's just a little bit, tell me yes.'

'You have no right to do this.'

'My love gives me the right. I've dreamed of this moment for so long.' There was a wild spark in her eyes, a heavy orange flickering of the sort one sees in animals through dense jungle foliage. Her voice was thick with emotion. 'I've loved you from the moment we climbed side by side at the Ta Chiu. I have slept with no man without dreaming of you. Their arms around me became your arms. And when they penetrated me, it was you I felt.'

'*Bliss.*' As he whispered her name again, Jake was aware that he had been wrong about her in the airport. She was not the sister coming to meet her older brother, but a woman hesitantly about to open her heart to her future lover.

She came towards him, seeming to float across the tile floor. He was fascinated, watching the play of her long muscles beneath that lustrous, smooth skin. He saw that she had the stride of a panther, a sinuous grace that was as powerful as it was erotic. She led with her thighs; she moved from the hips down with a low centre of gravity. With each step she took, it was obvious that she drew strength upwards from the ground upon which she walked. It was this elementalism that gave her innocence an erotic resonance.

At the moment their bodies touched, Jake gasped out loud. It was as if he had been brushed by an electrical current. He felt the nerves beneath his skin bristle as if they had been lying dormant for years. Something inside himself had been brought alive by her.

He felt her arms come around him, her face tilt upwards on its long neck. He was aware of her whole body lifting up, propelled by the arching of her feet. And because of this, her flesh slid against his.

At the instant his mouth came down over hers, he felt the heat of her groin pressing inwards, felt with a kind of lunatic tingling the brush of her pubic hair against his lower belly.

He groaned into her open mouth as he tasted her. She was like a sweet liquor of which he could not get enough. His head swam and he felt the tension in his legs burst into muscle spasm.

With this, he recognized that he had been thinking of her since the night of that first dream in the hospital. He had wanted her then and ever since, but his guilt and then his mourning for Mariana had not let him feel it fully.

He clasped her to him, feeling her warmth stealing through him, thawing his icy insides. At that moment he thought he felt his heart cry out, and he slipped down to his knees. His palms caressed her muscular flanks. His face was very close to her essence. Her innocence stirred him profoundly as he, too, thought of that children's night on Cheung Chau.

He could feel her heat on his cheek. His nostrils flared with the scent of her arousal. He opened his mouth and felt his tongue being drawn into the core of her. He licked softly and gently in long, loving swipes, and was amazed to find how quickly she opened to him, layer upon delicate layer.

Above him, Bliss thrust her fingers in his thick hair, holding on as she rocked her pelvis in towards him. Her heart beat like a triphammer as she felt her own secret flesh flowering open. Her insides had turned to water and she felt a fine filament of sensation arcing downwards from her navel to the spot where Jake was making love to her.

As his tongue moved, so too did the filament, filling out and intensifying into a ribbon of pleasure beyond anything she had ever felt. Her lower belly fluttered with its movement, out of her conscious control.

Without quite knowing what she was doing, Bliss reached down and took Jake's hands, drawing them upwards until she could press his palms against her breasts.

She moaned when she felt him grasping her there. The feel of his calloused flesh brushing back and forth over her distended nipples was almost more than she could bear. Now the ribbon extended itself upwards, fluttering through her breasts. Now she felt connected to him in all ways, as if, truly, he had entered her.

Bliss felt an energy building within her. Her intensive lifelong training with intrinsic energy caused her to be open to it, to embrace it rather than fear it, for she was immediately aware of its power.

'Ahhh,' she cried, panting. 'Ahhh!'

Bliss was crouching down, spreading her thighs as much as she was able in this position. Her openness increased her pleasure. Her neck arched and she threw her head back. She stared sightlessly at the ceiling, lost in the web of ecstasy Jake was weaving within her. Her eyes fluttered closed. Her breasts heaved within the confinement of his palms.

She could not stop her hips from flipping forward against him. She wanted him inside her, but even more, she wanted this ecstasy to continue.

She cried out sharply as she felt her engorged flesh being drawn into a liquid place. Heat suffused her and then the licking commenced again, but this time with the added sensation. She looked downwards, saw that he had taken part of her into his mouth.

'Ohhh,' she gasped. 'I can't stand it. I can't . . . Oh!'

The heat struck her across her chest, suffusing her shoulders, ribcage, and heart in a bath of liquid fire. It rushed up her neck and into her face.

Her breath shuddered through half-open lips, her nostrils flared. The tension in her muscles reached epic proportions. Then it all gave a final outward thrust as her orgasm overwhelmed her. She shuddered and shook within his embrace, crying out in Burmese in her release.

She collapsed into Jake's waiting arms, her head bowed, her eyelids flickering.

Jake lowered her slowly onto himself. He drew on what control he had left; he was mad to soak himself inside her. He was so hard he hurt, quivering with the burning images of her in the throes of her intense climax.

All the breath went out of him as he felt her streaming wetness engulf the tip of him. 'Oh, God!' The words were expelled from him like steam from an engine.

Bliss's hands were on his shoulders, and he felt them grip him as she came down on him. Her head bent forward

457

into the crook of his shoulder. Her open lips bit into his flesh.

'Take me.' Her voice was a ragged whisper. 'Take me, oh, please.'

Tentatively he pushed himself upwards, felt himself sink another half-inch inside her. Her warmth was almost too much for him to bear. His lungs were working like a bellows. Sweat streaked him. It pearled her long, night-black hair, strands of which clung to him like tiny arms.

'Oh, Jake!' It seemed that she had no breath left. He felt her hand moving downwards beneath their connection. Her strong fingers cupped him gently, squeezing rhythmically.

It was too much for him. With a deep moan, he slid all the way into her, hilting himself. Then he felt her lifting herself away from him. He slid all the way out and she hovered, brushing against his tip for as long as they could bear it. He hilted himself again.

Jake grabbed her, certain he could not hold out for much longer. He did not want this feeling to end, yet the ecstatic friction was ascending to such a height within him that he knew it could not be long sustained.

With every stroke he felt the core of her fluttering nakedly around him, felt her high mount pressed against his belly, her fingers squeezing gently but urgently at him.

He felt the weight growing inside him, the gentle pulling at his loins becoming ever more urgent. With a lurch, his anal sphincter tightened. He grew inside her, trembling.

Bliss sensed his ending and she rode him more rapidly now, pressing the top of herself against him as he pistoned in and out. Their flesh slapped together faster and faster, and as that happened, Jake felt a kind of ecstatic merging. He felt floodgates opening inside him, felt his vulnerability to Bliss and did not shy away from it. He embraced it.

And with great force and heady emotion, he jetted into her with an abandon he thought beyond him.

Merged with him, Bliss felt the building of her own

inner forces. His trembling ardour fuelled her own, so that she was on the brink when he came. The force of his explosion transferred itself to her and she exploded again, a quick, sharp burst quite different from before, but no less pleasurable.

Perhaps it was not only the hot water still running in the shower that steamed the room, but the force of their mingled emotions.

Outside, the moon had risen, huge and oblate, dimming the gemstone lights from the Peak all the way down to the harbour. The water glittered like a pathway to the stars in the new light.

David Oh was on the run.

Night. In his city. He would be all right, he kept telling himself.

He knew he had to get to Jake, tell him what he now knew. No place inside the Quarry was safe.

At his shoulder, the Singapore hotel rose up like a glass beehive, its room lights bright and inviting. Not for him. He hurried on down Lockhart Road. In brightlight Wanchai, full of late-night bars, dance halls, and cinemas, he felt safe. Then why was he shivering?

Remembering himself hunched over the GPR-3700 computer terminal, in the process of finding out that Stallings's missions somehow coincided with KVR missions of unknown objective; that shortly after his aborted missions, opposition leaders had been terminated, not killed as published reports indicated.

Except for Mahmed Al-Qassar, a secret CIA double whom the KVR had cheerfully allowed Stallings to mistakenly terminate.

Perhaps all of this had made no sense to Stallings. Perhaps if he had lived a bit longer he would have reasoned it out. David Oh had a leg up on that: the knowledge that someone inside the Quarry had ordered Mariana Maroc's termination before the official 'seek and terminate' directive had been given.

More time at the computer and a greater knowledge of the software programming allowed him to extract another vital piece of the puzzle. All the opposition terminations had been traced back to one source: Nichiren.

Nichiren was being run by the KVR. That meant General Daniella Vorkuta. The 'contrary' directives from inside the Quarry all benefited the Soviets. Vorkuta again.

That was enough for David Oh. As soon as he had come up against the stone wall of the *EYES ONLY, QUARRY DIRECTOR* graphic, he had made a hard copy of all the intelligence he had unearthed, including that.

Vorkuta had penetrated to the very core of the Quarry. She was attacking from inside and out. David Oh had no idea how far she had already got, but one thing was certain: he could trust no one. No one but Jake.

He slipped into the Grey Shark, a sleazy dive where the lights were low, the drinks two parts water, and the girls totally without a memory. The place was filled with noise and smoke. The noise was coming from sixteen loudspeakers girdling the enormous room. Billy Idol was spitting out the words to 'White Wedding'.

Red, green, and gold spots roved the rafters, swinging down every so often to brush the swaying dancers' shoulders. Sailors. David Oh saw lots of sailors. An American aircraft carrier was in. Piles of money would be made in Wanchai tonight, three-quarters of it illicitly.

He went to the neon-trimmed bar and ordered a whisky and soda. It tasted like water, which was okay with him. Now was not the time to get a buzz on. Except for the raised octagonal dance floor, the place was filled with tiny tables. To one side, near the bathrooms, a steep flight of metal gridwork stairs led up to a second storey.

David Oh's eyes scanned the room, but he saw no one

he knew. Out of the corner of his eye, he watched the door. Outs he ignored. It was the ins he was concerned with.

Within six minutes of his arrival he saw three possibles. All men, they caught his eye because of their faces. They had been trained by a large, disciplined organization. Their eyes swept the room, piercing to a different quadrant every eight seconds. There was no deviation. In a moment they were gravitating towards him.

David Oh grabbed a girl and, pulling her close against him, moved away from the bright aurora of the bar.

It had been a risk, using the computer in the manner he had over the past several days. Because of the peculiar nature of the software, he had picked up Stallings's trail. He suspected that General Vorkuta's contact inside the Quarry hierarchy had done so as well. That was why he had been sent back into Japan. Not to terminate Nichiren, but to be terminated himself.

David Oh knew in the back of his mind that the same fate could very well be in store for him. Still, he had continued with his unearthing. Once begun, he could hardly back off. He'd never be able to live with himself.

Now he knew that he had been discovered.

He took the girl up the stairs with him. In his ear, he heard her breathing the grocery list of prices. Did he want it straight or would he like to make it a threesome? did he want oral or anal sex? did he want to spend a half-hour, an hour, longer? Very romantic. He didn't even bother to tell her to shut up.

They went into one of the two dozen or so rooms upstairs, above the disco floor. Inside, he threw her from him, ignoring her 'Hey, S-and-M will cost you plenty more!' and jerked the small window up. Music permeated the floorboards, the heavy thump-thump-thump of the bass setting his teeth rattling.

He peered out. Drainpipes galore. There was no time to think about how long they had been there or how sturdy they were. He wriggled like a cat through the aperture and grasped the pipes, filthy with encrusted dirt and rust. Shinnied down into the gloom of the back alleyway.

He took off into the night, thinking, My only chance now is to find Jake. Three blocks later, filling his lungs with much-needed oxygen, he remembered Bliss. He had suspected from the first that Jake had slipped out of Hong Kong with her connivance.

Now she might be the only link he had. He dug in his pocket for a coin and began to run again. Looking for a phone.

Sir John Bluestone knew that he had an edge over his competitors as soon as the other man came into the room and began to report.

It was interesting, Bluestone thought now, stretched out on his leather sofa. Like a prince. A prince of commerce. That was how he thought of himself. Partially. He had his secret life as well, which warmed him every hour of the day and night. Working for a cause, that connected with him. He had been born into England's upper class. In India, then in the smaller countries of Southeast Asia, he had seen how the arrogance of the white man had turned a series of exquisite paradises into the dust of destruction. The wanton disregard for life that his people exhibited had filled him with disgust and, more importantly, disquiet. He had begun to make his feelings known. And had been contacted, vetted, recruited. Then he had been sent to Hong Kong and eventually had risen to his current level as one of the five *tai pan* of Five Star Pacific.

It was interesting, Bluestone thought again, watching the Chinese give his report. His study, in which he now reclined, was a reflection of himself. It was composed of a series of patterns – all variations on the theme of black and Chinese red. The ceiling was black lacquer, the walls

462

papered in a black-on-black, gloss-and-matte pattern, with a scattering of tiny chrysanthemums in red.

The leather couch on which he reclined was red, the chairs black. The floor was covered with plush wall-to-wall carpeting in black with red pin-dots. Ebony bookshelves climbed the wall behind the ebony desk and the black lacquer and red metal chair. There was a Chinese altartop sideboard in red, on which stood the only splash of another colour: a priceless Qing vase that was so translucent it could be said to contain either no colour or all colours at once.

In all, it was an overpowering place. Which was precisely Bluestone's intention. No one who crossed this threshold had ever failed to be intimidated by the place. This included the Governor as well as a handful of lordly ministers from the English Parliament.

Peter Ng was almost finished with his report. It was interesting, Bluestone thought, how all the birds eventually came home to roost. Here was a man who had been part of Bluestone's network for five years or more, ever since Bluestone had discovered, through his agents, that Ng had been clandestinely keeping a separate set of Sawyer and Sons' books which showed that over 23,000 shares of the company's stock had somehow come into his possession over the years. He had never been of much use to Bluestone, just a tidbit here and there. Until now.

'The bottom line,' Ng was saying, 'is that Andrew Sawyer's into Pak Hanmin to the tune of thirty thousand shares. Tomorrow he plans to go for another hundred. He thinks the issue's tremendously undervalued.'

Now I have something, Bluestone thought. Though I have T. Y. Chung buying for me, I need that last bloc of a hundred thousand shares to ensure my control over the company. I haven't enough money to cover that, though, and that hundred thousand might come very dear if Sawyer and I fight over it, which seems likely. It's the last major bloc up for sale.

Now is the time, he thought, to contact my new partners. The local banks with which he did business had kept him abreast of the buy-up of his short-term debt over the past several days. Through any one of them, he knew, he could get a message to his benefactors. If they had money for that, surely they'd have more to ensure Five Star Pacific's control over Pak Hanmin and the fruits of the nearly complete Kam Sang project.

He dismissed Ng, then picked up the phone. He opened his address book, quickly looked up the number of the president of the Hong Kong and Asia Bancorp. Never mind the late hour. He needed to get a message off. In order to fight off Sawyer and Sons, he needed promise of capital before the Hang Seng opened in the morning.

Bluestone listened to the quiet burr of the phone line, and when the male voice he recognized answered, he began to speak.

All the way from Wanchai on foot, using plate-glass windows as mirrors to check his flanks and behind him whenever possible, David Oh watched for brackets, box tags, all the subtle variations that ticks could take. He doubled back, switched sides of the street against the light, shied away from the wide avenues.

Then he hopped on a bus.

It was going in the opposite direction from his final destination. That was all right with him. He was determined to give this run plenty of time. If ticks were going to show themselves, he wanted to allow them the opportunity. He also wanted to know how the three of them were being employed. That would give him a clue as to their overall expertise.

He was clean when he made the call. His heart had leapt when Bliss put Jake on the phone. So much to say, so little time in which to say it. It was the wrong place for sentiment, and he had kept himself in check. He'd set up the rdv at the top of Victoria Peak. Near enough to Jake, but away from Bliss's safe house, out in the open – known territory. It'd be okay.

He got off the bus at the third stop, waiting until the doors were about to close. No one came after him. Swung aboard a bus heading the other way. Thirteen stops, an inauspicious number, but it was time to get off. He walked two blocks west to Queensway. It was after dinner, and the Colony's main arteries were crammed with people. The neon nightlife beckoned just a ferry ride away in the throbbing heart of Tsim Sha Tsui.

David Oh waited patiently for the bus that would turn up Cotton Tree Drive. It was becoming more and more difficult to tell whether he was clean. So many people packed into so small a space. But at least he had made visual contact with his ticks. He'd have no trouble spotting them again.

A bus came, but it was so overladen with passengers that he decided to wait. It gave him a chance to get an in-depth feeling about his immediate environment. Directly behind him was a shop emblazoned with the three-dimensional logos of four or five top Swiss watch manufacturers. As was usual, this kind of establishment drew a multitude of tourists, both those with enough wealth to buy the solid-gold-and-diamond-encrusted timepieces and those content merely to gawp.

Down the street a band of young Chinese strode purposely away from him, mingling in the crowd. He turned away. Across the busy thoroughfare a brace of sailors grabbed a taxi, heading down towards the pier and the Star Ferry.

The happy, raucous babble of dialects only served to make him feel apart from the hurrying crowds. His situation had made him disassociated enough as it was. The red double-decker swung into view. On its side was a tiger-striped poster for a new film. A woman reclined with her head upturned. The torso of a man loomed over her, half-shadowed. In blood-red script: *The Ninja – The Movie*.

The crowd that had formed for the bus began to surge forwards even before it came to a full stop. David Oh felt himself borne along on a tide of rushing human flesh. Chinese screamed in his ear, cursing an Australian for his slow-footedness.

The dark funnel of the bus's door seemed to suck the crowd up into its depths. David Oh followed along. He was acutely aware that he had had no chance to inspect everyone who crushed in behind him.

He slipped off the bus at the stop where Cotton Tree Drive and Garden Road came together. He waited for the light, then crossed to the Peak Tram kiosk. He bought a ticket for HK $4 and slid into the shadows just beyond the cones of light surrounding the small structure.

Mist was building. Already it was difficult to see farther than halfway up the Peak Road. He glanced at his watch. It was very near midnight, the time when the tram stopped running. No one else was about. It was not the most popular time to take the steep journey up the mountain.

He put his head back against the damp wall. He wondered what he would say to Jake when he saw him. He knew, over and above the information he now possessed, that it was important to right things between them. He realized with a plangent pang of sadness that neither he nor Jake had been much of a friend to the other during the past months.

Even at this moment his anger at Jake was a palpable presence. Something had happened to him at the Sumchun River. It was natural, perhaps, for Jake to clam up about it during debriefing. Maybe it was none of the Quarry's business, that part of it. But David Oh had to admit that he had been disappointed, then hurt, that Jake had not confided in him. Did their friendship mean so little? Didn't Jake trust him? Resentment had smouldered within him like a lit fuse. It did not change what he would do for Jake – just his perception of Jake. He had thought friendship was more important to Jake. As important as it was to him. Sacrosanct.

There was much to be accomplished this night, and the Peak was, perhaps, symbolic of that. The highest point in the Colony.

Up above the clouds, the rails began to sing. The tram was coming. Wires were vibrating. David Oh felt the movement.

As he swung aboard the dimly lit car, he felt his longing to return to friendship as a physical sensation. Startled, he realized just how much he had missed Jake.

He sat near the front of the car. Far off, he heard the muffled hooting of a barge and, closer to hand, the soft hiss of traffic passing across wet tarmac. The doors began to close.

David Oh looked around. A young Chinese in a black lightweight raincoat and hat sat at the opposite end of the car. He carried a tightly rolled umbrella, perhaps unconsciously imitating a British gentleman. He did not look at David Oh.

David Oh's gaze swung away. The doors sighed shut, and with a soft lurch, the tram began its tedious trek up the side of Victoria Peak.

Six stops. No one got on or off. They were halfway up now, completely enclosed in cloud. The night took on a softly luminescent glow. It was neither dark nor light, and it seemed now as if they travelled through an unchanging clime, suspended partway between heaven and earth. David Oh shifted to get his sticky shirt away from his back. He was thinking about Jake.

At the seventh stop, the tram ground to a halt. A Chinese

stepped into the car and the doors slid shut. They were on their way again.

The man looked around. He glanced at the Chinese with the umbrella, then towards the front of the car.

Then they both came after David Oh.

Outside, the moon had been obscured by the mist.

After the call had come in, Bliss asked no questions, as a Westerner surely would have. Nevertheless, she seemed to have picked up Jake's melancholy mood. Her hands were dug deep into her coat pockets.

'It might be best to walk to the Peak Tram station,' she said, starting down the sidewalk.

Jake nodded. 'Try to cover every possibility.'

'Trouble is, one rarely does.'

It had begun to drizzle. The perfectly clear night had disappeared as if it had never existed. Jake held them back in the shadows of the dripping wisteria. Just in front of them, the sidewalk stretched away. 'I want to listen,' he said, 'and look.'

The night was doleful. The misty cloud cover held the street and apartment lights, turning shadows grey. Every hiding place glowed with accumulated luminescence. Jake heard nothing and saw no one. Crickets beat a hidden racket. The sound, caught between the high-rises lower down on the slopes, reverberated, setting the night shimmering.

Jake was absolutely certain of his tradecraft. He had been trained by the best: Henry Wunderman. It was Wunderman who had approached Jake in Hong Kong more than twenty years ago. They had met for lunch at the Peninsula Hotel's grandly curving dining room.

Wunderman, his face shiny with sweat, had scraped his chair legs against the carpet in getting his bulk to the table. He had ordered bourbon and had made a face on taking the first sip.

'I understand you're out of work.'

'That's right.'

Wunderman made a great show of studying the menu, but had ended up ordering the blandest items. 'I'm not used to this part of the world,' he said. He waited for Jake to order, then put his elbows on the table.

'What are your interests?'

Jake wondered who this large American was. It would not have been good manners to ask. 'Martial arts, Chinese, *wei qi*.'

'*Wei qi*, what's that?'

'It's a game. I'll teach you how to play sometime. That'll take seven minutes. I can also teach you how to win. That'll take seven years.'

Wunderman had laughed at that. 'You're perfectly right,' he said. 'Some skills take a long time to develop.'

They had liked each other immediately. Wunderman found Jake smart enough so that he felt certain he could learn from him. For his part, Jake was intrigued by Wunderman's mystery. It was his opinion that this man represented a kind of sub rosa world, apart from Hong Kong or any one city on the globe. Jake, feeling apart from the world, felt an immediate attraction to this as yet unnamed society. It did not appear to be against the law, as the triad society was, but rather beyond the law.

As if reading his thoughts, Wunderman said, 'I understand you have triad connections.'

Jake nodded.

'Why aren't you working for them?'

The food came and they both waited until the white-jacketed waiter was gone.

'I am *gwai loh*,' Jake said. 'A foreign devil.'

'Only half.' Wunderman's soft brown eyes looked into Jake's. 'Sure, I know you're half Chinese, kid.' He looked away for a moment, stirring his drink with his forefinger. 'Tell me, why are you still on this rock?'

'It's my home.'

'Think there's something for you here, then?'

Jake's eyes held his.

'What d'you suppose that something is?'

'I don't know.'

'It wouldn't have anything to do with some crazy notion you might have about trying to find out what happened to your father, would it?'

Jake knew then that this man was someone special.

'Tell me,' Henry Wunderman said after a pause, 'if you were not . . . a foreign devil, but were fully Chinese, would you work for them then?'

'No,' Jake said, 'I'd find a way to make *them* work for *me*.'

Wunderman went back to his eating. He seemed wholly concentrated on that. After a time he said, 'Suppose I can show you a way to do that. Would you be interested?'

Jake looked at him. It was easy enough to give an answer, but he understood the gravity of the moment. A question such as this should not be answered in an instant.

'How long do you plan to stay in Hong Kong?'

Wunderman shrugged. 'How long will it take you to say yes?'

It had taken three days.

What had happened to them both since that time?

'All right,' Jake said now, leading the way down the path and out onto the street. Without the insects' clatter, the world would have been utterly silent around them. Even the airport across the bay was beginning its nightly shutdown procedures.

His mind was alight with David Oh's words: 'The Quarry's been penetrated.' So many questions; no time for even one. As he should have, David had set up the rdv and then rung off.

'There's a possibility,' Jake had said as he began to get dressed, 'that David will have visitors with him.'

470

'So?' She was drawing on her dress.

'What is this, "monkey see, monkey do"?'

'If there's going to be trouble, I'm going with you.'

'You're staying here.'

'Jake, there's no time to argue.'

'Right.' He buttoned his shirt. 'You're staying.'

'You can't stop me from following you.' She zipped up, searched for her shoes.

'Do you think you can run in high heels?'

'I was looking for these.' She held up a pair of dancer's thin-soled shoes. 'They make no noise.'

He looked at her, then turned and went into the living room.

'What is it?' she asked, coming after him. 'Do you think I can't take care of myself?'

'Maybe.' He slipped into his loafers.

'I studied with Fo Saan.'

He looked up. 'Fo Saan.'

She nodded.

He came over to her, so close he could feel her heat. He stared into her eyes. 'I'll make a deal with you.'

'What kind of deal?'

'You can come with me, hear whatever David Oh has to tell me, get your head bashed in, too, if it comes to that. But afterwards you tell me everything there is to know about you.'

She hesitated and he said, 'It's the only way, Bliss, that I promise you.'

She scooped her thick hair out of her eyes. 'I want you to trust me.'

'I wouldn't have suggested this if I didn't.'

'Then why do you – '

He put his hand on the door. 'Take it or leave it. I've let you keep your secrets too long as it is.'

'I can't.'

He opened the door. 'If you follow me, I'll know and I'll lose you. You know I can.'

She was unsure enough about that to acquiesce. 'All right. It's a deal.'

'Everything.'

'*A mi tuo fo*, yes! Everything.'

'Almost there,' Bliss said now.

Up ahead they could see the lights, glowing in the mist, of the Peak Tram station.

'It looks deserted,' she said.

'Let's make sure.'

Within seven minutes they met at the station, after having circumnavigated the perimeter. They could see the result in one another's eyes: nothing.

Together they stood in the close night, waiting. It was impossible to believe that an hour earlier the moon had shone clear and stark. The drizzle pattered all around them. The leaves on the trees at their shoulders bowed beneath the weight. Now he would never see rain without thinking of Mariana.

'Jake.' It was a breath beside him. He stirred. 'What we did earlier, we did out of love.'

'Bliss – '

'Please, I must say this.' Her fingertips touched his. 'No matter what I felt inside, I never would have approached you that way, had it not been . . .' She paused, momentarily flustered, took a deep breath, as if she were about to plunge off a cliff. 'If Mariana and Ting had not been dead.'

His head jerked away from his vigil down the steep incline of the tram tracks. 'You know about my first wife?'

Bliss nodded. Her eyes were filled with sadness – his sadness. 'I know that she took her own life.'

Jake said nothing. Bliss thought his face was hard enough to have been chiselled from stone.

She forced herself to go on. 'I didn't bring this up to

472

hurt you. It was to reassure you. I love you too much ever to upset your life.'

He looked down at her then. He could feel the familiar film growing over his heart, protecting his core. She had pierced him, back at her apartment. He had been open and vulnerable for the first time in three years. That was something, at least.

He knew that she was making an attempt to make permanent what was now only temporary. He wanted to respond in kind. He knew that in the most absolute sense. But it was too soon. Or he was no longer capable. He did not know which, and that knowledge was like a crippling blow to his heart. He wondered now just how deeply the Sumchun River had damaged him. Wondered, too, if he would ever recover.

He was about to say something when he heard the tension coming into the rails. Overhead, the tram wire began to sing. He glanced at his watch.

'Time,' he said. 'Let's get going.'

David Oh was slowed by his disbelief. He knew the three. Taiwanese. These two were Shanghainese. By all the gods great and small, he thought, how many have they sent after me?

Reflexively he managed to kick a heavily muscled leg outwards, connecting with one of the Chinese. He felt the impact as the toe of his shoe caught the man on the inside of his thighbone, along the line of the nerve meridian.

The leg collapsed underneath the man and he grabbed it, his sunglassed face grimacing in pain. The second Chinese held the tightly rolled umbrella before him like a lance.

David Oh heard a sharp click through the heavy rumbling of the moving tram car. It drew his eyes to the twenty-centimetre steel blade protruding from the end of the umbrella.

He twisted his upper torso at the last possible instant, feeling the hot wind of the mini-swordblade as it shot past his left ear. He struck immediately upwards with the edge of his hand in an attempt to crack the weapon. He felt it bend, not break.

Then the Chinese was yanking it backwards for another stab. David Oh heaved himself off the seat. Sitting, he had been at a serious disadvantage. As the Chinese rushed at him, he slammed his foot down on the man's tensed instep, using all his weight, centring his body over that one spot. He ground the steel-tipped heel of his shoe in a tight arc until he heard the crack of the metatarsal splintering under the pressure.

At once he clasped his hands together, swung them upwards from his right hip. They slammed into the Chinese just below his armpit. It was a little high to break a rib, but it got him off balance.

David Oh followed him down, keeping his foot on the other's foot until he heard the snap of the ankle. Used his elbows just under the Chinese's chin, digging for the windpipe and the cricoid cartilage.

The Chinese twisted desperately, aware that should his opponent find his mark, he would be dead within seconds. His fingers abandoned the now useless umbrella-sword, scrabbling between the rolling bodies to find a neural plexus.

David Oh felt the telltale burning and he knew the Chinese had hold of a major nerve centre. But now he had forced his elbow beneath the man's jaw. In a moment he would crush the cricoid artery. It was dangerous to ignore the other's attack, but David Oh made the decision instantly. There was simply no question of his giving up his advantage. He doubted that the Chinese would allow him back within his guard.

There was a buzzing filling up his head. Bees, like lead weights, swam through his brain. His coordination was slowing. He knew what he had to do, but getting the commands down the line to his extremities seemed more and more of a Herculean task. Spots danced before his eyes as the Chinese, knowing the end was nearing, exerted all his strength in this one desperate bid for life.

A viscous blackness hovered at the edges of David Oh's vision. He could no longer feel his legs, and he knew the creeping paralysis would soon rise into his arms. When they were too heavy to support, his elbow would come away. David Oh felt close to collapse. His sense of dissociation was now so acute that he seemed able to differentiate his inner self from the husk of his body. He no longer knew what he was doing.

Sweat stung his eyes, bringing him back to a semblance of reality. He felt his heart struggling to maintain his adrenaline level. He felt the hot breath sawing in and out of his painfully heaving lungs.

He knew then that he was in trouble. Concentrate! he ordered himself.

Saw the sharp point of his elbow jammed into the interstice between the Chinese's chest and chin, and with an awesome rush it all flooded back at him.

Leaned the full weight of his upper body in behind the elbow attack, felt it plunge downwards suddenly into soft flesh and cartilage.

He felt the easing of his nerve centre at once, but he lacked the perspective to understand what it was. He was panting in the heavy air, still filled with fear and excess adrenaline. There was a trembling inside him at the knowledge that he had almost died, and that he had killed a man.

'Buddha,' he moaned, beginning to massage the burning welts around his solar plexus.

With a great animal grunt, David Oh's head jerked backwards as the steel wire whipped around his neck. He had forgotten about the other Chinese! He began to cough as the oxygen flow was severely restricted.

The panic that tore through him caused him to bring both hands up to try to pull the wire away from the soft flesh of his throat. He was doing just what he had been trained not to do in this kind of situation. It was a waste of time to try to pull the garotte away. He had been trained to forget the garotte entirely and concentrate on the assailant. Disable him, and the garotte would come away.

The panicked animal knew only that something was choking it, and that it must pull it away at all costs.

Perhaps it was the muted laughter in his ear that snapped David Oh back into the mind-set of a veteran intelligence officer. He smelled the garlic and liquorice breath in great, foul pants and it made his stomach heave. The real problem was that the nerve damage he had suffered had not yet fully dissipated. He could barely drag his legs along. They felt like dead weights.

With a grunt, he tore his hands from their useless task at his burning throat. He willed himself to ignore the fact that there was now no oxygen at all coming in. His windpipe was on fire. His lungs strained for a new breath. He was strangling on his own carbon dioxide. He heard a singing in his ears, the siren song of his own desperately pumping blood. Sound became distorted. His eyes began to bulge.

The only thing that saved him was the braking of the tram. It came unexpectedly, and his assailant loosened his hold for an instant.

Half of that time was past before David Oh recovered enough to take advantage. He reached painfully behind him, grabbing the tail of the other's jacket. With all his remaining strength he jerked downwards. As a result, the garotte tightened against him so hard that he gurgled in agony. But then the Chinese lost his balance completely.

Dimly, David Oh heard the thump. He had to remind himself twice that it was the sound of a body falling.

476

Slowly, painfully, he collapsed to his hands and knees. He was gasping like a fish out of water. All colour had drained from his face. His oxygen-starved brain felt as if it were about to explode.

On the floor of the tram, he scrabbled at the wire constricting his throat, desperate to remove the cincture. Then he felt himself pulled down, a dog on a leash. The Chinese had regained hold of the ends of the garotte, and now, face to face with David Oh, he began again to exert pressure on the larynx and windpipe.

David Oh had scarcely enough strength left to resist. He met the garlic and liquorice head on, and he almost drowned on his own gorge as he gagged heavily.

He was so dizzy he no longer had any sense of up or down. He felt weightless, suspended as he had earlier, between earth and heaven. Only now he felt much closer to heaven.

He knew he was close to passing out – knew, too, that death lay on the other side of that slumber. He was determined that should not happen.

With great ham-like fists, he pounded against the Chinese face, harder and harder until the blood began to flow as he tore through skin, bruising the flesh beneath.

The Chinese was blind with his own sticky blood, but still he refused to let go of the garotte. All his energies were concentrated down that narrow line; his only thought was to pull the wire as tight as he could. Death was in his heart, not survival.

Still, David Oh fought on. He was no longer aware of time or place. There was only life and the void that succeeded it. He turned his thumbs outwards like spoons, dug them viciously into the Chinese's eye sockets. The man only grunted, where any other would have howled in pain and begged for mercy. The Chinese had inured himself to all consequences. He knew his job and he was doing it.

With a last desperate effort, David Oh leaned forward

and, hunching his shoulders so that all his muscles bunched up with effort, plunged his spatulate thumbs downwards through the soft sockets. The eyeballs burst apart as David Oh, howling in terror and rage, dug his nails through tissue and cartilage as far as they would go.

Death came, and the Chinese whipped under him in galvanic response. There was nothing left inside him but residual nerve flow and the reflexive convulsions of muscles carrying out the fiercely concentrating brain's last command.

The fists, white with effort and strain, remained pulling at the ends of the garotte. Even in death, the Chinese would not give up. He was killing David Oh just as if he were some undead fiend risen up out of a grave in some lurid horror film.

Jake knew something was wrong inside the car of the ascending tram even as it was slowing to head into the Peak station.

He saw the humped forms through the windows, recognized the black spatters flung across those same windows for what they were: blood.

'Jesus Christ,' he whispered, sprinting towards the cab. The tram rose at him out of the mist of the mountainside. It was shining, beaded with rain. Lights were flickering inside. Tendrils of fog clung to its sides.

Slowing as it entered the station proper.

Jake was running alongside, slamming his fist against the door. Bliss right behind him. 'Open this thing!' he shouted in Cantonese. '*Dew neh loh moh*, open the doors!'

At last the tram reached its berth. The doors slid open, Jake and Bliss rushed inside. The short hairs on the back of his neck tingled. The interior stank of blood and the sweet foulness of death.

Without thinking, he ran the length of the car, leaping over the prone body of a young Chinese. Slammed the heel of his shoe into the second Chinese's face and bent, dragging the man's clamped fingers one by one from their death grip on the ends of the garotte.

'David,' he gasped. 'Oh, my God! David!'

Bliss got the wire from the dead man's hands and began to unwind it. David Oh groaned as it came away. Blood leaked from the centre of the purple-black welts. The neck was already swollen to double its normal size.

Jake tried to hold David still as the younger man gasped for air. It appeared as if the severe swelling was preventing air from getting through the windpipe. He used the end of the garotte to make an incision in the flesh. Opened it with a small splinter of wood to allow the air unimpeded flow.

'Take it easy,' he said. David Oh was shaking all over. His hair was plastered against his skull by sweat and blood. He was gagging and crying all at once.

Jake lifted his head while Bliss went for assistance. In a moment she returned to tell him the ambulance was on its way.

'David.' Jake tried to lift him, but David Oh screamed so piteously that Jake eased up. 'David,' he whispered.

David Oh's eyes were filmy, their rich black turned watery. Their heads were touching. Jake cradled the younger man in his arms. David Oh was struggling to marshal his energies.

'Listen . . .' His voice trailed off and his lids fluttered closed. With a great effort, he looked into Jake's eyes. 'Beridien, Donovan, Wunderman. One of them knows . . . did this to me . . . to Stallings . . .' His lids fluttered, and when they opened, his pupils were dilated with pain. It was so difficult to speak. The taste of blood and bile was metallic in his mouth. His throat was filling up.

'Missed you, Jake . . . No one around to talk to . . . Taking off like that without telling me . . . anything . . . I thought you trusted me more.'

'It wasn't trust, David. It was personal, for me to do alone.'

'Like what happened . . . happened to you at Sumchun River.'

He was quiet for a moment, his breathing harsh and irregular. Blood leaked from the corner of his mouth. 'I feel like I'm filling up.' He was crying. 'I'm sorry, Jake. Whatever happened to you . . . there . . . Wish it had never happened. You're my friend. My friend . . .' A rigidity coming into his musculature. All at once, the onset. Jake had seen it before.

'*A mi tuo fo!*' Broken fists like claws digging into Jake's arms. 'Oh, Buddha!' His eyes snapped open and Jake saw the finiteness of the pain, the edge of death, coming.

'David – '

'The *huo yan*! Remember the *huo yan*, Jake!'

In death there was no more pain. That was the only sense Jake could make of David Oh's passing.

As he held the lifeless body, his thoughts were far away from the added revelations David Oh had given him. For seven years, Jake had been David Oh's mentor. He had taken care of the final phases of David's training, had protected him from the treacherous eddies of political manoeuvring inside the Quarry. Jake had been aware of all this, but in all those years they had never gotten around to talking about it. Now they never would.

It was terrible to know that this man had died while they were estranged from each other. There was an incompleteness to the equation that could never be filled. It was, not so oddly, just as it had been with Mariana.

Oh, David, Jake thought now, I've missed you, too. I'll always miss you. You were like my brother. Because you were so close to me, I hurt you the most. Like Mariana. Sumchun River did that, you were right. I began to die there. Mariana's death, the *dantai*'s, now yours. Piece by piece, until I seem more dead than alive.

At that moment he felt Bliss moving against him. Even in this situation, her flesh was like fire where it touched him. His pulse raced. Bliss.

Jake could, and would, spend the rest of the night mourning the loss of David Oh. But he wondered whether it would be a futile gesture on his part. Mourning was meant – insofar as the living were concerned – to bring about resolution to a relationship, a definite ending. All that he should have said to David, he had not. He had wronged his friend as he had wronged Mariana – and Ting as well, if he was to be brutally honest with himself. Now it was too late. Their relationship would forever remain incomplete.

He was engulfed in grief.

'I think we'd better get out of here,' Bliss said. 'The ticket taker's coming.'

Her urgent words pulled him into the present. In a moment his mind was filling up with David Oh's last words. *Remember the* huo yan. The 'movable eye' in *wei qi*. What did it mean?

And where was the material David Oh had unearthed from the Quarry? It was not on him, and a quick search of the other Chinese confirmed that they had not taken it from him. That was not surprising. David had been too good an agent to have come to an rdv with written material of that sensitivity.

'Come on! Come on!'

Bliss took his hand, pulling him upwards. As they raced out of the car, another thought struck him a savage blow. Now that the Quarry had found and sanctioned David Oh, it was a certainty that he would be their next target.

Shanghai/Hong Kong–Central
China–Shanghai/Japanese Highlands

For ninety-odd years, the foreign *tai pan* had ruled Shanghai. Now the rats and the mongrel dogs had the run of the rubble- and corpse-strewn streets. The *tai pan*, who, in years gone by, had made their fortunes in teas, opium, silk, shipping, rubber, real estate, and silver, depending on the decade, retreated to the rooftops of their white buildings along the Bund. There, binoculars in hand, they watched as their city was destroyed.

As they had been in 1932, the Japanese were on the march. Generalissimo Chiang, who had at that time been so successful in defending Shanghai's twisting streets and narrow back alleys, its array of bridges and canals, confusing to all but seasoned residents, had decided to make his stand in the city rather than face the invaders in the Kaoliang fields to the north. Besides, he knew that in Shanghai he would return to the international spotlight.

Quite naturally, the *tai pan* did everything in their power to keep the Chinese from fighting the Japanese, knowing that this war would certainly destroy Shanghai – and their futures – for good. But in these dark, militaristic days the *tai pan* had lost almost all their power. Once again they had forgotten that they stood on foreign soil. The illusion given them by the existence of the International Settlement had increased their arrogance. This time the Chinese ignored them completely.

Japanese and British gunboats rode at anchor in the great harbour. Ten thousand Chinese troops, handpicked for the job by Chiang himself, had dug in throughout the city, erecting barricades, unrolling barbed wire. Twenty-one Japanese warships began to sail up the Huang Pu; their blue-jacketed army was on the march.

On August 13, the first shots were fired across the Yokohama Bridge, at the northern tip of the Settlement.

The Chinese had bombers – American-built Northrops, as it happened. Their pilots were young, inexperienced, and short-tempered. For hours, the day following, they tried repeatedly to destroy Japanese factories and stores. Failing in that, they turned their attention to the huge battleship *Izumo*, lying at anchor in the Huang Pu. Bombs exploded in the river, along the wharves, destroying a line of *godown*s. The flagship of the Japanese naval forces remained unscathed.

Gritting their teeth in frustration, the pilots turned their planes and, heading lower, overflew the Bund. The impeccably dressed *tai pan*, field glasses to their eyes, gasped to see the bombs begin to fall over the Settlement's busiest crossroads, the intersection of the Bund and the Nanking Road.

The first plunged through the roof of the Palace Hotel, swarming with foreign and Chinese guests. The second detonated in the street just outside the entrance to the Cathay Hotel. The devastation was staggering. The road was jammed with people. Most of those in the immediate area never knew what hit them. Others, hit by spinning debris or caught in the flames spreading from the epicentres of the targets, stumbled screaming in pain and terror. Children eating ices were torn apart, young women crashed through plate-glass windows, or were crushed by collapsing mortar and brick. In all, 729 people were killed. Another 861 were seriously wounded. All within the space of ninety seconds.

Athena and Jake, safely away from the site of the terrible carnage, felt the shudder of the bombs. Athena, if she thought about the moment at all, assumed an earthquake had hit. Her inner-directed mind did not translate the roar her ears had picked up.

Ever since the night of the incident with Zilin's mistress, she had been a changed woman. Horrified at what she had done to another human being, she had taken Jake and retreated to Zilin's study at the rear of the house. While she had waited for him to return, she had had much time to contemplate her actions and her conflicting emotions.

It was the first time she had seen, firsthand, that intense fear could turn to hate. The expression of her own aggression terrified her.

Athena's Hawaiian mother was no more capable of hating than she was able to be unkind. It simply was not in her nature. Athena had always believed that she was like her mother in this. Until now. Her mother could not have done what she had done to Zilin's mistress, no matter what the provocation.

How do I know that? Athena had asked herself over and over. My mother never had her family threatened.

She had never felt so alone and frightened as she did during that long night. The arms of destruction were sweeping south towards Shanghai. Always, this teeming city had been the nexus of Chinese trading. It had been one of the world's richest cities. For years it had held the largest concentration of silver on earth, and one of the largest of gold. Certainly more opium passed through this port than any other. China was poor; China had always been poor. But Shanghai had always been rich.

Until now this wealth had provided a blanket of protection across the city, as if it were exempt from all ill as well as all law. The war of 1932 had been viewed, at least as far as the Western community was concerned, as a minor aberration never to reoccur.

Yet now the fall of Shanghai was assured. The Japanese were at the gate, and China, always inimically divided, seemed powerless to stop them. In contrast to the intensely militaristic and highly disciplined invaders, the Chinese were callow, ill-trained, and, with Chiang's German tacticians, ill-advised.

Shanghai had essentially been a hugely profitable boomtown since the day, ninety-five years before, when the British warship *Nemesis* steamed up the Huang Pu to blow apart the Wusong forts, crumbling China's last line of defence against the foreign devil. But it had been an unusually stable one, due to its international significance and the amount – one billion taels in silver – of foreign money invested in it.

Now war was bringing that all to an end. Shanghai's days of glory were being swept away like ashes into a trash heap. The stench of cordite and blood hung in the air like a pall. Masonry dust, borne by hot summer winds, turned the air dry and choking. Corpses lined the streets and alleyways while the rats and dogs feasted. Disease ran rampant.

Athena had waited hours for Zilin to return home. How many times had she planned the speech of contrition for his benefit and her expiation!

He never came. The servants, terrified by the onset of the fighting and the rumours of the city's imminent defeat, failed to return. The heart of the large house beat on, but Athena was already deaf to its pulse.

In the pale light of the grey morning, even Sheng Li was gone. Dumbly, Athena saw the smears of blood caking the floor, marring forever her husband's expensive rugs with their indelible brown tattoos. The iron poker lay where she had dropped it, discoloured at its tip. At sight of it, she murmured, 'God in heaven,' wheeled, and, with her hand pressed hard against her mouth, ran to the bathroom, where she vomited into the white porcelain sink.

She spent the next ten minutes bathing her face with trembling hands in ice-cold water. She returned to Zilin's study to find Jake playing on top of his father's desk. In his small hands was a stiff oversized envelope. Jake looked up at her approach, stuck a corner of the envelope into his mouth, chewing it with teething gums.

When she took it from him, though she did it gently, he began to cry. Athena picked him up and, kissing the top of his head, held him against her hipbone. She turned the envelope over, saw, 'My Dearest Athena,' written in Zilin's careful English script. Now she began to weep, knowing that she held the confirmation of what she had, in her nighttime terror, suspected: that her husband was not returning to her.

Her hands shook so badly that she cut her finger trying to get the envelope open. Inside, she found a note three lines long, directing her to Zilin's hidden safe. The last line was the combination.

Setting Jake down to crawl underneath the desk, a favoured spot, she crouched, opening a lacquer cabinet. Behind false doors, she found the safe and, using Zilin's combination, opened it. Inside, she discovered fifty taels of gold, one hundred ounces of silver, and a tiny silk-wrapped packet.

This last was marked as Jake's inheritance. She unravelled the silk until a shard of lavender jade lay revealed in her palm. It seemed to be part of a carved beast, though it was surely no creature she had ever come across.

'This *fu*,' read a card attached to the shard, 'is the birthright of my son and must stay with him no matter what may befall him. In the distant future, when he comes of age, he may have occasion to make use of it. If he ever does, my Athena, it will mean that I have succeeded in what I have set out to do.

'I love you, but, alas, I love China more. Perhaps you can understand this. Not now, I suspect, but later. Broken hearts may mend in time.' It was signed in vermilion ink with Zilin's chop.

But in this last, at least, he was wrong. Nothing could

mend Athena's broken heart. Zilin had been her life. But for him, she would have soon left China far behind, drawn to its allure but nonetheless wishing to contemplate it from a safer distance.

Now she was trapped by the war. The Japanese were laying siege to the city. She had been here in 1932 when their atrocities proliferated. So highly regimented and controlled in their daily life, the savage animal that lurked within every man was loosed in awesome intensity within the Japanese soldier by the pressures of war. That horrific, mindless carnage could and would happen again, she knew. She no longer thought about herself but only of her baby.

For two months she hoarded the wealth that was her only reminder of Zilin's departure. She kept to herself as much as she could, venturing forth from the house on Rue Molière only infrequently to shop for food and clothes. All around her, the evacuation of the city had begun. The families of the Western *tai pan* were removed to safety while the men stayed on, secure in the knowledge that the British destroyer *Duncan*, with its contingent of marines, was waiting for them, docked at the Shanghai Club.

In their dimly lit, wood-panelled sanctuary at Number 3 the Bund, distant in atmosphere if not in physical proximity from the sandbagged barricades where Chinese and Japanese shot, stabbed, and clubbed each other to death, the *tai pan* discussed the end of the world. *Their* world. It did not matter to them who won this stupid war. The Japanese would attempt to kill them if they won, and if the Chinese were, by some miracle, to emerge victorious, they knew that Chiang would push them into the sea. Their time in this foreign clime was over in any event. That, however, did not deter them from lifting their sparkling stemware and, with great quaffs of Scotch and brandy, toasting the end of an era.

Misery dogged Athena's life. During the day she marshalled her strength to keep Jake busy and happy. At night she lay awake in a semidarkness lit by constant fires. The smell of smoke was never out of her nostrils, and the crackle of small-arms fire was a dulling litany.

One day Athena took Jake shopping. It was the better of two choices: she would never have left him alone in the house. She chose the noon hour, since the ravaged city was most alive then, the Nanking dense with shoppers. She had just emerged from Sincere's and was heading across the road to the Wing On department store when her ears caught a peculiar buzzing sound.

It was the same noise that haunted her restless sleep through nights filled with the sweat of the heat and of fear. She knew instinctively what it was before anyone else around her did. Mutely she grabbed Jake off the street and, holding him tightly against her breast, ran through the jumble of rickshaw and truck traffic. At every step, it seemed, she was thwarted, and later, in the visions of these moments that were to engulf her, she would feel again as if she were trapped within a dream.

Time became elastic. She tried to elbow people aside. She ran into the dusty side of a car. People shouted at her, hurling Chinese epithets her way. Her feet felt stuck in mud, her leg muscles sapped of energy. And all the while the terrible metallic buzzing tore at her, increasing in volume until it filled up her brain. Death was coming.

Athena screamed in inchoate terror. My baby! she thought. Oh, God, save my baby, at least!

The great shadow of the plane shut out the yellow sky at the same moment the bomb fell. Athena could recall through her visions that one instant of deathly silence when everything on earth seemed to cease breathing.

Then the world collapsed.

Sincere's disintegrated into a flaming, spitting inferno. Athena heard the howling of the shoppers like a chorus of the damned. The earth erupted at her feet and she was hurled sideways by the tremendous concussion of the explosion. The entire wall against which she was thrown was scarlet. Blood and bits of pink matter drooled down the brickwork, just as if all human flesh in the immediate vicinity had been instantaneously liquified.

Athena curled herself into a protective ball around Jake, smashed one shoulder and knee against the wet brick. The stench of hot blood and faecal matter made her gag. It was a physical presence in this place, an abhorrent spectre striding through the city.

Jake cried out, choking on the fumes, and Athena instinctively put her hand over the top of his head. She whispered into his ear.

Then the wall of Wing On's against which she had been thrown started to crumble. Athena heard the rumbling far above her head, but could make no sense of it. Her instinct was to get up and run, but she pushed down the fright and stayed where she was. Had she moved, she and Jake would have been buried beneath the collapsing brick wall.

Athena felt the rushing of masonry. It seemed to her as if the sky were falling. A terrible grinding split apart the tie beams, and without support the wall caved outwards like the arc of a tidal wave.

Those still in the street, crushed together and spinning drunkenly away from the utter devastation of Sincere's, were crushed beneath the tonnage. An avalanche of brick, masonry, splintered wood, and shattered glass descended on them with lethal rapidity. There did not even seem enough time to understand what was happening to them.

Athena's curled position at the base of the wall was the best she could have taken. She was spared the fate of hundreds all about her who died of broken necks, crushed windpipes, shattered sternums, and multiple fractures that severed their arteries, nerves, and organs.

A stray brick struck her a glancing blow on the temple, its corner leaving a long, deep gash all the way from her scalp above the hairline to the ridge of her brow just above her right eye.

Blood coursed down her face, terrifying Jake. At first she was so dazed that she did not understand it was her own blood that was flowing now, and not more of the muck that had coated the wall in the last moments before its collapse.

'What?' she said. 'What?'

Thought seemed difficult. She did not know where she was for many minutes. She seemed to be breathing in water. Rescue crews working through the mire of the rubble finally found her. Two of them drew her gently out of the little pocket within which she lay. Even then she would not relinquish Jake to them so that they could check the child for wounds.

They took her to a hospital, where her laceration was cleaned, sutured, and dressed. The overworked doctors asked her to stay within the precincts of the hospital overnight, because they wanted to check for signs of concussion. Not, of course, in a room or a ward, which were all filled to overflowing with more seriously injured people, but out in the corridor where bandaged patients milled about, dizzy and teetering.

Athena escaped this bewildering asylum with Jake on her hip, certain that her baby should not be subjected to such an environment a moment more than was necessary.

The brick had left more of a mark on her than just the bandaged gash. All around the wound, her flesh turned black and blue, puffy and oversized, until the right side of her face was unrecognizable. Jake was terrified at the sight of her, and nothing Athena could do seemed to calm him.

He would not let her hold him, or even sing to him, the thing he had always loved most. It was as if he felt that someone pretending to be his mother had slipped into the house with him. Athena was not aware that the swelling was affecting her vocal cords; even her voice had changed into a deep-throated rasp.

At night she held her swollen head, ticking off the seconds by the throbbing. It seemed to her as if the only sound she could hear at those times was the coursing of her own blood through her veins and arteries. Sunk deep within the working plant of her own body, she was unaware of how distant the world was becoming.

There were times during the days when she could remember nothing. She would awake, on her feet, staring at Jake or out of the dusty window. She was a tabula rasa. No thought flickered inside her brain, no emotion. Then, just as if a master switch were being thrown, all her life would flood in upon her: memories, intellectual thoughts, emotions. The input was far too intense to absorb all at once. She would weep uncontrollably for hours.

Jake, sitting upon his father's desk as if it were a great winged steed of imagination, would watch her silently. He was no longer frightened of her. He saw, as the swellings subsided, that this indeed must be his mother. But somehow the emotional connection that had bound them until the moment the wall of Wing On had collapsed around them was gone. He watched her with the same intense but dissociated curiosity with which he observed all people when he was outside. He wondered who she was.

One night, Athena awoke. She sat bolt upright in bed. She felt as if she had been awake and was now asleep. An odd, timeless quality filled the bedroom. It was the night of the full moon and, unlike the weather of the last week or so, the sky was perfectly clear.

She found that she was staring at the window opposite her bed. Not through it but *at* it. A shaft of silver moonlight pierced the darkness, shimmering onto the floor, illuminating the rug at her feet. Its monochromatic light created new colours from old. The moonlight seemed to waver before her eyes as if its substance were not visual at all, but rather aural. It seemed to sing to her, a song so familiar it brought tears to her eyes. What was it?

As if in a trance, Athena climbed out of bed and, barefoot, padded across the room. She stood by the window. Slowly she put a hand on the sill, bathing it in silver.

With the same deliberation she lifted her eyes, her gaze following the band of light upwards. She saw the glowing disc of the moon. The heavens around it were absolutely pellucid.

She cried out as the first of her visions struck her with the power of a physical blow. She staggered, falling backwards. She sprawled in the moonlight while her mind recreated in painstaking detail the devastation in the Nanking from the moment she had first heard the plane until the wall collapsed around her.

When she came out of it, she stared unseeing up into the beam of moonlight. Its song was so loud in her inner ears that she was deaf to all else. A hymn, she thought. It's singing a hymn.

It was the same hymn her brother, Michael, used to sing at home when he came back from the seminary. She used to be so derisive of him, deliberately disappearing from the house on Sundays so that her mother could not ask her to go to church with him. She had hated religion, then. She had not understood the calling.

Some inkling of its power had dawned on her in, of all places, China. She saw how Michael's faith had made him happy, impervious to the heartbreaks of the vast, unknowable continent.

At last Athena understood why she had been reluctant to leave Shanghai even when the evacuation had begun. Her vision had shown her the answer. Her destiny lay here, in helping the sick, the poor, the injured. The doctors were there to bind their physical wounds, but someone had to take God's light and bind their inner hurt.

In her euphoria, Athena thought she could grasp God's larger design. Michael's death had to have a meaning. She was convinced this was it. His example was now made manifest inside herself. Michael's spirit would live on in his beloved China, through her.

The warmth of the moonlight, which she had only begun to feel, flooded through her. The soul-wrenching ache with which she had lived since the long night when she had branded Sheng Li was gone.

She had sinned, had paid her penance, and was redeemed in the calling of her dead brother. The world was now hers. She was no longer alone, directionless, afraid. Her epiphany of faith had healed all those agonies even as it had absolved her of her guilt. She no longer felt weighed down by terror or remorse. She was cleansed of hate.

For the next three months, Athena took to the streets as before she had huddled, terrified, within the confines of the house her husband had built for her. She preached her healing gospel to anyone who would listen and to many who did not.

There was no loss of work for her. Shanghai had become a hollow shell, echoing dully to the daily cannon and small-arms fire. At night, shells brushed the undersides of low-lying clouds before bursting in thunderous detonation within the Settlement. By day, the Japanese sent in more and more reinforcements. Little by little, Chiang's valiant but outmanned force was pushed back through the litter and rubble of what had once been the continent's greatest city.

Disease, pestilence. Athena remembered the Four Horsemen of the Apocalypse brought into existence by war. The skies were ashen, the once snow-white office buildings along the Bund now streaked with soot and blood.

Shanghai was a corpse, as raw and bleeding as were its many wounded inhabitants. Athena often crossed Sugiao

Creek to the south, to attend to the Chinese. Many were dying. It was merely a matter of increment: were they dying slowly or quickly? Athena tried to comfort them all. They seemed surprised that she could speak Cantonese. Others ignored her words, finding it impossible to believe that a foreign devil could speak their tongue with such fluency. None, however, failed to be moved by her ministrations.

She kicked at the persistent dogs and rats that patrolled this part of Shanghai as if it had become their own. Jake learned to take a piece of wood with him to beat them into bloody pulps.

The autumn was dying, as surely as was the city. Winter was coming, and with it the end of the Generalissimo's defence. In November, Chiang ordered his troops to abandon their long-held positions. They fell back rapidly and the Japanese began their triumphant march into Shanghai. Ninety thousand strong, they forged up the Yangzi in pursuit of the fleeing Chinese. They entered a city seemingly bereft even of breath. Smoke curling from smouldering fires hung in the still air. An awful silence enveloped the city now that the batteries which had been at each other for months had ceased their bombardments.

Extensive areas of the city had been devastated. Streets down their entire length had ceased to exist. Thousands of houses and factories had been levelled. The corpses were piled, rotting where they had been flung by the massed explosions.

From Brenan Road to the Garden Bridge, six thousand Japanese troops paraded in their dress uniforms. All of them wore sanitary masks to keep out the rampant pestilence. By order of the new garrison commander, soldiers with megaphones exhorted the observers within the defeated city to accord the victors their proper measure of respect 'by giving a gentle bow and wishing us good morning.'

Athena, with Jake beside her, watched this moment and felt a terrible pang to see her Chinese bow, murmuring, before this horde. She heard the ghosts of a billion Chinese ancestors cry out in horror and dismay. Their pain lanced through her so that she herself cried out. In a moment she had collapsed at Jake's feet.

Jake had never seen his mother so pale. She smelled funny. He did not want to approach her. He watched silently as the man and woman hanging back at the furthest edges of the crowd of spectators worked their way towards his prostrate mother. He observed them as they crouched over her. The man, who seemed very old to him, held her wrist in a funny way. His lips moved in time to some internal rhythm. Perhaps he was singing, but Jake did not think this moment was cause for even a hymn.

'Come on,' the man said to the woman, 'let's get her back home.' He lifted Athena up in his brawny arms. The woman held out her hand to Jake. He slipped his hand into hers. It was warm. He walked close beside her. She smelled good. He liked that.

In their house, Jake became aware of the loud noises his mother was making. She lay on a bed. Her face was shiny and tight. Her chest heaved. The woman attended to her, putting a wet, rolled-up cloth on her forehead. Once she tried to feed Athena something from a bowl. The liquid ran down Athena's chin and neck, wetting her clothes even more.

The man, who wore a strange six-pointed star around his neck, put his huge hands on Jake's shoulders, turning him away. 'Are you hungry?' He had an odd accent that made Jake giggle. Jake nodded.

In the night, they woke him gently with whispered words.

'Your mother wants to see you,' the woman said. She smelled sweet. Jake took her hand and went with her.

Athena smelled worse than ever. He wrinkled up his

nose and tried not to breathe. This made him gasp within the space of thirty seconds, so that the woman squeezed his hand.

He saw the sweat streaming down his mother's face. Why was she so hot? Didn't these people have a towel to dry her? Suddenly his mother's eyes flew open. In the light of the single oil lamp that the man was holding up, Jake could see the colour of her eyes, as pure and clear as ever.

At that moment their connection returned, and he threw himself upon her heaving bosom, sure now that something terrible was about to occur.

He felt the woman's hands pulling him back, holding him now, stroking the back of his head as he remembered Athena used to do.

'Jake.' It was a sandpaper rasp. He heard his name but could not recognize her voice.

'Mama.'

Athena was weeping. Her thin hands searched beneath her soiled dress. She was thwarted. Her eyes looked from Jake to the woman. 'Please,' she whispered, and her hand pulled away part of her dress.

The woman saw again the small bag hung by a leather thong from around her neck.

'Give it to him,' Athena said with some difficulty. 'Please.'

The woman let go of Jake and, bending over Athena, removed the bag. She loosened its drawstring and drew out some papers. She inverted the bag over Jake's hands. Out rolled a piece of lavender jade.

'See that he keeps it with him always,' Athena said. She sighed deeply, liquidly.

Jake stared down at his mother's blank face. In a moment the light swept away, plunging her countenance into darkness.

He heard the man's voice rumbling. 'It's time we left here. We will go to our friend's in Hong Kong.'

In the darkness, Jake felt the woman's acquiescence. He reached up, taking her hand in his.

The way to Mao led through Hu Hanmin. Zilin had known this from the moment he left Shanghai for the peasant fields of destitute Hunan, where, his sources told him, Mao had returned after thirteen years, to conclude the process of winning over the populous central provinces to his cause.

Zilin knew that he could not simply approach Mao with his ideas. In fact, at this point he had no desire to make himself known to the rising Communist leader. He wanted first to sink into Mao's organization and then, once entrenched, spread his philosophies slowly.

It was crucial that Zilin sell himself to Hu as a zealous Communist. If he could not accomplish that, Zilin knew he had no hope of continuing in his long-range plan. He did not relish using someone who had been a friend in other days, but he reminded himself harshly that he had already done far worse to those he loved even more than Hu.

He could have come with money – a commodity of which Mao was in desperate need. But that, he knew instinctively, would have been a grave mistake. For one thing, it would have called immediate attention to him. For another, it would have made him suspect. Zilin had no desire to have his background checked; he had lived too much of his life as a capitalist.

What Hu and Mao had in common – what had drawn them together in the first place – was their love of philosophy. Zilin knew, therefore, that he could approach them in the same manner, but using different cant.

For Mao, it would be Sun Tzu's *Art of War*, which he called on constantly in fighting his continuing guerrilla war against Chiang. For Hu it was Laotse, a philosopher whose writings Zilin had studied extensively, but with whom he had become disenchanted.

For one thing, Laotse's thinking was far too formularized. Early on, Zilin had learned that formularization was second only to rote in ossifying creative thinking. It was one of the roots of his disagreement with communism. Dogma, he thought, was all well and good for displacing anarchy, but as an ongoing structure it was no solution at all.

He found Hu without difficulty. He was out in the fields, working side by side with the peasants. He looked older, his wide face somehow greyer. Lines had appeared in his flesh, as if each day with Mao had marked him with the blade of a worker's crude knife.

'Ah, Shi Zilin!' Hu exclaimed when he recognized his long-time friend beneath the dust and the simple clothes. 'So you have come, after all.'

Zilin smiled. '"To be orphaned, lonely, and unworthy is what men hate most,"' he said, quoting Laotse.

Hu wiped the sweat from his brow. He stank of hard labour. His eyes narrowed. 'The war in Shanghai has devastated you? Is that why you are here?'

Zilin shook his head. 'I had divested myself of all my holdings some time ago. I urged my brothers to come with me, but their philosophical leanings lay in another direction. They had not been married to Mai, they had not sat with Sun Zhongshan and absorbed his faith.' He shrugged. '"Sometimes things are benefited by being taken away from,"' he concluded, quoting again.

Hu smiled cautiously. 'In that case . . .' he said, hefting a farm implement. He held it out to Zilin. 'When the callouses begin to form, I may begin to understand.'

Five months after Zilin entered into Mao's camp, the forces came under the first serious attack by Generalissimo Chiang's troops. Until this time, Zilin supposed, Chiang had been too busy licking his wounds from the Shanghai debacle – news of which had reached them somewhat belatedly – recruiting fresh soldiers from the provinces not already under Japanese domination.

He had had his one bad moment, then, seeing in his mind's eye the destruction of his adopted city. But he knew both Athena and Sheng Li were, in their separate ways, strong women. In his absence he had left them what he felt each needed to survive. He knew they would do all in their power to protect his children.

The onset of the rainy season had already begun, turning the ground marshy, flooding the many-tiered rice paddies. Mao's forces were currently occupying ground that, in Sun Tzu's opinion, would be considered 'encircled'. That meant access to it was strictly limited, where the way out was tortuous and constricted. It meant, in a nutshell, that should Chiang's troops catch them there, they could easily defeat Mao. Chiang, using intelligence from his spies, knew that and was coming as swiftly as was possible.

Accordingly, Mao had ordered a full retreat. If he could get his people across the wide-open fields and through the narrow defile before Chiang got there, they would be safe. The problem was the swiftness of movement. Mao's forces were tired. They had spent twelve-hour days in the fields with the peasants, putting aside their weapons for the time being and, in his words, picking up ploughshares.

Zilin, making a detailed estimation of Mao's men, felt certain that fatigue would slow them sufficiently so that Chiang's fresh forces would catch them either in the defile or just emerging from it. Either way, they would be on 'death ground', that is, one in which, in Sun Tzu's opinion, the army would survive only if it fought with the courage of desperation. Even assuming that, the casualties would be horrendous.

'There must be a better way,' Zilin said to Hu as they crouched on their haunches, eating boiled rice.

'The men follow Mao,' Hu said, stuffing rice into his mouth. There was little time before Mao's orders would come for the men to move out. 'They have done so from the beginning. They believe in him implicitly. He has never been wrong.'

So far, Zilin thought. He squinted up at the lowering clouds. It had been raining all morning, but the precipitation had ceased about an hour ago. Still, the weather was not good. The sky was so dark it might have been an hour past sunset instead of near noon. Zilin, who had been taught to read the portents of wind, humidity, and barometric pressure by Three Oaths Tsun, knew that more rain was imminent. Heavy rain, by the feel of how low the pressure was dropping.

He looked morosely out at the enormous expanse of fields they must cross in order to get to the head of the defile. He watched one or two peasants still at work, bent over, their filthy cotton skirts pulled up to their thighs. They were calf-deep in the mud, and as one moved off, Zilin saw that she sank down to the level of her knees. We'll never make it through that in time, he thought. It's like quicksand.

He sucked in his breath so sharply that Hu stopped his eating and stared at him.

'What is it?' Hu said, concerned. 'Are you ill?'

'On the contrary,' Zilin said. His heart was beating so fast he was obliged to concentrate on his breathing for a moment to slow it down to an acceptable level. Still, he felt the adrenaline pumping through him. He stood up.

'I may have discovered a way to save our men.'

Now Hu stood up as well. His bowl of rice was forgotten. 'What do you mean?'

'Listen to me,' Zilin said. 'You believe that Mao's strategy is correct, *heya*?'

Hu nodded. 'I do.'

'Tell me, then, what will happen if we engage Chiang's forces while we are still partially in the defile, or even if we have just emerged.'

500

Hu's face looked even more tired than usual. 'There will be many casualties. Many good men will die. But the cause – '

'They needn't die,' Zilin said.

Hu was quiet for some time.

Zilin pointed. 'Watch the women there in the paddies. Do you see how slow their movements are?'

'They are women,' Hu pointed out, 'not men. And soldiers at that.'

'Those women,' Zilin observed, 'could carry twice the field load of any of our men without complaining. Still, they are having difficulty in the field. It's become a quagmire.'

'Yes, I see.' Hu nodded. 'Bad for us. It will slow us down terribly.'

'And there is more rain on the way. I can feel it.' Zilin turned to face Hu. 'But if the field will be bad for us, think of how it will be in six hours' time, when Chiang's troops – at the end of their long day's trek – must slog through it.'

Hu looked at him blankly.

'And they *will* have to slog through it, my friend, if we do not move from here. If we hold our position until they have waded out into the paddies. Then we fall on them with all our strength.'

Hu was silent, absorbed.

'Besides,' Zilin said, administering the *coup de grâce*, 'we will be fighting in front of the peasants. They will see for themselves how we defend the land that we have been helping them till, all these long months. How do you think they will react to that? It will galvanize them to our cause. Mao will become legend in these provinces.'

Hu nodded slowly, thinking through all that Zilin had given him. 'It's true enough.' He pulled at his lower lip meditatively. 'It's an excellent plan. Come, I will take you to Mao.'

Zilin shook his head. 'It is only an idea I have passed

on. You and Mao are close. There is little time. He might not listen to me, but he surely would to you.'

'All right,' Hu said. 'But I'll tell him whose idea it was.'

'Tell him about the plan,' Zilin said, watching Hu hurry off. 'That will be sufficient.'

In the months after Mao's decisive victory over the force that Chiang had sent against him in Hunan, his prestige and power increased tenfold. Again and again, the tale of his military prowess was told over smoking fires in peasant villages all through the central provinces. And, as was the nature of such things, the actual details of that day's battle became more and more grandiose. Chiang's force swelled from six to nine hundred and thence to fifteen hundred. The count of Mao's army, of course, always stayed the same, so that the victory increased in importance in the retelling.

Mao was well aware of this, and was delighted to let the story grow out of all proportion. All men seemed happiest when grappling with outsized numbers. He would let them have their fun and, in the process, do his recruiting for him.

But he was also well aware that the plan had not been his. No one else within his army knew this, save Hu. And the man with whom the plan had originated. For, despite Zilin's admonition, Hu had felt honour-bound to mention his name to Mao.

For some time after the victory, Mao was in a quandary as to what to do. To acknowledge the man right away would be to lose incalculable face. But to ignore him was boorish and, worse, stupid. The man obviously had a keen and calculating mind. Such a one, Mao finally decided, could be of enormous value to him.

In due course, Zilin was summoned before Mao. Hu took him to the Communist leader but was dismissed immediately by Mao.

'Shi Zilin,' Mao said, 'I have begun hearing about you of late.'

'I am perhaps unworthy of so much talk.'

Mao nodded absently. He keenly wished to impart to this man that his interest in him was minimal at best. It was ill-advised to allow others to see that which you needed.

'Hu Hanmin thinks highly of you.' After their introduction, Mao had not once looked directly at Zilin. Instead, he paced the room he had made into his study. He had, Zilin had observed, the true revolutionary's restless spirit. Since he was never content to be in one place for any length of time, it must have taken extraordinary control for him to remain in the fields at Hunan for so long. Now they were in Yunnan, cave-dwellers like bats. 'I rely on Hu Hanmin.' Mao waved a hand. 'Perhaps he can find a place for you on my permanent staff.'

'As you wish, Comrade,' Zilin said, thinking, Two can play at this as well as one.

Mao glanced at him. 'We will speak again. Perhaps, if you have an interest in military matters, we could play a game of *wei qi*.'

'I would like that,' Zilin said, giving no outward sign that he had understood Mao's oblique reference to the plan he had created, which Mao had used as his own.

As Mao's stature grew, so too did Zilin's. More and more, those who sought an audience with Mao and could not get to see him were directed to Zilin. After a time, they asked to see him instead of Mao.

Zilin found the solving of these problems fascinating. Athena had read enough of the Bible to him for him to be able to draw a parallel with Solomon. It was not ego that led him to this comparison, but merely his particular bent.

On a windswept day when the cave had become a

503

howling hive, driving many of the men down the mountain-side, a woman entered Zilin's chamber.

It was near twilight. The lamps were lit, but their flames, whipped by the eddies of wind, flickered disconcertingly so that reading became impossible.

Zilin's aide, a young, intelligent man who shared many of his ideals, introduced her.

'This is Qing Ming, Comrade,' the young man said. He stood by her side until her intense stare obliged him to withdraw. When he had gone, the woman came across the room to where Zilin stood.

Zilin looked hard at her, but the unsteady light made definition difficult. She seemed no more than twenty. He thought she was exceptionally beautiful. She has been well named, he thought. Qing Ming meant Pure Brightness.

She wore the dusty clothes of the country folk to the south, and it occurred to him that perhaps she had come a long distance to see him.

'Would you like to sit down?' he asked her.

'Thank you, but I prefer to stand.'

'Tea?'

She seemed grateful for the offer, nodding mutely. As he poured, Zilin called for his aide, and when the man came, he asked him to bring in some food.

He smiled at Qing Ming. 'It has been a long, tiring day for me. I have not had a chance to eat since early this morning. I hope you will not think it mannerless of me to take food while we speak. My aide will bring enough for us both. Are you hungry?'

'Not really,' she said.

But she ate ravenously. Zilin picked at his food, not being hungry at all. He had divined this woman's intense pride. He suspected that she would never have asked him for food, even had she been starving to death. Watching her eat now, he wondered from how far away she had come.

504

After a time she wiped her mouth. She had sat down when the food arrived. Now, as Zilin poured her more tea, she sat on the edge of the chair, as if its full comfort was not for her. She seemed extraordinarily tense.

'This is difficult for me,' she said without preamble. 'For a time, after I heard of you, I thought that I would not come at all. It shames me to sit here before you.'

Zilin said nothing; it was the best he could do for her at the moment.

Her head came up and he saw the lamplight flickering in her ebon eyes. 'I am the granddaughter of the Jian.'

Jian. The word hit Zilin like a splash of cold water.

'The Jian,' he murmured. He remembered the garden, the solitude, the utter peace of the old man's environment in Suzhou. He thought of all he had learned from him. He thought of trying to find him. But he had only been a child then. The Jian had disappeared into the adult world.

He looked anew at this beautiful woman. He knew that he did not have to tell her his relationship with the Jian. In her eyes he already saw that knowledge.

'My grandmother loved the Jian. She was his mistress.' She looked at him. 'I have no one, and nowhere to go. My husband was killed three months ago in the fighting near Canton. His family has no use for me because I am not from their village. His mother spits on me. In these evil times, I have become a burden to them.

'I care little for myself. If it were just for me, I would not have come here to beg like a street urchin before you. But' – she put the palms of her hands against her belly – 'I have someone else to think of now. My unborn baby is all that matters to me.'

Her eyes dropped to her lap. 'The one story that came down to me from my grandmother was of you. Grandfather spoke of you all the time to her. To him, you were the son he never had. But I do not . . . in coming here . . . that is,

505

it is presumptuous of me to present myself here on the strength of what he felt.'

Zilin studied her for some time, marshalling his thoughts. 'My time with your grandfather,' he said, 'was the most important in my life. Without him I cannot think where I would be today.' He looked around. 'Certainly not here.' And, he thought, my grand design for China assuredly would not have been created without the lessons he taught me.

He got up and stood over the young woman. 'Your grandfather's love for me was certainly reciprocated. I am glad you screwed up your courage and came to me.' He pulled her to her feet. His open hand touched her lower belly.

'Your child is important to me. A descendant of the Jian is a member of my family.' He took her to the opening of the chamber and called for his aide.

'Tonight,' he said, 'you will sleep here in all the comfort we can muster. You will eat well. I do not want you or your child wanting for nourishment.

'Tomorrow I will begin making arrangements for your journey. It will be long and arduous. Without doubt, your child will be born before you reach your final destination.'

Qing Ming looked up at him. All of her tension had dissipated. 'Where am I going?'

'Through Burma to Hong Kong,' Zilin said softly. 'To a man named Three Oaths Tsun. I will give you a letter of introduction.' He smiled down on her. 'And, of course, a present for the baby.'

Every January 18, Yumiko – Sheng Li had begun, from the moment she joined the Japanese civilian evacuation of Shanghai, calling herself by the name her father had given her – took her son to the tiny *bochi* on the outskirts of the small hillside town of Kamioka.

The cemetery was within walking distance of their house.

No matter the weather – more often than not at this elevation there were more than a few inches of snow at that time of year – Yumiko would bundle her son up in warm clothes, throw on a quilted *haori* coat over her winter kimono, and walk with him on an undeviating route.

Their *geta* would crunch through the crust of the newly fallen snow. Silence draped the trees. Even the glossy black birds seemed to shiver on their perches within the bare crowns of the trees.

At the *bochi*, Yumiko would let go of her son's hand and, producing incense from inside her kimono, place the sticks in the frozen ground. He watched her, silent, as she knelt. The sound they made stayed with him for hours. She lit the incense and began her prayers. She never knelt in front of any one marker, and he had no idea who she was praying for until many years later.

In fact, when he was old enough to reason clearly, he assumed that she was remembering the *kami* of his father, long dead, she had told him in answer to his question, in China.

That he was mistaken in this was due more to Yumiko's reticence than to his erring in divining the signs. It was true that she was mourning. What else could he think?

By the spring of 1947, the World War was over. Japan was tired, humiliated, and occupied by American troops. For weeks, while the wild plum, among the earliest of blossoms, sprang up along the hillsides in bright patches of colour, Yumiko had been at work sewing a cloth pennant in the shape of a fish.

On the fifth day of the fifth month, it was hoisted atop a slender bamboo pole that Yumiko planted to one side of the entranceway to their house, just beyond the *engawa*. Mothers and fathers in this small town were doing the same – as they were throughout the islands. It was the *koinobori*.

Aki – this was the name Yumiko had given him, a rough

507

Japanese translation of his original Chinese name, which meant 'beginning of autumn' – asked his mother about the festival. During the war years the *koinobori* had not been celebrated.

It was the Boys' Day Festival, she told him. A pennant flew for each son in the household, smaller pennants for the younger children, larger ones for the older sons.

Aki was pleased to see that the pennant Yumiko had made was, in his estimation at least, quite large. He watched as the stiff spring breeze snapped the fish smartly. He saw each scale she had so painstakingly painted upon its side; he stared into its face, kind yet fierce, which she had lovingly created.

'It is a carp,' Yumiko told him. 'It was chosen as the symbol of *koinobori* because of its unquenchable courage. The carp is known to swim up waterfalls and to face the carving knife unflinchingly. It is said that schools of carp were enlisted by Empress Jingu when she led an armada of warships on an invasion of Korea.'

Yumiko took Aki's hand and sat with him at the edge of the *engawa*. It was still cool, winter's aftermath not yet having been entirely laid to rest by the warming sun. The air was very clear, so that the very peaks of the Hida-Sanmyaku range to the east stood out in sharp relief. Like the edge of a great avenging sword, Yumiko had always thought. Perhaps that was why she had chosen to settle here.

She looked at Aki. His black hair fluttered in the wind. His golden face was upturned as he continued to stare at the floating carp. The poignancy of the moment was not lost on her. Even in its moment of darkest defeat, Japan managed to celebrate the lives of its young. It was a symbol she had prepared just for him. He was almost ten now. It was time, she thought, to begin his real education.

'Aki-*chan*,' she said softly. 'Did you know that these carp pennants were not always used in *koinobori*?' He said nothing, but she knew he was listening. He always listened to her, and he retained everything. She had been concerned about him at first. What with all his infant sicknesses, his seeming inability to speak had terrified her.

Doctors had assured her that nothing physical was amiss. But these were men whose minds were on the war, on more important matters, and Yumiko remained afraid.

There were few things in life that could frighten her now. Since she had crawled in agony from Zilin's house in Shanghai so long ago, returning home to find the packet of gold and the shard of lavender jade for her son, she had vowed that fear would have no more place in her world. For had she given into her fear then, she would have died on the spot and her son with her.

Yet the prospect that he would somehow not grow into a normal, healthy child haunted her. Whether it was because she could not erase from her mind how he had come into the world so prematurely or whether, superstitiously, she felt he was cursed by her own bad *joss* in having fallen in love with Zilin, she could not say.

At fourteen months, Aki should have spoken his first words. In fact, he said nothing at all until his third birthday. Then, when he did open his mouth, what came out was an entire sentence.

'Mama, can I go and pick plums?'

Yumiko was so filled with astonishment and relief that she laughed and cried, hugging him to her for the longest time. When she had recovered, he asked his question again.

'Of course you can,' she had said. She accompanied him, watching him, amazed. From infancy, one of his favourite foods had always been *umeboshi*. These plums were harvested in the spring and put up for pickling so that they would be ready as a refreshing midday snack during summer's first heat wave in early June. It was perfectly clear why he wanted to go picking plums, but

Yumiko had not expected such sophistication from her three-year-old.

'Tell me about the carp,' Aki said now, looking from the pennants to her face.

Yumiko roused herself out of her reverie. 'In the 17th century,' she said, 'the *samurai* were the only ones allowed a display at Boys' Day. Then they would take out their *katana* and their armour, polished and shining in the sunlight, to honour their sons.

'Some of the common folk, as a joke, I expect, made paper carp to display on this festival day. Since they were forbidden to own swords, they chose these valiant fish to show the *samurai* that even commoners had their worth in the world.'

'Does that mean we are not *samurai*?' Aki asked with characteristic insight.

Yumiko looked at him for a moment. 'I do not know the answer to that, Aki-chan. It is possible that we are samurai, I suppose.'

'I think I'd prefer to believe that we *are samurai*,' Aki said thoughtfully. Then he stood up. 'Is it all right if I go and pick plums?'

'Of course,' Yumiko said. A single tear slipped down her cheek as she watched him run, long-legged, down the path to the street.

Over dinner that night, with the *koinobori* carp still fluttering outside, Yumiko told him why she took him to the cemetery each winter to pray. 'You're growing up quickly,' she said. 'It is time you knew the story of my life in Shanghai.'

'Will you tell me about my father?'

'There is nothing to tell,' she said curtly. 'He's dead. Long dead. It is much better that way.'

'But he was a brave man,' Aki persisted. 'A *samurai*.'

'In the war fought at Shanghai,' Yumiko went on, 'the bravest and the purest of spirit were the first to perish.'

Her eyes turned thoughtful. 'Perhaps it is always thus. Purity, in any of its forms, has no place, it seems, in this imperfect world. Perhaps those who find it – and live by its absolute precepts – are punished for their audacity.'

'If I was pure,' Aki said, 'I would not be punished.' He picked up one chopstick, brandishing it as if it were a weapon. 'I am a *samurai*. I would destroy those who would seek to punish me.'

Yumiko, who was about to admonish him for such talk, stayed her tongue at the last minute. She thought on what he had said. It was as if her own avenging spirit had somehow crossed the boundary between them; it was as if her *kami* had entered into his.

'We go to the *bochi* each January 18,' she continued, 'because on that date in 1932, five Japanese priests were attacked in Shanghai. One of them was killed. Murdered by the Chinese. He was the first to die – the first of many. We must honour his *kami* always.'

'Who is he? A *samurai*?'

'No, Aki-*chan*. I told you. He was a priest.'

'But why was he in China?'

How perceptive children could be, Yumiko thought. And above all others, her son. 'Because he was a member of a rather militant sect of Buddhists.'

'There are many Buddhists in town,' Aki said. 'Was he one of them?'

Yumiko smiled and touched her son. 'I don't think so. They have lost much popularity since that time. I doubt that any of his sect live around here.'

'What is their name?'

'Nichiren,' Yumiko said.

Aki learned from his mother that the real Nichiren had lived during the 13th century. He had believed in the *Lotus Sutra*, which, unlike the other major forms of Buddhism, Esoteric, Zen, and Amidism, considered the three forms

511

of the Buddha – Universal Body, Eternal Body, and Transformation Body – to be one and inseparable.

He had spent much of his life railing against these more prominent sects and criticizing Japan's rulers for patronizing what he considered false forms of religion.

Nichiren was not, of course, his real name. He had adopted it because it fitted his purposes. 'Nichi' meant 'sun', symbolizing both Buddha's Light of Truth, which Nichiren was dedicated to promulgating, and the Land of the Rising Sun, which he was dedicated to keeping pure. 'Ren' meant 'lotus', the symbol of the one and only righteous Buddhism.

Because of his endless militancy, Nichiren was at last sentenced to death by the ranking members of the Hojo regency in Kamakura. But as the executioner's sword descended upon his neck, a bolt of pure blue lightning struck the blade, shattering it.

This divine intervention caused the Hojo regency to reconsider his punishment. Eventually he was banished for life to a tiny island in the Sea of Japan, where he was the only inhabitant.

There he wrote, 'Birds cry, but shed no tears. Nichiren does not cry, but his tears are never dry.'

No one knows how long he stayed there, but one thing seems clear: he did not die there. Rather, a giant carp swam up to him while he was bathing in the sea and carried him away on its scaly back.

Aki thought about the story of Nichiren for a long time after he went to bed that night. Its message would not let him sleep. It seemed to him that Nichiren was pure; and for his purity of purpose he was punished. Yet, unlike his followers in more recent times, he had not been allowed to die. Hadn't Buddha intervened on his behalf, sending down that bolt of pure blue lightning? If so, why hadn't he done the same for the priests in Shanghai?

Perhaps it had not been Buddha after all. In that case,

the lightning was an act of nature. That made more sense to Aki, since it was a giant carp – another of nature's pure creations – that had spirited Nichiren away from his lonely exile.

Satisfied with his reasoning, Aki fell asleep. When he awoke in the morning, he helped his mother take down the bamboo pole from in front of their house.

When she moved to untie the pennant, he asked her if he could do it. Free of the cord that had bound it to the bamboo, the carp lay fluttering as if alive in Aki's outstretched hands.

He took it inside and carefully wrapped it up in their best rice paper. Then he knelt by the side of his *futon* and gently slipped the package underneath his pillow.

From her vantage point just beyond the doorway to his room, Yumiko looked on with glittering eyes.

That year, Aki received two presents on his birthday. The first, from his mother, was the boxwood bow and quiver of slender, finely fletched arrows he had been asking for all winter. He threw his arms around her excitedly, jumping up to string the bow outside.

'Aki-*chan*,' Yumiko said, 'haven't you forgotten something? You have another present to open.'

'I do?' He came back to where she knelt beside the low table. 'But how could that be? Who is it from?'

'There is a note for you, I think,' she said, handing him the gift. It was exquisitely wrapped in seven layers of handmade rice paper. Each had a different weave, a different hue, a different texture. The outermost layer was rough and ruffled, the innermost was as smooth as satin.

Aki was careful in unwrapping the present, sensing, perhaps, the importance of what lay inside by the complexity and care given over to its binding.

Inside he found a kimono. It was very shiny and unlike

any he had seen before. On the centre of its back was a charcoal grey *kamon*, an unfamiliar family crest.

Aki saw the heavy sheet of rice paper on top of the kimono. It was folded in precise thirds, sealed with a blob of vermilion wax. He took it up and broke the seal. It was handwritten in large brushstrokes by a forceful hand. It read:

Aki-*chan*. It has been almost ten years since you and your honourable mother settled here. I have watched you grow in that time. On your birthdays, I gave your honourable mother money because you were not yet old enough, in the grammar of my world, for me to give you a token directly. This year is different.

It was signed, 'Mitsunobe Ieyasu.'

'The *sensei*.' Aki breathed these words. Mitsunobe had been their only close neighbour. Though he had seen the old man speaking to his mother many times, Aki had never actually met him. There had always been a peculiar aura of unapproachability about Mitsunobe that had kept him away. On the other hand, he felt a fascination whenever he saw the old man, with his shock of thick white hair, striding down the road or leaning on his carved, gnarled walking stick while talking to Yumiko. Then he would crouch on the *engawa*, his arms tight around the wooden post, as if fearful that he would somehow be drawn down the last steps to his house and out towards the *sensei*.

Sensei meant 'master', and that was certainly what Mitsunobe was. He was the most celebrated *go* master of his time, and of course this alone would have been enough to earn him the title of *sensei*. But the old man was purportedly *sensei* in a number of other disciplines as well.

Aki unfolded the kimono. He tried it on. It was so gossamer-thin that he felt as if he had donned the wings of a dragonfly. It was unlined, which was odd in such a dress

514

garment made out of *habutae* silk. Aki, curious as always, commented on this.

Yumiko shrugged delicately. 'Then you'll just have to ask Sensei yourself. Perhaps one dons this kimono only on special occasions.'

'What occasion?' Then he turned to her, laughing. 'I know, "you must ask Sensei yourself."' Then his face darkened.

'Is something the matter, Aki-*chan*?'

He shrugged, abruptly mute.

'Don't you like Sensei's gift?'

'Oh, yes,' he said sincerely. 'Of course I do. It's just that . . .'

'Go on.'

'Well . . .' he looked up at her. 'It makes my heart pound to look at him.'

Yumiko smiled, put her hands on his shoulders. She felt his strong bones and muscles through the veiled layer of the ineffably smooth silk. It felt to her as if he was already taking on new form. 'That is only natural, my son. Sensei wields enormous power. I take it as a good sign that you can feel his power from such a distance. But you should not allow that power to frighten you or keep you away. It is a power to protect you, not to harm you.'

She began to walk with Aki to the front door. 'Now I will tell you a secret that will help you with Sensei on your first meeting. I know that he is waiting to hear from your own lips how much you like his gift. But it happens that today is also Sensei's birthday. I think that is one reason why he was drawn to you when we first moved here. He has no true son, only young and glib disciples. His wife died many, many years ago.

'Today, Aki-*chan*, is Sensei's *beiju*, his eighty-eighth birthday. Today begins his "age of rice".'

'Why is it called that?'

Yumiko took him back to the table, handed him a sheet

515

of paper and a brush. 'You know your *kanji*,' she said. 'Write the number eighty-eight.'

Aki did as she bade.

She took the brush from him. 'Now,' she said, using the brush, 'if you break down the character, you get three characters.' She drew them. 'What does this say now?'

'"Age of rice",' Aki said. He clapped his hands with delight. 'Is there more, Mother?'

Yumiko tousled his hair. 'In Japan, we begin celebrating old age at the sixty-first birthday, because an old proverb has it that "Life lasts only sixty years." But, further, our calendar gives remarkable emphasis to the sixtieth year. It is the time when one's birth signs are repeated wholly in the new calendar. Thus we see that year as marking a kind of rebirth. Special presents are given.'

'Have we given Sensei a special present for his *beiju*?'

For a time, Yumiko said nothing. She gazed down at her son's upturned face with loving eyes. She felt closer to him at this moment than she had to anyone on earth. How her heart was filled up with love for him.

'I thought I would leave that up to you,' she said softly.

'Me? But, Mother, how could I possibly know what to get Sensei?'

'Look to your heart,' she said. 'That is all that matters.'

Aki's face screwed up in concentration for a moment, then he said, 'Do you think Sensei likes *umeboshi* as much as I do?'

'Thank you for this gift.' His voice rumbled off the fine-grained cedarwood ceiling. It was as if the whole mountain-side were speaking.

Aki, his hands and forehead pressed hard to the *tatami* of the *Sensei's* entranceway, murmured, 'It is my favourite thing in the whole world.'

He heard the sound of paper unwrapping. Their rice paper was not nearly so fine as that in which Mitsunobe had swathed the black kimono, but it was the best quality he and his mother possessed.

'Ah,' the deep voice rumbled again, '*umeboshi*! How I love pickled plums. Even in the beginning of autumn!'

Aki ended his deep, respectful bow. His muddy *geta* had been neatly placed on the concrete slab just below the first cedar steps up into Mitsunobe's entranceway. On his feet were clean white *tabi*.

'Come in, my boy,' Sensei said. 'Welcome!'

His face was powerful. It was square, with his great shock of white hair, like a lion's mane, adding to the effect. His jaw was wide and firm. Deep lines were scored down from the sides of his nose to the corners of his broad mouth. His white eyebrows floated startlingly just above eyes like chips of flint. He was dressed in a wide-sleeved white linen blouse and a pale blue *hakama* skirt that Aki recognized as being similar to those he had seen the Zen archers wear when they practised their mysterious art.

Sensei's house gave an impression of great expanse. The ceilings were exceedingly high, massive cedar beams crisscrossing eyrie-like. He had directed the house to be built so that it faced the mountains. One could kneel and sip tea while gazing out at the almost limitless view that ranged up two miles or more through turreted crags, snow-driven slopes, and rising fields alternately sun-drenched and clouded over.

Mitsunobe made tea for Aki just as if he were an adult visitor. In fact, Aki was struck by the fact that Sensei did not seem to treat him as other adults did – save his mother. He did not talk down to Aki or feel that he had to be in some way amused just because the boy was ten years old.

'I am sorry that my gift is not as special as yours was to me,' Aki said, after sipping first at the frothy tea.

'On the contrary,' Mitsunobe said, 'I delight in pickled plums, and it is a rare day indeed when I am able to get the homemade kind.'

'As rare as the "age of rice"?' Aki asked in his straightforward way.

Mitsunobe laughed, the sound seeming to shake the bare rafters of the room. 'Oh, my goodness!' He shook with mirth. 'Yes, yes. As rare as *beiju*.' He unscrewed the cap of the jar. 'What do you say to sharing a portion of *umeboshi*?'

Night descended, but Aki did not notice until Mitsunobe rose to light the lamps. There was no electricity in the house. The illumination came from kerosene lanterns. Sensei fixed them a substantial though simple dinner of broiled fish and sticky rice.

Afterwards, they retired to the main room where no lights were lit. It was a clear night and, as Aki arranged himself on the *tatami*, he felt himself bathed in a kind of ethereal illumination. He looked up, saw the skylights set in a wheel pattern that seemed similar to the crest on the back of the black kimono.

In the silence of the upland night, starlight spilled into the house, lighting up the space with an extraordinary pinpoint glow.

'This is my time of contemplation,' Mitsunobe said, 'bathed in the Light of Buddha.' His face was only partially illuminated. Only patches of his features showed, so that Aki was obliged to use his memory and his imagination to fill in the dense shadows. In this atmosphere, Sensei's countenance took on chimerical characteristics.

'There was once a mystic badger,' Mitsunobe began. 'He was an exiled wise man who had transformed himself into the forest animal to escape the threats made against his life by an evil magician in the pay of a fierce and unjust warlord.

'In the transformation, he had left his human body behind. The warlord before whom the lifeless corpse was brought was satisfied that his enemy was indeed dead. But the magician, whose mind was far more devious, remained unconvinced.

518

'He ventured forth from the castle keep in order to prove his suspicions. The wise man, sensing that the magician was near, quickly ran. But he knew he could not run forever. Hiding in a cave or in the nearby stream was useless, for the magician had ways of discovering him.

'Accordingly, the badger sought out a floating forest of lotus he had heard of, and, plucking two, wrapped himself in the larger one, placing the smaller one atop his head like a cap. Thus he stood, his golden eyes like beacons searching for the magician's approach.

'At length he felt the chill one always feels with the onset of evil. He tried not to shiver inside his musky cloak, for any movement might dislodge his armour against evil.

'The magician passed over the badger on batlike wings. The hissing of his breath silenced the usually noisy nocturnal predators of the forest.

'In a moment he was gone. The lotus had protected the badger. After a time the badger returned to where he had shed his human form. Now that the crisis was past, he wanted to return to his natural body.

'But of course it was gone, having been brought before the evil warlord and burned in his presence. Now an ineffable sorrow gripped the badger's heart. He spent the next year hovering about the fringes of human society in a vain search for his body.

'During that time, however, he made many friends; foxes, stoats, rabbits, even the much-maligned weasels had their good side, he discovered.

'But not so with mankind. During that year the badger was able to observe human society as he had been unable to all his life, in total objectivity. He saw the cruelty that man inflicted on man. He saw wars, death, and blood running freely at the edges of the forest; he saw the victors exult, the vanquished collapse in despair.

'He saw, in short, that it was pride which separated man

from the animals. Pride was a sin which animals were incapable of committing.

'So, at the beginning of the summer solstice, when, in the innermost reaches of the forest, its creatures gathered to celebrate the new year, the badger abandoned a search for which he no longer cared, and returned to the circle of his new-found comrades. But it was the time of the hunter and, unknown to the badger, he had been seen by human hunters and followed deep into the forest.

'With their bows and arrows, they fired into the shadowed glade where all the creatures had gathered. The last to die was the badger, having had to see the death of all his new-found friends before at last an arrow pierced his chest.'

For a long time after Sensei's story was done, Aki said nothing. He listened hard. He heard the trill of a nightbird, and at inconstant intervals the scratching of a bough against the side of the house.

'I would like to be a badger,' he said at last.

'Indeed.' Mitsunobe was moving around in the dark. 'The danger is great.' Starlight glinted off his shoulders, making it seem as if he were appearing and disappearing through a dense forest.

'If I become clever enough, I can outwit the danger.'

At last Aki heard the soft susurrus of a *fusuma* sliding open. He felt almost immediately the slight chill of autumn's night wind on his cheek and throat.

'Let us see whether you are brave or merely foolish. Bring your bow and arrows.' Mitsunobe's voice reverberated out into the night. 'And follow me into the starlight.'

Aki rose and, grabbing up the present he had brought to show Sensei, scrambled across the *tatami*. At the lip of the doorway, he stepped down onto a broad flat stone. Its cold penetrated his thin *tabi*.

'My *geta*.'

'No clogs,' Mitsunobe said. His voice was like thunder. 'Only the kimono.'

'But it is thin,' Aki said. 'And it is cold out, this time of night.'

Sensei put his powerful arm across Aki's shoulders. 'Remember,' he said, his voice like thunder traversing the clear, star-laden sky, 'the mushrooms.'

Aki wrapped the *habutae* silk of the black kimono tighter around himself.

From somewhere far away, a mist was rising.

When he returned from his first round of lessons with Sensei, Yumiko found him changed. He was no longer Aki-*chan*, and she went to get her books. She summoned her son into the room in which she had had constructed the altar to the fox goddess, whom she had taken as her personal protectress.

Here she lit a multitude of candles and twenty-seven *joss* sticks in a semicircle around the plumeria wood altar. Her ancient books were spread open before her. She settled her son in the centre of the light. His face glowed with a special illumination. She saw the flickering flames reflected in his eyes. His strength filled up her sere heart, her withered soul.

They sat cross-legged on the reed *tatami*, and she felt his breath on her cheek, a fan of immortality. She might die soon, she knew, but he would live on and, through his power, her revenge on Athena and Zilin.

Nichiren was her logical choice. The historical Nichiren had killed in the name of a holy cause. Was her cause any less holy? Yumiko thought not. Beneath her kimono, her body burned along the meridians of the scars she bore, a physical manifestation of her shame. Nerves had been irrevocably severed, the Japanese doctors had told her. She should feel no pain in those spots, no sensation at all. Yet she burned. How she burned!

521

Only the knowledge of what she was about to do would assuage that agony. Aki-*chan* was Zilin's issue, as much as she wished it were not so. But it would be she who would mould him. She and the Sensei would assure that. Together they would make of Aki-*chan* something that Zilin would never recognize or tolerate.

His philosophy was one of ultimate reason and order in the world. Therefore, Yumiko had devised the ultimate revenge for him: to turn his son into the supreme anarchist. One drop of chaos into Zilin's precisely ordered world. His own son. It was only fitting. The irony pleased Yumiko.

Now she began her chants, raising ancient *kami*, the wildfire of desire resurrecting the ephemeral substance of spirit. Outside, the night had clouded over. The piercing starlight by which the Sensei had guided Aki-*chan* through the first of many years of lessons was gone. In its place, low, racing clouds, gravid with rain and electrical energy, dominated the atmosphere. Aki looked briefly out of the window at the refulgent night, and was reminded of the badger. He wondered if his mother had lotus leaves in which he could wrap himself. He felt something coming, and thought of batwings against the blackness of the sky.

The semireligious chanting of Yumiko gyred in the room, seeming to create patterns of light. Perhaps it was only the wind, seeping in through cracks in the walls and windows, that caused the candles' flames to flutter, then flare in incandescent brightness.

The incantations.

Yumiko had been quite correct. Aki-*chan* was no more. The child had been suffused with the spirit of the man. A certain man, iron-willed and hungry for life.

In Yumiko's mind, she had brought Nichiren back to life. He lived again inside her son. And who was there powerful enough to convince her that she was wrong?

Certainly not Aki-*chan*.

Book Four
KO*

* In Buddhism, the length of time exceeded only by eternity; In *Nei gui*, the point where the contending forces have reached a microcosmic stalemate

Summer, Present

Moscow/Hong Kong/Beijing/Washington/ Macao

'There is something I wish to know.'

Yuri Lantin lay on the rumpled bed, surrounded by the thick-striped Yves St Laurent sheets. Perfectly nude, he was smoking a thin cigarette of foreign manufacture. His long legs were flung carelessly out, crossed at the ankles. He seemed quite relaxed.

'There have been rumours,' he said, staring up at the groined, cream-coloured ceiling, 'of an increasingly disturbing nature.'

'Regarding what?' Daniella asked. She sat beside him with her back against a pair of goosedown pillows. She was wearing part of a three-piece Albert Nipon outfit that Lantin had bought her at the Beryozka store just three blocks from Dzerzhinsky Square. Though the place was within walking distance of her office, Daniella had never once gone in there. Though she possessed a coveted red plastic card that allowed her entrance to the restricted stores selling imported luxury items from the West, she had never used it. Since she had begun her affair with Yuri Lantin, he had taken her there three times.

Tonight she wore the gorgeous gored Nipon skirt, made of luminous deep blue synthetics that hugged her hips in a sexually inviting way. She wore black silk stockings; she was bare to the waist.

Lantin often dressed her thus for their long bouts of lovemaking. He loved inventiveness – loved, too, to see her nakedness through layers of half-open clothes and degrees of shadow.

She studied his nakedness now much as a fine painter

studies her nude model. With her eyes she traced the clean lines of his chest, free of the hair she despised on so many Russian men. His belly was flat and lean: she could see the outline of every muscle there. His groin was half-shadowed, just the head of him visible, curled on his thigh, waiting. He had very muscular legs, wiry like a runner's. Daniella found that she loved this body with an amazing passion. The galvanizing mind atop it was another matter.

At last Lantin finished his cigarette. He leaned over, stubbing it out, and in the same motion picked up a water glass containing three fingers of Starka. He liked to smoke occasionally, especially after sex, but he detested the taste it left in his mouth.

He swallowed some of the Starka, and said, 'The rumours concern Kam Sang. The nuclear power plant the Chinese are building in Guangdong.'

'What of it?'

'Rumours,' he said again. His gaze swept over her and he thought, What extraordinarily fine legs she has. If I could choose the method of my death, that would be it, to be strangled by those magnificent legs, my face buried in her snatch. 'Rumours that Kam Sang harbours a secret; that it is more than it purports to be.'

'But the rumours are true,' Daniella said, amused at how completely she had captured his attention. 'Do you think the KVR is ignorant of what is going on in Hong Kong or Southern China? I already know Kam Sang's secret. It was passed on to one of my agents. It's nothing to concern you.'

'I want to hear it anyway.'

'Kam Sang is going to be a radically different design in nuclear power generators. The engines will also be desalinizing sea water. Hong Kong's always had a water shortage problem. This will alleviate it.'

Lantin closed his eyes as if drifting off to sleep. Daniella contented herself with watching the rhythmic rise and fall of his chest and stomach. He even breathed like an athlete.

She, too, wanted something, and she was deciding how best to get it. Once she had seen a Western film depicting the Mafia. In it, the hero had to go to the boss, the godfather, to get permission to take action. Daniella wondered whether the Western term 'godfather' fitted Yuri Lantin.

'Are you certain of your intelligence?' he said.

'Concerning Kam Sang?' Her mind was far away.

'Yes.'

'Tell me, Yuri, have you had much experience in interpreting intelligence from the field?'

'I was in the army,' he said shortly. 'That was my field.' He said it as if no other field meant a damn.

'It's not like reading auguries,' she said. 'Poring through goats' entrails to divine the future. A network is an entity one sets up over years, allowing it time to settle in, to become, like an insect or a blade of grass, part of its environment. As that happens, over time, one evaluates the incoming intelligence, testing each bit like a chemist.' She pulled her golden hair back from the sides of her face. 'But that is where the analogy ends. There is nothing empirical about espionage.'

She said nothing more for a moment. She put her head back on the pillows, luxuriating for just an instant in the softness of the down. 'One tries never to leave anything to chance. From the first, I've had a vigil on each section of the network. Those observers report back to me. They are absolutely independent of the network. There are also specific backups for certain links in the chain. Each of these reports back to me independently to help verify the main body of intelligence.'

'This is all in aid of telling me that you are certain of the reliability of your intelligence.'

'No,' she said, 'it is to show you *why* it is reliable.'

'I think,' he said, 'that is why I was first attracted to you.' He turned to look into her grey eyes. For the first time he saw the tiny constellations of brown flecks there. 'You are not afraid.'

'It is stupid not to be afraid, sometimes.'

He reached out to touch her, as he rarely did, merely to make contact that contained no carnal component. 'That is not what I meant.'

'Fearless Daniella,' she said, wanting to draw him out. 'Having simultaneous affairs with a *sluzhba* general and a Politburo godfather.'

'A what?'

'The man with the ultimate power.'

'Not me,' he began. 'Premier – '

She had put the flat of her hand across his lips. He pulled her fingers away. 'Don't ever do that again!' he snapped.

She was not sorry that she had angered him. He was always in a more receptive state when he was angry.

She slapped him. 'Try to be civil, will you?' Her outrage seemed genuine enough to him.

He grabbed her wrist, twisting so far that she was obliged to curl away from her position. One half-clad thigh came down over his legs. She could feel his knee between her calves.

She cried out, her thick hair obscuring her face, the gold catching the light, glinting softly metallic as if it held hidden secrets.

'Perhaps it is also because you are so physical that I am attracted to you,' he said in her ear.

'You're hurting me.' She liked him to believe this, to hold him at a level that was tolerable to her. She suspected that, given free rein, his violence could easily slip across the boundary to become dangerous.

'Yes,' he said thickly, loving the sound of those words. He leaned in, bit the side of her neck. It was a spot that

528

made Daniella hot. She pulled away so that he would come after her as he desired. More and more, she felt caught up in his game, in deceiving him but slowly getting him to understand that she enjoyed what he was doing to her. She did not know why, and from time to time she found herself thinking about it. Generally, it was while she was at work. After a time she realized that it concerned her. Learning to like his kind of sex was somehow akin to taking drugs. It was different and addictive. It altered one's perception of reality. She did not know what to make of that.

Only knew she wanted more.

She beat him back with the heel of her hand against his pectorals. She loved the feel of him, the resilience and the hardness at once. When she aroused him he became hard all over. This, she had discovered, made her wild.

Her hair flew between them like a golden curtain. He took a handful and pulled her prone atop him. His knee began to part her thighs, flesh against silk. His hard thigh jammed against the fulcrum of her legs. The contact pushed all breath from her lungs.

She gasped and whimpered. Her eyes watered and he licked away her tears. Her nether lips were flowering open. Her heart was hammering hard. All she could hear was the rushing of her blood in her inner ears. She was making him wet.

'So hot,' he said, assaulting her anew. He flipped her over with a powerful twist of his upper torso. He circled her wrists with his hands, pulling her arms up over her head. Her heavy breasts thrust out towards him, and he shoved himself between them. The contact was dry and unpleasant, so he freed one of his hands to stimulate her roughly at the apex of her thighs. Daniella's eyes fluttered closed, she moaned to the sensation.

Then his hand came away and her eyes flew open. She watched him stroking himself, coating his long shaft with her fluids. Then he was between her breasts again, poling up and down.

His knees pushed her prominent breasts tightly together, forming the sheath. He was getting redder and redder.

Daniella lifted her head and, at an upstroke, enclosed the tip of him in her mouth. Swiped with her tongue. She felt him tremble and quickly let go.

He gasped, continuing to pole up and back. 'I need your lips,' he whispered. His face was contorted with his effort.

'I want you in me,' she sighed. 'Please.' His stroking was feverish. She whimpered and he could not refuse her.

He pushed the skirt aside, buried himself on the first thrust. They groaned simultaneously. Daniella's inner muscles massaged him until she felt the fluttering of his lower belly.

'Oh!' He sounded as if he were being stabbed to death. 'More!'

She gave him more, in tiny increments, increasing the friction from moment to moment. She thought he was going to have a heart attack.

Lantin convulsed atop her, the force inside him gathering and releasing, gathering and releasing. Daniella had never been with a man who came so long and so deeply.

This time she did not reach orgasm herself, though she came close. Her mind was filled with Karpov.

Later, at the edge of sleep, when it was so still within the apartment that she could discern the tiny increments of time being ticked off by the clock in the living room, he said into the space beside her ear, 'Tell me about your day.'

This was not an idle question, and she knew it. He had already digested the report copies she had smuggled to him. She resisted an urge to ask him about the conversation she had had with Tanya Nazimova. It had been odd to be on the phone with Chimera, her holiest of holy secrets, and to be the subject of a vigil at the same time, life ticking away like a time bomb, suddenly very dangerous indeed. But to the man following her, she was only on the phone, a call to a friend or relative, so what?

Defensive thinking. That was bad. If she could not manage to gain the offensive now, she would be finished in both a professional and a personal sense. She would be Lantin's, body and soul. Might as well slit her wrists right here in bed, mess all the new clothes he had bought for her. Hollow gifts, anyway, she knew. They were for his pleasure, not hers. She'd played that game many times before; she'd give him no cause to worry about her now.

She recounted the march of meetings she had had today, allowing him into her innermost thoughts regarding the fantasies she had of him, the comments of the other women officers at lunch about her smoking and new hairstyle, gulling him with the truth so that when she lied he would not spot it.

'Did they like the new you?'

His voice was soft and dreamy, lover to lover. But Daniella was not fooled. He did not care about that. *He* liked the new Daniella; that was all that mattered to him.

'They were fascinated,' she said, as if she were happy about it. 'They wanted to know what had come over me.'

'And what did you tell them?'

'That it was time for a change. That was something they could appreciate.'

'How do they feel about change?'

Having worked to get him to set the framework, Daniella could feel the edges of the topic that she wanted to discuss coming into view. She had deliberately kept away from it. It was important that Lantin came upon it without suspecting he had been helped.

'It depends on who initiates it.'

'Generally, then.'

'Generally, you know. They were not trained to take changes in their stride. Change upsets their ordered world.'

He thought about that for a moment. 'What else did they talk of? What gossip?'

They were close now. Very close. 'Oh, nothing exceptional. Who's sleeping with whom. What lieutenant came out of the closet this week. The usual stuff.'

'I've begun to hear some reports, leaking back to me.'

'About what?'

'I was wondering whether you had heard the same thing.'

'I don't understand.'

'I think you do.' He was being very clever. 'You're still loyal to Karpov.' There, it was out. 'He's been the one behind your career, pulling all the strings.'

'What about Karpov?'

'I think you know.' He turned, stroking her arm. 'You know, I think you're going to have to give up that particular loyalty.'

'I have my career to think about.' Just what he'd expect from her.

'Karpov is stealing my thunder.' His eyes were closed, his breathing calm. Sweat was a salty-slick film across him.

'Karpov has an ego the size of the Ukraine,' she said.

'Yes, I know.'

'Egotists are like blackmailers. Once they start, they never have sense enough to stop.'

'Is that your opinion of Karpov?'

She said nothing, quite deliberately.

'He was the original architect of Moonstone.' Lantin still had not opened his eyes.

'Karpov, I think, had one good idea in his life.'

'What was that?'

'Making me head of the KVR.'

He laughed at that and his lids popped open, surprising her. He stared at her thoughtfully. After a time he said, 'What am I to do about Karpov?'

'Why ask me?'

532

'You've known him a long time. You know him . . . intimately.'

'And you think I'm privy to all his secrets.' It was important that he work hard for this. 'Why don't you ask his wife, then?'

He chose to ignore her facetiousness. 'His wife, perhaps, loves him. Also, she does not possess your mind. People in the position Karpov is in are not so easy to bring down. As head of the First Chief Directorate, he has many friends. More in the military. One needn't muddy the waters to catch fish.'

She laughed. 'I almost think you're serious.'

'I am.'

Now that he thought of this as his idea, she could get on with it. 'This is not a small task.'

'I would think not.'

'Then I have something to ask of you.'

'What is that?'

'Your permission,' she said.

He looked at her breasts, so firm and rich they stirred him again. He felt himself growing, the breath quickening in his throat.

You're looking at the wrong place, Yuri, Daniella thought. She moved minutely so that her breasts quivered just enough for him to pick up.

'You are *sluzhba*,' he said. 'I am not. What would you need my permission for?'

She leaned over, grasping his erection at its base. She squeezed slightly. At the same time her pointed breasts dragged against the muscles of his lower belly.

'You are the power. Without you, there will be nothing.'

He sighed and she echoed him.

'Oh!' she whispered. 'So big!'

He closed his eyes, his breathing already ragged. He thought of how strong his hold on Daniella was. She would never speak a word against him. She might be devious, but she was a woman; she knew her place in the *sluzhba*. His intelligence on her assured that. Just as it assured that she would obey his every command.

Zhang Hua hurried across Tian An Men Square. Again, he was late for his meeting with Wu Aiping, and he was not looking forward to the withering comments the senior minister would subject him to.

He went quickly up the wide steps of the Historical Museum, opposite the National People's Congress Building. In the cool, dim interior, such a contrast to the devastating heat outside, he hurried past the enormous relief map of China hanging on the wall, with its quotations from Mao and its chronological history of the dynasties. He turned left, then right until he found the space filled with the ten-metre-long dugout canoe discovered in Jiangsu in 1958. It was presumed to be old, but like the majority of the 'artifacts' housed within the museum, it could just as well be a restoration or a wholesale copy. China had been too well plundered over the centuries for much to remain, even in the largest museum in the country.

'A thousand pardons, Comrade Minister,' he said as he came up to Wu Aiping.

The senior minister had been studying a replica of the calendar used during the Shang Dynasty, between the 16th and the 11th centuries B.C. To Zhang Hua's relief, he did not return an acid comment. Instead, he continued to stare at the chart on the wall.

In a moment he had moved on to the first of a series of large glass cases. As Zhang Hua followed him, he saw that the case was filled with weapons used long ago.

'Do you realize, Zhang Hua,' Wu Aiping said, 'that all the hafts of these knives, spears, and axes have been cleverly reproduced by modern artisans, using the designs garnered from ancient pictograms of the period? It makes one feel proud of modern China.'

534

It makes me sick to my stomach, Zhang Hua thought privately, to know just how much of our past has been stolen or ruined by the *faan gwai loh*. Now there is nothing left of our long and glorious past but these sad restorations that merely look like what they are not. But he said only, 'I understand, Comrade Minister.'

They moved on to the second case. Here were displayed a list of ancient grains, gleaned from characters found in archaeological inscriptions, as well as agricultural tools such as a bronze spade, purported to be real, stone hoes, and shell sickles. To Zhang Hua they looked no different from the weapons in the previous case.

'Now that it has been done, I don't mind telling you,' Wu Aiping said. 'In fact, I prefer to. You who are loyal to Shi Zilin, you whom I own. To pay for that loyalty, I would have you twist in the wind while you watch your mentor's destruction.'

Wu Aiping's tone of voice was the same as if he were strolling with a friend, idly enjoying the museum.

'The last of the cables has been sent to Hong Kong,' he continued. 'The *qun*, dipping into our various ministries' funds, has bought up all of Five Star Pacific's short-term notes. That makes a total investment of just over twelve million dollars. Now we control Five Star Pacific. Shi Zilin's main link in his *ren* has been neutralized. Now that the *qun* is Sir John Bluestone's partner, Shi Zilin is a thing of the past. He has no more leverage with which to sabotage Kam Sang.'

'Kam Sang could kill us all,' Zhang Hua said hotly. 'I feel as Shi Zilin does. Its secret is far too dangerous for – '

'Silence!' Wu Aiping's hissed warning served as well as a shout. 'I have no stomach to hear this weak-hearted drivel. Surrounded on all sides, China is besieged. If we do nothing to destroy the Soviets, they will certainly crush us. This war in Yunnan is but the first step of a concerted campaign designed to destroy us. Kam Sang's power will ensure that never happens!'

Zhang Hua recognized the lurid light of the zealot behind Wu Aiping's eyes. He was terrified by the power the senior minister wielded. His shoulders slumped against the glass case and he thought, If Kam Sang is activated, none of us will survive.

'Speaking of Sir John Bluestone,' Wu Aiping said, calmer now that Zhang Hua had ceased to verbally oppose him, 'I received a cable from him via the Hong Kong and Asia Bancorp. He wanted more capital to buy up all the remaining outstanding shares of Pak Hanmin.' Wu Aiping was savouring the knowledge that Bluestone was now *his* agent, unwitting or no. 'Last night I called the *qun* together, and though the risk to us is now high, I persuaded them to borrow further from our funds. Since we are assured of a quick return on the money, we wired out the money early this morning. That was the last nail in Shi Zilin's coffin.'

'But Comrade Minister,' Zhang Hua protested, 'Shi Zilin was about to advance them the money.'

Wu Aiping smiled. 'Of course he was. I just beat him to it. The pattern. I have broken it. Now that I control the *faan gwai loh* Bluestone, I can control the flow of events. You, good *lou sin*, Minister Mouse, will inform me the moment Shi Zilin sends his next coded message to Mitre.

'At that moment, I will set my hearing with the Premier. At last we are in position to destroy Shi Zilin. As soon as he sets the final phase of his Hong Kong plan in motion, he's a dead man. Once he is gone, we will weed out the generals who are loyal to him, replace them with our own men. Inheriting the axis of power that has been his for decades, we will actively use it as he has cravenly chosen not to.

'The time of swift action is upon us. A rising bubble of power that will sweep all my enemies from before me.'

Zhang Hua, walking beside Wu Aiping, heard this change in emphasis. He said nothing.

Jake watched Bliss, asleep, half hidden by the floral bedcovers. At the window, sunlight struck him a heavy blow across the shoulders. His back was to Hong Kong. He watched her with intimate absorption.

He felt the same standing here as he had moments before, asleep-awake next to her. He had dozed with unrestful deliberation, acutely aware of her presence beside him. The silken slide of her skin, her perfumed breath on his neck, strands of her hair, light as air, fanned across his chest.

He had felt the rhythmic rise and fall of her deep, even breathing, believing himself several times to be immersed in the South China Sea, off Cheung Chau island, Fo Saan's voice coming from nowhere and everywhere at once: *Bamahk, find the pulse.*

Rapt in her aura.

Deep slumber eventually took him, a clear, utterly restful time such as he had not felt in years. He had awakened just before dawn, aware of what had befallen him and so guilty that he had been obliged to get out of bed immediately. Never mind that he wanted to remain where he was, by Bliss's side.

That guilt, so Western in nature, must have been a genetic product of his mother. Certainly it had not come from his father. Jake rarely thought of his father. When he did, it was most often of David Maroc. His *fu* shard was his only link with the couple who had created him. His memories were full of David and Ruth Maroc, the people who had raised him as their own.

Carefully, in the light of the new day, Jake unwrapped the *fu* shard that Kamisaka had given him. Nichiren's piece. Yes, his eyes and mind confirmed, it was part of the same *fu*, the same Chinese emperor's seal. How was this possible?

Jake's gaze returned to Bliss's sleeping form. Who was she, really, besides his childhood friend? She had long outgrown that role. Or had she? He knew that he must get her to fulfil her promise to him. Jake was surrounded by mystery. He disliked unanswered questions. That trait, too, must be from his natural mother. Athena Nolan Shi. Even in her lunatic ravings just before she died, Athena had refused to give up that name. Jake Shi.

He had become Jake Maroc, but now, with the *fu* shard lying heavy in his palm, he suspected that there were others in the world who knew his real name. Who were they? How did they know? To his knowledge, only the Marocs had been aware of his origin. Not even Mariana, not even Ting.

The *fu*. Ever since his raid on O-henro House, events seemed to have revolved around the *fu* shard: Mariana's disappearance, Nichiren's actions, even Bliss's. She knew of the *fu* shard, had told him to go after it. Why? What did she know about this artifact that he did not?

He crossed the room. As he did so, his shadow fell across her face. Bliss awoke, staring into his eyes.

'Jake.'

She did not move. She slept naked. Her shoulders and the tops of her breasts were visible above the rumpled top sheet.

'You slept well last night.'

Causing another stab of guilt to go through him, sleeping better with her than he ever had with Mariana. 'I tossed and turned,' he said. 'I dreamed constantly.'

'I woke twice,' she said softly, 'to make sure you were all right. You slept like a child, unmoving. All the worry lines were gone from your face.'

He sat on the bed. He felt a flood of emotion. Just by

538

talking, she could melt his heart. How was such a thing possible?

She watched his face as a mother will watch the face of a troubled child. She sat, drew her legs up to her chest.

'I'm holding you to your promise, Bliss.'

Her thick hair was like dark wings shadowing her face. She rested the point of her chin on her knees. 'When I was a child,' she said, 'my father used to tell me the story of the fox who was forced to forage for himself and his mate, pregnant and ill with an unknown disease. It was winter in the northern provinces, a hard, mean season when frost rarely left the land. Because of this, the fox was obliged to stray farther and farther afield to find sustenance.

'One night he came to the edge of a farmer's land and, slipping through a gap in the reed fence, found the henhouse. Thereafter, every night the fox slipped into the coop and dragged out a hen. The farmer set traps, each night a different kind, each one more cunning than the last. The fox, desperate and determined that his mate and still unborn cub should not die, evaded them all.

'This went on for ten days until finally the farmer determined that he would have to go after the fox himself. Taking a broad-bladed axe, he sat in wait for the fox inside the henhouse.

'Eventually the fox arrived, but he scented the farmer's presence. He tried for a hen, but the farmer deflected him with the axe. He wounded the animal but it managed to escape the coop. The night was clear and the farmer, following the tiny droplets of blood, black in the moonlight, tracked the fox back to his lair.

'Using his axe, he set about to destroy the lair, but the bottom of the tree bole was hundreds of years old and as big around as the farmer's shoulders. It resisted his attack, and this exertion combined with the numbing cold to defeat him.

'Still, he wished to ensure that the fox would never again

kill one of his chickens, so he made himself as comfortable as he could in front of the lair's entrance. When the fox emerged, as he knew the animal must in order to eat, his weapon would make certain of that.

'All through the night the farmer kept his vigil, and into the following day. Morning turned into afternoon, afternoon into dusk, dusk into night. Numb and hungry – he had eaten only several scoops of snow – the farmer swung his axe back and forth in front of the lair.

'At last he heard a stirring, and turning as still as a rock, he waited for the fox to appear. His axe, honed and lethal, was at the ready. The farmer saw the beginning of the black muzzle, the whiskers. He could see the eyes. He prepared himself for the kill.

'And at the last instant he stopped his swing in midair. For what had emerged from the lair was not the fox who had been raiding his henhouse but a tiny cub, his fur matted down with his mother's saliva, his legs weak and unsteady.

'The farmer knew that this cub must be an orphan, for his parents would never have allowed him out of the lair. His father must have bled to death, his mother must have died as well.

'The farmer hefted his axe, setting it on his shoulder. He bent and took the trembling fox cub into his hand. Pressing it against his side to provide it warmth, he returned to his farm.

'The farmer, trained never to allow anything to go to waste, raised the cub, and when it grew up, he trained it to guard his henhouse from nocturnal intruders, which the fox did to the best of his abilities, which was very good indeed.'

Bliss put a hand up, stroked Jake's cheek. 'Patience, my love. The righteous have learned that patience is one of their most potent weapons.'

'I am hardly righteous, Bliss.' He took her hand away from him. 'I want some answers. Now.'

'Now. Now. Now. How Western you often are.'

Jake went very still. 'What do you mean?'

'Oh, Jake, I knew about the *fu*. Do you think I don't know that you are half Chinese?'

'The Marocs – '

'The Marocs took you out of Shanghai when your mother died.'

He stared at her. 'How do you know that?'

'My father was in Shanghai at the same time. He knew your father. Your real father.'

Jake got off the bed. He drew Bliss with him. They stood, naked, bathed in the morning light. All of Hong Kong stretched away below them. Above, the Peak was wreathed in mist.

'Bliss, you're a spook. You said as much.'

'That makes us the same.' Her head, tilted up so that she could look at him, was golden in the sunlight. Her blue-black hair was like a curtain separating them from the rest of the world.

'The *fu*. What is it?'

'The *fu* is the key to the *yuhn-hyun* in Hong Kong.'

'The circle? What circle?'

'The ring,' she said. 'Set up by your father, long ago.'

'I don't understand.'

'None of us inside the *yuhn-hyun* understand all of it. Pieces fit together to form the whole. Like the *fu*.'

'This is not my piece of the *fu*. It is Nichiren's. Mine came from my parents. My real parents. Do you know where his came from?'

'If I knew that,' she said, 'I would know everything.'

'Nichiren and I – ' He broke off, turned away towards the expanse of the city and the harbour. 'It disturbs me that he has this. That we share something . . . as unique as the *fu*.' He turned back to her. 'He is here in Hong Kong.

541

I'm told he comes here often. Do you know who he sees? Formidable Sung.'

'Your friend.'

'You know that, too. Whom do you work for?'

'I've never asked you that.'

'I suspect that you already know.'

'Whether I do or not,' she said simply, 'I've never asked you to abrogate your trust. Why do you ask me to?'

'Because of your promise. You said you'd tell me everything.'

'And so I shall.' She touched him again. 'In time.' She lifted up on her toes, pressed her warm lips against his. 'Patience, Jake. I am working to keep us alive. Will you allow me to do my job?' Her dark eyes met his with such force that he was shocked into silence.

It took Three Oaths Tsun more than twenty minutes to establish radio contact with Beijing. Atmospheric disturbances to the northeast were causing his signal to waver like a flame in the wind, so that when, at length, contact was made, the voice was stuttery and often indistinct.

Three Oaths Tsun, sitting in the stern of a five-metre lorcha, had anchored his craft along the shore of an estuary approximately sixteen nautical miles upriver from Hong Kong. He varied the exact point from night to night during his thrice-weekly rendezvous. But he was invariable as to the general area. He knew this topography intimately, and not wanting to keep his long-range transceiver on board his junk for obvious security reasons, he felt this to be the optimum recourse.

'Five Star Pacific has bought up all the outstanding shares of Pak Hanmin,' he said morosely into the microphone.

'Good,' the familiar voice said. Out of habit, they spoke Mandarin.

'By the spirit of the White Tiger, there was a fight over

the last one hundred thousand shares. Bluestone and Andrew Sawyer went at it tooth and nail before Bluestone prevailed.'

'Even better.'

'Better? Fornicate "better"!' Three Oaths Tsun cried into the mike. 'I've lost control of my company!'

There was a garbled response and he had to fight to remember that they switched frequencies every sixty seconds. He dialled furiously and asked for a repeat.

'Have no fear in that regard. All is going well in Hong Kong. My plan is on schedule, despite all the recent setbacks. Unfortunately the same cannot be said for events on this end. I am being sorely pressed by a clique of ministers here.'

Three Oaths Tsun hunched in front of the transceiver. 'How serious is the threat?'

'It's possible it will be lethal. I cannot say as yet. Have you scheduled *zui-hou-kai-ting*, the final meeting?'

'The day after tomorrow. Is there anything any of us can do here? Anything *I* can do?'

'Have you heard from Bliss?'

'She is with Jake.' He took a breath. 'David Oh, his friend, has been terminated.'

'By whom?'

'The Quarry.'

'Ah, Chimera has arisen. We are in the end phase now. You must get word to Bliss. Jake will be Chimera's next logical victim.'

'It's all coming down to one fine point,' Three Oaths Tsun said, 'isn't it?'

'That was the original design.'

'But there are so many variables.'

'Variables have already entered into play. They have changed nothing.'

'Nothing? Is Mariana Maroc's death nothing? Is David

Oh's death nothing? How many other deaths have there been of people whose names I do not know?'

'We are speaking now of the future of China . . . perhaps even of the world. How can you equate this with the death of a handful of people?'

Three Oaths Tsun shook his head. 'There must be some humanity left inside you. Do you see everyone as a piece in your game, to be manipulated at your whim?'

'I see the future of China. That is all.'

'And your family?' Three Oaths Tsun had promised himself that he would not bring this subject up. It was improper and, worse, disrespectful. But he found that he could no longer hold his tongue. There was Bliss to think about. And Bliss's emotions. 'What is left of your family? *A mi tuo fo*, look what your obsession has done to them!'

Silence.

The crackling of the ether, evidence of storms, far away and violent.

'Hello, Henry,' Antony Beridien said, looking up from his crowded desk. He always said that he felt most at home surrounded by dossiers. Files were the lifeblood with which he directed his agency. 'Is it time already?'

Wunderman nodded. 'Just past, really. I knew how busy you were. I wanted to give you as much time as possible.'

Behind Beridien, the White House shone like alabaster in the waning hours of a long, drab afternoon. The rose-bushes in full bloom were visible, but the crowds filing along the pavement past the President's office were hidden by the building itself.

Beridien stretched. 'You know, I've gotten almost no work done since you and Rodger instituted this red-level security scheme of yours. Why, you've even got the doctor's office rigged with videotape monitors.'

'Just a precaution, sir,' Wunderman said easily.

'Precautions, shit. I can't even take a piss without

cameras and agents taking a peek at my pecker. Christ almighty, man, even Ike didn't have this much security during the war.'

Wunderman smiled as they went down the clay-coloured corridor. 'Maybe that's because General Eisenhower didn't have Daniella Vorkuta to contend with.'

'Fucking KVR,' Beridien said. 'I'd like to get Vorkuta and Karpov in one room together. I'd give them something to contend with.' His palm pressed against the wall plate, calling for the private elevator.

'I've activated Apollo,' Wunderman said. 'He's my asset; I have full and complete integrity over him. He's been inside the Kremlin for years, under deepest cover. I think matters have come to a critical enough point that we must take the chance of his being discovered.'

Beridien looked at him as the brushed-bronze elevator door opened and they went inside. He pressed the lower button. 'Our queen for theirs, is that it?'

'If it comes down to it, yes, sir. That's precisely it.'

'You've nurtured Apollo for a long time, Henry. Are you certain that you want to sacrifice him in this manner?'

'It may not be a sacrifice, Antony. Apollo is clever. He may get away with terminating Vorkuta without incriminating himself.'

Beridien was shaking his head. 'Inside the KVR? He's not KGB, Henry. The risk is great.'

'Right now we need Vorkuta dead more than we need Apollo's intelligence.'

'I wish to Christ you'd come to me first.'

'Why, so you could order me to keep Apollo away?'

'We lose Apollo, Henry, and we lose our highest-level mole inside Russia.'

'And if we allow General Vorkuta to live, she'll destroy us.'

They passed by the double squad of guards and entered

the medical facilities wing. In the examining cubicle, Beridien began to undress. 'Either way, I'm afraid we'll lose something valuable.'

Dressed in the hospital gown, open down the back, Beridien got up on the table. He hissed as the cold hit him. 'You'd think they'd be able to heat these damned things in this day and age,' he said crossly.

Presently the doctor came through another door. Her brown hair was tied back in a tight bun. She wore only a hint of lipstick. Her high Slavic cheekbones needed no artificial aid. Wunderman watched her long legs as she walked across the room to where Beridien lay.

The checkup she gave him was complete but routine: eyes, nose, throat, heart, lungs, blood pressure, kidneys. Wunderman continued to watch the play of the muscles in her legs as she moved and especially when she bent. She must play tennis, he thought. Like Donovan.

'You're basically fine,' the doctor said after a time. Wunderman could hear the scratching of her pen as she completed her findings on Beridien's chart. 'But you've got the beginnings of a bug. A flu, perhaps. Nothing serious, but I'm going to give you a vitamin shot nonetheless. I don't want your long hours depleting you. I know better than to order you to take some time off.'

Beridien grunted.

'You can sit up now,' she said.

Wunderman became interested in her buttocks.

The doctor was at the gleaming stainless-steel crash cart. She inserted the end of a syringe into a vial, turned it upside down, drew the clear liquid into the body of the syringe. With a tiny squeak, she unplugged the vial.

'Just a moment,' Wunderman said. He crossed to where she stood, and took the vial from her. He studied the label, his gaze flicking over the list of vitamins. He looked hard into the doctor's brown eyes and nodded. 'All right.' She smelled of hand-milled soap.

The doctor watched him as he went back to his spot against the wall. When he was still again, she took a cotton ball soaked in alcohol and swabbed a spot on the fleshy part of Beridien's upper arm.

Beridien was looking away when the needle went in, otherwise he would have seen the doctor smile thinly as she depressed the plunger.

'This won't take long.' The doctor's words seemed to reverberate in the stillness of the room.

Beridien turned his head back when the doctor said, 'Not more than three minutes.'

'Not more than three minutes until what?' Beridien asked.

'Why, until you're dead, Director.'

Wunderman was already moving across the room.

'What? Is this a joke? I – ' But the venom had already begun to attack Beridien's central nervous system and he no longer had any control over his vocal cords. His mouth worked comically.

'As you can see,' the doctor said, 'it's no joke.' She put a hand on Beridien's head, flicked up one eyelid, then the other. 'Uhm, pupils already highly dilated.' Her voice had the crisp, detached tone of an automaton.

Wunderman pushed her aside. 'Antony!'

'Who are you talking to?' the doctor asked. 'He's dead.'

'What?' Wunderman looked into Beridien's eyes. They were clouded, bereft of intelligence. He bit his lip until he broke through the skin and could taste the salt of his own blood. 'What the hell – !'

'Poisoned,' the doctor said. 'I am his Livia, you see.'

Wunderman whipped a small-calibre pistol from beneath his jacket and fired three shots point-blank into her face. She reeled back into the crash cart. The black holes marred her look of total surprise.

Then he lunged for the red alarm button that was part

547

of every room no matter how small or insignificant in the Quarry building. He snatched up the phone.

'Emergency!' he shouted down the line. 'This is an emergency, not a drill! The director has been assaulted! I repeat, there is an emergency in the infirmary!'

In a moment the doors had crashed open. Agents streamed in. Above their heads, the video cameras silently recorded every movement in loving detail.

It was drunken shrimp time.

Sir John Bluestone had been introduced to the Chinese delicacy some years ago in Taipei by a young woman with a healthy appetite for sex and food. Drunken shrimp had been her favourite meal. Just as some people crave a cigarette after making love, this woman was happiest digging into this particular dish.

These days, in a kind of private remembrance of those faraway days of rash youth, Bluestone ordered drunken shrimp whenever there was an event to celebrate. Taking the controlling interest in Pak Hanmin was certainly one of those, and he had wasted no time in dragging T. Y. Chung off to a festive lunch.

The two *tai pan* were seated at the best table in Jumbo, the largest of the three floating restaurants permanently anchored in Aberdeen harbour, on the south side of the Island. This was not on the third deck, where all the *gwai loh* tourists were led, but down on the first deck. From this position they had an excellent view through a large window of the busy harbour, the town, and, beyond, the Peak. Jumbo's great fish tank was just a stone's throw away on their other side.

Bluestone lofted his glass of Johnnie Walker Black and clicked it against T. Y. Chung's. He would have much preferred champagne for this occasion, but he wanted to seem as Chinese in spirit as possible.

'To the man without whom I'd never have gotten Pak Hanmin.'

That was, of course, not strictly correct. It was true enough that T. Y. Chung's bidding and buying had been tremendously helpful, but really, Bluestone had to admit that it was his new-found benefactors to whom he owed his thanks.

At first, when his banks had contacted him to say that someone was buying up all of Five Star Pacific's short-term notes, he had become suspicious. Especially when he could find out nothing about the company, Yau Sin-Kyuhn Services, H.K.

But then the banks had assured him that it was not owned by either Three Oaths Tsun or Andrew Sawyer. In fact, they informed him that a document was being pre-pared by Yau Sin-Kyuhn's lawyers that would allow him to repay the loans at fourteen per cent interest, fully four points lower than what he had been paying. In exchange, the firm was asking for ten per cent of Five Star Pacific.

Bluestone, who had for some months been in a financial bind, could have thought of several more odious alterna-tives. After all, ten per cent was hardly enough to influence policy, and if Yau Sin-Kyuhn's intervention brought an end to his financial crunch, it would be a blessing in disguise. For months he had been putting off communicat-ing his problems to his source.

Then he had come up with a way that Yau Sin-Kyuhn could be of further use to him. He had hit them with the final bill for Pak Hanmin. Why not? They wanted part of the profits of Five Star Pacific. Why not get them to work for it?

And it had worked. Less than twenty four hours after he had sent the telegram to YSK, he had received the money, along with a simple loan contract, calling for repayment through Pak Hanmin's profits. He couldn't say no to that, even though he still had his suspicions about who was really behind Yau Sin-Kyuhn. He knew that he had done all he could to discover the identities of the owners. He would have to accept the situation as it was now. But he was determined to keep searching for clues to Yau Sin-Kyuhn. One day he would unearth its secret. Until then, he would use it in any way he could.

But there was no point in telling T. Y. Chung that. The less the Chinese knew about Bluestone's affairs, the better. After all, it was Bluestone himself who was in partnership with T. Y. Chung, not Five Star Pacific. The Pak Hanmin deal was something he had put together on his own.

'Without your help and the Hak Sam's intervention in the New Territories, my fortunes would be quite different.'

T. Y. Chung smiled thinly. '*Joss*, Mr Bluestone. The Hak Sam, the Chiu-chow triad with which you are affiliated, was no doubt pleased to resolve your contract problems in the New Territories. Utilities are their bread and butter. In that region, work is still difficult, and though this agreement with the Communists gives us some breathing room, people are still jittery, especially there.

'As for myself, new business opportunities are always welcome when they involve trading houses the size of Five Star Pacific.'

The waiter came with the food. First, *abalone* in blackbean sauce, then *garoupa* steamed with bamboo shoots and tiger lily buds. The men ate silently, with quick, jerky movements of their chopsticks. Tea was for later. Now, Bluestone continued to pour the Scotch.

At length the waiter arrived at their table with what appeared to be a small aquarium on a rolling cart. Inside, the pair could see two dozen outsized prawns, swimming lazily in the sea water.

With deft, economical movements, the waiter reached under the aquarium, producing a large metal bowl. He set this on the centre of the table. Into it he poured two full bottles of white wine. Then, one by one, he fished up the prawns with a bamboo utensil and placed them in the bowl of wine. When he had transferred all twenty-four of them, he took his cart and departed.

Bluestone saw T. Y. Chung staring out of the restaurant's window, not at the buildings of Aberdeen but towards the floating city of the Hakka. Bluestone thought he was looking for Three Oaths Tsun's junk.

'We've really stuck it to him this time.'

T. Y. Chung turned his head. 'I beg your pardon?'

'Three Oaths Tsun,' Bluestone said. He was slightly put out that his culinary *pièce de résistance* had not taken centre stage. 'We've dealt him a severe blow. Pak Hanmin was one of his pet projects. Now we've taken it away from him. You and I.'

T. Y. Chung smiled again, but in such a way that Bluestone had absolutely no idea what was in his mind. 'Yes,' he said. 'A severe blow, to be sure.'

Bluestone returned his gaze to the metal bowl. He pointed. The swimming of the prawns was beginning to falter. 'Look,' Bluestone said, 'they're getting drunk.'

T. Y. Chung lifted his glass. 'Just like us.'

Bluestone smiled, but he felt vaguely disquieted by the notion. He stirred the wine as if he were a chef.

'Now that our partnership has been firmly cemented by Pak Hanmin,' T. Y. Chung said as he watched the prawns dance, 'I think it's time we set up a three-way meeting with Sharktooth Tung.'

Bluestone looked pensive. 'He is a busy man.'

Don't I know it, T. Y. Chung thought. But you're not going to keep him all to yourself. Building a friendship with the dragon of the Hak Sam triad is one of the main reasons I am sitting here today. 'We're all busy men, Mr Bluestone. But in business, I find, there is no substitute for personal relationships. If our partnership is to flourish, we must enter into it with a joined spirit. If we do not, we are wasting one another's time.'

'I'll see what I can do, then.'

But by his tone, T. Y. Chung knew that Bluestone would do nothing of the kind. I'd better whet his appetite, he thought.

'I have something specific in mind,' he said. 'Something that perhaps Sharktooth Tung can help me with.'

'What does it concern?' Bluestone asked.

Now I have him, T. Y. Chung thought. 'Not *what*, Mr Bluestone. *Who*. Three Oaths Tsun. I've another acquisition in mind. In the New Territories. Local management, I am told, is riddled with Hak Sam.'

Bluestone thought, The sooner we can bring Three Oaths Tsun down, the better. There will be an entire rainbow of choice companies ripe for the picking. Together, T. Y. Chung and I will scoop them up in the same manner we did with Pak Hanmin. After all, that's one of the main reasons I agreed to go into this partnership. Right now I need this man. Five Star Pacific is cash-poor. T. Y. Chung's capital is a blessing. But all marriages must end, and when this one does, I want to be on the winning end.

'Perhaps, after all,' he said, 'I can prevail upon Sharktooth Tung to have lunch with us sometime next week.'

'Splendid,' T. Y. Chung said.

Sir John Bluestone glanced down into the metal bowl. He rubbed his hands together. 'I do believe our meal is now at the proper degree of drunkenness.'

So saying, he reached in and, plucking up a dazzled prawn, bit off its head. With great relish, he began to munch in earnest on the tender white flesh.

Formidable Sung, the 489 of Hong Kong's 14K, was a busy man. That was only to be expected, since he was the leader of the Crown Colony's largest and most powerful triad.

For years the 14K had fought a pitched and bloody battle with the Shanghainese Green Pang triad through

Hong Kong's twisting streets for control of the Colony. An uneasy stalemate of sorts had been broken by Jake, who went in search of Formidable Sung a month or so after he had been assigned to head the Quarry's Hong Kong Station.

What Jake had proposed was a mutual protection and assistance pact between the 14K and the members of the Quarry and their families. The idea was for the members of Formidable Sung's triad to keep the Quarry agents and their families safe within the precincts of their homes. In return he promised to pass on any intelligence directly affecting the triad that came the Quarry's way.

Six months after the 14K, under the direction of Sung, had begun their Quarry liaison, the balance of power began to swing inexorably in their direction. As a result a strong friendship had sprung up between Jake and the triad leader.

Sung Po-han was the youngest 489 anyone could remember within the triad, hence he had been renamed Formidable. He had done more for the reorganization of the triad in his first seven years of tenure, so it was said, than had been accomplished in the previous seven decades. That meant a schedule that would have crippled most other men within a year.

But as busy as he was, he always made time for Jake Maroc. From their very first meeting, Formidable Sung had been impressed with Jake, though he had taken pains not to show his feelings to Jake's face. That would have put him in a disadvantageous bargaining position.

Jake had looked for him first at his office in the toy factory. He had been referred here. Formidable Sung, involved in many businesses, had a number of offices around the Colony. Now, as Jake was ushered into the office off a tiny side street in Wanchai, Formidable Sung stood up. He wore an armband. It was white, the Chinese colour of mourning.

They bowed to each other across a space of not more than five feet. 'My condolences, Mr Maroc.' In the Colony, among Chinese as well as among the *gwai loh*, there was unyielding formality between business associates. 'I am happy that you are looking so much better than when we last were together, but I am sad, as well. I heard about the unfortunate and untimely demise of your wife. *Dew neh loh moh* on all Russians, and especially on all of their fornicating agents.'

'Thank you, Honourable Sung.' Jake's head was still bowed. 'I appreciate your concern.'

'It is, without exaggeration, the concern of all 14K in this locality,' Formidable Sung said fiercely. 'Let one dung-eating KGB agent reveal himself to us, and he will be squashed like the insect piddle he is!'

'It is good to know that one has such loyal friends,' Jake said, lifting his head up.

'*A mi tuo fo*, these are evil days. First your honourable *tai tai*, then David Oh. The honourable Oh was well known to us.' Formidable Sung shook his head sagely. 'Friends are important during the best of times. But in bad weather they are to be treasured.'

'Unlike taels of gold, however, friends sometimes have a way of reversing themselves.'

'Yes?'

Jake knew he had the other's attention. 'David Oh, it seems, was not murdered by KGB agents.'

'Chinese, weren't they? Terrible, terrible.'

Jake nodded. 'Especially so since these Chinese were agents of the Quarry.'

In the outer office, someone was typing up a storm. The tapping was abruptly distinct in the heavy silence.

'My dear Mr Maroc,' Formidable Sung said, 'if this is the case, I fear we are being presented with something of an enigma.'

'Only temporarily,' Jake said. 'David Oh solved it and

554

so will I, given a little time. Someone deep inside the Quarry has turned against it.'

'Oh, dear.'

Jake almost laughed. Formidable Sung sounded like an old woman. But there was nothing amusing about the situation and they both knew it.

'*Dew neh loh moh* on all traitors!' Formidable Sung spat into one corner to show the seriousness of his curse. 'Spies are like rabid dogs in the street, infecting all who come close to them. Who is to be trusted nowadays?' He clucked his tongue. 'Foul weather indeed.'

'Yes,' Jake agreed. 'We must both be on our guard. I am on the run from my own organization.'

'What?'

'Certainly I am their next target.'

'Then by all means we will take you off the streets. I know a place – '

Jake held up the palm of his hand. 'A thousand thanks, Honourable Sung, but such an imposition is not necessary.'

'Nonsense! Friends are friends. True friends know the nature of their obligations. They do not turn their coats inside out with the changes in the wind.'

'Undoubtedly so,' Jake said. 'But I cannot afford to go to ground now. There is, however, another way in which you might help me.'

Formidable Sung spread his hands. 'Anything, my friend.'

'Explain to me why Nichiren comes to Hong Kong.'

In the breathless moment after Jake had uttered those words, Formidable Sung saw how neatly he had been trapped.

'Why would I know anything about that?'

'Because,' Jake said, completing the trap, 'Nichiren comes here to see you.'

Formidable Sung felt no anger. Rather, he was filled with admiration. What a Chinese heart this man has, he thought. If I had any sense I would hire him as my chief negotiator at the summit.

'Nichiren, perhaps, sees many people in Hong Kong. I am just one.'

Jake had no time for this fencing, but he knew he had no choice in the matter. Formidable Sung had never in his life told anyone anything he knew was important to him without exacting a price. Negotiation. The Chinese never felt anything was worthwhile without it.

The trick here, Jake knew, was to divine what the 489 wished in return and offer him something of less value. Then it would become a question of who needed what the most.

'It seems to me,' Jake said now, 'that your triad has lately run afoul of the police in Stanley. Is the *h'yeung yau*, the fragrant grease, insufficient to protect you?'

'Great Pool of Piddle McKenna is the new chief there. Australians are always difficult to get at right away. We'll wear him down.'

Jake shrugged. 'Perhaps eventually. But it's a gamble. And in the meantime, how many taels are you losing day to day?'

'Not enough to bother about.' There was just the right note of nonchalance in his voice.

Jake tried another possibility. 'How is the *godown* war going?'

'Fornicating Green Pang. They're nothing more than a nuisance. We'll take care of them.'

He said this with even greater ease, so Jake thought, This is the one that's really a thorn in his side.

Jake waited a minute, then said, 'This information on Nichiren is important to me, Honourable Sung.'

The 489 was shaking his head. 'Confidences, Honourable Maroc. You would ask me to betray confidences.'

Jake was reminded of his conversation with Bliss this morning. 'Between friends,' he said, 'anything is possible.'

Formidable Sung nodded. 'Even doors with locks can be opened with the right key.'

'True. Even recalcitrant Australians can be persuaded by old friends.'

'You and Great Pool of Piddle, friends? I can hardly believe that.'

'I've known him since he was a corporal.'

Formidable Sung scratched behind his ear. 'Well, I don't think we can do business there, really. To be honest, we're on to something with him. I don't want to deprive myself of the pleasure of presenting it to him.'

'Which little boy is it this time?'

'Ah, I see you *do* know him!' Formidable Sung spread his hands again. 'Well, some intelligence is too dear for anyone to afford.'

Jake smiled, but not because McKenna's distasteful predilection was about to put him under the 14K's thumb. 'I suppose you'd like the *godown* war to end.'

'I'd also like to win every race at Happy Valley for a week, but one often has to settle for the possible.'

'Suppose I make it possible.'

Formidable Sung tapped his forefinger against his lips. 'Truly, Honourable Maroc, I do not see how this can be done.' But Jake had fired something within the 489. If I can bring an end to the *godown* war, Formidable Sung was thinking, I will be the hero at our summit the day after tomorrow. I will have gained immeasurable face. His confidence soared. He had a decision. 'I accept your proposal under one condition. The war must end within thirty-six hours. Agreed?'

'Agreed.'

Formidable Sung grinned. When he did so, he became a different person. Perhaps a hint of the old Po-han peeped out then; the free-spirited, even somewhat wild teenager who had sought out the triad society as a substitute family. His father had been a stern and unforgiving businessman who found it impossible to say a kind word to any of his sons. He had believed that contention, strife, and, most importantly, anger – he would say the control of it – were the most important moulders of a young man's character.

Sung Po-han had disagreed with him. Violently enough for him never to want to return. Within the precincts of the 14K he had found that he was quickly rewarded for his agile mind and his strong arm. He had risen quickly within the triad hierarchy. Now it was his only family.

'Tea is brewing,' he said. 'Then lunch. One cannot satisfactorily speak of important matters on an empty stomach, as you well know.'

Jake nodded. 'We've had many memorable meals together.'

'A sign of trust in this uncertain world, *heya*?'

Jake tried to make himself relax. 'Just so.'

In his mind's eye he conjured up a *wei qi* board. *Lian jie* liaisons were being made – that is, stones of the same colour in a line. Opposing stones were *chi*, eaten, as these liaisons surrounded them, depriving them of their breaths. Further, *dan guan*, routes that encircled a territory by means of liaisons, were forming.

His eyes snapped open. The only problem was, he did not know the identities of the contending forces. He was on one side. That was the only certainty. At first it had appeared that Nichiren was his opponent. Now it was the mole buried deep inside the Quarry. Were the two linked? At first glance it seemed likely, since Nichiren had managed to spirit Mariana away and take Jake's *fu* shard. But then the KGB had arrived in Tsurugi in an attempt to terminate him.

Then, at Kamisaka's, Nichiren had failed to show and, further, had left his piece of the *fu* for Jake. Why? Was it a peace offering?

It came back to Nichiren. 'Honourable Sung,' Jake said. 'About our bargain.'

'Ah, yes.' Formidable Sung put down his teacup. 'As soon as I have proof of your pledge, I will provide you with what you desire.'

'That's a day and a half away,' Jake said, keeping his anger carefully in check. Patience, Bliss had counselled.

'Only if you take that long to stop the *godown* war.' Formidable Sung smiled. 'It is up to you, Honourable Maroc.'

Jake was about to respond when the door burst open. Bliss came in, followed by three or four triad members.

'You were followed here,' she said, a little breathlessly. 'It took me this long to find a way in here without alerting them.'

Jake rose. 'How many?'

'Three.'

'Mr Maroc – ?'

'I think, Honourable Sung, our lunch will have to be postponed until we complete our bargain.' He looked around the room. 'How many ways out of here?'

'Three. Two above ground, one beneath.'

Jake chose the tunnel.

Antony Beridien was dying. Frame by frame, as the video-tape was advanced in super slo-mo, life drifted out of him in infinitesimal increments. Movements were slowed to such an extent that a single eye-blink took several seconds to complete.

'Christ on a crutch!'

'Maroc,' Wunderman said. 'Maroc is taking his revenge on us.'

Donovan stirred. He sat as a kid would, his legs crossed, ankle on knee. His fingertips tapped the toe of his Top-Sider. He was wearing a blue-and-green striped Ralph Lauren polo shirt and khaki polished cotton hiking shorts.

The two of them were sitting in the lead-insulated room one hundred and fifty feet below the basement of the

Quarry building in Washington. They were within a heart-beat of the White House. The President had viewed the tape; he had made his decision. It was like wartime, but only Wunderman was old enough to remember what that was like.

They had viewed this unfolding scene a dozen times. Here was Wunderman pushing the doctor away, bending over Beridien. In slo-mo there was no intelligible sound. They had to return to speed for that.

Wunderman's hand had disappeared inside his jacket. With excruciating slowness he drew out the gun. Shot the doctor in the face: blam! blam! blam! Blood and gore all over the place, the wall behind her coated with bits of skull and her exploding brains.

Donovan swivelled in his chair. 'You're the boss now, Henry. You don't have to answer this, but I'll ask it anyway. Why did you shoot to kill? If it had been me, I'd have wanted to interrogate her, get some answers. Now we have none.'

Wunderman passed a hand across his eyes, dug in for a moment. 'I don't know how to answer that question. It was instinctive, I guess. I realized what she had done to Antony, after all our added precautions. I hadn't slept in three days, worrying about security. This was the last place . . . Ah, what's the use. I have no good explanation. Rage, frustration, the blind need for revenge.'

'I understand all that, Henry,' Donovan said softly. 'But your training should have restrained you. You're a thirty-seven-year veteran. This never should have happened.'

'The whole goddamned thing never should have hap-pened!' Wunderman cried. 'Damn Jake Maroc!'

Donovan stood up and stretched. He turned off the VCR and the room glowed with indirect rose light. 'Maybe not Maroc at all.'

'What do you mean?'

'Our iceberg.'

'Vorkuta?'

'Vorkuta. Yes, I think she's a distinct possibility. The doctor might have been a Soviet sleeper.'

'One who got through our vetting process?'

'It's happened before.'

'At Central Trashies, not here. Never here.'

'Are our procedures so different from the CIA's?'

Wunderman grunted. 'That's not your area, so you wouldn't know. But yes, they're much different. Frankly, I think Jake would have had a better chance of getting to the doctor than Vorkuta would have.'

Donovan fished in a pocket, pushed a communications flimsy across to Donovan. It was pale yellow, indicating that its origin was inside the Soviet Union.

'From my most recent monitoring of that new polar cipher network,' Donovan said as Wunderman began to read the decoded report, 'I think we'd better find out more about this Kam Sang project the Communist Chinese are working on.'

'Why? I already know about it. It's a joint project with Western firms based in Hong Kong. What could be going on there?'

'Plenty,' Donovan said. 'At least plenty that we don't know about. As the flimsy points out, the KGB's just got word from a worker at Kam Sang. By accident, he stumbled on a restricted area. Naturally he thought it was part of the atomic pile for power generation.

'Then a squad of Chinese Army soldiers converged on him and he spent the next eighteen hours in solitary, being interrogated.'

Wunderman shrugged. 'Nothing too sinister about that. Any kind of a leak in that area could endanger millions of civilians.'

'True enough,' Donovan said. 'But this guy was interrogated by a pair of intelligence colonels. What does that tell you?'

'That it wasn't a routine security matter.'

'Nothing about Kam Sang is routine, Henry. Nothing is what it seems on that project.'

'You think there's a military component to Kam Sang?'

'If there is, we'd damn well better find out about it before the Russians do. With this more aggressive attitude they've been taking of late in Asia, the slightest sign of escalated retaliation on China's part would set the spark for a major confrontation.'

Wunderman scrubbed his face with his palm. 'I've got a bastard of a headache.'

'Yeah,' Donovan said, 'I know what you mean. And I've got a feeling it's going to get worse before it gets better.'

Zhang Hua almost passed out while leaving the office. He saw a sweep of cyclists rushing by below him at the foot of the steps and lost all equilibrium. It had been an incredibly hot, humid day, and Shi Zilin's offices had been stifling.

Zhang Hua took three tottering steps to the metal banister and sat down heavily. The concrete burned his flesh inside his trousers. He was hyperventilating and he knew it.

I'm just not cut out for this life, he thought, holding his head. Below him, the cyclists whirled by in dusty clouds, on their way home. The daily Beijing marathon. They blurred into grey wisps of smoke as he watched.

He felt his heart beating too fast, and his gorge rose at the thought of having to meet with Wu Aiping again. Zhang Hua was so terrified that he had given up sleep as a state of being far beyond his present lowly abilities. Exalted slumber was for the gods, and Buddha knew he was only one frightened man.

I've forgotten my briefcase, he thought woodenly.

In a moment he forced himself to stand and, on wobbly legs, return up the steps. Back to Shi Zilin's office. He felt as if he were split into two parts. His brain was on fire. He could no longer remember which lies he had to tell to which person. He wanted to crawl into a cave and disappear for a decade or so.

He was as white as a ghost as he drifted back into the office. He sat, muddleheaded, while Shi Zilin fetched him cool tea. He drank thirstily and almost immediately felt better.

He became aware of Shi Zilin peering at him from close range. The old man had pulled up a chair, and they now sat practically knee to knee. He felt himself shaking as if with the ague, and wondered idly if he was actually ill.

'Is there anything I can do, old friend?'

Zhang Hua put his head back. What was he to say to that? I want to end all this deceit, he wanted to cry out. But he could not. He thought of Wu Aiping and he could not. He closed his eyes and sighed a little.

'It is nothing, Comrade Minister. The heat. Nothing at all.'

'I see.' Zilin continued to study him. 'What we have to do every day is difficult. We all have our duty, Zhang Hua. Duty is what we survive on.'

'For you, perhaps.' Something snapped inside Zhang Hua. 'You who were born to the gods.' His eyes flew open and they were as wild as a fire-panicked horse's. 'But not for me. I am only a poor mortal. I have nerves that fray, teeth that clench, a stomach twisted into knots. I have a mind that refuses to shut down and let me sleep. Because this is so, I feel this terrible burden is crushing me into the ground. I am not the Celestial Guardian of China. I am not Jian.'

Zilin looked at his friend. He thought of Three Oaths Tsun's words: *A mi tuo fo*, look what your obsession has done to them! My family. Jian I might be, Zilin thought. But I am mortal. The cold pain in my bones tells me that, if nothing else.

The burden of separation from my family is something

for which I could not have planned. If I had known then of the pain it would bring me, could I have done what I did? Youth made my mind strong; my righteousness brought me through the trial of fire, leaving my women and my sons far behind me.

But I was raw then, despite my supposed sophistication. I had been witness to but a fraction of the atrocities man will perpetrate on his fellow man.

'Forgive me, Comrade Minister,' Zhang Hua said, his head lying limply against the chairback. 'I cannot think in this heat.'

'After all our years together, you are allowed to speak your mind, old friend.'

Zilin leaned to his right, swiped a forefinger along the windowsill. It came away with a light-coloured coating. Not dust. Sand from the Gobi Desert, on the far side of the Great Wall.

He rubbed the sand across his palm, feeling its abrading quality. At this moment, seeing Zhang Hua so close to a breakdown, hearing Three Oaths Tsun's words in his mind, knowing how he had lost two daughters-in-law, fearing that now that his two sons were together in the same city, the one fine edge of which Three Oaths Tsun had spoken would bring about the destruction of either. Or both. Was even the prospect of the *ren* worth that risk? If I can so callously risk their deaths, he wondered now, can I be any better than the bloodthirsty kinsmen whom I abhor? Men who have a vision and sacrifice all their humanity to obtain their power and their pitiful concept of immortality: the State.

I have seen the State change, firsthand. Because I have been the creator of that change. But after I am gone, will it all devolve into this same dust, as it did for those who came before me?

Sand from the Gobi. It was here before I was born. It will be here still, long after I am gone. Is this what I spent

564

fifty years of my life searching for? Sand? Dust of the ages? Colourless, featureless, is this the sole substance of my life? The end product of my *ren*, my harvest? No, no. It cannot be.

Who would be foolish enough to harvest sand?

Not the Jian of China, Zilin thought. Certainly not him.

'Tell me.'

'Three Chinese,' she said. 'One's in grey slacks, dark blue striped shirt. He's got a scar on his cheek. The second's just walking away from him now. Slight, wiry, wearing a white muscle shirt and black jeans. The third's across from them, older, ears like a bat, brown slacks, pale green sport shirt.'

'Got 'em,' he said.

They were head-high to the sidewalk, hidden in the dankness of the subterranean alley into which Formidable Sung's passageway had debouched. Jake could smell the vestiges of dried fish and urine. Garbage was piled everywhere.

'It would help to know who's behind all this,' Bliss said. 'As it is, if we slip these, there'll only be more.'

'David Oh knew.'

'But he didn't tell you.'

'He told me as much as he was able,' Jake said. '*Huo yan*.'

'The "movable eye"? But that's a strategy in *wei qi*. What's that got to do with the person who wants to kill you?'

'I don't know,' Jake admitted. He was watching the three men redeploy themselves. They were seasoned professionals, all right. 'But David knew what he was doing. If he had discovered something inside the Quarry, he would have made a hard copy of it. Since he didn't have it with him when he was killed, it's logical to assume he hid it somewhere.'

565

'But, where?'

'That's the puzzle.'

'*Huo yan.*'

'Trouble is, that doesn't ring a bell. It should mean something to me, but it doesn't. Meanwhile, we've got to get to Venerable Chen without any ticks tagging along.'

'Why do we need to see the 489 of the Green Pang?'

Jake told her quickly about the deal he had cut with Formidable Sung.

'Now I know you're insane,' she said. 'After what you did to help the 14K triad, you're lucky Venerable Chen hasn't cut off your legs. Now you're going to ask him for a favour.'

'Yeah. It does seem an impossible task on the surface.'

She snorted. 'Impossible any way you cut it.'

'Let's just say I like challenges.'

Bliss looked at him. 'Just as long as you don't have a death wish.'

'If I did, I'd be walking straight out into the street.' He had not taken his eyes off the three Chinese. They had taken up stations along Wing Cheung Street, using the striped shadows within which to curl like nocturnal predators. They all possessed that quality of extraordinary stillness so rare in a human but so necessary for their trade.

'The thing is to get them to move,' he said after a time. 'In motion lies confusion. Right now they've got the whole Morrison Hill area down like a gridwork map. We'll never lose them unless we get them into violent motion.'

'As long as it's not *too* violent.'

He gave her a silent laugh, looked down to the opposite end of the alley.

'I already checked it,' Bliss said. 'Dead end. We're in a box.'

'It depends on how you look at it,' Jake said, eyeing the piles of garbage. 'You carrying matches?'

'Sure, why? Planning a nice quiet smoke while those three close in on us?'

Jake ignored her sarcasm. 'Go light up those bags of garbage, will you?'

Bliss took a hard look at them. 'I don't think they're dry enough to give off much in the way of flames.'

Jake nodded. 'That's just what I'm hoping for.'

Bliss waited a moment, working it through. Then, crouching, she crossed the alley, struck a light within the cupped palm of her hand. She went through half-a-dozen matches until she got it going.

Then, abruptly, there was a great deal of smoke. It stank so much it made them cough, but it was thick enough. And noticeable.

The two younger men, Muscles and Scarface, slipped through the shadows, passing through darkness and light. Crossing Wing Cheung Street.

'You know the swim building off Oi Kwan Road?' he whispered. And when Bliss nodded, he said, 'If we get separated, that's where we meet. East side. The zinc-faced door.'

Muscles and Scarface came cautiously down into the alley. They did it well, one behind the other, point and backup. Jake went into Scarface low, bringing him down in a tumble. He felt Bliss high-jumping over the tangle, slamming Muscles high.

He went down but, twisting, grabbed her arm so that she fell heavily onto her left hip. She stifled a cry and Jake, swinging the point of his shoe into Scarface's throat, leaned forwards, chopping with the calloused edge of his hand. The kite caught Muscles in the nerve plexus just above and to the left of his right kidney. It took all the breath out of him, and Bliss was up and running, with Jake just behind her.

Full out down Wing Cheung Street, past Bat-Ear, taking a hard right onto Oi Kwan Road. It described a roughly hexagonal path around Morrison Hill and the buildings of the swimming pool.

Seeing the structures lit up, Jake veered away into the shadows. Walls rose up all around him as he made his careful way to the east side of Morrison Hill and the zinc-faced door.

Nestled against the concrete wall, Jake allowed his breath to return to normal. He still felt slightly dizzy whenever he ran or was subject to violent motion. He kept his gaze on that door, his ears open for the slightest sound of pursuit. Humidity, condensed on the rough, painted concrete, wept against his skin beneath his thin shirt. The buzzing of the cicadas was a metallic wash.

Jake searched in the bottom of his trousers pocket, opened up the paper clip. He took a deep breath and silently rushed the open space between the wall and the door.

Put the end of the clip in the lock and went to work. He was sweating more than usual, and he was aware that the fear factor was high. He was totally unprotected here.

Heard the snap of the lock and pushed the door inwards. Just then he heard a tiny rustling from over his head. He tensed, bending his knees to gain momentum, and broke concentration just in time as Bliss slipped down from the eaves. Angry with himself because he should have felt her presence, he pushed her inside, closed the door after them.

Echoes. The whisper of a vast emptiness stretching away. The thick chemical stench of chlorine.

Darkness.

Jake took her by the hand, edging her through the locker room. They sat on an unpainted wooden bench.

'This isn't smart,' she said. 'They'll find us here. We would have had more of a chance on the rooftops.'

'The moonlight's too bright,' Jake said softly. 'There are a lot of ways out of here. On a roof, the street's a long way down.'

'Shhh! I hear something.'

Jake strained his ears. 'Nerves.'

She pulled at him. 'Let's go.'

They went quickly out of the other end of the locker room. The soft lapping of the water was distinct, breaking up the silence into discrete segments.

Jake felt a presence behind him and whirled just in time to feel something slam into him. He went off the edge.

The pool was cold. And dark. The water, so devoid of light, seemed inordinately heavy, pressing in on his chest like a fist. He fought the bare arms and knew it was Muscles. He kicked out violently, and they went down into the deep end, tumbling end over end until pressure filled his ears with insects' incessant clamour.

Muscles must have been used to this slow-motion combat, water-drag on all limbs. He got a stranglehold around Jake's throat and refused to let go. Darkness descended into a dreadful night. Airless and as chill as a morgue.

Tried two *atemi*, percussion blows, with his elbow. Muscles only tightened his hold. Bubbles flew from the corners of his grinning mouth.

Fire in Jake's lungs, and he began to fight in earnest the instinct to inhale. His head was aching, the edge of the concussion insinuating itself on him again, and he knew he had little time.

Using a mantis, Jake extended his arms forward, moving into the hold rather than away from it. This made it necessary for Muscles to move with him, coming forward. Jake used the motion, combining his momentum with Muscles's, twisting to the right and, as he did so, straightening his right arm, using it as a battering ram against his assailant's left side.

Used the heel of his hand, massing the power from his shoulders and pectorals, allowing a straight line through his arm and into his hand. Felt the ribs give, heard nothing but the rushing of blood in his ears.

Clenched his teeth now in order not to open his mouth and gulp water, raised his right arm and slammed it down hard onto the point of Muscles's shoulder, the socket collapsing, his strength enormous even through the drag of the water.

The body slipping away from him and Jake kicking powerfully upwards with his legs, rushing to the surface in a welter of bubbles. Sucking in air in deep bursts.

He swam to the side of the pool and, dripping, levered himself from the water.

'Jake.'

Turned into the muzzle of Bat-Ears's automatic.

'I should blow your brains out right now.'

Just the slightest instant when he became more interested in Jake than he was in Bliss. A fatal mistake. Jake watched as Bliss translated motionlessness into motion.

The blur she became cracked down on Bat-Ears, catching him between targets. He wanted to squeeze the trigger on Jake, but he sensed the acuteness of the danger.

Bat-Ears was in the process of swinging around to meet it when Bliss tramped hard on his instep, pinning him. His motionlessness left him helpless as she slammed the sole of her shoe into the partly turned crease of his knee. Kneecap and shinbone splintered. Bat-Ears let forth a piercing scream, echoing in the vastness of the pool room as she hit the kidney meridian.

His splash was heavy. Wavelets came up over the side, inundating their feet. Jake was still panting. For a long moment they stared into each other's eyes.

This was the first time either had seen what the other could do in a violent situation. The moment was certain to stay with them for the rest of their lives.

* * *

Seven minutes later, they were on Hennessy Road. Though dishevelled, they did their best to look just like all the other window-shoppers crowding the Wanchai streets. Jake used the shop windows as mirrors to give him a sense of what was going on behind them and parallel to them, across the street.

They joined a long queue. The third bus that came was a Number 24, and they swung aboard. It was one of the crimson double-deckers with an open rear egress that many Chinese used to sneak aboard at the last minute when the conductor was otherwise occupied.

'It's a long trip,' Bliss said. 'We might as well go upstairs.'

But Jake shook his head. 'We're getting off before Cotton Tree Drive. If we haven't shaken them, I want to know it before we take the Peak Tram. I'm not about to lead them to your apartment.'

They stood in the crowded lower level, and as the bus proceeded, making its stops, they inched their way unobtrusively towards the rear. He did not have to tell her that he wanted to be near the rear exit when their stop came.

They went onto Queensway, heading towards Central District. The bus changed to an inner lane, began to brake. Two stops farther on was Cotton Tree Drive. Jake took a quick look around, not only to orient himself one last time, but also to fix in his memory those within lunging distance of him.

Bliss was just in front of him, standing at the edge of the steep steps down to the exit. Jake's quick but encompassing glance had taken in a fat, middle-aged Chinese woman, two Chinese teenagers with slicked-back hair and dark glasses, a slim businessman carrying an expensive leather attaché case. He was European or possibly Australian. A young Chinese woman carrying a baby wrapped in a pink blanket in one arm, holding on to her four-year-old son with the other hand. A pair of thickset Chinese in slacks and short-sleeved silk shirts. A young American girl with pretty eyes and a noticeable case of acne.

The bus slowed to a stop. Several people climbed aboard through the front entrance. No one wanted to get out. Jake took a look at the line of people filing onto the bus. When no one was left on the sidewalk, he nudged Bliss.

Immediately she went down the rear stairs. Jake followed after her. Jake saw her step off, and at that moment a Chinese teenager ran out from the crowd, swinging onto the bus, hoping for a free ride. He ran right into Jake, who by that time was halfway down the steps.

'*Dew neh loh moh!*' Jake shouted. 'Out of my way!'

The kid froze, stunned. At the same moment Jake felt a fierce tug from behind him. He whirled and was astonished to find the Chinese mother. She had abandoned her little boy, who was, he saw in a flash, probably not hers at all. For the baby she carried so tightly wrapped in the pink blanket was in fact a Lyson TY-6000, the mini-machine pistol manufactured expressly for the Quarry. Her hand was beneath the blanket, closed around the pressure-sensitive trigger lever.

At close range he could see the anger in her eyes. Jake estimated she could be no more than twenty-one or twenty-two.

The bus lurched as it started up. Everyone shifted to compensate for the force of acceleration. In that moment, Jake grabbed hold of the Chinese teenager and swung him into the woman.

She kicked out instinctively, and the kid went down on his hands and knees. Jake lifted his free elbow, slamming the barrel of the Lyson to one side.

Behind him, the kid bounced down the stairs, tumbling onto the road. Bliss, who had begun to run after the bus, smashed into him, scraping the heel of her palm and one knee on the macadam. She got up, running again.

Quickly, Jake turned his full attention on the Quarry agent. The Lyson swung downwards, the muzzle scoring a line from his temple to just beyond the extreme edge of his eye socket. Blood welled up, temporarily blinding him. He was immediately dizzy, the blow bringing back whatever vestiges still remained of his concussion. He staggered, felt the Lyson come away from him. He did not need his eyesight to know what that meant.

Desperately he reached for her, grabbing on to the haft of the machine pistol. Both of them were oblivious to the screams from the nearby passengers.

The girl, divining his intent, pushed violently forward with the Lyson so that it slammed into him underneath his chin. He gagged and, choking, went down on all fours. In doing so, he fell, as the Chinese teenager had before him, down the steps.

The girl followed him, bending her knees and bringing the Lyson down to the aim position. She got the aluminium stock against her side. She was at such close range there was no need to sight. Jake was all too familiar with the Lyson's muzzle velocity and its round-per-second capacity. He knew that if he allowed her to pull the trigger there wouldn't be much of him left intact to bounce along the road.

The only hope for him now was *jō-waza*. He was in the wrong position, and the weapon facing him was a machine pistol rather than a staff or a *katana*, but he had no other choice.

He slammed into her oncoming shin with the arch of his foot, lifting his upper torso painfully as he did so. The essential thing was to get his right hand between hers as she held the Lyson. She would be looking out for that, so he had distracted her first with the kick-feint.

As she reacted, his left arm shot out, his fist closing over the barrel of the Lyson.

On his knees, he twisted sharply to the right in the

severely limited space of the exit well. Continuing to use her forward momentum against her, he drew her towards him by twisting himself back to the left. At the same time he rotated his fist, turning the Lyson from the horizontal to the vertical.

Now he had pulled her two steps down into the well. She was at his level. Completing the *jō-waza*, Jake simultaneously rose up and bent forwards, taking her down with him. But she surprised him. She let go the Lyson, mounting an immediate double kite to his exposed left side.

He grunted in pain, threw the Lyson out the exit. That gave her enough time to deliver a hard blow to the side of his head. He careened into the steel wall of the exit. His head was ringing. Through the haze, he knew that he had misjudged her, believing the *jō-waza* sufficient to subdue her.

She crowded in on him and he collapsed down another step. Then another, until he was crumpled on the bottom step. He was half a metre from the blurred macadam of the road. The steel toe of her shoe shot into his thigh, and now he was half off the bottom step.

The girl crouched over him, pummelling him with lightning blows that sent shock waves of agony through him. He could not breathe, he could not see; he could barely think.

Blindly he attacked her face. She blocked him easily and through her gritted teeth he thought he heard a gurgling laugh. Got a handful of her blouse while she was doing that and bent her far forward over him. His other arm was still high, where he had allowed her to take it with her block.

His fist crashed down onto the bridge of her flat nose where it bisected her eyes, the force of gravity and momentum, along with his strength, combining to crush the cartilage.

Immediately she could not catch her breath. A torrent of

blood poured from the wound. Jake jammed a thumb into her eye. Pressing his fingers against the side of her face, he slammed it against the well's steel wall. He felt himself tipping over the edge of the bus. Diesel exhaust billowed up from beneath the bus. He made one last attempt to arrest his fall and failed.

Tightening his grip on the Quarry agent, he tumbled out of the back of the bus, pushing her under him to break his fall. He heard a snap, then another as they made contact with the macadam. Their momentum spun them end over end. He heard the heavy squeal of brakes, the sounds of cursing, a long string of Cantonese.

Then he got his breath back. He was lying by the side of the road, half-stunned. Someone was kneeling over him, but he was aware of a large knot of people hovering in the middle of the road like a gigantic bundle of flies.

'Let me through!'

He thought he was imagining her voice.

'Let me through, please! I'm a doctor!'

Someone moved slightly away, and he saw Bliss crouched over him. 'Buddha, you look a mess!' she whispered. Then, in a loud voice, 'Just keep back, please! Give him room to breathe!'

'I want to get up,' he told her.

She put her hands beneath him and they did it together. Jake felt a brief wave of nausea racing through him. He closed his eyes for a moment, licked his dry, cracked lips.

'Are you okay?'

He nodded. That was a mistake. It set off an intense wave of dizziness in him. Despite that, he got to his feet. He could taste blood; it was all over him. He wondered whether it was his or hers. His head hurt and he put his hand up to his temple.

'The kid all right?'

'Nothing serious,' Bliss said in his ear. He could feel her supporting him.

'What about the girl?' he asked.

'Is that what she was?'

He turned his head in the direction Bliss was looking. The knot of black flies was looser now, and he could see through their legs to the misshapen lump lying twisted and broken on the macadam. Behind her was a long smear, silver and scintillating like tinsel in the harsh highway lights.

'Lots of blood,' Bliss said.

They both heard the sirens at the same time.

'Let's get out of here,' Jake said, and then, 'We'd damn well better make sure we're clear before we go home.' He seemed out of breath again and he waited, panting, as he limped with her arm around his waist into the concealing darkness past the corner to the brightly lit Admiralty Centre.

'Your house is getting to be the only safe place in the Colony.'

Early morning was given over to a formal tour of the Serbsky Institute's newly completed psychosensory wing. The Institute was a potent arm of the *sluzhba*, housing many of the most important political prisoners and – in its softer rooms – defectors from the West.

The purpose of the Institute was to probe the minds of these dissidents and turncoats to discover the truth: what they believed; whom they knew; of what networks they were cognizant; whether or not they were whom they claimed to be; and so on.

The doctors at the Institute spent a lifetime devising new ways to penetrate to the shadowy depths of the human mind. The new section had been named the Andropov Wing by Karpov, who had led the two-and-a-half-year fight for appropriations from the Kremlin. It contained the most sophisticated and highly advanced digital hallucolography equipment at the Soviets' disposal, a good deal of it highly experimental.

This tour of the site of Karpov's newest triumph would have been hollow had he not invited Daniella to accompany him. They were met by a committee of three behavioural psychotherapists. Everything at the Institute was done by committee. They were fanatic about security here. The embarrassing theft of the visiting commissars' fur hats from the KGB offices last winter could never have occurred here.

These doctors all held the military rank of lieutenant-colonel or above. They appeared a very formal, dour lot. It seemed the seriousness of their work had left its mark upon them.

Silently, they escorted the two generals through deliberately antiseptic anterooms, down long corridors gleaming with stainless steel and copper, through high-ceilinged laboratories filled with banks of computerized hardware bristling with dials, toggle switches, faders lit up by colour-coded pinlights.

Past the laboratories were the doctors' lounges. It was explained that though three shifts of physicians and lab technicians were assigned, doctors often stayed through many shifts if they were working on a difficult patient. In that event, they would use the lounges for an hour's catnap when they could.

Another corridor. This one was constructed of rough concrete painted a dull institutional grey. Harsh fluorescent light hurt the eyes as it created lurid purple shadows of their passage.

A double-locked chromium steel and wire-reinforced glass door was opened on pneumatic seals by a pair of mud-eyed guards with pistols prominently displayed on their hips. Here were the holding cells, the committee explained. They stopped before one of a series of lead-lined steel doors. It looked like the entrance to a bank vault. The cells were escape-proof.

'We took the designer into one and locked him up,' said

one member of the committee. 'A week later we opened the cell door. He was dead. Then we were assured of the cell's absolute security.' The members of the committee laughed. It seemed to be an oft-told joke.

The generals continued their tour. They were told that the Andropov Wing contained a number of different kinds of cells, depending on the nature of the prisoner and his or her disposition. There were the so-called 'soft rooms' reserved for defecting members of foreign espionage and diplomatic services. Pastel-painted walls, lushly upholstered furniture, and opulent wall hangings all made the place seem part of a Western luxury hotel.

'They are brought here,' a member of the committee said, as they went inside, 'because we can make one of two assumptions about them. Either they are genuine in their change of political heart and will help us to the best of their ability, or they have been planted on us, in which case it is to our benefit to catch them off guard.'

They moved on to another section of the holding area. 'Here we have a "hard room".' Another member of the committee took over. The generals looked inside. Here was a stone cell with a thick wooden board inserted partway into the wall as a bleak and uncomfortable pallet. There was a hole in the stone flooring, the most primitive of toilets.

'Look upwards.'

The generals directed their gaze as instructed. The high ceiling, painted an almost blinding white, was studded with floodlights. The committee member snapped his fingers and they were bathed in an awesome and painful onrush of incandescent light.

'It helps to do this,' the committee member said, snapping his fingers again so that the lights went off, 'at six-minute intervals. Our extensive research has shown us that that time interval is perfect for interrupting the human sleep pattern and for causing the maximum amount of psychic anxiety in the subject.'

They stepped out of the room, resumed their walk down the drab hallway. The odd fluorescent lighting was disconcerting after the demonstration, and Karpov took his wire-rimmed spectacles out of his breast pocket, hooked them on. He disliked wearing them, but he felt uncomfortable with the black spots in front of his eyes.

'Now we come to the crowning achievement of the Andropov Wing.' Still another member of the committee had taken over. Another gleaming steel door was opened and the five of them stepped into a room that on first inspection was identical to the 'soft room': settees, fabric-covered chairs, rugs, bookcases, pleasant pastoral paintings. The walls were a pleasing shade of pale peach.

'This is a cell for our most recalcitrant prisoner: the ideological traitor,' the committee member intoned. 'For many years this particular kind of dissident was simply put to death in the basement of Lubyanka after a short and fruitless interrogation session. Nowadays we have more modern methods of handling such people.'

Karpov frowned. 'I don't understand.'

'Certainly, Comrade General,' the committee member said. 'A demonstration has been planned. Please sit down.' He indicated a reproduction of a gilt Louis XIV chair.

Karpov sat and the doctor snapped his fingers. Steel bands snapped into place over the general's wrists and ankles.

'What is this!'

A roaring filled Karpov's ears. The wall directly across from him began to crumble and a surge of water rumbled impossibly towards him. At the same time, the bookcase dissolved into a tentacled creature that humped swiftly across the floor to encircle his ankles. The rugs were shredding before his eyes until a raft of coiling serpents,

579

their wedge-shaped heads lifted and pointing in his direction, came slithering towards him. The striped settee was a tiger, roaring as it caught sight of him.

He tried to free himself, but he could not. 'I can't stand restraints! You must not – ' But he never finished the sentence, for the room canted over on an angle, spilling him in his chair into its lowest corner. Sprawled with his back against the wall, he groped in vain for his spectacles, which had been dislodged by his fall.

Now he felt the pressure of the ocean against his chest, and as he did so, the light in the room turned aqueous. Water continued spilling into the room through the rent in the wall. He felt cold and wet, though when he reached out his trembling hand, he could not be certain whether he encountered water or air.

Within the water now swam the various creatures of the sea. Sharks and giant squid. Stingrays and barracuda. It was the stuff of nightmares.

Karpov opened his mouth to scream, but cold water, bitingly salty, filled it up. His eyes were rolling wildly, his brain refused to function. He vomited all over himself.

In the adjacent room, fitted with one-way glass, Daniella watched this gruesome spectacle.

'So this is hallucolography,' Yuri Lantin said. He moved out of the shadows to stand beside her. 'From here it doesn't look like much.'

'You can't really appreciate its true worth unless you're in there with it,' Daniella said. 'The subject becomes the centre of the image-generation field.'

Lantin grunted. 'Our friend General Karpov seems to be getting the message.'

'With such a simultaneous all-out assault on the five senses,' the committee member explained, 'it is not surprising. The holograms generated by our new laser-imager are far beyond anything we have been able to come up with before this. Believe me, inside that room, they are real.'

Daniella and Lantin, their gazes fixed on General Karpov's cringing frame, could only agree.

'But our true breakthroughs have come with the olfactory and tactile stimulators. The human brain has learned that the eyes can be tricked, but it cannot cope with the same thing being done to the other senses all at once.'

On the other side of the narrow pane of glass, Karpov was trying to curl up into a foetal ball. His powerful muscles strained against the steel bands until he bled. It was clear, even though the microphones in the room had been turned off for the moment, that he was weeping uncontrollably even while he was gagging.

Lantin paid him no attention whatsoever. He was looking at Daniella, thinking he'd never before encountered so desirable a woman. What he told her was 'You were right, you know. I could never have asked Karpov's wife to dredge up his secrets. Sometimes the most extreme measures are the only effective ones. Still, it takes guts to follow through with them — what I believe the Americans call "true grit".'

Daniella saw his eyes burning with lust for her, and for the first time in her life, she felt embarrassment at such sexual outpouring. In this setting, with Karpov going slowly insane just a pane of glass away, with these three behavioural psychotherapists grouped a foot away, as cold as their arcane machines, Lantin's intimate emotion struck her as obscene.

It made her think again of the sexual drug he had offered her and of which she had willingly partaken. I must destroy him, she thought. If only to save myself.

Thus the two of them, their secret selves locked within the ringing silence of their skulls, stared through the window that the doctors of the Serbsky Institute had obligingly provided into a hell neither of them could have imagined.

On the other side of the small room, the committee

members continued to monitor the increasingly erratic life functions of General Anatoly Decidovitch Karpov, co-commander of the '56 Hungarian revolt occupation forces, hero of the Ukraine uprising of '66, patriot of the Revolution.

Andrew Sawyer was at the ghost wedding the *sam ku* had set with the Hu family when he found his world crashing down all around him.

It was odd how it happened. Truly odd, because it was the last thing on his mind. His thoughts had been wholly with Miki and her ghost-husband-to-be. The Hu family was large: seven sons and six daughters. The eighth son, Duncan, had died in an accident when he was six. A careening car driven by a motorist with one too many ounces of liquor inside him.

The *sam ku* that Peter Ng had found had put Sawyer and the Hus together. The spirits of their dead children cried out for a happiness denied them in the corporeal world.

Sawyer liked the Hus immediately. They radiated a warmth and goodwill he found invigorating. The pain in his heart that had stayed with him ever since Miki had come to him in the dream had at last begun to fade as he and the Hus had discussed the exchange of wedding gifts. These would consist of clothes, electronic household items, a king-sized bed – all miniatures made out of paper. They also agreed upon the amount of the dowry, payable in Hell Banknotes that Sawyer bought at a shop specializing in such arcane paraphernalia.

The *sam ku* chose the Taoist temple on Ladder Street in the Island's Western District. The day and the hour were important also, she had informed him. Here, before an altar specially prepared by the *sam ku*, she began her incantations, aimed at the brightly clothed paper dolls representing the bride and groom. Grouped around them were models of all the gods and goddesses of Hell, who, in their witnessing of the ceremony, gave their blessing to the couple.

Incense filled the air with clouds of orange smoke. The ritual, complex and totally impenetrable to Sawyer, ground on hour after hour until those in attendance felt giddy with the incessant drone of the unfamiliar words.

Magic was afoot. Even a *gwai loh* such as Andrew Sawyer could feel it, stealing along the wooden floorboards with the billowing of the incense and the *sam ku*'s litany.

After a time it felt to Sawyer as if the old woman's words had taken on a life of their own, as if she were not actually speaking but only now opened her mouth for the words, like three-dimensional objects, to issue forth of their own volition. It was as if the spirit of his Miki and the Hus' Duncan dwelled now within the *sam ku*'s convoluted incantation.

Towards the end of the ceremony, Sawyer was certain that he glimpsed Miki within the billowing shadows of the temple's towering interior, grown up and smiling at him as she linked her arm with that of a strong, handsome young man. Idiotically, he pointed the Kodak Disc camera he had brought with him and squeezed off a shot.

It was when he was standing immobile on the steps in front of the temple at ceremony's end, taking a picture of the Hus, that he caught a glimpse of a hurrying Peter Ng.

Sawyer was stunned. He had sent Ng across the harbour to Tsim Sha Tsui in Kowloon on important business that would take all day to conclude. What, then, was Peter doing rushing up Ladder Street on his way to Hollywood Road?

It had taken Jake and Bliss all morning and most of the afternoon to locate Venerable Chen's whereabouts. Jake was on his own in this; for obvious reasons, the Quarry's facilities were off limits to him, and because the rivalries between triads were so intense, the 14K's conduits came up with nothing but dead ends.

Naturally, then, it was Bliss who got the break. She had been making calls every half hour from public phone booths. Jake never asked her who she was calling.

At a quarter past four, she emerged from one such and said to him, 'He's in Macao.'

'Macao? Why there? That's not Green Pang territory.'

'Apparently it is now,' she said. 'Twice a week he goes to the Hotel Partita; he's got a piece of it.'

Forty-five minutes on the Jetfoil. There were three ways to get to Macao; it just depended on how much of a rush you were in. When Jake and Bliss were children, there was only the ferry. That took three hours. The more recent hydrofoil took about an hour and a quarter. The Jetfoil, the most recent addition to the Hong Kong–Macao route, was by far the quickest.

Strapped into their airline-type seats, Jake and Bliss rode across the Pearl River Estuary towards the distant spot of land that was Portuguese sovereign territory.

Macao was unutterably seedy. Jake had often thought that if Anthony Burgess had set *A Clockwork Orange* in Miami Beach rather than England, his vision of the world's bleak future would look like Macao.

The world's most tenacious touts rimmed the landing quay. The taxis were broken down, the once-smart hotels were shabby and flyblown, as if they had not been cleaned since the 1930s. Even the palm trees were dusty and listless.

Despite what the guidebooks claimed, there was nothing much for the tourist to see. What drew the crowds of Chinese were, of course, the casinos. The only legal form of gambling in the Crown Colony was the horseracing at Happy Valley. In Macao almost all forms were legal.

The casinos were jammed day and night, filled with the brown-grey fog of cigarette smoke, the body odour of

584

thousands of Chinese hungry to lay down their money at *fan tan, sik po, pai kau* as well as the Western games of roulette, blackjack, and craps.

The Partita was a round, pink-façaded affair just down the road from the Sintra. In places its stucco had faded to the colour of an old undershirt. It had been built in the 1920s, but Jake doubted that it had had any charm even then. Now it resembled nothing more than a boil on a fat man's bottom.

They found Venerable Chen busy playing 'dice treasure.' *Sik po* was played with three dice enclosed in a glass dome with an opaque cover. His face was flushed with the fever of gambling, and his round button eyes stared fixedly at the dome.

Jake hung back on the edge of the throng. Even though he had a deadline to meet, he was loath to interrupt Venerable Chen. This was going to be a difficult enough confrontation as it was. There was no sense in adding to it.

He took Bliss upstairs, where they had an indifferent Portuguese meal. Outside the window, the lowering sun beat upon the open sea with a sledgehammer fist. They were the only customers in the restaurant. Everyone was in the casino. Even the beach was empty.

Forty minutes later they returned to the casino. Venerable Chen was just where he had been before. He was wiping his sweating face with a handkerchief. Jake wondered where the challenge lay in winning from yourself.

As he watched the Shanghainese, he began to think there was nothing he could do to break the hard sheen of devotion to the dice, put up like a mask over Venerable Chen's face.

There are many ways into the enemy camp, Fo Saan had counselled him time and again. *But only one that will enable you to emerge unscathed*. As usual, Fo Saan was correct. This was not a matter of getting Venerable Chen's attention, but rather of keeping it.

Jake reached into his pocket, put a roll of bills into Bliss's hand. He looked into her eyes. 'How are you at *sik po*?'

He waited for them in the lounge. It was a dark and gloomy place located on the mezzanine level. He sat at a booth near enough the front to give him an excellent vantage point on comings and goings.

Through the open archway Jake could see the sightseeing counters, so deserted that the clerks had begun playing mah-jongg. The rapid click-click-click of the tiles travelled all the way into the lounge, where Jake, leaning against the wall, drank a club soda with lime; he was unprepared for alcohol. The place smelled of mildew and lost dreams.

In the twenty minutes he sat there alone, three women, two Cantonese and one Eurasian, passed close enough to murmur their price. All were overly made up, as appealing as wax dummies. On her second pass, the waitress propositioned him. Her price, at least, was more reasonable. He took another club soda instead.

Jake saw them coming up the wide corkscrew stairs from the main floor. He slid out of the booth and bowed formally as Bliss brought Venerable Chen across the room.

'I have heard of bizarre methods of introduction, Mr Maroc, but the one you have chosen is certainly the most intriguing. If nothing else, I have met this charming young woman.'

'Won't you sit down?'

The other nodded. Jake looked at Bliss, who nodded and went out. It would not do to have her at this meeting. Jake might understand, but Venerable Chen most assuredly would not. In Asia, women had their place. It was not in affairs of business.

Venerable Chen's bright little eyes searched every fissure of Jake's face. It was as if he could divine the nature of this meeting there, like a *feng shui* man reading the portents in the drift of the wind or the shape of the land.

'Mr Maroc,' he said now, after having declined Jake's offer of a drink, 'you have cost me a great deal of money, manpower . . . and face.' Not to drink with a companion, even if one was not thirsty, was a deliberate affront. It meant, more clearly than any words could, that this was not to be a friendly meeting. 'Now you have come across the Pearl River Estuary to seek me out. I must say quite frankly that I cannot imagine what you might have to say to me. But audacity, even in a devious barbarian, is to be acknowledged even if it is impossible to admire.'

He seemed to have said his piece. He folded his small hands one over the other, as if compactness were a religion with him. He seemed like a midget in his ill-fitting suit.

'Business is business,' Jake said. 'There was nothing personal in what I did. I saw an advantage to be gained and I took it. But Honourable Chen needs no explanation of the obvious.'

'But I do need an explanation of why you are here.' The Shanghainese glanced pointedly at his watch.

Jake was about to tell him, when the wall of the lounge nearest them ballooned inwards with a roar that shattered the glasses and bottles on the other side of the room.

Bliss had seen the two Taiwanese climbing up from the lower level of the casino. She had remembered their faces from when she was playing *sik po* by Venerable Chen's side. What had interested her then was that they did no gambling.

Upstairs in the main lobby, one had stood at the foot of the curling staircase up to the mezzanine while the other began a slow and thorough circumnavigation of the area. The first man had one hand on the wrought-iron handrail, and Bliss took a good look at it. Hard, yellow callous covered the lower edge.

She ducked back just before he glanced upwards. Though casual, the sweep of his glance took in the entire angle open to him. Bliss moved along the mezzanine to another location with a better view. She saw the second man return and speak quietly to the first. Together, they came up the stairs.

Bliss was on the verge of moving when she felt the fuzziness she associated with a nerve blockage. She had just enough presence of mind to turn, and saw a blurry face, thought, *Dew neh loh moh*, a third Taiwanese, and passed out.

The shattering of concrete, glass, and steel brought her around. She groaned, hanging her head to clear it of cobwebs. Then she got to her feet, stumbling down the mezzanine. Smoke, ash, and concrete dust filled her lungs and she thought, Oh, Buddha! Jake!

There was a breathless moment after the first shock wave before the wall caved in.

Just enough time for Jake to grab Venerable Chen by the shirtfront and haul him underneath the overturned table. The shield of the tabletop was what saved them as the wall broke apart, hurling itself like a mighty fist into the lounge. That and Jake's reflexes. The combination was not lost on the Shanghainese.

'Mr Maroc,' he said from his position curled inside Jake's protective shell, 'a barbarian you might be, but you must also be part tiger. Your quickness is what saved us.'

Jake unwound himself from around him and they stood up. Plaster was still pattering down around them. Save for the wall and the immediate area around their table, there was remarkably little damage to the lounge's interior. Someone was screaming hysterically. The waitress who had propositioned Jake was on her knees, rocking back and forth, sobbing. Plaster dust had turned her hair as white as a great-grandmother's.

Venerable Chen looked at the rubble. '*A mi tuo fo*, one of us has dangerous enemies.' They could hear sirens wailing, growing louder. The Shanghainese turned back to Jake. 'I wonder which one?' Then he laughed. 'What does it matter as long as our sacred members remain intact, *heya*?' He shrugged. 'Insurance and *h'yeung yau*, Mr Maroc. In the end, they're the same.' He gestured. 'This way, please.' He seemed quite unconcerned now about the damage.

In the mezzanine they met Bliss. Jake ran to take her into his arms. 'I'm all right,' she said, then put her head against his shoulder and cried. 'I'm sorry,' she whispered. 'I had two of them covered. I never expected a third one. He came up behind me. I turned, but by then it was too late.'

'It's all right,' Jake said, stroking her hair.

'Jake,' she said, 'I was so frightened for you.'

He held her more tightly. What was there to say?

He became aware of Venerable Chen at his side. 'Is the young lady all right?' the Shanghainese inquired.

'The young lady is fine,' Bliss said, wiping away the last of the tears with her knuckle.

'Good.' He gave a quick nod. 'Now, if you will follow me. There is no point in my having to listen to stupid questions for which I have no answers. The fornicating police will be here at any moment.'

He led them to the far end of the mezzanine, through a door marked PRIVATE.

'Now,' he said, slowing his pace as they entered a quiet, spacious office, 'I do believe, Mr Maroc, that I owe you a drink.'

Mystified, Sawyer said a hurried good-bye to the Hus. He hastened down the temple's stone steps. He could just see Ng nearing the top of the street. Sawyer was himself more than halfway up when he saw Ng turn right, disappearing around a corner.

He quickened his pace and, puffing slightly with the unaccustomed exertion, reached the summit in time to see

Peter Ng enter a warehouse. The sign at the front told Sawyer that the place specialized in ginseng root.

Sawyer immediately slowed his pace. He mopped his brow with a white linen handkerchief, thinking, It's damnably hot to be chasing all around the Western District after my *comprador*.

The front of the warehouse was open. A large Isuzu truck was backed up to the opening and two young men in headbands and sleeveless shirts were busy throwing cartons from a stack inside into the back of the truck. As he came abreast of them, Sawyer could see a third man, quite a bit older, with a clipboard and an abacus. He tallied the cost as the young men loaded.

Sawyer took the opportunity to step out of the brassy sun. In the shade and relative coolness just inside the corrugated-steel awning of another warehouse just across the narrow street, he could smell a pleasant mixture of spices. The men went on with their work. Good *joss* had delivered to him an excellent vantage point; because of the Isuzu they could not see him.

From here he could see Ng speaking in low tones to the man with the salt-and-pepper hair. Sawyer squinted through the sunlight in an attempt to focus on the other's face.

It was broad and flat, a Cantonese peasant face. There was something about it. Sawyer did not know what it was, but the more he looked at that face, the more certain he became that he knew it. But from where?

Ng and the Cantonese were huddled together. The two young men ignored them, moving back and forth like powerful automatons, delivering their cartons.

In that moment the Cantonese gave them a quick glance and, with a jerk of his head, moved off to the left with Ng. Deeper into shadow but closer to Sawyer. Their angle changed and Sawyer felt his stomach give a sick, queasy roll.

A mi tuo fo! he thought dizzily. I don't believe it.

As the Cantonese shifted, the left side of his face came partially into view. The outer corner of his eye was dragged down by a livid scar.

White-Eye Kao, Sawyer thought.

Several years ago there had been a problem at one of Sawyer and Sons' limited-access electronic facilities. Plans for two prototype systems disappeared. Working on his own, Sawyer had had plans drawn up for a dummy prototype. Setting infrared photography equipment in place, he had taken pictures of the spy.

Rather than having him arrested, Sawyer had hired a firm of excellent and absolutely discreet surveillance operatives to follow the man. The firm reported to no one but Sawyer himself, and the *tai pan* had kept all written material on the case locked in a vault to which only he had the combination.

Sure enough, the firm had traced the dummy plans back to a source. Sawyer could still remember the moment of holding the black-and-white photo, grainy from the high-speed film, the image unrealistically flat from the long lens. He'd remember that odd scar anywhere.

Sawyer was trembling now, but he did not know whether it was from rage or fear. The thing about White-Eye Kao was that he was a high-level Soviet agent.

The *tai pan* shifted his gaze. He could see a white-painted metal staircase running up the right side of the concrete wall from the loading platform to offices high up. Bamboo shades were partially drawn across dusty windows, but he could make out a figure moving behind them, lit from behind by fluorescent light.

Sawyer mopped at the back of his sweating neck. Buddha protect me, he thought. What is the *comprador* of Sawyer and Sons doing talking with a Soviet spy?

The *tai pan* had taken no action against White-Eye Kao, figuring that the enemy he knew was far less dangerous than the one unknown. Six months after the last theft, he had had to lay off thirty or forty people. He had made certain that the spy inside the facility was one of them. Now, however, he wished he had delivered up his evidence on White-Eye Kao to the Special Branch.

There was movement, and suppressing his shock, Sawyer concentrated his attention. The door above the two men was opening; a shadow was emerging, coming down the staircase. Sawyer could not make out who it was, the gloom was so dense in the warehouse's interior.

He heard a voice raised, and Ng and Kao broke off their conversation. Now Sawyer noticed an odd thing. The demeanour of the two changed radically at the third person's approach. It was clear from their stance and their expressions that they were in the presence of a *tai pan* of sorts.

My God, Sawyer thought. I know how high up White-Eye Kao is in the Soviet hierarchy. This must be the *tai pan* of Russian spies for all of Hong Kong.

Of course, Sawyer did not expect to recognize the person, and when he did, as they came into partial sunlight, his palsied hands rose in pure reflex, using his Kodak Disc camera to take shot after shot after shot. His mind was so frozen that he kept depressing the shutter long after the disc had been used up.

Peter Ng. Snap! White-Eye Kao. Snap! Sir John Bluestone. Snap! Snap! Snap!

'What you ask is patently impossible.' Venerable Chen stood up. There was a small porcelain panda on his desk. He picked it up, warming its cold, smooth skin in the palm of his hand. 'Besides, the *godown* war is between Formidable Sung and myself.'

'It affects all members of the Green Pang,' Jake pointed out. 'If just one man dies because of the wars, there is his family to consider.'

'They are adequately recompensed,' Venerable Chen said shortly. 'We know how to take care of our people.'

'But even one life lost is too many,' Bliss said from the corner of the sofa. 'Wouldn't you agree, Honourable Chen?'

The Shanghainese turned and regarded her. She was curled up like a cat, knees to chest, a double old-fashioned glass filled with Scotch clasped between her hands. He was about to remind her of her place when he remembered that he had been curled in just such a position after the explosion in the lounge. It made him think twice about reprimanding her.

'Death is in the nature of who we are,' he said evenly. 'No one can change that.'

'Of course not, Honourable Chen,' Jake said. 'But strictly from a business point of view, one finds that streamlining often results in a leap in net profit.'

'Any good businessman knows that, Mr Maroc.'

'Streamlining can also encompass compromise.'

Venerable Chen went behind his desk and sat down. He set his panda back in its place atop a pile of envelopes.

Jake took the silence as an invitation to him to continue. 'One compromises every day of one's life. The *h'yeung yau* that one pays policemen to stay away from one's operations, the intimidation one employs among shopowners, the infiltration of the Special Branch that allows one to make one's smuggling runs of guns, gold, and the poppy's tears – all these things, which are sometimes taken for granted in business, are forms of compromise.

'One must give up either money or manpower in order to get what one wants. Why should it be any different with the *godowns*?'

'Because, Mr Maroc, I want all of the *godowns* for the Green Pang. It is our hereditary right. I have my duty to perform.'

'When it comes to hereditary rights, then surely the Hakka, Hong Kong's true residents, should control the *godown*s. When it comes to duty, I agree absolutely. But tell me something, Honourable Chen. How much money have you taken in from the *godown*s since the start of the war?'

'None.' Venerable Chen said it without emotion of any kind.

Jake got up and stared out of the window at the South China Sea. 'Were I the *comprador* of the 489 whose triad was in the midst of this war, this is what I would counsel him to do. Contact the chief Hakka and make this proposal to him: let all the sons of the Hakka who can no longer tolerate spending all their lives on shipboard take to the land, as is their wish; let them manage all the *godown*s currently under contention; assign them an administration fee of, say, fifty per cent. The other fifty would be divided equally between the Green Pang and the 14K.

'My 489 would get his money every month without tying up manpower in running the *godown*s and in fighting a war that can, realistically, never end. Further, it would put the Hakka forever in his debt, since the problem with their current generation is reaching epidemic proportions. It would be ideal for the young men *and* their fathers. It would give them a new business on dry land and would keep them close enough to their ancestral home so as not to break up the family unit.

'Ah, the face he would gain by instituting such a sweeping reorganization!'

Venerable Chen stirred after the longest of silences. 'Mr Maroc, I was wrong about you. You are a devil, but not in the way I had at first thought. *A mi tuo fo*, you are as deviously cunning as a Chinese.' He laughed now, an infectious, boyish sound.

'I think in you I have found my secret weapon!'

Nichiren lay within Pearl's slender arms. He listened to her gentle snoring, smelled the faint trace of liquor on her breath, mingling with the soft scents of her perfume and her sexual oils. The windows were wide open and he could hear the sleepy drone of the nocturnal insects. He felt the light down on her velvet arms as she stirred, in the midst, perhaps, of some kaleidoscopic dream.

All these sights, sounds, smells, and touches were as familiar to him as the certain array of colours on an artist's palette. Each time before, when he had come to Hong Kong, the confluence of these sensations had served as a powerful palliative to send him off to a deep and dreamless sleep from which he would invariably wake ten hours later, refreshed and relaxed.

Tonight, sleep seemed as far away from him as the shores of Japan. For it was not of Pearl he thought.

It was of Kamisaka.

Something deep inside him was growing out of season. Kamisaka found him in the bars of spectral moonlight, which, at last breaking through the heavy cloud cover that had turned much of the night heavy and clammy, penetrated the open window, throwing themselves in reckless abandon across their entwined legs.

Though Pearl's prowess in the pillow ways remained undiminished, Nichiren had felt incapable of entering her licentious world. Try as he might, something inside him had remained adamantine, unshakable. It was as if a barrier not of his own manufacture had somehow been built inside him during a moment of unconsciousness. He had awakened to find himself irrevocably changed.

And, lying here in the semidarkness with these hedonistic comforts strewn in satiated abandon all about him, he knew that it was Kamisaka who had erected that wall inside him.

His dislocation here was a physical manifestation of her. For he felt called back to Japan not only by his innate love of his adopted land but now, too, by a human spirit. He saw for the first time that the power this *kami* could wield was greater than any other on earth.

This revelation shook him to his core. The fact that his feelings for another human being could supersede all his arduous training, the seeds planted within him long ago by his mother, stunned him into immobility.

It was odd. He felt as if he were lying in a perfect hammock, beneath perfect towering pines whose crenellated branches allowed the perfect amount of sunlight through to warm him. There he swung in short, languid arcs.

Content.

How could that be? Hadn't his mother told him that true contentment did not exist? Just as perfection in man's world did not exist.

Now he began to suspect that she was wrong.

Because now he knew how it felt to *belong*, knew as surely as he was lying here in Hong Kong that Yumiko had never belonged in that way, that she had had no conception of what that might mean to her spirit. He had lived his life until now as the outcast – as she had – either having it thrust upon him by circumstance or, after a certain period of indoctrination by his mother, opting for it actively. There had been, he had found, a certain degree of spiteful satisfaction in engendering in others exactly the reaction he had learned they would choose to put on him anyway. His control of the circumstances of his pain and anger seemed important at the time, even necessary for his survival.

And yet, oddly enough, this journey to revelation, which had begun with Kamisaka, had only come to its full fruition through the catalyst of Mariana Maroc. Mariana had been the first person to show him that he could be liked for himself. A friendship had sprung up between them as unmistakable as it was strong in the short time they had known each other. Something inside her had touched him deeply, perhaps because of how she had come to feel about him, despite her predisposition to hate him.

Her death had struck him across the heart. He realized that it brought to light secret emotions inside him. He had found at last that he could feel.

He thought about his Source. *I am your saviour*, the electronic voice had said in his ear time and again. Nichiren had never met his Source; he believed that he never would. That was all right. He had been given the most compelling reasons during his recruitment. By obeying the Source, he would save himself, and in working clandestinely for China, he would be helping to destroy the Soviets.

Nichiren's love for Japan was well known to his Source. The Soviets were inimical towards Japan. That had been enough.

Now Nichiren was not so certain. He stood in the centre, it seemed, of a vast, darkened theatre. Before him was the image of Yumiko. But he saw her now as if through an insect's multifaceted eyes. She was his mother whom he loved; she was a scarred woman whom he pitied; she was the presence who had begun him on his training; she was the creator of a terrible, vengeful demon she had bound into him through some arcane ceremony.

He saw before him now Yumiko's flesh. She who had been so beautiful was now hideously disfigured. For a moment, then, Nichiren heard the chanted words his mother had spewed out during the calling forth of his namesake.

Abruptly he felt strangled. Even his closeness to Pearl grated on him as if her arms, so soft and dreamily around his lap still, had turned to writhing tentacles, sucking him to her.

With a great gulp of breath, he swung his legs out of bed. He got up and silently crossed the dappled room.

In a moment he was dressed, slipping out of the front door like a wraith arisen from the mist of the land. When he reached the street, the moon was already down, and in the depths of the night, the blackness was complete.

In the end, it was Yuri Lantin who decided his own fate. He overruled Daniella, who had said that she would like to go back to her apartment for dinner. Death, she said as a joke, always tired her out.

At Lantin's, she sat in his plush leather wingback chair. His house was large enough to contain a study. If he had a child, Daniella supposed, this would have been its room.

It was lined with massive mahogany shelves filled with the literature of the world. Whatever else Yuri Lantin was not, he was certainly well-read.

There was a mahogany drop-leaf table on which was perched a thick-framed portrait of Lantin when he was much younger. He was smiling into the camera. His uniform, and perhaps his expression as well, made him seem dashing and somehow innocent. Beside it was another table, less aesthetic but sturdier, on which sat a high-domed typewriter. The walls were painted a deep luminous blue, the ceiling and mouldings cream.

Daniella was dressed in a side-slit Dior gown of pure satin silk. She had never even seen a gown except in photos, let alone worn one, before Lantin had bought this for her. Its sheen was tactile, especially because she was naked beneath its clinging wrap. Naked save for garter belt and sheer silk stockings.

Lantin had chosen her wardrobe, but Daniella did not complain. She felt precisely as if she were taking a steaming bath, and she was luxuriating in the experience.

Before he went into the kitchen to prepare dinner, Lantin had selected a volume from one section of the bookcase that was glassed-in and locked. It was bound in calfskin and had gilt edges. It was *The Story of O* by Pauline Réage. It was in the original French. Daniella had never told him that she spoke and read eight languages fluently. One of them – her favourite besides Russian – was French.

She had never read or heard of *The Story of O*, but after twenty or so pages she was beginning to get the idea. Mozart was playing on the stereo. Every fifteen or twenty minutes Lantin would appear and either turn over the record or change it. Always Mozart. It was difficult to get foreign pressings of such astounding virtuosity and aural clarity.

The subtle combination of the silk gliding against her flesh, Réage's heady prose, and the gorgeous music was beginning to dizzy her. It was almost possible to believe that she was in Paris, her old recruiting ground, rather than in drab Moscow.

Lantin came in to flip the record. Mozart began again, drenching the room in glorious melody. Lantin, wearing Calvin Klein cords and a cowboy's denim workshirt, walked barefoot across the Oriental carpet and popped *foie gras* in her mouth. It melted as she chewed, and she made a sound deep in her throat.

That was when he offered her the opium. It was as dark as night, filling the tiny bowl of a long-stemmed pipe of Chinese ivory the colour of a chrysanthemum. The bowl was carved and felt odd beneath her fingers.

Lantin lit the redolent opium, and Daniella inhaled. She had never experienced drugs of any kind firsthand before. Of course, her training in the *sluzhba* had included an extensive programme on drugs of all kinds, including their effect on different parts of the brain, nervous system, coordination, and so on.

She and Lantin shared the opium, and when the pipe was cool he returned to the kitchen. Through flared nostrils, she could smell fresh coriander and preserved chili

She resumed reading. The opium gave her the ability to absorb what she read and think independently at the same time. The leather, initially so cool on her bare buttocks, was now as deliciously warm as a lover's lips. She squirmed in the chair, aware of her body's flush. Réage's story was turning her on despite herself.

The smell of leather, so manly, mingled with the cooking scents to create a kind of wholeness that Daniella could not explain, but only wonder at. *Yin* and *yang*.

Her resolve to break irrevocably away from Lantin flickered like a candle in the wind. The truth was, she enjoyed the things **he** bought her, the luxury within which he immersed her. **He** was decadent and, oddly, that thrilled her. This gown was decadent. With every breath she took, she could feel the silk caressing her flesh. Mozart's sublime music caressed her ears, Réage's French caressed her mind.

She was filled up with emotion, soaking in discrete moments of desire. There was no yesterday, no tomorrow. Only an endless now.

She read steadily until she heard Lantin's voice.

'Get up.'

She obeyed.

She was wearing the high-heeled pumps he had bought her. Through half-glazed eyes she saw his gaze of lust as it glided over the thrust of her breasts, the stiff peaks of her nipples, the shallow bowl of her belly. The heels made her legs seem endless; the stockings gave them a sheen as if they were coated with oil

Lantin changed the record. 'Are you hungry?'

'Yes.'

'Walk across the room.'

She began, but he redirected her until she stood beneath the glassed-in bookcase.

'Hold out your hands.'

She did so, and before she knew what was happening, he had slipped a pair of gleaming chrome-plated handcuffs over her wrists. She heard with an odd kind of echo the *snik-snik* of the ratchets closing over her flesh.

Daniella was slightly dazed. If he had said 'Hold out

600

your wrists,' she might have had some inkling as to his intent, especially considering the book he had given her to read. As it was, she stood staring stupidly at him. There was already a great bulge in his jeans. She wondered whether the constriction was very painful.

'Turn around.'

She seemed incapable of any movement. She felt his hands rough on her shoulders, spinning her so that she faced the glassed-in case. He took her wrists by the manacles and slipped the chain linking them through an eyehook screwed into one of the higher bookshelves. This drew Daniella upwards until the heels of her shoes barely touched the floor.

'We will eat in a moment.'

She felt her Dior gown being pulled aside. The scrape of the jeans zipper abraded against the gently flowing Mozart, a scar disfiguring an otherwise exquisite face.

Daniella became aware of what he was going to do a moment before it happened. She thought of Réage's character and what she had been asked to do for love: to prove her devotion. This debasement was the first of many.

She cried out at the invasion of his hot, oiled penis. It seemed to have grown to four times its size. Her back arched instinctively, but this only presented her buttocks to him more completely.

His carnal heat was on her like a blanket. She felt as if she were being penetrated by a horse; there was nothing pleasurable about it. The shame and sickly tear served to evaporate the euphoria of the opium. Mozart's ephemeral stateliness now seemed hollow and mocking.

She thought of O. Of how her lover had taken her thus, how his friends had availed themselves of her in the same manner. How she had been whipped and then made love to. How the ring her lover had selected and which bore his initials had been put through her labia as an eternal symbol.

She thought of how O had endured all this for the love of her man, and she wondered whether this was what Lantin ultimately had in mind for her. Certainly this was the beginning of what he saw as a learning process. She saw that he had given her the book to read so that he would never have to say to her, 'Daniella, this is what is to come.'

Yet he had missed the essence of the story. O had been asked at every stage if she would accept what was to come. And at each stage she had agreed. Until the strength of her commitment, and the knowledge it lent her, had freed her of woman's traditional chains, giving her an extraordinary power over others.

Lantin had asked Daniella nothing. He had never sought her consent. He had gleaned from Réage's story only the most superficial emotions. Male dominating female. He had not recognized O's submission as strength, but rather had seen it erroneously as weakness. He saw weakness in all women.

Thus he made up Daniella's mind for her.

She let him have his grunting, sweat-sticky orgasm inside her. She turned her defilement into a rite of passage, a search for self, as Réage meant O's to have been. In the end she would have to thank Lantin, for it was through his cruelty that she began to see herself as a free creature rather than as a woman who was dependent on the more powerful men around her to scale the heights she desired for herself.

Still rampant from his rape, Lantin reached up and slipped the chain off the eyehook. He unlocked the handcuffs so that they fell away from her red wrists, landing at her feet. They felt hot against her toes, as if they burned with her shame.

He was deep inside her. Daniella felt as if she had dysentery. She was beset by cramps. She wanted to cry with the pain but she would not allow herself that release. Not in front of him.

He did not want to come out of her, but her calf muscles were trembling so hard now that he had no choice. He withdrew, and to Daniella it felt as if a swordblade were slicing through her bowels. She put her forehead against the glass case until it fogged with her panting breath.

Sweat drenched her, and she could smell the musk of sex swirling in the room along with the Mozart.

The music followed her as she staggered into the hallway, into the bathroom, where she fell against the door and vomited all over the tiles.

Twenty minutes later, after she had cleaned up, taken a chilly shower because as usual the hot water wasn't working properly, she stood before the medicine chest. She looked at herself in the mirror on the door and quickly opened the chest to rid herself of the sight.

It took her several minutes before her vision concentrated enough for her mind to understand what she was looking at. A bottle with a fairly new prescription. Sleeping pills.

She took them out, and while Lantin was busy in the kitchen completing his preparations for dinner, she went into the bedroom and threw all the pills into the bottle of Starka he always kept by his bedside. Twenty.

Gingerly she sat on the bed, watching fascinated as the thin coating slowly dissolved in the alcohol. Soon there was no trace of them. The bottle was less than a quarter full. She thought of the concentration of chemicals inside that bottle. Like swallowing poison, she thought. Almost.

It was so painful to sit on the hard dining room chair that she had to bite her lip through most of the meal. Lantin did not notice, or perhaps if he did, he felt it best to make no comment. He spoke as if nothing untoward had happened.

Daniella was astounded. It was as if he was unaware that she might have some feeling one way or another about being taken, or as if he did not care. She did not know which was the worse reality.

As was his habit, when he got into bed he drank three fingers of the Starka out of a water glass. In the airless dark, Daniella waited, feeling the sweat congealing on her flesh. Being so close to him now gave her goosebumps, as if he were a bear or a great cat who, though ostensibly trained, might strike her down at any moment.

At last she could stand it no longer. 'Yuri?' she said. Then, in a somewhat stronger voice, 'Yuri.'

No answer.

She turned over. She could just make out his profile. He looked like the Devil.

She reached out and, breathless, poked him in the ribs. She made a fist, beat down on his chest above his heart. She slapped him hard across the face.

Then she clambered across his still body and, reaching back, dragged him out of bed. This was no time, she thought, to take a chance.

Grunting with the effort, she took him up under the arms and pulled him across the room. The rug proved a bit of a problem. His heavy heels dragged it over the polished wooden floor, adding to his weight, until she dropped him and untangled it from beneath him.

Down the silent hallway they went. Daniella could hear the stentorian ticking of the clock on the mantel. Her breath was hot in her throat, and the stooped position she was in caused a return of her cramps.

In the kitchen, she opened the oven door and blew out the pilot light. Then she turned Lantin over on his belly and slid him up onto the Bakelite lip. Shoved head and shoulders into the aperture. Then, already gagging on the fumes, she turned on the oven full blast.

It took her fifteen painful minutes to dress, break into his cache of secret files, and remove all traces of her presence, including prints, from the apartment. By then the place was so thick with gas it was possible to hallucinate.

How many wars had he fought? The war against Chiang; the war against the capitalists; the war against the *faan gwai loh*. But the greatest toll of all had been taken in his war against himself.

Like a mountain climber who, after a long, exhausting ascent, stands wreathed in cloud, Zilin was now increasingly absorbed by his thoughts.

His secret life, dedicated to the fruition of the *yuhn-hyun*, had been kept from everyone. Every day had been a battle with security. On the surface he had to seem to be working towards the goals set by each succeeding regime. Of course, he had had his say, he had pulled the strings at which time had made him adept. But it had not been enough. Despite his work, present-day China was a shambles of political quicksand, indecisive priorities and allocations, and, above all, inability to devise a long-range plan and stick to it.

Perhaps, Zilin thought, it was not inability but unwillingness. Ever since Mao's disastrous five-year plans, there had been a reluctance within the governmental hierarchy to return to that kind of thinking, no matter the urgency of the need.

We are an unwieldy nation, he thought dispiritedly. We are too many people, too little educated in a quality fashion. Our Communist cant shackles us to an unsupportable economy. Our continued fear of Western 'contamination' dooms us to an endless infancy in the modern business world.

Time and again, Zilin thought about the examples of Chinese initiative and business acumen in almost every country of the globe. In most cases, they paid the price for it. Philippine-born Chinese were still denied citizenship in that country, even after their families had lived there for many generations. In the 1960s, thousands of Chinese were slaughtered in Malaysian and Indonesian race riots, principally because of their business dominance in those areas.

A decade later, the socialist regime in Hanoi had forced Vietnamese Chinese into the South China Sea, rather than harbour such potentially destructive capitalists in their midst. Today, the two most successful business tycoons in Jakarta were born on mainland China. But rather than risk the racial consequences, they had renamed themselves Soedono Salim and Surya Wonowidjojo, Indonesianizing themselves.

Today, while the Chinese in Indonesia are not subjected to mutilation and death as they once were, they are still persecuted in a way. The government has decreed that the Bumiputras, the sons of the soil, Islamic native Malays, have first rights on all new business enterprises. Further, 'foreign' businessmen are 'encouraged' to take on Bumiputras as business partners.

In America, however, the Chinese flourish. Among many, En Wang, an emigrant from the Mainland, had shown his genius in designing computer networks. Zilin regretted now that he would never see America for himself.

But in these days of pain and fear, he regretted most his decision to leave his wife and his mistress. For the first time in his life, doubts about himself had begun to assail him. He was, after all, just a man. Nowadays his youthful dreams, in which he had believed himself to be the reincarnation of a Celestial Guardian of China, seemed farfetched indeed. His increasing pain made him aware with every breath he took that he was merely a man, as mortal as those around him.

And now he felt the closing presence of Wu Aiping all around him. Fluttering wings of death beat in the shadows of his office and villa. At night the darkness closed around him like a cloak clutched in the senior minister's hands, bearing down on him. The sweat rolled off his emaciated body.

There were times when he wished he could weep. He wondered, then, how he had ever been able to leave Athena and Sheng Li. In the past he would have called it strength. Now he suspected that it was sheer callousness. How could he have been so unfeeling? How could he have left his two sons, one a child, the other merely an infant?

He had been driven by his dream. By the haunting vision of the *yuhn-hyun*, which had been born so many, many years ago in the Jian's garden in Suzhou. Artifice in the appearance of nature. That was what had sustained him for so long. It was what had kept him alive, but he suspected now, in sorrow, that it had also warped him beyond his own understanding.

He was Jian. The creator.

But for the first time he questioned the nature of his creation. He wondered whether the future of China was truly more important than his own happiness and the happiness of those he held dear. He had been witness to such cruelty, such stupidity, such inhumanity in his climb to power. He had done what he could, but it was, of course, never enough. He could never have stopped the evil flow. The eternal fluttering of the ring's banner had not let him. He had had to blend in, to seem to go along with those who had grasped the power. He could not have survived otherwise. Mao would have killed him. Later, he would have been destroyed along with Mao, the Gang of Four, all the others.

Increasingly he had begun to suspect that he was unable to feel any emotion, after all. My sons, my sons, he thought. I must have my sons back! Not even China means as much to me as they do now.

A chime sounded softly in the villa, and Zilin rose, sighing. He went to his transceiver and flicked on the power. With half his mind still immersed in deep thought, he went through the rituals to ensure security.

Contact.

They performed the recognition codes without a hitch.

'Report,' he said.

'I . . .' The voice faltered and Zilin came out of his reverie.

'What is it? What is the matter?'

'I do not know,' Nichiren said from a far-off place. 'Something seems to have changed.'

'In Hong Kong?'

'Inside myself.'

'Explain yourself,' his Control said with a calmness he did not feel.

'How? I was never taught to understand my own . . . emotions.'

'I thought I had accomplished that by breaking you away from your mother's control.'

'I wonder whether that is enough.'

'I do not understand.'

'I want . . .' For a time there was only the crackle of the ether. 'I want an end to this.'

'An end to what?'

'To obeying orders, to being under discipline, to being a part of the *yuhn-hyun*.'

'What are you saying? This is impossible! Do you have any idea how long it took me to set you up in just such a way, so that you would become irresistible to Daniella Vorkuta? As long as she was running you, you reported to me everything she said or did. I already had a line on her recruitment of Chimera, the Soviet mole inside the Quarry. That was my reason for ordering you to get Mariana Maroc and the *fu* shard out of Hong Kong. Chimera had somehow found out about the *fu* and had sent out a "seek and terminate" directive on Mariana.

'Daniella Vorkuta has been a primary element in the

yuhn-hyun, though she is totally oblivious of the fact. She has taken care of General Karpov for me; if I know her at all, she will have found a way to do the same with Yuri Lantin. Once that happens, we can move without fear. Lantin is our most feared enemy inside Russia. It was he who ordered the termination squad up to Tsurugi. It is he who seeks to strangle China by provoking her into a war he feels certain she cannot win.

'Listen to me. I have saved you from the utter anarchy and nihilism of your youth, and in so doing, I have furthered the *yuhn-hyun*. The positive ring. Without it, Buddha only knows what would have happened to you. You must think about that. You have your duty.'

'I believe I have a duty to myself also. That has been weighing heavily on my mind of late, something I learned not long ago. A lesson given by Jake Maroc's wife.'

'You will listen to me – !'

'I want my own life!' The cry was that of a lost child, and it froze Zilin. 'I want my own life and I will have it!'

Then the connection was gone. Just like that, such a slender thread, from father to unknowing son.

Zilin's hand trembled as he replaced the microphone and shut down the power. The *yuhn-hyun*, he thought. Fifty years of planning. The sacrifices he had made to become Jian.

I want my own life!

A cry in the night. Raw emotion that Zilin himself had felt growing inside him for weeks now. His longing to see his sons face to face, to let them know that he was alive, that he loved them, that he had always loved them even as he was abandoning them, was so intense that it over-powered the pain lighting up his body like lightning.

He shook where he sat, trembling with emotions he had pent up, it seemed, for almost an entire lifetime. What matter that he was Jian? His sons been lost to him for all these years. He saw now that one could not equate the one with the other.

Abruptly he tasted the dust of his life, understood its barrenness. He felt the alienness of his own self. Being Jian, so far from any human frailty, he had not laughed nor cried in decades. Nothing had been able to move him. In a vacuum, he had planned the intricacies of the *yuhn-hyun*. Like a great general, his manipulation of people had of necessity inured him to their pain and sorrow. Instead he was focused in only on their fears, for in knowing them, he could motivate them to make the moves he required of them.

I want my own life and I will have it!

He had never been there when his sons needed him. Now it was clear that Nichiren at least, lost and alone, could no longer survive in his current state. A woman could comfort him, but who could set things right but a father?

Oh, Buddha, help me! he thought. What should I do?

At last Zilin began to weep tears of such bitterness that they stung his flesh as they spilled out of his eyes.

It was strange how a telephone bell sounded as loud as a klaxon at night. Perhaps it was because the noise was so penetrating, or again perhaps it was because, like Pavlov's dogs, humans have been trained to expect only bad news at night.

In any event, the telephone woke Henry Wunderman out of a sound sleep. At once he sat up and grabbed for the receiver. With his other hand he reached out and gentled the stirring shoulder of his wife. With his hand over the mouthpiece, he whispered, 'It's all right. It's nothing. The kids are all asleep, go back to sleep yourself.' He waited until he felt her relax. With the kids in their teens, she never quite got used to the unbroken silence of the night.

At length Wunderman said, 'Yes,' into the phone.

'The Nightclub's open for dancing,' a familiar voice said in his ear.

'Right,' Wunderman said. 'Twenty minutes, tops.' His feet were already swinging over the side of the bed.

'The Nightclub' was Quarryspeak for Asian Theatre communications. 'Dancing' was the code word for 'top priority.'

Driving through Washington at night always reminded Wunderman of Paris. Both formed the essence of power on their continents. Cities of light. Also Washington, in its overall structure, was very European in nature, with its main streets radiating out from the nub of the Capitol. It was a city, Wunderman had been told, that was easy to defend.

Paris had a special place in Wunderman's heart. It was where he and Marjorie had gone on their honeymoon. A package tour, all he could afford at the time, since he had turned down the money from Marjorie's family. The busman's special. No matter. Paris was a place to fall in love, not just for the rich, but for everyone. He tried to think of what Rodger Donovan had been like, striding along the Parisian boulevards in his Izod shirts, white duck trousers, and Top-Siders. A quintessentially American figure amid all the Gallic charm.

The Parisian women must have gone mad for him; the Russians must have run for the hills. He was a one-man July Fourth celebration.

Wunderman went through security in five separate stages. Even though everyone knew him by sight, he was pleased to see there was no letup or exception made.

He was met on the eighteenth floor by the O.D., a young, earnest man named Rhones, whom Wunderman had handpicked out of the Washington talent pool.

'What do we have?'

Rhones didn't bother to apologize for getting his boss

out of bed at this late hour; he knew his job and did it to perfection.

'Computer call.'

That checked Wunderman. 'Are you kidding? Night-club's not computer.'

'That's right, sir. Communication came in from Hong Kong Station. It was automatically computer-routed because of the code.'

'Rhones, all our communications, overseas and other-wise, are ciphered.'

'I know, sir, but this is in GASP.'

Garbled Agraphic Speech Parts was a cipher that Dono-van had come up with some time ago. He had told Wunderman that it was essentially a joke, hence the name, which revolved around the word *agraphic*. Wunderman had had to look it up. It meant a pathological inability to write.

What Donovan had done in GASP was to take speech *sounds* rather than words and translate them into a represen-tational word-phrase alphabet. Then he had garbled it all to hell. Hence it was a cipher only the Quarry computer could translate.

Donovan had brought up the existence of GASP in the most offhand way, but Wunderman and Beridien had immediately seen its application and they had had Dono-van program it into the GPR-3700 memory bank.

Consequently the Quarry now had the only unbreakable code Wunderman had ever heard of.

Wunderman sat down at the computer terminal and Rhones left him. An unspoken quality of GASP was that it was Eyes Only, Director and Clearance Personnel.

He punched his first set of access figures into the computer. When the **GO FORTH** graphic lit up, he gave the recognition code for the GASP-cipher communication.

WORKING, the GPR-3700 told him.

It was hot in the windowless room, and Wunderman

called for Rhones to put up the air, which was on minimal at this time of night.

GO FORTH.

Wunderman picked out the second set of access codes.

CONFIRMED AND VERIFIED: JAKE MAROC RESPON-SIBLE FOR TERMINATION OF THREE QUARRY AGENTS, HONG KONG, DURING LAST TWELVE HOURS. REQUEST RECLASSIFICATION TO 'LETHAL ROGUE'. ORDERS?

The words rolled over Wunderman like a chill tide. He felt the breath go out of him just as surely as if he had been punched in the solar plexus. He glanced down at his hand, noticed that there was a slight tremor.

How could he give the order?

I brought Jake into the Quarry. I'm his mentor; I guided him through training, let him loose in the field.

But, my God, three agents killed, and Jake responsible for all of them. Wunderman thought of his wife and kids, asleep, safe in their house in rural Virginia. I've got to bring him back, he thought now. At all costs, I must stop him. He's running amok.

Jake's my responsibility.

Wunderman was about to stab out at the keyboard when the RUNNING graphic lit up the top of the screen. Another top-priority message was coming in. Wunderman hastily cleared the screen, typed in GO FORTH, followed by his access code. This is what came up:

RUMOUR CONFIRMATION ON RED ROSE: – Red Rose was Quarryspeak for Russia – NEW HEAD OF FIRST CHIEF DIRECTORATE, KGB, GENERAL DANIELLA VORKUTA. ANNOUNCEMENT FORTHCOMING WITHIN 48 HOURS. UNCONFIRMED REPORTS INDICATE WITHIN WEEK GEN-ERAL VORKUTA WILL BE FIRST FEMALE TO BE APPOINTED TO POLITBURO. ENDIT.

'Oh, Jesus Christ!' Wunderman breathed.

He thought, I've got to contact Apollo immediately. There was a pay phone he used on the way home. He did not like to do any security calling at all inside the Washington environs.

He cleared the screen and tapped in his command via GASP.

DIRECTOR TO HK STA: CONFIRM MESSAGE RECEIPT. MAROC HEREBY RECLASSIFIED 'LETHAL ROGUE.' REPEAT: 'LETHAL ROGUE' RECLASSIFICATION CONFIRMED.

Wunderman turned away from the screen, after shutting down the terminal. Now, he thought wearily, they'll shoot him on sight.

What else could Andrew Sawyer do but deliver the photographs to Venerable Chen? He himself had been wronged. Peter Ng was Sawyer and Sons' *comprador*, but he was Venerable Chen's nephew. Sawyer, attuned all his life to Chinese philosophy and customs, knew that family took precedence over business. It did not matter how many secrets Peter Ng had stolen from Sawyer and Sons. The only important point was that he was family to Venerable Chen.

'You know the man with the scar?'

Venerable Chen nodded. 'White-Eye Kao.' His face was filled with an unutterable sadness. 'A dung-eating lackey of the fornicating KGB.'

'They're all in it together,' Sawyer said. 'Ng, Kao, Bluestone.'

Venerable Chen looked up. 'You have taken no action?'

Sawyer shook his head. 'As I told you, Honourable Chen, it is to you I came first. Peter Ng's position in your family made that my duty.'

'I see.' The Shanghainese stared at the *tai pan* for a long time without saying anything further.

They were in the study of Venerable Chen's house in the Sai Ying Pun district of the Island.

When Venerable Chen spoke again, it was seemingly on

614

an irrelevant subject. 'I am told that you recently attended a Ghost Wedding.'

Sawyer nodded. 'For my daughter, Miki. She died when she was eighteen months old.'

'*Oh ko*, such a sadness. The burden is heavy for such a little one. But now, through the Ghost Wedding, her spirit is happy.'

'At last.'

The two men looked at each other appraisingly, as if a new light shone on them both.

'It would seem obvious, Mr Sawyer, that my nephew has done you and your firm great harm.'

The conversation was suddenly as delicate as crystal. 'I think,' Sawyer said, 'that it is as nothing compared to the disappointment he has brought you.'

'I appreciate your concern, but my first thoughts are of the damage to Sawyer and Sons.'

'It will take time,' Sawyer said carefully, 'to accurately assess the full extent of the loss.' He paused. 'I may need help.'

Venerable Chen had been waiting, it seemed, for just those words. 'Then it will be given to you. You have only to ask.'

Sawyer bowed. 'I am honoured by the thought, Honourable Chen.'

The Shanghainese looked up. 'And the punishment?'

'The crime was against Hong Kong. The punishment should fit the crime. At least that is my belief.'

Venerable Chen peered hard at Sawyer. 'Then you see no need to inform the Special Branch?'

'I leave that up to you.' Taking a big chance, his heart in his throat.

The other gave a quick nod of affirmation. He went on his tiny feet to sit behind his desk. He placed the photograph he had been holding at the end of a line of all the others. He stared at them one last time, then lifted his gaze to Sawyer.

He saw a kind man with open features, as Chinese read such things. It seemed at that moment to be filled with intelligence and more. Heartfelt emotion. For the first time he recognized the face of an ally.

'My judgment is this, Mr Sawyer. Let the Chinese take care of the Chinese. Let the *tai pan* take care of the *tai pan*.'

Sawyer took a step towards the tiny man. He bowed. 'With respect, Honourable Chen, I would like to make a suggestion.'

'You may.'

'Let us punish together. Let the punishment we devise between us be the first bond of many in business and personal life.'

Venerable Chen allowed a smile inside himself, through his grief at what his nephew had inexplicably become. And he thought, *Dew neh loh moh*, I may come to like this barbarian, after all.

Formidable Sung's main office was in a toy factory. The place manufactured tiny, articulated *samurai* warriors constructed of red, green, yellow and blue plastic, bright colours favoured by the Chinese but wildly inappropriate for the subject.

Aisles as straight as arrows were bounded by gigantic bins in which resided literally millions of arms, legs, torsos, and heads. Swords and bases were kept in a separate section of the factory because they were added last.

Lines of Chinese girls somewhere between thirteen and sixteen, dressed alike, sitting on hard, uncomfortable stools, their shining black hair tied up in thick cotton swatches, assembled the furious-faced warriors piece by piece along a kind of conveyor that moved at a speed that gave them no margin for error.

While there was perhaps enough money to turn this factory, and others like it, over to the gleaming robots of the 1980s, it was not practical. Human labour in Hong Kong was still far cheaper than converting to automation.

A bristly-haired triad member picked Jake up a hundred yards from the factory. He met him at the door and escorted him through the noisy chaos of the interior.

Formidable Sung was waiting for him. There was tea brewing. The twin gold and green dragons, their arched and flaming backs forming a symmetrical shape over the altartop of a camphorwood cabinet, stared crimson-eyed at him. *Joss* sticks were burning, adding to the confluence of intangible smells within the cramped space.

Wooden-slatted windows allowed thin slices of sunlight into the interior. Plastic dust floated like plankton in the semidarkness. Lights were lit within this room, Jake knew from experience, only at night. Even then, the shadows in the corners were inky and impenetrable. The dragons who inhabited the earth beneath this spot, Formidable Sung had once been advised by his *feng shui* man, preferred the darkness. He happily acceded to their wishes. *Dieh loong*, the earth dragons, were the 489's personal protectors; he believed in their existence with an almost febrile intensity. Those who were not aligned with *dieh loong* he refused to see or to do business with. He was adamant on this point, consulting the *feng shui* man before entering into any business deal, large or small.

'Ah,' he said, as Jake was ushered in, 'Mr Maroc.'

It was not the Chinese way to compliment or to touch in pleasure. It would have been especially unseemly for an older man such as Formidable Sung to show such emotion to a younger man such as Jake.

Instead he had brewed tea himself.

Jake was alone with the 489, which was rare enough in itself. In China, one learned to glean emotion from the most minute source, just as one learned in the desert to get water out of the most unlikely places. In either case, it was a survival technique.

They drank the tea in silence, both of them taking pleasure in the moment so that the ritual became almost an intimate kind of interplay. During this time, Jake knew, the façade of the 489 was down. Now Jake, if he wished, could take advantage of the other, ask him anything. But he also knew that although the other would answer, it would be the end of their relationship. Politeness dictated that Jake be content with the knowledge and accept the moment for what it was: a quiet time between equals.

There was ironbound honour between these two, and that was what was being displayed now. Neither of them wished to disturb the forces at play, invisible lightning ringing a park in summertime.

At last there was nothing in the earthenware pot but moist leaves. It was then that Formidable Sung said, 'The *godown* war is at an end.'

'I am pleased that no more lives will be lost.'

That simple exchange was all that marked an acknowledgment of Jake's victory.

They sat facing each other, the sounds of the factory engulfing them in a kind of dangerous noise. The aura of both men was very strong, their intrinsic energies meeting in the centre of the room like the confluence of two powerful rivers.

'Nichiren,' Formidable Sung said, opening the topic.

'I want to know why he comes here to see you.'

'He and I are in the midst of discussions. But he sees not only me when he comes to Hong Kong. He also sees Venerable Chen, Sharktooth Tung, head of the Hak Sam, the Chiu-chow triad. He sees all the dragons, in fact.'

'Separately, I imagine.'

Jake had said it lightly, but Formidable Sung took his time replying. 'That is not the way he has wanted it to be, but after two abortive efforts to gather us together in a summit, he has been forced to make the rounds. Does that answer your question?'

The breath had gone out of Jake. 'A triad summit? But why? How?'

The 489 cocked his head, and now there was a look of genuine puzzlement on his face. 'Has your friend not told you?'

'My friend?'

'Do you have another way to describe the woman?'

'Bliss?'

The other nodded.

'What does Bliss know about this?'

'My dear Mr Maroc,' Formidable Sung said softly, 'she is part of the *yuhn-hyun* and so are you.'

'How do you know about the *yuhn-hyun*?'

'How do you think? I, too, am part of the ring. So is Nichiren.'

'Nichiren?' Jake was dizzy. He felt as if the ground had given way beneath his feet. 'Nichiren works for the Soviets.'

'Not quite.' Now the other was smiling. 'The Soviets *believe* he works for them. His first allegiance is to the *yuhn hyun*.'

'I don't even know what this *yuhn-hyun* is.'

'That is not for me to tell you.'

'After what I did for you – '

'Mr Maroc, you know very well the parameters of our bargain. The *yuhn-hyun* was never mentioned.'

'All right,' Jake conceded. 'Nichiren, then. What is the purpose of the triad summit?'

'I thought that would have been obvious. To unite all triads behind one cause.'

'Don't tell me. The *yuhn-hyun*.'

Formidable Sung said nothing.

'How did you get into this? It was my understanding that all dragons were independent.'

'Independence, Mr Maroc, depends almost wholly on history. Allow me to tell you a story that is historical in nature. It goes back many years. A somewhat rash youth

619

ran lorchas with a man. Together they knew every inch of the waterways in and around Hong Kong where they plied their trade. Some things in China never change. I think you know that well. The tears of the poppy is one of those things. Smuggling opium was and is enormously profitable.

'Because that was so, the competition was – how shall I put it? – intense. Suffice it to say that the rash youth, in a moment of heady euphoria, bragged to people he thought were trustworthy. The prospect of wealth, it was later brought home to him, bores holes in the concept of trust. It was a painful lesson he never forgot.

'So it was that the rash youth and his mentor were ambushed one day, after picking up a rather large shipment. Four men were eventually killed, the youth was wounded quite severely. His mentor took care of him, healed him, and never once reprimanded him for the incident or the loss of the opium. The youth, by his own decision, worked for his mentor a full year without compensation to atone for the payment the mentor was obliged to make to cover the loss.

'The mentor was a most unusual man, and when, in time, events dictated that he move out of that business, he bequeathed it to the youth – who was now not nearly so rash.'

Formidable Sung was removing his suit jacket. He hung it carefully on a coat tree in the corner of his office. Then he undid the buttons of his long-sleeved shirt. Pushing his tie out of the way, he exposed his chest and right shoulder. The skin there was puckered and white with a series of thick scars, an abstract pattern across his hairless flesh.

'As you must have guessed,' he said, buttoning up, 'the rash youth was me. My mentor, Mr Maroc, was Three Oaths Tsun. He is the dragon of the *yuhn-hyun*. We are tied in business; in this also.' He shrugged. 'But I forget, you already know of his involvement in the *yuhn-hyun*.'

Jake was puzzled. 'Why should I?'

'Because, Mr Maroc, your friend Bliss is his daughter.'

The soldiers of the Premier's guard presented themselves at precisely nine o'clock in the morning at Zilin's office cubicle. There they went through Zilin's files, gathering up all information pertinent to Mitre, Hong Kong, and the *ren*.

Zilin looked on impassively, but Zhang Hua, who had followed the soldiers into the room, stood shaking, white with terror, as he watched the systematic rape of the office.

After the soldiers had finished their work, one of them, the commander, read them a precisely worded document that coldly called for their immediate presence before a tribunal of the Premier's calling. There was absolutely no question of not complying.

Zilin gathered papers into his briefcase and handed it to Zhang Hua. A tense look passed between them.

'Courage, my friend,' Zilin said softly enough so that the Premier's guard could not hear.

Together they went slowly down to the street. A dense, zinc-coloured rain was falling. It washed all colour from the greenery.

Ducking his head, Zilin climbed into the waiting car. He sucked in his breath at the pain the motion engendered in him. Zhang Hua sat by his side, the slim briefcase across his knees. He held on to the handle with white-knuckled fists. Zilin could feel the tremor shivering his body. He wanted to make a gesture to reassure his assistant, but he knew they were being watched.

The commander sat beside them. There were three more – one was the driver – in front. Privately, Zilin thought that excessive to fetch two old and tired ministers.

Zilin put his head back against the plastic seat and closed his eyes. Pain laced his consciousness like a web. It became more and more of an effort each day to separate the pain from his quotidian duties. It took time to compart-mentalize his mind, storing away the pain that whistled through him with the constancy of breath.

Zilin opened his eyes. Through the mist of his pain and the steadily drumming summer rain, he observed his Beijing. His love for it overflowed his heart, for a moment, at least, easing his agony.

He remembered, as a man of middle years, being taken to Zhoukoudian, southwest of the modern city, to inspect the site of the discovery of the remains of Peking Man. He had felt such excitement and such – what would one call it? – pride, perhaps, as he squatted in the ancient dust.

The centuries had rolled back, returning him to the dawn of man. It had been here, along the most strategic route on all of the Asian continent, that man had made his early mark.

Here, at the confluence of the vast Yellow River plain and the darkling mountains to the northeast, traders made their arduous way on this important north-south route. And here was where they had to cross the Yongding River, at just this spot, downstream of the mountains to the west and the dense, overgrown marshes to the east. Here the settlement of what was to become Beijing began.

Under the Zhou, during the Warring States period, somewhere between 403 and 221 B.C., it was known as Ji, 'the reeds.' After the fall of the Tang Dynasty, it lost its status as a frontier province. Incorporated into the northern empire in 936 A.D., it became known as Tanjing by the Khitan, founders of the Kiao Dynasty.

By the beginning of the 12th century, when the Jurched succeeded the Khitan, the name had been changed to Zhongdu, 'central capital'. One hundred years later, the Mongols razed it during their war with the Jurched. But the importance of its position was not lost on the victorious Khublai, who, in 1261, decided to make it his home. It was Dadu, 'the great capital,' to the Mongols. But to the visiting Marco Polo it was Cambaluc, a corruption of the Mongol word Khanbaliq, 'the Khan's town'. By that time, it was already vast.

When, in 1368, the Yuan were defeated by Zhou Yuanzhang, this founder of the Ming Dynasty renamed the city Beiping, 'northern peace'. It was inherited by one of his sons, later titled the King of Yuan. When he came to power in 1403, he decided to move the country's capital back from Nanking. Beiping became Beijing, 'northern capital'.

Under this ruler, the city took on roughly the shape it has today. To the north, new walls were built inside the old fortifications, excluding a large portion of the Yuan town. To the south, a wall of earth was built in 1524 and later, in 1543, rebuilt in brick, enclosing much of the former Mongolian sphere. This gave Beijing the appearance of being a double city, the one roughly square, the other rectangular.

Zilin turned his head. The rain battered against the windows as the limousine sped through the wide boulevards of the city. There was almost no traffic, and they were well away from the bus and trolley routes.

How he loved every year of this great city's rich history! How he relished having been born Chinese, having lived his life here! But in the West, the future of China lay waiting. Like a poisonous creature that was nevertheless essential to the continued existence of civilized man, the technology of the West had made Zilin walk a death-defying tightrope almost all his adult life. Now, he knew, it was time to either master it or to see that in reaching out for it, he had been fatally bitten.

The foul weather had turned the vast hall of the Premier as chill and dank as a grave at the bottom of the sea. Oddly, the room had the same smell as Zhoukoudian, where Zilin had crouched in the dust of the aeons so long ago to observe the place in the earth where Peking Man had been found, enwombed by the ages.

It was, after all, a certain scent that by its very existence smacked of petrification. In Zhoukoudian, it was as if the world had not advanced even one day since the living Peking Man made his stooped way over the same terrain so many aeons ago. Here, in this enormous space, it was not, Zilin thought, very much different.

As he approached the far end of the room in the company of the trembling Zhang Hua and the four guards who had escorted him from his office, he could see that Wu Aiping was already present.

He sat folded up in the same carved ebony chair in which he had sat during their first confrontation only weeks before.

The Premier was at his accustomed station behind the high wooden desk. His face was surmounted by the mask of power: that network of lines and sunken hollows that turned young men old, that turned old men's hearts into ash.

At that moment the procession passed a mirror set into a wall, and Zilin chanced to look into it. What he saw there shocked him. He saw the mask of the Premier clamped tightly onto his own face.

All the great love that had surrounded him like a comforting blanket during his ride through the streets of Beijing evaporated. Now he felt only the chill walls of the corridors of power, down which he had trod for so many long years. He thought of all the time he had spent watching and waiting for just the right moments to play his strategy out, spinning his complex webs of intrigue, patiently searching for the right set of circumstances that would, he had been certain, bring him the openings he needed for the final phases of his plan. It all came down to this one moment in time.

Yet his mind was filled only with the pain he had caused

those who had loved him. He shrank from their sad, floating faces, from their tears, from the unutterable loss of the severing.

Then he thought of his sons. How he longed to see them both, to look at them, to see the sun in their eyes.

Zilin and Zhang Hua sat.

'We are here today,' the Premier began, 'to hear charges of the most serious nature, which are being brought against one of our most respected senior ministers.'

Out of the corner of his eye, Zilin saw the slight smirk spreading across Wu Aiping's face. This is the moment, he thought, that my enemy has been waiting for since he insinuated himself into the *qun*.

'Wu Aiping,' the Premier said solemnly, 'please stand and face me.'

'With pleasure, Comrade Premier.' The man rose to his full, imposing height. Clasped in his left hand was a sheaf of papers. The incriminating evidence, I shouldn't wonder, Zilin thought.

'Shi Zilin,' the Premier said, turning his round head slightly, 'due to your advanced years, I will not require you to stand during this hearing.'

'That is quite all right, sir.' Zilin took Zhang Hua's hand in his, felt the other man's strength levering him to his feet. 'I am quite capable. I am not yet an invalid.'

The Premier nodded. He fixed his attention on a middle ground between the two. 'Last night I received, by special courier, a set of documents.' He ruffled some papers. 'I have them here with me now, having spent all night with my advisors cross-checking their validity.'

Wu Aiping could not suppress the glint of triumph in his eyes. 'You found everything in order, I trust, Comrade Premier.'

'Indeed I did.'

Wu Aiping nodded. 'Any additional questions you may have can be answered by Shi Zilin's aide, Zhang Hua.' He turned his head so that he could gaze upon Zilin when he said this last. 'Zhang Hua has been in my employ for the past months.'

'Zhang Hua,' the Premier said heavily, 'will you affirm this statement?'

Zilin had not moved at all. At Wu Aiping's pronouncement, he had evinced no outward reaction. This, at least, had angered Wu Aiping, who, in delicious anticipation, had longed to see his hated enemy squirm beneath the blade of the knife he had prepared for him.

However, when Zhang Hua struggled to his feet, it was the supposedly infirm Zilin who steadied him with a hand and forearm which, when the lesser minister grasped them, communicated great warmth and power.

Zhang Hua straightened himself and, gaining courage from the old man next to him, said in a clear, firm voice, 'I deny the allegation, sir.'

'What!' Wu Aiping took a step towards him, but was frozen in place by a gesture from the Premier.

'Please explain this, Shi *tong zhi*,' the Premier said.

'I will do my best, sir.' Zilin took a deep breath. 'I had suspected for some time that a group of ministers whose radical philosophy was antithetical both to mine and to that of the current regime was gaining in power. When it became known to me that Wu Aiping had become the head of this group, I determined to set about trapping him and exposing the entire *qun* once and for all.

'To that end, I used my assistant. With his consent, I set him up in a clandestine and quite illicit sexual liaison. This was extremely difficult for Minister Zhang Hua, since such an indiscretion is not in his nature, and further, the secrecy of the operation obliged us to keep the truth even from the members of his family.

'It was a dangerous ploy, but it worked. Wu Aiping, searching for a way to infiltrate my office, discovered the false liaison and, using photographs, commenced to blackmail Zhang Hua into delivering to him information of the most sensitive nature.

'Naturally, Comrade Premier, Wu Aiping was delivered only information I wished him to have.'

Wu Aiping was white with rage. 'I will no longer stand by and listen to this!' he cried. 'These lies are a mockery of — '

'Silence!' roared the Premier. He loved using a voice that, for the most part at least, was soft and pleasingly modulated, as another occasional manifestation of his ultimate power. He leaned forward so that his tunic-clad chest pressed against the high wooden banc. 'Do not dare speak out of turn, Comrade Minister. Not with these confirmations I have here in my fist of the embezzlement of funds for which you must hold yourself and your so-called *qun* accountable!'

'But, Comrade Premier, that is easily explained,' Wu Aiping said with a touch of desperation in his voice. 'You see, the money I borrowed from my ministry has been funnelled into the Hong Kong firm of Five Star Pacific.'

'Oh, I know, Wu Aiping,' the Premier said. 'I know all about you and Five Star Pacific.' The tone of his voice chilled Wu Aiping's blood. He knew at that moment that his life had become worthless. But how? *How?*

'The documents I and my staff pored over so assiduously last night were not your poor excuse for evidence, but an entire dossier compiled by Shi *tong zhi* and Zhang *tong zhi*. They show conclusively your involvement with Five Star Pacific, a company which has for some time been infiltrated by Sir John Bluestone, who, through Shi Zilin's diligence, we have discovered to be the KGB's highest-ranking agent in that part of Asia.'

'The *Soviets?*' Wu Aiping said in a strangled voice. 'But this is impossible! The *faan gwai loh* is Shi Zilin's agent; he is deeply involved in Five Star Pacific.'

'On the contrary, Wu *tong zhi*,' the Premier said with

finality, 'it is you and your compatriots who are involved in the company controlled by the Soviets. Twelve million American dollars deep. Can you deny making these money-draft transfers?'

'No, but – '

'Do you deny that your plot against Shi *tong zhi* was to be the first step in the furtherance of your own power within this government?'

'With all respect, I reject the notion – '

'You will answer this court truthfully, Wu *tong zhi*, or suffer the consequences.'

'My loyalty is beyond reproach. I must protest – '

'Do not speak to this court of loyalty! You are hereby stripped of all rights and privileges. Furthermore, you are remanded to the political prosecution detention centre pending further action.'

'This is all a terrible mistake, Comrade Premier. You have been traduced.'

'Almost, Wu *tong zhi*, almost. But through Shi *tong zhi* and Zhang *tong zhi*'s diligence, you have been trapped within your own game.'

At that moment, Zhang Hua, who, during this discursive and highly charged interchange, had been trembling more and more, gave a little cry. With a convulsive shudder, he broke away from Zilin's clandestine hold and pitched forward onto his face.

'Ah, Buddha!' Zilin breathed. With difficulty, he got down on his knees, though the pain was excruciating.

'Zhang Hua,' he called. 'Zhang Hua!'

The Premier signed to his guards, who rushed to aid the stricken minister. In a moment the Premier's personal doctor hurried into the hall. He knelt beside Zhang Hua's immobile body, turning him over with such care that Zilin began to weep. Until the moment of his death, Zilin would remember this instant with crystal clarity, the unknown

628

doctor's gentle hands turning Zhang Hua so that his ashen face was raised towards the ceiling high above.

His mind told him that this was *joss*, bad *joss* for them both. But his heart cried out in anguish. What matter his moment of ultimate triumph over the *qun*, after eleven years? It was meaningless now that Zhang Hua was not here to share it with him. Zhang Hua, who had known his duty and had turned his life inside out for Zilin.

Is this a hero's end? Zilin asked himself.

He felt the loss of his long-time friend with the same acuteness as that with which he would feel the amputation of a leg. He was a true cripple now. Perhaps, in a way, he had been a cripple all his life.

He did not know where to begin in attempting to encompass this well of sadness. Rushing back at him were not merely the years spent in the company of this man, but the moments when he gave up Athena, Jake, Sheng Li, and the infant who had become Nichiren.

The grief was too much for him to bear. His head bowed beneath the weight and his heart felt like lead, throbbing in his chest like a wound that would not heal.

Joss, he thought. *Joss*.

And then, I must not let this happen to my sons.

'I'm afraid there is nothing I can do,' the doctor said to the Premier a moment later, needlessly confirming what Zilin had felt the moment Zhang Hua pitched away from him. The doctor stood before the Premier like a prisoner in the dock. 'His heart simply ceased to beat. I suspect a massive myocardial infarction, but without an autopsy there's really no way to be certain.'

The Premier gestured to his guards. 'Come and take Wu *tong zhi* away,' he said. 'The look on his face is unsettling my stomach.'

Dazedly, Wu Aiping allowed himself to be led out of the room. He said nothing. His eyes were glazed.

Now the Premier climbed down from his banc. He was a

629

tiny man, smaller by far than the wizened Zilin. He stood very close to his senior minister. His old eyes watched as Zilin held Zhang Hua's head in his lap.

At last he bent down, helped Zilin to his feet. 'Come,' he said. His voice was now as soft as velvet. 'Come with me.'

Behind their backs, Zhang Hua was taken away in a litter. 'The loss is great, my friend, I know,' he said softly. 'But it is tempered by the knowledge of your success. The other members of the *qun* are being rounded up now. As to the Party Chief and the Defence Minister, warrants are being drawn up now. We have to be circumspect with them, still. The amount of power they have been amassing is extraordinary.

'Until I myself read through the evidence that you and your office clandestinely accumulated, I would never have believed that these people – this *qun* – could have such deep-rooted strength.'

'They rose on mighty wings to power heretofore unimaginable.'

The Premier nodded at Zilin's use of his own words at their previous meeting. 'Modern-day Boxers, yes. They were bent on the destruction of this regime. You were correct in that also. We needed your plan to trap them, to get down through all the layers of deceit. The *qun* was composed of many more comrades than I thought possible.

'Once again, I owe you my life. How many times must you save this unworthy self before you are satisfied?'

'It is my job to be your stalking horse, Comrade Premier,' Zilin said. 'Those who would seek to destroy you have in me an implacable enemy. They expend all their energy on bringing me down.'

'All roads in Beijing lead through Shi Zilin.' The Premier touched his long-time friend on the shoulder. 'It has been so, I suppose, for longer than we both care to remember, old friend, *heya*? We all have sacrifices to make.'

'I fear that this time the price has been far too high.'

'We will do what we can. Zhang Hua will be remembered as a Hero of the Revolution in a public ceremony. His eldest son will receive the medal that – '

'Comrade Premier, with all due respect, I beg of you, no ceremonies. Allow the dead to remain at rest.'

'Shi Zilin, the country should know.'

'*We* know, Comrade Premier. Perhaps that is too much already.'

They were at the far end of the Hall of Supreme Harmony now. Windows rose above their heads, long and narrow, like crystal swords.

'How is your pain?'

Zilin shrugged. What was the point of answering?

The grey rain beat against the windows, desperate to be heard.

'Only the elements remain, in the end,' the Premier said. 'So Buddha tells us.'

'What place has Buddha in our modern state?'

The Premier smiled slowly. 'It is Buddha who has sustained you all these long years, Shi Zilin, has he not?' It was a rhetorical question, and Zilin had better sense than to say a word. 'Did you think I was ignorant of your climbs into the Temple of the Sleeping Buddha? Or of your hours of meditation there?'

'It is antithetical,' Zilin said.

'*You* are antithetical, Shi Zilin, if the truth be told.' The Premier put his hands behind his back, clasping them loosely. 'I must confess that I envy you that – what shall we call it? – that perfect peace your meditations at Wofosi bring you.'

'Not perfect.' Zilin shook his head. 'Without my sons, now I cannot feel even a semblance of peace.'

'What can be done?'

'I must go to Hong Kong.'

There was a great silence between them, then, that the rain attempted to fill up with its anarchic drumming.

'Did you plan this all the time?'

Zilin gave a wan, ironic smile. 'Some things, Comrade Premier, even I cannot plan.'

'Then you will go. What then?' the Premier asked. 'You know it cannot end there.'

'It can, if Buddha wills it.'

They were out of all sight, enwrapped by the mist of the ages. It clung to them like tiny spectral hands. In China, the past had a way of remaining very much alive.

'And if he does not?'

'You know the rest,' Zilin said. 'I shall not return to Beijing.'

Somewhere, it seemed, the spirits of all the ancestors were crying out as one. 'Whatever am I going to do without you?' the Premier said. His voice was muffled by the mist, or, perhaps, by the spirits' calling.

'The wind will still ride the mountains; the Yellow River will still ebb and flow.'

'What will China do without your guidance? We are still children here, despite – or more accurately, *because of* – how passionately we cleave to the notion that we are the only truly civilized nation on earth.'

'We have been bloodthirsty in the pursuit of our civilization.'

'We have only done what we thought most prudent.'

'That, I believe,' Zilin said, 'is the most telling indictment of our political system.'

'Perhaps,' the Premier said distantly. 'Perhaps.'

Zilin felt tired. And he had not yet begun his journey. 'Yuri Lantin, our great enemy, is gone. And General Karpov, the mastermind of Moonstone, as well.'

The Premier was shaking his head. 'You were right about Daniella Vorkuta all along. I must admit to having doubts about your plan, Shi Zilin. I myself find the personalities of *faan gwai loh* impenetrable. I cannot fathom how you understand them. And besides, she is a woman.'

'As Laotse taught me, Premier, I use each person in accordance with his or her talents. There is no such thing as a useless individual. I spent over a decade studying the lines of power within and without the Soviet spy apparatus known as the KGB. It was my desire from the first to allow them to do for us that of which we ourselves were incapable.

'Towards that end, I studied my files. I came upon Daniella Vorkuta. Her unique mind, coupled with the circumstances of her advancement – that is, that she was a woman – gave me the germ of the idea.'

'I am still at a loss to see how you could create the situation of the killing ground for Anatoly Karpov and Yuri Lantin.' He had some difficulty with the foreign names.

'In this case, I created nothing. I merely saw a latent pattern among them and, with a certain amount of doctored intelligence funnelled in to Daniella Vorkuta, set that pattern into motion. The kernel was always there, waiting to be let loose. I thank Buddha that General Vorkuta possessed the strength of spirit and the consuming ambition that I saw nesting inside her. She acted, yes, she acted. I had nothing to do with that. I merely set her upon the stage.'

'But only you, Shi Zilin, could see the way to the killing ground. You have created victory out of the very ether around us. I understand now why it is known as "stealing the light".'

'I did only my duty, Comrade Premier,' Zilin said softly. His mind was on the loss of Zhang Hua, and this praise was, he felt, unseemly.

'You have made the Tao powerful once again,' the Premier said. 'I am most grateful. With Moonstone hanging like a sword over us, it was impossible to move against the *qun* outright. It had given them much added support. I am relieved that that particular threat is ended.'

633

'Perhaps one day we shall have to be as afraid of Daniella Vorkuta as we were of the two men,' Zilin said. 'Though I have convinced her that the way to undermine us is through Hong Kong, and though we control her through her Hong Kong network, one can never tell what power will do to the soul of even the hardiest individual.

'But soon we will have Kam Sang. Its dangerous secret is safe for the time being. Soon, I think, we shall have to allow our allies and our enemies a glimpse into what we have created in Kam Sang. But we must always remember with the utmost clarity our bloodthirsty past. The purpose of Kam Sang, after all, is to have it, not to use it.

'In that respect, Yuri Lantin and Wu Aiping were cut from the same cloth. They both wished to goad us into a conflagration, the one to prove our inferiority, the other to prove our superiority.

'You and I know that China's future lies down another path; through Hong Kong. It is the only way for us. Now I must be off, Comrade Premier.'

The other man came out of his thoughts. 'Of course. How unthinking of me.' He took Zilin by the arm. 'I will hear from you at journey's end.'

Zilin looked into the Premier's eyes. 'Either from me or from them.'

'Do you really think that's wise?'

In the end, the Premier looked away from that magnetic gaze. He felt humbled by the old man's power. His voice echoed in that vast, ancient hall, though it was only the two of them who could hear it.

'I accept your judgment, Jian.'

Jake and Bliss were on a vigil outside the factory that manufactured *samurai* warriors. He hadn't spoken in more than two hours, and Bliss was becoming concerned.

'I don't even know what we're doing here,' she said.

Jake said nothing, but continued to stare at the factory

entrance. After he had left Formidable Sung, he had taken a close look at every point of the building's exterior. Because of its position, wedged between other such structures, there was no possible egress other than the one Jake had used. Even the back of the factory abutted the windowless wall of a warehouse in the next street. Above it was a solid block of doll-sized apartments.

'Jake?'

Three of the young girls were leaving. Their hair, free of the cotton bands, shone in the streetlights.

'Jake, what's the matter with you?'

'Why didn't you tell me your father was Three Oaths Tsun?'

'Because, first, you never asked, and second, he's not my real father. He adopted me when I was very young. I never knew my real father or mother. Three Oaths Tsun told me that I was born in Burma, while my mother was on her journey south from the Mainland.'

Her head turned and she watched his profile, so strong and powerful. 'Why? Is it important?'

'I would think so,' he said distantly, 'since Three Oaths Tsun is the dragon of the *yuhn-hyun*.'

Bliss seemed startled, and for the first time he divided his attention between the entranceway and her face. 'Who told you that?' she asked.

'Formidable Sung.'

'He's wrong.'

'Really?'

She felt the tension building uncomfortably, and turned her head away. 'Let's not talk like this,' she said softly. 'It disturbs me.'

'I'm sorry about that,' Jake said with a hint of sarcasm, 'but think how I feel. You promised to tell me everything. You've told me nothing.'

'I learned nothing from David Oh,' she told him simply.

'All he said was *huo yan*. I don't know what that means, and neither do you. It may mean nothing at all.'

'I didn't guarantee that you'd learn anything from him when I allowed you to go to the rdv.' Jake was very angry now, and it was all Bliss could do not to show her fear of his rising intrinsic energy. She felt as if she were out in the open, facing the onset of a typhoon.

'You weren't ready to know – ' She stopped abruptly, aware of how wrong her words were. She thought, Ah, Buddha, I've done it now.

Jake's face was dark with rage, and now Bliss felt her heart shrivel beneath this onslaught.

'*I wasn't ready?* Who makes that decision? Your father? The dragon of the *yuhn-hyun?*'

Bliss knew that she had absolutely no choice now. Not if she wanted to keep the lid on this thing a moment longer.

'Yes. The dragon of the *yuhn-hyun,*' she said. 'But he isn't my father.'

'You'd better tell me who he is, then.'

Bliss took a deep breath. 'He's your father, Jake. Shi Zilin.'

Her words rang in his head. But in their iteration they lost all meaning.

In the stunned silence, Jake almost missed Formidable Sung. The 489 was emerging from the factory's entrance along with three of the triad.

'My father . . .'

'Why are we here, Jake?'

'My father is alive? But how? Why hasn't he contacted me to let me know?'

'He's Shi Zilin, Jake. Shi Zilin. What do you think it would have done to your career had the Quarry known that one of the most senior ministers in Beijing was your father?'

'Buddha, he's alive!'

Jake felt elation, fear, and apprehension all struggling

636

for supremacy in his mind. His father, alive! For so long he had been utterly alone in life. In a sense, he saw now, he had made himself that way, turning away from the women who loved him. Why? Was it an insane form of atonement for having been left an orphan whom the Marocs, out of pure human kindness, had taken in and loved until the moment of their deaths? Did he think that this statelessness, this limbo in which he had no family ties, was his *joss*, that he could do nothing to overcome it?

At this moment he felt the *fu* shard like a living coal against his thigh. Nichiren's piece, but from the same source. That link, he felt certain, was what had brought his father back from the dead.

My father, my father, my father. He even loved the sound the words made in his mind. They played a melody there of his own invention.

His father. One of the senior ministers in Beijing. Did that make him friend or foe? Just as important, what did that make Jake? Bliss was part of the *yuhn-hyun*. So, she said, was he. What did that make him? Wasn't it obvious that the *yuhn-hyun* was a Communist Chinese operation? And that he had been an unwitting part of it? For how long? he wondered.

It was incredible, really. He and Nichiren, mortal enemies locked in a global chase, were, unwittingly or not, working within the same operation, on the same side. And that side was the Communist Chinese!

What have I become? Jake asked himself. Merely a piece in a gigantic game of *wei qi*. And Mariana, David Oh. What did they die for? Have I any real idea?

He realized that he did not.

'Formidable Sung.'

Jake snapped out of his shock. 'What?'

'Is Formidable Sung why we've been on this vigil?'

Jake followed her glance, saw the 489 and his guard. He nodded. 'He's the reason,' he said.

He began to move, Bliss with him, as constant as a shadow. 'Formidable Sung's going to lead me right to Nichiren.'

Because of the incident at Lantin's, Daniella had failed to make two successive telephone rdvs with Chimera. Following the incident, she had been too busy poring over Lantin's cache of documents to think of anything else. Only questions from the brace of bloodhounds assigned to the investigation of Comrade Lantin's death interrupted her. They had found the note she had typewritten on Lantin's machine, outlining the precipitous decline of General Anatoly Karpov's state of mental health; how Operation Moonstone had been created by someone who, in effect, was already a madman; how Lantin had been gulled by the madman and how much it had cost the Soviet Union.

'Only now,' the note ended, 'do I understand that Moonstone put us a mere heartbeat away from a nuclear war. I cannot live with that knowledge.'

Daniella had adorned the bottom of the sheet with an excellent forgery of Lantin's signature.

That was that. The bloodhounds were idiots, which hardly surprised her. But even if they had been as canny as Lantin himself, there would never have been any suspicion cast on her. The neatness of the package she had presented to them had drawn them to the proper – if false – conclusions, as a flame will a moth. It appealed to their anal-retentive minds. Bureaucrats.

As for the dossiers, she was astonished not by the plethora of minor and not-so-minor peccadillos of Moscow's elite ministers, but that Yuri Lantin had managed to amass so much physical evidence on all of them.

The nature of his power base had become clear to her at once, and she had lost little time in establishing herself in the breach left by both Lantin and Karpov. Considering her skills and the fortune in intelligence she had filched from Lantin's apartment, it was not particularly difficult.

It merely meant that several days went by before she had a chance to reestablish communications with Chimera. When she did, it made her sorry that she had been so wrapped up in her internal affairs for that long.

What he had for her was the most promising intelligence yet. Kam Sang's secret, it appeared, was not the water desalinization plant encompassed within it.

'It is military in nature,' Chimera's electronic voice buzzed in her ear. 'And certainly inimical to us. Its secret should be breached as soon as is practicable.'

Yes, Daniella thought, breaking the connection well before the ninety-second limit, it will be breached. But for that we have time now.

In bed, hours later, she closed her eyes and sighed deeply. Now she was doubly relieved at Lantin's death. That insane Moonstone operation was her first order of business. Tomorrow morning it would be closed down, as would the puppet war the Vietnamese were waging with the Chinese.

I was right all along, she told herself. Hong Kong is the key; it always has been. Now I'm right inside the Colony. Just where I want to be.

She thought of the danger lurking like a dark-eyed adder within the heart of Kam Sang, and shuddered. What Lantin and Karpov had almost unleashed on the world, no one would know but she. The unknown weapon within Kam Sang was still asleep.

Daniella determined that whatever it turned out to be, it would sleep for all time.

The oily water lapped drowsily against the wooden pilings. Fittings creaked aboard the floating city of the Hakka. Just beyond the conglomeration of junks, the crimson, yellow, and emerald lights of Jumbo spangled the water. The last of the motor launches was bringing the late-night revellers back from its bejewelled decks.

Three Oaths Tsun was up near the bow of his junk. He had just mounted the companionway from the cabin belowdecks where he had finished making love with Neon Chow. She had wanted him to stay by her slick, sticky side, melded by the heat of sex. He had complied up to a point, feeling her thigh heavy across his knee, until her breathing had slowed and deepened rhythmically. While she slept, he left her.

Turning his eyes to the stern, he could see three or four of his children talking in low tones while they strung lines and rewebbed the thick trolling nets.

They are good children, he thought as he watched them. I do not want to lose even one. He turned his head quickly away, so that only the water could see. By the spirit of the White Tiger, that does not make me a selfish man. Just a loving one.

He heard a movement and simultaneously felt the minute change in the motion of the junk as someone came aboard. He looked around, saw the shadow approach. He did not need illumination to recognize the walk.

'Dangerous to be here like this,' he said when the figure was close enough.

'On the eve of the summit, I knew you could not meet me in our assigned place.'

'He is coming,' Three Oaths Tsun said. 'After all these years, he is leaving Beijing.'

'Our brother,' the other man said. 'It is almost impossible to believe.'

'Tomorrow there will be an ending of the *yuhn-hyun* as we have come to know it over the years.'

The figure moved slightly, so that the coloured lights from Jumbo picked out several of his features. 'That means all the *fu* pieces will come together at last,' T. Y. Chung said. 'There will be no more need for this business war we created.'

'We have spent fifty years in the pursuit of this ruse,' Three Oaths Tsun said passionately. 'This war was necessary so that the other *tai pan* should not suspect us of collusion. I could never have been able to begin Pak Hanmin otherwise; and Sir John Bluestone would never have become your partner. We never would have been able to purchase so many companies: Tang Shan *godowns*, Donelly and Tung's tankers, Southchina Electronics, Fan Man Metalworks. While everyone was centred on our feud, we acquired all the outside resources we needed for our part of the *yuhn-hyun*.

'Now the only question to be answered is what will happen when the *fu* pieces are united. Even I do not know the answer to that. It is obvious that the *yuhn-hyun* is not yet complete.'

'Who owns the fourth piece of the *fu*?'

'Until tomorrow, it is Elder Brother's secret. But it is already clear that we need all four pieces or we have nothing.'

T. Y. Chung looked out to sea. His face was filled with sadness. 'Nothing,' he echoed his brother, 'is what we may yet end up with. And in the meantime, look what the *yuhn-hyun* has done to us. Two brothers, never able to acknowledge our kinship, let alone share our lives and our families.

'Instead you put your adopted daughter in the gravest danger, and I have to spend my evenings with that viper, dunghill Bluestone.'

Three Oaths Tsun sighed. 'If we did not know the meaning of duty, my brother, we would be nothing better than the barbarian *gwai loh*.'

T. Y. Chung turned his head, spat heavily over the side. 'Then I must tell you that there are times when I hate being civilized.'

'We should feel only elation now that our Elder Brother has defeated his enemies in Beijing. It means the *yuhn-hyun* will work. You and I and everyone in Hong Kong must pray that it does work, because otherwise the Colony is doomed, despite this fifty-year respite that Elder Brother rammed through. The battle is not yet over. I am certain that there are others in the north who wish to see our Fragrant Harbour subsumed by communism.'

T. Y. Chung came and stood beside his brother. Their shoulders brushed as if by accident. 'We must guard him well here from both the dragons and the fornicating authorities. If his identity were to become known to either, it would mean the destruction of everything for which we have worked for half a lifetime.

'His protection is paramount. Our Elder Brother is an ikon. He is jade itself. Perhaps, as you have said, not a man at all. I think that he has made himself over the years what he believed himself to be as a child: a Celestial Guardian of China.'

At the head of the companionway, Neon Chow held her enormous excitement in check. When she had crept, scarcely daring to breathe, up the companionway just after Three Oaths Tsun, she had wondered what T. Y. Chung, Three Oaths Tsun's bitter rival, was doing here. Now she knew.

Dew neh loh moh, she thought. Who would have suspected that Three Oaths Tsun and T. Y. Chung were brothers? Buddha, what fantastic knowledge this is!

Three hours before, when Peter Ng had failed to make his rendezvous with Sir John Bluestone, she had been called into service. As Daniella had told Yuri Lantin, her networks had backup measures built into them.

Neon Chow remembered back several weeks to the first coded message she had sent off. As she had been instructed, she had used the blind postal box drop the morning after dialling the local number she had memorized.

Months ago she had overheard Three Oaths Tsun and Bliss talking about the *fu*. Neon Chow knew what a *fu* was, she just could not fathom its significance in the modern-day world. Less than a week later she had observed Three Oaths Tsun slip off the junk and, via a tiny tender, climb aboard a lorcha.

She withheld her excitement and was patient. She had discovered his routine: twice a week on nights when the moon was down or obscured by clouds. In making her decision to follow him, Neon Chow knew that she dared not attempt such a dangerous action more than once.

She had seen the long-range transceiver and had heard every word Three Oaths Tsun spoke in Mandarin. There were few dialects Neon Chow could not understand; that was part of her worth as an agent.

The *fu*. Three Oaths Tsun and the unknown contact spoke of the *fu*. They spoke of power. Power that could encircle Hong Kong like a ring and bring to him who held the whole *fu* incalculable wealth.

That night she had made her call and spoken the one word, 'Mitre', into the mouthpiece. The next morning her report was in the post box.

Neon Chow was in a faceless, essentially contactless world. She often wondered whether her report had been acted on. Once or twice, when she was feeling particularly depressed, she wondered whether it had even been read. There was no way for her to know whether what she had discovered was important or trivial.

This was one of the oddities of her world.

It was hard to do nothing but watch. He had been doing that for so long now. Eight hours ago it had been evening, and he and Bliss had been at the plastic *samurai* factory.

Using a rental car, they had followed Formidable Sung and his retinue to the 489's villa along the Peak Gap Road. The centre of Hong Kong, midway between Central

District and Aberdeen. Perched high in the territory of the predatory kites, large black flesh-eaters that swung through the evening skies in ever-decreasing spirals.

No one had gone inside after Formidable Sung had settled in for the night. No one had come out. That was unusual. The triad dragon liked the Colony's nightlife.

When Jake had told this to Bliss, she had said, 'Something's up.'

'Something like that triad summit.'

Bliss shook her head. 'They'll kill each other.'

'Unless Nichiren gives them a compelling enough reason not to.'

'But why would they even listen to him? He's Japanese. There's a natural enmity there.'

Jake recalled Mikio's files, which showed that Nichiren had emigrated to Japan with his mother when he was less than a year old. Where had he come from? Why *would* Chinese listen to him? Unless . . .

'What if Nichiren's Chinese?'

Bliss had stared at him. 'What?'

'That's the only way it makes sense, this triad summit.'

'I thought his mother was Japanese.'

'She was,' Jake said thoughtfully. 'But who knows if she was his real mother. Besides, even if she was, his father could have been Chinese.'

'He's not Japanese, not Chinese, either. They would hate him even more then.'

'Not necessarily. He's part of the *yuhn-hyun*, so we must assume that he's being run by the Communist Chinese, not the Russians. He's being doubled, and quite cleverly so.

'Somehow, I don't think my father would want the triad dragons to get wind of where the power of the *yuhn-hyun* ultimately lies. Formidable Sung himself believes that Three Oaths Tsun is the ring's dragon. I think it's safe to assume that the rest of the dragons have the same notion.

'Nichiren's involvement continues the ruse, but adding an international skew to it. How do you think they'd react to knowing that perhaps the single most important Soviet agent is secretly in league with them?'

'It'd be a great incentive to go in,' Bliss admitted, 'despite their bickering.'

'Exactly.' Jake thought a moment. 'Who else is involved in the *yuhn-hyun?*'

'I don't know.'

Jake looked hard into her eyes. 'Is that the truth?'

'Yes.'

'All right.'

Above their heads, a cloud, luminescent with moonlight, pierced the utter darkness of the heavens. But for a lack of discernible eyes, it might have been a coiled dragon.

'Jake,' she said, 'each day we're together, there must be a thousand things I feel we've forgotten to say to each other. Time goes by so swiftly. When I look at you sometimes, I see a man with his hands tied behind his back. Does that make any sense to you?'

He said nothing, staring out into the night. But Bliss felt a subtle stirring within him. If only she could get him to spew out the poison that had been inside him for so long. What was the dark secret he felt unable to share with anyone?

He will destroy himself one of these days. The thought came upon Bliss with breathtaking suddenness. She knew that she must deflect him somehow. She remembered a poem that Fo Saan had often spoken when she could not articulate what was troubling her. She wondered whether he had done so with Jake. To see, she spoke it now.

'"Down the well – echoing a plover's cry. That is all."'

Jake settled himself into their rock niche. 'I remember that,' he said quietly. 'It's been a long time since I recalled its meaning.' Bliss felt the softening inside him as keenly as if it were her own emotion. She said not a word.

At last, when Jake felt the core of him re-forming in the centre of his beating heart, he began. 'You know that I have been married twice. The first time, I was very young. In those days, as in the following ones, the Quarry came first. But Ting was even younger than I. She could understand everything but why I was never with her.

'Marriage makes no sense for the young, I have learned. When one is still searching for the key to oneself, it is no time to take on the responsibility for another life. Or lives.'

Here Jake paused, passing his tongue across his dry lips. His mouth felt full of cotton. He continued to force himself into deep, even breathing.

'Those were foolish days for me, Bliss. I wanted it all: a wife, a family, a life inside the Quarry. It was an impossibility.

'Ting was Chiu-chow, but she was well versed in the ways of the *gwai loh*. We had a daughter. As Lan grew, so did the rifts between myself and my wife. We were both in the grip of growing pains. Especially me.

'Naturally, Lan was affected by our quarrels, the friction between us. She did not – *could* not – understand that my absences were not actually directed at her.

'In any event, she became rebellious. Unhappy at home, she fled. This was in Hong Kong, of course. She reached out and found the anarchic wildness I had possessed as a child. She made it her own.

'The triads would not have her. They laughed at her. She was only twelve. She was female. And she was half *gwai loh*. Thus she was forced farther afield.

'Three years ago I was sent on a highly classified mission. My destination was a tiny village on the Sumchun River. Something went wrong, terribly wrong. Perhaps we were traduced. There was a pitched battle. It was like a war. In microcosm.' The closer Jake came to the heart of it, the shorter and choppier his sentences became. His breath felt hot and he had begun to sweat profusely.

'In the midst of it, I knew. Operations mounted against us all have a different feel. Depending on who has devised them. Like a fingerprint. In code signalling, it's called a "fist".

'It dawned on me that a master had planned the defence. A strategist. It had about it the precision of a *wei qi* endgame.

'You must understand that our attack was like lightning. The counterattack was the same. We were unprepared for that strategy. It unnerved some of the men under me. It hampered their effectiveness. We were being defeated. And defeat, of course, meant death.

'There was blood all around, seeping into the ground, soaking the heavy foliage, floating out into the muddy middle of the Sumchun River.

'Nichiren was there, directing the opposition as if he were placing his pieces onto the *wei qi* board. Yet he did not hold himself aloof. He killed two of my men. It appeared as if it was going to be a rout.

'Then I became aware of another element entering the battle. Chinese. I recognized some of them as a highly radical splinter triad who worked the border, bringing people out from Communist China.'

Jake swallowed. His eyes watched Bliss's with a kind of manic intensity. 'I suppose I was looking at her for some time before I knew who she really was. She had changed so much. And yet. She was still my little girl. My Lan.'

For a long time, then, there was silence. Jake was lost within the chaotic litter of his own thoughts as he saw it reproduced across Bliss's beautiful face. He did not begin again until Bliss stirred, refocusing him.

'I watched as she slit the throat of one of Nichiren's men.' When it resumed, Jake's voice had taken on an odd, detached quality. 'She did it with great skill, with the kind of animal fierceness a lioness shows when her cubs are threatened. I could tell there was no real pleasure in it for her. Just duty. It was something she believed in. Something neither her mother nor I could give to her.

'And in the next moment, blood flew from her. She twisted like a reed in the wind. Bullets broke her. Tore through her flesh.

'Nichiren ran from what he had done. And I. Ran after him.

'Not very far, of course. The jungle had swallowed him whole. When I returned, my dead daughter was gone, taken by her triad cohorts.'

Bliss stared unblinking at Jake for a time.

At length he closed his eyes. With the moonlight filling his eyelids with phosphorescence, it seemed as though he were still watching her.

The Taiwanese was in a lousy mood. His brother had been drowned in the indoor pool at Morrison Hill two days ago, the bomb he had set in Macao had failed to terminate his target, and to top it all off, he had been crouched here like a bear for more than eight hours, awaiting his chance.

He put the infrared nightscope up to his right eye and peered through it again. Bliss's head, then Jake's, came into focus. Stupid of the man, he thought, to take a woman into a situation like this. No wonder he was going to die.

The Taiwanese had traced them through the rental-car firm they had used. As easy as falling off a log. He should have been home by now. In Taipei he had a blind girl named Mo who could make him come just by walking across his naked back with her bare feet. She was other-worldly, that one, he thought now. He missed her. He had not had sex since he had taken on this assignment, and his testicles were tender, hard with their load. The Taiwanese thought that he would take the Chinese woman after he had terminated his target. She would not be as good as Mo, but she would have to do.

That was all right. The Taiwanese was aware that the

smell of blood increased his ardour during sex. He'd make certain there was some of that when he took this woman. That would make up for the fact that he was not home with Mo. At least she wasn't Occidental. Occidental women set his teeth on edge.

The Taiwanese shifted slightly and he felt his testicles weighing heavy between his legs. He took another look at the girl through the scope. It was attached to the Lyson TY-6000 submachine pistol. It was rather a new toy for him. He had been using the Swedish Kulspruta because he knew it to be the most powerful submachine gun in the world. That was before his new masters had introduced him to the Lyson. It shot eight hundred and fifty rounds per minute of the kind of ammunition he liked best: Parabellum.

The Taiwanese thought about his instructions: shoot on sight. But that was before his brother had been held underwater to drown. His target was fully in the cross-hairs now, illuminated in ghostly fashion by the infrared. All he needed to do was squeeze the trigger, and inside of three seconds there would be nothing of the man and the woman but twin smears across the rocks. So easy to do.

But the Taiwanese would never consider such a thing. Not now. He was a black belt in *tae kwon do*. The man in his sights had killed his brother. There was a matter of honour to be avenged now. It was a matter between men, face to face. It had nothing at all to do with eight hundred and fifty rounds of Parabellum ammunition a minute.

The Taiwanese set the Lyson aside. He slid off the rock on which he had been crouching.

This time Jake felt the approach. He had been deep in *chahm hai*, sinking into his surroundings. He had become part of the humid night, filled with drifting cloud, cicadas buzzing, nocturnal animals prowling, the night wind through the trees.

649

Fo Saan had taught him to do more than listen to the night. He had instructed Jake on how to become one with it.

Consequently, Jake felt the Taiwanese's approach. To his heightened senses it was as if a dark, inimical tunnel had appeared – a blackness deeper than the night.

He turned. But he was obliged to climb over the rock face he had carefully put at their backs. At this time of the night, it was slippery with dew. He lost fractions of a second. In that brief span of time he heard the slight whirring and, rather than protect himself, kicked back at the startled Bliss as she rose, knocking her off her feet and out of harm's way.

Jake knew a *nunchaku* when he heard it. The weapon had a distinctive sound, a trilling of a diurnal lark, out of character with the night.

His concern for Bliss cost him, and perhaps the Taiwanese had been right about him. It would have been different had he been alone up here among the hawks' nests and the eyries of the wealthy.

The working end of the chain-and-metal-bar *nunchaku* struck him across his hip and his entire right side went numb. He fell on his face in the wet grass.

He saw Bliss make a lunge for the shadow, take hold, and bring it down. Faint moonlight, inconstant through the sliding, silent clouds, illuminated the Taiwanese. His flat, shining face was intent on his work. It gave him the appearance of a stone god.

A coldness had invaded Jake's body and he struggled to overcome it. He did not waste time in trying to move. That would have been foolish. He concentrated instead on flushing the numbness from his system.

The Taiwanese was on top of Bliss. Her legs were splayed open beneath him just as if they were coupling. The intensity of their struggle held sexual implications as well. Out in the night, with only the moon and the clouds as mute audience, the sight was surrealistic.

Jake saw Bliss use an *atemi* to the Taiwanese's liver. He rolled half off her, at the same time striking upwards with his knee. Bliss, still partially pinned beneath him, could not avoid that blow to her pelvic bone. Jake heard her moan.

The Taiwanese took the initiative immediately, raining a series of percussion strikes across her chest and abdomen with his knuckles. Karate, Jake thought.

It was important now that his concern for Bliss not deflect him from what he had to do. This was not idle time for him. He needed to get a sense of the Taiwanese's style: his strengths and weaknesses, his spirit.

Feeling in his extremities was coming back. He concentrated on his breathing, slowing and deepening it all the more. It was important to help his system by oxygenating it.

The Taiwanese seemed to want to end his struggle with Bliss quickly. She was more tenacious than he had anticipated. She had seen Jake's incapacitation, knew that it was incumbent on her to delay him long enough for Jake to recover.

As the Taiwanese became more desperate to break away, he stepped up his attack. He was angry that this woman seemed to have the power to keep him here against his will. And it was this anger, perhaps, that saved her. Anger had no place in hand-to-hand combat. Emotion impaired judgments that had to be made at split-second intervals.

He put more effort into his strikes, but they were more erratic and somewhat easier to defend against. He was, of course, unaware of this, and his inability to make a winning blow only increased his anger.

Beneath him, Bliss felt the pain and swelling trebling every few seconds. The Taiwanese was very strong, and he knew his karate. He was hurting her badly, even through every defence she threw at him. Once, Bliss thought she had passed out. She had lost all sense of time, and that was bad. She seemed to be adrift on a sea of agony, as if she had been thrown into a pit of flame. Her nerves screamed at her to stop, to break away. But she thought only of Jake and she kept going, fighting against this powerful foe with all her waning strength.

Jake rolled over. He was barely a metre away. It seemed as if it were a mile. He regained his feet and sucked in the moist air. He was panting like an out-of-shape runner. He thought of what Kamisaka had said to him.

Launched himself at the Taiwanese. Used a double *atemi*, the heels of both clasped hands into the soft flesh above the man's kidneys. The strike went deep. It had all his strength combined with his momentum behind it.

Bliss saw the Taiwanese's face screw up in agony, his teeth draw back from his liver-coloured lips in a terrible grimace. He made no sound at all save an involuntary wheeze as all air escaped him. His hands ceased their attack. He rolled all the way off her, and the release of tension brought spots before her eyes.

The Taiwanese came after Jake. He was unmindful of the pain. He didn't bother to look for the *nunchaku*. His eyes were filled with the image of his brother's bloated face, the eyes dull and filmy with exposure to chlorine.

Jake went into *sumi otoshi*, grabbing the outside of the Taiwanese's extended right arm. As soon as he made contact, he pulled towards him, pivoting to his left as he did so.

This brought the Taiwanese off balance and Jake was able to bring his right arm up above the other's shoulder and, slamming it against the side of his face, pulled sharply down on the right arm. The resultant vectors of force were inescapable. The Taiwanese found himself thrown to the hard ground.

Immediately he kicked out, connecting with Jake's ankle. Jake fell and the Taiwanese struck him in the face.

Blood gushed from Jake's nose, and the Taiwanese brought the edge of his calloused hand down on the point of Jake's shoulder.

Jake collapsed and the Taiwanese, grinning with the onset of the victory adrenaline, scrambled after him. Right into an *atemi* that broke three ribs. The grin froze on his face. His eyes opened wide in astonishment as Jake rose as if from the dead, chopping down with a vicious *atemi* that broke the Taiwanese's neck. He died still thinking that he had won.

At dusk, Formidable Sung emerged from his villa and the tail began.

Jake and Bliss had held each other until long after dawn. Jake was dizzy, wracked with pain. He was astounded to discover that he was more concerned with Bliss's pain.

He had been patient, going over her body inch by inch, assessing the damage. There had been nothing broken, by what miracle he could not imagine, but much of Bliss's extraordinary golden skin was marred by bruises growing darker and more tender by the hour. Burst blood vessels traced themselves like grasping hands across her belly and breasts.

She had sat curled against him, her head against his chest while he made his examination. Her thick, glossy hair fluttered against his neck and chin.

She had made no sound even during his deepest probings around her ribcage, where he knew that the pain must be extreme. Still, he was aware of her deep breathing and knew what she was attempting to dispel.

She had spoken his name after he was finished, as if to assure herself of his closeness. He had kissed her forehead, the tip of her nose, her tender lips. He had been over-whelmed by the relief he felt at her safety.

They stayed like that through most of the cloudy day. Except for the brief times when one or the other rose to urinate into the trees or to stretch their legs, they remained locked together.

They had long since finished the food they had brought with them. They were content to drink the lukewarm water from the canteen by their side. It was odd that Formidable Sung had not gone to the office, that he had gone nowhere at all during the daylight hours.

Twilight had brought an end to their cramped waiting.

The sleek maroon Mercedes 500-SEL wound with great alacrity across the mountainous roads along the centre of the Island. Jake had trouble keeping up in the four-cylinder Nissan, and was grateful that there were few straightaways for the Mercedes, with its powerful V-8, to open up an insurmountable lead.

Now and again he could see Formidable Sung's silhouette in the front of the Mercedes on the passenger's side. The inside light was on, as if the 489 were reading as his driver negotiated the twisting, hairpin turns.

Jake drove the Nissan without lights. That was dangerous, but not as dangerous as alerting Formidable Sung that he was under surveillance.

Darkness crept over the outflung surface of the South China Sea far below their rushing bulk, and here and there a ship's sapphire and ruby running lights burned like living jewels.

The Mercedes raced with almost reckless abandon, as if it were late for a vital rendezvous. The driver was very good, which was fortunate, for these roads, under construction during the day, were a maze of sawhorses, swinging lanterns, and minor detours across dusty shoulders overgrown with wild foliage.

They were climbing the north side of Violet Hill. Just beyond the crest, the Mercedes suddenly went off the road.

Jake slowed, but even so he almost missed the turnoff. It was at a ninety-degree angle from the main road.

It was paved for perhaps a hundred metres. Soon enough it turned into a dirt track, but one that was obviously well used. Jake was crawling along. The dense woods on either side made it seem like the middle of the night.

He stopped the Nissan and, sticking his head out of the open window, listened intently. He could hear no other engine running. He went ahead cautiously, and when he found a gap in the trees, he pulled the Nissan in and shut off the ignition.

They approached on foot. The trees gave way almost immediately. They found themselves next to a villa roofed with azure tiles and set into the side of the cliff that dropped down to Repulse Bay.

Jake took Bliss's hand and they worked their way around to a point where they had a clear view of the front door. A few steps farther on, they caught a glimpse of a wide, wood-beamed veranda built out from the back of the house. It wrapped around the right side of the house, beyond which Jake and Bliss crouched, half-hidden by chrysan-themum and peony bushes. Jake saw that there was easy access to the veranda from a rock promontory not more than a metre from them.

The maroon Mercedes was parked in a gravelled offshoot of the shallow, semicircular driveway. In a moment, lights came on along the front of the villa and across the expanse of the veranda at the back. Jake saw two men come out and stand in the semidarkness.

Then he heard more cars coming, and he took Bliss farther back into the protection of the shadowed bushes.

'It's him!'

The triangular, feline head with its huge obsidian eyes, bobbing like a lethal stalk at the end of his swan's neck.

The small, flat ears barely visible through the long black hair.

Moving along the slate path to the house with the dangerous, liquid grace of a cat loping through the jungle floor.

Nichiren.

Bliss, so close beside Jake, felt the tension flooding through him. Her fingers closed down on the corded muscles of his upper arm.

'Don't!' she whispered fiercely from their place of concealment. 'There are others coming. You've waited too long to jump the gun now.'

Jake knew she was right. But it was not easy to crouch here in the shadows when his nemesis was less than a hundred yards away. A shadow he had been chasing over all the continents of the world for the past three years. With a vengeance, ever since the Sumchun River.

Now, with the last of the crimson and deep yellow light fading from the west, Jake saw Three Oaths Tsun and T. Y. Chung standing side by side on the veranda.

'I don't get it,' Jake said. 'Your father and Chung are bitter enemies.'

'That's what *I* thought,' Bliss said, thinking, How much has my father kept from me?

Off to one side, Formidable Sung and Nichiren were speaking in low tones. A pair of cars drew up. Out stepped Venerable Chen and Sharktooth Tung, the dragon of the Hak Sam triad.

The two stared at one another for several moments. They moved at the same time towards the front door, stopped together. It was a comedy act, despite the circumstances.

At last, Three Oaths Tsun came outside and engaged Venerable Chen in conversation, thus allowing Sharktooth Tung to go in first without loss of face to either man.

In a moment, Three Oaths Tsun took Venerable Chen inside.

'They're all there,' Jake said. It was odd, though. None of them was making a move to begin discussions. There was about the scene an air of waiting.

Bliss felt it, too. 'Something's going to happen.'

They watched while the sky went dark and the spangle of tankers' lights twinkled on the water like fallen stars. Along the beach, lovers strolled hand in hand, their faces to the rising moon.

Jake felt the vibration and turned his head. A black limo was emerging from the forest. It seemed to be coasting, so slowly was it going. It drew abreast of the front door. Its engine idled while a thin Chinese in a shiny blue suit opened the driver's door and got out. His back was rigid, and Jake recognized the bearing: army.

Intuition fluttered the muscles in his lower belly. He felt a heat rising in his neck and throat.

The thin Chinese was bending slightly to open the rear door. He reached in, apparently supporting something.

Then the old man emerged, and for the first time in his adult life, Jake looked upon the face of his father.

There was absolutely no doubt in his mind as to who this was. In the eyes, the brow, he saw himself reflected, as, with a tiny thrill, a sculptor will when gazing on the face of his first creation.

It was true, he thought. Everything Bliss had told him was true. Not that he had really doubted her. But the shock of the reality was breathtaking nonetheless.

'Buddha,' Bliss whispered, 'it's Shi Zilin! Why has he come here? His presence could destroy the entire *yuhn-hyun*. If the triad dragons get a hint of who he really is, everything will fall apart. What was so urgent that it required his physical presence? He's in great danger here. If the authorities knew . . .' She did not need to complete that thought.

The thin Chinese had pulled a walking stick from the

657

interior of the limo. Now, upon handing it to Zilin, he retired to the car. The old man was left to make his way across the slate.

No one inside the house made a move to help him. Such a gesture would have meant an enormous loss of face for the old man. But all were aware of his presence. No one spoke now, no one drank. No one looked out to sea or to the high-rises below.

Now, as Zilin negotiated the stone stairs, Three Oaths Tsun broke away from the others to stand just in the centre of the veranda. Jake, who was most attuned to Nichiren, saw the other stride away from Formidable Sung. At Three Oaths Tsun's side, he began to talk.

At first the older man made no reply. Then, as Nichiren became more insistent, he began to talk. Jake could not hear what was being said, but he could see well enough the expression on Nichiren's face.

'*Dew neh loh moh!*' Jake breathed. 'My father is Nichiren's Source!'

As Zilin appeared on the deck, there was a moment of absolute blankness on Nichiren's face, and that was when Jake detached himself from the shadows and hurled himself across the lawn. He hit the rocks with an elastic bound.

Bliss screamed after him, but he blocked out the sound. He was concentrating solely on that peculiar expression. He had seen it once before, when they had faced each other in O-henro House. Jake had been struck by it because it had presaged Nichiren's leap into aggressive action.

What had he asked Three Oaths Tsun? What had the older man replied? Jake did not know; he was only certain that he was already too late.

In a blur, Nichiren had gone from absolute motionlessness to violent motion. He had slammed into Shi Zilin, whirling the old man off his feet before Jake was three-quarters of the way to the veranda.

* * *

'I want to know who that is,' Nichiren had said at Three Oaths Tsun's side.

In truth, Three Oaths Tsun had not even heard him the first time he said it. He was engrossed in the sight of his brother, whom he had not seen in fifty years. It was the moment he had been dreaming of for decades. A reunion of the family. He was trembling with the advent.

His silence, however, had angered Nichiren. Nichiren repeated the question, and this time Three Oaths Tsun heard him. He knew an answer was needed. Now was certainly not the time to tell Nichiren that this man was his father, and knowing that Nichiren was dangerous enough to spot a lie, he told him another truth.

'He is your Source.'

That was when the blank look had slid over Nichiren's face like a Noh mask. What Three Oaths Tsun could not know was that Nichiren's mother had had an old, frayed photograph of Zilin, and she had carried it with her to Japan. She had been reluctant to throw it out because, over the intervening years, looking at it had renewed her desire for revenge.

On her death, Nichiren had found it and, along with her diary, had made the connection.

Now, many decades later, Three Oaths Tsun had inadvertently provided the next step in the connection: that Nichiren's father was also his Source. The knowledge had galvanized Nichiren.

I know everything there is to know about you, Source had said to him.

All the suppressed rage and humiliation he had absorbed from his mother, that unconsciously he had felt for the father who had abandoned him and his mother to their dark fate, boiled up in him. Red rage shook him to his core, to think that for years he had been blindly obeying the orders of the one man in the world whom he had hated all his life. The indignity of it! The bitter irony caught in his throat, threatened to choke him.

Nichiren found that he could not breathe, could not even think clearly. He wanted to be free, to return home to Kamisaka, to be his own person. Abruptly he knew such a thing could never be, so long as his father was living. There was no chance of breaking discipline yet again. The man was a magician to have sought him out, to have used him in such a manner. The scale of the deception that was involved staggered Nichiren. It frightened him as well. He knew that he was powerless against such deviousness.

He wanted so much to be free. Free of all the psychic weight with which he had grown up. He shook with his rage and his terror of this man. Fright was almost unknown to Nichiren, and it made him hate his father all the more that he could engender such an emotion in him.

Kamisaka's beautiful body mingled in his mind with the image of his mother's scarred flesh. He felt a burning inside him as if it were he who had been marked.

And, indeed, he had been marked. He saw that now. It was the only thing he saw clearly. His lungs were bursting with unnatural heat. His heart hammered wildly in his chest. Rage engulfed him like a flash fire.

He was burning out of control.

With a guttural growl that felt like the onset of some terrifying elemental force, Nichiren bounded past Three Oaths Tsun and, before those present could overcome their shock, had Zilin by the throat.

'Now you will join my mother. Only this ultimate atonement can heal her mutilated spirit.'

Three Oaths Tsun heard the words and they made him shiver. They seemed to have been uttered by an inhuman larynx.

Involuntarily, Jake's mouth opened. From deep inside him came the roaring of the *kiai* yell that Fo Saan had taught him.

It was an animal's call brimming with power and aggressiveness. It shivered the trees. It rooted everyone on the veranda to the spot. It made Nichiren pause long enough for Jake to make up the last of the distance between them.

He saw the old man's body being twisted, saw the face that reminded him so much of his own, passing through the violent air like a waning sun. He felt the extraordinary force of Nichiren's intrinsic energy.

Jake used an elbow *atemi*, the percussive force falling full across Nichiren's shoulder. The important thing was to get Zilin away from him. There was nothing more in Jake's mind at the moment, but as he peeled Nichiren off the old man, as he stumbled, locked in Nichiren's embrace now, across the slick, polished boards of the veranda, Lan became unsealed inside him.

He knew he had been walking on thin ice ever since he had witnessed her death at the Sumchun River. Perhaps his retelling of the incident had caused it, or again perhaps it was the touch of Nichiren's body against his.

Whatever the cause, the world narrowed down to one sharp point. Gone was the thought of the exchange of the *fu* pieces; gone was the thought of Kamisaka's kindness and love. Revenge rode like a great kite in his mind, blotting out a horizon of possibilities.

Only Jake and Nichiren existed – not this villa, not the people standing on the veranda, not Repulse Bay glittering in moonlight far below. Not even Bliss.

There was a terrifying animal inside him now, and it had extended its paws, its gaping jaws, its unthinking mind, leaping into the firelight. It had been born in the well of his unsharable sorrow and guilt. He was a father who had failed. A father who, in his own mind at least, had been just as much responsible for Lan's death as had Nichiren.

Within the last glint of intelligence in her eyes, he had

seen reflected his neglect of her. Mariana, an adult, might learn ways to deal with his long absences in the field. A child could not, and in the ending of her life he had seen one terrible, tragic result.

Like hammer on anvil, it had flattened his heart. It had twisted his soul all out of shape.

Since then, he had been in the process of dying. Withdrawing from the world of his own manufacture.

He had loved Lan so much, and had never found the ways to tell her.

Love twisted into hate.

Jake and Nichiren.

Tumbling across the veranda. Fetching up against the guardrail. Nichiren's left leg kicked out in a lethal *atemi*. Jake rolled and the guardrail splintered beneath the force.

Jake landed two rapid *atemi* of his own before Nichiren uncoiled. Like a panther he sprang, pinning Jake against the rail. With a grinding of split wood, it gave way. They both went over, tumbling into the night.

Nichiren stretched, twisting. He reached upwards, grasping the lip of the veranda. Jake, just below him, locked his legs around Nichiren's hips. He was blind to their situation. He only knew that he had found Nichiren. His mind was filled with Lan: her voice, her blood-flecked face, his own tear-streaked image reflected in her shining eyes.

'*Ba-ba.*' Daddy.

Her last whispered word. He had not been able to tell that to Bliss. Even now it was too much for him to bear to repeat it.

'*Ba-ba.*'

He beat at Nichiren as if he were the Devil himself. Jake no longer cared whether he lived or died. He only knew that he was haunted by the ineffably sad face of his daughter. He might dream of Mariana, but Lan would follow him every day of his life.

Above the struggling men, the Chinese were turned

immobile by the force of the combatants' hatred. Zilin might have sought to intervene but he was lying near the centre of the veranda. Three Oaths Tsun and T. Y. Chung knelt beside him, tending to him.

It was Bliss, leaping onto the veranda, following Jake's route, who seemed unaffected. She ran through the staring men and grasped the back of Nichiren's shirt. But his weight combined with Jake's was too much for her.

She screamed at Jake to stop. Then, seeing that Nichiren was busy using his legs to kick Jake off, she screamed at him as well.

Neither would listen to her. Perhaps they were *both* determined to die.

Jake had managed to crawl slowly up Nichiren's body. Now they hung together, Jake using his hands, Nichiren his legs and feet.

They stared into each other's eyes, close enough to feel their breaths merge. What strange spark passed between them? What clash of emotions? Each was locked within the past, a tiny, grimy room, long unused but certainly not forgotten. Nichiren was remembering the humiliation of his mother's scarred flesh; Jake was consumed by the image of the first rays of the sun rising above the treetops, illuminating in death a young face he had failed to understand in life.

Then the endless moment was broken. Nichiren, holding on to the edge of the veranda, was at a distinct disadvantage. Because of this, Jake was able to climb over him. He gained purchase on the boards and managed to lever himself up onto the veranda. He turned and slammed the edge of his hand into Nichiren.

The other man swung away and Jake, panting and sweating, thought it was over. In a moment he found out how wrong he was. Nichiren had used the momentum of Jake's attack to swing himself inwards. He stretched his legs as far as he could to gain momentum. Rolling his body into a ball after he reached the apex of the outward swing, he flipped up onto the veranda.

He landed and moved all at once. He caught Jake off guard and was atop him instantly. Two vicious liver kites brought Jake to the edge of unconsciousness.

Bliss, terrified, kicked out with all her strength. The toe of her shoe caught Nichiren on the point of his chin. His teeth clacked together madly and his head jounced on his neck. He coughed blood.

Jake immediately used a two-handed *atemi* across Nichiren's windpipe. Nichiren's body arched backwards. Still, he kicked out, slamming into Jake's thighbone.

Jake rolled, unthinking, his body wanting to get away from the pain. Nichiren, hoping for this, brought the edge of his hand down across Jake's back.

Writhing in pain, Jake shot his left leg out. It connected with Nichiren's hip, sending him flying backwards. Jake was already up, blinking back tears of pain. He was in the process of striking again, his arm outflung. But Nichiren was not stopped by the rail. Already splintered, a sharp end of wood brushed his side and nothing more.

Jake lunged for the killing blow. His fingers hit something and involuntarily closed around it. He heard a sharp snap, and then there was nothing in front of him but the glittering South China Sea. A dank wind blew in his face. Not even the shadow of a kite moved there.

Jake leapt to the edge of the ruined rail. Eventually he heard Bliss's soft voice calling to him as if from a great distance.

'He's gone, Jake. Nichiren's dead.'

'*Bah-ba.*'

Was it the night wind or Lan he heard calling to him?

In a moment he became aware that he was trembling violently.

Bliss pulled him away from the abyss. Light flooded across him as he came to the centre of the veranda.

Formidable Sung had led the other triad dragons into the house.

Shi Zilin was surrounded by Three Oaths Tsun and T. Y. Chung. The old man's skin seemed as delicate as rice paper. Blue veins patterned his countenance as lines scored others'.

'Nichiren?' His voice was as thin as his skin.

Jake could not answer. The muscles at the corners of his jaw were knotted.

'He's gone, *gaau-fuh*,' Bliss said. How long she had wanted to speak to him face to face. Her godfather.

'Gone.' In that one word was conveyed a lifetime of loving lost.

Shi Zilin put his head against the shoulder of his brother. 'Ah, Buddha, protect what is left of my family now.'

Jake took a step forwards. He wanted to say something, but his mind was a whirl of emotions. The hulking beast of his own manufacture was still running rampant inside him. After three years of being bottled up, it could hardly be otherwise.

Zilin's gaze rose, alit on Jake's face. For a long time those bright black eyes drank in the sight wholly. For fifty years he had dreamed of this moment; for much of that time he had not believed that it would ever come about. He was like a man who has not eaten in weeks and now finds before him the most delicious of feasts. His heart was filled up with love.

Zilin was utterly absorbed in his son. So brimming with genuine emotion was it that the others around him were held rapt by that absorption.

He wanted to speak but the words caught in his throat, jumbled by these feelings, so strong yet so strange to him. At last he said softly, 'Get me to my feet, Younger Brother, if, you would be so kind.'

Gingerly, with T. Y. Chung aiding him, Three Oaths

Tsun lifted the old man up. He was trembling heavily, as if a current were galvanizing him.

'Jake,' Zilin said.

Jake, still filled up with Nichiren, said, 'Why did you ask about Nichiren?'

'It was not meant to end this way,' the old man said. 'I did not foresee the depths of the hatred his mother had implanted within him. I thought I had exorcized it.'

The mists were clearing slowly. Jake felt a great fist clamping down on his heart, squeezing. 'I don't understand.' But he did! He did!

'Nichiren was also my son,' Zilin said. 'He was your brother. Or, more accurately, your half-brother.'

Squeezing.

Jake felt as if he were dying. A black wave of despair such as he had never felt washed over him. First Lan, and now Nichiren. He could not breathe. His heart seemed to have ceased to beat. There was a roaring in his ears.

'Jake?'

'I've murdered my brother,' someone was saying.

It was only after he had fled from them all, disappearing into the forest beside the dirt track, that he realized who that someone was.

Much later, in the silence of her apartment, Bliss brought Jake a *wei qi* board with two shallow dishes filled with black and white stones.

Frankly, she did not know what else to do. He had been there when she returned home, sitting on the sofa, staring out at the coming of dawn. Lights were still on here and there, haloed by the mother-of-pearl glow brushing the darkness of the night away.

Though he had not slept in forty-eight hours, he did not appear tired. Bliss had made him some food, but he had not eaten. He drank nothing but water. Now, as she set the *wei qi* game down in front of him, she opened the slip of paper Zilin had handed her as she rushed off after his son. It contained a handwritten local phone number.

'Jake,' she said, 'your father has called several times. He wants to see you.'

Jake said nothing.

Bliss had been sympathetic to what he was going through, but as the hours wore on, she became increasingly angry. This psychic retreat was self-destructive. He was so wrapped up in the past that he had lost touch with the present. This frightened her, and at last, as it began to get dark again, she determined to do something about it.

The L-shaped sofa had a low, wide back. In the shadows and silence of the apartment, she carefully undressed. Naked, she climbed onto the sofa back. Like a giant cat, she approached Jake's unmoving figure.

She pounced like a predator on its prey, tumbling both of them onto the carpet in front of the windows. Sprawled atop him, she' bit his ear, dug her nails in his chest, wrapped her ankles around his calfs.

'Bliss, no.' The first words he had spoken in almost a day.

'Yes,' she whispered. 'Yes, yes, yes.'

She bared her teeth at him, her eyes flashing. Her long hair flung itself like a living being down his belly. With her fingers, she tore open his shirt, and when he moved to stop her, she slapped him across the face.

'Bliss, goddammit!'

That's right, she thought, using her elbows and hips, give me a reaction, *any* reaction.

Their faces were so close he could feel her lashes when she blinked. She smelled of lemon and musk. Jake's mind was clouded with memories, chittering like hungry animals, crying to be fed at once. He resented this intrusion on his living nightmare. He had been quite content to wallow in his guilt – the atonement of despair.

Bliss's hardened nipples scraped across his bare chest.

She dipped her head, her hot lips enclosing one of his nipples. Her tiny pink tongue darted out. She made a deep sound in her throat as she felt the thickening bulge between his thighs.

'Leave me alone,' he panted. 'I don't want to.'

'Yes, you do,' she said in his ear. Her fingers were busy at his belt. 'What you mean is, you don't deserve this now. That's very Western of you, Jake. I hate you when you get like this.'

He stopped fighting her. His extraordinary copper-coloured eyes were almost orange in the twilight. But it was Bliss's, into which he stared, that were feral.

'Do you really hate me?' His voice was thick.

'Yes.' Her gleaming lips were half-parted.

Jake reached up, and taking her head between his hands, brought it down. His mouth enclosed hers, and when their tongues twined, a great shudder rippled through Bliss's entire frame.

Her fingers unfastened his trousers, pulling the material down his hips and thighs. She was wild to climb on him. Her pelvis squirmed and he gasped at the feel of her liquid heat.

Reaching down while their lips were still pressed together, she plunged him into her molten core. He reared and went all the way up.

Bliss, gasping, felt the air rush from her lungs. She panted against the side of his neck. Tears filled her eyes. She possessed him as he possessed her. The connection was so exquisite that she passed into another realm. She had never believed that she could feel so close to another human being.

Jake was more than her lover.

The feeling of him deep inside her, massaging her intimate flesh, engendered a completeness she had believed only Buddha could possess. She stroked her hips against him, moaning. Her hair covered them in a fan, filaments of feeling.

And when her orgasm opened up inside her, it radiated all the way to the top of her head.

The heat of him, spurting.

'Jake, oh, Jake! Yes, yes, yes!'

Her head curled on his heaving chest, she listened to his heartbeat as if it were the pulse of the sea. She kissed his damp flesh, her fingers stroking. When he, softened at last, popped out of her, she cupped him in her palm, reluctant to let go.

He could still feel the place on his skin where she had slapped him. A plover's cry, echoing down the well. He knew that she had not sought to hurt or to shock him, but merely to remind him of all that he was.

'Bliss,' he said. 'Bliss.'

And she wept, knowing that she had him back.

Still, he was adamant. 'I don't want to see him.'

'Jake, he's your father.'

'Do you think I want any part of his *yuhn-hyun*? It destroyed Mariana and David Oh. I killed my brother because of it.' He pocketed the slip of paper she had handed him, without looking at the number.

'Aren't you even curious as to what the *yuhn-hyun* is?'

'It's a Communist Chinese operation.'

'You're half right. It's a *Chinese* operation.'

He stared at her. His hand came out of his pocket. When he had shoved the slip in, his fingers had encountered an object. They both looked at it now.

'Where did you get that?' Bliss asked.

'When I grabbed for Nichiren at the very end, it came away from him.' Jake held a small, worn chamois pouch in his palm. He undid the drawstring and out popped his piece of the *fu*.

They both stared at it wordlessly for a time. Jake took it

to the table on which Bliss had set up the *wei qi* board. He reached into another pocket, placed the two pieces together. The fierce foreign tiger.

'It's one side of the *fu*,' he said. 'I wonder who has the other two pieces.'

'I thought you weren't interested in the *yuhn-hyun*?'

Jake made a face at her and she went across the room. He watched the play of her golden flesh. From behind, all the puffy bruises were hidden.

When she returned, she put her closed fist down on the table. Slowly she opened her fingers. There between them lay a shard of carved lavender jade, the head of a great dragon: the third piece of the *fu*.

'Buddha!' Jake said. 'How?'

'I am Shi Zilin's goddaughter. Long ago, when he was still a child, your father had a mentor. A Jian. You understand? That man was my great-grandfather. It was under Shi Zilin's protection that my mother journeyed out of China, through Burma, where I was born, to Hong Kong. She was very ill by then, but she managed to get me to the destination Shi Zilin had given her: Three Oaths Tsun.

'It was my mother,' Bliss said, fitting the third piece with the other two, 'who gave me this.'

'Then they all came from one source: my father.'

Bliss looked up at him. 'Yes.'

'Who holds the last piece?'

'I do not know. I think only Shi Zilin can tell you.'

He turned away. 'I am finished with him. I am finished with shadows and lies.'

'I do not believe the *yuhn-hyun* can work without you.'

'I don't care, Bliss.'

'And what of the Quarry's infiltration?' she said angrily. 'We have been hunted like dogs for the past four days. Do you think that will change? You must care about that.'

'Whether I do or not is immaterial.' He sat down on the

sofa, began absently to arrange the opening of a *wei qi* game. 'I don't know what got David Oh killed.'

'But the evidence exists.' Bliss drew on a pair of jeans and an amber V-necked blouse. ' "*Huo yan.*" '

'The "movable eye",' Jake said. 'Nichiren used it as part of his game. So do I. Don't you think I've been trying to figure out what David meant by that?'

'It must mean something.' Bliss came over and sat down next to him. 'You knew David a long time.' Jake nodded. 'Perhaps it has some meaning from out of your past.'

'But I can't think of what.'

'Did you and David play *wei qi* together?'

'Are you kidding? David hated board games of any kind. He was the eternal bachelor. Loved to spend his free time prowling after the girls. He used to tell them he was an intelligence agent. They didn't know what he meant until he said "spy". Of course, they never believed him. They'd giggle, peering under his armpits for the pistol they knew wasn't there.'

'Still, you two spent plenty of time together over the years. What did you do then?'

Jake was pushing the white and black pieces around the board, creating liaisons. 'Oh, we did a lot of things.'

Bliss laughed. 'Like what, chase girls and play *wei qi* at the same time?'

It was meant as a joke but it galvanized Jake. '*Dew neh loh moh*, I have the memory of a sea slug!' He jumped up, buckling his belt and thrusting his arms into his shirt. 'Come on!' he yelled.

'Where are we going?'

'*Huo yan*, of course. *Huo yan!*'

In Wanchai, where, less than a week before, David Oh was running for his life, Jake and Bliss hurried down the same jammed streets.

'There was this one place we used to go to that we both

671

liked,' Jake explained. 'It had the girls David Oh liked best: clean and young enough to still be interested. It was owned by a man named Mok. Bald, ring in his ear. A Mongol, maybe. I never knew his background, but that was how he looked.

'Mok was the meanest goddamned bastard either David or I had ever come across. We twice tried to recruit him, but he wasn't interested. Even the triads let him alone.

'He fooled around with the girls some, which was why they were clean and young. He also was a *wei qi* fanatic.

'His favourite endgame was invariably based on *huo yan*. David would be finished with his girls before the game was over. Even he didn't have the kind of stamina Mok possessed, so he'd be around for all of the endgames. *Huo yan* was the only move in *wei qi* he knew.'

'So you think he gave the evidence to this Mok.'

'We'll soon find out.'

Mok's establishment was in a seedy ground-level building on Luard Road. It looked like the kind of place only a horny sailor on leave would tolerate. Inside, coloured spots in red, blue, and yellow drifted over an octagonal dance floor. Uniforms and slit skirts dominated, along with blaring R-and-B music from the early sixties: the Temptations and the Supremes.

Jake took Bliss by the hand, led her over to the bartender. After speaking to him, they were shown to the back of the room.

Bliss picked out Mok immediately. He was just as Jake had described him, except that he appeared to weigh in excess of 250 pounds. Muscles bulging. *Very* mean. But when he saw Jake he beamed like a lighthouse on a foggy night. He rose from the *wei qi* board and pounded Jake on the back. He leered good-naturedly at Bliss when Jake introduced her.

'Come back after all this time for a game?' Mok had a

voice that was all basso. He seemed to be tattooed in the style of an American sailor.

'Not exactly,' Jake said.

The two men looked at each other for a moment.

'David's dead.'

'Shit and perdition,' Mok said, and spat heavily. 'In that case, I know why you're here.'

It took Jake just under three hours to read and analyse the data David Oh had extracted from the Quarry computer. By that time he knew that Gerard Stallings had been killed for the same reason that David Oh had been. He also understood that a Quarry extraction team had been sent to terminate Mariana on the night of his raid on O-henro House.

'If they only wanted your piece of the *fu*,' Bliss asked, after he had outlined the pertinent data to her, 'why kill Mariana?'

'Because someone in the Quarry knew that the *fu* shard was hidden. Whoever ordered the extraction team in knew me and knew Mariana well. He was aware that Mariana would never willingly divulge the *fu*'s location. They were sent to torture the information out of her. Then, of course, she would have to die. Otherwise, she would be able to identify an unsanctioned Quarry operation.'

The stupidity of Mariana's death appalled him and he said, 'Christ,' very quietly.

Bliss put her arm around him. In a moment she said, 'Donovan or Wunderman. Which one is the traitor?'

Jake, staring at the starlit Hong Kong night, felt weariness sweep through him. His race was almost run.

'Unfortunately,' he said, 'there's only one way to find out.'

There was a storm building over Washington. The weather turned the Washington Monument slate grey and the Reflecting Pool in front of the Lincoln Memorial gunmetal.

673

In Great Falls, farther away by fifteen miles from the Chesapeake, the clouds had begun to roll in. The humid day turned clammy, as if all the heavy foliage were sweating at once.

In Greystoke's cool third-floor study, Henry Wunderman was plugged into the Quarry's teeming storehouse of knowledge. The security precautions he and Donovan had instituted since the assassination of Antony Beridien did not satisfy him. Slowly he was becoming obsessed with Jake Maroc and the growing threat Jake posed to the worldwide organization he now controlled.

The overcast day did not stop Rodger Donovan from working on his 1963 Corvette. He had pulled it up beside the rose garden at the side of the large house. In amid the somnolent drone of the bumblebees, fat and lazy with midsummer pollen, he felt comfortably alone – detached, even, from the changeable weather. Here his mind was free to drift, working on ever more complex software programs for the Quarry's GPR-3700 mainframe.

When he heard the voice say softly, 'Hello, Rodger,' he stopped what he was doing. He was wearing gardener's gloves. In his right hand he held a grease-coated wrench. He held a sparkplug in his other hand. Just behind him was a bush with blossoms the colour of peaches.

He stood up straight now. He was clad in a purple Ralph Lauren cotton polo shirt, a pair of old, smeared white ducks, and scarred Top-Siders without socks.

'Jake,' he said, without turning around. He seemed quite calm. 'You seem to have as many lives as the hero of a novel. I knew we couldn't kill you.'

'It didn't stop you from trying.'

Donovan winced at the tone. 'Of course not. What do you take us for, amateurs?'

'No more talk,' Jake said. 'Take me to Wunderman.'

'Ah, Wunderman. I imagine he'll want to know how you evaded all our security measures.'

'Then he'll be disappointed. Come on, let's go.'

Now Donovan turned around. 'Do you believe I'll simply guide you to him? He's the Director now. And you've been classified "lethal rogue".'

'I won't bother to ask how that came about.'

'It wouldn't do you much good, I'm afraid. That's classified information.'

Jake's face hardened. 'Wunderman.'

Donovan spread his arms wide. 'Kill me, why don't you, with one of your hand-to-fist speciality items.'

Jake moved in so fast that Donovan did not even have time to blink. Just a blur with a hardened cutting edge on the end of it.

Donovan crashed into the rosebushes, his nose drooling blood. Thorns tore through his polo shirt, scratching like cat's claws. Tears came to his eyes, and dropping the wrench, he lifted a hand, wiping away the blood. 'My God,' he said, 'I believe I had better stop joking.'

Jake pulled him to his feet. 'Against the wall, Rodger.'

The other complied and Jake patted him down.

'That was hardly necessary,' Donovan said. 'I never carry a weapon.'

'Let's go,' Jake said. 'I need the two of you together.'

Donovan's face was apologetic when it poked into Wunderman's study. The nose and the upper lip were already beginning to swell, and he had had to stuff a wad of Kleenex in the left nostril to control the bleeding.

'Jesus,' Henry Wunderman said when he saw him, 'what the hell happened to you? Fall into your engine?'

'I'm terribly sorry,' Donovan said, sniffing.

'For what?'

Jake pushed him all the way into the room and came in after him. 'I think he means me.'

'Oh, Christ.' Wunderman's eyes bugged. He sat in his shirtsleeves before the computer console. Only his head

675

moved now as he followed Jake's progress around the room.

The walls, painted a robin's-egg blue, were covered with a plethora of preserved butterflies, all in miniature mahogany frames. Spread-eagled side by side, they looked like a series of inkblot cards. Above them, fluorescent strip lighting leached all colour from their delicate forms.

Jake had not taken David Oh's printouts with him. He did not intend to bring them up here, either. What was the point? The traitor would lie to save himself, and the innocent man would lie to protect the Quarry. In this respect, Jake realized, there was no difference between them.

In battle, Fo Saan had told Jake over and over, *words are meaningless. Men will say anything if they think it will give them an advantage. Only action has any meaning. Action is distilled intent.*

'You've broken every tenet of the Quarry's bylaws.' Wunderman sat with his hands on his thighs. He had changed since he became the Director. Not physically but emotionally. 'Don't expect us to make excuses for our actions, or to apologize for anything.'

'Henry believes you're going to kill us.' Donovan stood where Jake had pushed him. He had not attempted to move. 'He's convinced that your Chinese half has taken precedence. He thinks you've got nothing but vengeance on your mind.'

By the manner in which he spoke, Jake could tell that he was asking the questions for himself as well. Wunderman might be convinced of these things, as Donovan said, but Donovan himself was on the verge of believing them as well.

Jake said nothing. It was not his intention to engage these men in debate.

'Jake,' Wunderman said in the exaggeratedly reasonable tone a doctor will take with a madman, 'you've got to understand that the tragedy of Mariana's death has combined with the trauma of the Sumchun River and the death of the *dantai* at O-henro House.

'So many deaths to have on one's conscience is too much for anyone . . . even you. If you give yourself up now, before anyone else gets hurt, I promise you'll not be charged. We'll debrief you, bring you back to health.'

Jake could hardly recognize the man who had recruited him for the Quarry, the man who had led him through his training in these same rolling Virginia hills. The power to which Wunderman had aspired, the power that he had now achieved, had warped him. Perhaps the responsibility had been too much for him; better men than he had buckled beneath the enormous strain. Or, then again, perhaps it was his dual life that was ageing him before his time.

Donovan kept his mouth shut, which was just as interesting to Jake. Like Wunderman's, his eyes never left Jake, but there was no fear in them. He was as calm as if he were still rummaging through his car's engine.

Jake's hard gaze, on Donovan for some time, flicked back towards Wunderman. In that space, as his peripheral vision took over, he had a fraction of an instant to react. He saw the pistol in Wunderman's hand and he had to make his decision.

Action is distilled intent. And his own thought: *Whoever ordered the extraction team in knew me and knew Mariana well.*

Wunderman.

The pistol discharged, but Jake was no longer in the spot where Wunderman was aiming. He was a blur in the air, landing a blow with his leading foot across Wunderman's chest.

The two of them flew backwards with a crash. Wunderman's head struck the floor. The gun flew out of his hand, skittered across the carpet in the centre of the room. Jake struck with a pair of liver kites powerful enough to make Wunderman's eyes flutter.

'Hold it!'

Jake paused. Donovan was pointing the pistol at him.

'I should shoot you where you are!'

'There's a traitor inside the Quarry,' Jake said. There was no emotion inside him. He had imagined this moment, Mariana and David Oh's faces swimming before him, their spirits crying out for vengeance. But there was nothing compelling about what he was doing now. It all felt like nothing. 'I imagine you might have come to the same conclusion. David Oh was terminated because he found information buried in the computer memory banks. The same with Stallings.'

Jake registered the shock in Donovan's eyes. With it was confusion and a measure of disbelief.

'Henry thinks you're the traitor.'

'Henry thinks I'd kill David Oh?'

'We know you've terminated four Quarry agents in as many days.'

'They murdered David while he was on his way to an rdv we set up. Then they came after me.'

'With a "lethal rogue" directive out on you, it's no wonder.'

'Who ordered the directive?'

Donovan did not answer, but for an instant his eyes flickered towards Wunderman. 'Christ on a crutch,' he breathed. He waved with the muzzle of the pistol. 'Get away from him.'

Jake obeyed.

Donovan knelt down, loosened Wunderman's collar so he could put two fingers against his jugular. There was no pulse to feel.

After a long time of staring at the grey face, he said, 'Henry, you bastard.'

* * *

The two of them went out to dinner, to an inn serving French country food, not far from Greystoke. Moths buzzed in the lights and young girls swung in with their dates, bright-faced and clear-eyed. Donovan's nose was lightly bandaged, but even in this state he had managed to make himself look rather dashing. It was at him that most of the young girls glanced, not at Jake.

Donovan ordered the best wine in an excellent cellar, and together they toasted the Henry Wunderman who had once been.

Jake was thinking of the moment at the Peninsula when Wunderman had recruited him. 'To absent friends,' he said, just as if Wunderman were missing in action, which, in a way, he was.

'To Mariana,' Donovan said. 'For what it's worth, I'm awfully sorry.'

They finished more than half of the bottle before the food arrived.

'I suppose we'll never know exactly what happened,' Donovan said, over coffee and brandy, some time later. 'What made him turn.' He had ordered and demolished the pheasant. Jake had chosen shrimps, but the sauce, larded with clarified butter and glossy reduction of juices, did not appeal to his palate, and so they lay before him mostly unfinished. He was grateful when the waitress took the plate away.

'It's clear, however, that Wunderman was the bottom of Antony's iceberg.' Donovan poured his brandy into his coffee, stirred it absently. 'Speaking of which, have you heard that Daniella Vorkuta, the mastermind behind the iceberg, has just been elevated to head of the First Chief Directorate?'

Jake said he hadn't.

'She's also due to become the first female Politburo member.'

'Why are you telling me this?' Jake said. 'Isn't it classified information?'

Donovan made a noise into his napkin. 'I was hoping I could persuade you to return to the nest.'

'That's an interesting way of putting it.'

'I'm merely asking you to think about it,' Donovan said, calling for the bill.

But it was not of the Quarry that Jake thought when he returned to his hotel. The room, typical of hotel rooms throughout America, had the heavy blackout curtains pulled shut so that the space had the aspect of a womb.

Jake crossed the room and yanked open the drapes. He saw a courtyard filled by a mature plane tree. Its light-speckled branches were dipping slightly in the summer wind, but because the windows were closed, there was no sound at all. He might have been peering at a silent movie screen.

Through the branches Jake could see, a small café, set with striped umbrellas and tiny marble-topped tables. The scene looked curiously European. As he watched, a couple, middle-aged, but totally enraptured with one another, strolled hand in hand between the empty tables. To Jake, the observer, it was a melancholy sight.

Over dinner, he had thought Rodger Donovan's offer an ironic joke. But now, peering out at the spangled darkness, he saw what Donovan must have seen in him: that he was the same as he always had been. He was no different from the other men who played this deadly game.

When he looked again, the courtyard was deserted. In a moment the lights in the trees went off. Jake glanced at his watch. It was after midnight.

He went to the bed and sat down on it. He stared at the phone for some time. Then he drew out a slip of paper, unfolded it. He picked up the receiver, asked the hotel operator for an overseas line to Hong Kong. When she informed him that this was a direct-dial area, he gave her his room number and did as she bade him.

The line rang hollowly for the longest time. In the instant before he was about to hang up, a voice said, '*Wai.*' Hello.

So many emotions raced through Jake at the sound of the voice that he almost failed to speak.

Then, taking one deep breath, he said, '*Bah-ba.*' Father.

Epilogue

Summer, Present

Hong Kong/Washington

A dog barked as it ran along the waterline. Leaping for a red ball, it extended itself, arcing in the air like a missile. When it landed, it came near enough to Jake to leave a sandy mark on his trouser leg.

Jake and Zilin, walking slowly along the shallow crescent of the beach at Shek-O. It was midmorning. The hazy sun made the ocean seem as if it were coated with cream.

Zilin had just finished telling Jake about his life in China. He had taken the news of Chimera's death with characteristic equanimity. 'Now you know more about me even than my brothers.'

Jake looked at the old man, thinking, He'll always be full of surprises.

'I was wrong to leave you and your mother,' Zilin said. 'Just as I was wrong to take a mistress. But I was blind, you see. I was consumed with what I felt I had to do. I made decisions and never once conceived of the consequences.

'I was like a monk, Jake, who, after many years in the service of his god, is set loose in the lay world. I operated by an entirely different set of precepts.'

'The *yuhn-hyun*.'

Zilin nodded. 'In a way, yes.' They made a wide circuit around a brown child making sand castles at the edge of the water. 'I could not see that my actions would have repercussions on those around me. Or perhaps I did, and discounted the effect.

'You have told me what befell my Athena after I left you. I know, from what I gleaned from Nichiren over the years, how I hurt Sheng Li. The *yuhn-hyun* killed them, or rather my obsession with it.'

They walked for a time in silence. The clouds were piling themselves along the horizon above the black smudges of tankers. With a sweep of silver spray, a pleasure boat raced by them. A young blonde in a bikini raised a hand and waved at her admirers on shore. She was very sure of herself.

'I must rest,' Zilin said after a time. He sat by the edge of the water, parallel to the child's sand castles. Jake, standing beside him, watched as he took off his shoes and socks, rolled up his trousers. He stuck his feet into the curling end of the rolling waves. The sight brought tears to Jake's eyes.

Zilin, watching the child at play, did not notice.

Jake crouched down beside his father. They had not embraced when they had met here; not an intimate word had passed between them. That was not the Chinese way. Perhaps they had spoken to each other with silence.

'I will stay here now,' Zilin said. He turned his gaze out to sea. 'I was never a Communist. I love my country, but I do not relish what has become of it. I embraced communism many years ago because of pragmatism. And I was correct. Communism did unite China. I think, still, that it was the only way to stop our history of internecine warfare. History, as you may know, is rather difficult to break away from.

'But I, like many of my brethren, never knew the right time to disentangle myself from communism. It has served its purpose. I think all of us knew that some time ago. We continued to use it – for ourselves, I suspect, and nothing more.

'Now communism is what ties us to the past. It is what prevents our emergence into the future. That is how the *yuhn-hyun* was really born.'

Jake, waiting for his father to continue, watched the

people on the beach as he had been trained to do. Even in this atmosphere, he could not forget who he was.

'The *yuhn-hyun* came about when I became convinced that Hong Kong was the saviour of all China. If I could control Hong Kong absolutely – and now I am not speaking about the Chinese government, but rather about myself or someone like me – I could control the future of all of China. I could channel great sums of money into heavy industry, I could promote free enterprise as I strengthened the bonds between the *tai pan* houses here and sources of supply on the Mainland. I could, within fifty years, effect the unification of all China.

'That was the *yuhn-hyun*'s goal.'

Jake thought about this for a long time. He remembered Bliss's words: *It's a* Chinese *operation.* She had not lied.

'But to control all of the Colony,' he said now. 'I don't see how you could do such a thing.'

Zilin smiled, but there was no humour in that fragile face. The network of blue veins crisscrossed everywhere. 'I am Jian. What I create, lives. Such a thing *is* possible, I assure you, my son. In fact, it was within my grasp.'

'Even now?'

'Not that much time has passed. Yes.' The sun caught his eyes, turning them from black to white. Jake could see a pulse beating in his temple. 'But it won't happen now. Too many people have died because of my callousness. I am tired. Even a Jian must have his time of rest.'

To their right, the sea came up, dissolving one wall of the child's sand castle. The boy stared at the levelled place for a moment, before his eyes began to ooze tears. Then his sister came out of the water and stood looking at him.

She dropped to her knees, the sand coating her honey-coloured skin. 'Here,' she said. 'Here.' And began to build the ruined wall back up again. After a time her brother stopped crying and began to help.

Jake, who had been observing this scene, smiled.

'Father,' he said, 'would you talk to me about the *yuhn-hyun*?'

Zilin nodded. 'If you wish. But first I must tell you something. It was on my orders that Nichiren brought Mariana to Japan.'

Waves crashed along the shore as they always had, but to Jake the sounds seemed as loud as rifle shots.

Mariana, white-faced, the storm beating her back against the muddy rock. Slipping down and away.

Mariana! No!

'I wish to continue.'

Jake barely heard his father's voice. 'Why would you spirit Mariana away?' His voice was a hoarse croak.

'Chimera found out about the power of the *fu*. He sent a termination team to your apartment on the night you so rashly raided O-henro House.'

Jake barely registered the rebuke in his father's voice. 'I know that, but I still don't understand. Mariana would never have gone anywhere with Nichiren.'

'Of course not,' Zilin said softly. 'Not with what she knew or surmised about the long-standing enmity between the two of you. It was essential that she be convinced otherwise.'

Zilin stared out to sea, but his eyes saw nothing. 'Nichiren phoned her. He warned her of the team's approach. It was necessary to cut it quite close. Still, she did not believe him. Why should she? The Quarry was on your side.

'So he told her the name of the group leader. He was someone she knew well.'

'Evans.'

'Evans, yes. Chimera apparently was not aware that Mariana knew what Evans did for a living. She hid outside the building, and when she saw Evans lead his team in, she had no choice but to believe Nichiren.'

There was silence between them for a time. The high

688

spirits along the beach seemed far away. At length Jake said. 'But why Nichiren?'

'I didn't see any other choice. I had to protect Mariana, and do it at once. I had very little advance warning. I knew that the termination team would find her if she stayed in Hong Kong. I had to get her out.

'I thought the safest place for her would be with Nichiren. I believed that no one inside the Quarry would think of looking for her with your enemy.'

'But they did,' Jake said bitterly. 'They found out.'

Zilin nodded sadly. 'And a power struggle within the Soviet hierarchy sent a KVR team to Tsurugi as well. I am sorry, my son.'

Jake felt the tremor running through the old man beside him. His heart broke. We're all a little bit to blame, he thought. But mainly, it's the life I chose to lead. My violent world destroyed her. A world I love.

In time, he gathered himself together. 'Tell me about the *yuhn-hyun*, Father.'

Zilin accepted this ending because it was what his son wanted. 'All right. You already know about Three Oaths Tsun and T. Y. Chung. You're the only one. Even Bliss does not know that they are my brothers. I want it kept that way. The consequences of that particular bit of information are far too dangerous.

'You know that under the guise of their feud, they have been acquiring companies. They have been doing so under my direction, so that all these new firms are now part of the ring.

'As part of this ruse, T. Y. Chung has entered into a business partnership with Five Star Pacific. Within six months, thanks to the machinations of one of my enemies in Beijing, we will have a clear majority control of that house.

'The triads are ours as well. Three Oaths Tsun, as you

know, has a friend in Formidable Sung. That gives us the 14K. Sir John Bluestone is affiliated with the Hak Sam.'

'That leaves the Green Pang,' Jake said. 'You won't get far without the Shanghainese triad.'

'Quite true,' Zilin assented. 'That means Andrew Sawyer – and Venerable Chen, who controls virtually all gold trafficking in and out of Macao.' He turned now and stared into Jake's eyes. For a moment the years sloughed off him and Jake glimpsed the young man his father had once been. 'You have three pieces of the *fu*, my son. Andrew Sawyer has the fourth.'

'Sawyer. Buddha!'

There was a small Buddhist shrine hidden away along the slopes above Shek-O. Late afternoon found the two men entering its cool, musky interior. The scent of cedar mingled with the curling smoke of the *joss* sticks.

Zilin spent a long time at prayer. Jake, by his side, thought of other things more worldly but no less important. He was still getting used to having a father, to being next to a human with whom he shared the same bloodline. Often he found himself trembling. He thought it might be with relief.

'The *yuhn-hyun* is useless now,' Zilin said as they sat in the shade of the shrine's painted bamboo overhang. 'Without someone to sit at its heart and run it, there is nothing.'

The westering sun spilled its golden light all across the South China Sea. Even the gathering clouds at the horizon were, for this moment, obscured.

'You are speaking now of the *tai pan* of all *tai pan*,' Jake said carefully.

'In effect. He would control all of Hong Kong . . . all of China, eventually. Because without international trade and the vast revenues it brings China is nothing.'

'You have me, Father.'

Zilin was shaking his head. 'Your life has already been intruded upon enough, my son.'

'I am qualified.'

Zilin hesitated, debating with himself. 'In all the world, Jake, you are the most uniquely qualified to be the centre of the *yuhn-hyun*. That had been my original intention. You and eventually Nichiren in Japan, extending the ring.'

'Then it's settled.'

'No. Nothing's settled. For many years, we on the Mainland used the tenets of Marx and Engels to achieve a form of order and freedom from the *faan gwai loh* who, not content to rape our country, threatened to swallow us up whole.

'Communism was a means to an end. It has been clear to me for some years that we have reached that end. We have a sense of stability now. But we are still mired in feudal thinking. In Beijing there is a plethora of backward philosophy.

'What has also been clear to me is that China's future lies now with capitalism. Hong Kong – and through it a united China, including Taiwan – will be able to feed itself by employing a market economy. That is what capitalism can provide us with now.

'But the way is fraught with danger, both in Beijing, where powerful Maoists still exist, and inside Russia, where the Kremlin lives in fear of our true independence. This, too, is part of the fearful legacy of the *tai pan* of all *tai pan*.'

'Father, when I went back to Washington, I learned something vital about myself. My life is what *I* have made of it.'

'Even though you know now that Fo Saan was part of the *yuhn-hyun*.'

'Yes. Even so. Fo Saan trained me, but it was my skill. He could not, and indeed *did* not, seek to influence my interests.

'In just the same way, my life today is what I choose to make of it. When I say it's settled, I mean it.'

'This must be something that you want.'

'Of course.'

Zilin watched the sun coming down. He had been struck by how different the world was outside of his home. He had to continually remind himself that this, too, was China. Strange, he thought now, but even the sun looks different here. It would take some getting used to, the world. He knew that he would not have the time to assimilate it all. But after he was gone, there would be Jake. He was astonished at how important that thought was to him.

At last he nodded.

'So be it. I have already spoken to Andrew Sawyer. He owes me a debt he can never truly repay. He is *tai pan* because of me. That is why he was given the last of the *fu* shards. Remember that well.

'Sawyer gave me some interesting information, which I will pass on to you now. Sir John Bluestone is the KGB's top operative in the Asian theatre. Sawyer's own *comprador* for years, Peter Ng, was Bluestone's agent. He has already been dealt with.

'Bluestone, however, is another matter entirely. When you go to see Sawyer, I think it would be prudent to keep Bluestone in place. He is in direct contact with Daniella Vorkuta, and I believe it would be in our best interests to keep things that way, at least for the time being.'

'I agree.'

'Good. The only question still remaining is how Chimera found out about the *fu*. That information was not leaked by any source I have been able to run down.'

'That means there's someone out there, on the loose.'

'An agent we are ignorant of, yes.'

'I'll find him.'

Jake was thinking about all the people lost to him. For how long had he believed that he had no family? Now he had his father back. And with him had come uncles, nephews, and nieces. He felt like a man who, after years of wandering in the desert, had stumbled upon King Solomon's Mines. His new wealth astounded him.

Zilin closed his eyes. He felt the sun on his face, but it was his son sitting beside him who warmed his flesh. He felt a hand on his, and despite himself, he was electrified by emotion. So much so that he thought to himself, For this moment, it's all right.

He was dreaming of Paris. The molten summer light spread itself like honey across the boulevards. He was in his second-storey apartment in the brownstone building in the Sixteenth Arrondissement. The flock of high windows looked out onto a back courtyard that seemed grey even at this time of year.

The dream, which he had at regular intervals, always began with a quick flash, like an Impressionist painting, of that courtyard. Grey it might have been, but it was always filled with birds.

He heard their calling. Always their sounds were inextricably mixed with the rapping on the door. His pulse quickened as she came into the foyer. He was consumed by her cool grey eyes. They were flecked in precisely the same way as one particular spot in a Seurat painting he coveted. He could watch that spot for hours as the dots of colour swirled, forming and reforming, creating new hues.

How he loved that painting; how he loved those eyes, and the thick honey-blonde hair that cascaded down around her face. When she spoke English, it was with no discernible trace of an accent. In his dream, her voice was a visual rather than a sonic presence. Like the grey, bird-filled courtyard, it held a magical quality. Like the painting. Like Seurat.

She came three times a week, never on the same days from week to week, never at the same hour. Always she called him during the day to set the time. Always she spoke English, though his Russian was flawless.

His dream ended with one particular image. She was naked, standing or sitting; he was never quite certain which, because of the light. It was an artist's light. He was painting her. Instead of a brush he used his penis, swiping the tip of it against her white, white flesh. He did this until she was completely covered with the modern runes of computer language.

Always he awoke, as he did now, with an erection so tight it was painful. The dream was like an opiate. He rose from it dizzy with delight.

In a shower filled with steam and the scent of patchouli, he spoke her name as if that would recreate her out of the smoke.

'Daniella.'

Towelled off, he shaved, staring at his face in a mirror clouded around the edges. He dressed in midnight-blue linen slacks and a cream-coloured Ralph Lauren polo shirt.

Slipping his feet into his worn Top-Siders, Chimera thought about how he, in his own way, was an artist. How, with the programs he created for the Quarry's GPR-3700 mainframe, he could make people see what was not there.

Whistling, went out to make his report. He dreamed of Daniella only on the days when he was scheduled to speak with her.

Then the whole day glowed. Just like the painting by Seurat.

Glossary

a mi tuo fo – literally, 'take refuge in the merciful Buddha.'

ama-gasa – an umbrella.

amah – housekeeper or nanny. Traditionally from the lower classes of Chinese society.

asagao – literally, 'the face of morning.' A Japanese morning glory, earlier blooming than its Western counterpart.

atemi – any one of a number of percussive blows used in *jujutsu*.

ba-mahk – literally, 'feel the pulse.' A state of mental preparedness where aspects of one's surroundings previously hidden become apparent.

bah-ba – Cantonese for 'daddy'.

beiju – literally, 'the age of rice.' The eighty-eighth birthday.

Boxers – the colloquial name for Yi He Tuan, said to be the oldest of the Chinese secret societies from which the modern Triads of Hong Kong are descended. Certainly the Boxers were the most violently reactionary. In 1900, during what is commonly known as the Boxer Rebellion, the Yi He Tuan defied their Empress Cixi's orders and attacked the 'Legation Quarter' of Peking, trapping the foreigners inside for fifty days. The foreigners were eventually rescued by a combined mission force of Western and Japanese soldiers.

bushido – the way of the *samurai*; a stringent moral code of honour.

chahm hai – literally, a 'sinking in'. A meditational state in which one becomes one with one's surroundings.

chano-yu – the art of the tea ceremony.

dantai – a group of individuals so closely knit that there develops a communal consciousness.

dew neh loh moh – Cantonese epithet meaning 'fuck your mother.'

dieh loong – earth dragons thought by many Chinese to be powerful protectors.

dim sum – literally, 'to touch the heart'; Chinese dumplings, steamed or fried, usually eaten for breakfast or tea lunch.

dōjō – the physical place of martial arts practice.

dōmo arigatō – thank you very much.

engawa – a porch. In Japanese culture, the meeting place between the homeowner and those of the outside world.

faan gwai loh – Mandarin for 'foreign devil'.

fan tan – Chinese game of chance using buttons.

feng shui – the art of geomancy: the art of divining the portents from the elements, earth, fire, air, water. No Chinese enters into any major business deal or personal change, i.e., moving, getting married, etc., without consulting a *feng shui* man.

fu – in China's past, an Imperial chop or seal – usually made of jade or ivory – which the Emperor gave to his most trusted aides in his absence. Use of the *fu* was the same as wielding the Emperor's power.

Fuji-yama – Mount Fuji.

fūrin – Japanese wind chimes, used primarily in summer because their peculiar music is said to lift and cool the spirit in the face of high heat and humidity.

furo – a hot bath.

fusuma – a sliding door, usually opaque.

futon – thick, foldable cotton batting used by the Japanese for sleeping.

gaijin – a foreigner.

geisha – one trained in the arts of entertainment.

geta – wooden clogs.

giri – the complex concept of moral duty or obligation.

go – the Japanese name for a game of strategy using black and white stones on a gridded board; see *wei qi*.

godown – a warehouse.

gwai loh – Cantonese for 'foreign devil'.

haiku – a traditional Japanese poem of seventeen syllables containing the maximum of emotional resonance in the minimum of space. Often, a profound reflection of an aspect of the culture.

hakama – the traditional divided skirt used in a number of the martial arts, including archery. See *kyūjutsu*.

hara – to be grounded within oneself, to possess force of spirit, inner strength; therefore, to garner respect. Most prized by Japanese. *Hara* resides in the lower belly.

huo yan – literally, 'the movable eye'. An 'eye' is formed in *wei qi* in order to prevent your stone from being surrounded. *Huo yan* is a defensive strategy in which the player forms two 'eyes' adjacent to one another.

h'yeung yau – literally, 'fragrant grease'. A bribe.

irezumi – the ancient art of Japanese tattooing.

iteki – a barbarian; derogatory term.

janomegasa – an umbrella of oiled rice paper.

Jian – in Mandarin, this word has many meanings, among them, 'general of the army', 'grand champion of *wei qi*', 'creator'.

jō-waza – in *aikido*, performed while holding a stave; various methods of defence.

jōdan-uke – in *aikido*, a high-handed attacking motion.

joss – the Chinese concept of luck or destiny.

kami – a spirit, familial or otherwise. The Shintoists believe *kami* can, and often do, affect the lives of the living.

kamon – a family crest.

kanji – Chinese characters as used in Japanese writing.

karma – the Buddhist concept of destiny. See *joss*.

katana – a traditional *samurai*'s long sword.

keibatsu – the traditional bond between blood relations or those marrying with that family.

kenjutsu – the martial art of swordsmanship.

kiai – a scream used to startle and terrify the enemy.

kimono – a traditional Japanese robe, usually of silk or cotton.

koinobori – Boys' Day Festival.

kumi-uchi – a kind of battlefield *sumō* based on offensive throws mainly involving legs and hips. One of the most ancient methods of hand-to-hand combat.

kyūjutsu – the martial art of archery.

lou sin – Mandarin for 'mouse'.

lu – one of the 361 intersections on a *wei qi* board.

manrikigusari – a weapon consisting of a length of heavy chain weighted at either end.

marumono – tanned hide over cotton batting wrapped around a thick wooden dowel. One of the three traditional targets in *kyūjutsu*.

meinichi – although its two ideograms form 'life day', it is known among Japanese as 'death day'. On the anniversary of the ancestor's death, the family assembles at the burial site and by thought and deed 'brings the ancestor back to life' through memories.

nawanoren – a neighbourhood pub.

nunchaku – a weapon consisting of a short length of heavy chain with metal bars attached to each end.

o-nigiri – rice balls.

oyabun – chief of a *yakuza* clan.

qi – the driving force of will combined with intrinsic energy. The essence of power.

qi – in *wei qi*, each player's stone has four *qi*, or breaths. When it is surrounded, it is deprived of all *qi* and is taken off the board.

qun – in Mandarin, 'the group'.

ren – literally, Mandarin for 'harvest'. Here, it is used colloquially for 'master plan'.

sakē – traditional Japanese rice wine.

samurai – member of the highest level of the Japanese caste system.

sarakin – a moneylender, especially one catering to wage earners, usually at high-interest rates.

sensei – a master; usually, although not always, limited to the martial arts.

sentō – a public bath.

shioyaki – roasted fish coated with salt.

shōji – a sliding door, made of translucent rice-paper panels stretched across a wooden screen.

sluzhba – 'the service'. Used internally by its members as shorthand for the KGB.

sumi – coloured ink made from pressed charcoal; see *irezumi*.

sumi otoshi – in *aikido*, a projection technique known as the 'corner drop'.

sumō – Japanese wrestling or a practitioner of the sport.

sushi – raw fish wrapped around sticky rice and a dab of hot green horseradish.

Ta Chiu – the Spirit-Placating Festival.

tabi – Japanese socks, usually made of fine cotton or, sometimes, silk, with a separation between the big toe and the others.

Tai He Dian – in Mandarin, the 'Hall of Supreme Harmony.'

tai pan – the head of any of the large trading houses in Hong Kong.

tai tai – a *tai pan*'s wife.

tansu – wooden chests originally used by merchants in the Edo (1603–1867) and Meiji (1868–1912) periods.

tatami – a straw mat used as flooring in traditional Japanese rooms.

tetsu no kokoro – an iron spirit.

tian yuan – a section in the middle of the *wei qi* board known as 'the belly'. A most strategic area to occupy.

ting – a summer pavilion in a *yuan*, a garden.

tokonoma – an alcove with a raised platform in a traditional Japanese room. During the Kamakura (1185–1392) and the Muromachi (1392–1568) periods, art works, especially hanging scrolls, imported from China became popular in Japanese households. Mobile displays soon became fixed features, thus the *tokonoma* was born.

tong zhi – 'comrade', in speech. Mandarin honourific used after the family name.

tsuyu – literally, 'the plum rains'. Heavy rains in late spring and early summer.

umeboshi – fermented pickled plums.

usagigoya – literally, 'rabbit hutch'. A tiny apartment in modern Tokyo.

wakizashi – the shorter of the two traditional *samurai* swords; see *katana*.

walla-walla – small, engine-driven vessel plying the harbours around Hong Kong to transport people from place to place.

wei qi – literally, 'to surround'. A Chinese game of military strategy, identical to *go*. The object of the game is to surround your opponent's stones. It is played on a board with nineteen vertical and nineteen horizontal lines. Stones are placed on any of the 361 intersections. It has a heavy philosophical bent. As in the martial arts, a player's *wei qi* strategy is an extension of his view of life.

xing – literally, 'stars'. Nine strategic *lu* on the *wei qi* board.

yaba – an archery range.

yakuza – members of the Japanese underworld bound by a strict moral code; see *giri*.

yan – in *wei qi*, 'eye'. When a player surrounds an intersection with his stones, this prevents the opponent from taking certain key pieces.

yin-yang – the Buddhist concept of the duality of nature. Everything, everyone requires two sides to be whole. The darkness and the light, combining to achieve a perfect harmony.

yuan – a formal contemplation garden built in harmony with the tenets of Buddhism.

yuan lin – a Chinese villa surrounded by an ornate garden. See *yuan*.

yuhn-hyun – Cantonese for 'ring' or 'circle'. Here used as the secret ring of people in Hong Kong involved in Zilin's master plan.

The world's greatest novelists now available in Panther Books

To order direct from the publisher just tick the titles you want
and fill in the order form.   GF781

All these books are available at your local bookshop or newsagent, or can be ordered direct from the publisher..

To order direct from the publisher just tick the titles you want and fill in the form below.

Name _____

Address _____

_____

Send to:
Panther Cash Sales
PO Box 11, Falmouth, Cornwall TR10 9EN.

Please enclose remittance to the value of the cover price plus:

UK 45p for the first book, 20p for the second book plus 14p per copy for each additional book ordered to a maximum charge of £1.63.

BFPO and Eire 45p for the first book, 20p for the second book plus 14p per copy for the next 7 books, thereafter 8p per book.

Overseas 75p for the first book and 21p for each additional book.

Panther Books reserve the right to show new retail prices on covers, which may differ from those previously advertised in the text or elsewhere.